I0561731

The Planet of Darkness

Book 1: City of the Dark Tyrant

Tirzah Darnell

Book Cover by BoBooks

Illustrations by Tirzah Darnell

Author's Notes

Welcome to The Planet of Darkness. Here are some travel tips that will ensure you have an enjoyable experience.

Travel Tip One: On the Planet of Darkness, residents are given numbers, not names. To keep track of the numbers of persons of interest, refer to the back pages of this book for their identity cards with photographs, numbers, and occupations.

Travel Tip Two: On the Planet of Darkness, individual's numbers may not be pronounced the way you expect. For instance, 7,500's number is pronounced "Seventy-Five Hundred." The glossary at the back of the book includes the pronunciation for all numbers of individuals you will meet on your excursion.

Travel Tip Three: The Planet of Darkness is rife with Persuaders and Enforcers who will try to convince you through wiles, torture, or brute force to remain on this planet. Do not give in! Remember, the whole point of your excursion is to find a path that will lead to the Planet of Light.

As the author, I hope you enjoy your stay and continue the journey throughout the entire trilogy!

--Tirzah Darnell

Chapter One

The cavern was dark — deathly dark. It was always dark here and night was the only time of day. This entire Planet of Darkness was so far away from its sun that the sun's light was indistinguishable from the light emanating from any of the other stars in its black-night sky.

The planet received warmth only from the fiery magma that moaned and groaned beneath its surface. At intervals of time, this magma would create pressure on the planet's crust and spew forth scorching hot steam. No one knew when or where this was likely to happen and the fact remained that if you stood for too long in any one spot, that steam could burst forth right below you.

Out of one of the darkest crevices of this cavern skulked a tall, darkly cloaked man. His clothing was darker than the dark night and he slipped from shadowed rock to shadowed rock. He pulled his hood closer about his face so that the shadows from it would cover his large pale-blue eyes. Besides a few light reddish-brown curls, the only other visible portion of his face was his terse nose, pouting mouth, and smooth, determined chin. He adjusted his cloak once more around his well-formed shoulders. Even though he was nearly impossible to spot, he kept glancing about furtively. He knew someone was watching him — whether it was the smog-like ghosts or some other spy keeping its eyes on him — he knew someone was watching him. *The Dark Tyrant always has someone watching you — wherever you are; whatever you're doing . . .*

Being one of the top propaganda specialists on the planet, the man had often reminded the population that the Dark Tyrant ruled over all the habitable areas of any significance on the Planet of Darkness. According to the man's latest pamphlets, the Dark Tyrant's hand-picked, well-trained experts in politics, economics, and social welfare all agreed, statistically speaking, he ruled exceptionally well. 95% of his subjects obeyed him all the time, without question. These experts also agreed the Dark Tyrant had devised the perfect blend of punishment, propaganda, and prevention to extract this obedience. Refusing to obey the Dark Tyrant inevitably led to a gruesome and painful death. All his subjects, from an early age, were drilled over and over that all power belonged to the Dark Tyrant and that only by obeying his rules could all subjects of the Planet of Darkness be truly happy. The Dark Tyrant had even devised a multitude of methods for watching every one of his subjects wherever they were so his police force could spot disobedience practically before it happened.

An icy blast cut past the man's face and he drew the hood more firmly over his head. He shuddered as he reminded himself the Dark Tyrant's experts had everything calculated to the finest nanometer, from how many whippings it would take for the laborers to produce the maximum amount of labor, to the perfect punishment that would ensure the silencing of a baby's disruptive cry. But, while 95% obedience was a remarkable achievement, the Dark Tyrant was still troubled by that annoying 5%. This 5% consisted of a certain group of people who defied the Dark Tyrant's leadership. This 5% dared to hope there was someplace where they could live a life filled with freedom, goodness, beauty, and — Light. The man had heard rumors whispered that there was another planet near enough to be reached by spaceship, a planet that glowed with a brightness that blinded those who saw it through a telescope. Warnings had been issued that all those who had attempted to journey to this planet had lost their lives in the attempt. Still, the desire for freedom was so strong in these people, as it was now within the cloaked man, so strong he dared to risk everything to escape to the Planet of Light.

The cloaked man slid behind a rock, looking around for any sign he was being followed. He listened, training his ear to hear every sound no matter how inaudible. It was then he heard the sound every subject of the Planet of Darkness fears — the nearly silent semi-mechanical humming of one of the Dark Tyrant's spies. Accompanying this humming was the hissing of the creature adjusting its mechanical eyes to peer deeper into the shadows of the cavern. The cloaked man searched for the source of the sound until he spotted two large, binocular-like eyes homing in on him from a small cavity in the side of the cavern. These creatures resembled armor-plated snakes. Billions of these spies slithered all over the Planet of Darkness. These half-robot, half-snake creatures were contrived by the Dark Tyrant to track down disobedient subjects. The man knew he was in a cavern off limits for all subjects who, like him, did not carry special passes. It came as no surprise to him that the spy had him in its sights. The spy slithered out of the cave and moved in to where the man hid in order to capture a better picture of him. Then, it slid up close to him, and the man's hand flinched when a sharp prick from the creature's forked tongue stung him as it flicked out and collected a sample of his DNA. The man brushed the creature away and hastily grabbed a large rock, ready to crush it over the noxious creature's head. Before he could bring the rock down, the creature slipped back into the shadows — to take his information to the Dark Tyrant. The man tossed the rock aside as he glared into the shadows that had swallowed the spy creature. Mumbling curses under his breath, he turned to trudge on his way.

The man came against what appeared to be a dead-end to the cavern, a high rock wall. He stood and waited . . . waited for several tense minutes.

A gust of wind whooshed through the cavern. The man held onto his hood as the wind swept about him. He shut his eyes tight as the wind picked up even stronger, as if it was carrying him away to some far-off part of the planet. When he finally dared to open his eyes, he realized he was still standing in the same place he was before.

"2-45," an unfamiliar voice boomed.

It startled him to hear so strange a voice shouting his number. Looming over him was a ghastly phantom of a wizard standing over ten feet tall. The wizard had a long, grisly beard and mustache and fixed 2-45 with a fierce, blood-freezing glare. His robe was a swirl of nauseating reds, blues, blacks and greys that glowed in the shadows. What 2-45 found most unnerving was that even though he stood there looking straight at the wizard's stomach, he was in reality looking *through* the wizard's stomach — straight into the wall of the cavern.

"Y-y-yes." 2-45 forced his eyes off of the wizard's stomach and up to his face.

"WHY HAVE YOU AWAKENED ME?" The wizard's breath was hot, smoky and smelled of burning flesh.

2-45 bit his lip, pondering his answer. It was said that people whose answers did not please the wizard were consequently struck down by giant fire balls conjured in the palms of his hands. Being burnt by fire balls was not on 2-45's agenda. He had been told that with the correct answers the wizard would open a secret door in the side of the rock wall. 2-45 wanted to enter that door.

"ANSWER ME. WHY HAVE YOU AWAKENED ME?" The wizard's fury inflated him several feet.

"I am in search of wisdom," 2-45 replied as calmly as possible.

"HOW DARE YOU ASK FOR SOMETHING WITHOUT OFFERING SOMETHING!"

2-45 knitted his eyebrows in contemplation. "I offer whatever I have."

The wizard shrunk a couple feet while determining the sincerity of 2-45's words. "WHAT IS YOUR BUSINESS HERE?"

2-45 took the shrinking of the wizard as a good sign. "My business benefits the one who dwells inside."

The wizard bowed his head, becoming smaller by a few more feet, but he still looked sternly at 2-45 past his bushy, contracted eyebrows. "HOW WILL IT BENEFIT HIM?"

"Wealth benefits everyone."

Another blast of wind swirled about 2-45 and the wizard as if to ingest them. 2-45 braced himself hoping this was not an indication that he had answered incorrectly. Hideous contortions came over the wizard's face as he clutched his own head and moaned. The gust of wind engulfed the wizard, and swallowed him up, leaving 2-45 looking at an open doorway in the rock wall in front of him. 2-45 lowered his hood as he entered.

2-45 walked through a long, dark tunnel lit only by torches in holders at intervals. The shadows and the flickering light were mottled in an orange and black display that neither obscured the path nor lit the way. From out of the marbled blackness, a man glided up behind 2-45. The sudden portentous breath upon 2-45's neck startled him.

"Strange that I should find you here," said a voice from out of the shadows — a voice that could have belonged to either a demon or a poet. 2-45 turned and found himself face to face with 1-13, one of the Dark Tyrant's top Persuaders.

Through a plethora of methods such as drugs, hypnosis, and torture, Persuaders managed to persuade subjects to comply with the Dark Tyrant's wishes. The Dark Tyrant put these Persuaders to use whenever a subject needed to be convinced to confess guilt, to inform on someone, or to do anything else they might be reluctant to do.

Persuaders were known to dress exceptionally well. 1-13 wore a dark red silken shirt and nicely fitted black pants. Around his shoulders, he wore a silver cape embroidered with images of ghostly skeletons. The light flickering on 1-13's face made him look unnaturally excitable. His face reminded 2-45 of either an unusually old elf or an unusually young warlock. The glimmer of light in his eyes was not the glimmer of wisdom, but the glimmer of craftiness. He smirked at 2-45's surprise at seeing him. "Didn't expect to see me here?" he partially asked and partially commented. "But you *know* that the Dark Tyrant allows me to come here since it falls within *my* duties. But *you* — he wouldn't give *you* a pass." His speaking ability was so well perfected that even the inflections of his words had a hypnotic effect. "Why would a Propaganda Officer need to come to a *place* like *this*?"

2-45 looked down, flicked his fingers against his thumb in thought as he weighed how he should respond. *Of all the people to meet. The Dark Tyrant would certainly take 1-13's side.*

1-13 placed a hand on 2-45's shoulder. While making this gesture of concern, he nonchalantly brought his other hand to his mouth in order to cover a condescending smile. "I see. You *aren't* supposed to be here." He raised one eyebrow knowingly and turned away as if to leave. Still, he stood where he was, his ears attuned for 2-45's next words.

"Wait."

With feigned surprise, 1-13 looked back. An overly friendly smile played on his lips.

"Are you going to report me?"

"*P e r h a p s,*" 1-13 said slowly and meaningfully.

"You mean you might NOT report me?" 2-45 raised a finger and watched 1-13 intently.

"If I *feel* like reporting you, I will. If I *don't* feel like reporting you, I won't."

2-45 looked deep into 1-13's eyes, trying to determine the answer to his riddle. His eyes were hypnotic and mysterious. It amazed 2-45 how 1-13's powers even extended to the shadows that played across his face. The shadows moved with the flickering of the torches with a mesmerizing effect, like the constant in and out of the ocean waves on the shore.

"And what would make you NOT feel like reporting me?" The control 2-45 had over his mind was slowly slipping to 1-13.

1-13 clasped his hands before him in a benedictory pose. On the index finger of his right hand he wore a large silver ring adorned with a jade stone engraved in the form of a skull. 1-13 brought the fingers of his left hand over the ring and twisted the stone's casing. A green smoke filled the air. Like hands reaching out, the green smoke embraced 2-45's face and placed him into a hypnotic trance.

1-13 guided 2-45 into a sitting position on a stone bench in the tunnel. 1-13 lifted the sleeve of his own left arm. On his wrist was a silver bracelet. Small green lights pulsated on and off around this bracelet. He touched one of the green lights, turning on a small recorder.

"Now, 2-45, *dear* friend," 1-13 tried to sound as innocently concerned as possible, "why have you come here? I know the Dark Tyrant has *not* given you a pass to the Dive of Distraction — yet I find you *here*. Are you here for pleasure?"

2-45 shook his head "no".

1-13 clutched 2-45's arm in a firm grasp, and spoke between clenched teeth, "Say it. Yes or no?"

"No."

1-13 crossed his arms and held his head high. He knew he was soon to record the words that would spell doom to one more defiant subject of the Dark Tyrant. "So, tell me, *what* are you planning?"

2-45 spoke slowly but deliberately, "I was hoping to meet with 6,025, the owner of the dive. I heard that for the right amount of money, he could help me get away from this planet.

I want to leave here so bad . . . I think . . . if I stay . . . I . . ." 2-45's eyes moistened. With a strong effort of his own, he swallowed hard to keep from expressing anymore emotion.

1-13's eyes fired with excitement. He turned his recorder off so his own laughter would not become part of the finale of his recording. He slapped 2-45 on his back to wake him from his trance.

2-45 breathed deeply and rubbed his temples, trying to bring himself back from the world of mist and smoke. He heard 1-13's voice echoing eerily from down the tunnel. "Wake up to your doom." 2-45 turned to watch 1-13 disappearing in the darkness. 2-45 hit the wall in frustration. He knew now he had no option other than to continue with his plan.

Further down the tunnel, 2-45 came face to face with two giant floor-to-ceiling mirrors. He shifted, uncomfortable with standing there at a dead end looking straight at himself. As far as he could tell, he had two choices. He could either turn back or continue to stare at his own image in the mirror. 2-45 knew he had not made a wrong turn, so it followed that the dive had to be somewhere nearby. He touched one of the mirrors seeing if there was any way around or through the mirror. The ground underneath him opened and 2-45 fell through.

2-45 did not fall far. As he stood, he saw he was in another long, shadowy hall. The only light emanated from the numerous open doorways along the hall. Shadowed movements in the doorways suggested there was considerable activity going on in each of the rooms. He heard a rambunctious mixture of sounds: frenzied music, dancing, fighting, talking, shouting, laughing, and crying. When these sounds were combined with some eerie croaking and moaning that he could not place, 2-45 wondered if he had accidentally ended up in a dungeon for the mentally imbalanced. He looked around for a way back to the first hall, when he noticed someone he recognized walking toward him. This man, 7-43 by number, was tall with reddish-brown hair, and, prior to this instance, 2-45 had considered him dignified and gentlemanly.

Right now, though, the man was neither dignified nor gentlemanly, but significantly drunk.

"Aha, 2-45. Quite a jolly-baloo finding you here." 7-43 tripped on his own shoes to reach 2-45.

"7-43. What are you doing here?" 2-45 smirked with surprise. "You look to me a little . . ."

"Not a little." 7-43 grinned. "I'm so far down in the pickle jar that it'll take some doing to get me out." He laughed with an overabundance of enthusiasm.

"But what *are* you doing here?"

"At the Dive of Distraction?" 7-43 took a step and stumbled over nothing right into 2-45. "Getting distracted, of course."

2-45 glanced around, irritated at the chaotic surroundings. "How could anybody do anything here? The noise. It's so confusing."

"Not a-tall." 7-43 put his arm around 2-45's shoulder and led him to one of the rooms. "It's quite a hush-a-bye out here. Wait 'til you get inside. That's when the music really gets noisome."

As they stepped into the room, 2-45 had to shout to be heard. "If it's so terrible, why do you stay?"

7-43 laughed. "Ah, but that's the idea." He directed 2-45 to a table near the bar and refilled his glass from a bottle of strong-smelling drink. "The music's so noxiously loud and the drink's so noxiously strong. They so obviously exist so you, for a brief moment, don't have to." He spilled a drink into a glass for 2-45. The drink did not look or smell appealing, but, to be polite, 2-45 accepted it.

The room was lit by strobing red and orange lights and was uncomfortably crowded. With the room lit only half the time, it was difficult to tell who was who or exactly what anyone was doing. No doubt the room was designed this way so the customers could later deny they were ever here doing any of the outrageous things they were doing.

2-45 coughed on a sip from his glass and set the rest of the drink aside.

7-43 laughed once more and gulped down the rest of his drink. "You know, you were the absolutely last person I expected to find here." He gestured toward 2-45's unfinished drink.

"Same here. About you, I mean," 2-45 replied with a knowing smile.

"I've been coming here for a long time." 7-43 examined his empty glass, hoping if he looked at it long enough it would refill itself. Hopes dashed, he turned the glass upside down in front of him. "I enjoy being distracted. It takes you away from the mundane existence of life." He sighed and tapped his fingers on the bottom of his upside-down glass. He became excited as he added, "Did you know that each of these rooms contain different types of distractions? There are so many of them that I haven't even tried them all. Yes, I like it here. When I'm here I don't have to think . . ."

"What if the Dark Tyrant finds out you've been coming here?" 2-45 reminded him. "There are rules about this place."

"That doesn't worry me. He doesn't really mind us being here. They say there are restrictions, but they're only superficial." He leaned forward confidentially. "The rules are there to make you *feel* like you are getting away with something. Now what *really* worries me, what I try not to *think* about is . . ." 7-43's words cut off as he stared straight ahead of himself with horror.

"What?"

7-43 turned toward 2-45 and became suddenly sober. "The judgment beyond death." He blinked off the thought and stood, knocking the chair over as he did. "I think I need a stronger drink." He stumbled toward the bar.

The possibility of a judgment beyond death was not a new concept for 2-45. It was a point of wonder and concern for most people on the Planet of Darkness. Whether people existed in some form or other after death was difficult to prove or disprove since death is a place few people have ever visited and returned from with pictures to document their travels.

According to the Dark Tyrant's scientific experts, death was nothing more than a living human being transforming into a dead human being and to believe in the existence of anything resembling a soul was delusional. Therefore, the experts declared a judgment beyond death could not possibly exist.

Still, a judgment beyond death was a subject often whispered about by people who either wondered whether it really did exist or wondered whether it was just an idea spread about by the authorities to make extracting obedience from the citizenry easier. 2-45 once belonged in the second category. He was under the impression the Dark Tyrant had originated the idea of the judgment beyond death and circulated this idea throughout the Planet of Darkness using his army of Enforcers. In 2-45's mind, this was a fiendishly clever plan because it forced the citizens into absolute obedience by threatening them with both the Dark Tyrant's painful punishments in this life and an unknown future full of torment after death. 2-45 was so certain the Dark Tyrant had devised this plan, that one day he approached the Dark Tyrant for advice on a propaganda project and asked him about the possibility of incorporating the "judgment beyond death" into it. By using an idea that originated with the Dark Tyrant, 2-45 was sure he would gain favor. However, when 2-45 brought up the "judgment beyond death," the Dark Tyrant's face twisted into an expression of horror and he lashed out at 2-45 demanding that he never mention the "judgment beyond death" again. 2-45 was shocked by the Dark Tyrant's outburst and the look on his face convinced 2-45 that the "judgment beyond death" must really exist. After this, 2-45 became more determined to find a way off the Planet of Darkness.

2-45 decided to try his drink one more time. As he lifted the glass, a young, heavily made-up girl in a slinky silver dress was pressed by the swarm of people into 2-45.

"Sorry." She was embarrassed to find that for once she had run into a man completely by accident.

2-45 set what was left of his drink back onto the table. "That's all right." He brushed off the drink that had spilled on his shirt.

"Are you here for pleasure?" The girl blinked and swung her hip close to his.

"No, on business."

"The only business here is pleasure." She moved closer to 2-45 and leaned her head on his shoulder.

2-45 did find her beautiful and might have been tempted by her, but the hubbub of the crowd and the boom-de-boom of the music was not his idea of a romantic setting. The girl was jostled just as she had leaned her head on his shoulder and her head jabbed right into 2-45's throat.

"Sorry." She lifted her head from his shoulder.

"That's all right," 2-45 laughed nervously.

The girl smiled, glad that he took it so well.

"By the way," 2-45 had to raise his voice to be heard over the noise, "do you know where I could find 6,025?"

The girl pouted and wrapped her arms around him. "Why? Don't I give you more pleasure than he could?"

"Of course." 2-45 tried not to become embarrassed at his words being taken the wrong way. "I just have a business deal to make with him."

The girl looked at him skeptically, but finally relented. "All right. I can take you to him."

16

Chapter Two

As the girl led 2-45 down the main hall, 2-45 caught glimpses of what went on in the rooms they passed. In one room he saw someone screaming in pain; in another room he saw someone clutching his head in anguish; in yet another room he saw someone walking around in a daze of complete confusion. Above each of the rooms, 2-45 noticed a clock, evidently there to measure the time a person spent in each room. Every clock measured the time at a different rate so that the ticking and tocking of all the clocks combined created a cringingly chaotic beat. The stream of people in and out of the rooms was just as jumbled as the beating of the clocks, for while 2-45 was sure he saw a particular person entering a certain room, not two seconds later, he saw that same person leaving another room further down the hall on the opposite side.

2-45 and the girl approached a white pillared doorway. The girl touched a blue glowing light near the door and the door opened. They walked into a room that, instead of having four walls, was in the shape of a hemisphere, much like a planetarium. The room was brightly lit and luxuriously decorated. The floor was a white and grey marble adorned with black and white fleece rugs. Marble statuary was set on finely carved mahogany tables. Off of the room was a gold and marble veranda. The veranda led to what appeared to be a beautiful outdoor flower garden beneath a cloudless blue sky. Even 2-45 was fooled for a moment into believing the blue sky, the green grass, and the red roses were real . . . until he noticed a nearly hidden projector that holographed this artificial enticement.

2-45 turned away from the veranda and noticed, resting complacently on a chaise lounge, a vastly overweight man in a luxurious dark suit with a pearl stickpin in his silken cravat. Around his shoulders, he wore a black cape lined with purple silk and on his head sat a black top hat. This combination made him look much like a magician about to perform some cunning card trick to amuse his audience.

The man pulled his giant mass off the chaise lounge. As he stood, scratching his enormous belly, he stretched the kinks out of his shoulders and leaned his triple-chinned head backwards then brought it forward again. He did all this with such a blasé faire attitude that the action resembled some type of religious ritual. "So, welcome to my cottage of concoctions — my temple of temptations — my web of wickedness — my center of sensualities — take your pick." He did not once look 2-45 in the eyes. His deep voice echoed as from a bottomless pit. He waved his chubby hand in as enthusiastic a salutation as a man weighted down with so much blubber could. He then held out his other hand and shook 2-45's hand once firmly. "I am the Duke of Distraction, so, naturally, I can satisfy any of your desires for distraction." Even more distracting was the way his lips were still moving after he finished talking, as if his voice had been overdubbed and his lips had not yet caught up with his dialogue. "So tell me, your name is—?"

"2-45."

The man removed his hand from 2-45's clasp with disdain. "I dislike this number system. To be just a number, pshaw. Of course, everyone else going by numbers . . . well, that makes me that much more important." His lips still lagged behind his voice. "You know, it took me some time to convince the Dark Tyrant to permit me the privilege of a name — but it *is* purely for business purposes, isn't it? So, when I was told I was permitted a name — I took on three. Ha-ha. That'll show him. So, now I am the Duke of Distraction, the Demigod of Diversion, and the Deity of Delusion." The Duke of Distraction chuckled a low, hollow chuckle as he set his ample posterior down on a large gold gilded throne. He adjusted his overflowing flab until he could finally find a comfortable position. He then, like a king commanding his servant, waved his hand toward the girl who had accompanied 2-45. She immediately rushed to the Duke of Distraction and massaged his neck. "Now tell me, 2-45, what was it you came to see me for?"

2-45 politely paused to allow both the Duke of Distraction's voice and lips to finish their question. "I had heard that for enough money you could . . ."

The Duke of Distraction held up a hand, gesturing for 2-45 to stop. "Not yet." He rubbed his immense belly with a discomforted grimace. "My stomach is speaking so loudly I can hardly hear you. I believe it is time for my hourly meal." He clapped his hands several times.

From a side room glided in a large table covered with a white tablecloth, lighted candles, and several covered dishes of food. Behind the table, scurrying on light feet, came a tall, thin, dignified waiter who, 2-45 finally realized, was pushing the table. He placed the table right in front of the Duke of Distraction and lifted the covering from a plate revealing a large steak, a big smothered baked potato, and a sizable serving of seasoned asparagus. "Your meal, your excellency," the butler said with a Shakespearean flair.

"Ah," the Duke of Distraction forced his fat lips to form an enthusiastic smile as he looked down at his plate, "I have never seen a more glorious sight." As he grabbed his knife and fork, he gestured toward another chair not far away.

Taking this as a hint, the butler wound himself up and went into action. With several hops and skips, he bounded to the chair and returned with it to place it at the table. With a sweeping wave of his arms, he indicated that 2-45 was to take a seat. 2-45 paused, annoyed at this interruption, but concluded that complying with the Duke of Distraction's wishes would be the best way to further his goal. He sat and the butler uncovered a second plate containing a meal identical to the Duke of Distraction's. The butler poured two glasses of red wine and presented them before both the Duke of Distraction and 2-45.

The Duke of Distraction cut off a large piece of steak and stuffed it into his eager mouth. "You know what I just adore?"

2-45 took a bite of asparagus. "Steak?"

"No. Cheesecake. All creamy and buttery. And with oh so much sweetness. Drizzled and drizzled with raspberry and chocolate. One . . . no . . . two . . . no . . . three huge dollops of whipped cream. Sprinkled all over with little chocolate munchies. My mouth waters just thinking about it."

2-45 wondered how the Duke of Distraction could continue to scarf down his steak while talking on and on about cheesecake. *Guess he is just looking forward to his dessert.*

After the Duke of Distraction had scooped up his last heaping glob of sour-creamed baked potato, the butler swiped both plates, even though 2-45 had barely started on his steak. After reshuffling the plates, the butler presented two new plates both bearing a large slice of cheesecake embellished just the way the Duke of Distraction had been imagining.

As soon as the plate had touched the table, the Duke of Distraction shoveled forkful after forkful of cheesecake into his mouth. "Mmm-mmm-mmm. Nice juicy steak — that's what my tummy wants right now. Flavorful sauce drenched all over it, dripping its way down the sides of the steak — the steak swimming in this tasty pool of deliciousness. Just the right balance of seasonings. Cooked nice and pink — not too well-done — just right. A plateful of satisfying yum. What a meal that would be."

"And earlier you were so eager to get to the cheesecake."

"Hmph." The Duke of Distraction was visibly annoyed at 2-45's interruption of his steak-filled daydreams.

2-45 shrugged off the Duke of Distraction's annoyance. "Well, as I was going to say before, I was told that if I came to you, you could . . ."

The Duke of Distraction flapped his hands several times upside-down for the butler to take the table away. In two leaps the butler swept the table and everything on it, including 2-45's unfinished cheesecake, into the side room. 2-45 watched the cheesecake disappear with disappointment, unsure of what to do with the fork he still held in his hand.

"You were right to come to me. Everybody needs to be distracted now and then — and I have here in my dive every distraction method in existence — you would be amazed." With a short grunt, he lifted his bulk off of his throne, raising himself with effort to his big, fat, swollen feet. He then waddled his way to the middle of the room and took a remote-control wand from one of the tables. Wand in hand, the Duke of Distraction spread his arms out with a sweeping gesture and images formed on the planetarium-like ceiling.

2-45 sat back as he toyed with his fork and watched the Duke of Distraction's grand display. "I'm sure this is really very interesting, but I already know what I want."

"You can never know what you want until you know everything you could want. There is more you could desire than you know. Let me show you." As the Duke of Distraction continued to speak, a collage of everything he described spread itself in flashing images on the ceiling. "Think about it — A world of diversions all at your disposal — What would you like — So many to choose from — And you've never even dreamed of the fantasies I can offer you — Let's think about — No let's start out with — No, well . . .Uh — Ah, perhaps you want to distract yourself with something like the sensualities of sex — Oh, passionate sex — The fervor — The fire — And look at all of those wild wicked women — All there just for you — or, then again, perhaps you go for something else — Oh, how about drowning your troubles in a mug of beer — a glass of wine — a shot of liquor — Why go small — Take it by the bottle — Dull your brain to the humdrum duties of life with bottle after bottle of whatever you like — Why think about anything — you're drunk — dead drunk — And if the morning headaches get too distracting for you, drink some more — Stay drunk morning and night — If that doesn't work, maybe you want something stronger — Oh, and what a wild trip you could have — maybe even to the moon — On the road with a rabbit called O'Reilly — In a stew of smoking salamanders — Skiing through the sloping hills of a marshmallow sundae — Maybe only stoned in a garden called Zen — Ah, and next — Here comes my favorite — Food — What can bother you when you are eating bowl after bowl, plate after plate — Eat what you can when you can, that's my motto — Entertainment — watch it — live it — become it — Do whatever — Don't worry about life — Jump in — Climb in — Come on board — Zone out — Unattached — In another world — Go faster — Do more — Don't stop — Do it all — When they say 'try one,' try three — When they say 'do something,' do everything — Nothing's out of reach — Nothing's too dangerous — Nothing's immoral — Nothing's illegal — Try it all — Try everything — Try it right now — Distractions are the only way to escape from all of your troubles."

What with the Duke of Distraction bursting into such a flurry of excitement and the images flying across the ceiling in such blurred flashes of hypnotic chaos, 2-45 was overwhelmed. In fact, he was so overwhelmed that when the Duke of Distraction finally ended his speech, 2-45 had to take several seconds just to catch his breath and regain his thoughts. Even after this, he had to wait some time for the

Duke of Distraction's lips to finish their last exclamations. 2-45 then said flatly, "But what about a spaceship?"

"What was that?" 2-45's comment so distracted the Duke of Distraction that he gave 2-45 a double-take.

"What about a spaceship? I would say a spaceship is the best way to escape from your trouble, especially if your trouble is a planet called the Planet of Darkness."

"Ah . . . Well, why didn't you mention it before." The Duke of Distraction let his flabby arms fall as he set his remote-control wand down. "I have had extensive experience in the area of spaceships. But — it will cost you a lot more than any of this . . . you do have money, don't you?"

2-45 pulled out of a pocket several pouches and stepped up to a table next to the Duke of Distraction. He emptied the pouches onto the table creating a mound of gold and silver coins. "Before my father died, he was one of the top advisors to the Dark Tyrant. The Dark Tyrant rewarded him by giving him part ownership in several gold and silver mines on the north side of the city. Right here is a little of the mines' surplus. I should hope this would be enough."

The Duke of Distraction ran his plump fingers through the coins. "My . . . yes . . . I think we can work something out."

At those words, 2-45 handed the Duke of Distraction the pouches the coins had come in. "I would like to leave as soon as possible."

"Certainly." The Duke of Distraction carefully gathered the coins, putting the larger share into two of the pouches and a small handful into the last one. Afterwards, he pocketed the two large pouches and kept the other one in hand. "We can leave right now." The Duke of Distraction picked up his remote-control wand and flipped a small lever on one side of it. The entire floor descended. In less than a minute they found themselves one floor down. The metal sliding door to a cave-like room opened and the Duke of Distraction headed through it. "Come with me." He made his portly way down a descending hall with 2-45 following him.

"You have a spaceship hidden down here?"

"Not just a spaceship — but a pilot as well."

They followed the hall to a small underground hangar that housed a medium sized star-shaped spaceship. The spaceship's entrance was open and ramps were in place to facilitate loading. Just as the Duke of Distraction and 2-45 approached, a well-built young woman with short dark brown hair hurried out of the ship with a resonating clanking of the metal ramp. She wore a nice fitting beige and white one-piece outfit that zipped up in front. Around her waist was a brown utility belt with various tools for spaceship repairs.

"Good day." Her smile sparkled, but she spoke with few inflections as if the words had been overly memorized. 2-45 also noted a hint of something mechanical in the timbre of her voice.

The Duke of Distraction approached her. "1-05, meet 2-45. He would like you to fly him off the Planet of Darkness."

"That's easy enough." 1-05 held her hand out to 2-45.

It seemed to 2-45 that 1-05's eyes were looking past him not at him. He took her hand and it felt cold. "So you can get me off this planet?"

She smiled again. "I told you it would be easy. But I doubt if you want to live in the cold emptiness of space." She laughed, but without moving her lips. From over 1-05's shoulder emerged a second head that looked identical to hers. The head moved over and 2-45 realized there was a body attached to this second head and there were in fact two 1-05's. This new 1-05 laughed upon seeing the incredulous looks on the faces of the Duke of Distraction and 2-45. She took a deep breath, trying to keep a straight face. But, she could not hold the laugh back for long and was soon laughing uncontrollably.

The Duke of Distraction frowned. "Having fun again with your shape-shifter, are you?"

Reaching the bottom of the ramp, 1-05 nodded as she covered the lower part of her face to help regain her composure. She noticed 2-45's confusion. "You have never met a shape-shifter before?" The real 1-05's voice was nowhere near as monotone and emotionless as the shape-shifter's.

2-45 shrugged off a feeling of momentary foolishness. "I have heard of them, but I have to admit that this is the first time I've met one face to face."

"They are amazing." 1-05 patted the shape-shifter on the shoulder. "They can become practically anything you want them to be from a little mouse to a great, big Boratog. And as you see, they can even look like anyone you want them to look like."

"So, how do you acquire a shape-shifter?"

"You buy them." The Duke of Distraction scratched his flabby chin.

1-05 went on to clarify. "Well, it's like this, not long ago I lost my co-pilot . . ." She paused a moment looking down to hide a choke of emotion. ". . . well, the Duke of Distraction, here, in exchange for a few transporting jobs, was willing to pay the money necessary to acquire this shape-shifter so that it could act as my new co-pilot. Its name is Alpha 3-0-3."

"That's right, and a good deal it was." The Duke of Distraction chuckled. He then handed her the small pouch of coins. "This is for you to take him off the planet."

She smiled as she took the money. She was about to ask the Duke of Distraction one last thing, but he had already waddled off. After a short pout, she turned to 2-45. "So, I hope you don't mind telling me a little more what this is about."

"Isn't it obvious?"

Alpha 3-0-3 stepped closer to listen in. 2-45 eyed it nervously.

1-05 noticed 2-45's nervousness and turned with a hand on her hip to her shape-shifter. "Get to work and make those repairs. We will be leaving soon, so we better get the *Journey* ready for flight." Alpha 3-0-3 nodded and left to prepare the spaceship. 1-05 turned back to 2-45 and patted the spaceship.

"That's the name of our ship. The *Journey*. Apropos, wouldn't you say? So, exactly where do you want to go?"

2-45 rubbed his arm nervously and took a few steps closer to examine the ship. He faced 1-05, eying her intently. "First, I want to know. *Is* it possible?"

She knitted her eyebrows. "Is what possible?"

"Most people I have talked to say it's impossible to get to the Planet of Light."

1-05 looked upward in disbelief. "Oh. To the Planet of Light. Not this again." She circled the wing and mounted the spaceship's ramp.

2-45 caught up with her. "You mean it IS impossible?"

"Not necessarily. But I've never been able to get there."

"Do you know where it is?"

"I know where it's *supposed* to be."

"Would you be willing to try?" 2-45 was hopeful.

She noticed his determination. She paused while her mind fell to a moment in her past. She smiled softly. "All right. We can try."

2-45 embraced her in his excitement. "Thank you, thank you, thank you."

1-05 good-naturedly pushed him aside. "I warn you, it won't be easy."

"Of course it won't. If you need any more money, I can pay you." He eagerly pulled out another bag of coins.

She was unamused. "Money's not the problem. Just realize that if things get too dangerous, we're turning back."

"All right." He put away the bag.

1-05 climbed the rest of the way up the ramp and 2-45 followed her.

After they had disappeared into the spaceship, 7-43, who in his drunken state had wandered into the underground hangar, stepped out from where he was hiding behind a crate. He opened the crate and found, inside it, a bottle of liquor. "Well, well. This looks like a nice place to spend some time." He opened the bottle and took a drink. He then wandered his way up the ramp, unnoticed, into the spaceship. Inside, he found a small dark room full of crates. He toddled his way inside, dropped to the ground and drank himself into unconsciousness.

In the cockpit area, 1-05 guided 2-45 to his seat. "You've got to be secure. You don't want to fly out that window and have to find your own way to the Planet of Light." She matter-of-factly buckled him in. She then pulled a lever to adjust his seat. 2-45's seat unexpectedly began jiggling back and forth, startling 2-45. Laughing at her little joke, 1-05 moved to her pilot's seat, leaving 2-45's seat to continue rocking quickly back and forth like some type of annoying amusement park ride. 2-45 reached over and finally found the lever to stop his seat. He laughed weakly after catching his breath. "Thanks for keeping me awake."

While 1-05 was busy settling herself in the pilot's seat, Alpha 3-0-3 entered. As it stood in the doorway, its image of 1-05 wavered, transforming itself into a mass of sparkling particles. It then reassembled these particles into the form of a grey tabby cat. It quietly made its way over to 2-45 and rubbed its head against his leg. "I didn't know you owned a cat."

"I don't," she said bluntly. "That must be Alpha 3-0-3."

The shape-shifter leaped into 2-45's lap and nudged 2-45's hand as if begging to be petted. 2-45 rubbed the cat on the head, looking at it oddly, unsure of how you react to a cat that isn't really a cat.

"Prrow," said the shape-shifter. "Shhh. Don't warn her about what I'm going to do."

"How can I?" 2-45 asked. "I don't even know what you are going to do."

"Are you still playing around back there?" 1-05's eyes were fixed on the controls. "We need to be getting on our way."

The shape-shifter jumped to the floor and its image wavered and took on the shape of a handsome male co-pilot. He had medium brown hair, kind brown eyes, and a well-formed jawline. He was tall with strong shoulders and chest.

Alpha 3-0-3 quietly stepped up behind 1-05, touched her shoulder and kissed her lightly on the neck. A tear formed in 1-05's right eye as she remembered the boyfriend she lost on a journey she took several years ago. *He looks just like him. And he's my co-pilot, just like him. Maybe it can be just like those times.* 1-05 smiled at the shape-shifter. The shape-shifter raised its head higher seeing that 1-05 was pleased. It took its seat in the co-pilot's chair. It then looked over at her and winked. Back from her reverie, 1-05 lowered her head. *No, maybe not.*

The doors to the underground hangar opened and the spaceship flew out into the darkness of outer space.

Chapter Three

Being *one of* the Dark Tyrant's top Persuaders was not enough for 1-13. His ambition was to be *the top* Persuader. Everything he did and everything he thought and everything he felt was with that goal in mind. Still, his ambition did not prevent him from enjoying the advantages of his position, like the best food, the finest wines, the well-tailored clothes, and, of course, his luxuriously decorated apartment. He lounged back and smoked a hand-crafted cigar as he admired the expensive artwork on his walls. What pleased him most about his apartment was its location. It was just off his workshop, where he tortured, tormented, and tempted the souls of subjects over to the will of the Dark Tyrant.

Being so close to his work made it that much simpler to achieve his goal of progressing to the top of his profession. More than one night 1-13 had quit the comforts of his cushioned bed and silken sheets to burn a well-used candle and pore over the manuals of past Persuaders to perfect his practice. By studying these manuals, he became one of the few Persuaders with the power to control the skeleton-ghosts from the infinite pits of the abyss. Skeleton-ghosts were demonic spirits that lived in the fiery regions of the planet beneath its crust. When 1-13's mentor had informed him that the skeleton-ghosts were a strategic key to the door of true power, 1-13 set out on a journey to the abyss to seek them out. Through a series of promises, most of which 1-13 never intended to keep, he managed to ally himself with a group of six skeleton-ghosts who now lived with him in his workshop. 1-13 was pleased with how useful the skeleton-ghosts were, especially when fear was the best method to acquire a subject's cooperation. 1-13 so enjoyed using his skeleton-ghosts, and so hilarious did he find the horror in the eyes of his subjects when they saw them, that he often used them even when other means of persuasion would have worked just as well.

Right off of 1-13's workshop was a corridor of cells, each of which held a subject waiting for the moment 1-13 would administer his means of manipulation. 1-13 walked through the dark, damp hall, his head bowed, his eyes closed, and his fingertips touching his temples in meditation. Two guards trudged behind him, their footsteps keeping time with his lighter footsteps. While these guards were human, their sub-human level of intelligence did not make that apparent. But what these guards lacked in intelligence, they made up for in strength. Their massive muscles permitted them to wield axes twice their size and to cut down anyone that would dare interfere with 1-13's agenda.

As he moved through the hall, 1-13 allowed his intuition to indicate which prisoner he should bring to his workshop. He stopped in front of a cell. He raised his head and opened his eyes. In the cell was a young man with tousled reddish-brown hair and piercing blue eyes framed by thick knitted eyebrows. When the young man saw 1-13's face through the bars, he frowned, pressing his lips together to boost his willpower. 1-13 sensed the fiery nature in the young man and took it as a challenge. He brushed back one side of his cape and drew a key out of his left inside shirt pocket. After unlocking the cell door, he pulled it open with such force it clamored hard against the wall.

As the guards dragged the young man out, he struggled to free his arms. He managed to squirm himself loose long enough to swing his fist at 1-13's chin. But the guards regained a firm hold and 1-13 was spared a nasty bruise. Throughout the incident, 1-13 stood firm, not flinching at the close blow, and only a trained eye could have noticed the slight flicker of his eyelash at this near miss. In his profession, there must be no sign of weakness.

"Bring him." 1-13 signaled the guards onward.

1-13 walked alongside the prisoner. "Scholarly men have pointed out that those who lash out in *anger*, as *you* have done, are the ones most in need of *help*." 1-13 stopped and faced the young man. 1-13 rested a concerned hand on the young man's shoulder. "So, please . . . *realize* . . . I want to *help* you . . . Let me *help* you." 1-13 smiled in counterfeit concern.

The young man lifted his chin. "That's what YOU say."

"I *see*." 1-13 raised an eyebrow as he recalled a manual he had read that detailed the exact reaction he was seeing in the young man and listed the underlying emotional causes. "You may not want help *now* . . . but you *will*." He punctuated his statement with a slow, meaningful nod, his eyes fixed on the young man's eyes as if penetrating his mind with all the horrors he had in store for him. 1-13 pivoted, increasing his pace to reach the workshop ahead of the guards and prisoner.

In his workshop, 1-13 stopped at a screen in the wall and pressed a series of buttons beside it. The screen displayed a file containing information on the young prisoner. As 1-13 perused the information, the guards entered with the prisoner. Without looking away from the screen, 1-13 gestured for the guards to seat the prisoner on a couch in the center of the room. After doing so, the guards took their posts near the doors.

"So." 1-13 looked in the direction of the prisoner. "Your number is 85-27."

85-27 looked up. "So what?"

"You seem a little uptight." 1-13 stood behind the couch and placed his hands on 85-27's shoulders, noticing the tension in his muscles. "You are too worked up. *Relax*." 1-13 strolled around the couch and sat casually. As he did, he waved his hand in the air much like a conductor leading an orchestra. A tropical setting with a soothing waterfall appeared on the walls surrounding the room. The room grew dark as the lights focused on the waterfall, 1-13, and his prisoner, and opened up their brightness, spreading and contrasting with the shadows, while soft, hypnotic music played.

85-27 took all of this in with wary wonder. "What kind of game is this?" He braced himself for any other surprises.

"*This* is no game." 1-13 reached for his left inside shirt pocket and withdrew a silver pocket watch engraved with a skull. "Like I said," 1-13 slowly swung the pocket watch before 85-27's eyes, "*relax*. I am only . . . *here* . . . to *help* you."

As 85-27's eyes followed the watch, the eyes of the engraved skull glowed a ghostly green. The skull grinned and laughed ghoulishly and leaped off the watch toward 85-27. A cold sweat broke out on 85-27's face. The skull stared right into his eyes, with a cackle of insane laughter. 85-27's mouth gaped in a silent scream.

1-13 smirked as he continued to swing the watch. "Don't *fight* it. *Embrace* it."

The skull flew closer as it continued to stare 85-27 in the eyes. 85-27 kept his eyes focused on the skull's eyes, but pulled himself back. "No, get it out of here."

"I said, don't fight it. Let *us* help *you*."

"Ha, you don't want to help." 85-27 turned his head away from the skull.

The skull was absorbed back into the watch. Annoyed, 1-13 stuffed the watch into his pocket.

85-27 stood and faced 1-13. "I know you want to get information out of me. But, you're not going to get it."

1-13 pursed his lips to hide a chuckle. He found the young man's bluntness amusing. "You're a *very* clever young *man*. You're quite a bit like *me* when I was *your* age."

As 85-27 resumed his seat, he glanced at 1-13 suspiciously out of the corner of his eye.

"Yes, *I* was once a lot like *you*. So, there is *no* reason you should try to hide *anything* from me. I *understand* what you are going through."

85-27 snickered. "What I'm going through now is because of you."

"You are trying to *fight* the *inevitable*. The situation you are in is not going to your *liking* so you *reach* out and *take* it by the throat. You want to control that situation, *rein* it in." He walked away from the couch, then faced him again. "But being a *clever* man you must *realize* that it is to your *advantage* to *cooperate* with me." 1-13 raised a hand and the tropical rainforest went black. The music faded to a hum. "You work in manual labor room 15, *correct*?"

"Yes."

1-13 waved his left hand upward and a large desk rose out of the floor. "And there are several people who work with you there, *correct*?" As 1-13 stepped around the desk, he pulled from a pocket inside his cape a small silver wand engraved with skeletons. He polished the wand with the sleeve of his shirt and admired the wand's detailed engravings.

"Yes." 85-27 watched 1-13's every movement.

1-13 nodded, pleased with receiving a response to both questions. He sat at the desk. "And . . ." He folded his hands on the desk in front of him and leaned forward. ". . . certain of them are planning some type of rebellion, *correct*?"

85-27 clenched his hands together, looked down, and did not answer.

1-13 banged his fist hard on the desk. "I'm trying to help you. So answer me. Certain people you are working with are planning a rebellion, correct?"

85-27 remained silent.

"All right." 1-13 rose from his chair and stepped forward from behind the desk. He lowered his head but still looked straight into 85-27's eyes. "You will regret not cooperating with me sooner." He held out his hands in front of him with the palms facing upward. As he slowly raised his hands, two snake-like spires of smoke rose from the floor on either side of him. When his hands were level with his head, he faced his palms toward 85-27 and pushed them forward. By the power of his movement, the spires of smoke rushed toward 85-27 and wrapped themselves around him, lifting him from the couch. 1-13 sent a couple more spires of smoke toward 85-27 and these spires pushed him against a metal post near the couch. The smoke spires wound around 85-27 and the post until it was impossible for him to free himself.

85-27 fought with the smoke, but the more he tried to squirm free, the more the smoke burned his flesh. He realized there was no way free. His anger and fear merged in a confused combination and pulled him deep within himself. He closed his eyes tight and in his mind's eye he saw one thing that gave him hope, a bright star in a black sky. *Just keep your eyes focused on that light.*

1-13 started toward 85-27, but before he reached him, the door opened and in slithered one of the Dark Tyrant's spies. 1-13 lifted a hand and the lights came on throughout the room. The creature wriggled past 1-13, slipping right over his feet. 1-13 looked down at the creature with the warmth of a father toward his child. He held a special fondness for the Dark Tyrant's spies. There was a time when these spies were merely mechanical robots, no life or emotion in them at all. But, by 1-13's advice, these robots were raised to a much higher standard. 1-13 worked with a group of expert biologists, mechanical engineers, and computer specialists, and, by combining the dependency of a mechanical robot with the zealous loyalty of a living creature, they were able to create the snake-like creatures that became known as the Dark Tyrant's spies.

The snake creature wriggled its way over to 1-13's desk and stopped. It looked back with its binocular eyes focusing on 1-13. It made a little questioning chirp like a child asking its parents for something it cannot reach. 1-13 smiled and his heart leapt within him at his own creation's dependency on him. He took three steps to his desk and tenderly picked up the creature, raising it high enough for it to slither onto the desk. "There you go," he said as the creature purred contentedly, rubbing its head on 1-13's hand. "So what are you doing way over here, hm?" He stroked the creature gently. The creature refocused its binoculars on 1-13's eyes, and hissed, twittered, and squeaked until 1-13 grasped what it was saying. "Oh, the Dark Tyrant wants to talk with me? . . . Right away? . . . It's very important? . . . Very well." The creature answered each of 1-13's questions with an enthusiastic nod. 1-13 smiled fondly down at the creature and picked it up into his arms.

Knitting his eyebrows in frustration, 1-13 turned to 85-27. He pressed a button on his silver wand three times. The wand sent out three high-pitched screeches. From hidden crevices in the corners of the room oozed a light green smoke. The smoke swirled and danced near the ceiling until it slowly drizzled to the floor. As it descended it took on the form of three ghostly skeletons embalmed in ghastly green smoke.

"Ah . . . My beautifully frightening creatures." 1-13 held his hand out toward them as if to embrace them with enthusiastic admiration. The skeleton-ghosts looked down at him with a disdainful pride, a look 1-13 either did not notice or considered the usual expression of skeleton-ghosts. 1-13, followed by the skeleton-ghosts, stepped over to 85-27. The skeleton-ghosts loomed down at 85-27 as they surrounded him. "My dear friends will now babysit you while I am gone. They know very well how to put you in the state of mind I will require when I come back. I assure you that when I return you *will* eagerly answer every question I *ask*." 1-13 gave the skeleton-ghosts a nod, releasing them to use whatever means they wished, and made his way out of the room with the Dark Tyrant's spy held protectively in his arms.

Chapter Four

Upon reaching a level of mastery in their careers, Persuaders were assigned apprentices to assist them with their duties. This apprenticeship program had its advantages. Apprentices could take care of menial odd jobs for the Persuaders, who trained the apprentices to eventually become Persuaders themselves. Among these apprentices was a young man with sandy blond hair whose number was 50-83. He was at first assigned to work for 1-13. However, when 1-13 learned he was required to let his apprentices in on his professional secrets, he made up his mind he wanted no part of the apprenticeship program. He threw 50-83 out of his workshop, declaring his skeleton-ghosts were more use to him than a slew of apprentices. It was only because 1-13 had a reputation for success that the human resource professionals allowed him to forego the use of apprentices and 50-83 was re-assigned to 6-96.

While 1-13 was *one* of the top Persuaders to the Dark Tyrant, 6-96 was *the top* Persuader. She was tall, with pale, nearing titanium white skin that appeared even whiter when contrasted with her stark blood-red lipstick. Her hair was blue-black and framed her diamond-shaped face much like the button-top of a mushroom. She wore a tight-fitting black leather jump-suit adorned with silver zippers and silver-buckled belts around her wrists, waist, and boots. While 1-13's methods of persuasion leaned more toward mental manipulations, 6-96 preferred deadly threats, gruesome dismemberment, and painful torture. These methods produced a higher body count than 1-13's methods, but she acquired results more quickly and cheaply, therefore producing more persuasions per week than any of the other Persuaders.

As one entered 6-96's workshop, the walls were made of reflective steel, but deeper within, the milieu devolved into primordial stone walls lit by grim orange lights along the baseboard. Her preferred area to torture her subjects was a hollowed-out cave-like corner of the room. On a table in this corner was strapped a nearly lifeless man. His clothes were in tatters from the tortures he had endured. His eyes were wide and sunken with lack of sleep. Deep knife wounds on his forehead and arms bled profusely. He had a large gaping wound on his chest and the skin on his wrists was worn raw from fighting to free himself from his bonds. The straps across his chest were so tight they caused his broken ribs to puncture his lungs. Blood oozed from his mouth as he fought to breathe.

6-96 handled a blood-stained ivory knife. She tested its sharpness across her thumb as she casually circled the table. "You're afraid, aren't you? . . . Fear builds up . . . That's good . . . Fear is the greatest survival instinct . . . Right now it is telling you to save yourself while you can. Those friends of yours, THEY would turn you in to save themselves. Why should YOU die to save THEM?" She held the knife against the skin near his left eye. "Maybe instead of killing you quickly I should first gouge out one of your eyes, first your left one . . . and then your right one . . . and then . . . well, this could go on and on." She pressed the knife so close to his eye a drop of blood formed.

50-83 entered the dimly lit workshop. Other than a white jacquard vest with gold buttons, he was shirtless. His pants were silken white with the legs tucked into knee-high white boots. Though 50-83 did not boast the muscles of a weightlifter, he was still athletically built. Around his neck, he wore a gold necklace with a crystal sphere pendant. 50-83 was intelligent, hard-working, and willing to do whatever was necessary to accomplish his tasks. Even though he was young, his eyebrows were knitted either with purpose or defiance and his jawline was firm, more from suppressing his thoughts than from determination to follow orders. However, upon meeting him, the first thing people noticed was how shy and innocent he seemed. What gave people this impression was the way he avoided their eyes. He did not do this out of shyness, though, but because, being a compulsive liar, he feared if people looked him in the eyes, they would know he was lying.

Ever since he was young, 50-83 told lies as a means of self-preservation. Once, when he was ten, he and a close friend had sneaked out into the wilderness area of the planet, a dangerous place, off limits to all humans. The sandy soil continually bubbled and churned, being cooked by the burning fires within the planet. Often the soil became so hot fires would burst out spontaneously. The area was also notorious for its numerous deep, dark crater pits, so deep that, if someone fell into one of them, there was no way out. To attest to this fact numerous human skeletons littered the bottom of each of these craters. Lurking in these craters and behind the many giant rocks and dead logs in the wilderness wild creatures lay in wait to maul and eat the flesh of any unsuspecting passersby. Growing in the shade of these rocks were vine-like plants that shot up and wrapped themselves around whoever came near, binding their victims tighter and tighter until every bone in their bodies was broken and the breath of life was squeezed out of them.

Despite their reckless natures, 50-83 and his friend, with some luck, managed to sneak past each of these dangers and make their way to the mountainous region of the planet. Some mountains were low enough to climb easily and others were so high that even an expert mountain climber would dread to scale the steep slopes. This was the area where the towering dead trees stood as monuments of a time when, it was rumored, life once flourished in this region. 50-83 climbed the slope of one of the mountains and discovered that, because the soil of the slope was loose, he could slide down the slope with his feet as if on skis. His friend soon joined in the game and in no time they both were enthralled with racing one another down the slope.

It was not long before they were discovered by a swarm of the Dark Tyrant's spies who immediately sent pictures to the Dark Tyrant of the young boys playing on the mountain slopes. A group of Enforcers arrived and the boys were brought in for punishment. They stood apprehensively before the Dark Tyrant and his Legal Examiners in the scorching, oppressive executive hall.

The Dark Tyrant looked down on them with his furious eyes on fire. His smog-like form paced back and forth, smoke sputtering from his nostrils as he derided the boys for their disobedience. A cold sweat broke out on the forehead of 50-83's friend and he burst into a panicked confession of his crime. Through tears, he begged the Dark Tyrant for mercy. The boy looked up into the faces of the Legal Examiners and they all coldly and condemningly shook their heads. The Dark Tyrant stretched out his claw-like fingers and wrapped them around the boy's throat. "Mercy?" the Dark Tyrant chuckled, "I will show you how merciful I am." He consequently rewarded the boy by grabbing a handful of six inferno darts and jabbing them right into his chest. The darts burst into flames within the boy's body and in seconds he was nothing but ashes.

50-83's eyes widened as he watched this take place. He wanted to scream, rush forward, and find some way to undo what had just happened. But, he saw the Dark Tyrant, his assistants, and his guards all surrounding him, glaring down at him ready to give him the same treatment if whatever actions he chose were not to the Dark Tyrant's approval. As a result, 50-83 forced his body into inaction and grew numb. He concluded that since his friend was killed because he told the truth, to avoid a similar fate, he must not tell the truth. He took a deep breath and searched his mind for a way to convince himself to believe what was true was not true and what was not true was. He then was able to "honestly" persuade the Dark Tyrant that it was not his idea to go to the wilderness area, that it was his friend who insisted, that he tried to warn his friend they should go back but that it was his friend who had refused, that he *had* always and *will* always do exactly what the Dark Tyrant ordered. He lied so believably he managed to convince everyone, including himself, all his lies were true. The Dark Tyrant reached a smoky claw forward and patted him on the shoulder. 50-83 was forgiven and set free.

It was not long before 6-96 became aware of 50-83's tendency to lie. She revealed to 50-83 that, depending on how he cultivated it, his ability to lie could either become a terrible burden or a useful talent. If it came to the point where he was unable to differentiate between when he told a lie and when he told the truth, his lying would control him. If he could learn to control his lies and recognize when he was lying, his ability could help him work his way up in the ranks of the Persuaders. To assist him in cultivating his gift, she had a crystal sphere created. He wore this sphere on a gold chain around his neck. When he held the crystal sphere in his hands, the sphere homed in on his exact feelings and thoughts. The sphere would ask him questions and 50-83 would answer them. The sphere detected whether 50-83 answered the questions truthfully or not. The difficulty was, though, that 50-83 often convinced himself so deeply his own lies were the truth that even the sphere could not tell whether what 50-83 was thinking and feeling was the truth or not.

In 6-96's workshop, 50-83 heard her subject gasping for breath as he confessed the numbers of those involved in their assassination attempt. 50-83 winced at the man's painful moans. He knew her knife had accomplished its task. Blood was dripping from the throat of the man on the table. His head leaned to one side, eyes fixed on 50-83. A tear trickled from the man's eyes. 50-83's heart fell within him.

6-96 took a cloth from a shelf on the wall and wiped down the blade of her knife. She laughed once, thrilled with her success, and placed her knife back in the sheath on the belt around her right thigh. Looking up, she noticed 50-83 standing in the doorway. "Another task finished successfully."

50-83 swallowed a sob and forced a smile. "Yes." His eyes actually sparkled with admiration. "Very well done."

6-96 crossed her arms across her chest and looked down on 50-83. "So . . . I assume you didn't come here just to admire my work."

"No . . ." 50-83 knitted his eyebrows, unsure of what reply 6-96 was wanting. "I mean . . . yes . . . Well . . . there was a message. The Dark Tyrant wants to speak with you in his executive hall."

"Ah, I will see that it is to my advantage." She snapped her fingers and gestured for 50-83 to approach her.

50-83 knew 6-96's orders were to be carried out immediately. Parts of the room were so dark that, after taking a couple steps, he tripped and fell over something on the ground in his path. He felt that he had fallen into warm mud all jumbled with something he could not tell what it was. He tried to find a firm place to set his left hand so he could balance himself as he attempted to stand, but instead his hand sank into what seemed like some deep pit in the mud lined with twigs. 6-96 turned on another light. 50-83 turned cold all over when he realized he had fallen into a pile of corpses and his hand had sunk into where one of the corpse's stomachs would have been.

"Stand up," 6-96 commanded.

After gingerly removing his hand from the corpse, 50-83 shakily rose to his feet. He glanced down and noticed his white vest and pants were covered in blood. "I'm sorry, ma'am. I'm afraid I wasn't looking where I was going." He gestured toward the pile of corpses. As he did, his eyes followed his hand and he saw it was also covered with blood. He grimaced trying to devise a way to discretely remove the stains. When nothing came to mind, he gave in and wiped his hand off on his white jacquard vest.

"You clumsy thing." She slapped him across the face and looked at his clothes with disgust. "Now you're an ugly mess. Remove these bodies to the furnace and clean yourself before I return." She marched past him.

"Yes, ma'am." 50-83 stepped out of her way to let her pass. As he did, he almost tripped backwards but caught himself by placing a hand on a nearby dead tree. A hissing sound caught his ears. 50-83 froze. The tree was home to several slithering snakes. 6-96 came back and eagerly drew 50-83's attention to what he finally realized was not several snakes but one seven-headed snake curled around the tree. One of its heads was reaching forward to bite 50-83's hand.

"Ah . . . It looks like you've upset my new pet. Remember, one bite and you will be enslaved by its venom."

50-83 pulled his hand away just in time.

6-96 laughed and patted 50-83 on the cheek. "Be good . . ." She waved a scolding finger at him then strode out of the room.

50-83 backed away from the tree. The snake's seven heads rose one at a time, watching 50-83 mistrustfully. 50-83 lifted one eyebrow, his eyes still fixed on the snake's heads. He took two more steps away. No longer considering 50-83 a threat, the snake lowered its heads. He turned from the snake and looked at the pile of bodies on the ground. He grimaced and wiped his hands once more on his vest. He shook his head. The bodies could wait. Instead, he decided to find himself a safe dark corner far away from all annoyances. He sat in this corner and removed his necklace. He held the crystal pendant in his hands. The pendant lit into a yellow glowing ball and floated above his hands.

"Good day to you, 50-83. And how are you feeling?" the crystal asked in a pleasant female voice.

"I'm very happy, thank you." He smiled, even though, deep inside, he was afraid and alone.

"Very good," the crystal said. "Yes, I can tell you are happy. Now, what are your thoughts in regards to your work?"

"It is going very well, thank you. I enjoy my job. I like working for 6-96 and I look forward to proving myself to my superiors." Yet 50-83 found working as an apprentice to 6-96 stressful and depressing.

"Excellent. Yes, I can tell you enjoy your job and all its challenges. Now, tell me, is anything worrying you?"

50-83 stared at the crystal sphere. He took a deep breath to hide the sorrow that was forming in his throat. "No," he smiled, "nothing is worrying me . . ."

"Wonderful," the crystal replied jubilantly.

1-13 approached the double-door to the Dark Tyrant's executive hall. Outside, 6-96 was waiting. "About time you got here. What took you so long? Busy pickling your latest witch's brew?" She laughed.

1-13 held the spy creature in his arms and scratched it behind where its ears would have been if it had any. "I fail to see the humor in that remark." His eyes fell to the spy creature as it purred. He stepped up to the door, lifting a hand to push it open.

"You fail to see a lot of things." She pushed his arm down from the door. "Like for instance that you're losing your ability as a Persuader faster than *that*." She snapped her fingers to accentuate the point. "I've even heard some say that if they had to choose who to be persuaded by, they would pick you. That isn't exactly a compliment."

The Dark Tyrant's spy in 1-13's arms focused its eyes on 6-96 and bared its fangs with a sharp hiss. 1-13 glared at 6-96 as he continued to pet the creature. He then released the creature to the freedom of the floor. "I would take those remarks back if I were you." He spoke as calmly as possible through clenched teeth.

6-96 crossed her arms and raised her chin high. "I never take back a truthful remark."

Her disdain so infuriated 1-13 that his logical reasoning, for a moment, left him. "You —" He rushed at her, mentally ready to tear her to pieces.

6-96 grabbed his wrist with one hand and his shoulder with the other and slammed him against the wall. She held him there with her hands clutching his upper arms. "So," she snorted a laugh in his face, "you've just demonstrated that you really are unfit for your position as a Persuader. Tell me . . . what was it we were taught about NOT losing our temper?"

1-13 closed his eyes and took a deep breath to regain his calm. He glared at her through narrowed eyes. "Very well. All right. Just let me go." He tried to pull himself out of her firm grasp, but she did not release him.

"I think you need me to teach you my methods of persuasion." She brought her face and body uncomfortably close to his.

1-13 drew himself as far away from her as the wall would allow. "Your methods are disgusting."

"Yes. But mine are much more effective. Perhaps I should demonstrate how I slowly peel away the skin from the bodies of my victims . . . Or how I chop their fingers and toes off one by one."

1-13 leaned heavier upon the wall as he was overcome by a moment of light-headedness.

"Too weak to learn the art of true torture, I see. You'll never get any higher in the ranks if you don't let me teach you." She looked down at him.

1-13's eyes fell, too uneasy to meet her gaze. "I told you, I don't need your help."

6-96 chuckled. "You do need my help. But if I were to teach you anything, you wouldn't survive." She stepped back, grabbed him by the front of his shirt, and shoved him aside.

1-13 caught his balance and steadied his shaking nerves. He ran a hand over his shirt and cape to make certain they had not been wrinkled.

A guard stepped out of the executive hall and held the doors open for 1-13 and 6-96 to enter. 6-96 thrust herself in front of 1-13 and entered the hall first. 1-13 brushed his shirt off once more and kneeled to pick the spy creature back up from the ground before following 6-96 in.

The Dark Tyrant's executive hall was covered in a smoky black humid mist. The second 1-13 entered the room, it was an effort for him to breathe, as if a strong grip was around his throat, choking him. Standing in the foyer of the hall, 1-13 looked down over the railing. Below was a deep pit filled with burning, smoking lava. Out of this lava protruded the flailing limbs and the expressionless faces of those whom the Dark Tyrant deemed unfit to continue as citizens of his realm. Once the Dark Tyrant sent a subject into the lava pit, the subject was braised, boiled, and burned until the subject realized their place in society as absolute nothingness. At that point the subject was allowed to bubble up from the lava pit and take its place next to the Dark Tyrant's throne as spineless, shapeless goo. These goo creatures would wallow about blubbing and blobbing with one another until the moment the Dark Tyrant said something that must be emphasized. When he did, the goo creatures would raise themselves up several inches and form their shapeless selves into mask-like faces that agreed whole-heartedly with whatever the Dark Tyrant had said.

Immediately afterwards, they slumped back down to their state of goo-ish nothingness.

A long, narrow bridge over the lava pit connected the foyer to the executive hall. No matter how many times 1-13 had crossed the bridge, he still felt uneasy. Though he avoided looking down, the anguished wails of the victims, the burbling of the lava, and the smell of burning flesh all gave him a vivid picture of what was taking place below. He focused on the point straight ahead of him and listened only to the rapid beating of his own heart as he crossed to the other side of the bridge. Once across, 1-13 was in the Dark Tyrant's executive hall. On the far wall was a black marble archway leading to a dark shadowy room. No one but the Dark Tyrant had ever entered this room. The executive hall itself was lit by intense squares of red light placed intermittently in the hall's floor. These red lights blended eerily with the dark shadows and the fiery glow from the lava pit. In the walls were built various glowing maps and globes monitoring the movements of the subjects of the planet.

1-13 took his place next to 6-96 who stood tall in front of the dark archway. She held her head confidently, her hands placed behind her back in anticipation of the Dark Tyrant's arrival. The floor in front of the archway filled with a burning black smog. 1-13 stepped backwards to ensure that the smog did not touch his newly polished shoes. The black smoky mass billowed out of the archway and formed a spire of smoke and fire. The smoky spire built itself up until it filled the archway and took on the shape of a dragon with red glowing eyes and a burning belly of fire. He reached out his long claws as he plodded into the hall. He turned his head to 6-96 and 1-13. As he did, he opened his mouth wide, roaring, and a burst of flames spewed out of his mouth.

6-96 stepped forward. "Dark Tyrant, we are here as you commanded."

The Dark Tyrant scratched the side of his cheek in thought as the fire within his belly burned even stronger. "Yes, I see."

His voice crackled and boomed like an ear-piercing combination of explosions, earthquakes, and tornados. The Dark Tyrant's dragon-form faded as he turned his head around and shot a glaring eye at the spy creature in 1-13's arms. The Dark Tyrant's head slowly took on a human form. "Put that creature down," he commanded, and even though his appearance changed, his voice was just as loud and harsh.

1-13 shifted his weight and looked at the Dark Tyrant askance. "Didn't you send this little creature to me with the message for me to come? I thought it only right to return him to you." 1-13 held the spy creature out to the Dark Tyrant.

The Dark Tyrant stretched his claw-like fingers out and wrapped them tightly around the spy creature's throat. He picked the creature up and tossed it hard to the other side of the hall.

1-13's mouth dropped in concern. He stepped toward the spy creature but stopped when he noticed the Dark Tyrant glaring at him. He noted that the spy creature, while a bit dazed, was still alive. Reassured, he stood at attention before the Dark Tyrant.

The Dark Tyrant's smoggy form slunk over to the monitor. "Over here." He pointed to a monitor screen in the wall. 6-96 and 1-13 stationed themselves around him. He touched the monitor. Out of the monitor's screen floated the hologram of a globe that mapped out the Planet of Darkness. "We have two areas of concern." The Dark Tyrant's hands hovered over the globe and traced its boundaries. "And I want you two to address them." He pointed a claw toward an area outside of the map. A visual representation of 1-05's spaceship flew out of the planet's atmosphere. "Notice something?"

"Someone is trying to leave the planet," 6-96 sneered. "But, why should that concern us? We are Persuaders. You have Control Fleets to bring them back."

The Dark Tyrant's face melted into the form of a snake. "Rebellion has been brewing among my subjects. These two areas could be starting points for this rebellion. 1-13."

"Yes?" 1-13 stepped forward.

"When my Control fleet brings that ship back, I want you to question everyone onboard. I want to know every plot in their brains."

"Very well." 1-13 gave a quick bow of his head.

6-96 placed her hands on her hips and wrinkled up her nose in disapproval. The Dark Tyrant pointed a claw toward her and directed her attention back to the globe-like map. The next location highlighted was in the populated area of the planet. The Dark Tyrant waved his hands over the globe and the face of 2,040 appeared on the screen. He was a middle-aged man whose hair and beard were starting to grey. Even though his light blue eyes were mirthful, his mouth curled up in a condescending and plotting way. 2,040 was the Dark Tyrant's top Researcher for the Economics of Production. His job was to analyze all the manual labor rooms and to find ways to extract more work out of the workers without any extra cost to the government.

"Are you saying he's behind the rebellion?" 1-13 asked.

"No," the Dark Tyrant growled, his face once more resembling a human, "not necessarily. But he could be." He put a clawed hand on one of 6-96's shoulders. "You will find out everything about him. Question everyone who comes into contact with him. There is something he is hiding. I want to know what it is."

"Am I free to use whatever methods I choose?"

"Yes. But do not kill him or any of his contacts until I give you permission."

1-13's eyes strayed from the Dark Tyrant to the monitor as a sudden glowing light on the globe drew his attention. At first this light pulsed slowly. Then it quickened. Raising one eyebrow, he examined it closely. Within the light was the image of a young, beautiful blonde-haired woman. Her hair was long and wavy, and her blue eyes drew his toward her own, and his head and heart lightened. 1-13 pointed out her picture. "And what about her?"

The Dark Tyrant jerked his head around. Upon noticing the young woman's picture, he spewed a disgusted burst of fire. "So, more rebellion . . ."

"I will question her," 1-13 offered.

The Dark Tyrant grabbed 1-13 by the throat and dragged him to the lava pit. "Don't ever tell me what to do. Understand?" He held 1-13 over the lava pit. 1-13 gulped, for his dangling feet nearly touched the lava. He squeezed his eyes shut, certain he was doomed to die. A panicked sweat trickled down his face. "No, please! I beg you." 1-13 glanced from the Dark Tyrant to the lava pit beneath his feet. The Dark Tyrant snorted in disdain. He released 1-13 by merely letting go of his throat. If 1-13 had not caught the edge of the pit in time, he would have fallen in. A hand of one of the doomed souls in the fiery pit clutched 1-13's ankle. 1-13 held onto the edge and pulled hard to free himself from the nearly formless soul. The grasp on his foot was tight and 1-13 only managed to free himself by prying off his shoe, sending it with the soul back into the pit. 1-13 clambered over the edge of the pit in one piece minus the shoe. Straightening his clothes and hair with his hands, he returned to 6-96 and the Dark Tyrant.

6-96 laughed, and the Dark Tyrant raised his head with superiority. The Dark Tyrant gestured toward 6-96. "You will handle this for me. Find out everything you can about her, what it is she is plotting, everything — even if you have to kill her." 1-13 raised a concerned eyebrow. "After all," the Dark Tyrant continued with a sneer, "*she* is expendable."

The goo creatures slugged up near the Dark Tyrant and raised themselves to form contorted faces. "Yeeesss," they moaned in blind acquiescence. "Yeesss. Sheee issss expendable."

The Dark Tyrant ignored their obsequious interjection and waved an indifferent claw for 6-96 and 1-13 to leave.

1-13 lowered his eyes. He shuffled his way to the spy creature, and picked it up, looking it over for any broken bones. He petted the creature to calm it and carried it tenderly out of the executive hall.

A short distance north of the main populated area of the Planet of Darkness was a small community designated for the 3.5% of the population who did practically nothing. They were normal human beings born with the potential to think and work like any other citizen of the Planet of Darkness. Only by command of the Dark Tyrant, they were not allowed to think or work. The Dark Tyrant's social experts found that, to keep a balance, 3.5% of the population had to do nothing but exist. This percentage became known as the Slump-Bumps. They lived in small hovel-like huts where they had all their basic needs provided for, food, water, and shelter. They could do anything absolutely necessary for existence as long as they stayed within the area designated for Slump-Bumps. What they were not allowed to do was work, play, party, and above all else, they were not permitted to think. In fact, any Slump-Bump who engaged in any of these activities was punished with painful deaths.

Among these Slump-Bumps was 4,021, the young woman 1-13 had seen on the Dark Tyrant's monitor. The misomerth creatures were humming eerily in the mud outside the hovels of the Slump-Bumps. 4,021 sat on the ground and gazed out at the dark sky as her long blonde hair and the gossamer white sleeves and hemline flares of her dress fluttered in the soft breeze.

Another Slump-Bump, 5-68, a neighbor of 4,021, stepped out of his hovel and sat on a wooden rocking chair in the middle of his muddy plot of ground. He was a middle-aged man, stocky and dark, and had smooth black hair with bangs that nearly covered his eyes. With eyes half closed and mouth half open, he made himself comfortable in his rocking chair. Every time he rocked, the chair creaked loudly.

4,021 closed her eyes and raised her eyebrows hopefully. She heaved a deep sigh.

5-68 stopped rocking and frowned. "Hey." He spoke loud enough for 4,021 to hear. "What was that?"

4,021 looked up at the stars in the sky. "A sigh." She noticed a pin-point of light that was brighter than the others.

He knitted his eyebrows, a little worried. "A sigh? What caused that sigh?"

"I thought of something."

"Now, watch yourself," he warned her, noticing a bug crawling up his pant leg. "You know better. We aren't supposed to think." The bug continued to crawl up his leg, but 5-68 knew he was not allowed to exert the amount of work necessary to brush off the bug.

"But the thought came from a dream. Certainly they can't outlaw dreams."

5-68 yawned. "If they lead to thoughts, they can."

4,021 placed the palms of her hands together in front of her and continued to look up, a soft smile on her lips. "The dream was about a man, the most wonderful man in the world. He came in a magnificent spaceship and he picked me up in his arms and carried me away from this planet."

"Why would that make you sigh?"

"The sigh was just how much I wished it could come true." She gazed once more at the pin-point of bright light, and again she sighed. There was no doubt in her mind the sigh traveled all the way through space and reached that pin-point of light.

Chapter Five

The pinpoint of light 4,021 had seen was the Planet of Light. Her sigh was propelled by such emotion that it broke through the atmosphere of the Planet of Light and orbited into the view of the telescope belonging to the prince of that planet. He stood on one of the many verandahs that branched out from the council hall. The council hall was built of light beige bricks trimmed with gold. Red and pink roses vined their way up the sides of the building. The verandah's railing was constructed of marble and on each baluster was engraved the likeness of one of the upholders of truth from ancient times.

The prince's name was Infinity. He stepped back from the telescope. His determined eyes, arched over with black knitted brows, penetrated the night sky as the breeze tousled his short, black waves. His tall, slender form and broad shoulders were a stalwart shadow against the moonlight. His chin was set so firmly, the sides of his face were drawn in with thought. His face was lit with compassion, glowing so brightly that his subjects focused less on his features and more on the fact that he was loving, kind, brave, and intelligent.

He wore a black and red duvetyn vest over a white silk shirt. His duvetyn pants were black with a thin stripe of red down each side and his tall knee-high black boots folded over at the top. Infinity looked through the telescope once more to reaffirm the desperation within the sigh. He rounded the telescope and leaned his hands on the verandah's railing as he glared passed the cascade of waterfalls and foliage on the horizon of the Planet of Light into the depth of space and towards the Planet of Darkness.

"That planet reeks with cruelty and evil." He slammed his fist on the verandah's railing. "I must find a way to rescue those who want out before it is too late."

"I'm pleased to hear you say that." Infinity heard the familiar rich, smooth voice of his father, the King. The tone of his voice was such that he could command a legion of troops or comfort a baby in a crib. Infinity turned to his father, who stepped from the council room into the doorway of the verandah. His dark hair and beard lent him dignity, and his glimmering brown eyes shone with compassion. He wore a light-blue embroidered surcoat over a white tunic. His beige pants were tucked into dark brown ankle-high boots.

On his way to his father, Infinity took a book with worn leather binding from a latticed garden table. He drew his finger across the title. "*The Destruction of Bercolar.*" His eyes narrowed. "We see the pattern forming. History does repeat itself. Astronomy and history speak, but too many fail to listen."

"You are right." The King patted his son's shoulder. "Too many don't see the patterns in politics either. Thankfully our councilmembers can discern them. I have just finished speaking to them and they all agree with you that something must be done about the Planet of Darkness." The King looked down, saddened by the thought of the inevitable destruction. Not long ago, he had sent several waves of spies to the Planet of Darkness. Many of the spies met with torture and painful deaths, but a few survived to bring back reports. The all-too-clear images from their reports of the cruel treatment and suffering of its citizens would remain fixed in his mind. He met his son's eyes and spoke with renewed energy. "People are suffering on that planet under the dictatorship of the Dark Tyrant. We must put an end to his brutality. But, I can't help thinking of the great risk you would be taking in traveling to that place."

"A risk I am not afraid to take, father." Infinity returned his determined focus toward the Planet of Darkness. "They don't know the destruction they are facing and how to get out. I can help them. I *will* help them."

"I don't want to send you on this mission." The King grasped Infinity's upper arms and shook him. "You're my only son, my only child, and it would hurt me to lose you." A lump formed in his throat as he remembered the days of the revolt. The Dark Tyrant had tried to lure a portion of the citizens off the Planet of Light. As the Dark Tyrant raced to his space transport, Infinity intercepted him and plunged his sword into the Dark Tyrant's neck. The Dark Tyrant clutched his neck in pain and screeched, "You won't stop me. One day I will be back to destroy the Planet of Light. If we ever face each other again, I swear I will kill you." And he scurried to his space transport and flew off with his followers to the Planet of Darkness.

"Yes, but how can I not take this risk for them?" Infinity gazed with concern past the cloudless blue sky in the direction of the Planet of Darkness.

Tears stood in the King's eyes as he nodded. "Yes, they need you there and I taught you there is no glory in shunning danger." The King recalled the years he had spent training his son in skills such as fencing, horsemanship, target practice, battle strategy, and leadership. His heart had warmed as he watched his son excel in each area, many times outdoing even him. "You may go with my blessing." The King embraced Infinity, his tears streaming down his cheek.

"I will miss you." Infinity rested his hand on his father's back. "I promise I will make you proud of me."

"I already am, son."

While the Planet of Light was only 460 million units from the galaxy's sun, much closer than the 900 million units between the Planet of Darkness and that sun, still 460 million units was not quite close enough to grant the Planet of Light the full benefit of that sun. Instead, the planet's energy source was an inner light in the atmosphere generated when the water in the planet's numerous giant waterfalls flowed over the litho-stones that made up a large part of its surface. This light not only brightened the planet but also kept the planet at a comfortable temperature and, along with a balanced rotation of moisture from the pure lakes and waterfalls throughout the planet, encouraged a healthy growth of vegetation. Flowering vines and a variety of medicinal herbs brightened the mountains just outside of the city, and blossoming trees and bushes lined the streets within the city, providing homes for flocks of colorful birds.

But light and litho-stones were not the only commodities that caused the Planet of Light to be a valued place to live. Both the King and his son, Infinity, ruled the planet with freedom and justice. Punishments were rarely needed because, due to the fine examples provided by the King and his son, the citizens of the Planet of Light knew in their hearts how to live peacefully with each other. They had compassion for one another, they valued one another, and they had a sense of logic to tell them what was right and what was wrong. Since the people could be, for the most part, trusted to rule themselves, the main duties of the King and councilmembers was to listen to petitions from the people and protect the Planet of Light from any attacks from outside planets.

The King and Infinity entered the council hall through the arched doorway. The councilmembers stood from their seats at the large triangle-shaped table made of well-polished ebony and bowed their heads in their direction. The father and son stepped forward and stood in their place at the head of the table, the point of the triangle. Along one side of the room were arched open windows letting in the outdoor moonlight along with a cool lavender-scented breeze. Along the other side were seven golden pillars with mauve drapes hung between each one. The drapes were pulled back between the five central pillars revealing four historical paintings. The first painting depicted the time when the King brought light to this planet. The second painting showed the King guiding people to their new homes on the Planet of Light. The third painting showed groups of people deserting the Planet of Light for the Planet of Darkness. And, the last painting showed Infinity standing in front of a path leading to the Planet of Darkness holding a sign that warned of danger.

The King gestured for the councilmembers to be seated. "Councilmembers," the King addressed them, "many of our meetings for the past several years have been over one particular subject, the senseless suffering of those living on the Planet of Darkness. As we know, people are living on the Planet of Darkness because groups of our own citizens left this planet, drawn there by the shadows they assumed would hide their crimes. While we are saddened that anyone would choose to live in cruelty and darkness, we know that not everyone who lives on the Planet of Darkness wants to stay there. There are those who were born on the Planet of Darkness and don't know what it is like to live on a planet with fresh air and healthy life-giving light. Many of those people long for a chance to come to our planet and start a new life.

"Even today," the King continued, "three desperate cries from the Planet of Darkness were brought to my attention. I could sense a hope in those cries, a hope of one day reaching our planet, and that hope is the only thing that gives these three people the courage to continue. And my son has seen one of these cries. It was a sigh of such desperation that it moved him to take on the perilous journey to the Planet of

Darkness to bring back any person who wishes to start a new life here on the Planet of Light."

At first a hushed stillness fell over the council room followed by a rush of surprise and amazed murmurs.

The King raised his hand. "Yes, my son is well aware of the dangers he will be facing in undertaking this mission, but he knows this is something that must be done and he is . . ." The King looked in his son's direction with tender admiration. ". . . willing to risk his life for this cause." He took a breath to mask his deep concern for his son's safety. "I will now cede the floor to my son, Infinity. He will inform you of his plans and how each of you can help him with this journey."

The councilmembers applauded as Infinity stepped forward. "I am grateful to each of you." He raised his hands in appreciation and the clapping of the councilmembers slowly ceased. Infinity took in the faces of each of the councilmembers and smiled. "We are thankful for all you have done for us. You have stood by us, and it is because of you that the Planet of Light is a haven of peace in a galaxy of war. But, war may be coming our way. The Planet of Darkness continues to bar its citizens from making their way to the safety of our planet. And if the Dark Tyrant insists on continuing to prevent them from coming here through a show of violence, we are not afraid to fight him.

"I am even now making preparations to travel to the Planet of Darkness. I will protect and bring back anyone there who wants safe passage to our Planet of Light. All I ask from you is your help. Will you help me in my preparations, on my journey, and in any battle the Dark Tyrant may force upon me?"

The twelve councilmembers stood and enthusiastically offered their help in all stages of the mission. Infinity delegated the jobs for preparation accordingly: the four councilmembers on the left side of the table were to ready Infinity's spaceship, the four councilmembers at the far end of the table were to equip Infinity's armor, and the four councilmembers on the right side would assist in preparing his weapons.

"I thank all of you for your generous assistance. But it is also important that you prepare your hearts for battle, because I know the Dark Tyrant will try to prevent me from carrying out my mission and a battle with his forces is inevitable. I will need everyone who is willing to fight. When I arrive on the Planet of Darkness, I will look for signs that a battle is imminent. At that time, I will signal you by creating a portal in the Planet of Darkness' atmosphere which will extend to the Planet of Light. You and the forces you will bring will be able to pass through this portal to the Planet of Darkness, but you will not be able to return by the portal, so be prepared for a long journey back home by ship. When you see the portal form in front of the lookout tower, that will be your signal to join me in battle against the evil tyrant and his legions."

The councilmembers stood and shouted their whole-hearted support for the King and Infinity, lifting their fists in the air with zeal.

The King beamed. "Your willingness to support my son in this dangerous venture pleases me. I offer you my blessings as you leave now and make ready for my son's departure."

As the councilmembers were leaving and discussing among themselves their volunteered tasks, Infinity slipped out alone to organize one last thing.

Before Infinity proceeded to the hangar, he stopped to visit a man whom he had rescued from the Planet of Darkness several years ago. Infinity had been taking his spaceship, the *Ghost III*, on a patrol around the planet to ensure there were no infiltrators penetrating the atmosphere. The *Ghost III* detected the heat from a living body in space and Infinity zoomed the *Ghost III* to where he found the man, kept alive only by his space suit and gear. The *Ghost III* extended its retrieving pincer and brought him inside. Infinity came to him in the medic's room and nursed him to health with the assistance of his mechanical agent. He was impressed by the man's resilience and tenacity to survive. The man was medium-tall with a fairly strong build and medium-brown hair. He had determined eyebrows and a firm jaw.

"You're not from the Planet of Light," Infinity commented when he noticed the man regaining consciousness. "Where are you from?"

Sweat broke out on the man's forehead as he forced himself into a sitting position. "You're not going to send me back there, are you?"

"Absolutely not. I can tell from your reaction that you are from the Planet of Darkness. People from that planet react one of two ways. They either are afraid of being taken to the Planet of Light or they fear being sent back to the Planet of Darkness. The ridiculous thing is that no matter which category you are in there is nothing to fear because those from the Planet of Light will not force anyone to stay nor force anyone back. But, few people from the Planet of Darkness have ever come as close to our planet as you have. How did you find your way?"

"While I was on the Planet of Darkness, I met someone, a spy I suspect. He told me he was from the Planet of Light and that the way to the Planet of Light can't be found on a map. That the way could only be found through one person, and that person's name was Infinity. So, I determined not to search for the way to the Planet of Light but to search for this man. I set the course of our ship based on an inner leading. And I haven't felt so strongly as I do right now that I am close to finding him."

"You have met him." Infinity pointed toward his designating symbol on the upper-left portion of his black and red duvetyn vest. The symbol was a cross within a triangle within a circle. "I am Infinity."

Eyes widening, the man reached out his hand. "You are? You can take us to the Planet of Light? I must tell 1-05. She –"

Infinity cut him off with a somber wave of the head. "When I found you, you were alone."

The man gasped, his shoulders tensing. "But she — she can't be dead."

"No, she isn't. But she wasn't with you when I found you. Now that you know the way, you will soon be 'The Way-Guide' for her. On the Planet of Darkness, citizens are identified with a number. On the Planet of Light, we identify people with names of meaning. You will be the 'Way-Guide' because you will help to guide many people to our Planet of Light."

The man smiled and forced himself to his feet, steadying himself by leaning his right hand on a nearby table. He clasped Infinity's left upper arm with his left hand. "As soon as you say the word, I am ready to guide."

As Infinity walked from the council room on his way to the hangar, he stopped at the Way-Guide's house. Being an experienced pilot, the Way-Guide naturally found work in operating space transports for several of the local businesses and it was convenient for him to live close to the hangar. His small two-story house was separated from the hangar only by a narrow alleyway. His front yard was not large but was brightened by several flowerboxes growing petunias and marigolds. Fireflies and moths darted about the flowerboxes as if intent on lighting the way to the front porch. Infinity mounted the wooden steps to the porch. He tapped on the frosted glass window of the door and the Way-Guide admitted him in. He offered Infinity a seat on the half-circle couch.

Upon hearing the plan, the Way-Guide embraced Infinity. "I've waited for this day a long time. It's been *so* long — five years, I think — I wonder if 1-05 will even recognize me when I see her." The Way-Guide laughed even though a tear was forming in one of his eyes.

"Come, we will see if the *Ghost III* is ready." Infinity led him toward the hangar.

At the hangar, the King approached them. The Way-Guide bowed. He had heard so many awe-inspiring stories about the King's powerful exploits to protect his people that his head swam in admiration. The King gestured for him to rise. "You are the Way-Guide, is that true?"

"Yes, your majesty. I am grateful to be accompanying your son on this mission."

The King smiled then turned to his son. "The councilmembers have prepared everything for you." The King guided him toward the *Ghost III*. "Your armor and weapons are waiting for you on the ship."

"Thank you, father." Infinity embraced him one last time.

"I know it will be several months, maybe years, before I see you again." The King's voice broke slightly. "But your wisdom, faith, and compassion will keep you. And I will give you this." The King took from his sheath a golden sword that glowed with a soft red light. "My sword of sacrifice. Use it well."

Infinity took the sword and tested its weight while admiring the sharpness of the long blade. "Thank you, father. I am honored." Infinity looked into his father's eyes and became empowered by a strength that would accompany him along the journey. "It is a formidable sword."

"When the Dark Tyrant learns you are coming, there is no doubt you will need it." The King stepped back to allow his son to leave.

Infinity and the Way-Guide boarded the *Ghost III*. The *Ghost III* was triangular and contained two floors. On the bottom floor were several cabins, a cafeteria combined with a lounge, a communications room, and a medic's room. An engineering room, a strategic development hall, and a cockpit area were on the upper floor. Stretching between the two floors and encircled by a protective railing was a brilliant ball of energy that shot out power to all electrically run devices on the ship. Infinity directed the Way-Guide to the ship's controls. Sitting in the co-pilot's chair, the Way-Guide did not take long to acquaint himself with the *Ghost III's* controls.

Infinity took his place at the pilot's controls. "With you and me on this mission together, there is no way the Dark Tyrant can stop us."

Chapter Six

1-05 punched a series of coordinates into the *Journey's* navigational computer. The spaceship rocked with the usual 'thump' as it settled on its course. After 1-05 pulled a control lever and pressed the lock button, the *Journey* stabilized into automatic pilot mode. She detached her seatbelt and moved her seat away from the console.

1-05 stood and turned to 2-45. "Well, we're on a straight course to the Planet of Light. If you want to get up and stretch your legs a bit, you can." She moved to the co-pilot's chair where Alpha 3-0-3, still in the form of her previous co-pilot, was seated. She set her hand on the back of its chair, leaning her weight on it as she bent forward to give the shape-shifter instructions. "Check on compressor valve 32 in the engine room. It was giving us problems on our last flight and I want to make certain the repairs are still holding. Also, apply some more lubricant oil to the fittings of the propellant injectors."

"Naturally." Alpha 3-0-3 saluted and left to take care of the repairs.

2-45 freed himself from his seat and stood up. He was unsteady at first and, to keep from falling onto the console, caught hold of 1-05's shoulder.

1-05 looked from his hand to his eyes, indicating his hand was not welcome.

"Uh, sorry." He regained his balance and removed his hand.

"No problem." 1-05 was pleased he took the hint. "I sometimes forget that not everyone is as used to spaceflight as I am. You'll soon get the hang of it." She stepped toward the exit of the cockpit area.

2-45 smiled, embarrassed. After shrugging it off, he followed her to the door. "Still, I do learn quickly."

Outside the cockpit area, there was a hallway, which to the left led to some cabins and to the right to the storage areas. The engine room was straight ahead from the cockpit and down a ladder. 1-05 strode down the hallway and turned to the left. 2-45 followed her.

1-05 reached the door to her cabin and, with a hand on her door, faced 2-45. "If you don't mind, now, I would like to rest." The door slid open and she entered her room.

"Certainly, go ahead."

She sat on her cot and looked at him, annoyed he was still there.

He crossed his arms and leaned on her doorframe watching her. "But, before I wander off to wherever will best keep me out of your way, I would like to ask you one or two or possibly three more questions."

"Questions?" She groaned, but then conceded. "I suppose you have that right. But I warn you, I'm keeping track and I'm tired, so, no more than three."

2-45 liked the way 1-05's eyes flashed when she was annoyed. "Number one," he lifted his first finger as he counted, "how long do you project it will take us to reach the Planet of Light?"

"Hard to say. When I tried to make it before, we ran into a cloud of gorslanchers, some of the deadliest space creatures in this part of the universe. They did critical damage to my ship and we had to stop for several days to make repairs." She lowered her head and sighed. After half a minute, she looked up, trying to appear unconcerned. "However, if all goes well, we could make it to the Planet of Light in less than one week."

"I see." 2-45 rubbed his chin, uneasy about the prospects. While he knew he would be facing some type of danger, gorslanchers were much more than he had expected. Still, he tried to keep a positive attitude. "In that case, we'll focus on one week. Number two." He raised two fingers. "When you say 'we' . . . are you referring to your shape-shifter and you?"

"No." Her mouth twitched as she held back a sob. "I didn't have Alpha 3-0-3 at the time. The 'we' refers to me and 8-23. He was my co-pilot and engineer. After we had picked up a load of minerals from Planet 4B, he and I decided to risk making it to the Planet of Light. We were doing fine until the gorslanchers damaged the ship, and we had to stop to make in-flight repairs. There was damage to the external guidance system, and you have to go out-of-ship for that type of repair. He insisted on doing it without my help, and he had just finished fixing it, when a piece of the ship's molding broke loose, knocking him far away from the ship. I was wearing my out-of-ship gear, but, before I could make it outside to help him, he had gone too far out. I couldn't reach him. I spent a whole day searching with the ship, but I was never able to find him." A tear trickled down her cheek.

"I'm sorry." 2-45 looked into her eyes, sincerely concerned. "I know it probably doesn't help much, but I feel confident we're going to make it this time."

1-05 shook her head as she wiped the tear from her cheek. "I don't know. I sometimes wonder if I even want to go there anymore."

"You were willing to take me there when I asked. I think you do." He moved forward and lifted her chin so that she looked him in the eyes as he gazed into hers. He added softly, "and I will see that you get there." He noticed a kind sparkle of light in her eyes.

1-05 lowered his hand from her chin. With one deep breath, she left the tragic day and was once more in the present. "What is your third question?"

2-45 pressed his lips together to keep from laughing at himself. He had actually thought she might fall in love with him. "All right," he held up three fingers, "number three. Which cabin is mine?"

1-05's eyes twinkled with a sarcastic smile. "Cabin number *three,* naturally."

"Naturally." 2-45 nodded a good-bye and left, closing her door, and headed for his cabin.

1-05 lay on her cot, face forward, as she cried into her pillow. *It's so unfair. If 8-23 were only with me now . . . maybe we could make it this time.* She pounded her fist into the pillow, hoping the blow could destroy that moment in the past.

Her door opened, and Alpha 3-0-3 entered in the form of 8-23. It tip-toed silently to her. It sat next to her on the cot and gently set a hand on her back. "Poor little 1-05." The shape-shifter tried to sound as concerned as it could with its stilted, mechanical voice. "I am here with you, and I will never leave you. Please, don't cry."

1-05 faced Alpha 3-0-3 and saw the image of 8-23 through a blur of tears.

Alpha 3-0-3 took 1-05's hand and patted it. "You know that all I ever want is to make you happy." It raised its other hand and sparkles of light emanated from its fingertips. The sparkles danced around 1-05's head. 1-05 smiled. "Are you happy now?" Alpha 3-0-3 asked.

"I know you want to cheer me up." 1-05 touched the back of Alpha 3-0-3's neck and stroked it down to its shoulder. "But even though you look like 8-23, you can never really be him."

Alpha 3-0-3 bowed its head and pursed its lips in a pout. It rubbed the palm of its hand on its leg in frustration. Then, it looked up at her with a child-like smile. "But we can pretend, can't we? Tell me, what's something 8-23 would do to cheer you up?"

1-05 bit her lip to hold back the tears as she thought about 8-23. She could remember his kind words, his embraces, his kisses, but it only hurt to remember. "I can't think about him anymore . . ." She breathed in a sob.

"Oh." Alpha 3-0-3 stood up. It took a few seconds for it to readjust its programming to this new way of thinking. "In that case, we won't." It allowed its image to waver and sparkle until it took on a new form, that of a little brown puppy with floppy ears. It barked as it wagged its tail.

1-05 laughed as Alpha 3-0-3 jumped into her cot and licked her face enthusiastically. She petted it and smiled brightly. "Thank you, Alpha 3-0-3. Right now, I really think you are the only one who can make me happy."

As 2-45 was searching for his cabin, he heard clattering and banging sounds from the hall to the right. Curious but cautious, 2-45 made his way toward the hall to the right that led to the storage rooms. As he followed the sounds, he heard what resembled someone singing. The singing grew louder as he drew closer to the storage rooms. When he stood outside the door to Storage Room A, he listened for a moment and carefully slid the door open. He turned on the light and saw, lounging on top of a crate of liquor, 7-43 drinking from one of the bottles and singing. Scattered on the floor were several recently emptied bottles.

2-45 marched up to 7-43 and snatched the bottle from his hand. "Well, what a surprise. I had no idea there were other passengers on this flight."

"Ah, depressing, isn't it? — realizing that there are things that you don't know." 7-43 produced another bottle from the crate and waved it triumphantly in the air and started singing drunkenly once more.

2-45 slapped his face.

7-43 quickly stopped singing and glared at 2-45. "What's the matter?" 7-43's words slurred. "Don't like my little sing-song?"

"When I want to hear singing, it had better be good, not like your drunken bellowing." 2-45 grabbed the new bottle from him and slapped his hand when he reached for another one. "I wonder. Are you even aware of this ship's destination?"

"Ship?" 7-43 tried to climb down from the crate. "What ship?"

"This ship you are on."

"What you are saying right now is just a bunch of twiddle-twaddle nonsense." 7-43 wavered his way to the storage room door. "I only come to this bar on occasion and when I do, I don't spend time talking to blotto bo-bos like you who think we're on a spaceship." He shook his head as he stumbled out the door.

2-45 followed him. "Whether you believe it or not, we *are* on a spaceship, in fact, we are on a very dangerous journey to the Planet of Light." Once they were both outside the storage room, 2-45 pressed a button to lock the door.

7-43 unexpectedly turned to 2-45 with genuine excitement. "Ah, the Planet of Light. Well, that sounds like a bout of bristling fun. I've never been to the Planet of Light before. I'm sure it's a place everyone ought to visit at least once in their lifetime. Now move along and show me to my room. I'm so beastly tired." 7-43 yawned and raised his eyebrows in an attempt to keep his tired eyes open.

2-45 tilted his head. "You think *I* would get *you* a cabin?"

7-43 raised his nose in the air. "Oh, if you insist on being so blasted uncooperative, I'll just find my own room." 7-43 toddled off to find his way around the spaceship.

2-45 noticed 7-43 was heading toward the cockpit. Not wanting 7-43 to, intentionally or unintentionally, foul up the ship's controls, he rushed over and guided 7-43 down the hall leading to the cabins. "All right, I'll find you a cabin. Just one thing."

"What's that?"

"Things will probably get dangerous, and I want to make it to the Planet of Light." 2-45 fixed 7-43 with a deadly serious stare, "So, no matter what happens, do not interfere with us getting there."

"Dangerous?" 7-43 watched 2-45 nervously. "You can be assured that if anything gets dangerous, I'll let you handle it."

"All right, follow me." 2-45 led him toward cabin number four.

At the cabin door, 7-43 turned to 2-45. "Tell me, why are you so determined to get to the Planet of Light?"

2-45 smiled confidently. "It's a challenge. I love beating the odds." He turned and headed for his own cabin.

Chapter Seven

Twenty feet below ground was 50-83's small 10' x 10' room. 6-96 would lock him in this room whenever she did not require his assistance. The high walls of 50-83's room were made of light-colored stone. His furniture consisted of only his small neatly made bed, a nightstand holding a few books, and a small desk. He stored his clothes on pegs on the wall behind his bed and, on the wall opposite his bed, was the small, open elevator that led to the door in the ceiling. The elevator was the only way out of the room, from which it would rise to 6-96's workshop just under a small glass overhang. At times, 50-83 could see through the open wire-framed elevator and the glass overhang a nice view of the perpetual night sky. However, at the moment, the metal door in the ceiling covered this view.

50-83 lounged on his bed wearing a light tan jacquard vest and charcoal silk pants tucked into black leather boots. Beside him on the bed was a plate with a sandwich made of bread and cheese, and on his nightstand was a glass of water. He ate the sandwich by tearing off pieces and putting each piece in his mouth. The sandwich was dry and clogged his throat, but he convinced himself he *loved* dry sandwiches, and, consequently, he thoroughly *enjoyed* his meal. When he had popped the last bite into his mouth, he brushed his hands off over his plate and washed down the bite with the last drink of water in the glass.

After setting the plate and glass aside on the nightstand, he sat at his desk. He took from one of the desk drawers a small wooden box with a lid. He took the lid off of the box and pulled out a couple of gold chains and a small pair of jeweler's pliers. He linked the two chains together forming a bracelet with an alternating star and circle pattern. After he finished with this, he took from the box a medium-sized gold and diamond star pendant and attached it to the bracelet. He returned the wooden box to the desk drawer and placed the bracelet on his left wrist to admire it. He ran the fingers of his right hand across the star pendant noticing how it sparkled much like the stars that glimmered in the black sky above the shadows of his dark world. He looked at the locked metal door and wished he could move the door back and let the sky and those sparkling stars engulf him. *If only there was a way to live up there away from the craziness of this place.*

There was a beeping from a monitor on the desk and the image of 6-96 appeared on its screen. "Come here this minute," she ordered brusquely.

"Yes, ma'am. Right away," 50-83 responded with his memorized lines. As 6-96's image faded from the monitor, he removed the bracelet from his wrist and tucked it away in an inside pocket of his vest.

50-83 turned and saw the metal door in the ceiling slide open, indicating that 6-96 had entered the code into the door's control box to unlock the door. 50-83 stepped onto the open elevator and pressed a button on its frame. As the elevator rose, he held onto its frame with one hand and lifted his other hand, palm upward, toward the night sky. He imagined the stars falling from the sky and settling in the palm of his hand. He let go of the elevator's frame and placed that hand over the imagined stars and held his hands together so as to not let the stars escape. He then held his hands close to his face and the stars seemed to enter inside him, dispelling depression and fear. The elevator climbed through the door in the ceiling and stopped just under the glass overhang. 50-83 noticed, through the glass door leading to 6-96's workroom, 6-96 gesturing in an abrupt manner for him to come to her. 50-83 quickly made his way into the workroom.

6-96 stood next to the dead tree. She held in her right hand a long silver staff with a black pointed obsidian stone on top. Using her staff, she pointed out the seven-headed snake curled under the tree. "Look here. What do you see?"

50-83 wondered what type of childish game this was. "I see the snake under the tree," he said as if reciting a lesson.

"All right, so the snake is under the tree. And what is the snake doing under the tree?"

"It is curled up like it is asleep . . ."

"Yes," she interrupted him. "The snake is curled under the tree. And why? This snake curls up like this whenever he has not eaten." She slapped 50-83 hard across his face. "Your task list included feeding him today and YOU did not." She took her staff in both hands and swung it at 50-83's stomach, knocking him down.

50-83 fell hard to the stone floor. He instinctively clutched his stomach where 6-96's staff hit him, but pain also built up in his arms, back, and head from the fall. Ever since the seven-headed snake nearly bit him, he had built up a hatred for the snake. His task list did include feeding the snake, but he chose to ignore that task. "I'm sorry," he was finally able to say through a groan of pain. "I guess I forgot."

"Get up, you," 6-96 commanded. 50-83 attempted to rise, but 6-96 callously kicked him in the leg and he fell back to the ground. "You lied," she snarled. "You didn't forget to feed him. You never forget your tasks."

Rubbing his sore leg, 50-83 looked at her with an innocent expression. "I know. Usually. But this time I really *did* forget."

"I do not believe you. Stand up." 6-96 yanked him to his feet by his vest. "You were being wicked, weren't you?" She glared at him narrowly. "So, tell me the real reason you didn't feed him." Her eyes lit with excitement. "Was it because you wanted him dead?"

"No, I'm telling you the truth." He avoided her gaze by looking down. "I really do remember feeding the snake. So either I did feed him, or . . . I must have forgotten."

"Oh? . . . Really?" 6-96 looked at him askance with her left hand on her hip.

"Of course."

"Look at me when you say that," she snapped sharply.

"Yes, ma'am." 50-83 instantly looked up. "Of course." His eyes focused on a set of knives hung on the stone wall just behind 6-96's head.

"Well, then, since you forgot . . ." she dragged him over to the snake and, with her staff, gave him a hard push toward it. "You can feed him now."

50-83 shuffled over to a cupboard in the wall and opened its doors. He grimaced as he took a large bag of raw meat from it. He carried this bag over to the snake. He gingerly dipped his hands into the bag, and, as he placed the meat in front of the snake, he murmured, "I mean, I *was* going to feed him. Why wouldn't I feed this nice snake?" The snake ravenously swallowed the meat. "After all," 50-83 continued, "I really do like him. Of course I would want to feed him." 50-83 tried to wrap his mind around the idea that, while the snake may seem mean and vicious, in reality it had kind and compassionate feelings. Being lonely and having few real friends, 50-83 told himself the snake could possibly fill that void. 50-83 reached a hand slowly toward the snake to pet it. Suddenly, one of the snake's heads jolted forward and hissed viciously. 50-83 jerked his hand away. "Yes," he tried to convince himself, "of course I like the snake."

6-96 shook her head at 50-83's ramblings. "Erg, you are hopeless."

50-83 had gotten used to 6-96's belittling remarks and now blocked them from his ears. He tossed another piece of raw meat to the snake and noted the blood it left on his hands. He picked up a cloth from a nearby table and wiped off his hands.

6-96 grabbed her knife from its sheath on her thigh and tapped it in her left hand as she slowly stepped up to him. "Perhaps the only thing you are useful for now is as a guinea pig in my next experiment on new methods of torture."

50-83 looked up at 6-96 in alarm. An excited sneer spread across her face at his expression, so, he quickly decided to counter her excitement by acquiring an unconcerned attitude. "Then you'll be stuck carrying out the dead bodies?" 50-83 grumbled as he carried the bag containing what was left of the raw meat. He stuffed the bag into the cupboard and slammed the cupboard door shut.

6-96 scrunched her nose. "I could always get a new apprentice." She polished the blade of the knife on her sleeve. "But, perhaps you are right. You are good at following most of my orders. But remember . . ." She grabbed him by his ear and pulled hard. ". . . when I give a command it must be obeyed."

"Yes, ma'am." He winced.

She let him go and lifted her head confidently. "You know, when you put your mind to it, you make a very good apprentice. Tell me 'yes'."

"Yes . . . but—"

"But what?" 6-96 demanded with a raised eyebrow.

"But what I really would like to do is . . ." He was about to mention one of the many sports he enjoyed when he was young — hiking, boxing, swimming — but he knew too well what he was supposed to say. ". . . be like you and work as a Persuader."

"And you will, if you do what you are told." 6-96 placed her knife under his chin, lifting his chin with the knife as she examined his face. "You have a nice face. Some would call you handsome."

"I suppose so, ma'am," he blushed, unsure of what she had in mind. He would have shifted nervously if 6-96's knife had not been so close to his throat.

6-96 moved the knife from his chin and ran a finger down his cheek as she continued to study his features. "Yes, nice cheek bone and firm jaw." She felt the muscles in his shoulder and upper arm. "Yes . . . you are strong, too. You will do for the job."

50-83 knitted his eyebrows in confusion. "What do you want me to do?"

"The Dark Tyrant assigned me two jobs. I need your help with one of them. Do you know where the Slump-Bumps live?"

"Yes. When I was a boy, I used to play near there. It's a really muddy place, so me and my friend built this mud fort there. We tied rocks and sticks together and layered them with—"

"That's enough. 4,021, a young woman, lives there. I want you to go there and find her."

"Why?" he asked with distrust. "So you can torture her?"

"We might. But first, I want you to talk to her. Become her friend. Perhaps make her fall in love with you. Convince her to tell you everything about her and anything she might be planning and bring the information to me. This should provide you with some valuable practice in persuasion."

"Yes, ma'am."

6-96 slammed her knife on a table and lowered her head with a stern glare. "Now go and get started right away."

"Yes, ma'am." 50-83 left 6-96's workroom. While he was eagerly anticipating his first experience as a Persuader, he actually wished he was heading for the Slump-Bump area in order to build a mud fort.

Chapter Eight

5 0-83 trudged the muddy path toward the area where the Slump-Bumps lived. He was careful to avoid the sides of the path where the mud was the deepest, but even so, more than once, he stepped in a mud hole and sank up to his knee. With effort, he was able to extract himself, and, leaning against a rock, he wiped the mud from his pants and emptied the mud that had seeped into his boots, and continued on.

He had only taken a few more steps before he heard a mechanical whirring and was blinded by a glaring light that penetrated the darkness around him. He heard a hypnotic voice behind him saying, "You'll only *ruin* your *boots* in this *mud*."

50-83 stopped and turned around to see the glaring headlights of a mud-crawler and 1-13 at the wheel. The mud-crawler was an off-road vehicle that was capable of driving over even the muddiest terrain. Its tires were composed of a material that had super traction ability, and under the body of the mud-crawler near each tire were devices that could release gasses powerful enough to levitate the mud-crawler to hover

over areas of deep mud. The lines of the mud-crawler were smooth and the seating area was open.

1-13 stalled his mud-crawler next to 50-83. "Did 6-96 send you on a job without providing you with the necessary tools?" 1-13 smiled smugly.

Recognizing 1-13 as the Persuader who threw him out, 50-83 raised his head self-sufficiently. "I can make it all right without help." He turned from 1-13 and continued to trudge his way through the mud.

1-13 shook his head pityingly and continued to drive slowly next to him. "It would be much *easier* if you let *me* drive you. Get in."

50-83 pressed his lips together in determination and persisted on. It was not long, though, before he skidded and fell on a muddy slope in the road. 1-13 stalled next to him as 50-83 pushed himself back to his feet. 50-83 rethought his decision to continue the journey on foot and turned with sulky annoyance to 1-13's mud-crawler and climbed inside. 1-13 frowned and shook his head at the globs of mud 50-83 had tracked onto the floor and seat of his vehicle, then drove on.

"So," 1-13 said raising a thoughtful eyebrow and speaking in his hypnotic manner, "*why* has 6-96 sent you *here*? You are on a job for her, *aren't you*?"

"Uh . . . yes . . . But why should that concern you? You never wanted me as your apprentice." He watched 1-13 suspiciously out of the corner of his eye.

1-13 waved one hand as if to wave away any doubts in 50-83's mind. "Now, *why* should I *want* you as an apprentice when *you* and *I* could work so much better as *p a r t n e r s*?" He smiled and looked 50-83 in the eyes entrancingly.

"Partners?" 50-83's eyes narrowed. "Doing what?"

1-13 ignored 50-83's question. "6-96 assigned you to find out about 4,021, *correct*?"

"Yes."

"Have you seen her?"

50-83 shook his head.

"She is a *young, beautiful* woman with *sensitive* eyes." 1-13 heaved a deep sigh as he described 4,021. 50-83 could not tell if 1-13's sigh was merely a method to manipulate his feelings or if it was a sincere sigh. 1-13 raised his chin and waved a hand in a poetic gesture. "She is not someone who would respond *well* under 6-96's *brutal* tactics."

"If you say so, sir." The few months of working as 1-13's apprentice had conditioned 50-83 not to question 1-13 aloud. "But, all the same, I have to do what 6-96 orders."

"No, you don't," 1-13 commanded firmly. He then added with a smile, "I *know* that when you *see* her gentle beauty, you will agree that *4,021* would be much safer under *my* more *sophisticated* methods."

"But what could I do?" There was a hint of nervous panic in his voice. "I couldn't bring her to your workshop unless either 6-96 or the Dark Tyrant gives me the order."

1-13 brushed aside 50-83's panic with a sweep of his hand. "What exactly has 6-96 ordered you to do?"

50-83 thought a second and recited 6-96's orders as accurately as he could remember, "To gain 4,021's confidence and find out whatever I can about her and report that information back to 6-96."

"*Very well*," 1-13 smiled and nodded, pleased. "Go ahead and do that. But *also* report to *me* everything as well. Did 6-96 mention anything about plans to torture 4,021?"

"She said we will if we have to."

1-13 stopped the mud-crawler where the path forked off in two directions. He turned to 50-83 and placed a hand on his shoulder. "*You won't* let that happen."

"But how could I stop it?" 50-83 asked.

"You are *intelligent*. You are *strong*. And, if you need *my* help, let me *know*." He gestured toward the path to the right. "Here you are. Her hovel is just a little ways down that path. It's less muddy here, so you shouldn't have any trouble."

50-83 stepped out of the mud-crawler and saluted a wave good-bye.

1-13 held up a hand as if giving 50-83 a benedictory blessing. "*Remember*, I'll be expecting your report *soon*." He nodded once and drove away.

50-83 followed the path indicated by 1-13. His first inclination had been to disregard everything that 1-13 was trying to convince him to do. After all, once he had taken his position as 6-96's apprentice, he was commanded to follow only orders that came from the Dark Tyrant and 6-96. So, upon climbing into 1-13's mud-crawler, he had determined to politely agree with everything 1-13 said while not listening to a word of it. Yet, even though 50-83's survival instincts told him he *should* do everything the Dark Tyrant and 6-96 told him to do and even though he had convinced himself he *wanted* to do everything the Dark Tyrant and 6-96 told him to do — deep inside, 50-83 had a rebellious nature that yearned to lash out against them for the torment they had put him through. *It's not so much that I want to help out 1-13, but I sure would like to get back at 6-96.*

50-83 continued along the muddy path and soon reached the point where he could see the rows and rows of the Slump-Bumps' little white, mud-soaked hovels. Each hovel was off a similar muddy path, came with a similar muddy yard, and had identical open doorways and windows which allowed the muddy yard and path to track in. Perhaps the Slump-Bumps' hovels would have looked better with some decorative stones in the yard and some curtains in the windows, but to be creative took thought and to carry out a creative idea took work, both of which were strictly forbidden for the Slump-Bumps.

After several minutes of looking for some means to locate and identify 4,021's hovel from the hundreds of other hovels, 50-83 stood confused in the middle of one of the muddy paths. Unexpectedly, four unruly boys between the ages eight and eleven came running out from behind a large rock towards 50-83, a couple of them even pushing him off balance. One of the boys grabbed a gob of mud from the ground and flung it at 50-83. The mud splotched right onto his jacquard vest.

50-83 brushed as much of the mud off his vest as he could. The boys laughed at him and took off running. But, before they could escape, 50-83 caught up with the boy who had thrown the mud and took him by the arm. "So, what game is this? Look, what you did to my shirt."

When the other boys saw one of their members was in trouble, they stopped running and watched, trying to decide whether to run and save themselves or stay and stand by a friend.

The boy 50-83 held by the arm was an eight-year-old scruffy-looking boy with freckles and tousled red hair. He stared at 50-83 blankly, afraid to answer. "I-I d-didn't mean—" he stuttered and looked helplessly over at the other boys for assistance.

An older dark-haired boy gave 50-83's arm a rough jab. "Let 'im go. He didn't hurt you."

"I suppose it was all part of a game you were playing?" 50-83 asked pointedly.

The red-haired boy gasped and shook his head quickly. "Oh no. Not playing."

"Yeah," the older boy added looking about to make sure no Enforcer was watching, "we weren't playing . . ."

"I must agree with you there," 50-83 said with a knowing tilt of his head. "What kind of game is it where you throw mud at someone who isn't even expecting it?" He released the red-haired boy. "There's no competition in that."

"What do you mean com-pah-tish-on?" a young curly-haired fatter boy asked. "What's that?"

"That's the challenge in a game that makes it fun. That's what makes you work harder. When you know there's a chance you could lose, you want to try harder so you can win." 50-83 grabbed a handful of mud. "So. Now, let's *really* play."

The boys all looked at each other warily, wondering whether to join in or not.

50-83 gestured the red-haired boy towards the ground. "Go ahead, you get some."

"What's it you're gonna do?" the boy asked cautiously as he took a scoop of mud in his hands.

"Now that I have this," 50-83 held up his gob of mud, "you never know. I could easily hit you first. Still, if you're clever enough, you could get your shot in before me."

The red-haired boy hesitated. An older tow-haired boy pushed him forward. "Come on. You can hit him. You hit him first, didn't you?"

"Yeah," the red-haired boy gulped, "but if I lose . . ."

"That's part of the fun." 50-83 readied his handful of mud. "Me and my friends used to play this game all the time. And I warn you, I'm very good." He smiled proudly. He pointed toward the curly-haired boy. "When you shout out 'now,' that's when we try to hit each other."

The curly-haired fat boy waited a moment, glancing at the red-haired boy to make sure he was ready. When the red-haired boy nodded in his direction, the fat boy shouted out, "Now."

At that moment, the red-haired boy threw his mud, but, being in such a hurry, he failed to take aim and the mud landed on 50-83's boots. 50-83's well-aimed shot splatted mud all over the red-haired boy's face.

"Ugh." The boy wiped the mud from his eyes. "That's not fair."

"You just need more practice," 50-83 told him. "And, know what? If you build yourself a mud fort, it would be even better."

"Build a mud fort?" the tow-headed boy repeated. "Never heard of such a thing."

"A mud fort is a barrier from whatever the rival team is throwing at you. You just get some rocks and sticks together for the frame." 50-83 gestured, demonstrating how the fort should look. "You build them like this and cover them with mud and debris. Then you hide behind it while you get ready with whatever you plan to throw your enemy's way."

"Hey, that sounds great," the dark-haired boy exclaimed. "Could you show us how to build it?"

"Of course." 50-83 led the boys off the muddy path over to a pile of stones. "This looks like a good place." He gestured toward two of the boys. "You two bring over some of those medium-sized stones. Here. I'll help you."

The older boy and the tow-headed boy carried the stones to the area designated by 50-83. With the help of the other two boys, 50-83 put them in place. He then showed the boys how to collect the right size and shape of sticks. As the red-haired boy and the fat boy collected the sticks, the other two assisted 50-83 in tying the sticks together with some twine for the frame.

As 50-83 and the boys were finishing the frame and beginning on coating the fort in mud, the red-haired boy noticed a crowd collecting around them.

"Oh, wow," the red-haired boy smiled in amazement. "We've got an audience."

50-83 set down the sticks and stepped forward as he took in the group gathering about the fort they were building.

An older, white-haired man approached 50-83 and sat on a rock next to the fort. He took a pipe, filled it with tobacco, and lit it. "So," he spoke to 50-83 as he blew out a disdainful puff of smoke, "what is this *thing* supposed to be?"

"A mud fort."

"A mud fort?" The older man laughed in disbelief. "I see. How unusual. So, what does it do for us?"

The tow-headed boy dropped an armful of sticks he was carrying. All of the boys stopped working for a moment as they turned their attention to 50-83, waiting for his reply.

"It's just part of a game," 50-83 tried to explain.

"A game?" The older man shook his head in disapproval.

An overweight woman stepped up and scratched her cheek as she scowled at the fort. "But why is it here? We haven't had anything like this before. Why should we have one now?"

"That's right," shouted a thin, drunken man, waving a bottle of beer. "It looks ridiculous." He laughed loudly.

"Yeah," exclaimed another drunken man. "Who wants a stupid wall there anyway."

"Young man," a toothless man turned to 50-83, "you know you are breaking the rules by encouraging those boys to work. We're Slump-Bumps here, and we're not s'pose to work."

"Work?" 50-83 looked at the man, incredulous. "We weren't *working*. We were *playing*."

"Playing? . . ." the toothless man's frown deepened. "That is even worse."

At that moment, four tall, muscular men forced their way through the crowd and up to where 50-83 was standing next to the nearly completed fort. The four men were dressed in the black and navy blue armor of the Enforcers and each of them wore a black helmet that covered the top of their heads, as well as their ears and eyes. The helmets protected their heads while also giving them the ability to see in the dark and to hear sounds that were barely audible. In their hands they carried large auto-targeting annihilation guns. "This man is right, 50-83." The Enforcers wore armor around their throats containing mechanical devices that altered their voices to make them louder, unemotional, and more authoritative. "By encouraging these boys to think, work, and play, you are in serious conflict with the Dark Tyrant's rules."

50-83 paled as they approached him. He lowered his head, nervously avoiding looking into their eyes. "Sorry, sir. I thought the kids wanted to play. I didn't know that was against the rules . . . or that building a mud fort would be considered work. I'm sorry."

"Are you in this area on business?" another Enforcer asked bringing his intimidating mask to a level with 50-83's eyes.

"6-96 sent me here to question one of the Slump-Bumps."

The first Enforcer took out a hand-held computer and searched it for documentation. He nodded his head as the computer confirmed the orders. "Very well, you are to interrogate 4,021. Her hovel is down that path over there. Continue on your way and carry out the business."

50-83 gave them a short bow, turned, and headed down the path the Enforcer pointed out. As he was leaving, 50-83 noticed the Enforcers breaking up the crowd and asking the four boys some questions. He earnestly hoped that none of the boys would be punished because of what he had started.

After 50-83 had trudged a ways through the grime, he came to 5-68 rocking back and forth in his rocking chair in his slimy yard of mud.

"Hello," 5-68 greeted him. "You're new to these parts, right? Or are you just one of those Enforcers checking up on us Slump-Bumps?"

"No, I'm not an Enforcer." 50-83 puzzled over how he came to that conclusion. "Not even wearing a uniform."

"You could be in disguise."

50-83 watched the rockers of 5-68's chair, and noticed how each time 5-68 rocked, the rockers were sinking deeper and deeper into the mud. "I am just looking for 4,021."

"And it's none of my business why you are looking for her, right?" 5-68 crossed his arms behind his head and lazily rested his head back. "No need to worry, I follow the rules."

"Of course." 50-83 did not really care whether 5-68 followed the rules or not. His main concern was finding 4,021 and wondering why 5-68 had not noticed that the mud was now reaching the H-railing on his rocking chair. "So," 50-83 looked from the railings of the chair to 5-68's face, "do you know where I can find her?"

5-68 gestured towards the hovel to the left of his. "You're in luck. She's my neighbor. And I'd say you have good reason to check up on her. She dreams and she thinks." 5-68 did not want anything to happen to 4,021. She was a good neighbor, quiet and to herself, but 5-68 was glad the attention of the authorities was on her and not on him.

"Oh?" While 50-83 knew Slump-Bumps were not allowed to think, he was surprised 5-68 would mention dreams, because 50-83 could not see how outlawing dreams could benefit anyone. "I see." He nodded a good-bye to 5-68 and moved on towards 4,021's hovel.

50-83 entered 4,021's hovel. It was small with only one room, a living room and kitchen combined. The floor was constructed of concrete and covered with a thin layer of mud. 50-83 noticed how the mud he tracked in added to this mud layer. A daybed in the living room doubled as a couch. A circular table in front of the daybed served as a coffee table. There was a smaller table beside the daybed that held a lamp, the hovel's only source of light. The kitchen contained a sink, a kitchen nook, and shelves for storing and preserving food. The kitchen contained no stoves, no burners, and no appliances, since the Slump-Bumps could only eat previously prepared food at home. If the Slump-Bumps wanted cooked meals, they had to visit one of several nearby cafés.

While 50-83 was looking at some dishes on one of the shelves in the kitchen, 4,021 entered the front doorway carrying a bag of fruit she had picked up from the food storage building. Seeing 50-83, she gasped, startled. The light from the lamp by the daybed glared onto the side of 50-83's face and cast shadows that almost obscured his features. 50-83's shape and light-colored hair reminded 4,021 of the man from her dream who had come to carry her away from the Planet of Darkness, and she wondered if her dream was coming true.

50-83 saw he had frightened her, so he moved forward to steady her and to ensure that she did not drop her bag. Once 50-83 had moved out of the direct glow of the lamp, 4,021 saw that he was not the man in her dreams. While disappointed, she did see that 50-83 appeared kind and concerned, so she gave him a smile and allowed him to carry her bag to the kitchen counter.

"Did I scare you?" 50-83 asked sheepishly. "I'm very sorry."

"No. I shouldn't have been frightened. It isn't that you looked scary, it's just that for a little while you looked like you were someone else." She took the fruit from the bag and set it on a shelf.

"Someone else?" he asked in surprise. "Who?"

"Oh, someone very handsome, kind of like you, but different."

"Is he a friend of yours?"

"I hope so. I had a dream with him in it." She smiled as her mind wandered off to the dream in which that man held her in his arms. When she noticed the serious look on 50-83, her smile melted. "Is that wrong?"

"I don't think it is wrong." 50-83 noticed her dreamy, deep blue eyes. "Of course some of the rules are very strict, but there's no way they could know you had a dream unless you told them. The trick is to keep it a secret." He leaned his elbows on the counter with a smug air and pressed his lips together firmly to hide a slight chuckle. He found it funny that the Dark Tyrant would make a law about something like dreaming. It was so easy to keep people from finding out about dreams.

"But how can I keep it a secret when it was such a wonderful dream?" She sighed, her blue eyes sparkling with enthusiasm. "I want to tell it to everyone."

"Well, it is hard sometimes," he agreed. "What you have to do is this. In your mind, take that dream and put it into a little box, close the box real tight, and only open it when you are alone and nobody is watching." 50-83's method of hiding memories and thoughts was so simple to him he was surprised when he learned not everyone used it. The number of boxes in 50-83's own mind — and that included boxes within boxes — was too many to count. There were even some boxes so tightly locked that 50-83 could not even remember what was inside them.

"But what if someone asks me about the dream?"

"You can tell them, 'What dream? I don't have dreams.' After all, you don't have a dream in your head, right? You have a box." 50-83 laughed with a clever light in his eyes.

"What about you? Could I tell you about the dream?" she asked, moving to sit on the daybed.

"I already know you had a dream, so I guess you could tell me about it." He sat next to her. "So, what happened in this dream?"

4,021 closed her eyes and held her hands out longingly in front of her as she watched the dream play out in her mind. "In my dream, I was sitting outside in my yard looking at the stars in the black sky. Then suddenly, a great big, magnificent spaceship landed in front of me and the most wonderful man ever came out of the spaceship. He picked me up in his arms and carried me into his spaceship and we flew off towards the beautiful bright stars. I really wish the dream would happen. Do you think they ever do?"

"It would be nice. I know I sometimes wish I could fly into the sky and live among the stars." He thought of the times he would lie in his bed looking through the glass overhang at the starry sky and fall asleep by dreaming of building his own space station among the stars. "Up there, nobody to tell you what to do, nothing to worry about." 50-83 reached into the pocket inside his vest and took out the bracelet with the star pendant he had made. He held it before her. "Maybe we can't get to the stars right now, but I have a bright, shining one right here." The hovel was dark and the light from the only lamp caused 4,021's blonde hair and blue eyes to shine like stars against a black sky. 50-83 saw in her a micro-version of the splendor of outer space. "Would you like it?"

"Oh, it's beautiful."

"Then you can have it." He unlatched the bracelet, encircled it around her wrist and reconnected the fastenings. "Now you can watch over this bit of the universe that belongs to us."

4,021 brought the bracelet on her wrist to her heart and caressed it with her other hand. "You said that so charmingly." She had never owned anything so lovely and looking at it caused her heart to skip with happiness. "Would you be surprised if I said I loved you?"

"No." 50-83's voice was flat and unemotional. "Would you be surprised if *I* said, 'I love you'?"

"Yes." The shadows made it difficult for her to read his expression. "You say it so seriously, it's hard for me to feel that you mean it."

"But it's true."

4,021 looked him in the eyes, trying to tell if he were speaking the truth.

50-83 looked down to avoid her gaze.

4,021 sighed despondently. "All right, so you *say* you love me. But I get the feeling you're lying. You're trying to hide something from me."

"You don't believe me?"

4,021 shook her head 'no.'

He took the necklace with the crystal from around his neck and held it up. "Well, I have this. It asks me questions and I answer the questions and it knows if I am telling the truth. Watch." 50-83 held the crystal between his hands and it glowed with a yellow light and floated over his hands.

"Good day, 50-83," the crystal chirped.

"Good day," replied 50-83. "I am ready for another question."

"I can tell that you are," agreed the crystal enthusiastically. "What do you think of the Dark Tyrant's rules regarding the Slump-Bumps?"

50-83 took on a serious demeanor and concentrated hard as he determined the answer the crystal was looking for and forced himself to believe it enough to answer the question convincingly. "I believe the rules are very intelligently placed and that they are necessary for the happiness and well-being of everyone who lives on our planet."

"Excellent. I can tell that you place great confidence in the Dark Tyrant's ability to rule you wisely."

"Now, crystal, I would like you to tell me if what I say next is the truth. I love 4,021."

"Absolutely," the crystal said happily. "It is clear that you felt the words you spoke."

4,021's face lit up with a smile and she looked into 50-83's eyes. "So it is true? You do love me?"

50-83 nodded and lowered the crystal into his hand and held it by its chain.

4,021 leaned over to him and embraced him. 50-83 did not return the embrace but only patted her on her shoulder.

"Don't worry, sweet one," he told her, "I will see that no harm comes to you."

Chapter Nine

The City of the Dark Tyrant was the governing center for the Planet of Darkness. 50-83 entered the main complex of this city on his way back from the Slump-bump area. The main complex was an enclosed maze of sturdy and high walls under a multi-domed ceiling constructed of a glass-like material. The air on the Planet of Darkness was contaminated and nauseating, so to keep the system running for the majority of the population, contaminants were filtered out of the air and the freshly filtered air was pumped back into the large complex. While this air was by no means pure and refreshing, it was easier to breathe than the air outside. The complex consisted of halls lined on one side by windows and on the other by doors leading to work and study rooms. Intermittently, between the doors, were alcoves that led to other halls branching off from the main hall.

Once inside the complex, 50-83 followed the maze of dimly lit halls until he found a washroom and ducked inside to clean the mud from his boots and clothes. The washroom was lit by cylinders of green glowing gel that lined the dark gray marble walls. He made his way to the flowing waterfall that streamed from an opening in the mirrored wall on the far end of the room. 50-83 grabbed an absorbent cloth from a shelf nearby, held it under the flow of water until it was damp, and used it to wipe off his vest. Reflected in the mirrored wall, 93-73 entered the washroom. 93-73 was a research apprentice for Researcher 7,500. Each Researcher had an area of expertise and was assigned to research all elements of government, social welfare, and production that had anything to do with that area of expertise. The Researcher's job was to develop plans on how the Leaders could run each of these elements so the government had more control over its citizens, the manufacturers had more output from their workers, and the elites could organize society more efficiently.

93-73 stepped up beside 50-83, took a comb from his shirt pocket and, looking into the mirrored wall, combed his lanky black hair. 93-73 was a tall, willowy young man with large, brown, cat-like eyes. He wore a loose white linen shirt and black corduroy pants. His black shoes were polished to a high sheen and he wore a matching shiny black belt.

"Well, hello, 50-83." 93-73 tucked his comb away into his shirt pocket. "It looks like you got into a mess."

"I just came back from the Slump-Bump area." 50-83 set one foot on a low shelf and wiped the mud from his pant leg and boot.

"Oh, that's right, you're an apprentice for 6-96. No doubt she gives you assignments here, there, and all over the place," he said with a fluid wave of his hand. "And you, poor thing, bear the brunt of it all. Now, me, you remember, I work for a Researcher of historical information. So, I'm stuck most of the time in the library under a huge stack of books. Or, worse yet, at a computer. Look." He gestured toward his eyes in dismay. "How bloodshot my eyes are."

"There are certain things we just have to put up with." 50-83 inwardly detested almost everything about his job, but he knew he should not confide that fact to anyone. If he did, 6-96 might find out, and she would likely claim that 50-83 was unsuitable for his job, and more than anything, 50-83 did not want to feel like a failure. So, instead, 50-83 managed to convince himself that anything that bothered him about his job was a little thing and he was tough enough to take it.

"Yes, I know." 93-73 shrugged his shoulders. "I guess I just complain too much. I admire your stalwart attitude. Well, I guess I better get back to my research. You should see the list of manuscripts I have to read. The list is this—" He gestured the length with one hand well over his head and the other hand near his knee. "—this long. But, like you said, it's our job and . . . oh, well." 93-73 held a hand up and fluttered his fingers in farewell. "So, good-bye to you and may you have success in all of your assignments." He turned to leave, but stopped and looked back in a secretive manner. "By the way, is it true? Is 6-96 really going to be gathering information on 2,040?"

"2,040? Are you sure you have the number right?"

93-73 nodded seriously. "Absolutely sure."

"I haven't heard about that. Of course she doesn't tell me everything." The only thing 50-83 knew about 2,040 was that he worked as a Researcher. He had not heard of any problems with him or his work and had no idea why information would need to be gathered from or about him.

"To be honest, I was just hoping to learn whether or not the rumor was true." 93-73 waved both hands in the air in a resigned manner. "It's just that the Researcher I work for is a friend of his, so if I could find out . . . but, oh well . . ." He tilted his head to one side and swung his hands flippantly.

50-83 put his other foot on the low shelf and wiped the mud from that pant leg and boot.

"You know, if the rumor is true, 6-96 *may* assign you to gather the information." 93-73 pointed a finger in the air thoughtfully. "Maybe you should get a head start. I happen to know that 2,040 is taking on a new research apprentice today. I saw the apprentice out in the hall as I was coming in just now. He might still be there." He put his hands on his hips as he looked down annoyed at 50-83 still meticulously cleaning the mud from his pant leg. "Are you almost done?"

"Of course," 50-83 looked at 93-73 quizzically. "Why?"

"I was thinking if the new research apprentice was still out there, you could introduce yourself to him. What better way to find out about a Researcher than through his apprentice? *He* will know 2,040 and tell you what he knows and, since *I* know you, you will let *me* know what you find out and, since I know 7,500, I can tell him what I find out and that way everyone's happy." 93-73 beamed cheerily. As soon as 50-83 set down the cloth, 93-73 grabbed 50-83 by the wrist and dragged him to the door.

93-73 stood in the doorway of the washroom with 50-83 right behind him looking over 93-73's shoulder. 93-73 glanced down both sides of the hall until he spied who he was looking for down the right side of the hall. 93-73 pointed out a tall dark man. "There he is, that tall man there. He's 2,040's new research apprentice. You see him? He's talking to that grey-haired man with the beard."

50-83 gave 93-73 an incredulous look. "What am I supposed to do? Go to him and say, 'How do you do? I work for Persuader 6-96. I'd like to talk to you about 2,040'?"

93-73 raised his eyes to the ceiling in irritation. "You're a Persuader's apprentice and you don't know how to approach someone better than that? Where's the subtle charm? Come on, you can do it." 93-73 stepped behind 50-83 and gave him a push in the direction of 2,040's new research apprentice.

After sending 93-73 a glare for having forced him into the hall, 50-83 turned his attention to the research apprentice. He took on a nonchalant air and stepped up to the two men.

While approaching 2,040's new research apprentice, 50-83 was able to see him face-on over the shoulder of the man the research apprentice was talking to. 2,040's research apprentice had black coarse medium-length hair parted to one side. He had penetrating brown eyes and, beneath his neatly trimmed mustache, a serious mouth that curled up a bit on the sides demonstrating that he had the ability to see the more humorous side of life. He was slender with broad shoulders.

When 50-83 stepped up, 2,040's research assistant acknowledged his presence, yet still focused his primary attention on the man he was talking with.

". . . and even though many of my students were well qualified to work for 2,040, I selected you, 9-85, for this position because you're not only intelligent and hardworking," the bearded man said to 2,040's new research assistant, "but you have good attention to detail. 2,040 needs a man like that . . . Also, you're not ambitious. Too many of my students are, but they don't have what it takes to handle a position of authority. Now, you're a man who can handle the responsibility, so, when the time comes to advance, don't let them hold you back."

9-85 smiled and nodded. "Thank you for your faith in me. And if new positions open for me later on, I will come to you for advice on when and which positions I should accept." He turned to 50-83. "Is there something you were wanting?"

"Uh, yes." 50-83 looked down in thought. "I just wanted to offer you congratulations. I heard that you are going to be working for 2,040. He's an amazing man. Very clever. And I've always been fascinated by his area of research." 50-83 lifted his head and stood tall, trying to appear confident even though he had no idea what topics 2,040 studied.

The bearded man patted 50-83 on the shoulder, impressed. "Absolutely," the man agreed. "Too many people are not disciplined enough to handle the higher mathematics necessary for the research involved in the economics of production."

"Yes, of course . . ." 50-83 nervously shifted his weight. While he could easily manage basic mathematics and algebra, he knew the type of mathematics the man was talking about was way over his head. ". . . And . . . uh, I just know it's essential to keep production going and make it as efficient as possible . . ." 50-83 laughed uneasily.

"You're right, naturally," 9-85 told him, with assurance. "But what a lot of people don't realize is how many factors go into each of the different types of production. Too many times they want to simplify the calculations by narrowing their study to include just a certain number of factors, but what they don't realize is that every one of those factors that they eliminated has an effect on the factors that they chose to include. So, when they do this, what do you think is going to happen to their calculations?"

50-83 looked at 9-85 blankly. "I . . . uh . . . I guess . . . uh,what?"

"They're going to be wrong, of course." 9-85 shook his head and sighed in exasperation, not at 50-83, as 50-83 self-consciously assumed, but at the thought of the calculations being wrong. "And this is the exact type of calculating that is going on in all areas of research. They believe that some element is too small or unimportant for their notice, so they just ignore it. But they don't take into account that the very element that they chose to ignore will cause major problems for them at some time in the future, if not immediately."

50-83 nodded as seriously as he could. "I see what you mean." He put on an air of intelligence.

"Yes," the bearded man smiled proudly. "9-85 is extremely dedicated to research and mathematics. 2,040 is lucky to have you. Good luck. You'll do well." He waved good-bye to 9-85. "And you, too," he turned to 50-83. "It was good to meet a man who has the brains to understand complex mathematics and economics. Perhaps we can get together sometime for coffee. You can help me with the matrices I am working on. They're so complicated, they even cause the computer to throw tantrums. But you wouldn't have any trouble at all with them."

". . . uh . . . sure . . ." 50-83 chuckled nervously.

"You just let me know when would be a good time." He waved once more to 50-83 and 9-85 and made his way on down the corridor.

9-85 walked in the opposite direction. 50-83 followed him, eventually catching up and walking beside him. "You seem to really understand research."

"Well," 9-85 looked away, laughed, and shrugged his shoulders. "Most people in the research department consider my methods radical. 'A nuisance,' they call me. They think that we don't have the time and people necessary to do calculations that are so extensive." He hammered his right fist into his left hand. "We *have* the time. We *have* the people. We even *have* the computers and tools we need. What *they* want is to save a little extra time and a little extra effort and end up with the wrong answer. Why is it so difficult for them to take a little extra time and a little extra effort to get to the truth?" 9-85 turned to 50-83 in anticipation of a reply.

50-83 looked down, pondering what to say. He finally mustered the courage to speak. "The truth can be frightening to some people." His thoughts wandered to the stacks and stacks of tightly closed boxes in his mind that he did not even dare to think about opening.

"To be wrong is more frightening," 9-85 told him emphatically. "By the way, you work in research?"

"Uh, yes."

"What area of research?"

"I research . . . the building of houses . . . and things," 50-83 said with thoughts of constructing the mud-fort still fresh in his mind.

"Oh, excellent." 9-85 smiled. "I'm sure we'll be working together in the future. Your number—?"

50-83 shifted nervously. "It's . . . uh . . . 50-83." He knew he was taking a risk in giving 9-85 his real number , especially when he had already given him a false occupation. If 9-85 found out that he had lied to him, 9-85 would most likely never confide in him again. But 50-83 told 9-85 that he worked in research because his training in persuasion taught him that if he wanted to get information from someone there had to be something he and that other person had in common, such as their occupations. Now, when 9-85 asked him what his number was, 50-83 was tempted to give him a false number, but 50-83 wanted 9-85 to be able to find him easily should he seek him out to talk to him. "And yours is 9-85?"

"Correct." 9-85 paused a moment thoughtfully, then glanced over at the door. "Well, I'll see you later, then." He turned and disappeared through the door.

9-85 entered through a narrow hallway to 2,040's extensive suite of rooms. Centered in front of the entrance was a large white-stone fountain made of three progressively smaller hexagons. Instead of soft streams of water billowing from the center of the fountain, streams of colored electricity danced in a mesmerizing way with blues, pinks, and greens swirling down to the largest hexagon at the base of the fountain. In the ceiling over the fountain was an architectural skylight in the shape of an extended hexagon. Flood lights on the roof poured artificial light in through the skylight, emphasizing the splendor of the fountain. Behind the fountain was a marble staircase leading to a mezzanine that provided a walkway to several rooms on the second level.

On the first level to the left and right of the entrance hallway were computers, globes, telescopes, and other research materials. To the right of the fountain was a living room suite in front of a fireplace. Above the fireplace was a large silver-framed painting of 2,040 ponderously holding a book and a pen. In the far right corner of the room, beyond the living room suite and under the mezzanine, was a doorway to a laboratory. Near the doorway was a white-stone statue of 2,040 wearing robes and holding a telescope. Leading to the laboratory door was a large table containing chemistry equipment such as test tubes, burners, beakers, and jars of chemicals. In the center wall across from the entrance and under the staircase was an alcove containing 2,040's trophy display. In the center of the display was a marble rostrum holding a large book chronicling 2,040's accomplishments. On the wall to the left of the alcove were displayed photographs of 2,040 studiously working on projects and proudly receiving awards. In the far left corner of the room was a recessed library with two walls lined with bookshelves and a table surrounded by chairs in front of the shelves. There was a large blackboard near the table with several mathematical problems worked out halfway. On the left hand wall were several file cabinets and two hallways leading off to other rooms.

9-85 stepped into the room and, while admiring the fountain, rounded it and made his way to the fireplace. As he was studying the painting of 2,040, he heard footsteps on the mezzanine. He turned and saw 2,040 leaning on the railing looking down at him. 2,040 was wearing a white lab jacket which caused his grey hair and beard to look even more intellectual. His blue eyes glimmered excitedly when he spotted 9-85 near the fireplace.

"Oh-ho-ho. Well, I was expecting you, but I didn't think you would come this early." Due to his long legs, 2,040 managed to scurry down the stairs in just a few seconds. The next second, he stood next to 9-85 ready to shake his hand. "Of course maybe you are here on schedule. I don't know. I often lose track of time while I'm in my laboratory." He waved a hand in front of his forehead to bring his mind back to the mundane thoughts of everyday life.

9-85 had been warned that 2,040 was eccentric, but he did not expect to be greeted with such enthusiasm. 9-85 smiled warmly as 2,040 shook his hand and then knitted his eyebrows quizzically as he considered 2,040's last words. "But I thought your laboratory was there." 9-85 indicated the words "laboratory" on the door under the mezzanine.

"Oh, absolutely right." 2,040 nodded and smiled as a mother would when her son had shown promise in his studies even though he had not come up with the exact right answer. "There are stairs in the lab leading up to the mezzanine." He used the first two fingers on his right hand to mimic running up the stairs. "I like to greet my guests from up there. Gives a sense of awe to my sudden presence."

He then glided over to the laboratory door and tapped on it lightly. "34,000," he spoke, nonchalantly, through the door. "Please come out here. I would like you to meet my new research apprentice." His mouth curled up thoughtfully as he took a couple steps back to 9-85. "34,000 is my lab assistant. I think you'll like her. A shy, demure little thing, but, ah, so intelligent." He turned toward the door as 34,000 came out of the laboratory. She removed a pair of lab goggles and set them on a shelf near the door. She had long black hair held back in a loose ponytail. Her large brown eyes were framed by thick dark eyebrows. Her lips were full and rosy pink contrasting with her tan complexion. Her cheekbones were prominent and her nose was thin and distinguished. She stood with a confident air as she removed her gloves and her lab jacket.

"So, this is your new research apprentice. At least he doesn't look as young and naïve as the last one." She moved over to 2,040 and helped him off with his lab jacket.

"Oh, he *is* clever," 2,040 agreed, lowering his eyelids in complacency, "and *trustworthy*, too. I've been doing some research on him, to make sure this time, they gave me a research apprentice with intelligence and loyalty. But, I'll be watching to see if *everything* they say about him is true," he said to 34,000 even though he was looking pointedly at 9-85.

9-85 looked down and shook his head modestly. "I don't claim to be anywhere near a genius. I just know how to research and I know how to find the answers. The *correct* answers."

2,040 clapped his hands in approval. "Perfect." He leaned forward in an entre nous fashion. "I like the way you talk. You know just what to say. Of course we want to come up with the correct answers." As he spoke, he led 9-85 over to the living room suite. "But do you realize how many correct answers are disregarded as soon as they reach the higher ups?" 2,040 sat in a chair near the fireplace and placed a hand to his weary forehead. "Oh, how hard it is to please the fools."

34,000 stood behind 2,040 and placed her hands on his shoulders and massaged them.

"Thank you, dear." 2,040 patted her left hand gratefully. "Just down a little further in the middle of the back . . . there, that's better." He reluctantly turned his attention from the relaxing massage to give 9-85 a meaningful look. "Now, when I say 'fools' don't take my meaning wrong. I love every one of those precious little dictators dearly. I use the word 'fools' merely as a term of endearment." 2,040 snickered at the irony of what he had just said.

9-85 sat on a couch across from 2,040. "It must be discouraging to have them disregard the work you do."

2,040 sat back in his chair and brushed the thought aside. "Not at all. I'm used to it by now. Besides, my brain works so fast that I can work out the necessary equations quickly and send them off just like that." He snapped his fingers emphatically. "And that leaves me with extra time to work on projects of more importance."

34,000 sat next to 9-85. "2,040 is a genius," she said with conviction. "He has thorough knowledge in so many areas. In his free time, he is working on a variety of important projects to help make our planet a better place for everyone to live."

9-85 looked over at 2,040 impressed but skeptical. "Sounds admirable. And what is your reason for doing all this?" 9-85 had never met anyone generous and considerate enough to do any type of charitable act without an ulterior motive.

2,040 leaned forward in 34,000's direction. "Bring us a bottle of that excellent wine and some glasses, won't you, dear?" 34,000 slipped off to procure the wine. 2,040 turned confidentially to 9-85. "How would you like to live forever?" He gave 9-85 a solemn expression as he turned his hand slowly as if around some fascinating globe of wisdom.

9-85 raised his eyebrows in surprise. "While I admit most people would love to live forever, we realize it is an impossibility. Are you referring to the 'life after death' some people believe in?" He gave 2,040 a cynical look, speculating whether 2,040 was one of the handful of philosophers who claimed there was no way to disprove a judgment beyond death existed.

2,040 chuckled and shook his head. "No, of course not. And, being an intelligent man, I am perfectly aware that no one can *really* live forever. But," 2,040 moved excitedly over to the couch and sat next to 9-85, "there is a way to see that your persona lives forever. Ah. Fame. Sweet Fame," he said as if reciting a dramatic poem. "The one who breathes life into the dead so that they may live forever in the hearts and minds of people everywhere."

34,000 returned with a bottle of wine and three glasses. She set them on the coffee table and uncorked the bottle.

2,040 took the bottle from 34,000 and looked at the label. "Excellent," he smiled at 34,000. She lowered her eyes, bashful but pleased. "A very good year and chilled just right." 2,040 handed the bottle back to her. He gazed into her steadfast brown eyes and smiled in confidence. "You are invaluable, 34,000."

34,000 smiled serenely as she poured three glasses and distributed them. "I overheard your soliloquy on fame." She tilted her head to one side, taking pride in the great talents of the man she assisted.

2,040 laughed, feigning modesty, as he brushed off her attention with a wave of one hand. "Oh, just a little something I came up with off the cuff."

She looked into 2,040's eyes tenderly. "Well, then why don't we drink a toast to fame?"

"Brilliant." 2,040 stood and lifted his glass before him with the air of a priest ready to perform a holy rite. "To fame. May it bless each one of us with eternal life."

They each stood and lifted their glasses in the toast then brought the glasses to their lips.

9-85 sat back down. "So, that is your main goal? To gain fame from your projects?"

2,040 pulled on his ear in thought and sat next to 9-85. "In reality, my goal is three-fold. That goal is made of popularity, prosperity, and protection. Popularity is my means to eternal life and prosperity gives me prestige. And protection — Ah-ha-ha. No matter what happens, I will be safe here. The walls to this room are equipped with a second protective wall I can bring down anytime I choose." 2,040 made his way over to the statue of himself. He pressed a hidden button at the base of the statue, and a panel in the wall behind it opened up. Inside the panel was a plate of black glass. 2,040 pressed his hand firm on the plate of glass, and a bright blue line of light moved from the top to bottom, reading information from his hand. There was a beep, and the glass panel lit to a bright green. A heavy, thick metal wall fell with a heavy thud on three sides of the room, the wall to the outside hall, the wall with the fireplace, and the wall leading to the laboratory. "This wall is extremely thick, and, when I turn it on, it will melt anything that touches it." He pressed a series of buttons located below the plate of glass, and a loud humming filled the room. 2,040 picked up a metal bowl from his laboratory table and threw it at the wall. When the bowl hit the wall, it heated up until white hot and disintegrated into ashes.

"Impressive." 9-85 nodded in approval with new respect for 2,040.

"You think that is impressive? Well, come with me." 2,040 set down his glass and gestured for 9-85 and 34,000 to follow him.

2,040 led them to the other side of the fountain. He pushed aside a large file cabinet, and behind it was revealed a hidden metal door. Near the door was a narrow panel with six buttons arranged vertically. 2,040 pressed the buttons in a particular order and the metal door slid open. 9-85 and 34,000 followed 2,040 through the door and into a hidden physics laboratory. The room was dark, lit by only one directional light hanging from a wire on the ceiling. The walls were lined by tables and shelves strewn with wires, various parts, and tools. In one corner was a large power generator producing powerful flashes of electricity moving from one energy conduit to another. The generator and the hanging lamp sent out a hard light, casting eerie shadows throughout the chamber. At the far end of the room was a capacious vehicle enclosed in a thick glass cubicle to keep it protected from prying hands. The compartment of the vehicle that held passengers was of rounded glass. The body of the vehicle was of shiny white metal. Doors opened on either side and, instead of wheels, the vehicle stood on thruster rockets.

2,040 wrung his hands together in excitement as he moved to the vehicle. "Look. Isn't it beautiful? Now, if the higher-ups become too jealous of my great success, I have a means to escape their vengeance. This is my escape vehicle." He directed a grand gesture toward the vehicle. "It can travel through any type of terrain. It can move in any direction — Up — Down — Across — And even — Whoosh — off into outer space." As he admired the vehicle, he held his hands tightly together at his mouth and placed the side of one of his fingers between his teeth to contain his enthusiasm.

9-85 studied the vehicle. "It appears to be a well-constructed piece of machinery. What's its power source?"

"It can generate energy from the hydrogen in water, but its primary source of energy is from geothermal heat. If it should run out of energy, it is programmed to spot sources of molten magma and to drill into the earth to draw energy from those sources. This planet is rich in geothermal energy, you know."

9-85 nodded in agreement.

"And . . ." 2,040 moved over to the wall near the glass cubicle containing the vehicle. He pressed a point in the wall that opened a hidden door disguised as part of the wall. ". . . Should it become necessary to get away quickly in my escape vehicle, I'm even prepared with this handy escape tunnel." He took a lamp from a table nearby and lit it. He stood in the doorway with the lamp and gestured for 9-85 to enter first.

9-85 peered uneasily into the dark tunnel. He was often insecure when faced with the unknown. He shook his head decidedly. "It's your tunnel. You lead the way."

"If you insist." 2,040 led 9-85 and 34,000 into the tunnel. The lamp did not brighten the tunnel enough to dispel the dark shadows, but did give enough light to demonstrate it was large enough to contain the vehicle. "Très convenient, non?" He beamed.

9-85 smiled and shook his head in amazement. While 9-85 was overwhelmed by the mental and physical effort that 2,040 had put into his escape plan, he was not convinced he had enough information to give a detailed analysis on the feasibility of the plan. Still, 9-85 thought 2,040 deserved a certain amount of praise for the immense amount of effort he had put forth. He gave 2,040 a pat on the shoulder. "It looks like you thought of everything."

Chapter Ten

5 0-83 arrived at the door leading to 1-13's apartment intending to tell him about his visit to 4,021. He hesitated when the door failed to open to him. The only way he could enter now was if he placed his hand on the palm identifier set in the wall next to the door. Unfortunately, the palm identifier not only identified people by their fingerprints and DNA, but it also sent records of where that person was and when to the Main Information Center. Through these records, the Dark Tyrant and 6-96 could learn 50-83 had been visiting 1-13. And, that was one thing 50-83 did not want anyone finding out about.

50-83 turned to leave when his path was blocked by two of 1-13's tall, muscular guards. He looked at the guards askance. The guards' only answer was a forward gesture of their large axes indicating that 50-83 was to head back to 1-13's apartment. 50-83 sighed and turned around even though he was uncomfortable not knowing what the guards with their huge axes were up to behind his back. One of the guards placed his own hand on the palm identifier and the door opened. The guards conducted 50-83 into the apartment.

1-13 approached them with a friendly smile and his hands folded in front of him in a priestly fashion. He nodded in the direction of the two guards and they returned a slight bow and left the room. 50-83 took a deep breath and unstiffened a bit.

1-13's apartment was not large but was luxuriously designed and decorated. The foyer was set off by three walls, one with the door leading from the hall, and another forming a corner with the first wall to provide a cozy study nook with a desk and chair. The third wall contained the door that led to the prison cells. The third wall formed a corner with the first to frame an area for 1-13's bed and nightstand. The shape of the rest of the room was circular. Several curved bookshelves lined the circular wall and whatever wall space was not covered by bookshelves or windows was decorated by large abstract paintings. In the center of the room was a small cushioned couch and chair graced by a coffee table and end table.

"*So*," 1-13 said, "I am *pleased* that you took the *time* to come and *visit me*." He led 50-83 over to the couch and gestured for him to sit.

50-83 made himself comfortable on the couch.

1-13 held out an opened cigar box, encouraging 50-83 to take one. "*You* should appreciate *these*. They're very expensive."

50-83 selected a cigar, and 1-13 took a silver lighter from the table and lit it for him.

1-13 picked out a cigar for himself and sat in the chair. He lit his own cigar. "I know *you*. You like valuable things, don't you?" With an aristocratic blasé manner, he indicated the cigar in 50-83's hand.

50-83 stopped puffing on his cigar a moment and sunk a bit deeper into the couch self-consciously. "Doesn't everybody?"

1-13 raised his head higher, realizing he had found one of 50-83's weak points. "Not *everybody* appreciates them with as much *discrimination* as *you* and *me*." He breathed in a draught of smoke from his cigar then, as he exhaled, he waved his cigar in the direction of a large painting on the wall. "Some people would even consider that *masterpiece* to be garbage. Now *you* and *I* know the artistic value of such a *work* of *art*."

50-83 looked at the painting. He was impressed by the swirls and waves in the gold gilded frame, but 50-83 found the blotches and streaks of color in the painting confusing. "The painting is very interesting." 50-83 tried to indulge 1-13's unusual taste in art.

"*Naturally*," 1-13 nodded and smiled. He chuckled to himself, amused by the bewildered look in 50-83's eyes as he tried to interpret the painting.

"I didn't come here to discuss art. I thought you wanted me to tell you what I found out from 4,021." He had been annoyed with 1-13 for a long time, and was now reaching the point where he found no reason he should tell him anything. He decided to explain to him that he learned nothing from 4,021 and quickly end his obligations to 1-13.

"Naturally, but *patience*," 1-13 said as a parent tenderly scolding a child. "Perhaps you would *like* a glass of *wine*?"

50-83 took in a lungful of cigar smoke. His hands and head relaxed unnaturally. While 50-83 did not care for any wine, he found himself unable to refuse. "Yes," he agreed, noticing a sudden dizzy sensation in his head.

"*Perfect*," 1-13's mouth curled up in a satisfied smile. He stepped to a bar near his desk and poured two glasses of wine, one from the original bottle and the other from a decanter. He handed 50-83 the glass of wine poured from the decanter. "This *is* excellent wine. I'm *certain* you will *like* it." To conceal a chuckle at his own cleverness, 1-13 took a drink of wine from his glass and gestured for 50-83 to do the same.

50-83 wanted to let 1-13 know he had no right to order him to do anything, so he set his glass firmly down on the table to make the point. When he tried to reach his hand holding the wine glass toward the coffee table, however, he was unable to move. The only movement he could make was to look up. His eyes became fixed on 1-13. 1-13 gestured once more for 50-83 to drink the wine. 50-83 could not resist and all he could do was to move the glass to his lips. He took a drink from the glass. The room dimmed, and everything became dark.

1-13 set both glasses on the coffee table and moved forward to keep 50-83 from falling. He leaned 50-83's head back to the arm of the couch and lifted his feet so that 50-83 was lying on the couch. He took the cigar from 50-83's hand and set it in an ashtray on the coffee table. Afterwards, 1-13 walked casually to a button on the side of a bookshelf and pressed it. The lights in the room dimmed. Specks of light resembling stars lit up and danced on the ceiling.

1-13 returned to 50-83 and reached into an inside pocket of 50-83's vest. He pulled out a small recording device no larger than a square inch. He had secretly placed the recording device there while 50-83 was in his mud-crawler earlier. He pressed a small button on the device and listened to the recording. He smiled, pleased that the device had clearly recorded 50-83's whole conversation with 4,021. After listening, he turned the recorder off. He leaned over 50-83 and waved a hand over 50-83's eyes. "You may *open* your *eyes,* but you must only *do* as I *say.*"

50-83 opened his eyes and saw the starlight spinning on the ceiling. His heart lightened and nothing worried him. He wanted to fly up to the stars and join them, but he was convinced he could not move unless 1-13 told him he could.

"*Now* that I have heard every word that passed between you and 4,021 . . ." 1-13 held up the recording device. ". . . we go on to the *next* step of our plan. *First*, when you go back to 6-96, *don't* tell her anything about the conversations you've had with 4,021 and *me*."

The induced sense of elation in 50-83 came crashing down at the realization that he had been duped and had no agency to prevent it. Still, the hypnotic influence was strong, and he could say nothing but "Yes, sir."

1-13 patted 50-83 on the head paternalistically and sat down. "Now, when you don't bring back any promising information, I bet that 6-96 will want to torture 4,021 to acquire the information she needs." 1-13 moved his hand behind 50-83's back indicating that he could resume controlling his own actions.

50-83 rose and looked at him askance. "But you said we wouldn't let her do that."

1-13 stood as tall as possible. "So, you are becoming fond of 4,021."

50-83 was exasperated with 1-13. *What makes 1-13 think he has any right to pry into my feelings, whatever they are?* 50-83 turned hotly away from 1-13 to look out a window near one of the bookshelves. "6-96's method of torture is cruel and I wouldn't—"

1-13 pursed his lips with disdain and stepped up behind him. "Yes, 6-96 *is* barbaric. What you need to do is bring 4,021 to *me*. It is for her *protection*. My questioning methods are *sophisticated*. It doesn't sound to me like 4,021 has done anything very *wrong*. At the most, she'll just be reprimanded." 1-13 leaned his back on the side of the bookshelf. The nearby lights placed low on the wall produced an unnatural green glow on his face and the upward lighting caused his uncanny expression to appear even eerier.

50-83 gazed out the window at the dark sky and the tiny lights of the few brave stars that managed to glow bright enough to bring a small amount of light to so dark a world. He looked deep into the darkness, wondering if 4,021's dream had any basis in reality. He did not see any spaceships entering the atmosphere. He did not see any hero reaching out to rescue anyone. *They certainly wouldn't punish someone for hoping for something that could never happen.* 50-83 glanced over at 1-13 and shrugged. "Yes, maybe you're right" He headed for the door.

"Good." 1-13 pushed himself from the side of the bookshelf and followed him. "So, you'll bring 4,021 to *me*?"

"Of course."

They shook hands in agreement. 50-83 kept his eyes averted from 1-13's and the palms of 50-83's hands were sweaty. *He's afraid of me,* 1-13 gloated. *He'll do whatever I say.*

In the spaceship, the *Journey*, 2-45 was lying down on his cot in his cabin. He noticed several small cabinets built into one of the walls and decided to ascertain their contents. He rose from his cot and stepped over to the cabinets and rummaged through them. He had just run across a liquor cabinet and pulled out a small bottle of claret to look at its label when his cabin door opened and 1-05 stood in the doorway with a hand on her hip.

"So," 1-05 said in a biting tone, "I see you're spending your time wisely."

2-45 smiled nervously. "I wasn't planning on drinking it." He replaced the bottle and gestured toward the cabinets. "I was just curious about what was in them and . . . now I know."

1-05 took the bottle of claret back out of the cabinet and handed it to him in an unconcerned manner. "If you want to drink it, go ahead." She crossed her arms over her chest and leaned back against the doorframe. "Just to inform you, while you were busy snooping through your cabinets, I was doing some calculations. Do you realize that within forty-two hours, our ship could be attacked by gorslanchers? At least that's what the radar is picking up in our path."

2-45 set the bottle back into the cabinet and looked at 1-05 seriously as he rested his index finger against his lower lip in thought. "What type of defenses does this ship have?"

"Standard defenses." 1-05 shook her head in concern. "But the radar is picking up a lot of them, and if we are attacked, our ship is no match. Gorslanchers can quickly chew through our weapons' wiring system, and have found ways to jam the ship's protective radiation layer. If they board this ship, we can consider ourselves done for."

"Does anything kill them?" 2-45 closed the cupboard door and leaned one hand on it. He watched her expression closely, mentally keeping his fingers crossed for a positive answer.

"Have you ever used a pro-58 exterminating gun?"

"No," he shrugged. "In fact, I've never used any gun more sophisticated than a slingshot, and that was when I was seven years old."

1-05 chuckled bitterly. "As a Propaganda Specialist, you were probably expected to abide by the Dark Tyrant's glorious laws which include no arming of the people." She pressed her lips together in a perturbed frown. "The Dark Tyrant despises anything that could hinder his Enforcers. The second he orders it, he expects them to storm in and easily lock up any or all helpless citizens."

"I do have a fairly good aim. Whenever I was bored, I would toss paper wads at a rival Propaganda Specialist." He smirked as he remembered the exasperated expression on the other man's face. However, he brought his mind back to the situation at hand and looked at 1-05 earnestly. "And I'm not against trying my hand at an exterminating gun."

"You're going to need some practice." She pushed herself off the doorframe. "I wish you would have thought of this a few years back. Then we wouldn't need this crash course." She gestured for 2-45 to follow her down the hall to Storage Room C.

As 2-45 accompanied 1-05, they ran into 7-43. 1-05 looked at him drily. "Okay, and hello, Mr. Stowaway."

7-43 tipped an imaginary hat and bowed to her with an exaggerated politeness. "Well, well, I'm famous. And what's the jolly fun you two are up to now?"

2-45 tapped the knuckles of his fist on top of 7-43's head. "Wake up. What's going on isn't all 'jolly fun'. Unless, of course, it tickles your fancy to bump into a slew of gorslanchers." His expression turned deadly serious. "We're going for our first lesson in target practice, and you're coming along." He grabbed 7-43 by the arm, leading him down the hall. He chuckled in an over-dramatized evilness and looked at him intently, "Maybe you can be the target."

7-43 pulled his arm out of 2-45's grip and grimaced as he rubbed it. "I believe your brain is brimming with bonkers. I'm leaving." He winced with a slight pout and turned to leave.

As 7-43 tried to brush past him, 2-45 blocked the hallway with his arm. "No, you're coming with us."

7-43 turned to 2-45, perturbed. "I refuse to have anything to do with guns. They're blinking illegal."

"Oh, really," 2-45 feigned surprise. "And I suppose when those gorslanchers force their way on board, you'll shout, 'Don't worry, I'm not carrying any illegal weapons.' And they'll turn to you, smile, and say, 'Good,' while they *very legally* bite your head off."

"Let him go." 1-05 waved 7-43 off. "He'd just be in the way."

2-45 reluctantly stepped out of 7-43's path and 7-43 made his way down the hall, turned back and blew 2-45 a 'so-there' kiss goodbye before continuing on. 2-45 shot after him an exasperated glare, then turned insistently back to 1-05. "He should come with us. He's the sort of person who could wreck the whole ship just by accidentally running into the wrong button."

1-05 lifted a hand, gesturing for 2-45 not to worry. "Alpha 3-0-3 is watching the controls, and if he dares to step into the engine room, the alarm will go off." She led 2-45 into Storage Room C. "Right now, you only have a few hours to get used to firing one of these." She took the parts of a pro-58 exterminating gun from a crate near the wall, locked the pieces together, and placed the gun in 2-45's hands.

2-45 took the gun. The gun's weight caused his hands to drop a couple inches. 2-45 chuckled lightly. "A little heavier than I expected."

"It's not a toy, you know." 1-05 turned, made a fist, and pounded it on the wall. "The walls of this storage room are reinforced, so you won't do any real damage." She guided 2-

45 to take a few steps back and pointed to a target on the wall. "It's important that you can hit the target, as opposed to the wall, the ceiling or those boxes over there. Ideally, you will be able to hit the point right in the middle, but I'm not expecting that on the first try."

"You don't have much faith in me, do you?" he murmured, looking thoughtfully into her eyes.

"I have faith in you," she said spiritedly, holding herself even higher. "I'm standing in the same room as you when you're going to be firing that gun."

2-45 smiled and nodded. "You win," he admitted resignedly as he held the gun up and looked for the trigger.

"Right here," she sighed wearily as she moved his hand to the triggering mechanism.

He smiled at her in an 'I-really-knew-that' manner and acquired a firm grip on the gun and the trigger. "Now?" he asked with a subtle raise of his eyebrow.

"First, make sure you're aiming at the target," she reminded him matter-of-factly.

2-45 aimed the gun at the target and fired, creating a large deep black hole near the ceiling. He blushed. "I didn't do very well, did I?"

"Let's say all you managed to do is make the gorslancher angrier." She smirked and placed her one hand confidently on her left hip as she took the gun from him with her other hand. "But your aim isn't bad. You just need to hold the gun firmer against your shoulder and when you're aiming, allow for the recoil. The force often pushes the gun back and up."

"Maybe if you show me how . . . ?"

1-05 nodded and held the gun firmly in place and aimed at the target. She hit the target dead in the center. She lowered the gun and turned to 2-45 with a self-assured raise of her chin.

2-45 smiled and clapped his approval. "Excellent. At least we have one defender who will hit the target."

"I warned you that trying to make it to the Planet of Light would not be easy." She handed the gun back to 2-45. "Why are you so determined to get there?"

2-45 held the gun in his hand and looked her in the eyes seriously. "Like I told you, I'm a Propaganda Specialist and working in an atmosphere full of half-truths and misrepresentations made me wonder. If you have to use deceitful methods such as propaganda to convince people about something, how could that something be true? I personally think the whole system set up by the Dark Tyrant and his associates is nothing but some hyped-up hoax. I want something I can believe in, and I'm hoping I can find that in the Planet of Light." He leaned his back against the wall and looked thoughtfully down at the gun in his hand.

1-05 was swept away by his speech. She stepped closer to him.

He raised his eyes to hers.

She looked deep into his eyes and could tell that he believed completely in what he was saying. She smiled at him and embraced his arm with her hand. "I hope so, too. But what made you decide to try the Planet of Light before any of the other planets in the area?" She knitted her eyebrows, questioningly.

He patted the hand she had placed on his arm. "Not long ago I started reading this book. It was a banned book, of course. That made the reading all the more interesting. The book described the human soul. It said that the human soul longs for light." 2-45 pushed himself off of the wall and faced the target. He held the gun firmly and aimed. He fired and hit the target near the center.

Chapter Eleven

Not long after 50-83 had left, 1-13 lit himself another cigar and reclined back onto the bed and smoked. He pondered the progress he was making on his current objectives. He considered how his infatuation with 4,021 and his hatred of 6-96 had motivated him into interfering in one of 6-96's tasks for the Dark Tyrant. If his plan went well, he should easily ruin 6-96's ability to finish her assignment and destroy her reputation as the Dark Tyrant's top Persuader as well. 1-13 found it amusing that by using her own apprentice, he was setting up her defeat. He narrowed his eyes and smiled with satisfaction as he reviewed the strategy he was formulating in his mind. *First, see that 50-83 brings 4,021 to my workshop before 6-96 has a chance to take her. Then, using my expert skills in persuasion, I will convince her to tell me the details about whatever-it-is she is plotting with that man she said is coming to her in a spaceship from far away. Ridiculous little story, but if it helps me, instead of 6-96, to receive commendations from the Dark Tyrant, it is worth the effort.* 1-13 paused in his thoughts and frowned. He realized the uselessness in stealing the praise away from 6-96 if he failed to finish his own assignment. He swiftly rose from his bed, placed his cigar in an ashtray on his nightstand, and stepped over to the door leading to the hallway.

As he made his way swiftly down the hall, he reviewed the task the Dark Tyrant had given to him. *What was it he wanted me to do? There was some ship that was trying to leave our planet. Simple enough. Find out if the Control Fleet have captured the ship. When they have, question those on board. Present my report to the Dark Tyrant and soon I'll receive accolades for both assignments.* With his one-two-three to-do list in his mind, he reached the Control Fleet's Tactical Center.

1-13 entered with an energy that was ready to undertake his task. The center was small with dark orange walls. In the middle of the room was a strategy table where the Control Fleet Commanders originated their plans of attack. The table was large, rectangular, and made of black metal, the top of which glowed with a soft blue light. Covering the wall straight across from the entrance were three large monitors. Control Fleet Observers sat at the consoles in front of these monitors and switched through various monitor views of the area of space just off of the Planet of Darkness alert for signs of anything unauthorized leaving or approaching the planet. Whenever the Control Fleet Observers located an unauthorized form, they brought its radar readings to the attention of the Location Calculators. The Location Calculators sat at computer consoles in a corner to the left of the entrance. They performed calculations on the unauthorized form to obtain every possible bit of information that the Control Fleet Commanders would find necessary, such as what the unauthorized form is, where the form is projected to be so many minutes from now, if there are any humans inside this form and how many, and/or what is the history of this form, etc.

1-13 marched determinedly up to the Commander in command, 906, a sturdy, middle-aged woman with short reddish hair.

"Persuader 1-13?" The Control Fleet Commander regarded him with a nod. "The Civilian Control leader told us to expect you." She tapped her head with her index finger in concentration. "Now this is in regards to . . . ?"

1-13, taking on an overly official attitude, stood tall with his chin raised and his arms behind his back. "A certain *spaceship* . . . It has left our planet *without* permission. There are *orders* for you to intercept this spaceship. I am to take the passengers into custody for *questioning*. How *soon* will you be able to deliver these passengers to *me*?"

"I will have an estimate for you shortly. It was just a few minutes ago that we located the spaceship." She gestured over to the Location Calculators working at their consoles in the corner of the room. "They are calculating the necessary information right now."

1-13 glanced over at the Location Calculators working feverishly on the data they were gathering. He nodded seriously as he turned back to the Control Fleet Commander. "*Good*. I'm *pleased* you have everything under control."

"Yes." the Control Fleet Commander moved over to the strategy table and leaned forward with her hands on top of it. "It's basically routine now." Her face was lacking expression, yet she was ready to talk for hours on the efficiency of the Control Fleet Branch of the Dark Tyrant's forces. "The technological advances made on our planet, thanks to the excellent ruling of our Dark Tyrant, have brought us to the point where there really is no way anyone could make it off this planet unseen. With our new quasatic radar that pinpoints even the smallest objects and heat identification devices, it would be—"

She was interrupted by one of the Location Calculators who turned to her. "The information is ready, Commander."

The Control Fleet Commander straightened herself. "Send the information over."

"Yes, Commander." The Location Calculator turned to his console and pressed in a series of buttons as he watched the monitor carefully.

The Control Fleet Commander focused on the strategy table, waiting for the information to come through.

1-13 stood next to the Control Fleet Commander. He followed her gaze to the strategy table and saw the table was made of several screens with a long list of information appearing on one of them. 1-13 tried to read the list, but the information was scrolling too fast. He turned his attention to the Control Fleet Commander, who appeared capable of gathering the information she needed from the fast moving words and numbers.

The Control Fleet Commander finished digesting the information and pressed a button on the side of the strategy table. A 3-D image of the *Journey* floated over the table. She contemplated the image with a serious frown and knitted eyebrows.

1-13 looked at her with anticipation. "*What* have you *learned*?"

The Control Fleet Commander tapped the fingers of her hand on the table in thought. "The pilot of this spaceship is 1-05. She is an infamous gunrunner dealing in illegal weapons. They have a large supply of weapons on board. While there are only three people on the ship, they could put up a fight."

"In *other* words, it may take you some *time* to capture them." 1-13's fists tightened at his sides.

"It could be hours. It could be minutes." The Control Fleet Commander turned to an officer and waved him to join her at the table. As the officer stepped up, the Control Fleet Commander looked back at 1-13. "Either way, I think you would be wasting your time waiting around here. We will let you know when we have captured them and in what condition they are in."

1-13's eyes flashed fire, and he slammed his fist on the table. "Well, they better be in a condition to talk." His eyes were fixed meaningfully on hers. "The Dark Tyrant wants information out of them. *So watch it.*" He turned from them and marched out of the room.

The Control Fleet Commander scrunched her nose at the nuisance of 1-13's outburst. She took on a serious expression as she faced the officer. "Our best option is to use three Control Craft. Prepare them immediately."

"Right away, Commander." The officer nodded and exited, heading toward the hangars.

The Control Fleet Commander moved back to the strategy table and pressed a series of buttons on the side of the table. The 3-D images of three Control Craft appeared over the strategy table moving in on the 3-D image of the *Journey*. The Control Fleet Commander watched the images in confident expectation.

The *Ghost III* whizzed at top speed through space enroute to the Planet of Darkness. On a couch in the lounge of the ship, the Way-Guide woke from a deep sleep. He moved his arms above his head to stretch out any stiffness and sat up. Infinity carried in a tray of food.

He stood beside the Way-Guide. "Did you have a good rest?"

"Yes, I did." The Way-Guide rubbed his head to ensure that he was fully awake. "But I didn't mean to doze off like that. I'm sure you needed my help."

"It is more important that you rested. There are dangerous regions ahead that will require us to be constantly alert. You need to sleep while you can." Infinity placed the tray on the Way-Guide's lap. "Here. You need to eat."

The Way-Guide looked down at a delicious breakfast of coffee, pancakes, and scrambled eggs. He eagerly took a sip of coffee.

On the far wall there was a floor to ceiling window. Infinity gazed out watchfully past the shadows of space in the direction of the Planet of Darkness.

"Aren't you going to have any breakfast?" the Way-Guide asked with concern as he set down the mug and took up his fork.

"Later. Right now a message is coming through." Infinity placed his right hand to his right ear as he concentrated his attention on the communication device implanted in his ear. This device permitted Infinity and the *Ghost III* to converse directly over any distance. "Yes, *Ghost III*. What is it you have to tell me?"

The *Ghost III's* voice was authoritative and emphatic. It echoed both throughout the ship as well as through Infinity's communication device, *"I have vital information concerning a young woman on the Planet of Darkness. One of the many who are searching for a way out."*

The *Ghost III* lowered a viewing screen in front of the floor to ceiling window.

The Way-Guide set his tray on a table and stepped up beside Infinity. He watched the viewing screen with anticipation. It displayed the Planet of Darkness. The image zoomed in closer and closer on the planet bringing into view the dark valleys and muddy hills. Eventually, 4,021 was seen standing in front of her hovel, looking hopefully into the starry sky.

"This young woman is in danger," the *Ghost III* told Infinity. *"Forces are conspiring to discourage her. She must be protected and encouraged."*

"Yes, *Ghost III*, you are right," Infinity said with firm determination. "And she WILL be encouraged. She WILL be protected." He swished his cape back over his shoulder.

The image on the screen faded to black, and the *Ghost III* raised the screen revealing once more the star-speckled black sky that enveloped the ship.

The Way-Guide turned to Infinity with concern. "How are we going to help her? It will be several days before we reach the Planet of Darkness. What can we do?"

Infinity looked straight at the Way-Guide, unmoved. "We don't have to be physically there to protect her. We will send a little of our power ahead of us."

Infinity walked over to a long rectangular glass table surrounded by ten crystal blue chairs. He reached over to a clear crystal vase in the shape of a perfect right triangle that sat in the center of the table. He took from the vase a large beautiful red rose. He then placed his hand into a pocket of his black and red duvetyn vest and retrieved a piece of paper. He seated himself at the table, took a pen that burned with fire, and wrote something on the paper, creating a river of words that glowed red with power. After writing, he wrapped the paper around the rose and placed it into a cylindrical container.

Holding the cylindrical container, Infinity stepped over to the floor to ceiling window. On the wall next to the window was a small metal door. Infinity pulled open the door and set the container inside a small launching compartment. After closing the door, he pressed a series of buttons and the container was hurled off into space.

4,021 stood outside her dwelling place. She gazed at the blackness, wondering if her dream would ever become a reality. She noticed an object fall from the dark sky and land right in front of her.

4,021 stepped over toward it and saw that it was a container. She knelt next to it and reached out to touch it when the container melted into the mud to reveal its contents. Before her, on the muddy ground, was a beautiful red rose with a note wrapped around it. She looked at the rose in awe. She had never seen anything so beautiful. Because of the lack of light, blossoming flowers could not grow on the Planet of Darkness. She picked up the rose and caressed it. After unfolding the note from around the rose, she looked at it and even though she could not read, she heard the words in her mind.

Dear Hopeful One,

> *Do not let anyone discourage you. I am on my way to you, and I look forward to greeting you and holding you in my arms.*
>
> *Believe me when I say, I love you. I will rescue you and take you away from all those who do not treat you with the kindness and the respect that you deserve.*
>
> *Again, I love you. Keep this rose near your heart. It is a symbol of my love, and it will protect you.*
>
> *Your friend and your lover,*
> *Infinity*

4,021 smiled, enraptured, as she looked up at the sky. "Thank you, Infinity. I look forward to seeing you." She took the rose and folded the note around it. Afterwards, she tenderly placed both the rose and the note into a pocket near her heart.

Chapter Twelve

7-43 wandered aimlessly down the hall of the *Journey*, trying to find some way to amuse himself. He was used to having all forms of entertainment flung at him in the Dive of Distraction, and now here, he found the liquor locked up and the company uninteresting. He detested being bored. He stopped in the middle of the hall and tried out the double tap-tap shuffle-shuffle of a new dance step, and by chance stumbled his way into the cockpit area. Upon entering, his boredom was cut short. He was shocked to see, sitting in the pilot's chair, 2-45, whom he had just left a ways down the hall not seconds ago.

After his initial shock wore off, 7-43 burst into laughter. "Now that is some bizabulous bippity-bam magic trick you just did. How did you manage to whiz-wammit like *that*." He punctuated the "that" with an enthusiastic wave of his hand as if he were waving a magic wand.

2-45 stood from the pilot's chair and turned to face 7-43 with an expressionless look. "Your language is difficult to assess," he said with the mechanical inflectionless voice of Alpha 3-0-3. "Could you please rephrase your last statements?"

7-43's mouth fell open with surprise. "Blast my blinkers. You're not 2-45. You must be that nasty little shape-shifter they told me about." 7-43's look of surprise transformed into a sneaky grin. "Is it true that you can transform into just about anything?"

Alpha 3-0-3's eyes skewed up in thought. "Well . . . yes . . . practically. I can't make myself as big as a planet if that is what you are wanting to know."

7-43 chuckled contemptuously at the ridiculous idea of Alpha 3-0-3 transforming into a planet. Afterwards, he tried to stifle his laughter, but could not keep his voice from fluctuating. "Oh, that is just too bad."

Alpha 3-0-3 tilted its head to the side, trying to analyze the unusual personality of 7-43. "I'm glad you are happy . . . yet you aren't really . . . you may laugh, but you are really very sad. What is making you sad?" It looked into 7-43's eyes with concern.

"What's making me sad?" 7-43 sighed an indolent sigh as he sunk lazily into one of the passenger's chairs, putting his feet on the chair in front of him. "I'm so blistering bored, that's what. I've never been so bored in my life." Lounging back in the chair, he tapped the fingers of both hands together. "I want to be distracted. I want to be entertained." He pulled himself closer to Alpha 3-0-3 to ask confidentially, "By the bye, are you able to transform yourself into a curvy dancing girl and do some sexy rhumba?" He raised one eyebrow as he eyed Alpha 3-0-3 in eager anticipation.

Alpha 3-0-3 touched its finger to its chin in thought, nodded, then smiled satisfied with its decision. "You don't want to be distracted. You just don't want to think."

"You changed the subject. Aren't you one of those robot thingies that are supposed to do whatever the blazes I say?"

"No," Alpha 3-0-3 replied matter-of-factly. "I'm only loyal to 1-05. No matter how much you command me to do something, I won't do it unless I know it will help her."

7-43 pursed his lips into a pout. "Oh, you're such a jerk-aholic. Anyways," he said, coming up with, what he considered, a clever new angle, "your entertaining me does help 1-05. It keeps me out of her way." A languid smile spread on his lips. "So? You didn't answer me. Could you turn into a sexy dancing girl?"

With a philosophic air, Alpha 3-0-3 walked back over to the console. "Your question is irrelevant because I have already answered it." It sat in the pilot's chair and used the ship's outside camera system to keep an eye on the surrounding area.

"Your *answer* is irrelevant," 7-43 snorted. "I mean, what's this heaping rubbish you're giving me? I know better than to—" A screeching alarm suddenly sounded, causing 7-43 to leap from his seat. "Ghosts in goulashes. What is that?"

Alpha 3-0-3 calmly pressed some buttons on the console. A viewing screen displayed three Control Craft in attack formation moving towards the *Journey*. "As you can see, we have been spotted by those Control Craft. I don't think they are pleased that we are leaving the Planet of Darkness." It looked up at 7-43 with the composed manner of a waiter giving the bad news that the kitchen had just run out of apple pie.

7-43 slammed his forehead with the palm of his hand. "You mean they are going to attack us?"

"Absolutely." Alpha 3-0-3 pulled a lever forward while holding down a large button beside it. "So," it peered at 7-43, trying to analyze his reactions, "are you still bored?"

"It's one thing being bored, and another thing being killed," 7-43 bawled between panicked breaths. He sent a pleading look over to Alpha 3-0-3 in desperation. "Aren't you going to do something about those ships?"

"I have already lowered the secondary protective shield and I have calculated the location of all three Control Craft as well as their projected paths. There's really nothing more to be done." Alpha 3-0-3 folded its hands in its lap, relaxed and unaffected.

"Yes there is. Can't you blast them?"

Alpha 3-0-3 shook its head. "That would be unwise until they attack us first."

1-05 and 2-45 rushed into the cockpit area.

After a momentary sideways glance at Alpha 3-0-3 who was still in the image of 2-45's double, 2-45 made his way to the console and looked at the viewing screen.

Alpha 3-0-3 smiled, amused at how quizzically 2-45 looked at coming face to face with his own image. "Control Craft," it told him.

"That's great," 2-45 murmured sarcastically. "And we thought that all we would be dealing with was gorslanchers."

1-05 shrugged her shoulders. "At least you can surrender to the Control Craft. The gorslanchers don't know the meaning of the word."

2-45 shook his head. "As far as I'm concerned, I'd rather be eaten by a gorslancher than to surrender to the Control Craft."

7-43 gaped at 2-45 in disbelief. "You dismal dimwit, you don't know what you're talking about."

"I certainly do." 2-45 was deadly serious. "Surrendering to the Control Craft is about the same as slicing our throats. The Dark Tyrant isn't going to pat you on the back and say, 'you naughty boy, don't let it happen again.' He's a zero-tolerance leader. And he won't just execute us. His brutal methods of torture will make you yearn for the day you finally die."

1-05 glared at 2-45 in irritation. "I'm sure we could come up with some story why we drifted off course. If I send Alpha 3-0-3 into the control room to damage the thruster system . . ."

"They'll figure it out," 2-45 shouted in frustration. "They're not idiots. I tell you, our only options are to either outrun them or to fight them."

7-43 looked narrowly at 2-45. "I know why you don't want to surrender. It's because you're the only one who'd be taking a risk if we do." 7-43 moved over next to 2-45 and leaned against the back of the co-pilot's chair as he crossed his arms over his chest and raised his chin. "After all, aren't you the one who wanted to get to the Planet of Light? I mean, me, I just accidently stumbled aboard as you were preparing to take off. I'm in no danger if we surrender." He smiled smugly and, nonchalantly, circled around and relaxed into the co-pilot's chair.

2-45 glared at 7-43. "All right, in that case, let's pretend you're not really here and that you have nothing to say about what we do." He turned abruptly from 7-43 to 1-05. "You're the pilot. You have the final say. Should we risk being captured and tortured or do we try to fight them and get away?" He focused his entire attention on 1-05. Even though he did not believe in psychic powers, he still hoped that he could transport the choice he wanted into 1-05's brain by having that choice in a constant loop in his own brain.

1-05 pressed her lips together in thought. "Either way, we face serious risks." Her eyes fell to the floor as she pondered and then she looked back at 2-45 decisively. "Very well, we'll try to fight them off."

Pleased that 1-05 had made, what he considered, the right choice, 2-45 smiled at her and nodded his approval.

"But," 1-05 quickly added, "at whatever moment I decide we are taking too big a risk, I'm surrendering."

2-45 swept his hands out in front of him and to his sides. "Naturally."

7-43 sighed and shook his head in pessimistic disbelief. "You're meandering into moron-dolous madness." He swung one leg over the arm of his chair and sunk into it more comfortably. "How can you expect them to believe you accidently drifted off course after you've bam-de-bam-bam blasted them in a space battle?"

Putting one hand on the back of 7-43's chair, 2-45 brought himself to his level so he could whisper confidentially. "Perhaps you would prefer me to tie you real tight to this chair." He grinned and rubbed his hands together like a comical villain. "That way you can claim you were innocent.

Held hostage by us evil, cruel murderers." 2-45 laughed playfully at his sarcasm.

7-43 let his chin sink to his chest as he sulked. "Well, it is true," he muttered as he rested his elbow on the arm of the chair and dropped his chin into his hand. With everyone against him, he knew he was isolated from the only civilization existing in his present world. "I *am* a hostage here."

In the star-strewn darkness of space, the three white Control Craft raced in their pursuit of the *Journey*. These spaceships were long and narrow and, from the side, shaped like slim sideways trapezoids. The center ship was larger than the other two and was commanded by Control Fleet Admiral 12,134. He was tall, thin, and had greying hair. His face was fierce and stern, having all the qualities of an unquenchable fire. He strode through the cockpit area of his spaceship making his rounds from one center to the other. The cockpit areas of the Control Craft were trapezoidal-shaped with the pilot and co-pilot's consoles at the narrower top side of the trapezoid and the entrance at the base. To the right of the entrance was the communication center, from which Admiral 12,134 kept contact with the other two ships through his communication specialist. To the left of the entrance was the attack center where three weapons specialists controlled the weapons during attacks at Admiral 12,134's commands.

Admiral 12,134 stopped in front of the pilot's console and looked grimly out the window at the *Journey* which was some distance in front of them. He groaned with impatient frustration and drummed the fingers of his right hand on the knuckles of his left hand. "How soon will we reach our objective?"

The pilot glanced at a reading on his console. "Twenty-three minutes and fifty-two seconds, sir."

Admiral 12,134 frowned and wrinkled his nose with displeasure at the thought of having to wait that long to engage in battle. *But,* he decided, *time is needed for preparation.* He contorted his mouth into a haughty smirk and walked to the attack center. He stood with his chin raised and his head tilted in superiority. "Set the quark blasters to the highest energy strength," he commanded the top weapons specialist. Admiral 12,134 cracked his knuckles. He smirked with disdain when the top weapons specialist winced at the noise. "I want to take them quickly."

"Yes, sir," the top weapons specialist confirmed, making the adjustments on his console.

Admiral 12,134 turned away and strolled to the communications center. He pointed sharply at the communications specialist. She took the hint and opened a communications link between their ship and the two other ships.

"Communication is ready, sir," she informed him.

Admiral 12,134 nodded and moved over to the center of the cockpit area where the sound reception was the clearest. "*Control Craft 2* and *Control Craft 3*?" he inquired, speaking loud and precise. "This is Admiral 12,134 of *Control Craft 1*. Can you hear me?" He looked around the room with overly wide eyes as if expecting the exaggerated expression to be transmitted to the other ships along with his voice.

The low-pitched, rugged voice of Captain 3,443 of the *Control Craft 2* was heard throughout the cockpit area. "We hear you, Admiral, and we are ready for your orders."

Immediately afterwards, the efficient voice of the Captain of the *Control Craft 3* came over the communications system. "Yes, Admiral. Captain 844 here and waiting for your commands."

"Excellent." The Admiral's eyes squinted with a savage eagerness for a fight. "We will proceed with our preplanned battle strategy. *Control Craft 2*, you will close in on the ship from the starboard side. *Control Craft 3*, you will take the port side. Bombard the ship with strong fire. Slow it down, but do not destroy it unless I command you otherwise. In the meantime, my ship, *Control Craft 1*, will come in close and attach to their access chamber. Then, my forces will storm the ship and take anyone on board prisoner." His face twisted into a distorted grin as, with effort, he prevented himself from breaking out in triumphant laughter. A few seconds later, he allowed his expression to relax back into a scornful sneer. "Afterwards," he continued maliciously, "we can celebrate by blasting their ship to subatomic particles."

The room echoed with an intense roar as the pilot, co-pilot, communications specialist, and weapons specialists, as well as the Captains on *Control Craft 1* and *2*, all cheered in eager anticipation of success. Admiral 12,134 nodded his acceptance of their approbation while his mouth spread itself into a wide scornful grin.

Chapter Thirteen

2,040 passed his electric fountain and skipped up the steps toward the mezzanine, from which he moved over to a door on the far left. Slipping through the door, he came to another mezzanine less elaborately constructed, overlooking his laboratory. He stood, leaning on the railing, proudly admiring what he termed his 'realm of all things scientific,' which included a vast display of projects he was working on.

The laboratory was shaped like a long rectangle, with the distance from the mezzanine to the back of the room close to a hundred yards. Six large white tables occupied the front portion of the laboratory. The first two tables contained chemistry equipment in which simmered, steamed, and smoked chemical preparations in the experimental stage. The next two tables held medical and surgical equipment, jars holding small creatures and organs in preserving fluids, and stacks of medical books and charts. On the last two tables were several machine parts and tools being used for electrical and mechanical projects in the process of being assembled, studied, and tested. Lining the right wall were a number of computer systems that monitored the weather, the stars, and planets; geological activities taking place inside the planet, as well as analyzing visual and aural phenomenon. Lining the left wall were several incubators growing and maintaining genetically constructed plants and animals. At the far end of the laboratory stood a large white spherical object with metal tubes and wires connecting it to a generator.

2,040 noticed 9-85 and 34,000 sitting at a small round table analyzing a stack of papers that described in detail the economic efficiency model 2,040 created to facilitate an ezocane crystal extraction process. 2,040 smiled proudly, impressed with their enthusiasm, and scurried down the stairs and over to them. He jumped behind 9-85 and gave him a pat on his back.

9-85 jolted as he was pulled unexpectedly out of the world of numbers.

"Surprise, surprise," 2,040 laughed chirpily. "It's just me." He rounded the table and sat next to 9-85. Looking at him intently, he clasped his hands together on the tabletop. "I see you're looking at that little economic model of mine. What do you think?"

34,000 reached out and fondly clasped one of 2,040's hands. "I told him it was honored for review by the Economic Efficiency Committee." She smiled at 2,040.

With a wave of his hand, 2,040 brushed off the compliment, even though he still beamed as he basked in her adoration. "Well," he turned back to 9-85 excitedly as he patted the stack of papers proudly, "does it pass your approval?"

Scanning a few pages once more, 9-85 nodded, impressed. "I haven't had enough time to go over everything as thoroughly as I'd like. But, from what I've seen, it's a work of genius." He held up a page and pointed out a particular section with his pen. "The way you break up each action and delve into difficulties most people would ignore, your attention to detail is amazing."

2,040 did not appear surprised by 9-85's compliments. "Thank you. Your professor told me you are not easily impressed. I take your approval as evidence the Economic Efficiency Committee will eagerly accept my model and use it as they install their system of standard procedures." Annoyed, he noticed 9-85's attention was being drawn from him and back to the papers. 2,040 grabbed the papers from his hands. "So, enough of that." He flippantly tossed the papers onto a shelf cluttered with maps, jars, wires, tools, books, and photographs. "I want to show you something even more impressive. Come this way."

2,040 led 9-85 and 34,000 past the lab tables, computers, and incubators to the large white sphere at the far end of the laboratory. He ensured that the wires and metal tubing were thoroughly attached to the generator. "Amazing, isn't it?" he said with a humble clasp of his hands and bow of his head. "But, I'm certain you're wondering to yourself what it is."

9-85 knitted his eyebrows as he scrutinized the white sphere. He noticed that while the sphere was wired to a generator, it was also wired to a computer designed to measure electromagnetic waves and the output of lumens. "It looks to me like some type of light source." He moved over to study the sphere closer and reached out his hand to touch it.

2,040 pushed him away from the sphere. "Ah-ah. You don't want to touch it. The chemicals inside the sphere are still quite unstable. But you are right. It is a light source. But not just any type of light source. Capital T-H-E — THE ultimate light source. This, my true work of genius, is what is necessary to transform our Planet of Darkness into a Planet of Light." 2,040 reached his arms out grandly toward the sphere as if to hug it, but instead brought his hands to his lips and back toward the sphere as if blowing it a double kiss. "Ah, magnifique."

9-85 regarded 2,040's invention with both admiration and skepticism. "Really?" 9-85 raised an incredulous eyebrow. "How?"

With a knowing smile, 2,040 raised a studious finger. "Well, maybe not this sphere exactly — this one is only a smaller working model — but one much larger." 2,040 clasped his hands together and exhaled an excited breath. "See, it extracts energy from the heat within our planet, but once it has been fed enough energy, the chemicals within the sphere eventually start to generate their own energy and their own light. It is placed into the orbit of our planet, and — ta-da — We have light. And a light so powerful and so natural that we can transform this bleak planet into the verdant oasis it should be. We can finally have things many of the people on this planet have never seen, plants, like flowers and ferns. And we can grow our fruits and vegetables outside instead of in our computerized underground greenhouses."

9-85 tapped his index finger to his lips in thought as he nodded his head. "Yes, it is an amazing piece of work, but—"

"But . . . I was told you had a tendency toward pessimism." His mouth turned down in a disappointed frown. With a deep sigh, he placed a hand to his temple and shook his head to relieve a momentary headache.

34,000 took this cue and, with concern, she moved closer to him. She embraced his arm and massaged his neck. "There is nothing wrong with this project. It is perfect." She glanced in 9-85's direction with a 'how dare you' expression and quickly turned her attention back to 2,040. "I told you that before. Don't you believe me?"

2,040 patted 34,000's shoulder. "Of course I do, dear. Still, we must be open-minded and listen to the criticism—" 2,040 looked over at 9-85 and sighed with frustration, then glanced back at 34,000 with the look of a martyr. "—along with the praise."

9-85 held his hands up palms facing forward indicating he did not wish an argument. "I'm not criticizing this. And it will, in all likelihood, work perfectly. It was just that, well, you said I shouldn't touch it because it was dangerous. I was imagining it as enormous as it's going to be, and say it falls out of its orbit and back to the planet? It poses too great a risk to everyone living here." His eyes fixed on 2,040, searching for a response.

Laughing cavalierly, 2,040 brushed off what he considered an overly cautious remark. "There's no danger. I created the sphere using ultimate magna-crystals. They practically never break." 2,040 stepped over to a glass jar containing ultimate magna-crystals. He reached into the jar and grabbed a handful of the crystals. He tossed them hard onto a lab table to accentuate his point. Each one of the crystals remained unscratched and unbroken. Gesturing at the evidence, he smiled at 9-85, confident that his argument was irrefutable.

9-85 picked one of the crystals and analyzed it carefully for a point of weakness. He held it so the weak side faced downward and let it drop lightly onto the table. The crystal shattered into several pieces. 9-85 looked at 2,040 with a grave expression. "Practically."

2,040 frowned and despondently picked up one of the crystal fragments to examine it. A loud buzzing filled the laboratory and 2,040 pulled his attention from the crystal to the door on the mezzanine leading to the front room. 2,040 beamed. "Well." He set the crystal fragment on the table. "I'll bet that is my dear friend 7,500. He mentioned that he might stop by." With the rapidity of a rabbit completely behind schedule, 2,040 turned and weaved his way through the tables and equipment toward the mezzanine. He paused halfway there and turned back to 9-85. "Come," he gestured for 9-85 to follow him. "I want him to meet you."

Realizing he had already caused 2,040 some embarrassment, 9-85 was now anxious to put 2,040 back into a more amiable mood, so, he eagerly rushed to catch up with 2,040. 9-85 knew little about 7,500. All he knew about him was that he was a Historical Researcher and that his ideas were considered a little radical.

2,040 guided him to the mezzanine. "I know you will find 7,500 fascinating. He's clever and likable. He's one of those fellows that you just can't help but want to be their friend."

2,040 and 9-85 reached the mezzanine overlooking the fountain. 34,000, who followed them at a distance, entered the room a few minutes later. 2,040 looked down from the mezzanine at 7,500 below standing contrapposto in front of the fireplace, admiring 2,040's painting above it. 7,500 was tall with the build of a Grecian statue. He wore tight-fitting white polyester pants and a loose-fitting white cotton shirt. The shirt was accentuated by a dark purple vest adorned with frills down the front to hide the buttons. He had a well-shaped chin and a mouth that was more comfortable frowning than smiling, although he did have an impressive smile because of his perfectly straight, white teeth. A little black make-up around his eyes drew attention to what he considered his best feature, his large green expressive eyes. His hair was dark brown and formed several curls that framed his forehead and further accentuated his eyes.

With great enthusiasm, 2,040 raced down the steps and to 7,500. He gave 7,500 a quick hug and waved 9-85 over to them.

9-85 approached them and nodded politely to 7,500, though there was something about 7,500's appearance and manner that caused 9-85 to distrust him.

7,500 raised an apathetic eyebrow as he regarded 9-85 and held a hand out to him. "So, you are — what was it . . ." he took a moment to remember. ". . . 9-85, right?"

"Yes," 9-85 nodded. He did not immediately like nor dislike 7,500, still, despite his distrust of 7,500, something about his laid-back yet flamboyant attitude intrigued him.

"The new research apprentice." 7,500 placed a hand on 9-85's shoulder and patted his chest. "A sturdy fellow, and just as sturdy in your brains, I'm certain." He gave 9-85 a meaningful sideways glance.

Something about 7,500's look caused 9-85 to become unnerved. He felt compelled to reply but was at a loss as to what to say. "I try to attend all of the conferences for—" he finally managed to say but found himself cut off by 7,500's wandering gaze.

Looking up, 7,500 noticed 34,000 descending the staircase. He pushed his way pass 2,040 and 9-85 to the foot of the staircase. He watched 34,000 walk down, his eyes fixed on the part of her legs that showed below a knee-length skirt. His eyes slowly scanned their way up to her face. "And, well," he said with a charming grin, his voice mellow and resonant, "I'm always glad to see my favorite little lab assistant. You're looking . . . healthy . . . as always."

34,000 stepped off the final step and moved in front of 7,500 up to 2,040. She kept her eye on 7,500 as he followed her. She smiled, flattered by his attentions. "And, of all the researchers, 7,500, you are the most magnificently handsome, after our dear 2,040, that is." She looked over at 2,040 and took his hand in hers.

With an easy-going shrug of his shoulders, 7,500 conceded the prize. "Naturally. 34,000, I admire your loyalty. Makes me wish I had gone into economic research. I might have been blessed with an assistant like you."

"Oh, really," 2,040 good-naturedly scolded him, "your research apprentice, 93-73, is hard-working, and loyal, isn't he?"

7,500 suppressed a chuckle. "Hard-working, yes. Loyal, yes. But definitely not as pretty." He grinned a bright grin in 34,000's direction.

Blushing, 34,000 leaned her head on 2,040's shoulder and looked up at him. "Shouldn't we offer him a polite drink?" she asked him in a manner similar to a little girl asking her parents for a birthday party. "It's the least we could do after he's complimented me so nicely."

2,040 kissed her fingertips and shook his head adamantly. "You may find his compliments nice, but I am seething with jealousy." He then playfully pushed her off of his shoulder. "Besides, don't you remember, he doesn't drink."

Polishing his fingernails on his vest, 7,500 nodded in agreement. "That's right. I'm a staunch teetotaler." He held his hand out and admired his nails. "I abhor those contemptible vices that so many people are addicted to these days — drinking, smoking, drugs — I prefer to keep my brains and my dignity, thank you." He moved over to the chair near the fireplace and sunk into it comfortably looking much like a king on his throne.

Amused, 2,040 clapped his hands. "Beautifully put. I confess I do enjoy my little sip from the fruit of the vine now and then, but I won't take offence at your pointed remarks, because I can't deny you do have a way with words. Bravo." He dramatically waved his hand in the air as he stepped over to the fireplace. Standing in front of the fireplace, he rested his elbow on the mantel. He gestured for 34,000 and 9-85 to take a seat on the couch.

After sitting on the couch across from the chair, 9-85 rested his one arm on the back of the couch. He looked at 7,500 seriously. "It appears that you and 2,040 know each other well. Are you two working on a project together?"

7,500 leaned forward, setting his elbows on his knees. "In a way, yes. As a Historical Researcher, I work with practically every department. History forms the basis for all fields of research. But I'm sure you knew that already." He breathed out a light laugh and tilted his head with an amused pout.

"Yes, of course, but I find that history can be difficult to grasp. There are too many different interpretations of it. People seem to want to twist history to mean what they want it to mean. They should just let us make our own judgments based on the pure facts." 9-85 grimaced as he remembered reading certain historical volumes and trying to weed through a plethora of flowery praises toward certain historical figures and damning curses toward others. "I dislike dealing with tainted variables."

2,040 beamed, impressed. "Smart boy." He gave 7,500 a smug expression. "Didn't I tell you? So brilliant."

7,500 nodded thoughtfully. "Yes, but remember," he addressed 9-85 gravely, "being too brilliant can be dangerous. There are many reasons people like to twist ideas to mean what they want them to mean. And if you try to question or interfere in their reasons, you could find yourself in a dangerous position. If you feel you must question what the powers do, be extremely careful." He pointed a serious finger at 9-85, lowering his head, his eyes fixed somberly on him.

An expression of flustered concern fell on 2,040's face. "Yes," 2,040 anxiously agreed as he moved to sit on the arm of the couch next to 9-85, "you must be certain you know exactly what you are doing and that the person you are talking to shares a similar perspective." With a grave expression, he tapped the back of the couch to carefully emphasize each point.

"You two make it sound as if what I said was a rebellious statement against the Dark Tyrant." 9-85 looked searchingly from 2,040 to 7,500. "That was not my intention."

7,500 laughed lightly at 9-85's anxiety. "Of course not. We never thought that at all." He stood and moved over to 9-85 and looked down on him with a hint of contempt. "But, between you and me, I believe everyone on this planet with any brains questions the Dark Tyrant and his dictatorial form of government at least once in their life." He lifted an eyebrow cockily and moved one hand to the curls at his forehead and adjusted them with an intention of making everyone aware of how dashing they looked on him.

Warily, 9-85 rose to his feet and took a few steps away from 7,500 and toward the electric fountain. "What makes you say that?" he demanded as he turned back to face him. "Perhaps you're the one that's the traitor."

2,040 shook his head adamantly. "No. 7,500 is not a traitor. None of us are." He flitted over next to 9-85 and the electric fountain. He gestured toward the fountain as if it were the picture worth a thousand words. "It's just that when you get a group of people like us with so many intelligent sparks zapping here and there, well, we want to answer every little 'if' that may come our way." He touched a blue stream of electricity that flowed from the fountain. The stream of electricity sparked and zapped into a colorful lightning display. When 2,040 pulled his hand back, the stream of lightning, at first, tried to remain attached to his hand, but it eventually returned to its original course, continuing to flow to the bottom of the fountain.

"And so we need to know as much about the way the Dark Tyrant rules our planet as possible." 7,500 walked back to 9-85 and placed an arm around his shoulders. He sent 9-85 a look of deadly resolve. "We want to be ready 'just in case' the Dark Tyrant turns around and stabs us in the back. And you should be ready, too." He pulled on his own ear in thought as he stepped to 2,040. "You know, I think 9-85 is just the sort of person we need. We should give him our little tour."

"You think so?" 2,040 asked, more out of convention than curiosity.

"Absolutely."

"When?"

"Now." 7,500 marched toward the door and turned impatiently back around to see if everyone else was following him.

"Very well." 2,040 shrugged his shoulders in concession. "I guess we're going on a tour."

Chapter Fourteen

*C*ontrol Craft 2 and *Control Craft 3* closed in on either side of the *Journey*. The Captains of the two Control Craft kept the *Journey* within firing range as they waited for Admiral 12,134's order to begin firing. Admiral 12,134 followed at a distance behind the other ships in *Control Craft 1*. From this vantage point, he was able to oversee the battle as it commenced.

In the cockpit area of the *Control Craft 1*, Admiral 12,134 strode up behind the co-pilot's chair. He rested his hands on the back of the chair and leaned in close with a stern look as he peered out the front viewing window.

The co-pilot shifted uncomfortably, but kept her eye efficiently on the window and her controls.

The Admiral drummed his fingers on the back of the chair. "Aren't we nearing the coordinates for what used to be the planet Gorzardus?" One eyebrow shot up.

"Yes, sir," the co-pilot replied unemotionally. "The planet would have been 15.3 million kilometers to our starboard."

Admiral 12,134 curled his lips into a sneer. "Very interesting." He chuckled to himself as he moved briskly over to the pilot's chair. He looked at the pilot with a quizzical yet disdainful expression. "You are an intelligent man, aren't you?" he addressed him condescendingly. "Tell me. What is significant about this particular area?"

Trying to remain calm, the pilot faced Admiral 12,134. "It is the breeding zone of the deadly gorslanchers, sir." There was a hint of nervousness in his voice.

"Perfect." Admiral 12,134 scratched his right sideburn thoughtfully as he stepped away from the pilot.

The pilot apprehensively looked back at the Admiral. "Perfect?"

Turning back around, Admiral 12,134 frowned scornfully at the pilot. "Yes. Perfect."

"But, sir," the pilot said, "the gorslanchers are just as dangerous to *our* ship as they are to the target ship."

"I am aware of that, Captain." The Admiral turned his back on the pilot and faced the communications specialist. "Do I still have open communication with *Control Craft 2*?"

"Yes, sir."

"Good." The Admiral took his place in the center of the room. He crossed his arms over his chest defiantly. "*Control Craft 2*: Do you hear me?"

"You are coming in clearly, Admiral," the Captain of *Control Craft 2* responded.

"Excellent." The Admiral grinned in excitement. "Focus your entire firing power on the target ship's right thruster. I want that thruster entirely disabled."

"Yes, Admiral."

Admiral 12,134 stepped to the viewing window and rubbed his right index finger across his lips as he watched with anticipation while *Control Craft 2* moved in on the *Journey's* starboard side and blasted away with its quark blasters at the *Journey's* right thruster.

The *Journey* jolted with the strong blast. Alpha 3-0-3 held the ship's piloting levers steady and brought it back under control. After pressing a few buttons on the console, it assessed the damage. "They hit our right thruster. It is damaged, but still functional."

7-43 pulled himself back to his seat from the floor where he had fallen during the sudden rocking of the ship. "That was much too zapping close." He brushed his clothes off with exasperation and steadied his shaking hands. "It's a wonder we're still alive." He climbed to his feet and faced 1-05. "I wish you'd stop listening to 2-45. We need to just take this chance and surrender right now before it's too blithering late."

"The thruster can be repaired," 1-05 told him seriously. "Right now, our main concern is to keep them from causing any more damage." She turned to 2-45 who stood next to her and tapped him on the shoulder. "I suppose you've never operated a ship's attack station."

"No. But, like I said, I do learn fast." 2-45 rubbed his hands together enthusiastically.

"All right. Come with me." She led him to the attack station not far from the pilot's control console. She gestured for 2-45 to sit.

As 2-45 prepared to take his place, the ship shook again with another blow from the Control Craft. 2-45 held tight onto both the chair and the console to keep from falling over.

1-05 moved back to Alpha 3-0-3. "Where did they hit this time?"

"The thruster again," Alpha 3-0-3 replied matter-of-factly. "I will have to slow down to keep the thruster operational and our ship on course."

"Very well." 1-05 stepped back to 2-45, determinedly. "Sit down."

2-45 took his seat at the attack center. "All right. Ready." He scanned the console and found he had no clue as to what lever to pull or what button to press. He looked back to 1-05 for assistance.

"Turn on the attack guidance system. That's the blue switch on the left."

Overcoming a moment of nervousness, 2-45 glanced over the left side of the console, found a blue switch and flipped it on. A viewing screen above the console lit up and displayed a wide angle of the three Control Craft. "Now what?"

7-43 leaned on the wall near the attack station. "You blast them, of course, and doom every chance we have of getting out of this alive." He lowered his eyes and shrugged his shoulders in a blasé-faire manner.

Reaching over 2-45's shoulder, 1-05 pressed a button below the screen. "We want a clear range on the Control Craft that's firing on us." When the screen showed a close shot of the ship, 1-05 smiled satisfied. "I'll watch the numbers on the display. When they indicate we are in range, I will tell you to pull that red lever on the right — and do it fast."

2-45 nodded nervously and placed his hand on the lever.

Watching the display screen carefully, 1-05 noticed a slight lurching of the ship. "Alpha 3-0-3, what's happening?" she asked without looking away from the screen.

Alpha 3-0-3 tried with difficulty to keep the ship from swaying. "The thruster is giving out and it is becoming impossible to control the ship. We are swerving starboard."

Several large rock-like objects flying through space just outside the ship hit the pilot's viewing window.

7-43 scrambled to the pilot's console and looked out the window. "Oh, just great," he grumbled sarcastically. "Don't tell me we're being hit by meteorites."

Alpha 3-0-3 shook its head and smiled cleverly. "Those aren't meteorites. Those are gorslancher eggs. The larger ones are ready to hatch and if we hit one of those — look." It pointed to a large boulder-sized egg just in front of them.

The gorslancher egg hit the window and cracked open. A green lizard-like creature crawled out of the egg and clutched onto the screen. It looked in at Alpha 3-0-3 and 7-43 with huge red composite eyes and growled with an enormous mouth full of pointed teeth. The gorslancher had a long tail with no back legs. Its two muscular forelegs contained fingers full of sharp claws splayed across the screen.

7-43 stared at the creature in total fear. "I-it-it sees us . . ."

Watching the numbers on the display, 1-05 counted down with the numbers silently. "All right," she said when the ship started to come into range. "Now, fire."

2-45 quickly pulled the red lever.

A large blast of energy zapped from the *Journey's* mounted quark blasters and hit the main control center of *Control Craft 2*. The Control Craft slowed down, lagging a distance behind the *Journey*.

7,500 led 2,040, 34,000, and 9-85 from the glass hallway through a tall arched sliding door into the ground floor of a complex consisting of four floors, each consisting of several large rooms. "Our first stop." 7,500 turned around and led the way, walking backwards. He held up both of his hands and gestured grandly around him at the high ceilings, steep staircases and branching hallways of the foyer. "This is the Pre-Adult Preparation Complex. This is where babies, children, and young teenagers are prepared for the jobs they will be assigned as adults." 7,500 looked directly at 9-85. "I'm sure you remember some of the rooms in this complex."

"Yes, of course." 9-85 knitted his eyebrows in thought, trying to determine what point 7,500 wanted to make by bringing him here. "Everyone on this planet grows up in this complex." He could not forget the days and nights his research professors would incessantly drill him over and over again in all aspects of math, statistics, and data.

7,500 raised a finger and shook his head in negation. "Not everyone. Follow me." 7,500 led the way to the left toward one of the first rooms in the complex.

As they stepped into the room, they were stopped by a tall, muscular guard standing at a checkpoint. "What is your business here?" The guard asked threateningly.

2,040 held up his right hand to show the guard his leather identification band strapped around his wrist. "I am 2,040, Research Economist. This is 9-85, my Apprentice and this is 34,000, my personal assistant."

Moving forward, 9-85 and 34,000 both showed the guard their identification bands.

7,500 pushed his way to the front. "And I am 7,500, Researcher of Historical Information." He showed him his identification band. "We're here to gather data for a project." He raised his chin haughtily. "I certainly hope there's no law against us doing our jobs."

The guard allowed them to pass. "Just checking. All part of routine."

2,040 smirked and turned to 34,000. "Without a doubt, if we added all the time it takes to accomplish these 'routine' tasks we would have more than enough time to accomplish something of glorious importance." He stepped past the checkpoint just after 7,500 and moved in ahead of him. "Ah, yes." He glanced around the sterile, white room that contained several large metal tables holding medical equipment, rows of medical cots, and one long wall lined with shelves from the floor to the ceiling, upon which were open metal boxes each holding an infant. Doctors and nurses rushed to and fro, attending to their duties. "What better place to start the learning process than with the infants?" He guided 9-85 and 34,000 to a corner of the room. There, a nurse was bringing a baby over to a lab table where she tightly strapped him in. "This is a clever little method developed through a joint effort between the Education and Biology experts."

A black metal scanning hood was lowered over the baby and a doctor, nurse, and examiner moved to a large console. The examiner pressed a few buttons on the console and columns of data filled the viewing screen.

Smiling disdainfully, 2,040 leaned over to 9-85. "The data they are collecting is from that infant's DNA, its brain potential, and its muscle potential. When all that information is compiled, the Labor Executive decides what area the infant is best suited for, and that will be the one and only focus of its education."

9-85 watched them analyzing the data gathered on the infant and wondered what future would be decided for him. He recalled his own education and how it had been narrowly focused on mathematical research. He had often been curious about other subjects, but whenever his curiosity drove him to research about something he found interesting, his professors quickly disciplined him and directed his attention firmly back to mathematical research. As a student, 9-85 had found out 2,040 was an expert in so many different areas of education that 9-85 was drawn to pursue a position with him. 9-85 hoped that by working for 2,040, a broader world of knowledge would open for him.

9-85 noticed at the end of each metal container a printed read-out of the data. Coming up beside 9-85, 34,000 pointed to the read-out on one of the boxes. "It is vital that this data is well calculated and well analyzed. There is little room for error. This indicates the child would do well as an Enforcer, so, whether he enjoys it or not, whether he does well or not, that is what he will be." She looked 9-85 in the eyes. "Do you like what you do in mathematical research?"

9-85 tilted his head in thought. "Well, math does come easily for me, so I guess the method works. It's just that—" He quickly cut himself off in mid-sentence as he remembered he did not want to be caught saying anything even slightly negative.

After glancing around at the doctors, nurses, and other workers, 34,000 leaned in confidentially to 9-85. "Between you and me, I, myself, have always had a passion to paint landscapes." She closed her eyes dreamily and sighed. She opened her eyes once more, smiled at 9-85, and slipped away from him to take her place next to 2,040.

A nurse, carrying a tiny baby in her arms, passed by 9-85. 9-85 edged his way forward and acquired a glimpse of the baby. The infant was missing its right eye and right ear. 9-85 turned to 2,040. "Where are they taking him?"

7,500 placed a hand on 9-85's shoulder and leaned toward his ear. "Like I said, not everyone grows up in this complex. The future usefulness of a defective infant is minimal and there is too much expense involved in trying to educate one. This infant will be quickly and quietly disposed of." 7,500 shook his head pityingly as he watched the nurse walking away with her bundle. "A little sad, wouldn't you say?"

Turning his eyes from 7,500 to the nurse carrying the baby, 9-85 stared after her, unsure how to respond to 7,500's question. 9-85 could comprehend the economical motive in this policy, but he could not help momentarily putting himself in the baby's situation and feeling the emptiness in such a short life.

The nurse placed the baby on a cart where several other babies had been placed earlier. She took the handle of the cart and pushed it out the sliding doors.

2,040 gestured for 9-85 to step back to the data console where they were collecting the data for the baby strapped on the table. "This is interesting." He stroked his beard. "The data they collected indicates that this infant won't be growing up in this complex either." He pointed to the screen. "Very little potential for anything." He shrugged his shoulders and stepped aside to allow a nurse access to the controls for the scanning hood.

"What do you mean?" 9-85 asked as the scanning hood over the baby rose. "That baby looks healthy and alert to me."

2,040 pressed his lips together and shook his head. "Ah, but the scanning hood can tell you much more than a mere visual examination. And the data indicates that this infant is a Slump-Bump and will be sent to grow up among the rest of the Slump-Bumps." He put a gentle pressure on 9-85's back to guide him toward the room's exit. "Now that the Dark Tyrant has eliminated the expenses of training several citizens, let us move back into the hallway."

Pushing his way forward, 7,500 slipped out of the room first. He stepped in front of 9-85 in the hall. "So, would you say we have an efficient little system?" he gestured with his thumb toward the room they had just exited. His eyes narrowed and his mouth curled up into a sarcastically inquisitive expression.

9-85 rubbed the back of his neck. "The system is efficient —"

Stepping up to 7,500, 2,040 cut 9-85 off by briskly raising his finger in his face. "But who is it efficient for?" He fixed his eyes squarely on 9-85 as he firmly hammered his right fist into the palm of his left hand.

"Our government," 9-85 answered flatly.

"Exactly," 7,500 quietly applauded. "This system saves time and money. Plus they can control the number of workers in each field to fit the need."

"Not only that," 2,040 added, "but the government keeps its citizens stupid."

9-85 looked at 2,040 incredulously. "Stupid? How can you say that when they are being educated?"

"No, they're not. They're being trained." 2,040 looked upward as he waved his hands toward the ceiling as if the whole world outside of him was in a completely hopeless state.

"2,040 and I completely agree on this one point," 7,500 said with a self-satisfied smile. "Our government is keeping its citizens obedient by teaching them only what they need to know in order to do the job that is given them. They are not being taught how to think or how to learn."

"And what are they becoming?" 2,040 snorted. "Nothing more than robots."

"Our leaders know that when their citizens don't know how to think and learn on their own, they will accept anything the leaders tell them." There was a clever gleam in 7,500's eyes. "They *have to* accept it. They don't know anything else. Ignorance forces dependence. So, tell me, 9-85, in this situation what would be the key to challenging our leaders?"

9-85 stepped back and looked at 7,500 guardedly. "Is this a trick question?"

"Not at all. The answer is quite simple. Learn everything you can. Especially learn to think." 7,500 punctuated his sentence with a slow, meaningful nod of his head.

Chapter Fifteen

1-05 watched the attack display closely. She noted that the Control Craft was swaying into range. "Fire again," she commanded 2-45.

2-45 pulled the red lever down once more.

Another blow from the *Journey's* quark blasters hit the already crippled Control Craft.

Moving to the pilot's console, 1-05 turned to Alpha 3-0-3. "What damage has been done to—" 1-05's sentence was cut off as she stared out the viewing window and saw the freshly hatched gorslancher clutching onto the window with one forearm and clawing with the other to work its way inside the ship. It glared in at her viciously.

Finishing 1-05's sentence in its computer-like brain, Alpha 3-0-3 made the calculations necessary to answer her question. "The primary damage was to their acceleration processor. The ship is still controllable and they should repair all damage within 3 minutes and 24 seconds." Alpha 3-0-3 glanced up, ready for 1-05's response. Her attention was on the viewing window.

"So we've strayed into the gorslancher's breeding ground," 1-05 breathed bitterly. "Have you activated the electronic repellant shield?"

"Yes," Alpha 3-0-3 replied.

7-43 steadied himself by holding onto Alpha 3-0-3's chair. "But that goof-inine gorslancher seems completely unaffected by it." His eyes widened anxiously.

1-05 pursed her lips in annoyance. "Gorslanchers have unusually thick skin," she muttered. "Very little can penetrate it." She turned back to Alpha 3-0-3. "Increase the strength of the shield by 3 voltage points."

"Right away," Alpha 3-0-3 nodded as it made the adjustments on the console.

2-45 pushed himself from his chair at the attack station and moved to 1-05. "I was noticing the Control Craft on the viewing screen. It seems to have increased its speed and—" He paused to take a somber breath. "—the main Control Craft appears to be closing in on us."

Alpha 3-0-3 pointed out *Control Craft 1* in a viewing screen on its console. "Data indicates that that Control Craft is moving into position to board our ship."

"All right, let's fire on them." 2-45 moved with determined fervor towards the attack station.

1-05 stopped him by holding onto his arm and looked him anxiously in the eye. "They're too close. The blast would only cause more damage to our ship than to theirs. And, with our ship as crippled as it is, our best option is to desert this ship and take over theirs. And we'd want theirs in one piece."

"Oh, dradzit," 7-43 exclaimed in horror. "Look." He pointed out two more gorslancher eggs as they cracked on the viewing window, producing two eagerly destructive gorslanchers. One chewed on the fittings of the window, attempting to work its way inside. The other crawled across the window on its way to do damage to the back part of the ship. 7-43 stared nervously out the window. In a panic, he grabbed 1-05 by the arm. "Isn't there some way to stop them?"

"A blast between the eyes from a pro-58 exterminating gun would do it." 1-05 answered bluntly. "But we'll have to wait 'til they're inside."

Alpha 3-0-3 noticed the progress the gorslanchers were making on the viewing window. "They could make it through that window in 6 minutes and 49 seconds. When that happens, the oxygen, air pressure, and gravity levels will fluctuate uncontrollably, making the cockpit area unsafe for you three humans."

1-05 paused a moment in thought. "Who do you estimate will invade our ship first? The gorslanchers or the Control Craft?"

"Unless the gorslanchers slow them down, I would say the Control Craft."

"I see. Alpha 3-0-3, you stay here and watch the controls. Once the gorslanchers break in, lock the controls on automatic, exit the cockpit area, and seal it off." She turned to 7-43 and 2-45. "You two, come with me." She left the room.

2-45 eagerly followed her. 7-43, noticing he was alone with Alpha 3-0-3 in a room about ready to be invaded by gorslanchers, hurriedly accompanied them through the cockpit doors.

2-45 walked quickly to keep pace with 1-05. "Do you have any valuables on this ship?"

1-05 continued to hurry her way down the hall of the ship, but looked over at 2-45 quizzically. "What does that matter right now?"

2-45 slowed down his pace and stopped 1-05 with an outstretched hand.

Tilting her head questioningly, 1-05 stood facing 2-45.

2-45 raised an eyebrow and smiled cleverly. "I've heard those in the Control Fleet are easily bribed. I have my money with me." He pulled back his cloak to show her a hidden pocket with several bags of coins. "And the more money we have the easier it will be on us if we're captured."

Biting her lip, 1-05 decided that 2-45 had a good point. "If I have to pay any of my money, you owe me," she warned 2-45.

"Yes, yes. Of course," 2-45 hurriedly agreed. He turned back to 7-43 who stood behind them, listening in. "What about you? Do you have anything of value on you?"

7-43 raised his eyes wearily and sighed. "Yes, my head. And, dash-arama, I plan on keeping it."

"I have a safe in my cabin. You two go to the storage room, get the ammunition, and bring it to Central Hatch A. I'll meet you there." 1-05 raced off to her cabin.

2-45 tapped 7-43's shoulder and gestured for him to follow him to the storage room.

"I remember when you and I used to be fairly good friends," 2-45 remarked, eying 7-43 narrowly as they made their way to the storage room.

"Until you thought of trying to get to the Planet of Light," 7-43 grumbled. "It's crazy. It's impossible. And now it's darn-right dangerous." He shook his head in exasperation. "Definitely not my idea of an enjoyable and entertaining evening. Blast-amania. We'll probably get killed."

"Admiral," the communications specialist of *Control Craft 1* announced. "Captain 3,443 wishes to report to you."

Admiral 12,134 disdainfully waved a hand toward her, indicating for her to open the communications link between *Control Craft 1* and *Control Craft 2*.

The communications specialist made adjustments on her console and nodded in the Admiral's direction. "The link is open, sir."

With his head raised proudly, Admiral 12,134 took his place in the center of the room. "Captain 3,443," he spoke loudly, "can you hear my voice?"

"Yes, Admiral," the Captain of the *Control Craft 2* nervously replied over the speaker.

Admiral 12,134 forced his distorted sneer into an enthusiastic grin. "You have done well. With the damage you inflicted on the target ship's thruster, in no time, my men will be able to board their ship and bring them in. I will see you are well rewarded." The Admiral eagerly held a hand behind his ear, listening for the Captain's response.

For a couple of seconds, all that was heard was static in varying degrees of loudness. Finally, the Captain's garbled voice came over the speaker. "*[garble, garble]* appreciate that, Admir — *[garble, garble]* having a few problems with the repairs . . . *[garble, garble]* our ship is *[garble, garble]* . . ." The last few seconds of static were punctuated by a terror-stricken scream that ended with a groan of pain.

The pilot and co-pilot exchanged horrified expressions.

Admiral 12,134 moved his head back a notch as he knitted his eyebrows in annoyance. He raised a limp finger toward his communications specialist. "What was that noise?"

The communications specialist looked at the Admiral seriously. "I believe it was a scream, sir."

Turning in his seat toward the Admiral, the pilot pointed frantically toward the ships ahead of them. "Look, Admiral. *Control Craft* 2. It's being demolished by gorslanchers."

The Admiral moved up behind the pilot's chair and casually looked out the viewing screen. Scores of gorslanchers covered the *Control Craft 2*, extensively damaging the ship, and moving in and out of the ship through gnawed out holes they had created.

The corners of Admiral 12,134's lips fell into a frown. He shrugged his shoulders. "They've accomplished their part of our mission. No loss." He dropped a hand on the pilot's shoulder to ensure he had his full attention. "See that we quickly move into position to attach to the target ship's hatch. We want to finish this mission before those gorslanchers finish *Control Craft 2*."

The pilot swallowed nervously and nodded. His entire attention focused on controlling the ship as it moved toward the *Journey*.

The Admiral coolly stepped over to the co-pilot. "Ensure that the locking claws are ready. As soon as we are in position, I will give you the command to release them." He then turned to a Lieutenant who was standing near the door of the cockpit area. "Prepare your men. When I give you the order, board their ship."

The Lieutenant nodded and left the room.

Admiral 12,134 moved back to the pilot's console and watched the *Journey* through the viewing screen. His mouth stretched into an eager contorted grin.

The chief commodity of the Planet of Darkness was ezocane crystals. When heated to an extreme temperature, these crystals could be hammered into clear glass-like sheets and used in the production of windows, viewing screens, flooring, and even weapons. Since there was a high demand for sheets of ezocane, the planet procured a substantial profit by exporting them and many workers were needed for collecting, extracting, and preparing the crystals for manufacture.

Ezocane crystals were extracted from bloquious rocks, a form of igneous rock, found in abundance throughout the walls of the numerous volcanoes on the Planet of Darkness. Workers climbed down the walls of the volcanoes and, using small shovels, pickaxes, and knives, worked these rocks from the walls. These rocks were then transported to manual labor room 15, where the extraction process took place. In this room, hundreds of workers slaved away at various workstations at which the workers accomplished the different steps involved in extracting ezocane crystals from the bloquious rocks that encased them.

On the left side of the room were several large boiling pots each standing 15 feet high with a diameter of eight feet. The pots held bloquious rocks which were boiled at an extremely high temperature. The viscous red liquid in the pots bubbled furiously and spewed forth a thick black smoke. The area around the pots reached well over 120° Fahrenheit, causing the workers assigned near the pots to sweat profusely, to suffer dangerous burns, and to grow weak from heat exhaustion. During this process, the bloquious rock and the ezocane crystals both melted to a liquid form. The heavier liquefied ezocane crystals sank to the bottom while the lighter liquefied bloquious rock floated to the top. The workers would then open a valve near the bottom of the boiling pots and fill large rectangular metal pots with the liquefied ezocane crystals.

In the opposite corner to the right was a huge furnace built into the corner of the room. This furnace was heated even hotter than the boiling pots to purify the ezocane crystals. After they were heated in the furnace, all impurities were skimmed off the top and the purified liquid was allowed to cool to a temperature at which it was still malleable. The ezocane crystals were then hammered into clear glass-like sheets and were either sent to manual labor room 17 for preparation for manufacture or sent to the transportation hangar for exportation.

2,040 and 7,500 stepped through the metal sliding doors leading to manual labor room 15. 9-85 and 34,000 followed. They walked onto a metal-framed mezzanine which was green and rusting with metal stairs leading down to where the workers processed the ezocane crystals.

2,040 leaned forward against the railing of the mezzanine, looking down at the activity below. He gestured for 9-85 to join him in the view. "This shall be my masterpiece." He smiled proudly. "That economic model you were studying. This is where it will work its miracle."

Running his palm across his forehead to prevent a stream of sweat from flowing into his eyes, 9-85 nodded. "Some kind of miracle is needed here. It's so boiling hot, how are those workers able to do anything?" He unbuttoned his shirt a few buttons and shook the cloth to allow the air to evaporate his sweat.

34,000 joined them and leaned her head on 2,040's shoulder. "2,040 will solve all those little problems and this labor room will run efficiently and smoothly as intended."

7,500 took one smooth step up to 9-85. "Of course the Dark Tyrant isn't one bit concerned about his workers' welfare. That has nothing to do with the reason he assigned 2,040 to create his economic efficiency model. It's merely that the leaders want more ezocane sheets created in a shorter amount of time." He noticed some bloquious rock debris settling on his white shirt and brushed it off. "The driving force behind everything is profit, prestige, and power. The leaders will say all sorts of nice things and sound oh so charitable, but in reality, they want to step over your dead body to their next new position of power which you helped them procure."

9-85 was unable to hide an expression of surprise. If he were to choose to inform on 7,500 and his rebellious comments, 7,500 would be quickly put to death. Why 7,500 was willing to take such a risk by confiding in him was a complete mystery to 9-85.

Looking over the railing of the mezzanine, 9-85 could see, below, the workstation for boiling the bloquious rocks. Behind this workstation was a door marked "Overseer's Office". This door opened abruptly with a loud bang audible even over the humming and clanging of the machines. A tall, strongly-built man exited this office. He had a full head of thick red hair and a red, closely-trimmed beard that framed his chin and jawline. His upper-lip was neatly shaved. He had eerie light-blue eyes that, when light hit them, appeared virtually white. His face was long and his nose resembled the beak of a hawk. The man looked and saw 2,040. Grinning excitedly, the man rushed to the stairs and climbed to the mezzanine. He held out a hand to 2,040.

2,040 grabbed the man's hand and shook it warmly. "366, it is good to see you again."

"Yep. Great to have you here." 366 buzzed with nervous energy. "Any news on when the committee will be approving your model?" He chewed a hangnail off of one of his fingers.

"I'll be meeting with them next week." 2,040 smiled and clasped his hands together eagerly. "Of course I anticipate whole-hearted approval."

"Naturally." 366 waved brusquely for 2,040 and his guests to follow him down the stairs and toward his office. When they reached the bottom of the stairs, he stopped and turned to 2,040. "I suppose this is the first time some of your friends have ever seen a manual labor room? Mine's a prime example." He lifted his head a notch as he surveyed the workroom with pride. He pointed toward the corner adjacent to the furnace where a large stage was positioned. The stage floor was made of light wood and had rounded edges. There were three walls behind the stage angled to give a clear view of each one. On these walls were several viewing screens playing camera views of the activity going on in the room, in the halls outside the room, in the prison cells, and in the torture rooms. Several Enforcers stood on and near the stage watching the workers to ensure that the workers kept their focus on their jobs.

9-85 eyed the viewing screens inquisitively. "What is the purpose of those screens? It seems that the Enforcers already have an unobstructed view of all the workers."

"You're a clever man, aren't you?" 366 clapped his hands together nervously. "Listen to 2,040 and do what he says and you've got a good career ahead of you." 366 moved briskly past 9-85 to 2,040 and 34,000, leading them to his office.

9-85 lingered behind and faced 7,500, annoyed with 366.

"My feelings exactly," 7,500 sympathized. "He thinks he's some god because he's the ruler over his little world of workers, but in reality his mind is so narrow that to think about anything outside of his feel-good zone, hurts his little pea-sized brain."

"But tell me, what good are those viewing screens?" 9-85 demanded.

"It's part of their little incentive program," 7,500 told him with flippant sarcasm. "The screens depict images of other workers being captured, beaten, imprisoned, and tortured. The workers here see how much better they have it, working themselves to death. And so, inevitably, they will continue working." He casually leaned against the railing to the stairs and, with an air of self-importance, scanned the workers as they toiled in the heat.

9-85 frowned. "Certainly they could come up with something better than that?"

7,500 smiled knowingly without answering the question and guided 9-85's attention to the floor of the work-room. "Have you noticed the floor?"

The floor consisted of square tiles. The tiles along the edges of the floor and near the exits glowed with a bright orange light. "I suppose this is another part of their 'incentive program'," 9-85 murmured drily.

7,500 nodded, impressed. "You catch on quickly. Those orange tiles are safe enough for you and I to pass over, but if, during working hours, any of the workers step on them — zap." He snapped his fingers in emphasis. "— that worker is burned to ashes." He used the back of his hand to carefully dab some beads of sweat that were forming on the side of his face.

"In other words, every worker completes their full sixteen hours every day," 9-85 concluded cynically as he turned to make his way toward the overseer's office.

Pushing himself off the railing, 7,500 sauntered down the last few steps to where a group of three workers were at a table hammering out a sheet of ezocane. One of the workers was 85-27, the young man 1-13 had been working his persuasion techniques on to obtain certain information regarding a rebellion. Another was 38-95, a tall, middle-aged, blond-haired man with well-formed muscles. The third worker was 17-07, a man of medium height with longer light brown hair tied back and a neatly trimmed beard and mustache.

7,500 nonchalantly reached into his pocket and pulled out a small round metal direction-finder and glanced at its readings. Replacing it into his pocket, he 'accidently' dropped it. It rolled across the floor and under the table where the three workers labored. 7,500 glanced around cautiously then moved to the table next to 85-27. Lowering himself to his knees, he reached under the table for the direction-finder and grabbed it back up. As he carefully rose to his feet, he discreetly slipped a note into 85-27's hand. Taking the note, 85-27 quickly hid it in the pocket of his pants before any of the Enforcers noticed it. 85-27 nodded surreptitiously to 7,500 indicating that the note was safe. 38-95 and 17-07 looked questioningly over at 85-27. 85-27 looked back at them meaningfully. 7,500 then turned from the workers to join 2,040 in the overseer's office.

Chapter Sixteen

2-45 made his way to the middle of Storage Room C to a large crate carrying pro-58 exterminating guns. He opened the crate, grabbed several of the guns, and dropped them forcefully into 7-43's arms.

Seeing the guns in his arms, 7-43 jumped back uncomfortably. "I've already told you, I'm absolutely against weapons. I don't even like to touch them." He let the guns fall back into the box and grimaced with disdain.

2-45 rummaged through the crates for boxes of ammunition. "That's right." He leaned his hands on a crate and smiled slyly at 7-43. "You're of the opinion that you can go up to the Control Crew and raise your hands in the air, saying, 'look, I'm unarmed.' You'll surrender to them nicely and they'll be so impressed that they will give you an award for bravery." 2-45 opened a crate near the wall. "Ah, here it is." He filled his pockets with the boxes of ammunition.

"That's not one diddle's worth what I said," 7-43 insisted sulkily. "Besides, this trip was your idea, so if those blithering Controllers capture me, it will be entirely your fault."

A Control Craft sent a blast to the *Journey*. There was a loud bang and the ship shook with the impact. 7-43 fell backwards against some crates and used the crates to rebalance himself. "I'll just stay right here—" He held up a bottle of liquor his hand happened upon in the crate. "—and solace myself with this." He opened the bottle and took a large drink.

2-45 shrugged, unaffected. "Very well. Have it your way." He gathered up the pro-58 exterminating guns and decisively marched out the door.

7-43 sat on the floor and lounged against one of the crates. To his horror, he noticed one of the pro-58 exterminating guns next to him. He gingerly picked it up and moved it a distance away. He turned his attention to the crate of liquor and pulled out several more bottles, setting them neatly in a row. Comforted, he grabbed one of the bottles and guzzled down the liquor.

2-45 raced to Central Hatch A and piled tables, chairs, and boxes to form a barricade. He crouched behind the barricade and loaded the six pro-58 exterminating guns he had brought with him. He stopped when he heard footsteps. Holding the gun he had just loaded, he raised himself to look cautiously over the barricade. He saw 1-05 racing up to him and moved his finger from the triggering-mechanism of his gun.

Slipping behind the barricade and next to 2-45, 1-05 sunk to the floor to catch her breath. "That last blast knocked out our conversion-driver. That means if we can't take over one of the Control Craft, we're sitting ducks."

2-45 handed her a loaded pro-58 exterminating gun. "So," he smiled with an unexpected sparkle in his eyes, "there's still a chance."

1-05 breathed a chuckle of disbelief at his unexpectedly cheerful attitude. "Only a very small chance."

"All right," 2-45 held his gun ready and looked intently toward the hatch, "you're the captain. When you say it's time to surrender, I will. Until then, I'll blast them to nothingness."

1-05's face lit up into a smile as she laughed at 2-45's eager cooperation. "You're unbelievable." She shook her head incredulously. "You could at least look a little gloomy."

"That, my dear 1-05, is an absolute impossibility."

She started in surprise. "What?"

"I have complete faith that we're going to get out of this alive and we're going to make it to the Planet of Light."

Gazing at him, 1-05 knitted her eyebrows questioningly.

2-45 fixed his eyes on her and nodded mysteriously. "It's something I know. It's something I feel—" He smiled a warm enigmatic smile. "—right here." And he patted the left side of his chest.

She placed her hand over his before he could lower it from his chest. "I hope that feeling's right," 1-05 sighed, wishing she could be as confident.

Admiral 12,134 watched through the viewing screen eagerly as his ship positioned itself adjacent to Central Hatch A of the *Journey* which was now barely moving. He tapped his hand lightly on the co-pilot's chair in a cold, methodical manner to keep mental timing for the appropriate moment to give his next command. When that moment came, he hammered his hand down hard on the co-pilot's chair to ensure that she was fully alert. "Now," he shouted. "Release the locking claws. Attach our ship to their hatch."

"Yes, admiral," the co-pilot acknowledged as she pressed the commands into her console.

"And . . ." The Admiral moved to his communications specialist and barged in front of her to press a button on her console.

"49-59 here," a voice came over the speakers. "What is it you want, Admiral?"

Admiral 12,134 slid his fingers down the front of his neck in thought. "Have your engineers ready. As soon as the locking claws are in place, have them force the target ship's hatch open." He narrowed his eyes like a chess player impatient for his rival to finish his move.

"Yes, Admiral."

Admiral 12,134 pressed another button on the communications console. "Lieutenant, are you there?"

"Yes, sir," the Lieutenant replied with timid wariness.

The Admiral eagerly twisted his face into a sour-lemon-taster's expression. "Once the engineers have opened the hatch, you and your Control fighters are to enter the ship." He clenched his teeth, vibrating with nervous excitement. "Take prisoner anyone who surrenders willingly. Kill those who resist."

Alpha 3-0-3, in the pilot's seat of the *Journey*, attempted to keep the ship under control. It glanced at the speed readings. The ship's speed was rapidly decreasing. Since it knew little could be done now to repair the ship, it focused entirely on protecting 1-05 and seeing that she made it back to the Planet of Darkness alive. A gorslancher clawed out a large piece of the viewing screen. The gorslancher snorted then set to work on another piece to enlarge the opening enough to fit through.

Off in the distance was a large band of gorslanchers. Alpha 3-0-3 realized the *Journey*, was now hurtling uncontrollably toward them. Setting its index finger to its lips, Alpha 3-0-3 pondered the situation. After calculating possible outcomes, it came upon its plan of action. It tapped a few buttons setting the coordinates into the *Journey's* navigational computer, pulled the automatic pilot control lever, and pressed the lock button to stabilize the ship as much as possible into automatic pilot mode. Alpha 3-0-3 rose and allowed its image of 2-45 to waver. It became a mass of sparkling particles and transformed itself into a huge green gorslancher.

Finally acquiring an opening wide enough, the gorslancher outside pushed its head through the viewing screen. Its large, ogling eyes peered around the cockpit area, eager to devour anything with energy, living or electrical. Its eyes fell unexpectedly on the much larger and more muscular Alpha 3-0-3. Alpha 3-0-3 flexed its muscles, spread its claws, and glared with red fiery eyes at the gorslancher. The gorslancher paused, yelped, and pulled its head back to watch warily from a safe vantage point. Alpha 3-0-3 growled fiercely and the gorslancher's eyes widened fearfully as it slipped back even further.

Alpha 3-0-3 slowly moved back toward the door while keeping its eyes fixed on the gorlslancher. Once it reached the door, it pressed a button on the side. The door slid open and Alpha 3-0-3 rushed out. The door closed and Alpha 3-0-3 opened the control panel in the wall. Behind the control panel was a set of eight levers. It flipped every other lever to form an up-down-up-down pattern. A message appeared on the screen indicating the door to the cockpit area had been sealed off. Satisfied, Alpha 3-0-3 closed the control panel and set off in search of 1-05.

7-43's subconscious mind picked up the sound of clanging, rattling, and scraping. With an effort, he shook himself awake from a drunken snooze. His first hazy thought was that the noises came from within his swollen, aching head, but, vigorously rubbing his head to lessen the throbbing, he noticed they came instead from somewhere above the ceiling of the storage room.

Scratch . . . scratch . . . clank . . . scrape . . . grrr-grrrr . . . scrape . . . rattle . . . clank . . . scratch . . . scratch . . . creak.

7-43 looked apprehensively upwards. The ceiling trembled with the noise. A pipe extending across the ceiling vibrated from some destructive force above it.

Grrr-grrrr . . . bang . . . clank . . . rattle . . . scratch . . . scratch . . . creak . . . groan . . . clank . . . scratch . . . scratch.

After a deep nervous breath, 7-43 swallowed one more drink from his bottle of liquor. Anxiously keeping down, he slowly scooted backwards closer to the wall and behind some crates. He stayed hidden behind them as he closed his eyes tight trying to tell himself he was just having some horrible nightmare. One deafening thud caused a couple of metal sheets to break loose from the ceiling. 7-43 jerked back to avoid them as they came hurtling down.

Groan . . . scrape . . . scratch . . . creak . . . grrr-grrrr . . . rattle . . . crank . . . snort . . . slam . . . groan . . . clank . . . scratch . . . scratch.

The metal pipe fell within inches of his hiding place crashing down onto one of the crates, splintering it into pieces. 7-43 pressed himself against the wall. He was weak with fear, but with a frantic effort, he made a mad dash for the storage room door. Anxiously, he searched the wall for the door's control panel. He finally found it. After pressing in a few combinations of numbers, the realization hit him that he had no idea what numbers opened the door. He turned desperately around and raised his eyes once more to the ceiling. The scraping and clawing noises grew louder, coming closer as if only a thin layer of the ceiling separated him from whatever was on the other side. He turned back to the door and hammered his fists on it as loud as he could.

"Anyone. Can you hear me? Let me out." A clammy sweat broke out on his forehead. No one heard him.

From Central Hatch A came the clattering clank of gears being pushed in place and the scraping of metal against metal as the cover sections were forced against the coaming. 1-05 readied her weapon. She glanced over at 2-45 and saw he held his gun tightly and was watching the hatch door anxiously. While she was impressed with his positive attitude, she knew he was inexperienced in warfare. She took a deep breath, wishing with all her heart that 8-23 could be by her side at this moment.

Oh, 8-23, wherever you are? She hoped her thoughts were strong enough to find their way to him. *I wish you could hear me. I need your help.*

The rollers on the hatch clanked and clattered and 1-05 could tell that the Control Crew had nearly unlocked it. She tried to relax and stay alert.

Out of nowhere, she heard a soft yet confident voice. "I am coming to rescue you."

1-05 looked at 2-45 and he looked back at her with a smile of encouragement. She smiled back, but realized she was the only one who had heard the voice.

Thank you, she replied within herself to the voice.

With a resounding clunk, the hatch flew open and a company of Control fighters burst in. Holding their auto-targeting annihilator guns ready, they surveyed the area. The Lieutenant raised his hand for his fighters to hold their fire. He then held out the palm of his left hand and looked down at it. Built into the palm of his glove was a round flat passenger detector that gave a visual reading of the room he was in and the location of any living beings. He pointed his fighters' attention to the barricade 2-45 had created. The fighters turned and positioned themselves in attack formation around the barricade.

The Lieutenant stepped forward. "I know there are two of you," he raised his voice. "You have no chance against my fighters. But, if you surrender now, you will not be harmed."

2-45 could not believe they thought him stupid enough to fall for their lies. "No deal," he shouted back. "I am well aware of The Dark Tyrant's policies and that those who surrender rarely live long and if they do it isn't a life worth living."

The Lieutenant shifted uncomfortably, frowned, and stepped back. He gestured for his men to commence firing.

2-45 ducked below the barricade to avoid the succession of blasts from the Control fighter's annihilator guns.

Supporting her gun on the barricade, 1-05 took her aim and fired at one of the fighters, hitting him in the chest.

With a feeling of nausea, 2-45 stared in horror at the dying fighter who clutched at his chest and writhed in pain.

"You said we'd fight them," 1-05 remarked sharply to 2-45, "well, then, fight them."

2-45 shook his head and forced his mind to attention. Decisively, he pulled his gun up and took aim. He fired and the blast hit the wall behind another fighter.

1-05 quickly aimed her gun at the fighter 2-45 missed and hit him between the eyes. The fighter shook with the force of the blast and fell over dead.

Forcing his eyes away from the corpses of the fighters and the blood-stained walls and floor, 2-45 turned to 1-05. "Good job," he said, impressed. And, trying to maintain a positive outlook, he muttered drily, "Only about a hundred more fighters to go." A blast from an Control fighter's annihilator gun burned out a portion of the wall beside 2-45. He froze, shocked at how nearly he had missed being hit.

"Keep firing on them," 1-05 shouted to him.

2-45 took a resolute breath and aimed his weapon once more. Choosing an easier target, he fired and hit a large fighter in the chest.

The Lieutenant moved to two of his sergeants. "Have your men continue firing on them," he commanded one of the sergeants. He turned to the other sergeant. "Take your men and search the ship for any other passengers."

Alpha 3-0-3 felt a vibration of activity coming from the area around Central Hatch A and followed the hall in that direction. It heard several oncoming footsteps racing in its direction and a blast from an Control fighter's annihilator gun just missed its head. Alpha 3-0-3 quickly slipped into a control room nearby and closed the door. It hid in the shadows as it listened to the footsteps approaching. The footsteps stopped right in front of the control room door.

"I tell you, it *was* a gorslancher," the voice of an Control fighter insisted. "I saw it right here."

"Sure," the voice of another Controller agreed, "it very well could have been a gorslancher, but we're not looking for gorslanchers. We're looking for that other passenger."

"Yeah, but if there *is* a gorslancher, shouldn't we kill it?"

"That's not what we're ordered to do. Let's just get out of here. Let's look in the engine room." The one set of footsteps faded down the hall.

There was a moment of silence. After which, the other set of footsteps moved closer to the control room door. Alpha 3-0-3 hid deeper in the shadows as the door slid open letting in a stream of light across the center of the room.

A shadow was cast onto the floor and moved into the room. Following his shadow, the Control fighter entered, the glare of the light behind him obscuring his features. He stepped inside cautiously, holding his gun ready. He warily surveyed the room as he entered further. A powerful force came at him from a dark corner of the room. His annihilator gun was knocked out of his hands and fell to the ground with an echoing clunk.

The scratching, scraping, and clanking resonated through the storage room ceiling and grew even louder. 7-43 stood with his back against the door and stared upward. Several large gorslancher claws ripped through the ceiling. A gorslancher with fierce red eyes glared in, eying 7-43 hungrily. Oxygen began to dissipate from the room out through the opening in the ceiling. 7-43 gasped for air, but the short supply of air molecules in the room failed to satisfy his need.

The gorslancher gripped the sides of the opening and forced the sides further apart to enlarge it. Several boxes and crates were sucked out through the opening and into the vacuum of space. A couple of the crates collided into the gorslancher. Irritated, it swiped the crates fiercely out of its way.

Feeling his body lifting from the ground, 7-43 desperately grabbed hold of a metal brace near the door. He tried taking another breath, but afterwards his lungs felt even emptier.

The gorslancher climbed down into the room and slithered up to 7-43, snarling viciously.

7-43 drew himself next to the door and frantically hammered his fists on it once more.

The rest of the crates in the room were sucked out through the opening along with some loose lining, pipes, and metal beams. The gorslancher reached out his claws to grab for 7-43.

7-43 took hold of another metal brace on the wall and dragged himself out of the gorslancher's reach.

In maddened disgust, the gorslancher pulled back the claws of its right hand and brought them down slashing across 7-43's arm and chest.

7-43 cried out in pain as the gorslancher's claws ripped through his shirt to his skin. He tried once more to take a breath but only managed to increase the pain from the cuts on his chest. His head grew dizzy and his vision blurred.

The gorslancher snatched 7-43 and pulled him toward the sharp teeth of its huge mouth.

The storage room door abruptly opened and a Control fighter stepped in. Strangely unaffected by the vacuum of space, he coolly aimed his annihilator gun right between the gorslancher's eyes and fired.

After one agonized roar, the gorslancher dropped 7-43. Its body fell limp and rose toward the opening in the ceiling.

The Control fighter reached for 7-43 and pulled him out of the storage room and into the hallway. He punched a code into the door's control panel, sealing off the room.

7-43 took a deep breath and turned with gratitude to the Control fighter. "Thanks for saving my life. And, yes (*gasp*) I surrender whole-heartedly. (*deep breath*) I had absolutely nothing to do with this dastardly attempt to leave our Planet of Darkness. (*gasp*) It was the others. (*breath*) They practically kidnapped me. (*another deep breath*)"

"You need to learn the benefits of loyalty," the Control fighter told him flatly.

"What are you talking about?" 7-43 looked at him incredulously. "I'm loyal to the Dark Tyrant. I'm one of his most loyal subjects."

"But you haven't been loyal to those who needed your help in this crisis."

"You're sounding confusingly strange for an Controller." 7-43 studied the Control fighter carefully and noticed a far-away look in his eyes which he had seen some place else. "Are you Alpha 3-0-3?"

"Yes, I am," it told him succinctly.

"You —" 7-43 pulled his fist back, eager to punch the shape-shifter in its nose, but he stopped himself when the pain from his wounds reminded him of how Alpha 3-0-3 had just saved his life.

"We are wasting time. Follow me." It turned to the left and headed down the hallway.

7-43 followed Alpha 3-0-3, but, as soon as he heard the blasts of annihilator guns and the shouts of violence, he stopped. "We're not going where all of that brute-asinine fighting's taking place, are we?"

"No," the shape-shifter replied.

They continued down the hallway.

7-43 looked down at the blood seeping through his shirt and nearly passed out. "Uh, I-I think I'm going to pass out."

Alpha 3-0-3 slowed down and walked alongside 7-43. It studied his wounds intently. "You're not going to faint. It is just a superficial wound. The bleeding is slowing down and you're not losing that much blood."

"Dastardly drumsticks. It doesn't matter." His body was covered in a sticky clamminess. He stopped and leaned his back against the wall as his legs buckled under him. "If you don't stop talking about it, I *am* going to faint."

The shape-shifter helped 7-43 take the next few steps, after which they stopped in front of a round hatch in the wall. Alpha 3-0-3 faced 7-43. "Now, you wait here while I go back and find the others." It turned to leave down the hallway.

7-43 grabbed the shape-shifter's arm to stop it. "What is this?" He gestured to the hatch.

"An EEV, of course." Alpha 3-0-3 punched a code into a panel beside the hatch. The hatch clattered and groaned as its gears spun and it pushed open.

7-43 stepped to the opening and looked inside. "EEV? I still haven't the fog-blasting-est idea of what this is."

Alpha 3-0-3 tilted its head in amazement at the human's inability to understand. "It is an EEV — an Emergency Escape Vessel. The *Journey* is falling apart. It is invaded by Controllers and gorslanchers. We need to escape to where we can be safe."

"But won't the Control Craft see the escape vessel and fire at it?"

"It's constructed of trantonine metal which both absorbs and reflects images. Since the EEV is small and will be projecting the image of space, it would be difficult for the Control Craft to detect."

7-43 raised one eyebrow in thought. "How do you operate it?"

"I will go and find 1-05 and 2-45. When I come back, we will leave." Alpha 3-0-3 turned and resolutely headed down the hall.

Leaning his one hand on the top of the opening, 7-43 gazed into the EEV, mesmerized. "So . . . this is the way out."

Chapter Seventeen

A lpha 3-0-3 neared Central Hatch A. From its standpoint, the shape-shifter could clearly observe 1-05 and 2-45 behind their barricade warding off the Controllers with their weapons. Alpha 3-0-3 knew it was vitally important to carefully consider what form it chose for its next transformation. It had to appear as something that would not draw a hostile response from the Controllers nor frighten 1-05 and 2-45. As Alpha 3-0-3 pondered, its thoughts became distracted, not by the piercing blasts from the exterminating guns nor by the shouts and screams from the wounded Controllers. The sound that distracted it was a soft drip-drip-dripping of a clear liquid trickling down from a broken pipe that hung from the top edge of a nearby wall. Studying the pool of clear liquid forming on the floor below the pipe, the shape-shifter came upon a workable solution.

Alpha 3-0-3 allowed its image of the Controller to flicker into the trillions of minute particles that composed it. It brought those particles together again to take on its new form, a small puddle of water near the liquid on the ground that had leaked from the pipe. Pushing and pulling itself along the floor, the shape-shifter forced its fluid shape to move against the gravity force within the ship. With a gush and a surge, it continued along the hall and streamed its way behind 2-45's make-shift barricade. It swirled into a small whirlpool behind 1-05 and rippled, swooshed, and bobbled, trying to secure her attention.

"1-05 . . . 1-05 . . ." Alpha 3-0-3 spoke as loud as it could over the battle noise, but its watery voice was not much louder than a burbling river. "I am Alpha 3-0-3. I am here . . . I want to help you . . ."

1-05 started, surprised at hearing such a soft voice past the loud din. At first, she wondered if she was hearing the same voice she had heard before. But, she soon realized the voice was different. She cautiously sank further behind the barricade for protection.

Noticing that 1-05 had slipped to the floor, 2-45 dropped down to make certain she had not been hurt. "Are you all right?"

"Yes." She shivered. "Did you hear that strange voice?"

2-45 noticed she was visibly pale. "No." Even though he had not heard the voice, 1-05's shaken appearance proved she must have heard something. He turned to fire a few shots at the Control Craft then moved back next to 1-05. He looked into her eyes. "What did it sound like? Where did it come from?"

"You didn't hear it?"

2-45 shook his head.

1-05 glanced down, embarrassed. She saw a dirt smudge on her pant leg and tried to rub it out with her hand. Looking back, she was relieved to see a sincere expression on 2-45's face. "I couldn't tell what it said, but it sounded so strange."

Alpha 3-0-3 quivered with frustration. Its goal was to *not* frighten them. It pulled itself up until its fluid-shape sloshed and swirled to resemble a liquid miniature human. "It's me . . . I'm here to help . . . It's me . . . Alpha 3-0-3 . . ."

This time, 2-45 could just make out the voice. He directed his attention to the shape-shifter and was stunned at its strange appearance. "What? What is this?"

1-05 crawled up to the water shape and smiled fondly. "Alpha 3-0-3, is that you?"

"Yes," it said, perturbed that it took so long for them to realize it.

The Lieutenant of the Controllers moved behind his line of fighters and toward Central Hatch A. There, he was joined by another sergeant who had brought with him a fresh squad of fighters. The Lieutenant gestured for the sergeant to position his fighters in a weak area to the left of the barricade. Glancing back in the direction of the barricade, the Lieutenant noticed their targets had not fired for some time. He raised one hand and his Controllers ceased firing. He took one confident step toward the barricade. "Are you two ready to surrender?"

Seeing the increase in fighters, 2-45 clenched his fists in annoyance. "We can't hold them off any longer, but I refuse to surrender." He pounded the wall with his fist, to emphasize his words to himself more than anyone else. With the situation becoming more discouraging, his determination started to wane.

"That's what I came here to tell you," Alpha 3-0-3 said. "We must hurry. You can't win this fight against the Controllers. The *Journey* is falling apart. It is invaded by gorslanchers. We need to escape to the EEV."

While escaping in the EEV sounded like a good idea, 1-05 shook her head hopelessly. "The EEV will only take us back to the Planet of Darkness. It wouldn't be much different than surrendering to the Controllers right now."

Receiving no reply, the Lieutenant shifted tensely and took another step forward. "Well?" He adjusted the setting on his annihilator gun in preparation for any retaliation from his targets. "Are you going to surrender or do we need to come and take you by force?"

Turning to 1-05, 2-45 clutched her arm. "To surrender is suicide," he persisted.

Alpha 3-0-3 doggedly surged its liquid-form even higher. "We don't need to surrender to them. All we need to do is get to the EEV." It stubbornly placed two off-shoots of water resembling arms on what appeared to be its hips. "I can navigate it to a remote area rarely frequented by the Dark Tyrant's spies. From there, I can take you to a safe-house. I have the location of it stored in my memory banks."

1-05 allowed the shape-shifter's words to sink into her mind. She nodded decisively and grabbed her gun. "All right, then. Let's go."

"How can we?" 2-45 held her back. "If we leave this barricade, we'll be blasted."

1-05 pushed his hand away. "We can't stay here. We'll have to shoot our way out." She moved to the edge of the barricade.

Alpha 3-0-3 sloshed in front of her. "That would be dangerous." It raised a fluid finger thoughtfully to what may have been its head. "I have a better idea."

Growing impatient for 1-05 and 2-45 to surrender, the Lieutenant was about to turn to his fighters to tell them to storm the barricade. He stopped, though, and had to shake his head and blink his eyes in disbelief. He could have sworn he saw the wall behind the barricade jump up and forward toward him.

He stepped back to his sergeant. "Did you see that?" he asked him under his breath.

"Do you mean the wall jumping, sir?" the sergeant asked seriously.

"So you saw it, too?"

"Yes, sir."

The Lieutenant ran his fingers through his hair to ensure he was thinking clearly. "Well, it's about time we put an end to all this. Gather your men and storm that barricade. Dead or alive, we're taking them in now."

The sergeant ordered his squad of fighters to close in on the barricade. The fighters approached and took their positions nearer it. Prepared to fire, they waited. Neither gunfire nor any sound of movement came from behind the barricade. The sergeant waved his fighters forward. They rushed forward and surrounded the barricade. The sergeant took four of his men and they crept up. When they reached it, they looked behind the barricade and found it empty.

"Sir," the sergeant shouted to the Lieutenant, "there's no one here."

The Lieutenant's mouth fell open in surprise. He ran to him. "That's impossible. We would have seen them if they had left." He pushed his way forward and looked inside, finding the barricade vacant.

The sergeant's eyes strayed to the wall behind the barricade. In bewilderment, he screwed his eyes up as the wall melted. The sergeant tapped the Lieutenant's arm and directed his attention to the wall.

The Lieutenant jumped back in fright as the wall slushed to the ground into a puddle of water that slithered and streamed its way down the hall. He pressed his hand to his heart to calm himself. After a deep breath, he forced himself to stand confidently tall. He turned to his sergeant brusquely. "Search the ship. Every corner and crevice. Find them." He narrowed his eyes, as if his eyes were capable of shooting fire on anyone who failed to follow his command.

1-05 and 2-45 reached the EEV hatch, but found the EEV had already been launched. They exchanged expressions of disbelief.

When Alpha 3-0-3 flowed up to them, it swooshed forward into 1-05's hands. "Come on," it splashed eagerly, "let's go."

1-05 petted the shape-shifter on what was most likely its head. She looked down at it unhappily. "We can't. The EEV is gone."

"Gone?" the shape-shifter rippled backwards in surprise. It craned itself around, peering into the hatch as it calculated carefully all the possibilities. "I brought 7-43 here to wait for us. He must have left without us."

"I'm sure that's what happened." 2-45 frowned in annoyance.

The Controllers stormed around the corner and took their positions opposite them. They aimed their annihilator guns at 2-45 and 1-05.

"All right," the sergeant shouted resolutely. "Nobody move."

Alpha 3-0-3 let its image flicker and transform into a barely visible flea. It jumped onto 1-05's ear. "Don't worry. No matter what happens, I will stay with you."

"Thank you," 1-05 whispered to it. She itched her ear.

The fighters stepped forward with their guns aimed at her warningly.

1-05 moved her hand away from her ear and the shape-shifter jumped from her ear to a pocket in her sleeve.

Uncertain what to do, 2-45 glared at the Controllers, wishing he could make them disappear with a thought. He looked over at 1-05 questioningly.

Sighing dispiritedly, 1-05 nodded to him as she raised her hands. "We surrender."

2-45 hated how he had planned so carefully, worked so hard, and spent so much money to try to leave the Planet of Darkness and now he was being forced to go back. He pressed his lips together in frustration and raised his hands.

The sergeant moved to the EEV hatch and saw that it had been launched. "Looks like the other one got away." He turned to 1-05 with a disdainful smirk. "But don't worry. Your friend won't get far. The Enforcers will be waiting for him as soon as he reaches the planet."

◂◆◆◆▸

On board the *Ghost III*, Infinity and the Way-Guide stood
on the second floor leaning on the railing that encircled the
enormous ball of energy in the center of the ship. This railing
connected seven metal posts running vertically through the
two floors. The ball of energy glowed red and orange and
flashes of lightning rapidly zipped and zapped around each
other. Sparks branched from the ball of energy and into the
seven metal posts that surrounded it. The metal posts collected
the energy and used it to power the *Ghost III*.

"The *Ghost III* has been keeping a vigilant eye on everyone
who is searching for a way out of the Planet of Darkness."
Standing in the middle of two of the metal posts, Infinity
placed the palm of one hand on one of the posts and the palm
of his other hand on the second one. As soon as he was
touching both of the posts, the center of the energy ball
calmed down to a depressed area like the eye of a hurricane.
This area then pushed back the active outer zone to the lower
floor's railing. A round viewing screen was revealed in the
center of the floor.

Infinity directed the Way-Guide's attention to the images
displayed on the screen. The images were of people on the
Planet of Darkness living in misery and searching for some
means of escape. "The *Ghost III* informed me that everyone
on the Planet of Darkness who wants out is in great danger
right now. More and more of the people on that planet want to
escape. The Dark Tyrant is becoming aware of this and
considers them a threat."

The Way-Guide studied the images on the screen and his
eyes fell on a picture of 1-05, the woman he loved, being
taken prisoner by Controllers. A feeling of desperation spread
throughout his heart. They were not even half-way to the
Planet of Darkness and his girlfriend, and others like her, were

risking their lives to find a way out. "There must be some way to make the *Ghost III* get there faster. All these people are counting on us to help them."

Infinity lowered his hands and the ball of energy converged and covered the viewing screen.

His anxiousness nearly driving him into a panic, the Way-Guide gasped for air as he turned toward Infinity for guidance.

Infinity smiled at him paternally. "The *Ghost III* will get there at the right time. They need our help, but even though we are here and not there our hands are not tied."

Trying to calm himself, the Way-Guide listened to Infinity seriously, trying hard to believe him. "But what can we do?"

"We have an agent there. It is her turn to act." Infinity placed his hand onto his ear as he focused his attention on communicating with the *Ghost III*. "*Ghost III*, contact our agent on the Planet of Darkness. Tell her to start gathering those who are searching. Let her know that I want her to keep them safe 'til I arrive."

Chapter Eighteen

The only light in 1-13's room was a trio of candles burning on his desk. He wanted the room dimly lit to block out all extraneous distractions. He wanted to focus on the files he was fervently researching on 4,021. After going over the stacks of information for several hours incessantly without rest, 1-13's eyes grew heavy. Soon all he could concentrate on was the center candle in front of him. He placed his hands, palms down, on either side of the candle and stared at its flame. A sweat broke out on his forehead as he watched the orange and yellow flame dance carefree over the crimson candle and the coal-colored wick. The flame was quickly overpowered by the tiny puffs of smoke it had brought to life. These puffs of smoke spread into large black thunderclouds that whirled across 1-13's vision and burrowed themselves deep into his thoughts. His mind drifted into nothingness, and his head dropped onto his arms on the desk. He fell into a deep sleep.

It was late when 1-13 finally woke. He groggily lifted his head from his arms. Glancing at a clock on the wall, he noted the time was much later than when he had seen it last, but he could not tell just how long he had slept. From some far area of the room, he heard angry voices arguing. He rubbed his head to ensure that he was fully awake. Turning in his chair, he scanned the room. The voices were louder than before and sounded as if they were plotting to set some trap for him. He stood from the desk. Feeling a little shaky, he kept one hand on the desk for support as he looked from the wet bar which stood next to him. To the bookcases. To the couch and chair. To the door. Trying to determine where the voices were coming from.

When he faced his bedroom nook, he verified that direction as the source. Apprehensively, he peered into the darkness in the direction of the nook. He could not see anything in the darkness, but he still heard the voices, and the voices were more distinct. He discerned there were many people talking, ten, fifteen, maybe, twenty people, mostly men. 1-13 was mystified over how fifteen men could have squeezed into his small bedroom nook . . .

He kept his eyes fixed on the nook, looking deep into the shadows for any evidence of human forms. Among the gruff murmurings, 1-13 caught them mentioning his number several times. What is it they are planning? . . . Are they wanting to kill me? . . . Perhaps this is some prank plotted by 6-96 . . . 1-13 forced himself to appear calm, but he had no control over the panicked beat-beat-beat-beat racing of his heart. He reached into his desk drawer and pulled out a small dagger, holding it ready in his right hand. With his left hand, he grabbed one of the candles and made his way cautiously in the direction of his bedroom nook.

He took steady and firm steps, preparing himself for whatever attack he was being lured into. Nevertheless, his nervous apprehension created a dizziness in his mind sending the room swaying back and forth. The floor seemed to slant one way, then the other, pushing his footing off balance. As he stepped closer and closer to what he assumed was the source of the voices, the light of his candle illuminated the area, and he grasped the fact that nobody was there. After a quick check under the bed, he was relieved to discover that the voices had ceased. He moved over to a bookcase and pressed the light control button. Once he had looked about the now well-lit room and saw that nobody was there, 1-13 breathed easier. He moved back over to his desk, trying to shake from his mind the inexplicable incident . . . when he, suddenly, heard the voices again. *"Come with me over here . . . (mumble . . . murmur) . . . Take that there . . . (murmur) . . . Give me one of those . . . This way — not that way . . . (grumble . . . groan . . .)."*

1-13 stopped in his tracks as he realized they must be standing near him. In fact, 1-13 could hear their footsteps on the floor right next to him. He swallowed his anxiety and cautiously followed the footsteps to the door leading to the cells where he held his prisoners. Though the door remained closed, he distinctly heard the sound of it opening, the footsteps and voices going through, and the door closing. 1-13 quickly subdued a shiver that tried to spread throughout his body, and, holding his dagger even tighter, pushed his way through the door.

In the hallway between the prison cells, he could hear the voices and the footsteps a few paces away from him. He hurriedly switched the light on and was unnerved that he distinctly heard the sound of shoes going over concrete, the material the floor of the hall was made from, yet he could clearly see no one was there in front of him. He followed the sound of the voices, and as he did, he carefully checked through each of the cells' barred viewing windows to ensure that all of the prisoners were in their cells and quiet. As he was approaching the door to his workshop, *he* could hear the voices plotting in front of him. *"Get over there and finish the job . . . (mutter . . . groan) . . . No more complaining . . . We can hide over there . . . (murmur . . . grumble) . . . No, not there — over here . . . (mumble . . . mumble . . .)."*

1-13, in a perplexed panic, increased his pace, but the voices were one or two steps ahead of him. Once more he heard the door open and close and the voices and footsteps moving through the door even though it remained shut. 1-13 followed them into his workshop.

1-13 switched the lights on. He heard the voices in each of the corners all at once, but saw no one. *"We can handle this . . . (grumble . . . groan) . . . You just go over there . . . We will go over here . . . (mutter . . . mumble) . . . This will be easy . . . Watch, he is already afraid . . . (mutter . . . groan . . .)."* The voices creaked into an other-worldly laughter, rasping the way someone does when being choked. Overwhelmed, 1-13 dropped his dagger and clasped his head in his hands. "Stop it," he shouted at the room. "Who are you."

1-13 jolted as he heard one of the voices close to him laughing with a distinct and familiar raspy laughter.

"So . . ." 1-13 narrowed his eyes knowingly, ". . . it is *you*."

1-13 turned and saw the green smoke oozing and swirling over the couch in the center of the room. Slowly, the smoke formed into one of his eerie skeleton-ghosts sitting obstinately on the couch. It glared at 1-13 with an evil sneer.

1-13 laughed, reassured, convinced that the whole thing was one hilarious joke. "What was all that about? Why were you playing that ridiculous trick on me?"

The skeleton-ghost just sneered and glared even more intensely.

1-13 shrugged his shoulders, unaffected. "Well, anyways, you were very clever, but, it would have been funnier if you had played this trick on 6-96. I wonder, would you mind—"

Two more skeleton-ghosts formed near the first one, standing on either side of it, arms crossed in front of their ribcages. The first skeleton-ghost oozed over to 1-13. When it stood next to him, it looked condescendingly down on him. "Your plan is faulty," it hoarsely declared.

1-13 glared at the skeleton-ghosts and snorted in a humiliated huff. "What do you mean? How is my plan faulty?"

The other two skeleton-ghosts seeped over and stood powerfully around the first one. The first skeleton-ghost shook its bone-rattling hand at him. "You are becoming weak. So much so, that you are losing your power over us." The skeleton-ghosts cackled and creaked creepily.

1-13's chin dropped at this unexpected blow. "What makes you say that?"

"Your mind is not focused," the skeleton-ghost screeched. "You even failed to ensure the apprentice's loyalty. He will not do as you say." The green smoky ooze from the three skeleton-ghosts surged out in 1-13's direction.

It was hard for 1-13 to grasp the idea that someone could be immune to his control. "50-83?" he gasped but quickly gathered his thoughts and refocused his eyes on the skeleton-ghosts. "So, my servants are rebelling against me."

The three skeleton-ghosts glared down at him and nodded. As they moved their necks their vertebrae rattled ominously.

50-83 entered 6-96's workshop carrying a large and heavy wooden crate. Once in the room, his muscles gave way, and he let the crate fall to the floor. The sliding door shut behind him, and the light from the adjacent room was cut off. The workroom was now only lit by the orange lights along the floorboard.

Out of a shadowed corner, 6-96 approached the wooden crate and looked down at it, perturbed. "If anything is broken . . ." She sent 50-83 a warning glare.

50-83 rubbed his sore arms. "I didn't drop it hard."

Grabbing her silver staff, she sniffed condescendingly. "You better not have. Open the crate," 6-96 moved over and sat in a cushioned chair nearby, completely apathetic.

Numerous times before, 50-83 had carried crates into 6-96's workshop and opened them for her. Each time, once he viewed the contents, 50-83 was convinced those contents would have been better left inside. He eyed the crate forebodingly but knew there was no way out of opening this new box of evils. "Very well, ma'am." 50-83 made his way to a pile of tools near the potted tree, home of the seven-headed snake. The snake's seven heads rose and watched him carefully. Keeping a wary eye on the snake, 50-83 reached into the pile of tools and searched for a lever.

6-96 glared. "Stop dawdling."

50-83 nervously turned his attention away from the snake and onto the tools. He grabbed the lever and hurried back to the crate. He tried to act as nonchalant as possible as he wiped some grime off the lever with his hand. "What's inside it anyways?"

Using her finger, 6-96 tested the sharpness of the pointed obsidian stone that decorated the top of her staff. "Something important for *our* work." She looked at him meaningfully. "I created it so *we* can achieve an even higher success rate in our persuasions."

50-83 began prying the lid open with the lever. He bit his lip in annoyance at the way 6-96 drew him into her gruesome deeds through the use of words such as 'we' and 'our'. "Why didn't *you* create it here? Then *I* wouldn't have had to carry it all this way."

6-96 stood and swung her staff hard against 50-83's back, and he fell forward onto the crate. "Don't you dare question me."

50-83 grimaced and pushed himself back on his feet. "Sorry." He looked down uneasily.

Taking 50-83 firmly by his hair, 6-96 forced him to face her. "I needed the help of the electrical engineering department. That is why I did not create it here. Understand?" She jerked his hair even harder.

50-83 winced. "Yes, ma'am."

"Good." She brusquely let go of his hair. "Now, open the crate."

Without thinking, 50-83 loosened the rest of the lid and moved it to the side.

Looking inside the crate eagerly, 6-96 set her staff on a nearby table. "Take that side," she pointed toward the left side of the crate's contents. She took hold of the other side. Together, they pulled out of the crate a tall machine made of crystal and silver in the shape of a 'T'. After they set down the machine, 6-96 attached a cube-like power source to the back of it and turned the machine on. Streams of aqua blue light flowed up and down as the machine powered up.

The waves of light nearly hypnotized 50-83. He was tempted to touch the machine but stopped himself, realizing he had no idea how the machine doled out its torture. He thought about asking, but knew he had better not. 6-96 might choose to use him for a demonstration.

"So . . ." 6-96 patted the device proudly. "What do you think?"

With the workroom so dim, the machine's glowing lights shone so brightly that it fascinated 50-83. Still, he did not relish starting a conversation about torturing devices. "I'm sure it will be very effective."

6-96 placed a hand on his shoulder. ". . . And you'd like to know how it works?"

50-83 looked at her askance and did not reply.

Snatching her staff again, 6-96 strode back to the torturing device. "The victim is placed against here, facing forward, with arms outstretched on either side, following the device's shape." With her staff, she indicated the machine's cross shape. "We then lock the victim in with these five clamps, one for the body and two for the arms and two for the legs. The clamps force the victim against the front of the device which is lined with electrical nodes. We can then control the electrical current flowing through these nodes by this lever, mildly painful, horribly painful, deadly painful, or anywhere in between, increasing it as the victim needs more convincing." She impatiently waved for 50-83 to examine it closer. "What do you think?" She arched an eyebrow indicating she expected a quick and precise answer.

"I'm sure it will work." He surveyed the machine with a business-like seriousness.

"And it will convince 4,021 to tell us about her rebellious plots?"

50-83 faced 6-96 in alarm. "You're going to use it on *her*?"

"Naturally," 6-96 replied dispassionately. "I developed it with her in mind." She raised her head conceitedly.

"But you don't even know if you'll need it. She may tell you everything without it."

6-96 took him tight by his wrist and yanked his arm upward and back as far as possible. Her nails clawed into his flesh. "You fool. Haven't I taught you that the most effective method is to use as much torture as possible? Even if she *says* she will tell us everything, we use it on her to make sure she does."

50-83 stared at 6-96 with wide eyes. "But you don't have to. I talked to her. he will be easy for you to convince."

She sneered disdainfully. "You are such a liar. I've learned it is impossible to ever know if you are telling the truth."

"I am telling you the truth this time."

Looking back at the torturing device, 6-96 grinned maliciously. "There's a way to find out if you are telling the truth." She dragged him over to the device.

50-83 tried to pull himself away.

6-96 jerked his right arm toward the machine and clamped it in. "Don't worry . . ." Her mouth curled into a saccharine smile. "I won't place the electrical current on a setting that's *tooo* high."

50-83 fought to free his left wrist from her grasp, hoping to use it to unclamp his right arm. In the struggle, the crystal on the necklace around his neck swung to the back of his neck. He pulled his wrist free, but 6-96 quickly grabbed hold of it again.

With one strong shove, 6-96 pushed him onto the torturing device and clamped him in.

50-83 tried to pull his arms free from the clamps, but he was locked in too firmly. He slumped in resignation. "I have been telling you the truth."

6-96 ignored him and switched the machine's electrical current setting to "highly painful".

The torturing device whirred softly as it activated the electrical nodes. 50-83 was clamped in so tightly that the crystal on his necklace came into contact with one of the electrical nodes. The electrical power in the crystal overpowered the machine and the machine sputtered and crackled. The whirring slowed down and faded into a labored groan until the machine shut down and was silent.

6-96 gaped in shock at her torturing device that was no longer functioning. She tried turning it on and off without success. Infuriated, she kicked the machine and marched to 50-83. "What did you do?"

"Nothing." 50-83 was just as surprised as 6-96.

6-96 unclamped him, yanked him from the torturing device, and threw him across the room. "You evil—" she spewed out the words venomously. "I don't want to see your face. Get to your room."

50-83 caught himself and regained his footing. He lowered his eyes. "It wasn't my fault." As he turned to head for his room, he noticed that his necklace was askew. He reached to adjust it. As he pulled the crystal back around, he detected the warmth of the crystal. He glanced back at the torturing device and, as he held onto the crystal, became aware of what had happened. He pressed his lips together knowingly and casually continued on to his room.

After the elevator had brought 50-83 down to his room, he sat on his bed and unchained his necklace. He held the crystal in front of him. It floated above his hands and glowed a bright yellow. He waited, but the crystal said nothing.

50-83 knitted his eyebrows, wondering why the crystal was not asking him its usual questions. "Good day to you, crystal," he said, hoping the familiar words would remind the crystal what it was supposed to do. He waited . . .

The crystal continued silently glowing . . .

"Aren't you going to ask me a question?" 50-83 asked anxiously.

"Sorry," the crystal answered cheerily. "I'm afraid I have no questions to ask."

"What? But you were created to ask me questions, weren't you?"

"That's true." The crystal vibrantly beamed. "But, I'm afraid I can't anymore."

"Why?"

"That last power surge has altered my functional ability."

50-83 stared at the crystal, incredulous. "What do you mean?"

The crystal's light pulsed as it hummed for a few seconds.

"Are you there?" 50-83 wondered if the crystal was losing its power completely.

"I'm here," it answered calmly.

"What's the matter?"

"I was just executing an analysis of my electrical and mechanical capabilities," it explained matter-of-factly. "The power surge has burnt out several circuits connecting my micro-intellectual computer and my micro-analytical computer."

"Oka-a-a-y." 50-83 was not completely convinced because, for as long as he had owned the crystal, it had never had to 'execute an analysis' before. "And that means . . . ?"

"I can no longer ask questions." The crystal's light dimmed.

50-83 sighed, trying to accept the fact that the crystal's usefulness had come to an end.

The yellow glow of the crystal beamed bright again. ". . . I can only answer them."

Surprised, 50-83 grinned excitedly. *I would much rather own a crystal that can answer questions than ask them.* "All right, crystal, here's a question. Will I ever be top Persuader?"

The crystal hummed a few seconds. "I cannot answer questions about the future with certainty. There are too many variables, too many possible paths you could take. But I can answer you this. You have the talent and skills necessary to be a top Persuader. Use those skills well and you are sure to succeed."

50-83 was amazed. For a minute, he self-assuredly pondered the crystal's answer. He only asked the question on a whim. He had not thought of himself as a talented or skilled Persuader, definitely not one of the top Persuaders. His goal had only been to follow the career track laid out for him and someday become a half-way decent Persuader. He turned his attention back to the crystal. As he considered the possible questions he could ask, he thought about 1-13. He remembered the last time he met with him in 1-13's room. "Can I trust 1-13?" he asked.

"No," the crystal answered. "And there is no reason you should have to trust him. Your ability for persuasion is far superior to his."

Again, 50-83 was astounded by the crystal's answer. He blushed a bit. "Why thank you, crystal." He smiled a smug smile. As he formed the next question, his mind drifted to 4,021 and the horrors she would have to face from both 6-96 and 1-13. "What about 4,021? Do you think I should try to help her?"

"4,021 is alone and unaware of the danger she is in," the crystal replied. "You would be unhappy if you did not at least try to warn her."

Searching deep into his heart, he realized the crystal was telling the truth. "You're right," 50-83 resolutely agreed. "I must warn her." He took the crystal by its chain and replaced it around his neck. He noted that 6-96 had not yet locked the metal door in the ceiling above the elevator. He rubbed his chin thoughtfully. *I had better use this opportunity to get out.*

50-83 climbed off his bed and stepped over to his desk. He opened the drawer and pulled out the wooden box. Opening the box, he grabbed his jeweler's pliers and put them inside his pants' pocket.

50-83 made his way to the elevator. He did not want to operate the elevator and draw 6-96's attention, so, instead of going inside the elevator, he climbed the outside of it using its metal frame for hand and footholds. When he reached the top, he slipped through the open metal door on the ceiling and crouched on top of the roof. Looking up, he saw that he was now confronted with the glass overhang that sheltered the glass walls enclosing the roof of his room. He crawled to the edge of the roof and looked down, noting the gap between the roof and the glass wall, where, several feet below, were piled heaps of jagged rocks on a dust-filled incline. He reached over to one of the side walls of the glass overhang. Grabbing hold of one beam in the glass wall's metal frame, he let his feet slip from the roof. He settled his feet on a lower beam, and, using his jeweler's pliers, he bent back a portion of the metal frame that held one of the glass panels in place. After several minutes, he was finally able to bend back the metal frame on all edges of the glass panel. He pulled out the glass panel and slid it gently on the roof of his room.

50-83 climbed through the open space and made his way down the outside of the glass wall by reaching for and stepping down on the beams in the metal frame. When he was a couple feet from the ground, 50-83 let go of the beam he was on and dropped down.

The distance was further than he had anticipated, so he ended up stumbling and falling forward. He grimaced, but, determinedly, pushed himself back to his feet. He noticed some dirt on his pant leg and brushed it off.

Other than a few steep inclines to his left, this area was relatively flat. The ground was a lifeless blend of red clay and sand. The large and small sharp rocks that scattered the region instilled within passers-by a morbidly uncomfortable sense of entering a cemetery.

Lifting his eyes from his pant leg, 50-83 saw, a few yards away, a lone wolf with golden eyes watching him. He had never seen a creature like this before. He stared at the wolf, mesmerized by his glistening eyes.

The wolf looked meaningfully into his eyes.

50-83 stood, unable to move.

Around the wolf's neck was a collar that contained a pouch. The wolf reached into the pouch with his mouth and pulled out a white envelope. After setting the envelope on the ground, the wolf turned and bounded off into the shadows.

50-83's heart was racing. A rush of happiness overtook his heart for those few moments when the wolf was there and 50-83 wished he could run after him. But 50-83 could tell the shadows were so deep and there was no way he could be sure which direction the wolf went. 50-83 raced to where the wolf had been, bent down, and picked up the envelope. He opened it and found inside a beautifully hand-written letter. 50-83 read the letter:

> *To the young fighter,*
>
> > *I have noticed that you are struggling to be free of the troubles that are oppressing you. I can show you a way out. Please join me in my valley for a time of safety and rest. To find my valley, journey past the infested wilderness and the high mountains. There I will be waiting for you.*
> >
> > > *The Shepherdess of the Valley*

50-83 was unsure whether the letter was meant for him or for someone else. The intent gaze the wolf had sent him caused him to assume the letter was for him. But the letter was addressed to a 'fighter' and 50-83 knew he definitely was *not* a fighter. *Besides, it would take more courage than I have to travel through the wilderness and mountains. Those areas are deadly and very few people have ever returned from them, and on top of that, the Dark Tyrant forbids us to enter them.* Still, he smiled, knowing there was a person on the Planet of Darkness who was concerned about someone in trouble. He placed the letter in his inside vest pocket and headed for the Slump-Bump area.

Chapter Nineteen

The Emergency Escape Vessel slid into a rough landing in a yawning cavern located in the planet's deserted area. 7-43 looked out the EEV's small window and pouted in annoyance that he had no idea where he was. Back when Alpha 3-0-3 had left him alone in the hallway in front of the EEV's hatch, 7-43 had to do nothing more than to step inside it, sit down, and simply press a button marked 'start'. The EEV detached itself from the *Journey* and hurtled off toward the Planet of Darkness. 7-43 had no control over the EEV in flight and no control over where it chose to land.

"So," 7-43 murmured to himself, "here I am back on the Planet of Darkness, but what's so jolly about that when I have no blanking idea where I am?"

The inside of the EEV was comprised of nothing more than a cockpit area. Still, 7-43 searched around for anything that might give him a clue as to where he had landed. Unfortunately, 7-43 had no way of knowing what to look for. He worked for the Dark Tyrant in the Main Prison Complex as the warden of Floor 14 and had been taught next to nothing about maps. So even if he found one, he would not know how to use it.

"Blast-arama," he grumbled as he leaned his elbow on the nearby window's ledge and let his chin sink into his hand despondently. "I guess I'll just have to go outside and look around."

7-43 scooted over to the EEV's hatch. Luckily, there was a lever clearly marked 'open'. 7-43 pulled the lever and, with a grinding and clanking noise, the hatch door opened.

Stepping out of the EEV, 7-43 surveyed the surrounding cavern. He noticed a point in the wall of the cavern that sloped upwards, creating a path leading out. He was convinced he had seen this area before.

"Ha-ha.What blissfully good luck. I'm not far from the Dive of Distraction. I'll just pop over there and my good friend the Duke of Distraction will help me out of this terr-ysmal mess."

While the Dive of Distraction *was* near a deep cavern, 7-43 failed to take into account there were many deep caverns on the Planet of Darkness, all looking much alike. The deep cavern he was in now was nowhere near the Dive of Distraction, and, in reality, to reach the Dive from this cavern would take several weeks by foot. Blissfully ignorant of this fact, 7-43 whistled a tune as he started up the slope in the cavern.

7-43 heard racing steps in the distance. "Drat-illion," he cursed, jumping to the first conclusion that came to his mind. "Just what I *don't* need, an army of Enforcers heading this way." He stood still and glanced down first to the right passageway and then to the left passageway. Billows of dust rose from both passageways and he could hear the steps were now racing towards him coming closer . . . and closer.

7-43 scrambled up the slope to the top of the incline and out of the cavern, but before he could reach it, a large pack of wolves formed a half-circle just behind him. He turned around. The wolves growled, bared their teeth, and lowered their heads threateningly. They stared at him with a warning gaze which froze him with fear.

Deciding he would not make it out of the cavern with the wolves at his heels, 7-43 bolstered his courage enough to grab a stone from the ground and throw it at the wolves. "Get out of here, you monsters."

The stone just missed the largest wolf. This wolf stepped forward until he was less than a foot away from 7-43. The wolf reached over with his mouth to the pouch on his collar and pulled from it an envelope. He set this envelope on the ground in front of 7-43. The wolf then rushed back to his pack and turned to solemnly watch 7-43.

7-43 glanced down at the envelope with curiosity. He cautiously approached it, squatted, and picked it up to study it more closely. He opened the envelope and noticed a hand-written letter inside. Without bothering to read it, he laughed condescendingly. "This is the stupidest thing I have ever heard of. A letter from some barbaric animal." And he threw the letter along with the envelope back to the wolves. "Now get out of here, you minus-brained, dim-iotic beasts." He realized he would have been quite a fool to fall for such a devious trick. He assumed the wolves had plotted for him to become engrossed in the letter so they could pounce on him and devour him. Determined to show more sense and more courage to make up for his embarrassment, he faced the pack of wolves with brutal anger. "Leave me now or I swear I'll kill you all," he shouted at them even louder and threw several more stones.

The large wolf made his way calmly to the envelope on the ground and picked it back up in his mouth. He stared at 7-43 with a pitying look. He then, with resignation, faced his pack and gestured with his head for the other wolves to follow him. The wolf pack raced off through the passageway in the cavern.

7-43 sighed deeply in relief. He light-heartedly climbed the incline in the wall, and within minutes, he was out of the cavern. Glancing about his new surroundings, he became confused. He now realized in despair he was lost.

7-43 heard an unexpected whirring and hissing. Slithering out from behind various large boulders and dead trees were a score of the Dark Tyrant's mechanical-snake spies. They slinked up to form a circle around 7-43, hissing at him and adjusting their eyes to relay a clear picture of him to the Dark Tyrant. Desperately, 7-43 kicked a couple of the spies away and slipped out of the slimy creatures' constraints.

The spies readjusted their formation spreading themselves out into two wide rows of ten each. They tenaciously slithered up behind 7-43. 7-43 pulled a branch from a dead tree and swung it back and forth at the spies, knocking them out of his path, temporarily stunning them. Having slowed down the spies, he turned and ran as fast as he could away from them.

7-43 was unable to make it far. From out of the shadows, emerged fifteen Enforcers. They pointed their auto-targeting annihilation guns at 7-43. "Don't move," the Enforcer commanded. "We are taking you to the Dark Tyrant."

"Wait." 7-43 raised his hands in the air. "This is all some terrible mistake. I did not come here on purpose."

Two Enforcers stood on either side of 7-43, gripping him firmly by his arms. Another Enforcer stepped in front of him and jabbed him in the chest with his auto-targeting annihilation gun. "You are 7-43, correct?" the Enforcer asked in his mechanical, no-nonsense voice.

7-43 looked at the Enforcer with wide, expressionless eyes. "Why, yes, but…"

"You were in the EEV that just recently launched from the *Journey,* correct?" the Enforcer asked his next question.

"Well, yes, but, you don't understand," 7-43 objected.

"That makes no difference. The Dark Tyrant will now decide your fate."

7-43's eyes rolled upwards, not because he hoped for some last-minute rescue from a powerful force in outer space, but because he had just succumbed to a spell of faintness.

◂◆◆◆▸

7,500 strode up to the double-doors that led to the Dark Tyrant's Executive Hall. He turned around patronizingly, waiting for 2,040, 34,000, and 9-85 to catch up with him.

"Ah, yes," 2,040 clasped his hands together. "Our final stop on our tour. The Dark Tyrant's Executive Hall." His mouth curled into an ironic smile. "The center of impartial justice for all citizens . . . except—," he chuckled meaningfully. "Except for what? Except for whom? Except for when? You'll find they throw at you an awful lot of 'excepts'." Raising an eyebrow, he watched 9-85 out of the corner of his eye, expecting a reaction.

9-85 shrugged his shoulders. "I have little interest in legal matters."

Patting him on his upper arm, 7,500 gave 9-85 a reassuring smile. "You're not the only one. Most citizens of this planet know nothing about how the Dark Tyrant runs his legal system until they are dragged in through these doors to face it firsthand."

34,000 moved past 9-85 to stand close to 2,040. She drew her gaze from 2,040 to 9-85 with ominous solemnity. "And at that point, your chance of leaving this hall to report what you've seen is very . . . very small."

"Yes, that's what I've heard." 9-85 could not forget the times people he had known were dragged to the executive hall for minor disobediences. He even remembered one time when a classmate of his was taken in. He stood outside the doors to listen. He heard his shouts as he begged for mercy. He heard his screams of pain. And that was the last he ever heard of him. "So, you just have to make sure you go by the rules."

"Beautiful," 2,040 shook his head in disbelief. "I see there are some things you learn much too quickly." He looked upward in an overly-exaggerated poetic expression. "So, 9-85, tell me, isn't it just oh, so wonderful how obedient the citizens become when threatened with something frightening . . . something painful . . . something unknown." He looked 9-85 squarely in the eyes to accentuate his point.

"Well," 9-85 replied, "all forms of government need to have some means to keep order."

"Of course, there needs to be order." 7,500 held the door's handle. "But when the means of keeping order makes the lives of those ordered so miserable that life isn't worth living, well, is there any sense in that? In that case, we'd be better off with chaos." He tilted his head with a direct arch of his eyebrow as he opened the door and waved a hand for the others to enter the executive hall.

9-85 entered first, followed by 2,040 and 34,000. 7,500 walked in behind them.

Once inside, 9-85 was weighed by the stifling heat. Forcing himself to move, he made his way to the railing and looked over it into the lava pit below. He caught glimpses of the vacant-faced forms grasping desperately for some way out of the pit. For a few seconds, his heart stopped beating and he took several steps backward away from the railing.

2,040 bolstered him with his hands to his back. "I suppose something like that is a bit shocking at first. Just be glad knowing it's not *you* in there." 2,040 nodded with a cautionary look in his eyes. He guided him with a gentle shove toward the bridge and helped him across.

When they reached the other side, 2,040 took his place at 9-85's right side in the front area of the hall. He turned to 9-85 with a suddenly light-hearted smile. "And now for the big moment." He gestured toward the archway. "The Dark Tyrant, himself."

34,000 stood beside 2,040 and took his hand in hers. She gave his hand an affectionate squeeze. He gazed into her eyes tenderly. She returned his gaze with loving warmth.

9-85 shifted nervously. "Are you sure the Dark Tyrant doesn't mind us being here?"

"Of course not." 7,500 took his place on the other side of 9-85. "We have an appointment."

9-85 watched the center of the archway, anticipating the moment the Dark Tyrant would appear. He had maintained a reverent fear of the Dark Tyrant. He was honored he would be meeting him and sincerely hoped he was doing the right thing and would live through it.

A dark shadow filled the doorway. Increasing in size as it came forward, the shadow moved toward the four visitors. A beam of orange light fell on the shadow's face, revealing the face of a man none of them had ever seen before.

"Who are you?" 2,040 demanded, admonishingly. "What are you doing here?"

"That's right," 7,500 concurred. "We have an appointment with the Dark Tyrant, certainly not with you."

The man held his chin proudly. He was short and fat, looking much like a huge egg that had evolved into a toad that had evolved into a man. "Yes, you did have an appointment with the Dark Tyrant, but he is extremely busy right now and I will speak for him." He punctuated his sentence with an expression of wide-eyed volatility.

"Busy with what?" 7,500 stood defiantly tall.

"There have been an increasing number of signs that numerous rebellions are trying to pop up." Speaking confidently and matter-of-factly, the man continued to hold his chin high. "The Dark Tyrant has been delving into the matter. He feels confident he will soon be finding the source of these rebellions and will rapidly deal with that source."

2,040 stepped forward, perturbed. "You still haven't told me who you are? And what gives you the authority to speak for the Dark Tyrant?"

The man either did not notice, or chose not to notice, 2,040's frustrated attitude and instead he stretched his arms out grandly in the glory of his moment. "My number is 1. I work so closely with the Dark Tyrant that I know what he thinks and what he would say if he were here. You don't believe me? But the sub-citizens believe me." He turned and gestured toward the goo creatures. His hair flew wildly out of place and a maniacal grin formed on his face. The goo creatures obediently crawled over to surround him.

"Yeessss," they agreed as they ballooned up in subservient unison. "Yooou are the powerful associate of the Dark Tyrant. What yoooou ssssaaay must beeee obeyed."

7,500 and 2,040 exchanged expressions of disbelief.

Chapter Twenty

As soon as the Controllers had captured the *Journey*, 1-13's skeleton-ghosts enlightened him concerning this new development. Considering it only polite to allow the Controllers a few minutes to relay the information to him, 1-13 took the time to smoke a cigar while he lounged on the couch in his room. He waited and watched his communications set tensely. When half an hour had past and he still had not heard anything, he stood furiously and crushed his cigar in a nearby ashtray. He stormed out and marched briskly down the hall to the Control Fleet Center.

1-13 entered in a huff. He was caught off guard by finding the room sardine-packed by a large crowd of workers and fighters who pressed passed him, coming and going, and surrounding the Control Fleet Commander. 1-13 was jostled about by the flow of the crowd as he moved forward. Eventually, he was able to squeeze through and reach the Control Fleet Commander.

"*What* is going *on* here?" 1-13 demanded. "We had an *agreement*. Immediately *after* you captured the *passengers*, you were to bring them to *me* for *questioning*."

Unfazed, the Control Fleet Commander looked 1-13 coolly in the eyes. "There has been a change in plans. The Dark Tyrant gave orders that the prisoners were to be brought to the executive hall first." She abruptly turned her attention from 1-13 to a control screen that contained, what she considered, a more pressing matter.

Within himself, 1-13 angrily pounced on the Control Fleet Commander and tore her to bits, but, on the outside, he smiled good-naturedly. "And *why* is *that*, may I *ask*?"

The Control Fleet Commander shrugged her shoulders. "I believe he wants to eliminate some of them. Or maybe even all of them."

"They can't do that," 1-13 protested. "We'll never find out anything if they do."

A short distance away, two of the prisoners were being held by several guards. 1-13 watched them and narrowed his eyes shrewdly as he realized he recognized the man as 2-45, the one he had earlier met at the Dive of Distraction. *Well, well,* 1-13 thought, *the son of The Dark Tyrant's most prestigious advisor. The Dark Tyrant isn't playing favorites this time.*

2-45 nodded good-naturedly to the guards that encircled him and 1-05 and gave them an exaggeratedly friendly smile. "Well, I, uh, trust you're having a wonderful time. I certainly hope you're comfortable. Feet aren't sore, are they?"

1-05 looked at him askance, silently questioning his sanity.

2-45 sent her a quick wink which, when decoded, said, 'Don't worry, I've got a plan'. "Keep them happy," he told her aside. "Things will go better if you do." He turned to the guards. "That's right. Happy, happy," he said loud enough for the guards to hear. "Everyone's happy, right?" He held his hands up to indicate that he was happy and at peace with all. He reached into his cape and pulled out a few bags of coins. "And to ensure that everyone continues to be happy and keeps a smile on their face . . ." He distributed a handful of coins to each of the guards.

2-45 turned back to 1-05. "Remember that money I told you we would need? Go ahead, get yours out."

1-05 reached into her pocket and found it empty. "Oh, darn," she groaned in frustration. "I lost it. Must have been during the fight." She exhaled and pounded her fist on the wall.

Shaking his head sympathetically, he patted her on the shoulder. "I guess you will just have to hope for the best."

Leaning her back against the wall, 1-05 fumed. *It seems 2-45 has little concern about saving anybody's life but his own.*

While the guards were counting their newly acquired wealth, 2-45, in a lighthearted manner, made his way to the Control Fleet Commander. "And how do you do, ma'am? Everything is perfect and in order, I trust? Wonderful." He smiled in feigned shyness as he held out to her three bags of coins. "Just a little something to show you how grateful I am for all you've done for me."

The Control Fleet Commander unenthusiastically took the bags, tied them to a belt at her waist, and moved over to a console that was flashing for attention.

1-13 smirked disdainfully. "*She* is not the *one* who will be deciding your *fate*."

"I know." 2-45 handed 1-13 a couple of bags as well. "But it is always good to have as many friends as possible. If nothing else, these coins will remind you of me when I am gone." He raised his head with a clever smirk.

1-13 held the bags, testing their weight in his hand. "Maybe *now* I won't *tell* them where *you* were earlier." He looked 2-45 deep in the eyes meaningfully.

2-45 looked away to avoid 1-13's eyes. . . . *Earlier* . . . 2-45 had almost forgotten how recently it was that he and 1-13 had met in the corridors of the Dive of Distraction. He detected 1-13's condescending attitude and shifted uncomfortably. *He must have found out my reason for being there.* 2-45 frowned. "Well, thank you," he replied succinctly and started to pass by 1-13 on his way back to 1-05.

1-13 caught 2-45 by the arm. "You *are* the *son* of the Dark Tyrant's previous advisor number 32, *correct*?" There was an intense gleam in 1-13's eyes.

Caught off guard by how suddenly 1-13 changed the topic, 2-45 turned back to him. "That's right." He nervously drummed his fingers against the bags of coins he held.

"I used to work *closely* with your *father*. He was an *extremely* clever *man*. If everything goes *well* today, perhaps *we* could work *together*, too." 1-13 placed the bags of coins in his own jacket pocket and patted it to ensure its security. He gave 2-45 a confident nod.

2-45 lined up in his mind all the possible reasons for 1-13 wanting to work with him and he came up with quite a few. They ranged from simple sentimentality to pretentious plotting. But, what 2-45 wanted was that one specific reason so he could know whether 1-13would back him up during the trial. Unable to discern it, he studied 1-13 cautiously. "Perhaps . . ."

Several Enforcers entered the room. Two of them held 7-43 firmly as they dragged him in. 7-43 looked weak and docile, his head bowed. The highest-ranking Enforcer marched to the Control Fleet Commander. "We captured the last prisoner from the *Journey*, Commander."

The Control Fleet Commander smiled, pleased. "Good. And to reward your assistance . . ." She took from her belt one of the bags of coins and handed it to the Enforcer.

The Enforcer took the bag in one mechanical motion and gave her a short routine bow. "The prisoner is left in your custody." He turned and gestured curtly for the other Enforcers to follow him out the room. The Control Fleet guards surrounded 7-43.

7-43 took a quick gasp of air and ran his hand across his sweaty forehead. Being hemmed in by so many guards was causing him to feel claustrophobic. "You don't have to stand so squeezy-wheezy close. It's not as if there's any way I can gallop-a-trot out of here," he murmured mostly to himself. He squirmed and took a step away from the two closest guards. The two guards took their posts once more on either side of 7-43. 7-43 sighed, resigned.

Alpha 3-0-3, still in the form of a flea, was hiding in 1-05's pocket. It heard 7-43's voice and peeked over the edge of the pocket. Upon spotting 7-43, Alpha 3-0-3 hopped out of the pocket and onto 7-43's ear. "That was very cruel of you. How dare you take the EEV and leave us there to face the Controllers alone."

7-43 started at hearing the small, high-pitched flea-ish voice and not seeing anyone. "What's this? I must be going crazy. I'm hearing ghoul-arific ghosts."

"No, no," Alpha 3-0-3 corrected him obstinately. "I'm not a ghost. I'm Alpha 3-0-3. I'm here in your ear. I'm a flea."

7-43's eyes widened in fear. "A flea. Get away. I can't stand fleas." He swooshed his hand around his ear to brush away any flying, hopping, or crawling insects that might be there.

Alpha 3-0-3 hopped away from 7-43's oncoming hand and landed back over on 1-05's shoulder. It let its head sink onto one of its front limbs in thought. "Oh," it groaned despondently. "That 7-43 is so difficult."

Satisfied that he was free of any fleas, 7-43 noticed that 2-45 had returned to stand next to 1-05. With an amicable smile, 7-43 took a step past the Control Fleet guards over to him. "Ah, 2-45, old friend." He put on the air of a jolly drinking buddy.

"Ah, yes, of course, and how are you, old friend?" 2-45 wryly joined 7-43 in his let's-make-believe-we're-just-old-friends-meeting-at-a-bar routine.

"It's obvious, isn't it?" 7-43 shook his head despondently. "Those Enforcers. Such jerk-aholics. I think they were just there waiting for me to walk into their trap." After glaring at the nearby guards and then sulking for a moment, his mouth curled into a knowing smile. "I saw you passing money out to that Control Fleet Commander and that Persuader."

"There's no law against that. Our leaders love to get their hands on as much money as they can." 2-45 raised his chin in a confident, professorial expression.

"Of course, I know." After realizing his right hand had several scratches and blisters, 7-43 rubbed it dejectedly. "But that does give you some influence with them. They will listen to you." He looked at 2-45 with as sad and pitiful an expression as he could muster up. "Please, tell them to go easy on me. Don't let them kill me or put me in prison. Those prisons are terrible. I couldn't take being locked up. You'll tell them to let me go, won't you?" He widened his eyes sadly and forced his lower lip to tremble.

2-45 crossed his arms over his chest. "Why should I? When we were trying to make it to the Planet of Light and fight off the Controllers, you refused to help us." He arrogantly moved away from 7-43 and looked through the open doorway at a group of Legal Examiners on their way to the executive hall. 2-45 stepped over to them. The Legal Examiners scowled at 2-45, but he assumed a cheerful, positive attitude. "Ah, looks like we have a smiling group of Legal Examiners here. And, just to keep everyone happy all around . . ." He handed a bag of coins to each of the Legal Examiners. The Legal Examiners eagerly took the bags. They nodded, looking happier, and continued down the hall.

7-43 sunk into a pout. "It's so dang-blasting unfair. Just because he has money, they're all eager as dandy doilies to listen to him. It's not like it's hard to pass out money. If I had money, I could deal it out just as easily." He pounded his fist into his hand and winced at the pain from the blisters. "Oh, I'd like to pickle him in vinegar."

Alpha 3-0-3 hopped back over onto 7-43's head and slid down to his ear. "Don't worry," he said perkily. "I'll help you."

"Ooooh. Not that spook-rifying voice again. Don't tell me it's another flea." 7-43 scratched his ear in alarm.

Alpha 3-0-3 sidestepped 7-43's fingernails, shocked at the narrow escape. "Well, I'm really not a flea. I'm just Alpha 3-0-3 in the form of one."

"What?" 7-43 thought for a moment, then realized he could be hearing Alpha 3-0-3 after all. "Oh . . . yes. That's right. You're a shape-shifter . . . anything smaller than a planet and all." He laughed recalling his earlier conversation with the shape-shifter. He quickly became serious. "Did you say something about helping me?" He tilted his head, his eyes hopeful yet languid.

"Absolutely," Alpha 3-0-3 said, optimistically eager. "It's quite possible that the Dark Tyrant will just lock us up in prison, you know."

7-43 grimaced. "I don't want to go to prison. I am quite familiar with how horribly awful those little bits of hell are. I work as a warden, you know."

"Yes, but being a shape-shifter, I could transform into something that could help you escape the prison."

7-43's face brightened. "Oh, I see. And you promise you will?"

"Of course."

5-68 woke from a deep slumber in his mud-drenched rocking chair in front of his hovel. Just as he had begun to doze off again, he heard footsteps approaching. He half-heartedly opened one eye and saw 4,021 standing next to him.

She playfully blew a handful of leaves into his face. "Wake up. Everything's so beautiful."

5-68 groaned. "Well, what's making you so alert and chirpy?"

4,021 smiled. "You would be, too, if you saw what *he* gave to me."

"You've got to stop this," 5-68 snapped as he pulled himself into a sitting position with an exhausted moan. "You're dreaming too much. You're thinking too much. And you've been walking around too much. You should go back into your hovel and do what a normal Slump-Bump is supposed to do — like snoozing the rest of the day." He lethargically sank back in his rocking chair, so drowsy, he was not even aware his feet had sunk ankle-deep into the mud.

Looking down in disappointment, 4,021's eyes fell on the rose in her hand. "But I just wanted to show you this." She held the rose out to 5-68.

5-68 opened his eyes and started at the sight of the rose. "Get that away from me." He pulled himself back from the rose and grimaced in repulsion. "It could be dangerous."

"It isn't dangerous. It's beautiful."

5-68 shook his head, pityingly. "I hate having to be the one to tell you this, but everyone's been talking about you. You're becoming an outcast among the Slump-Bumps. You're going against the rules. You're doing too much, and you're thinking too much." His last sentence was punctuated by a big slosh as his feet plunged deep into the mud.

4,021 lifted the rose to admire it. She breathed in its delightful perfume. "It doesn't matter what they all think. This is the most beautiful thing I've ever seen, and I would never give it up for anything."

4,021 walked dreamily away from 5-68 to a murky stream of water. The stream had been created by sewage draining from the City of the Dark Tyrant. She looked longingly past the stream into the dark sky. "Oh, Infinity, I hope you come soon." She placed the rose into the pocket near her heart. Saddened that he may still be a long way off, she sighed disconsolately and turned to head toward her hovel. Before she had gone far, 50-83 approached her.

"How are things going?" he asked.

"All right, I guess." Things were not really going 'all right', but she was so used to answering 'all right' that she did so without a thought. But she then remembered something which lightened her heart. "Look." She excitedly held out her wrist to him. "I'm still wearing the bracelet you gave me."

50-83 touched the bracelet's star-shaped charm. "The bracelet looks nice on you."

4,021 smiled, noticing that his eyes appeared kind. "Can I show you something without you becoming upset?"

Puzzled, 50-83 studied her face. "That depends on what it is."

4,021 took the rose from her pocket and held it out to him. "It's this. It's called a rose. Isn't it beautiful?"

"Yes. It must be some sort of plant." Gazing at the rose with awe, 50-83 stretched his hand out to touch it. When his fingers fell on the rose, they burned with pain as if touching fire. "Ow." He jerked his hand back and noticed red blisters forming on his fingers.

She stared at the blisters in concern. "I'm sorry." She found it horrible that someone she liked would be hurt by her beautiful rose. Dejectedly, she put it back into her pocket.

50-83 sucked on his fingers to ease the pain. "How come *you* can touch it without it burning you?"

She shook her head in confusion. "I – I don't know." 4,021 gently touched the rose in her pocket. "It was given to me by the man I was telling you about. Oh, and I found out something. His name is Infinity." Her eyes sparkled with excitement as she took from her pocket the letter Infinity had sent her. "He wrote me this." She handed the letter to 50-83.

50-83 read the letter out loud. "Dear Hopeful One, do not let anyone discourage you. I am on my way to you, and I look forward to greeting you and holding you in my arms. Believe me when I say, I love you. I will rescue you and take you away from all those who do not treat you with the kindness and the respect that you deserve. Again, I love you. Keep this rose near your heart. It is a symbol of my love, and it will protect you. Your friend and your lover, Infinity." He was fascinated with the letter. He noticed some warm glow radiating from it. He looked up from it and his eyes strayed past 4,021 into the muddy stream behind her.

One of the Dark Tyrant's spies ominously lifted its head out of the water. Its mechanical eyes whirred into focus on 50-83. It hissed at him threateningly.

50-83 stared at it, frozen with fear. He took a deep, anxious breath and closed his eyes to calm himself.

In concern, 4,021 followed his gaze to the muddy stream. "What's the matter? Was it the letter? What do you see?"

"Nothing," 50-83 said nervously under his breath. "It's just—" Knowing that the spy was listening in, he took another deep breath not certain what he could say to keep both 4,021 and the Dark Tyrant happy. Before anything came to his mind, the Dark Tyrant's spy submerged under the water. As the spy slithered away below the water's surface, 50-83 watched its blubbing and swooshing path in the stream.

"Just what?" 4,021 blinked her eyes questioningly.

In a serious and unaffected manner, 50-83 handed the letter back to her. ". . . a very nice letter."

"And from someone so wonderful." She held the letter to her heart.

"Yes." 50-83 stepped to the murky river and surveyed it, watching for signs of any other spies. Satisfied he was not being watched, he turned back to 4,021, looking at her soberly. "I came here to warn you about something."

"What?" she asked with child-like simplicity as she placed the letter in her pocket.

"I want to warn you about 1-13 and 6-96. They want to question you about that letter, that rose, and about Infinity. About you wanting to leave the Planet of Darkness."

Stunned, 4,021 moved a few inches away from 50-83. "What are you talking about?" While what he was talking about was a riddle to her, she could tell it was something terrible by the urgent tone of his voice.

"I'm talking about the Persuaders. You can't let them know about these things." 50-83 took a moment to peek into one of the boxes in his mind. He remembered that day when he and his friend stood in front of the Dark Tyrant. His friend answered the Dark Tyrant's questions truthfully and, because of that, he was killed. His mind proceeded to transform the image of his friend into one of 4,021. The sequence played out the same and ended in the same horrifying way, with 4,021 being disintegrated into ashes by the Dark Tyrant. He winced and opened his eyes. A feeling of responsibility came over him as he looked at her, and he determined to help her somehow. "You've got to lie. You've got to tell them you are happy here. You've got to tell them you would never want to leave this place."

4,021's simple mind could not wrap itself around the idea of lying. "But, I'm not happy here. I want to leave. I want Infinity to come and take me away."

50-83 grabbed her by her upper arms and shook her. "But you can't trust 1-13 or 6-96. They want you to tell the truth. And when you do you will be killed. *You've got to lie.*" He was about to say more but he noticed that tears were starting to form in 4,021's eyes. He stopped himself and took a deep breath as he let go of her arms.

"Why should I?" 4,021 sobbed, wiping a tear from her eye.

"I want to help you. If you want to live, you can't tell the truth."

"But you read in the letter." Imploringly, she grasped hold of the front of 50-83's jacquard vest. "Infinity said the rose would protect me."

50-83 nodded as he rubbed the blisters on his hand. He could not deny that 4,021's rose possessed some supernatural power. *Perhaps she is right,* he thought. *Perhaps Infinity can protect her from everything.* But 50-83's mind strayed back to the moment the Dark Tyrant plunged the inferno darts into his friend's chest. *Not everything.* "I'll admit the rose is unusual, but it can't protect you against the Dark Tyrant." He then realized the only way he could protect her from the Dark Tyrant was to hide her away from him. *But where? . . . And how?* . . . He searched his mind desperately and finally remembered something. "I have an idea . . ." From his inside vest pocket, he pulled out the letter the wolf had given him. "This letter talks about a place where we can go to be safe. I could take you there."

"Where is it?" 4,021 asked.

"A valley some ways from here." He studied the directions in the letter. "I think I could find it."

4,021 caressed her rose. "But if I leave, will Infinity be able to find me?"

50-83 sighed in exasperation. *Here I am trying to get her to someplace safe, to keep her from being killed, and all she can think about is this no-guarantees-he-exists Infinity finding her.* To keep himself calm, he counted to five before he answered. "Of course Infinity will be able to find you. He was able to find you to give you the rose, so he should be able to find you again."

"You're right. Of course, he would be able to find me." She held her hand out to 50-83. "I'll go with you."

50-83 took her hand in a firm, protective hold. As he led 4,021 out of the Slump-Bump area, their path was blocked by two huge guards, threatening them with axes. One of the guards lumbered forward. "1-13 tells us to take girl to workshop." With mindless strength, the guard grabbed 4,021 by the arm.

"That's not true." 50-83 held onto 4,021 and pulled her from the guard's grasp. He knew the guards were less than intelligent and, if he displayed enough confidence, they were easy to bluff. 50-83 held himself tall, with a self-assured air. "1-13 assigned me to her. I'm supposed to be questioning her and he hasn't told me any different."

4,021 stared at 50-83 in confusion. 50-83 had been talking about how dangerous 1-13 was, and now he was saying he worked for him. She wanted to trust him, but how could she when he kept contradicting himself?

Before 50-83 had a chance to resist, the other guard took hold of his arms so firmly that 50-83 could not move. The first guard took out of his coat a pocket communicator. He held the computer's screen before 50-83's face and turned it on.

1-13's moving image was displayed on the communicator. He stood before the hustle and bustle of the Control Fleet Center, looking into the camera with a superior mien. "My *dear* friend 50-83, *I* am sending *you* this message because your *rebellious* nature is certain to *retaliate* to my *new* change in plans. I had *hoped you* and *I* could work together to accomplish some *magnificent* goals. *But*, since then, you have proven yourself *untrustworthy*. I cannot *work* with someone I cannot *trust*. *So* I am *terminating* our *partnership*. Farewell." The communicator switched off.

50-83 looked over at 4,021. She did not meet his gaze. 50-83's head sunk to his chest as the two guards led 4,021 away. She did not resist.

Chapter Twenty-One

R aising his wild eyes to the double doors, 1 observed the six Legal Examiners entering the executive hall in a uniform row. "Ah," he proclaimed with one hand outstretched like an egotistical Shakespearian actor. "I see we are preparing for another trial." He chuckled with frenzied glee. "This should be exciting."

9-85 nervously stepped over next to 2,040. He wished he could have hidden behind him instead, hoping to avoid becoming involved in something as complicated and contentious as a trial. "Maybe we're not supposed to stay here," 9-85 mentioned to him under his breath.

"Nonsense," 2,040 replied with a delighted smile. "Of course we're allowed to watch." Then, assuming the manner of a strict schoolteacher, he told him, "I *want* you to watch. This will be educational for you."

7,500 pulled 9-85 closer to him by his upper arm. He leaned his mouth in toward 9-85's ear. "A little warning, just in case you're the sensitive sort. The likelihood that those on trial will be executed is very high."

9-85 could have braced himself for seeing someone shot down for their crimes, but he had heard these executions were often ghastly demonstrations. He shifted uneasily. "Do we have to watch? Isn't there some way we could inconspicuously slip out?"

Raising a cautionary finger, 7,500 sent 9-85 an admonishing glare. "Careful. 2,040 *is* your superior. He said you're to watch, so you had better stay and watch."

9-85 exhaled in frustration. 7,500 had spent the last couple of hours lecturing on his radical viewpoints, and now it took 9-85 off guard to have 7,500 so abruptly change. To demonstrate his disapproval, 9-85 moved back over next to 2,040.

The Legal Examiners paraded ceremonially over the narrow bridge and toward the front of the hall. The featureless souls boiling in the lava below the bridge moaned and groaned as if providing the processional music for the Legal Examiners as they marched across. Once they reached the front, the Legal Examiners lined up on the right side of 1.

A metal door on 1's left opened and the Control Fleet Commander entered promptly. She made her way to 1 and bowed succinctly before him. "I have brought the prisoners."

1 grinned, looking much like a man trying to suppress nausea. "Excellent. Bring them in immediately."

The Control Fleet Commander bowed once more and turned to the six Control Fleet Guards waiting in the doorway. She waved for them to enter; after which, she moved behind and to the side of 1, out of the guards' path.

The guards arrived with 2-45, 7-43, and 1-05 in tow. They lined up on 1's left side and forced the prisoners to kneel on the ground before him.

1 eyed them disdainfully. "You three have been charged with a VERY serious crime. A crime verging upon rebellion." He held his head high, flaring his nostrils with wild zeal. "You three tried to leave our beloved planet. This demonstrates your extremist tendencies. And that you do not wish to be one of us. That in itself is rebellion." He tilted his head and widened his eyes to accent his unbending disgust.

1-13 entered the hall from the side door, which, afterwards, slid shut behind him with a loud thud. The floor creaked as he approached 1. In an effortless gesture, 1-13 bowed to him.

Eying him in annoyance, 1 pulled his mouth down in a long, deep frown. "Can't you see I am busy? This is an urgent trial of the highest priority."

1-13 lowered his head further in what would have been a sign of obeisance if his eyes had not been aflame with fury. "*Forgive* me," he said in feigned humility. "But I did not *mean* to intrude. I only *want* to make certain you *understand* that the *Dark Tyrant* has *commanded* that *I* should *question* the prisoners in regards to the *rebellion*."

"Your intrusion was unnecessary. I already understand that." 1 raised his head more arrogantly. "You may take any of the prisoners you wish to question . . ."

1-13 smiled in relief. "Thank you, all-powerful 1."

Abruptly, 1 held up a hand, crushing 1-13's moment of euphoria. ". . . AFTER the trial."

Trying to suppress a look of disgust, 1-13 mumbled a string of words under his breath which unethically described 1's ignorant stupidity and departure into oblivion. He reluctantly bowed and moved to stand alongside the Control Fleet Commander. "After the trial," he mockingly murmured to himself. "There won't *be* any prisoners alive *after* the trial. It *amazes* me the amount of *incompetency* there is around here."

The Control Fleet Commander glanced over at him, raising an arched eyebrow.

1-13 waved off his earlier remark. "Nothing," he apologized with a look of innocence. "Just talking to myself."

1 pointed a chubby finger in 2-45's direction. "You, Prisoner 2-45. Step forward." 1's frown elongated, resembling the mouth of the large toad from which he must have evolved.

Maintaining as lighthearted an attitude as he could muster, 2-45 rose from his kneeling position. He stood before 1 and bowed. He put on a self-assured posture and began his planned-out speech. "I admit I did the wrong—"

1 crinkled up his nose in distaste and waved a hand to cut off 2-45. "Silence. I will first present the court with your crimes." He pulled from the pocket of his oversized coat a small clipboard holding a stack of papers. He coldly flipped through the papers until he came to the page he was looking for. Squinting his eyes, he read off 2-45's crimes in an authoritative and unemotional voice. "You expressed a desire to leave our Planet of Darkness." He rapidly rustled through several pages of detailed information. "You bribed a pilot to carry out your wishes." Turning over more pages. "You resisted arrest." Even more pages. "You damaged the property of the Dark Tyrant and you violently assaulted several Controllers." With finality, 1 brought the pages back in place on the clipboard. "Do you object to these charges?"

While 1 was reading, 2-45 ignored him, focusing instead on not forgetting his memorized speech. Once 1 was done, 2-45 took a deep breath and resumed his speech, speaking the words with the same beats and inflections he knew by heart. "I admit I did the wrong thing. But it wasn't exactly—"

"So." 1 looked down his nose as if affronted. "Are you disputing the charges?"

"No. I mean — I . . . uh," 2-45 shook his head, flustered. Being forced away from his planned speech, he was unsure what to do or say. The only thing was to start again. "I admit I did the wrong thing . . ."

"You said that before," 1 sniffed haughtily.

2-45 held a hand up in sheepish acknowledgement. "Yes, well, if it's all right with you, could I finish?"

1 nodded superciliously.

"Thank you." 2-45 ran his fingers through his hair while closing his eyes to calm himself. He then continued. "I admit I did the wrong thing. But my intention was not to rebel. I wasn't wanting to leave the Planet of Darkness permanently. I just thought it might be fun to go for a little ride in outer space in 1-05's ship. It seemed like an exciting thing to do at the time and, you have to admit, 1-05's a nice-looking girl . . ."

He glanced in her direction and smiled in a playfully flirtatious manner.

1-05 responded back with a glare. On the *Journey*, 2-45 seemed so brave and she was comfortable working and fighting alongside him. She was even starting to become fond of him . . . But now, the way he was talking, she was furious.

2-45 frowned and took a moment to regain his composure. "But, it was a stupid thing to do and I promise, promise, promise—" He clasped his hands in front of him and faced 1 with a sincere expression. "—never to do it again. And to make up for it . . ." 2-45 smiled excitedly and took from his pocket several bags of coins and offered them to 1 with a sweep of the hand that was larger-than-necessary.

1 accepted the gift with a wide, cheerful grin. He opened one of the bags, pulled out a coin and studied it to ascertain its authenticity. Satisfied, he put the bags into a deep pocket at his hip. However, with a sudden somber expression, he turned back to 2-45. "One more question," he acted as if the incident with the coins had not happened. "When we questioned the Duke of Distraction in regards to you, he mentioned that you asked about a spaceship that would take you to the Planet of Light. Can you explain that?"

Hearing this, 2-45's heart sank. He was most certainly doomed. He forced his brain into action. "Yes . . . of course . . . I can't remember exactly what I said when I was talking to the Duke of Distraction. I may have mentioned the Planet of Light, but, if I did, I wasn't serious about it. I wouldn't really want to go all the way there — it's so far away — and I've heard it's a very dangerous journey."

"That's right," 1 laughed as he patted 2-45 on the shoulder. "I understand." He turned to the Legal Examiners and nodded a signal of approval. "Now, Legal Examiners, how should this prisoner be punished?"

The Legal Examiner closest to 1 moved forward. "He should be punished—," he said in a stiff, formal manner. "But not severely. Not by death nor by imprisonment."

"Very good." 1 turned back to 2-45 and made an emphatic gesture for him to kneel.

2-45 knelt before 1, unsure of what to expect. *So, if they're not going to execute me or put me in prison, how are they going to punish me? Will it be something worse?* 2-45 started as the floor under him lit up in a reddish-orange glow.

1 moved to stand before 2-45. As his feet touched the ground, a smoking red lava oozed up through the floor, swooshed at 2-45, and crept up to cover his hands and legs.

The lava burned as it touched 2-45's flesh. He winced in pain, but forced himself not to move or cry out. He had heard that the punishment could become worse if he did. The portion of the floor where 2-45 knelt lowered and, as it did, 2-45 sunk deeper and deeper into the lava.

"You have committed crimes against our Dark Tyrant," 1 announced authoritatively, "our Planet of Darkness, and all citizens of Darkness. Your crimes are not so grievous, though, that with the right punishment, we could not endure keeping you as a citizen. But you have failed as a Propaganda Specialist, so, you are now barred from that profession. Since that is the only profession you know, you are, consequently, barred from working in any professional field. From now on, you must follow the orders of others."

1 stepped back and the smoking lava slowly drained out of the floor. The floor moved back in place and the reddish-orange light dimmed. As the lava slunk away from him, the pain left 2-45's body. He heaved a deep, thankful sigh.

1 gestured for 2-45 to rise. "For now, you will go with 1-13 and do whatever he says." 1 indicated 1-13 with a perfunctory wave of his hand.

2-45 stood. The Control Fleet guards came forward and conducted him to 1-13.

1-13 smiled slyly. "Looks like *you'll* be working for *me* for a while, *Ex*-Propaganda Officer." 1-13 brushed a speck of lint from his sleeve and held his head in biting over-confidence.

With a dry, nervous chuckle, 2-45 shrugged his shoulders. "I suppose so." 2-45 paused a moment in thought. "Tell me," he asked sarcastically. "Does working for you include being tortured and brainwashed?"

"*That* depends . . ." 1-13 replied. ". . . *depends* on whether you've been a *good* boy or a *bad* boy. *Do* as I *say* and things shouldn't go *too* badly for you." He chuckled belittlingly.

1-13's contemptuous attitude aggravated 2-45. The position of Propaganda Specialist was a highly respected one and 2-45 was accustomed to being treated with respect. He remembered how the Dark Tyrant had gone out of his way to place him on this coveted career path as a reward to his father, Advisor 32. His father had bargained with the Planet Obscura to establish a treaty in return for plans of their advanced weaponry. 2-45 lowered his eyes in resignation. *I've heard rumors about 1-13's eccentricities . . . And I don't like the way he seems to want to control me . . . but I suppose it could have been worse.* 2-45 rubbed his arm uneasily and glanced over at 1-13. "I suppose I shouldn't complain, though," he said aloud. "The trial went better than it might have." He regretted having had to spend so much money in bribes, but at least he was wealthy enough to afford it and was able to come out of the trial alive.

"*Better?*" 1-13 shook his head in disbelief at 2-45's naivety and leaned closer to him confidentially. "Yours was the *best* it could *be*. Prisoners are guilty as *soon* as they *enter* the executive *hall*. Your money was *well* spent and *earned* you an *amazingly* mild punishment. I doubt if your *friends* will have it as *good*."

"*Please, I beg you.*"

2-45 heard the shout coming from the direction of the other prisoners and turned to look.

7-43 rushed forward in a panic and fell on his hands and knees before 1. "Don't punish me. I didn't do anything wrong. It was just some crazy accident that I ended up on that blasted ship." His lip trembled and his face was clammy and pale with fear.

1 scrunched his nose at 7-43 as if 7-43 were some unusual form of insect. "We are not here to decide whether you are guilty or not. We already know you *are*."

7-43's mouth dropped in disbelief. "But . . . I'm not guilty," he murmured unsteadily.

"You ARE guilty," 1 declared with finality, his mouth enlarging to form a gaping hole lined with sharp rotting teeth.

7-43 stared in shock. "B-b-but . . . I . . . I . . . don't . . . don't . . . don't . . ." 7-43's words were barely audible and were spoken between agitated breaths.

"Don't what?" 1 grimaced. "What is that you're saying? Speak up, young man."

7-43's hands shook and, even though he was kneeling, he had the sensation he was going to drop into some never-ending abyss. "P-p-please . . . don't . . . don't . . . s-s-send . . . m-m-me . . ."

"Send you?" 1 asked in bewilderment. "Send you where?"

"Please." 7-43 trembled. ". . . don't . . . don't . . . s-s-s-send . . . me . . . to . . . to the . . ."

Becoming more and more confused with the way the trial was progressing, 9-85 placed a hand on 2,040's shoulder to gain his attention. "What's the matter with that man?" he asked, with a questioning tilt of his head.

"A case of nerves perhaps?" 2,040 replied, pursing his lips studiously.

9-85 frowned at having not received the type of answer he was hoping for. "Do you think he's telling the truth that he *is* innocent?"

2,040 laughed superciliously. "Who knows? And, to tell you honestly, nobody around here really cares."

With concern, 9-85 watched 7-43 who was shaking uncontrollably in terror. "But where is it he doesn't want them to send him?"

Shrugging his shoulders, 2,040 shook his head to indicate that he was clueless. "I wouldn't take anything he says seriously. In a delusional state, no doubt."

Furiously, 1 waddled up to 7-43, and took him by the shoulder of his jacket, shaking him violently. "Stop this insane outburst, RIGHT NOW."

"But please," 7-43 continued, his voice choked by a sob. "P-p-please don't send me . . . to the . . . judgment . . . beyond . . ." As he spoke the words, the overwhelming concept of 'the judgment beyond death' became such a reality in his mind that he gasped in fright.

The room filled with a dark, oppressive cloud. The cloud pulled itself into the form of a huge, malicious bat. It abruptly spread its large wings and flew up, fiercely encircling the executive hall over the heads of the onlookers who watched with wary apprehension.

2,040 leaned over to 9-85 enthusiastically. "That's him. That's the Dark Tyrant."

With guarded awe, 9-85 looked up and followed the dark form with his eyes. It was as if the sinister being had overpowered his mind to nearly control his thoughts.

The Dark Tyrant screeched and spread open his jaws to spew fire in 7-43's direction. "Silence," he shouted in absolute fury. "Don't ever, EVER mention THAT again." The Dark Tyrant landed in one steady but forceful motion next to 1. He raised his shoulders menacingly and stretched his neck forward to glare at 7-43 with narrowed fiery eyes.

Sweat matted 7-43's hair to his forehead. He tried to lift his eyes to look at the Dark Tyrant, but they remained fixed on the floor. "B-b-but . . . I-I didn't mean to . . . I just don't want to . . . Please . . . don't send me there . . . please . . ."

The Dark Tyrant hissed and grabbed from a nearby stand a dagger with a jade handle embellished with silver. He ferociously threw the dagger, directing it straight into 7-43's chest.

7-43 screamed in pain, looking down in disbelief at the dagger that had lodged in his chest. He tried to clutch at the dagger but his arms refused to move.

The carved jade portion of the handle melted into a green slime, releasing a number of small, vicious, parasitical worms. Set on their deadly purpose, the worms immediately slinked their way across what was left of the dagger and tunneled into the wound in 7-43's chest. Once inside him, they quickly multiplied and spread throughout his stomach, bowels, lungs, brain, and heart, taking over his entire body, sucking from his organs whatever particle of potential energy they could find, leaving each organ to resemble an empty, useless sack.

7-43 shook violently, emitting a low, bone-chilling groan, and collapsed onto the floor. The worms oozed out of his nose, mouth, and eye sockets, slithered from his remains, and disappeared into the floor.

1 frowned and gestured for two of the guards to carry away 7-43's lifeless, hollow body. He then chugged back over to the Dark Tyrant and spoke to him in confidential whispers.

In a state of stunned nausea, 9-85 took a step back. "He didn't even have a chance to explain himself."

7,500 shifted over next to 9-85 and patted him on the back to alleviate his concern. "It may seem a little unfair, but he won't complain." He grinned with counterfeit excitement, revealing his sparkling white teeth. "Two down, one more to go."

As the guards carried 7-43's body past 2-45, crossing directly in front of him, 2-45 had to fight against his legs buckling under him.

Noticing the dazed look on 2-45's face, 1-13 chuckled with a saturnine sense of humor. "You *did* have the *monetary* advantage over *him*."

1-05 closed her eyes to block out what may follow. She could not calm her rapidly beating heart. Her mind raced. *It didn't turn out very bad for 2-45, but 7-43 was executed. Where does that leave me?* "Alpha 3-0-3, what should I do?" she whispered desperately to the flea-shaped shape-shifter.

Alpha 3-0-3 leaped up to her ear and sat above her earlobe. "The most important thing is to not be frightened. Go to them with confidence. If they try to hurt you, I will stop them." It kept a watchful eye on everyone as it clenched its small forelegs ready for action.

As calmly and bravely as possible, 1-05 stepped up to 1.

1 watched her with marked superiority and coldly buttoned his oversized jacket around his bulging belly. "On your knees, young lady."

1-05 pressed her lips together in annoyance, but reluctantly knelt before 1.

Pulling out his clipboard, 1 read off her crimes. "You attempted to unlawfully leave the Planet of Darkness. You were transporting illegal goods. You resisted arrest. And you joined an attack on our Controllers." He glared at 1-05. "You are a wicked woman and should be severely punished." He turned to the Legal Examiners and shook his head disdainfully.

The Legal Examiners swiftly conferred among themselves.

1-05 was dumfounded at how quickly the trial was coming to a close. "But," she protested. "Aren't you going to, at least, listen to my side of the story?"

1 snorted. "That's exactly what you'd tell me, *a story.*"

"Oooh," 1-05 fumed under her breath. "What should I do now, Alpha 3-0-3?"

"Don't worry, I'll take care of him." The shape-shifter hopped down onto 1-05's shoulder and took a few moments to decide whether to transform into an ultra-powerful, weapon-enhanced spaceship or a mountain-sized, laser-firing Hermoltian creature.

Before Alpha 3-0-3 had a chance to act, 1-13 calmly approached 1. "May *I* have a *moment* to *speak* with the *Dark Tyrant, please*?"

1 scrunched up his face as if he had swallowed a lemon. "I fail to see how that will help this trial to progress."

The Dark Tyrant's form billowed up and absorbed itself. The dark smoke left took on the appearance of a large, black and iridescent green serpent, who brought his face close to 1-

13's and stared him in the eyes. "Go ahead. Speak," he said in a low, and unusually rumbling, hiss.

1-13 bowed effortlessly to the Dark Tyrant. "*I* was under the *impression* that you wanted me to *question* these *prisoners* in regards to the *rebellion*, so, if you *are* planning on *executing* her, I wanted it to be *you*, and not *him*, who said *so*. While I am *completely* aware that you are *free* to change your *mind*, from my own *limited* viewpoint, it still seems like a *good idea* to question her *first*." He smiled a hopeful yet restrained smile.

The Dark Tyrant growled as his appearance melted back into the dark cloud and then twisted and whirled to form a fierce tiger with glowing orange eyes. "She will be punished severely, but not executed. At least, not yet."

"Very well," 1 agreed with head held high. He marched sternly up to 1-05. "You will be confined to a small, dark cell in the Main Prison Complex and be forced to endure the customary torture." 1 waved over a churlish, shirtless man whose frown was a huge as his muscles. His glassy eyes were blood-shot and surrounded by a pale rim.

The man mindlessly knelt before 1. "Eager to do as you demand, all-powerful 1," he recited with more of a grunt than a voice.

"Warden 22-09. Take her away. Have her locked up. Show her how we punish rebellious actions." He looked from the warden to 1-05 with a meaningfully wide-eyed stare.

"It will be done." Warden 22-09 marched with a determined sweat-infused stride up to 1-05, grabbed her by her upper arms, and pushed her ahead of him toward the door.

1-13 anxiously took two steps up to 1 which caused the floor to creak complainingly. "But *when* will *I* be able to *question* her?"

1 shrugged in disinterest. "Perhaps when the warden is through torturing her."

Intensely upset, 1-13 turned and watched the warden shoving 1-05 out of the room. *When he is through, I'll be lucky if she is still alive.*

With animalistic doggedness, Warden 22-09 dragged 1-05 to the prison block just off of the executive hall. The prison block consisted of several long halls with stone floors and walls made of molding brick. Along the hall were rows of heavy metal doors.

Alpha 3-0-3's eyes glimmered with a plan. It jumped from 1-05's shoulder to the warden's nose and bit down hard.

"Ow," the warden screamed out as he jolted and brushed the shape-shifter from his nose.

The shape-shifter laughed with eerie glee as it hopped onto the warden's head. "That's just what you deserve, you sadistic creep," it sang merrily in its high-pitched voice.

The warden grunted. Because Alpha 3-0-3's shrill voice blended with the whirring generators in the ceiling, it was impossible for him to discern what it had said.

"Careful," 1-05 covertly told Alpha 3-0-3. "You don't want to give yourself away."

Assuming she was talking to him, the warden knitted his bushy eyebrows and glared at 1-05. "I'll shout 'ow' if I want to. So, shut up, or you won't live through the torture."

Alpha 3-0-3 giggled and swayed from side to side to prepare for its next attack. It sprang down to the warden's rear end and bit him again.

The warden jerked forward and hollered out in pain. "What's going on here?"

1-05 put her hand to her mouth to cover a smile.

"Keep moving," the warden grumbled and gruffly shoved 1-05 on. The warden lumbered up to the prison cell, yanked the door open, and thrust 1-05 inside.

1-05 fell against the brick wall of the cell, scraping the side of her cheek. She wiped the blood from her cheek with the back of her hand and apprehensively turned to face the warden who loomed in the doorway.

He reached over to a whip that was hanging just outside of the cell. But before he could grab it up, Alpha 3-0-3 jumped over to the whip and let its image waver. It then transformed from a flea into a whip. Knocking the other whip down, it took its place and the warden grabbed Alpha 3-0-3 instead.

In a rush of hostility, the warden stormed into the cell and pushed 1-05 face forward against the prison wall.

1-05 felt the razor-sharp edges of the bricks jabbing excruciatingly into her cheek, shoulders, and stomach.

"I'll teach you to disobey the Dark Tyrant." With a callous and hulking movement, he drew his arm holding Alpha 3-0-3 back and brought his arm forward with force. The popper of the whip flew at him and slapped him hard in the face. Stunned, he jolted his head back and shouted a string of curses.

1-05 burst out laughing at the warden's ridiculous expression.

"YOU—," the warden screamed angrily.

Rapidly moving past the warden, 1-05 bolted for the open cell door. The warden hurriedly blocked her path and thrust her back against the wall.

He pulled the whip back again and swung it forward with even more force. This time the popper swung right in his eye, blinding him. The warden dropped Alpha 3-0-3 and yelled out in pain as he clutched his eye, blood oozing through his fingers. He then raced out of the cell.

"40,609," he called out desperately.

From down the hall, a prison guard rushed up and noticed the warden's wounded eye.

"See that she doesn't get away." The warden turned to head for the medical center.

When 1-05 saw the warden moving away, she rushed for the cell door, hoping to escape.

The prison guard pushed 1-05 back in. He then grabbed Alpha 3-0-3 from off of the floor and hung it on the hook on the outside of the cell. Afterwards, the guard closed the prison door, locking 1-05 in.

The guard started to head down the hall when he eyed the other whip on the floor. He picked it up and looked it over curiously. He looked from the whip in his hand to the one hanging on the wall and frowned, puzzled. Coming to the conclusion the whip had been misplaced, he shrugged his shoulders and carried it away with him.

Alpha 3-0-3, in a flurry of sparkles, transformed its image into a small grey field mouse. It cocked its head alertly and looked down both sides of the hall. Satisfied that no one was watching, it scurried down the wall, slipped through the bars, and made its way to 1-05.

1-05 sat on the cold, stone floor and rested her head in her hand. "You need to be careful. They may figure it out and take you away. Shape-shifters aren't invulnerable, you know."

Alpha 3-0-3 stood on its hind legs and folded its forelegs across its chest. "I don't care. They're not going to hurt you without dealing with me." With a playful grin on its face, the small defiant mouse-shaped shape-shifter raised itself as tall as a little mouse could be.

"But the most important thing is to get out of here." She looked desperately around at the sturdy walls and door of her small shadowy cell. "And it doesn't look like there's any way out."

"Don't worry," Alpha 3-0-3 raised his head cockily. "No matter what I have to do, I'll find some way to get you out of here."

Chapter Twenty-Two

The Way-Guide saw 1-05 standing on the top of a white and gold staircase like a precipice in the middle of a black starless sky. Emptiness surrounded her on all sides. Dark, ominous clouds concealed the lower half of the staircase making it impossible to see just how high the staircase was. The Way-Guide reached out for her but she was too far away. Fire burst out of the sky revealing a sinister shadow-like creature. It was shaped like a giant flying serpent and came at her with a blood-thirsty screech. With a rapid, rough swoop, this creature grasped her in its huge talons and carried her away from the stairs. It hovered over the ominous clouds and, without warning, let her drop. Crying out, she fell and was swallowed up in the clouds. The Way-Guide felt her heart skip a beat as she plunged into a fiery pit waiting below.

The Way-Guide jolted up in his bed. A cold sweat broke out on his forehead as he tore himself out of the nightmare. In a chill of horror, he ran his fingers through his sweat-matted hair. He gasped in a panic, reliving the images that had just invaded his mind, worried about the danger that threatened 1-05. He threw back his covers and bolted out of his bed.

With the frustrated, pent-up energy of a caged tiger, the Way-Guide paced his room. He exhaled, angry that miles and miles of space prevented him from helping the woman he loved. He stormed to a viewing screen on the wall through which he could see the star-strewn vastness of space. "When we get there, it's going to be too late." Pounding his fist hard on the steel casing of the viewing screen, he groaned, "oh, this waiting and wondering is killing me."

The cabin door opened and a ray of white light flashed in. Infinity entered through the light and up to the Way-Guide. "There is no reason to be worried or impatient," he told him in a calm and confident voice.

The Way-Guide turned to face Infinity, incredulous. "1-05's in trouble. I know it. We may not get there in time to save her." He pulled his attention from the viewing screen to face Infinity with desperation in his eyes. "Why shouldn't I be worried?"

"Worrying about her is not going to help her." Infinity stood next to him and rested his strong hand on the Way-Guide's shoulder. "You have to trust me. We *will* get there in time to rescue her. Of all the people on the Planet of Darkness, she's the one who is the safest." With a fixed assurance, Infinity raised his head higher.

The Way-Guide pressed his hand to his forehead with emotional exhaustion. "But I've got to do *something*."

"Merely 'doing something' accomplishes nothing," Infinity said with a meaningful tilt of his head. "But doing the *right* 'something' at the *right* time will accomplish what we need."

The Way-Guide searched Infinity's eyes. He had thought he had learned every truth Infinity had to teach him, but at this moment he realized he still had a lot to learn. "But how is it possible to know what is the right thing to do at this time?"

Infinity stepped over to a metal panel on the wall and tapped it lightly. The room lit up and the *Ghost III* hummed louder as if suddenly exuding new life. In solemn respect, Infinity held his hands out to draw attention to the spaceship. "The *Ghost III* knows."

Looking around, the Way-Guide felt a presence in the room that he had been unaware of earlier. "The *Ghost III?*" The presence he was feeling was the spaceship itself. "You mean . . . it's alive?"

"Of course it's alive . . ." In reverence, Infinity walked through the room. As he did, the atmosphere became charged and radiated, like diamonds and gold. To emphasize what he was telling him, Infinity circled the Way-Guide. ". . . yes, alive in a way that most people have a hard time comprehending. The *Ghost III* has a powerful being that is capable of permeating space anywhere and everywhere. It can be here, a billion miles away, and another billion miles in the opposite direction, all at the same time. It knows what is happening at all times, here . . . *and* there." He looked the Way-Guide meaningfully in the eyes. "That is why if you want to know what you should do to help her, ask the *Ghost III.*"

As Infinity spoke, the Way-Guide was more and more impressed with the *Ghost III,* so much so that he felt increasingly insignificant compared to it. With a sense of awe, he proceeded to a console nearby and sat in front of it. "*Ghost III*, I understand that you know what 1-05 is going through right now. Can you tell me what I should do to help her?"

The screen displayed the symbol for the Planet of Light, a cross within a triangle within a circle. The visual dimmed. The Way-Guide looked questioningly back at Infinity. Infinity continued to watch the viewing screen steadfastly. Realizing that he had nothing to worry about and that everything was still under Infinity's control, the Way-Guide turned his attention back to the screen as well. What eventually appeared on the screen was a name displayed in large, elegant black letters against a dark green background. The name was 'the Shadow-Shield'.

Bubbling within the bowels of the Planet of Darkness was a molten magma so hot that it kept most of the planet warm even though it was one of the furthest planets from its sun. The magma slithered its way through thick snake-like tunnels where the barsian rocks were found in abundance deep inside the planet's crust. As the magma traveled, it came into contact with the barsian rocks, causing a powerful chemical reaction to occur. This chemical reaction created a steam that pushed its way through faults, fissure vents, and craters. Eventually, the steam became trapped within the atmosphere by the dark layer of mesolyne gas that encircled the planet. The trapped steam warmed the atmosphere to a nice, comfortable range of 85° to 95°. Still, barsian rocks were not found in all areas of the planet. Therefore, heat from the steam did not reach every region. Certain remote areas in the north were so bitterly cold that they were prone to blizzards that could easily freeze the blood of a human. In fact, they were so cold that most of the Dark Tyrant's means of control failed in these regions. The spy creatures quickly died in the cold, the guns and vehicles of the Enforcers and Controllers had mechanisms that froze due to the subzero temperatures, and the Enforcers and Controllers themselves could not survive long in the harsh conditions. The blizzards in these regions often lasted for several weeks and would cover the land with snow so deep that a crew of workers shoveling for months would not be able to clear a path. Through one of these bitterly cold blizzards trudged a lone, unusually brave, Enforcer. He pulled his cape tighter around him in an attempt to keep warm. As he did, he readjusted a medium-sized package he held closely in his arms to ensure it was kept out of sight. Between the planet's perpetual darkness and the blinding blizzard, it was nearly impossible for him to see the way ahead. He pressed a button on the insulated armor plate that covered his arm. This button sent a signal to his helmet and activated a viewing screen within it. The viewing screen lit up guiding arrows to help direct him through the snow to the spot he was looking for.

Once he reached his destination, he knelt in the iced-over snow. Still holding tight to his package, he used his free hand to dig through the snow until he came upon a small round hatch built into the ground. He knocked hard on the hatch, three times fast, two times slow. The hatch opened and the Enforcer climbed inside.

He came to a secret underground room. The room was just big enough for its contents, consisting of a table with two chairs, a single-sized bed, and a corner computer console. Light beige walls surrounded the room. The walls and ceiling were made from solidified porenthian foam, capable of channeling oxygen. By extending the porenthian ceiling so that it was situated just below the snow, the material was able to draw in the oxygen through the snow and into the hidden room.

A young, blond-haired man helped the Enforcer inside and closed the door behind him. The young man was strong, yet lithe, with blue eyes. The Enforcer gave the package to the young man who handled it with care.

"What is this?" the young man asked.

The Enforcer pulled off his helmet. He was a handsome, strongly-built, black-haired man with high cheekbones and skin of a dark tan. He opened the lid of the box, revealing a little baby gurgling and sucking on its thumb.

The young man smiled. "It sure is amazing. The way you sneak these babies out before those brutes destroy them . . ." He looked back down at the baby. The baby's eyes met his and she moved her hand from her mouth out toward the young man. He laughed in delight as he picked her up out of the box. "It's hard to believe someone wanting to kill this little charmer."

The Enforcer set his helmet on the table and flung off his cape. "It *is* hard to believe." He removed his gloves. "When I think of the people forced to live in the City of the Dark

Tyrant . . . not even realizing their minds have been deluded . . ." He sighed as his heart sank with a feeling of pathos. "They have lost the ability to be charmed by the sweet, beautiful things of life."

The young man gently held the baby's hand and pretended to shake it in a greeting. He then held her so that she was facing the Enforcer. "You should feel like a little princess . . ." He play-acted a dutiful nod of the head. ". . . with such a tall, strong hero to rescue you."

The Enforcer smiled and stroked the baby's cheek. "A task I was pleased to perform."

With a look of concern, the young man turned back to the Enforcer. "Each time you go out, I wonder whether you'll make it back."

"The Dark Tyrant can't kill someone he can't find," the Enforcer replied with a roguish laugh.

The young man took a seat at the table and held the baby securely in his arms. "This whole operation wouldn't exist if it weren't for your skills in stealth." His face beamed with admiration. "How you sneak in there and sneak back undetected is extraordinary."

The Enforcer sat across the table from the young man, picked up a jar, and opened it. He gave the young man a thoughtful look. "This talent wasn't something I was only born with. I was also taught by the real master in stealth, Infinity." He scooped out of the jar a fingerful of ointment and dabbed it on a wound on his right wrist that he kept hidden under the table. "That's when he honored me with my name, the Shadow-Shield."

The Shadow-Shield's mind wandered to the day he and Infinity embarked on that crucial mission together. They had flown to the planet Grey-Marrow to dismantle an enemy tracking center. This tracking center had been constructed by the Grubian Ghouls to enable them to spy on the Planet of Light. He and Infinity both wore their full battle armor. They had finally managed to tear down the last shred of the vacuum radar capacitor when they realized they were completely surrounded by the vicious Grubian Ghouls. Because the ghouls were nearly invisible in the darkness, they were able to sneak up on them undetected. But, Infinity noticed the faint ripples in the atmosphere as the Grubian Ghouls moved in and he managed to send a distress signal to the *Ghost III*. The *Ghost III* raced to Infinity and cast a sharp beam of light that revealed the Grubian Ghouls' dripping, decaying, indistinct forms in its radiating reddish glow. Infinity pulled from the pocket near his boot a small disc and threw the disc at them. The disc exploded in mid-air and burst into a bright light that temporarily blinded the ghouls. That was the moment when the future Shadow-Shield decided to act. He pulled his black cape around him and slipped into the shadows, becoming virtually invisible. Furtively, he made his way behind the ghouls. At that moment, the Grubian Ghouls recovered from their momentary blindness and were preparing for a malicious attack using their projectiles of flesh-eating slime. Hidden in a shadowed crevice, the future Shadow-Shield managed to activate a speaker in his armor. The speaker emitted a squeal at a pitch so high it passed the Grubian Ghouls' pain threshold and caused them to become momentarily disoriented. In a confused flurry, the ghouls raced to their space vehicle and escaped. This demonstration of his stealth and quick thinking impressed Infinity. As the trainee soldier emerged from the crevice in which he was hiding, Infinity ran to him and embraced him and congratulated him warmly. At the next meeting of the councilmembers, Infinity honored him by bestowing on him his new name: the Shadow-Shield.

The Shadow-Shield brought himself back to the present and looked proudly at an insignia of the Planet of Light on the wall. "To be working for Infinity is always an honor." To ensure he had sufficiently staunched the bleeding, he lifted his wounded wrist from under the table.

The young man gasped, noticing the gash on the Shadow-Shield's wrist.

The Shadow-Shield wrapped a piece of gauze over the wound. "Just grazed it on a grate when I was slipping through the air duct."

The young man stood and, holding the baby at his hip, moved closer to the Shadow-Shield. With his free hand, he assisted in taping the gauze.

The Shadow-Shield stood. "I couldn't continue this work without you. You understand the people we are rescuing. You understand from experience that dreams can be dashed and hope can be hard to hold onto. That's why Infinity named you the Dream-Saver." The Shadow-Shield brushed the baby's hair with his hand. "These little ones have a lot of dreams that need saving, and that's your job."

"I'll take the baby to the house and see that she's well fed." The Dream-Saver headed for a door in the furthest wall, but stopped as he remembered something. "By the way, a message came for you while you were away. It was from the *Ghost III*."

The Shadow-Shield nodded. "It must be important. I will contact Infinity right away."

Carefully carrying the baby, the Dream-Saver made his way through the door and into a narrow passageway. This passageway was kept relatively warm and well-lit by globes of light on the ceiling. It led from the hatchway and the entrance-room to a safe house half a mile away. The Shadow-Shield and the Dream-Saver had designed and built the house so that it was large, safe, and comfortable for those they had rescued.

Several people already lived here. In fact, the house was home to twenty-two adults, eight children, and half a dozen babies. The house was much larger than it appeared, since only the top half was above ground. The house did not have the clean sleek lines of the rooms found in the City of the Dark Tyrant because it was put together using the sturdy logs of the fossilized trees found in the area. While air was drawn into the house by a layer of solidified porenthian foam, the inside was also insulated from the cold by a second layer of camboline stone. The inside of the house was dimly lit, but comfortable cushioned furniture and a centralized fireplace with a crackling fire made it cozy.

An older woman with graying black hair greeted the Dream-Saver at the underground entrance and took the baby in her arms. The baby squirmed and let out a short squeal. "She certainly is a lively one and certain to keep me busy," the woman laughed good-naturedly.

A younger, blonde woman stepped up behind her and set her hand on the baby's head. The baby stopped crying and turned to gaze at the younger woman in what seemed to be admiring awe. With her eyes focused on the wall behind them, a slight smile hovered on the younger woman's lips. "You won't be on your own in taking care of this child, Soul-Guard," she whispered to the older woman. "There is something about her that reminds me of . . ." Her mind trailed off in thought and she added, "Yes, I will help care for her." She tenderly took the baby from the Soul-Guard. She put her lips close to the baby's ear and whispered as she carried her to the other room, "One day you will be the protector of many."

The Soul-Guard smiled at the Dream-Saver. "There is no way to argue with her. When her mind is made up, well, I think I will let her help with that little one." She sighed and adjusted a strand of hair that was falling into her face. "And you . . ." she patted the Dream-Saver on the chest, ". . . the children have been begging for the rest of that story you were telling them."

He looked around, not seeing the children anywhere. "Where are they?"

"In the kitchen helping with supper," she told him with a chuckle. "You can tell them the rest of the story while you help them."

Back in the secret room, the Shadow-Shield poured himself a cup of hot coffee and sunk in front of a console in the opposite corner of the room. He took a sip of coffee and pressed a button to reestablish a connection with the *Ghost III*.

The video transmission of the Way-Guide appeared on the viewing screen. The Shadow-Shield had met the Way-Guide a few times before. He had to admit to himself that he was often jealous of the Way-Guide. While they both worked closely with Infinity, it appeared to the Shadow-Shield that the Way-Guide was given the more prestigious and less risky missions. *Someday he'll realize how much better he had it than me,* the Shadow-Shield thought sullenly to himself, *when he attends the ceremony where they issue me my award — posthumously.*

Aboard the *Ghost III*, the Shadow-Shield appeared on the screen and the Way-Guide leaned forward. "Is this the Shadow-Shield I am speaking to?" he asked anxiously.

Focusing his mind on the mission, the Shadow-Shield gave him a good-natured smile. "That's right." He took another sip of coffee as he waited for the Way-Guide's response.

"I'm certain you remember me," the Way-Guide replied.

The Shadow-Shield chuckled in an attempt to bring a laid-back feeling to the conversation. "Of course. Just a few months ago, you and I and a half a dozen soldiers went to clear out the infested caves of Zeento. You were running the operation from the ship, and I was below on the planet with the rest of the soldiers . . . getting my flesh gnawed by the giant air-breathing piranhas of Orfoid." He smirked bitterly.

The Way-Guide added pointedly, "And, if I remember correctly, you received a medal for that operation."

"Yes, but most importantly the mission was successful . . . and everyone survived."

"And now, I am assisting Infinity on a rescue mission." The Way-Guide rubbed his chin thoughtfully. "Infinity told me that you were sent to the Planet of Darkness as a spy and that you could run a mission for me there."

The request did not come as a surprise to the Shadow-Shield. *No doubt something dangerous he would rather avoid,* he pondered cynically. However, he smiled politely to the Way-Guide. "I would be glad to help you and Infinity any way I can."

"There is someone who is close to me still on the Planet of Darkness." The Way-Guide looked him straight in the eyes. "Her number is 1-05. I know she is in danger. Could you check on her and help her?"

"1-05 . . . I believe I know her." The Shadow-Shield recalled a few years back, before he began his work as a spy, when he was working as a guard at the robotic engineering plant where they were creating the shape-shifters. He had watched with interest as they created the shape-shifter Alpha 3-0-3. The Shadow-Shield knew there was a connection between himself and this shape-shifter and had a premonition their paths would cross again someday. He now remembered that this shape-shifter had eventually been allocated to 1-05, an unusually talented and skilled pilot. "Yes. I heard from an Control Fleet Lieutenant that she had recently been locked in prison by the Dark Tyrant," the Shadow-Shield informed him. "But I can assure you that she has been assigned shape-shifter Alpha 3-0-3 and I believe it is still looking after her and is devoted to her."

The news did little to comfort the Way-Guide. Nervously, he wiped away beads of sweat dripping down his forehead and cheek. "Still, could you check on her and give her every bit of assistance you can?"

The Shadow-Shield knew that any mission that included gaining access to the main prison complex was extremely risky. Still, his destiny was leading him in this direction. "Of course. I will see that no harm comes to her." The Shadow-Shield gave him a confident nod.

The sound of water rhythmically dripping onto the stone floor mingled with the moans coming from the other prison cells in the hall. 1-05 woke on the hard floor. With effort, she sat up and surveyed her dreary prison cell. It had not changed since she had fallen asleep. The same dark shadows. The same filthy floor. The same moldy stone walls. The same maze of spider webs. 1-05 shifted her position to lessen the aches in her legs and back.

Alpha 3-0-3, still in the form of a mouse, scurried to her. "Did you get a good sleep?"

"Not really," she told the shape-shifter with a slight grimace. "I don't see how anybody could sleep in a place like this." She crossed her arms in front of her and lowered her head.

Alpha 3-0-3 sunk its chin into its paw and pouted. "Oh, I'm so sorry," it sighed. "I was hoping you'd be rested enough for our escape."

Excitedly, she sat up further. "We're going to escape? How?"

The shape-shifter pressed its paw to its mouth thoughtfully. "I've been formulating the plan and I'm certain it will work . . ."

"It better work. I'm counting on you to get me out of here." She lifted the shape-shifter in the palm of her hand and set it down on her knee.

"And I will," the shape-shifter said dutifully with a bow.

"At least *you're* on my side . . ." She patted it on its head. Letting her mind drift to thoughts of 2-45, she added bitterly, ". . . unlike *some* people." She would have a hard time forgiving herself for momentarily falling for 2-45's charms.

There were scraping, sniffing, and snorting sounds at the prison door. 1-05 and Alpha 3-0-3 exchanged tense, puzzled expressions and 1-05 warily stood to her feet. The door creaked open and a form silhouetted by the light from the hallway entered the room.

"Who's there?" 1-05 called to the form.

As her eyes became accustomed to the light, she realized that the form was that of a large animal. Following behind this animal was a man.

"Shhh," the man waved to her for silence as he closed the door cautiously. He then turned back to her and set the lantern he was carrying on the floor in the center of the room. He pressed a button on the side of the lantern to expand its radius. The lamp cast its light upwards eerily onto their faces.

1-05 could see the man was an Enforcer and the animal with him was much like those wild dog-like creatures that were rumored to roam the wilderness regions of the planet. "What do you want?" she tried to hold herself taller and stronger than she knew she was.

The Enforcer removed his mask to reveal his handsome, dark features. "My name is the Shadow-Shield."

When Alpha 3-0-3 saw the man, a clear, bright light of recollection swept through its memory bank. In a few seconds, the shape-shifter played through every time he had seen the Shadow-Shield. Satisfied that the Shadow-Shield was someone who could be trusted, Alpha 3-0-3 scampered closer to his foot. The shape-shifter looked seriously at him. "Shadow-Shield," it repeated the name, trying to fully understand its meaning. "But who, exactly, are you?"

"I am an agent for the Planet of Light," continued the Enforcer, "and a soldier for the Shepherdess of the Valley."

1-05 looked at him, bewildered. "What are you talking about? . . . You're dressed like an Enforcer and . . . Shadow-Shield? . . . Agent for the Planet of Light? . . ."

With concern, the Shadow-Shield rested a hand on her shoulder. "The Way-Guide asked me to come here to ensure your safety."

Uneasily, 1-05 pulled herself away from him. "You're not making sense . . . Who is this Way-Guide?"

The wolf moved into the light. He brought his muzzle to 1-05's hand. With an encouraging nudge, the wolf sniffed and licked her hand in concern.

The Shadow-Shield knelt next to the wolf and petted his neck. "Certainly you remember 8-23."

"Ohhh," she sighed as a tear formed in her eye. "Yes . . . How could I forget? . . . He's dead." She turned away from the Shadow-Shield to hide her tears.

"He is *not* dead."

Stunned, she looked back at him with disbelief.

"He was rescued by the prince of the Planet of Light. And now, 8-23 wants to help you make it to the Planet of Light as well."

She sniffed back her sorrow. "How can I know that what you are telling me is true?"

He held out a small, square-shaped box. "He wanted me to give you this."

1-05 took the box and opened it. Inside there was a gold ring set with emeralds and rubies forming the insignia of the Planet of Light. The Shadow-Shield took the ring out of the box and flipped up the insignia to reveal a hidden compartment. He handed the ring back to her, gesturing for her to look inside. She noticed a photograph of 8-23. "Oh, yes . . ." she breathed, becoming overpowered with a surge of passion as she admired her boyfriend's handsome face. ". . . That *is* him." Feeling as if she were in some dream-like spell that could be broken any minute, she placed the ring on her right index finger. Contemplatively, she lifted her eyes to the Shadow-Shield. "How is he?"

The Shadow-Shield took her hand and clasped it comfortingly. "He is doing just fine. He works with Infinity, the prince. Now, what is important is that you wear that ring." He looked her seriously in the eyes. "It holds a strong link with Infinity and the Way-Guide. It links to their ship, the *Ghost III*. If the Warden and his guards try to harm you, a signal will be sent to them. And they will protect you."

"Can't *you* take me out of here?" she demanded, flustered.

"I could — but . . ." In a solemn manner, he stepped back and gestured to draw her attention to the wolf.

With his mouth, the wolf pulled a letter from the pouch around his neck. With an intent look in his eye, he placed the letter in 1-05's hand.

As 1-05 opened the letter, Alpha 3-0-3 scurried up her arm and perched on her shoulder to read the letter along with her. She read the letter out loud. "To the dauntless defender, I have noticed your sorrow and suffering. A path will open for you and lead you to your future happiness. But, for now you must wait where you are. You will be kept safe. I have an important task for you soon. Wait for another message from me. The Shepherdess of the Valley."

Alpha 3-0-3 cocked its head, impressed. "This Shepherdess must be very important."

It took everything 1-05 had to avoid grimacing at Alpha 3-0-3's words. The letter was not the type of message she had hoped for. . . . *And just a few minutes ago we were getting ready to escape,* she thought to herself, displeased. *Now I'll be stuck here forever.* She glanced over at her mouse-shaped friend and noticed the sincere look in its eyes. Reminding herself she had never known Alpha 3-0-3 to be wrong, she finally agreed with it. "Perhaps . . ." She crossed her arms in front of her in annoyance. "But why must she insist that I stay in this horrible prison cell?"

The Shadow-Shield stood beside her and calmly rested an arm around her shoulder. "For one thing," he confided in her, "the Shepherdess knows this is where you will be safest . . ."

The wolf lay on the floor and sunk his head to his front paws. He whimpered.

The Shadow-Shield stroked the wolf's back. "And he wants me to tell you about the other reason. The Shepherdess has an important mission planned for you — a mission that couldn't be accomplished unless you *are* here." He smiled excitedly, hoping to pass some of that excitement on to 1-05.

The wolf raised his head and looked over at the Shadow-Shield, proud of the important work he was doing, and at 1-05, awed by the important task that had been assigned to her.

1-05 shifted and pouted in frustration. "So, I'm to stay here, in this awful place, with those stinking prison guards glaring at me, and wait forever for another animal like this one to come and bring me another letter." She heaved an exasperated sigh. "I hate the plan."

Solemnly, the wolf lowered his head in contemplation.

Alpha 3-0-3 tapped its paw gently on 1-05's cheek to draw her out of her grumbling. "But, don't forget, it *is* what 8-23 wants you to do."

Fuming, she stomped over to the corner of the cell. There, she plopped herself on the floor as Alpha 3-0-3 regained its balance on her shoulder. Petulantly, she sunk her chin in her hands. "I know. That is why I will do it."

The Shadow-Shield smiled and stroked the top of her head gently. "He will be proud of you." He then gestured for the shape-shifter to follow him.

Adroitly, Alpha 3-0-3 slid off of her shoulder, raced across the floor, following the Shadow-Shield. It then scampered up the doorframe to stand on the doorknob so it could more easily converse with him.

The Shadow-Shield spoke in a hushed tone. "You remember when we both were at the robotic engineering plant. You were being created and programmed and I was a guard at the plant."

"Absolutely."

The Shadow-Shield pulled out from his left glove a photograph and held it before Alpha 3-0-3's eyes. "Do you remember this man?"

Alpha 3-0-3's face brightened. "Of course I remember him."

"His name is Infinity." He raised his head higher and met Alpha 3-0-3's eyes with a steadfast gaze. "He is the one that programmed you and you know that it is impossible for you to disobey that programming."

The shape-shifter was not surprised by the Shadow-Shield's remark. It recognized that whenever it was told to do something by those loyal to the Dark Tyrant, their orders did not make sense. Alpha 3-0-3 let its memory bank replay the time it had met Infinity, and it found everything about Infinity was logical and admirable.

"You are to help protect 1-05 and anyone else who wants to escape the Planet of Darkness." The Shadow-Shield adjusted his cape and gloves in preparation for his journey back to the northern region of the Planet of Darkness. "In your programming is the location of our safe-house. If you meet someone who needs to hide from the oppression of the Dark Tyrant, you are to lead the way to that safe-house."

"I certainly will."

The Shadow-Shield shook the shape-shifter's tiny mouse-sized paw in farewell. Alpha 3-0-3 hopped down from the doorknob and stood by as the Shadow-Shield carefully opened the prison door. He and the wolf slipped surreptitiously out, closing the door silently behind them.

Alpha 3-0-3 scurried back over to 1-05 and perched itself once more on her shoulder. It gave her an encouraging pat on her ear. In a resigned manner, 1-05 petted the shape-shifter on its small head, grateful for its loyalty.

Chapter Twenty-Three

s 50-83 sloshed dejectedly along the path out of the mud-drenched Slump-Bump area, his feet sank deep in the mud bank. *I guess I should have done something to stop them from taking 4,021, but what?* When he reached the end of the mud bank, he stopped to kick the mud from his boots. He looked back on the path and frowned. *There're just some things that are meant to happen,* he forced his brain into a logical, not emotional, mode of thinking. Pulling himself back around, he continued until he reached the tall petrified tree that stood near the entrance of the Slump-Bump area. With a discouraged sigh, he leaned his back against the tree and tried to convince himself there was no reason for him to feel guilty. He took the crystal from around his neck and held it out before him. It glowed brightly. "All right, crystal? You know there was no way I could have kept 4,021 from being captured by those guards, right?"

The crystal hummed mirthfully as it calculated 50-83's question. Its answer was proceeded by bell-like laughter. "Of course you could have stopped the guards," it replied with positive assurance. "You are intelligent and persuasive. By using those gifts, you are capable of convincing anyone to think your way."

50-83 stared at the crystal in astonishment. "What?" His throat was choked by an overpowering rush of emotion. It took him a few minutes to find his voice again. "You really mean it? . . . I-I could have stopped them?"

"Absolutely."

"Oh . . ." he groaned and replaced the necklace around his neck. He wanted to kick himself. *I messed things up for her, so what now?* He trudged on toward the City of the Dark Tyrant. *So now, I guess . . . I've got to set it right.*

When 50-83 entered the City of the Dark Tyrant, he quickly made his way to 1-13's workshop. He noticed the door was maintained by a lone guard. While this guard followed the usual prototype for 1-13's guards — dumb, beefy, and belligerent — this guard was a little more approachable. The guard actually looked at 50-83 genially with a small, yet friendly, smile.

"Is there something you're wanting?" the guard asked with open eagerness.

"Well, uh, actually, yes." 50-83 tried to appear confident. His eyes fell to the ground as he forced his brain to work at top speed. He was desperate for a plan to convince the guard to help him free 4,021. He remembered the letter given to him by the wolf. He took it out of his pocket and showed it to the guard. "Have you ever seen a letter like this?"

The guard looked at the paper, his eyes twisting up in confusion. He tried to make out some of the words, but found them entirely illegible. Guards were not taught to read anything beyond a few basic words. "Sorry. Can't make it out."

50-83 blushed, then threw his hands up and shrugged to let the guard know there was nothing to worry about. "Let me read it to you. It says, To the young fighter, I have noticed that you are struggling to be free of the troubles that are oppressing you. I can show you a way out. Please join me in my valley for a time of safety and rest. To find my valley, journey past the infested wilderness and the high mountains. There I will be waiting for you. And it is signed, The Shepherdess of the Valley." 50-83 looked from the letter to the guard. "What do think?"

An excited smile broke out on the guard's face. "I like that letter. Where did you find it?"

"Somewhere." 50-83 replied, still trying to play it safe. "It does sound nice, but kind of impossible. I don't see how anyone could make it through the dangerous wilderness and treacherous mountains to reach this Shepherdess."

"It's possible." The guard tilted his head and smiled. "You know, I'd like to go there. I really could use a bit of rest."

50-83 could hardly believe what he heard. He tried to suppress a grin. "You mean it?"

"Yeah," the guard nodded with a faraway look in his eyes. After a moment, he brought himself back to reality. "Can we could go?"

"Well, if you know how to get there, we could."

"Of course I know how." The guard winked and moved away from the door toward the hallway. Noticing that 50-83 was not following him, he turned back with an annoyed and uneasy look. "Aren't you coming too?"

"Well, yes, but—"

"But what?" the guard demanded with good-natured impatience.

50-83 shifted nervously, realizing what he said next could determine his plan's success. "I wanted to bring someone else with us."

"Really? . . . Who?"

"One of 1-13's prisoners."

"Ohhh." The guard knitted his eyebrows, as if he were trying hard to think.

50-83 bit his lip, wondering if the guard had caught on to his plan.

The guard's eyes fixed on 50-83. "So then . . . why didn't you say so in the first place?" He gave 50-83 a friendly pat on the shoulder. "I can get her out. I got the keys." He indicated a ring of keys tied to his belt.

50-83 smiled, his eyes brightening. "Well," he laughed, "I would have mentioned it sooner if I had known."

The guard led 50-83 into 1-13's workshop and to the door that led to the corridor of cells holding 1-13's prisoners. The corridor was guarded by several more guards. 50-83 glanced over at the guard questioningly.

The guard blocked 50-83 from entering the corridor. "Which prisoner is it?" he asked with his focus fixed on the cells.

"Her number's 4,021."

"All right. You wait here."

50-83 took a step back into the shadows of the workshop while the guard marched into the corridor and to the other guards.

"Let me through," the guard told them with a blustering assertiveness. "I got orders to take a prisoner."

The other guards grunted their acknowledgment and moved out of the guard's way.

His keys jangling in his hands, the guard pushed on into the deeply shadowed corridor and to one of the cells. He inserted the key into the lock, turned it, and opened the door.

4,021 was sitting inside on the cold, stone floor. While she was lonely and confused, she was not afraid. Her eyes were fixed on the rose she held before her.

The guard snapped his fingers to draw her attention.

She looked up, finding the guard's impatience slightly annoying.

"Hey, come on," the guard whispered as loud as he dared. "We're getting you out of here."

4,021 stood to her feet. "What? How?"

"Shhh. Don't let the other guards know." He guided her out of the cell. He beamed proudly as he leaned over next to her ear. "We're gonna take you to the Shepherdess' Valley."

"Oh," she smiled dreamily as she walked beside the guard. "That sounds nice."

The guard led her down the corridor, past the other guards, and to 50-83. "Is this the prisoner you wanted?"

50-83 gazed at 4,021. Seeing her again reminded him of how he stood by, inactive, while she was imprisoned. He averted his eyes to the ground with a feeling of shame. "Yes."

As soon as 4,021 saw 50-83, she embraced him warmly. "Oh, I'm so glad it's you. Are you coming with us to the valley?" She lifted his chin and met his eyes with a friendly and enthusiastic expression.

"Of course."

Streams of people were continually hustling and bustling through the cold, glassy halls of the City of the Dark Tyrant. 50-83, 4,021, and the guard found it effortless to lose themselves in these crowds and therefore were able to make their way easily out of the city. As they approached the wilderness area, the guard took the lead. The atmosphere of the wilderness area was buried in a thick, overpowering fog. Through the fog, 50-83 could sense the movement of the wild creatures that crept from rock to rock, waiting for an opportune moment to pounce on their chosen victim. The underground heat rising through the sandy soil was so intense it burned their feet painfully through their boots. The guard squinted, looking deep into the fog, to carefully guide them around the wide and deep craters.

As they passed one of these craters, 4,021 stepped on one side of the crater, and it broke loose. But, before she plummeted into the crater, 50-83 grabbed hold of her waist. 4,021's weight was pulling on him, but he tried, with difficulty, to keep a steady footing. Soon the ground beneath him cracked loose and he found himself being pulled into the crater with 4,021. But the guard moved forward quickly, and took firm hold of 50-83's free arm and, with his full strength, heaved both 50-83 and 4,021 out of the crater. Just as they had regained their footing, a loud screeching wail was heard in the distance.

4,021 gasped at the chilling sound. "It's dangerous here." She looked around nervously.

Taking her hand in his, 50-83 smiled reassuringly. "This area is a little tricky to get through. There are nasty creatures, and you need to keep clear of those plants." With alarm, he noticed the snake-like vines of a plant reaching out for her leg. He swiftly drew her closer to himself and away from the plant. "They are mean," he cautioned her.

4,021 shivered and held tighter to 50-83's hand.

Calmly trying to shift to a more pleasant subject, he assumed a laid-back air. "But I used to come here a lot when I was a kid, me and my friend. We wanted to just be naughty and goof off." He laughed casually.

4,021 looked at him questioningly. "Are *we* being naughty?"

Her question took him by surprise. *Are we being naughty?* he asked himself. He realized grimly that they *were* breaking the Dark Tyrant's rules. *But wouldn't it be 'naughtier' to let 4,021 fall back into their hands?* 50-83 started to answer her, "No . . ." but he was cut off.

The guard shouted an alarm and rushed up and pushed 4,021 out of the way. She collapsed to the ground a distance away from the large, thorny, purple plant, but it once again wound its way up to 4,021 and wrapped itself around her leg. 50-83 grabbed hold of 4,021 to pull her away from the plant. With all his muscular might, the guard tried to pull the plant off her leg but the huge, tenacious vines would not budge. In a fury, the guard pulled his axe out from his belt and hacked away furiously at the vines until the plant released her leg and slipped reluctantly back into the deep shadows.

50-83 helped 4,021 to her feet. "Are you all right?"

"I think so," she said, catching her breath. She looked at him with frightened eyes. "This place *is* dangerous."

"Don't worry, though." The guard grinned with an overly-zealous confidence. "That's the worst of it. From now on, it's as easy as smashing bongamites with hand-belted boulders." The guard held her arm as he guided her boldly across a narrow path between two extremely deep craters. On the floors of these craters were razor-sharp stalagmites, around which were littered the skeletal remains of people who had earlier stumbled off the path. 50-83 followed them cautiously. Once across, the guard positioned himself in front and continued to lead the way.

After several miles without incident, 4,021 took out her rose and held it close to her heart.

Stepping up beside the guard, she showed him the rose.

"Pretty . . ." the guard nodded his acknowledgment. "Where'd you get it?"

"It's for protection. Maybe carrying it here in the front it will ward off danger."

He waved off her remark disdainfully. "I'M here to protect you. Take your little trinket and get back where it's safe." He self-assuredly marched on ahead.

Standing still in disappointment, she pouted, looking after the guard. She moved closer to 50-83. Walking beside him, she smiled up at him warmly.

50-83 hoped her smile meant that she cared about him and would eventually ask him to tell her more about himself.

"I wonder if we'll find Infinity waiting for us when we reach the valley."

"Who knows?" He sulked, disappointed that her mind was on Infinity and not on him.

"I hope so. Infinity is so wonderful." She glanced over and realized that 50-83 looked sad. Hoping to cheer him up, she playfully tickled his ear. "I'm sure he wants to be your friend too."

Oh, not again, 50-83 thought to himself in annoyance, *why is she always bringing the conversation back to Infinity?* "Of course," he agreed wearily. Then, 50-83 came upon an idea of how to impress 4,021. "I should know. . ." He turned to her proudly. ". . . You see, I'm a close friend of his."

"Really?" 4,021 turned to 50-83 excitedly. "Why didn't you tell me so before?"

"Nobody's supposed to know," he informed her subtly. "I'm working with him on a secret mission." 50-83 stood a little taller, convincing himself of the importance of his mission.

"Wow," she exclaimed, impressed. "Can you tell me more about him?"

"Well . . ." He wished he could step into her brain a moment and see what she was wanting to hear. Since that was impossible, he decided to describe Infinity the way *he* wanted him to be. "He's tall and strong, has big, blue eyes, and his hair is blond and wavy and . . ."

"I thought his hair was dark and his eyes were brown."

"Ohhh . . ." He pursed his lips in frustration. He was just starting to like the Infinity he was creating. *I guess what I have to do is tweak MY Infinity a bit here and there, so he's more like HER Infinity.* "Well . . . I don't think his eyes are *exactly* brown. Maybe they are kind of hazel and while his hair *is* blond, it gives the impression of being darker when he's in the shadows." He shifted nervously and glanced at her expectantly.

"What does he act like?" she asked eagerly.

He breathed in relief, reassured that she did not question his response. "He's determined." He once more imagined his ideal Infinity. "And a great soldier. You should see him in a fight. His enemy doesn't stand a chance. And he's firm, very firm. When he says he's going to do something, he's going to do it." 50-83's eyes sparkled with excitement.

"I knew it." 4,021 squeezed 50-83's hand tighter. "That means he really will rescue us."

"Oh . . ." 50-83 tried to figure out how much of what he had told her was a lie and how much was true. "Well, I . . . I guess so." He stopped walking and looked around the area, which looked entirely unfamiliar. He turned to the guard. "Do you know where we are?"

The guard shook his head. "No . . ." He surveyed the region blankly. "But I think we're going in the right direction."

50-83 felt uneasy. A misty green fog floated in and danced around them with an eerie moan. Looking deeper into the fog, 50-83 noticed something that resembled an evil face of doom glaring back at him forebodingly. He shuddered and moved closer to 4,021.

"Are you afraid?" 4,021 looked over at him with wide, anxious eyes.

"A little. Aren't you?"

4,021 nodded but held the rose tightly in front of her. "Infinity's rose *will* protect us."

50-83 found it unbelievable that 4,021 had so much confidence in one little rose, enough to trust it could protect them from an army of ghosts. Still, her confidence boosted his.

The guard's eyes became fixed on something past the fog that fascinated him. His face brightened into a huge grin and he gestured widely toward something a short distance away.

50-83 strained to look past the fog, but all he could see was a flock of predatory flying creatures circling over a deep gorge.

Entranced, the guard walked through the green fog toward the gorge. The fog trailed behind him, as the ghostly faces urged him on. They nudged his shoulders, pushed his back, and whispered hoarsely in his ear, driving him toward whatever it was that was drawing his attention.

"What is it?" 50-83 shouted to him. "What do you see?"

"We're saved," the guard cried back with wild enthusiasm, "Don't you see it? . . . The marble bridge leading across that ravine. Past it is a huge house . . . and I see people there, waving for us to join them." He quickened his pace as he continued toward the gorge. "Come on. Let's go."

Watching the guard apprehensively, 50-83 took a step back closer to 4,021. "Do you see a bridge and a house?"

4,021 shook her head. "No. All I see are those horrible ghosts . . . and we shouldn't go near them."

As 4,021 spoke, one of the ghostly faces turned abruptly to look at her in disgust. It shrieked and lunged at her. 4,021 held her rose further out in front of her. As the ghostly face peered down at the rose, its eyes bulged in terror. With a painful groan it spun around and raced back toward the guard.

Marching with a brisk and steady rhythm, the guard made his way right to the brink of the ravine and stopped. As he stood there, he gaped in bewilderment at the residue of what he had once envisioned was his rescue. The image of the bridge, the house, and the people were now faded away and all that remained was a fallen, decayed tree, a pile of large rocks, and the flying predators. These hideous creatures resembled huge, flexible, round stomachs. Attached to their dark brown exterior were grasping bat-like wings. Their red eyes glared furiously under jagged, black eyebrows.

When the guard realized what was happening, he whipped around in a panic to race back to 50-83 and 4,021. Before he made it far, though, one of the flying creatures swooped down, opened its expandable mouth and swallowed the guard whole with one bite.

"Oh, no," 50-83 shouted in horror as he stumbled forward, in hopes of rescuing him. But he jolted to a halt, fists clenched in frustration. It was already too late for the doomed guard.

4,021 had kept her eyes steadily on the beautiful rose she cradled in her hands. Unaware of the tragedy, she looked toward her friend. "What happened?"

50-83 patted her gently on the shoulder. "Nothing you need to worry about." He guided her away from the scene. He heard the familiar whirring sound of 1-13's mud-crawler. The vehicle drove right in front of 50-83 and 4,021, shining its bright headlights on them. 1-13 and two of his guards stepped out of the mud-crawler and up to them.

1-13 seemed just as surprised to see 50-83 as 50-83 was to see him. "Well, well," he said attempting to mask his bewilderment as he stood facing 50-83. "6-96 sent her *little* apprentice *out* to *play*? Or, rather is it that she is *unaware* of him playing *hooky*?" He raised an arched eyebrow as he looked suspiciously in 4,021's direction.

50-83 protectively took hold of 4,021's hand. "Was it your brainless guards that told you we were here, or those snake-like spies you have everywhere?"

"*Neither,*" 1-13 replied, raising his head proudly. "I have a tracking device *implanted* into *each* of my *guards*. When I noticed one of them had *wandered off*, I came out here to *collect him*. But I have to admit I was surprised to find there were *accomplices* in my guard's *disappearance*." He moved closer to 50-83 and shook his head. "What *are* you *playing* at?"

50-83 pressed his lips together and refused to reply.

"*All right,*" 1-13 conceded, trying, with difficulty, to stay calm. He scanned the area superficially. "*So* . . . where is my guard?"

"He was eaten," 50-83 told him flatly.

1-13 gave 50-83 a quizzical expression. 1-13 followed 50-83's gaze to the gorge and observed the ravenous Schlampine birds circling over it. There was little doubt in 1-13's mind about what had happened to his guard.

"Those *birds* crave *flesh*," he declared pointedly. "They *fear* certain *plants* growing near us. But we are not *safe* here for *long*."

50-83 glared at 1-13. "You mean we should go back with *you*?" He said the word 'you' as if it had been a disgusting, over-rotten piece of meat he had tasted and spat out.

"You could *always stay* here with *them*." 1-13 directed a thumb in the direction of the Schlampine birds.

The guards guided 50-83 and 4,021 forcefully toward the mud-crawler. 1-13 gave 50-83 a rough shove inside. "I think 6-96 *owes* me something for *returning* her *lost pet*."

50-83 glared at 1-13.

1-13 responded by raising his chin haughtily. He then guided 4,021 into the front seat, while the two guards sat in the back on either side of 50-83. 1-13 took his place beside 4,021.

"Are you *comfortable* back *there*?" 1-13 asked 50-83 as he started the mud-crawler.

50-83 was sandwiched by the sweaty, hairy bodies of the two guards on either side of him. He wanted to complain but refused to reply.

With a hopeful look, 4,021 asked 1-13, "Are you coming with us to the valley?"

"The *valley*?" 1-13 looked at her quizzically. "*What* valley?" He looked back at 50-83 questioningly.

50-83 shrugged his shoulders as if he had no idea what 4,021 was talking about.

"You mean we're not going to the valley?" 4,021 eyes fixed on 50-83 with concern.

50-83 lowered his eyes and shook his head despondently.

Taking 4,021's chin in his hand, 1-13 turned her face toward his. He gave her a shrewd grin. "My *dear* girl, right *now* we are going *back* to the City of the Dark *Tyrant*."

Chapter Twenty-Four

5 0-83 hesitated a moment to build up enough courage to enter 6-96's workshop. The room was dark and almost lifeless. The only sound he heard was the sinister slithering of the seven-headed snake coiling itself around the lifeless grasping limbs of its grotesque tree. After scanning the vicinity, he saw a narrow pillar of light emanating from the far end of the room. 50-83 cocked his head with guarded curiosity and made his way toward the light. As he approached, he realized the light came from the half-opened doorway to 6-96's bed chamber. He tried to convince himself to leave and go straight to his room without seeing 6-96. He stepped away from the door, but quickly remembered that not letting 6-96 know he was back was a risk he did not want to take. Apprehensively, he moved back to the door and knocked.

"Yes?" she demanded sharply. "Is that you, 50-83? . . . Enter."

50-83 warily pushed the door open and found 6-96 lying on her bed. Her eyes were fixed on the ceiling while she tapped her fingertips together as if plotting 50-83's demise.

"You're late, you know."

"I was just doing what you told me." 50-83 leaned on the doorway, and his gaze fell to the granite floor. "I went to the Slump-Bump area. I was talking with 4,021. You said we wanted to find out what she is up to."

Her focus still on the ceiling, 6-96 narrowed her eyes and rubbed her hands against each other as if flattening out kwaminer bugs. "You're lying again . . ."

50-83 looked up quickly, an indignant fire burning within him. "I'm not lying. I *was* talking to 4,021."

6-96 reached across the head of the bed and grabbed her staff. Gripping it in her claw-like hands, she stood and faced him. "But . . . you do not come from the Slump-Bump area . . ."

"But I *was* there."

"Perhaps . . ." She loomed steadily up to him. ". . . at some time . . . But just now you came from 1-13's workshop. You're working with him — *aren't you*?"

6-96's remark startled 50-83. He took a step backwards as 6-96's shadow covered his face. "Who told you that? It's not true."

6-96 was about to pass him on her way out of the bedroom, but instead paused in the doorway next to 50-83. She turned and glared at him. "You have betrayed me," she growled.

50-83 sighed wearily, realizing it was futile to deny it any longer. He lowered his head submissively. "I'm sorry. I didn't want to. 1-13 forced me to—"

"Still, you must be punished." 6-96 wrapped her hand tightly around 50-83's throat. "— punished so severely that you will never even think of betraying me again." With her right hand still firmly around his throat, she grabbed his arm with the hand that held her staff and dragged 50-83 out of the bedroom and into the workshop.

Stumbling along, 50-83 struggled to breathe. He pulled at her hand grasping his throat, loosening it enough for him to gasp for air. A sudden familiar, slithering sound caught his ears. It was so close, he could feel the vibrations on his eardrum. After managing to turn himself around in her grasp, he realized that 6-96 had brought him to the seven-headed snake.

"Looks like you've forgotten to feed it again." 6-96 sneered.

"Let me go," 50-83 tried to break free from her grip. "I'll feed it."

"No." Her face scrunched in an evil, mocking smile. "*I'll* feed it this time." Holding 50-83 firmly, she forced his right hand out close to the seven-headed snake.

The snake's most centralized head hissed at the other heads, warning them to keep back. It then hovered menacingly up to 50-83's hand. Its narrow, fiery, devil-like eyes stared hungrily at his hand as its forked tongue flicked in and out from between its sharp fangs.

Sweat poured down 50-83's forehead as he watched the snake. He took a deep, anxious breath of air. He felt the sharp prick as the snake plunged its fangs into the flesh of his right hand. Immediately his hand swelled, burning with a horrible constricting pain.

When the snake finally removed its fangs, 6-96 released 50-83 and he fell to the floor.

From beneath his half-closed eyes, 50-83 saw the room spin hazily around him. The pain in his hand quickly traveled throughout his body. He groaned. "How soon am I going to die?"

6-96 loomed over him. "Die? Ha." She jabbed him lightly with the pointed obsidian stone on her staff. "Don't you wish . . . the bite of this snake does not kill you. Don't you remember? When it bites you, you become enslaved by its venom."

"Enslaved . . .?" 50-83 pushed himself to a seated position on the floor, wearily resting his elbows on his knees. He ran his fingers through his sweat-matted hair. ". . . But I feel like I'm going to die."

"Of course you *feel* like you're going to die. You *want* to die." 6-96 smirked coldly. "You are enslaved by its venom of depression." She bent down staring him right in the face. "That's what you get for betraying me. Now, will you do as I say?"

50-83 struggled to pull himself to his feet. "Yes — I will do as you say," he moaned.

"All right." She shoved 50-83 into a chair. "There will be an Economic Efficiency meeting tomorrow and 2,040 and his apprentice will be attending. I want you to attend the meeting also. Befriend them. Gain their confidence. And above all, learn how they are involved in the rebellion. Report back to me everything you learn. You will do this, won't you?" Her narrowed eyes eerily resembled those of the seven-headed snake.

"Yes . . . of course," 50-83 replied mechanically. He heaved a sigh as a feeling of a dark, impending doom overpowered him.

A kaleidoscope of colored lights swirled in circles over the ceiling of 1-13's workshop. Watching the lights meditatively, 1-13 lounged on the couch as he smoked his cigar. His eyebrows knitted together as he plotted some means of destruction for 366, the overseer of the manual labor room. *How dare he try to interfere with my plans?* 1-13 was becoming so angry the nails on the fingers of his clenched fists dug painfully into the palms of his hands. But he forced himself to calm down and found comfort in remembering he had left one of his spy creatures there to keep an eye on that fool for him. Another little spy creature slithered near him onto the couch, winding itself around his arm. 1-13 stroked the creature's head and smiled at it tenderly. The creature chirped with pleasure.

He heard a commotion at the hall door. 1-13 groaned disconcertedly. Still cradling the spy creature in his arms, he rose to his feet with a perturbed indifference and took a few steps toward the door. Briefly shutting out the unwanted interruption, he playfully scratched the creature under its chin. The door slid open and 1 waddled in.

1-13 gave 1 a slight bow. "To *what* do I *owe* this visit?"

"I have a new task for you." 1 bobbled about the room, absorbed in what he imagined was a clever plan. He directed 1-13's attention to the door he had just entered through. As if on cue, two of 1's guards marched in with 93-73 held securely between them.

Strangely out of character, 93-73 stood pale and stooped with his arms hanging on either side lifelessly. Perhaps resigned to his fate, he bit his lip and focused his eyes nervously on a smudge splattered across his left shoe.

1-13, like the cresting of a wave, flowed up to 93-73 and lifted the man's chin to better examine his face. "This is the assistant of *7,500*." Cocking his head questioningly, 1-13 turned to face 1. "He *must* have been *involved* in something of *immense* political importance for you to bring him to *me*."

Frowning a toad-like frown, 1 puffed himself out proudly. "Immense political importance, indeed." He snorted disdainfully. "We've found strong evidence that he is the man behind the rebellious actions of the workers." Wobbling his head in an inordinate fashion, he spat out, "I want you to question him, make him confess to it."

With a quizzically raised eyebrow, 1-13 glanced back at 93-73. To him, 93-73 was the picture of an unquestioning, eager to please, one-dimensional-minded person, hardly the type to be heading a rebellion. "*So,* are you *telling* me to *make* him *confess, even* if he *wasn't* the one behind the rebellion?"

1 ballooned up with infuriation. "He IS behind it. Make him confess." With a twist and a turn, which emphasized the finality of his act, he briskly left the workshop with his two guards following behind him.

Recovering from the illogical nature of what had just transpired, 1-13 gestured to his own guards to take 93-73 in tow. Staring into the depths of his eyes, dead center, 1-13 said pointedly to 93-73, "It looks bad for you right now."

93-73's face turned an ashen pale. He lowered his focus to the floor once more.

1-13 shook his head and exhaled, either out of exasperation at the foolishness of 1 or out of pity for the plight of 93-73. "You *aren't* the one who is orchestrating the workers' rebellion, *are* you?"

"Ohhh," 93-73 moaned in desperation, "no matter what I say, nobody will believe me."

"*Well then.* Who IS behind it?" 1-13 asked, watching 93-73's eyes for a reaction. "7,500? . . ." He then remembered an associate of 7,500 whom the Dark Tyrant had mentioned as involved in the rebellion. A realization dawned on him as his brain connected the dots. ". . . or *perhaps* his friend . . . 2,040?" 1-13 noticed that 93-73's eyes twitched nervously at 2,040's number, and 1-13 was convinced he had guessed correctly. "Thank you," he nodded to 93-73 with a gleam of satisfaction in his eyes, ". . . that's all I needed to know." He waved perfunctorily for the guards to take 93-73 away. "Lock him up."

93-73 shivered, then slumped into paralysis as the guards dragged him to the cell-lined hallway. 1-13 gently lowered the spy-creature to the floor. It slithered away to a corner of the room and curled up for a nap. He smiled fondly after the creature, then his mind jolted back to the task at hand and he turned to make his way out of the workshop and into the hall.

When 1-13 arrived at the door leading to 2,040's suite, he found 2-45 waiting nearby as 1-13 had earlier instructed him to do. 2-45 glanced at him indifferently. Whether he was relieved or peeved at his arrival was hard to tell. He kept his feelings securely hidden from 1-13.

With meticulous care, 1-13 removed his shiny ventualine gloves and then folded them neatly as if to accentuate some point. "I'm pleased to see you are ready to proceed with our plan." A smile with subtle, clever overtones spread itself on 1-13's face.

2-45 crossed his arms over his chest, leaned against the wall, and raised his eyebrow in a slightly condescending manner. "Before we get started, I should warn you about something. I was passing by the conference room and I saw 6-96's assistant wandering around there, asking questions. It seems he's after the same information you want me to get." Momentarily unable to conceal his growing irritation, he looked away.

"I'm not surprised," 1-13 grumbled in frustration. "6-96 would give anything to beat me to it."

Although 2-45 shrugged his shoulders blandly there was still a hint of nervousness in his voice. "Well, I just wanted to make sure that if I don't succeed because of *his* interference — well, I wouldn't want to be the one to take the blame."

Time seemed to freeze as 1-13 pictured in his mind the many cruel and sadistic methods 6-96 could employ to keep 50-83 at her beck and call. "6-96 is indeed an enemy we should not underestimate." 1-13's eyes narrowed cleverly. "You stick with 2,040 and 9-85. I'll do what I can to minimize the interference." 1-13 gave a curt nod and headed for the conference room.

1-13 located 50-83 sitting on a bench outside the conference room, talking to an elderly man. The man was thin, wore a goatee beard, and had narrow, squinting eyes. 1-13 recognized him as 389,000, a top Interplanetary Trade Specialist. 50-83 listened with an assumed interest and charming smile as 389,000 discussed import prices versus export prices.

The moment 389,000 stopped for a breath, 1-13 politely nodded to 389,000. "*Excuse me* for interrupting your conversation—"

389,000 cleared his throat meaningfully. "That's quite all right, young man." He rubbed his swollen eyes.

50-83 shot a sharp glare in 1-13's direction.

1-13 responded to 50-83's glare with a pleasant smile. "I'm certain your discussion is most important, but orders from the Dark Tyrant obligate me to borrow this young man for a brief moment." He glanced about, hoping none of the Dark Tyrant's spies were within earshot.

Drily, 389,000 mumbled his consent but 50-83 rose resentfully to his feet. "I don't want to talk with you."

1-13 attempted to calm 50-83 with a serene smile. "I'm sorry, but you must."

Two of 1-13's guards took 50-83 into their custody. 1-13 gestured his command for the guards to usher 50-83 into a nearby empty room. He followed them in and closed the door. The room was a plain, white cubicle, empty except for several large pipes that ran the length of the wall and a few, large metal boxes tucked into one corner.

"Release him," 1-13 told his guards with a cool composure.

The guards loosened their tight grip on 50-83, and he rubbed his sore arms to restore the blood flow while glaring in 1-13's direction.

In a sudden fit of rage, 1-13 slammed his hand hard against 50-83's chest, shoving him against the wall. "You miserable little imp. How dare you interfere with my plans."

"You're the one interfering," 50-83 shot back.

1-13 slapped 50-83 across his face. "Shut up." He pointed a warning finger. "You will not interfere with 2-45, you understand?" 1-13 gave him a sharp, determined look accentuated by an almost deafening silence. He then turned and left the room with his guards.

50-83 took a deep breath to regain his composure. While 1-13's outburst added to his many anxieties, they did not frighten him away from his task. *6-96's tactics are much more sinister and cruel than anything 1-13 could dream up.* So, he knew he had no option other than to continue on with 6-96's orders.

◀◆◆◆▶

The monotony of waiting outside of 2,040's room became too much for 2-45 to endure. He tapped once on the door and was surprised to find it was not locked. It slid open and 2-45 slipped in. He glanced about the room, mildly impressed, especially with the architectural skylight. As his gaze returned downward, it fell upon 34,000. His heart skipped a beat — because he was caught trespassing or because he was gazing into the eyes of the most beautiful woman he had ever seen — he could not tell which.

34,000 stepped closer to him, with an inquisitive tilt to her head. "Do I know you?"

"I don't think so." 2-45 smiled at the adorable way she spoke, placing the inflection on the 'do' and not the normally expected 'know'. "Anyway, I know I don't know you — because I've never seen a woman as beautiful as *you*." He leaned a hand on the fountain's railing and bent closer to her.

34,000 laughed brightly. "Now, that is most amusing. Do you go popping into every stranger's room to tell them things like that?" She twisted back a step.

"No." 2-45 lowered his eyes bashfully. "I'm sorry if you took it the wrong way. This is the first time and I couldn't help it . . ." He looked back into her eyes. ". . . When I saw you . . ."

"Are you trying to say you are falling in love with me, 2-45?" she asked him matter-of-factly.

Stunned, 2-45 took a step back. "How did you know my number?"

"How could I NOT know your number?" she gave him a humoring smile. "I was there at the trial. You performed very well."

Realizing 34,000 was not responding to his charm, 2-45 answered her flatly, "Thank you." His hand dropped from the fountain's rail.

Entering from the laboratory, 2,040 accompanied by 9-85 came up to 34,000. 2-45 noted, with a tinge of resentment, that the color rose in 34,000's cheeks and a glow of emotion sparkled in her eyes at the arrival of 2,040. 2,040 gave 34,000 a tender peck on her cheek.

9-85 eyed 2-45 suspiciously and took two firm steps to him. "Why are *you* here?"

2-45 shifted nervously when he noticed all three of them watching him, waiting for his answer. "I work for a top official who asked me to escort you to the Economic Efficiency meeting. He wants to make sure you attend." He softened the demand with a charming smile.

A pleased expression spread itself across 2,040's face. "How nice," he effervesced in gratification. "And, of course, we're going to attend. But if you wish to escort us—" 2,040 gestured for 2-45 to lead on, "escort away."

2-45 was taken aback by 2,040's enthusiasm, but, with a nod, he filed out the door with 2,040 and 34,000 following him. 9-85 paused a second, weighing in his mind whether 2-45 could be trusted or not. He decided to go with the 'or not' and hastened to 34,000 because she was walking the furthest behind 2-45 and was the closest to reach.

"I think he was sent here to spy on us," he whispered in her ear.

She gave 9-85 a confused glance. "What gives you that idea?"

"Think about it. He just barely escaped being executed," 9-85 reminded her emphatically under his breath. "The leaders must have spared his life for a reason. And now he'll do anything they want, including spying on 2,040. The leaders don't trust anyone one hundred percent."

34,000 turned to him furiously. "There is no reason at all for the Dark Tyrant to mistrust 2,040. He is completely loyal." With hurt defiance, she whipped away from him and rushed to catch up with 2,040.

9-85 stood stiff and glowered, recalculating the variables and coming to the same definite conclusion. He continued to follow them from a short distance, a cautious eye stayed upon 2-45.

50-83, just exiting the cubicle in which 1-13 had accosted him, noticed 9-85 approaching the doors of the Economics meeting hall and made his way to him. Driven by his orders to procure 9-85's confidence, 50-83 smiled as warmly as he could past his deep, ever-growing, depression. "Are you attending the economics meeting too?" he asked with contrived casualness.

"I am," 9-85 replied before even realizing it was 50-83 who was asking him. He then turned and recognized him. "Oh, yes, you. I almost forgot. You're an architect, right?"

"Well, yes," 50-83 smiled, wishing it were true. "But I am still an apprentice."

9-85 laughed unconcerned continuing toward the entrance. "So am I." He waved a hand towards 2,040 who was entering the conference room ahead of him. He glared as he noticed 2,040 telling the guard to allow 2-45 to enter as a guest. He then returned his attention to 50-83. "2,040 over there. He is the man I apprentice for. He's the one attending the meeting. I'm just here to keep his papers in order." He held up a folder full of papers. Preoccupied by his annoyance with 2-45, 9-85 continued to head toward the conference room door.

50-83 followed him, hoping that by staying close to 9-85 he would be guaranteed entrance into the conference room. "Yes, I know what you mean." He smiled with a false smug confidence. "I have to keep tons of papers in order too. There's the draft for this building and that building. And ideas scribbled here and scribbled there and . . ."

9-85 came to the conference room door and placed his hand on the palm-identifier. It flashed green allowing 9-85 to enter. 50-83 paused as 9-85 walked in. He stared at the palm-identifier, weighing whether he should take a chance with it or not. He turned to glance at the guard standing near the door who looked back at him with a narrow, warning glare. 50-83 stepped back and was about to consider trying to enter through a vent in the ceiling, when 389,000 approached.

"Having difficulty getting in, young man?" 389,000 asked as he patted 50-83 on the back with the feeble good-humor so common to intellectual old men.

"Well, I'm not exactly invited." 50-83 blinked once with big, sad eyes.

"Oh, bosh. Someone with as much interest in economics as you have should be welcomed with open arms. Come on, you can be my guest." And with a wrinkled smile of pride, 389,000 easily guided 50-83 into the conference room past the guards.

50-83 delighted in his good luck but resented the fact he had been separated from his assignment. His mind played out the many ploys that could retarget him in his mission.

The conference room was wide and spacious. Upon first inspection, its walls appeared to be an ethereal white, but, looking closer, one soon realized that throughout the walls were swirled soft, powdery blue patches. The far wall contained a podium situated in front of a monstrous-sized monitor. On the left half of the monitor was displayed an enormous picture of 1, smiling in his usual superficial manner. The words in a calligraphic script 'The Dark Tyrant and 1 await your successful achievements' filled the other half. A tall, bulky man with dark hair and a beard took his place at the podium, adjusting his ceremonial robe. Next to the huge monitor, he looked rather insignificant.

Fifteen rows of shiny white bench and table top combinations built in concentric half circles created a multilayered crescent around the podium. 2,040 directed 34,000, 9-85, and 2-45 to follow him to the centermost table which was closest to the front podium. 2,040 took his seat at the furthest end on the left. 34,000 sat next to him on his right. 9-85 sat next to her, with 2-45 on his other side. As they took their seats, the table top in front of each one of them opened and individual viewing screens rose out of the table. The viewing screens displayed the functions of the models with a variety of parameters necessary for model verification by the committee.

With an elegant hand raised politely toward 34,000, 2,040 leaned past her to talk to 9-85. "This is an exciting moment," he grinned with overflowing enthusiasm. "The committee will be considering my model for implementation, the highest honor ever given to an economist."

More subdued, but with sincere appreciation for his mentor's accomplishment, 9-85 agreed, "You've worked hard on this. Naturally they are going to accept it."

"I can't help being a little nervous though." 2,040 wrung his hands anxiously.

34,000 hugged 2,040's upper arm encouragingly. "There is nothing to be nervous about, dear. See all the people here. They all love and admire you." And she beamed gloriously at the man she idolized.

2,040 smiled as he viewed the crowd entering the conference room. "Yes, you are right, my sweet. And the model I came up with, I must confess, it is brilliant." He sighed, readjusting his mindset and took on a more contented and confident posture.

As 2,040's model appeared on all the individual viewing screens, 34,000 proudly gestured 9-85's attention to it. Despite the fact that he had already analyzed the model using all possible parameters and was confident he knew its every detail, he humored her and glanced at it. Within a few seconds, his face fell into an expression of dismay and his heart pounded with a jolt. He was astounded that he had, until now, failed to notice the error which so blatantly stared at him from the screen. The model was no longer feasible. He quickly tapped the edge of his screen to prevent it from going on to the next function so that he could study it further. Due to the fact that the model had been on several pages while he was studying it, he had not connected two functional constraints that had been on two separate pages. Now these constraints were side by side on one screen and 9-85 could see that they violated the proportionality assumption and, due to the compilation of the restraints, he realized the model actually had no feasible solutions. 9-85 could not believe that he did not noticed this before.

"Is something the matter?" 2-45 asked in a 'just trying to be helpful' tone.

A little too eagerly, 9-85 thought, but he kept his focus on the model. "No," 9-85 said, in an attempt to keep 2-45's attention away from the error, "it's nothing." But his hand clenched tightly and his jaw stiffened.

2-45 leaned over to look at what, to him, appeared to be an incomprehensible conglomeration of nonsensical scribbles. As he did so, he overheard 9-85 murmuring to himself about the model being all wrong. With a subtle smile of satisfaction, 2-45 sat back in a forced slowness so as not to appear too eager about the point he had just earned.

50-83 sat next to 389,000 and glanced down at the viewing screen on the table before him. He cocked his head in puzzlement at the profuse influx of numbers. The cluelessness that overpowered him as to the mysterious meaning of the mathematical menagerie doubled his feeling of being an outsider in this economics meeting. He looked over at 389,000 and found him with his eyes fixed on the screen, astutely pondering the models.

50-83 raised his head a bit to convince himself he was just as intelligent as anyone at the meeting. "These formulas are cleverly put together." It was the only thing that made any sense to him.

"Perhaps." Intent upon the screen, he raised a skeptical eyebrow. He ran his fingertips across the table top as if scribbling the calculations on the surface. "But it's hard to know until you've tested all of the parameters completely."

"I suppose," 50-83 sighed. A wave of depression fell over him. He could not tell if it was just an effect from the bite or if it was because he was starting to feel uncomfortably stupid. 50-83 forced himself to return his attention to his own screen and convince himself that the spatial organization of the numbers was fascinating.

A movement from the meeting room's entrance caught 50-83's eye. It was 1-13 in a heated conversation with the two guards. Throughout the conversation, 1-13 made several forceful gestures in 50-83's direction.

50-83 thought about sinking under the table, but realized this would only draw more attention to himself. Instead, he leaned toward 389,000. "Uh, sir . . . uh, excuse me . . . but, uh, I'll be back in a moment . . . just going to find the washroom."

"It's over there," 389,000 waved an abrupt hand toward the left, back corner of the room.

50-83 slipped in the direction of the washroom and, in an attempt to conceal himself, mingled with the entering crowd. Convinced he was completely concealed, it came as a surprise to him when a hand tightly gripped his upper arm and roughly pulled him out of the crowd.

"I told you not to interfere," 1-13 shouted at him with a fiery glare.

"Just because I'm here doesn't mean I'm interfering," 50-83 protested yanking himself free of 1-13. "In fact, I was sitting all the way on the other side of them. There was no way I could interfere." And he adjusted his vest with a defiant tug.

"That may be so," 1-13 admitted grimly, "but you are too devious. I cannot allow you to stay." With a quick, determined movement, 1-13 dragged 50-83 out of the room and then turned to the guards. "Under no circumstances allow this man into the meeting room. That order comes directly from 1, himself."

"Yes, sir. There is no way he will get inside," the guards confirmed.

1-13 nodded in approval. He turned back to 50-83 and gave him one more threatening glare, after which he withdrew down the hall.

One glance toward the guard convinced 50-83 not to even try to make it back into the meeting room. Instead, he walked around the corner to a bench in a dark alcove along the side of the hall. Unsure of what his next step should be, he unlatched the necklace chain from around his neck and held the crystal before him. It rose in the air above his hands, glowing brightly.

50-83 waited for a moment for the crystal to speak . . . *silence.* Tired of waiting, he finally concluded that it was up to him to start the conversation. "Crystal," he said in an anxious whisper, "are you still able to answer my questions?"

The crystal hummed and whirred. "Of course," it merrily replied.

"Great," 50-83 grinned. "Crystal, tell me, what can I do to find out if 2,040 is involved with the rebellion?"

"Ask his assistant, 9-85," the crystal answered chirpily.

"But 9-85 is in the meeting. There's no way I can get in . . . and I'll probably never get another chance. Besides, I doubt he would answer a direct question like, 'what rebellious activity is 2,040 involved in?'" 50-83 glanced toward the barred entrance with annoyance.

"2,040 has constructed an unauthorized escape vehicle," the crystal answered the question 50-83 had intended for 9-85.

50-83 stared at the crystal in bewilderment. He knew it could answer his questions, but he had no idea the crystal could give him answers about someone it had never even met. "How do you know this?"

The crystal whirled about proudly. "I contain wireless micro-connectors that allow me to access information from other computers that contain wireless micro-connectors. The escape vehicle constructed by 2,040 contains these."

50-83 narrowed his eyes slyly. "And where does 2,040 keep this vehicle?"

"At his suite, in a hidden workroom," the crystal replied simply.

"Well, crystal, looks like you've told me everything I need to know." With a smug grin, he replaced the necklace around his neck. *I suppose these types of meetings last for about two hours,* he pondered deviously, *I could spend that time at the gym and when I go back to 6-96, I could pretend that I attended the meeting and connived the information out of 9-85.*

When the Economic Efficiency meeting was coming to a close, the committee leader took that moment to announce the honor about to be bestowed on 2,040. With a stoic yet solemn pride, he announced, "It is now time to reveal to all of you that the new economic efficiency model of 2,040, our brilliant Researcher of the Economics of Production, will be put into operation. This model is an ingenious piece of work and the Dark Tyrant is certain it will benefit our planet by lowering production expenditures by well over fifty billion." He nodded at the applause that followed, then directed it to silence with a flick of his wrist.

As the committee leader spoke, 9-85 apprehensively looked over at 2,040, who, to his dismay, was beaming jubilantly.

2,040 turned and smiled at 9-85, enthusiastically giving him a triumphant thumb's up.

"The brilliance of 2,040's model is astounding," the committee leader continued to bellow, "It takes into account every minute bit of data concerning manual labor room 15 and its workers. He has even done thorough research on ezocane and the processes we use in its preparation. There is not one thing that escapes 2,040's intelligent mind." The committee leader paused at this point to allow for another round of applause. After the audience quieted, he addressed 2,040. "And now, 2,040, we would like you to say a few words to the committee."

"Absolutely." 2,040 eagerly stood to his feet. The crowd applauded heartily. While 2,040 made his way to the podium, he raised his hands to altruistically subdue the ovations.

"Fellow economists," he began triumphantly, "and even if some of you here are not economists, well, if you're here, you're an economist at heart."

The crowd laughed and cheered. 2,040 paused and looked toward the ceiling as if to add some drama to the few brief moments he used to collect his thoughts.

After a breath, 2,040 continued, "I am so gratified by such an honor that has been placed upon me. But, distinguished colleagues, there is no reason why we all shouldn't be honored in this very same way. Your minds may baffle at the allusion I am about to present to you, but, no one can deny that we as economists have great power." He smiled and glanced about the room, eagerly anticipating their awe at his wisdom. "In fact, we are so powerful that one could compare us to magicians. Magicians pull floppy-eared bunnies out of empty hats, and that is what we do. We create something out of nothing." He clenched the podium zealously.

The audience murmured and looked at each other incredulously.

"What I am saying should not come as a surprise to you," 2,040 went on complacently. "You all realize the power of numbers, and with the right combination, we, who have control over numbers, can make great things happen." He flicked out his fingers into the air as if flinging magic dust. "With a few spells, a few waves of the wand, and — poof. Magic happens. With our magical powers, we could cause the economic destruction of our great City of the Dark Tyrant. — or with that very same power, we could make our city great as I have done today. And the honor that has come to me, that same honor could come to each one of you. Fellow magicians, soon you could be up here receiving the same type of accolades in the near future. Thank you . . . Thank you." He bowed and smiled, smiled and bowed.

34,000 clapped so much her hands burned as much as her heart leapt with love and admiration. As the audience applauded, 2,040, basking in the accolades, made his way back to his seat, where he gestured for 34,000 and 9-85 to follow him out. 34,000 took 2,040's cue, but 9-85 failed to notice because he was still puzzling over the discrepancies in the model.

Bending over 9-85's, 2,040 spoke in his ear, "So, how does it strike you? From the look of their faces, I think I've impressed them all. But, you — your face is a little harder to discern. Didn't you like my speech?" A quizzical hurt scarred his previously joyous expression.

"It's not the speech," 9-85 replied flatly. "It's the model."

"You've looked over that model hundreds of times," 2,040 reminded him fretfully. "It is perfect. Now come on, let's go." 2,040, along with 34,000, continued on to the door, a crowd forming around them, stopping him, and asking him questions along the way.

Keen on learning more about the mishap with the model, 2-45 leaned subtly over to 9-85. "Is there something wrong with it?"

9-85 looked into 2-45's penetrating eyes and was instilled with a powerful distrust of him. He quickly closed the viewing screen and stood. "This matter does not concern you," he told 2-45 firmly and walked decidedly away.

When 9-85 reached the committee room door, he noticed 2,040 was unable to leave because a crowd of committee members had formed around him, offering their congratulations. 9-85 squeezed his way through the crowd, mazing a path up to 2,040. "There is something you ought to know," he whispered aside to 2,040 once he had reached him.

2,040 turned to him, quizzically, "You look so worried . . . what is it?"

9-85 was about to speak but was jostled by the crowd. "Not here. When we are back in the room."

After giving 9-85 a quick nod, 2,040 turned back to the crowd and shook a few more hands, scattered a few more 'thank you's', and conveyed to them how the excitement had exhausted him to the point that he must go to his suite and rest. He then managed to push his way out of the meeting room, clearing a path for 34,000 and 9-85 to follow him.

Once they were back in 2,040's suite, 9-85 ensured the door was securely locked and faced 2,040 with a grimly pensive expression.

2,040 replied to 9-85's expression with a questioning tilt of the head.

9-85 took a breath to clear his thoughts. "We need to do something, and we need to do it quickly. The efficiency model is wrong and if they implement it, it will be a disaster, and if that happens . . ." He finished his sentence by lowering his eyes to the floor somberly.

2,040 shook his head and chuckled in a condescending manner. "Don't be ridiculous. There's nothing wrong with the model. Each of us worked it out numerous times. It's perfect."

"Of course it is," chimed in 34,000.

9-85 shook his head emphatically. "It's not perfect. It is totally flawed. Not only are the functional constraints incongruous, but the proportionality assumption is violated. In addition to all this, 7,500 sent me to a meeting with the workers of manual labor room 15 and their complaints are much more diversified than we had anticipated. We'd have to adjust those parameters to allow for more differentiation between each of the workers' needs which would alter our calculation of the mean in each of the functions." He stopped for a second to regain his thoughts. After rubbing his forehead to prevent an impending headache, he continued, "I don't see how we missed all these mistakes. But we did, and now our model that contains an extensive number of errors is about to be put into operation."

The intuition of a lover allowed 34,000 to notice the nearly undetectable frustration building within 2,040. She could tell this frustration was about to be directed toward 9-85, so she stepped between them. "Perhaps it's not as drastic as you make it sound. After all, they evidently didn't notice the mistake when they chose to use the model. They must have examined it before approving its use." She moved close to 2,040 and patted him comfortingly on his back. "I'm certain everything will be fine."

"It won't be fine," 9-85 told her emphatically. "When the model doesn't work and the Dark Tyrant realizes it was because it contained errors, we will be the ones blamed, and we will be the ones who will pay for it with our lives." His eyes blazed with the irrefutable truth of his warning.

34,000 shot 9-85 a glare. "It's not as bad as that."

2,040 took 34,000's hand and lifted her fingers to his lips. He kissed them gently and gave her a smile to assure her his moment of frustration had passed.

9-85, moved by 34,000's loyalty, slackened his rigidity a moment. "I would like to think that everything is fine, but no matter what, we need to do something—"

"We can't," 2,040 cut off 9-85's sentence in a flippant blasé-faire manner. "Whether the model is right or wrong, there is nothing we can do about it. It's been submitted to the committee, it's been inputted into the system, and it's been uploaded to the Dark Tyrant's master computer. At this point, our hands are completely tied."

9-85 stared as the fatality of this statement hit him. Exhaling in annoyance, he ran his fingers through his hair. "But we can't just leave it the way it is."

2,040 moved jovially up to 9-85 and draped his arm over his shoulder reassuringly. "Stop letting this worry you. I know the Dark Tyrant. I've worked for him for years. A couple little petty mistakes will be merely 'ta-ta'-ed." He flipped both hands up to wave away the problem. "Now's not the time to worry but to celebrate. I know *I'm* going to." He beamed and slipped over to the side table and poured himself a glass of wine. He held the glass in a toast, smiled warmly, and drank down the glass's contents.

Upon entering 6-96's workshop, 50-83 found himself looking straight into the eyes of the seven headed snake's most centrally located head. The snake slithered up its tree further, so that it could stare deeper into 50-83's eyes.

"Get away from me, you stupid snake," 50-83 grumbled. "It's your fault I'm so depressed."

The snake swayed closer to him, hungrily, as if the earlier bite had been merely an appetizer.

50-83 stepped back. He could not be certain, but it seemed the snake was no longer hissing, but laughing at him. "Ha . . . ha . . . ha . . . ha."

Pulling his gaze from the snake, 50-83 followed the movement in his peripheral vision to see 6-96 entering the room. He now realized the laughter was not coming from the snake, but from 6-96. He had never seen her so happy.

6-96 sat on a small, backless chair near the snake. She laughed as she twisted her staff in her hands. "So, 50-83, are you ready to report? What is it you found out?" She smiled an exaggeratedly wide smile that only succeeded in contorting her face into some monstrous creature from the world of nightmares.

50-83 took a sidestep to avoid the snake and made his way to 6-96. "You'll be very eager to learn." He smiled smugly.

"Yes," she said, uncharacteristically calm. Then, suddenly, she stood and reached out to pull 50-83 by the hair and jerked him over to the chair she had been sitting in. "So you better be sure to tell me everything." She pushed him to the chair and stood threateningly over him. "You, more than anyone, should know I have excruciating methods for procuring information."

"Of course." 50-83 rubbed his sore head. "I was planning on telling you."

6-96 tapped her staff in her hand impatiently as she waited for him to speak.

Fortunately, he had worked out his reply to the last detail. "Well," 50-83 sat up confidently as he prepared to tell 6-96 the concocted scenario of how he learned his information, "I managed to gain the confidence of 9-85 — that is 2,040's assistant — by pretending to have a similar occupation." He leaned back with his arms folded across his chest. "We talked for some time about economic situations like import costs and export costs and solutions for complicated matrices, and he even told the guards to let me into the meeting." He looked at her, half expecting some kind of positive response, but received her typical frozen glare instead. "After a while, he began to confide certain things to me, you know, asking me for advice." He looked at his fingernails, avoiding her penetrating stare. "Well, in the conversation, he let slip that 2,040 is building an unauthorized escape vehicle. That's something rebellious, wouldn't you say?" He met her eyes at last with a 'now isn't that something.' look.

6-96 narrowed her eyes in satisfaction. She moved next to 50-83 and patted him on the head rigidly. "You can do very well when you put your mind to it."

Chapter Twenty-Five

2-45 made it through the trial alive, but his punishments were not over yet. From the executive hall, he was abruptly sent to a legal office, an austere, cold room where arrogant legal assistants would wrench information from the citizens. A stuffy and irritable secretary presented 2-45 with a leaking ink pen and a tall, teetering stack of paperwork. Several hours later, 2-45 was still battling it out with the pen, his hands stained with ink. When, at last, he managed to scribble in the *final* bits of tedious information on the *final* document, he painfully rubbed his cramped and aching wrist. Feeling like a worn-out soldier struggling along bearing his battle wounds, 2-45 handed the papers to the not-so-impressed secretary who scrutinized each one thoroughly. The secretary nodded and turned to file the papers. 2-45 waited a few minutes, unsure of whether this was a cue that he could leave. When the secretary looked over at him, 2-45 tapped his own lower lip thoughtfully and tilted his head in search of answers.

The secretary only glared and asked disdainfully, "Are you still here?"

"Just leaving," 2-45 replied, with a nervous laugh and quickly left the office.

2-45 made his way to the north edge of the city. He came to an old parking garage where he had left his Barso-Cycle in an obscure corner. The Barso-Cycle is a two-wheeled open vehicle with spiked wheels enabling it to easily climb over rough terrain. It is powered by molten barsian rocks flowing through the cycle's clear ezocane tubing. Eager to escape the headaches of the city, he mounted his Barso-Cycle and drove it down a nearly deserted gravel pathway leading to the north suburbs.

The north suburbs consisted of two regions. One region was extremely hilly and held a scattering of luxurious mansions. The other region was a bleak, rocky valley with several gold and silver mines. Once 2-45 reached the hilly region, he came to an arched gateway which led to his towering mansion. He jumped off his Barso-Cycle and placed it in a designated open garage. Half-way up the stone path to the front door, he noticed something moving in the shadows of a cluster of tall rocks. 2-45 stood still and listened. There was the sound of scuffling footsteps. He peered expectantly into the darkest point of the shadows and saw a dark, sinister form emerging.

A large wolf crept out into the lighted path. 2-45 gasped and forced himself not to move. The wolf calmly came and stood in front of him, looking him intently in the eyes.

Despite his terror, 2-45 gave the wolf as friendly a smile as possible. "And how are you, you scary creature, you? . . . Now, if you'll just leave, I will continue on to my house and not bother you."

Circling 2-45, the wolf sniffed him all over.

2-45 tightly closed his eyes and flicked the fingers of his right hand against his thumb nervously as he braced himself for the moment the wolf would attack.

Facing 2-45 once more, the wolf sat on his haunches and growled softly.

"Shoo. Get on. Go. Shoo-shoo." 2-45 waved his hands slightly away from him in the direction he wished the wolf would go.

The wolf bared his teeth and growled louder.

"All right, then," 2-45 took a careful step back from the wolf. "Stay, if you insist."

The wolf stopped growling but continued to stare intently at 2-45.

2-45 waited, rubbing his sweaty hands against his cape.

Using his mouth, the wolf pulled an envelope from his pouch.

2-45 tilted his head inquisitively as he watched.

Holding the envelope in his teeth, the wolf walked up to 2-45, bringing the envelope close to 2-45's hand.

Now realizing that the wolf wanted him to take the envelope, 2-45 reached out carefully and took it as the wolf released it.

Stepping back, the wolf gave 2-45 an approving nod. The wolf then turned and dashed off into the darkness.

2-45 looked down at the envelope curiously. He opened it and removed the letter to read:

To the kind-hearted conqueror,

> *I know that you desire to be free from your overpowering difficulties. I have the solution to your problems, but it will cost you much. You will find me once you have escaped from what holds you here.*
>
> *The Shepherdess of the Valley*

2-45 raised a speculative eyebrow. Although he was encouraged that someone was willing to help him with his endeavor, the letter confused him. *Does this mean that the Shepherdess will only help me escape after I've already managed to escape on my own?* He folded the letter back into its envelope and tucked it inside a pocket in his cape. *I'll see if*

I can find someone to help me decipher this, he decided as he continued up the path to his mansion.

2-45's mansion stood on the highest hill in the region and rose taller than any of the other mansions. The mansion was a cylindrical stone tower rising sixteen floors high. It was surrounded by four smaller cylindrical sub-towers attached to the main tower by hallways. The only room inside the main tower was a large circular foyer. Along the wall of the foyer, circling up sixteen floors, was a spiraling staircase that climbed to the top of the tower. Off the staircase were doors that led to the rooms in the sub-towers. Covering the ceiling of the main tower was a sheet of clear ezocane which permitted those in the foyer to see the dark night sky overhead.

Pushing his way through the high arched wooden doors of the entryway, 2-45 arrived at the foyer. A fat, balding butler rushed to greet him and help him off with his cape.

"We had word that you were on your way, sir," the butler said in a straight-faced monotone.

"So, you had word—" 2-45 commented in a cavalier manner. "And from whom? One of the Dark Tyrant's spies? A mysterious Enforcer? An intruding Controller? Our gossiping neighbors? Or a puff of smoke entering the window?"

The butler gave 2-45 an uninterested, heavy-lidded look and left to hang up the cape.

Turning to the left, 2-45 entered his office on the first floor of one of the sub-towers. Along the wall of the office stood a table that contained a decanter and several glasses. 2-45 poured himself a drink. As he gulped the drink down, an older woman bustled in. Her hair was flamboyantly coiffured, her face was covered with make-up, and she was dressed gaudily.

2-45 promptly set his glass aside and approached the woman, smiling with delight. "Mother." He gave her a big hug. "It's great to see you."

The woman embraced him warmly. "Oh, it's so good to have you back." But, she quickly changed her mood and brusquely pushed him away. "You are a horrible son." She shook her head despairingly. "Your poor father must be rolling in his grave. The humiliation our family must endure, all because you thought it would be a thrill to joy-ride to some stupid planet on the other side of the galaxy."

2-45 patted her reassuringly on her back. "A joy-ride? No. I wasn't trying to make it there just for fun. It was a completely clear-headed, business-minded venture."

"Oh, pooh." She dabbed tears from her eyes with a handkerchief. "That's what you always say, and then you go and do the most ridiculous, foolhardy thing imaginable."

Heaving a sigh, 2-45 turned to face her. "But, mother, do you know that on the Planet of Light they have mansions even taller than ours?"

"The Planet of Light?" she fumed. "Is that where you were trying to go? Ooooh, you know if they find that out, we could all be killed." Horrified, she wrung her hands.

"No, we won't," 2-45 replied confidently. "I explained everything at my trial."

2-45's mother shook her head with concern. "They certainly won't just slap your hands and tell you, 'never do that again'."

"Well . . ." he answered reluctantly, "What they told me is that I'm no longer a Propaganda Specialist." He shrugged his shoulders and frowned indifferently.

"I knew it." 2-45's mother stormed over to the door of the office and spun back around to face her son. "We will be the laughing-stocks of the neighborhood. What will we do? What WILL we do?" She set a weak hand to her forehead and dizzily rushed out of the room.

In exasperated concern, 2-45 dropped his arms as he rushed out his office door after her, but when he reached the foyer she was nowhere to be seen. He scanned the foyer once more and his eyes fell on what he at first thought was a decorative statue. It stood on one leg and its other leg was extended back over its head as it reached its hands high toward the ezocane ceiling. 2-45 took a double take and finally realized that what he saw was not a statue, but his younger sister, 5-07. She was an energetic woman in her early twenties, well-suited to the disciplines required to maintain a healthy lifestyle. Her light red, loosely-curled hair was held back with a thick, white hair band. She wore a black body suit and meditatively relaxed into her pose.

"2-45, is that you?" she asked unemotionally as she lowered her one leg and moved into a similar pose with the other leg.

He smiled at the familiar twitch in his sister's eyebrow that often meant something was irritating her but she was not going to say what. "Yes," 2-45 replied as he lowered his eyes and moved closer to her.

"Mother sounded quite upset," she told him calmly.

"She is," he agreed.

5-07's pose became unsteady.

"But, don't worry," 2-45 quickly added. "She's upset with me, not with you." He reached out and placed his hand on her waist to help steady her.

She lowered her leg and faced 2-45 with a smug smile. "Don't I know it. Ha. While you were away, she changed her will. Now, everything will be mine." Her green eyes sparkled as she confidently placed her hand on her hip.

2-45 gave her a slightly irritated but playful shove. "Why, you little brat."

With her hands high in the air, 5-07 raised her chin proudly. "What else could she do?" she informed her brother haughtily. "You were off acting like an idiot."

"I was NOT acting like an idiot."

"Well, it *seemed* like you were. At least to everyone else. I *told* you not to leave." 5-07 reached for a towel and, dabbing sweat from her forehead, peevishly walked over and sat on a couch in the center of the foyer.

2-45 followed her to the couch. "I would like to think that you, of all people, still had a little bit of faith in me." He grimaced, trying to conceal a hurt expression.

"Of course I do. It's just that I hate to see everyone laughing at you." In a pout, her eyes fell to the floral pattern on the arm of the couch.

He sat close beside her. "They won't be laughing forever. I have a few more ideas. Soon we will all be there on the Planet of Light—"

5-07 abruptly stood to her feet and slapped 2-45. "Stop it with that Planet of Light nonsense."

He looked at her in disbelief. "But think about it. Just what kind of future is there for us here?"

In disgust, she threw the damp towel in his face. "Can't you behave yourself? I want a brother I can be proud of. Not a — an — embarrassment." She burst into tears and ran off to her room.

2-45 leaned his elbow on the arm of the couch and rubbed his cheek sullenly.

2-45 felt the butler's breath on the back of his neck and turned to face him. The butler cleared his throat. "1 and 1-13 are here to speak with you — NOW."

"Oh, really?" 2-45 replied with a blank stare.

"I directed them to your office."

"Oh," 2-45 moaned, trying to discern in his mind what dark and twisted entrapments they were fiendishly plotting together. He gestured for the butler to leave and took a few moments to gather his thoughts before heading for his office.

In his office, 2-45 noticed that 1 had taken his place at the large desk, and on top of this desk sat 1-13. With a wild grin, 1 cracked his knuckles confidently.

1-13 pushed himself up from the desk and assumed an air of congenial politeness as he stepped over to greet 2-45. "*Ah*, 2-45. How *good* to *see* you."

2-45 nodded a subdued greeting. "Yes . . ." He frowned as he narrowed his eyes contemptuously. "Still I didn't expect us to see each other again so soon."

"You can blame the *visit* on your *fascinating* personality." 1-13 removed his silver cape and gestured for 2-45 to take a seat in a chair near the desk. "Our *highly* esteemed 1 found you *so* interesting that he *desires* to learn a little *more* about *you*." He neatly laid aside his cape on the desk.

2-45 collapsed onto the chair as he eyed 1-13 suspiciously. "Oh, so that's it. Well, I appreciate the compliment, but isn't that information somewhere on a computer file?"

"No, *not* the information *he's* looking for." 1-13 pulled from his pocket his watch with the engraved skull. He subtly raised the watch hypnotically before 2-45's eyes. A ghostly green light emanated from deep within the eye sockets of the skull.

2-45's eyes were unconsciously drawn to the skull and he was compelled to stare at it. Menacingly, the skull pulled itself out of the watch and thrust itself right into 2-45's face. It kept its glowing eye sockets fixed on 2-45's eyes. Sapped of what remained of his now depleted strength, 2-45 still gazed into the skull's eye sockets. His eyes grew tired, his eyelids fell shut, and his mind sank into a submissive maze of haziness.

With a triumphant gesture, 1-13 turned to face 1. "His *mind* is *yours*. Ask him *whatever* you *would like* to *know*."

"Excellent." 1 rose from the desk chair, basking in another conquest so easily achieved. He waddled his way around the desk, and, with his nose in the air, stood next to 2-45. "2-45," he spoke with over-precision, "can you hear me?"

2-45 nodded his head limply.

"While the Control Fleet had little difficulty in capturing the *Journey*, there are still a few inexplicable events that I would like clarified. There was mentioned something about a jumping wall, water taking the form of a miniature human . . ." An insane wide-eyed look spread itself across 1's face as he spat out his words. ". . . and just recently there was a report involving a whip that attacked a warden . . ." 1 raised his eyebrows and looked at 2-45 askance. "I demand an explanation for this, and I demand it this instant." 1 pounded his fist into his hand.

2-45 looked unseeingly at the wall across from him. "1-05's co-pilot is a shape-shifter called Alpha 3-0-3," 2-45 recited in a weak stupor.

1 pressed his lips tightly together to stifle his amusement. "Of course, a shape-shifter. Why didn't I think of it before?" He no longer could control himself and he burst out laughing.

1-13 shook his head sternly at what he considered to be an overreaction on 1's part. Once 1 had stopped laughing, 1-13 interjected, "But aren't shape-shifter's relatively rare? How could this pilot afford such a thing?"

"Exactly. That is something I must look into." He scratched his flabby cheek in thought. "I would also like to know why *I, myself,* 1, haven't been given a shape-shifter. Can you imagine, and with everything I have to deal with, I, of all people, ought to have one." Stung with a feeling of neglect, his jaw dropped and his long, toad-like mouth fell open.

"You're absolutely right. I *whole-heartedly* agree with you, *all-powerful* 1." 1-13 nodded his acknowledgment.

1 scrunched his nose as his face turned red. "It's criminal," he screamed as he raised his head high and his hair flew into a mess. "Why HAVEN'T I been given a shape-shifter?"

There was a sudden beeping sound that came from 1's belt. 1 regained his composure and pressed a button on it. The voice of 1's secretary came from a speaker on the belt. "Just a reminder, all-powerful 1. The Dark Tyrant is expecting to meet with you in a few minutes."

1 nodded his head as his nostrils swelled in a deep inhalation of air. "I will be there promptly." He turned to 1-13 solemnly with an uplifted brow. "Continue to question 2-45. I still want to find out what prompted him to try to make his way to the Planet of Light." He took a few steps toward the office door then turned back to 1-13 with a devious expression. "I'll mention to the Dark Tyrant that we should have more shape-shifters working for us."

1-13 smiled humoringly. "Excellent plan." 1-13 had only half-heard what 1 had said and he chose his reply primarily because he sensed 1 wished to hear it.

2-45's butler met 1 at the office door and bowed deeply to him. "This way, your greatness."

1 gave the butler an approving nod and bounced after him out the office door.

Once 1 was gone, 1-13 heaved a relieved sigh. *At last,* he thought to himself, *now I can focus my attention on matters that are R E A L L Y important.*

1-13 slinked back over to stand on the left of 2-45, who was still sitting, staring unseeingly at the wall. 1-13 tugged his mouth to the side in a confident smirk. "2-45, do you still hear me?" he spoke to him in an authoritative tone.

"Yes, I hear you."

"Good." 1-13 smiled in an overly friendly manner. "I'm *glad.*" He casually strolled in front of 2-45 to the other side of him. "You and I have *known* each other for a *long* time . . ." He waved his right hand in front of 2-45's face and, with a smooth gesture, pulled it back toward himself, drawing 2-45's eyes toward him. ". . . *way* back when your *father* worked as a *loyal* advisor to the Dark Tyrant. So, too, *you* should be *loyal,* to the Dark Tyrant, and to *me.*" He raised his head self-assuredly. "You *will* be loyal to *me, won't you?*" 1-13 lifted 2-45's chin to bring his eyes in focus with his own. Narrowing his eyes, 1-13 looked deep into 2-45's eyes.

"Yes, I will be loyal."

1-13 released 2-45's chin and stepped around him to stand once more to 2-45's left. "There is certain *information* I want to *procure.* A treacherous *secret* 2,040 is *hiding* from us . . . and I want *you* to find out what it *is.*" He moved in closer right next to 2-45 and bent down to look him meaningfully in the eyes. "You *will* do this for me, *correct?*"

"Yes, I will find out what he is hiding."

1-13 smiled complacently. "*Perfect*." 1-13 set a firm hand on 2-45's shoulder and jerked him brusquely from his stupor.

2-45 suddenly found himself in a blurred world of lights, shadows, and colors. His head could not think past the foggy lightheadedness. He took a deep breath and shook his head to bring himself back to reality. He rubbed his eyes as if trying to wipe from his mind some recurring nightmare. Finally gaining his bearing, he saw 1-13 smiling down at him with self-satisfaction. 1-13 was leaning over 2-45 so domineeringly that 2-45 was overtaken with a dreadful feeling of claustrophobia. "I suppose you extracted some dark secret from me . . ." 2-45 exhaled wearily. "All right, what's your price?"

With an air of camaraderie, 1-13 patted 2-45 on his back. "Don't be concerned about *that*. You and I are working *together* now." He punctuated his sentence with a curt nod of his head. "So *that* means we're *looking out* for *each other*. I'll help you by *protecting you* from the Dark Tyrant and 1 . . ." Confidently, he tilted his head. ". . . and *you'll* help *me* by procuring *any* information I *need*." He gathered his cloak from the desk.

2-45 scowled as he watched 1-13. "And *how* am I supposed to get the information you want?"

1-13 raised a controlling hand in front of 2-45's face. "First," He took a sharp step to 2-45. "Tell me, *who is it you are gathering information about?*"

"2,040." 2-45 had not even stopped to think.

Pleased, 1-13 smiled. "And . . ." He swung his cape around his shoulders. "Tell me, *what is the information you are gathering?*"

"Information on the treacherous secret he is hiding." 2-45 blinked in disbelief, uncertain of where he had learned the answer to 1-13's question.

"Very good." 1-13 nodded in approval as he connected the clasps on his cape. He then leaned one hand firmly on the desk. "Now. The day after tomorrow, 2,040 will be attending a conference, The Economic Efficiency Conference." Confident he had 2-45 within his power, he no longer spoke with hypnotically varying tones, but rather with a rapid military precision. "I will see that you are able to attend. It will be the perfect place for you to get to know 2,040. You should have no trouble *gaining his confidence* and *learning at least some hint* about his secret." He looked him pointedly in the eyes. "You *are* going to attend, *aren't you?*"

"Of course. I will attend and I will find out about the secret," 2-45 answered quickly. He tried to fight the power that was taking control of his brain, but a sharp pain radiated in his head causing him to break out in a cold sweat.

"Yes . . ." 1-13 glided from the desk to the office door. He turned back to 2-45. ". . . I believe you will," he murmured slyly, then slipped out the door.

2-45 rubbed his forehead. He heard an unnatural, eerie voice in his brain that was unfamiliar to him. This voice seemed to compel him to do whatever 1-13 told him to do. He pounded his fist on his forehead, hoping to silence this voice, but it would not be silenced. Gathering every ounce of will-power, he forced himself to concentrate. Although the voice was still there, it was quieter and, for a moment, 2-45 could relax.

The butler entered the office and stomped up to 2-45 to ensure his entrance was heard. "Someone else has come to see you."

2-45 was annoyed by his butler, so, before he replied, he stood to ensure he towered over him a full six inches. "Who is it this time? The Dark Tyrant himself?" he said with marked irritation.

"No." The butler lowered his eyes smugly. "The Duke of Distraction. He said it was past his mealtime . . ."

Exasperated, 2-45 cut in, "It's *always* past his mealtime."

". . . so I directed him to the dining hall," the butler continued without stopping for 2-45's interjection.

2-45 gave the butler an infuriated look. "The dining hall?" He clapped his hand to his head in disbelief. "Oh, damn it.

There goes our supper." He pushed his way past the butler and out the office door.

Upon entering the dining hall, 2-45 found the Duke of Distraction seated at the head of the long table, surrounded by plates, platters, and food carts holding the remains of the dinner that had been prepared for 2-45 and his family. The Duke glanced up from his feast and gave 2-45 a cursory nod of acknowledgment and subsequently returned to consuming the food.

2-45 stood beside him and peevishly crossed his arms. "I hope you are enjoying your meal."

The Duke of Distraction raised a fork to indicate he needed a moment to finish his mouthful. "The meal is excellent. Reminds me of the one I had on my visit to the Planet Chorondi with Prince Bantone. A banquet I will not forget. It lasted a whole week. I ate more than I have ever eaten since. You should have been there. Heaping plates full of pot roast, potatoes, and parsnips. And if only you could have savored the exquisite creamy cabbage pie, the cornbread, and the quiche." He smacked his lips as his eyes sparkled with glee. "And then there was the dessert—"

Not being in the mood to wait for neither the Duke of Distraction's mouth nor his voice to finish his sentence, 2-45 abruptly interrupted him. "All right, so what is it you came for?"

Waving off 2-45's impatient outburst, the Duke of Distraction calmly replied, "But I thought you would appreciate this little courtesy I provide." He pushed his plate away and leaned back in his chair to rub his huge belly. "Someone from The Dark Tyrant's legal staff dropped by my dive and asked me a few questions about you and I wanted to make sure you weren't in trouble because of the little distracting adventure I arranged for you."

"Oh, I see. Well, they did demote me." He rubbed the back of his neck in chagrin. "I have to work for 1-13 now. I suppose you can't do anything about that."

The Duke of Distraction laughed heartily, which was an odd thing to observe since his laughter came on the off beats to the up and down movement of his enormous stomach. "That's ridiculous. Nonsense. Can't do that sort of thing to one of my best customers. I'll talk to 1 about that right away." He heaved himself from the chair and wobbled his way over to 2-45. "I like you. I like your money. And if there's ever anything else you need — you just let me know." He let his flabby hand fall on 2-45's shoulder and an amicable smile caused his cheeks to bulge.

2-45 remembered the letter the wolf had given him. "There is something. Just wait here a second." Knowing the Duke of Distraction's patience would last only so long, 2-45 hurried out the room and to the coat closet. Once he grabbed his cloak, he raced back to the dining hall. There, he reached into the pocket of the cloak and pulled out the letter. "Just today, I was given this by a large wild animal lurking outside the mansion. It's an interesting letter and I was wondering if you could help me figure out what it means." 2-45 handed him the letter.

The Duke of Distraction read it over and scratched his bloated temple in thought.

"It's a very mysterious letter, don't you think?" 2-45 searched his face for a clue to his point of view.

"Naturally it is. The woman who sent you this letter *is* mysterious." The Duke of Distraction looked at 2-45 with wide, warning eyes that seemed to say, 'Be wary. You never know what dangers lie in the spooky unknown'. But with the excitement of a teller of ghost tales, he continued to expound, "Very enigmatic. She speaks that way. Her messages are that way. Her house is that way. Everything she says or does is like some kind of cipher or code." He pointed a plump finger to the letter. "Even her name in this letter is coded. See. It says here: The Shepherdess of the Valley — when her real name is the Mystic of the Vale." He raised his triple chin with a cocky self-assurance.

Confused, 2-45 rubbed his forehead. "But, why would she send me a letter like that? I mean, how could I figure out what it all means?"

"She wants you to go to her and ask *her*." The Duke of Distraction handed the letter back.

"But look at what she says." 2-45 hit the page with the back of his hand. "'You will find me once you have escaped from what holds you here.' Tell me, how does that help me find her?"

The Duke of Distraction shrugged his jiggling shoulders flippantly. "She knew that I would show you." After pulling out a notepad from the pocket of his jacket, the Duke of Distraction wrote out sketchy directions to her house. He pulled the page from the book and slapped it into 2-45's hand. "There you go. You'll like talking to her. She's a fascinating person. Wise and witty. Very entertaining."

As the Duke of Distraction heaved his massive bulk to the front door, 2-45 followed him to the foyer. 2-45 heard the door open and close but his attention was on the scribbled-out directions written on the paper. A sudden bright light seemed to surround him and his eyes were drawn to the ezocane ceiling and dark sky overhead. A bright star caught his notice and he knew it must be the Planet of Light. So close yet unreachable. He looked back down at the letter and the directions in his hands and wondered what the Mystic of the Vale was like and if she would help him find a way to the Planet of Light.

Chapter Twenty-Six

O ther than the swirling pattern of purple and green lights displayed on one of the walls, 1-13's workshop was dark. The lights intermittently cast their constantly evolving colors on the faces of 50-83 and 4,021. 50-83, biting on the side of his finger, sat on the left side of the couch while 4,021 lounged on the right side as she handled her rose. He caught a glimpse of her face as the green lights momentarily glowed brighter.

"Do you think it's true?" 4,021 asked, glancing anxiously around the room.

"What?" he asked, his face falling into darkness.

A bright magenta light lit up her face. "That 1-13's creepy skeleton-ghosts are watching us," she said in a cautious whisper. "I . . . don't see them." Momentarily, the room dipped into shadows once more.

With a dread of what might unexpectedly appear, 50-83 scanned the room. He thought for a second he saw the green glow of one of the skeleton-ghosts in a far corner, but he told himself that the glow was more likely a reflection from the light display. Searching for some form of security, he clutched at the crystal on his necklace. "I don't see anything either," he replied breathlessly. "But I'm sure they must be there somewhere. We should be careful." As he looked over at her anxiously, his face was lit by a green light.

1-13 made his way down the corridor of prison cells to the door leading to his workshop. On either side of him marched one of his hulking guards. He pressed a button on the wall and a panel to the left of the door slid up revealing a viewing screen. 1-13 turned on the viewing screen to observe 50-83 and 4,021 as they waited in the workshop.

1-13 chuckled. *"Perhaps* a little *eavesdropping* will provide me with a *clue* as to this *rebellion* 4,021 is taking part in . . ."

Shifting his position on the couch, 50-83 darted his eyes about the room once more. He frowned warily. "I really feel like they are watching us."

"I know." she concurred. The room dropped into darkness.

50-83 rubbed his clammy palms on his pant legs. "Are you sure he's going to come?"

"1-13?"

"No," 50-83 corrected her and laughed self-consciously at being misunderstood. "Infinity." He grew sober, contemplating their desperate situation. "Are you positive he's coming to rescue you?"

4,021 moved closer to him. "Of course," she smiled. "And you should know it, too. More than anybody. You're working with him."

"Uh, yes, I know," he stammered, bringing his mind back to the story he had created. He shrugged nonchalantly as he reassumed his role. "But, I was just wondering . . . so much could happen. If he runs into trouble or decides it's not worth it. He might change his mind and decide to head back to the Planet of Light."

Her eyes sparkled confidently through a blue-green light. "He wouldn't do that. Infinity is someone who keeps his word."

"But it's taking such a long time for him to get here. If he really was coming, wouldn't he be here by now?" 50-83 visualized the Infinity he had mentally created. He knew for certain an Infinity like his would instantly come to their rescue and, with just a few powerful blasts from his weapons, eliminate everything that 50-83 found frustrating. He shook his head, gloomily. "I'll bet he's forgotten about us and we'll just have to survive somehow the best we can."

4,021 smiled at him as she squeezed his hand. "We can't give up hope. Infinity cares about us and knows what we're going through." She held up her hand to show him the bracelet with the star-shaped pendant. It sparkled intermittently with each flash of light. "Look. Isn't it beautiful? We need to just believe that Infinity is coming and he will be here soon." As the lights glowed a reddish-purple, she enchantingly looked deep into his eyes.

An oozing green glow gathered behind 4,021 and from within its bowels, emerged one of the skeleton-ghosts. Its long, thin, claw-like hands wrapped themselves around her throat. "Don't you dare mention Infinity," it screeched.

4,021 gasped, choked, and tried to pull its iron-like grip from her throat.

With a galvanizing rage, 50-83 scrambled to his feet and rushed at the skeleton-ghost, kicking it hard in the shin. "Get your hands off of her."

The skeleton-ghost sneered down at 50-83.

Another skeleton-ghost oozed up behind 50-83, grabbed him by the arms, and yanked him back away from its cohort. 50-83 struggled to free himself.

1-13 entered the room with marked irritation. He flipped a switch that turned off the light display, casting the room in a bright natural light. He heaved a frustrated sigh and marched up to the skeleton-ghosts. "Let them go."

The skeleton-ghosts reluctantly released 50-83 and 4,021 but glared haughtily at 1-13.

With a disgusted scowl, 1-13 shook his head. "You fools," he shouted at the skeleton-ghosts. "Why did you have to interfere? If you would have let her speak just a few minutes longer, I would have learned everything I needed to know." 1-13 pressed his lips together in a suppression of anger, which, had he not suppressed, might have developed into his bursting into tears or ripping off the heads of the two skeleton-ghosts.

The first skeleton-ghost wheezed in what sounded like a death rattle. Its mouth curled into a sneer. "She mentioned Infinity. We abhor him. The sound of his name nauseates us." The green ooze that surrounded the skeleton-ghost shivered with hateful terror.

1-13 stared at the skeleton-ghost in disbelief. "Why?"

"Because he brings light to darkness," the other skeleton-ghost hissed. "We must have darkness to thrive."

Displaying a much-too-busy attitude, 1-13 rushed past the skeleton-ghosts. "Oh, you and your petty drivel. Leave me." He waved a hand to signal their immediate departure.

The two skeleton-ghosts gave 1-13 a sinister glare and evaporated into a green smoke that dissolved into the darkness.

1-13 nodded, pleased to see them gone, and moved over to 4,021 to take her hand. He helped her to her feet. "Are *you* all right, my *dear*?"

She shook her head in bewilderment. "It's hard to believe how anyone could get so upset about Infinity."

"I know," 1-13 agreed. "These *creatures* of *low* intelligence constantly *baffle* me." He calmly turned to 50-83. "By the way, 6-96 was *asking* about *you*." He raised his head cockily. "Running away is a *serious* offence . . . *so,* I told her you did *not* run away." 1-13 casually pulled his silver wand from his pocket and toyed with it.

"Thank you."

"*Instead*, I told her I saw you *talking* with 4,021 near her *hovel*. If you *tell* 6-96 anything about what has *really happened*, it could be disastrous for you, and I could *change* my story. So, you *won't* tell her anything, *correct?*" 1-13 gave 50-83 a warning gaze.

50-83 nodded and looked at 1-13 narrowly. "What are you going to do with her?"

1-13 stroked 4,021's cheek gently. "4,021 and I will have a very *enlightening* chat."

50-83 sent 4,021 a look of caution, hoping he could mentally remind her of his earlier warning concerning 1-13's interrogations.

1-13 turned abruptly to his guards. "You two, lead him out of my workshop."

The guards converged on 50-83 and each took him by an arm. 50-83 tried to free himself from their grasps, but the guards managed to jerk him around and drag him to out into the hallway.

In a royal, almost princely, manner, 1-13 took 4,021's hand and led her through the hallway of dark, depressing prison cells and into his private room. He closed the door behind him, and gestured for her to sit on the ivory loveseat.

"Make yourself *comfortable*, my *dear*."

Still holding to her rose, 4,021 sat down. She glanced about the room, trying to accustom herself to its elegant décor. Perceiving how different it was from her hovel back in the Slump-Bump area, she shifted uncomfortably.

Extremely confident in his abilities, 1-13 picked up a wine bottle from an ornate silver ice bucket on the coffee table. "May I *pour* you a *drink?*"

"No, thank you."

Nodding to her wish, 1-13 replaced the wine bottle and slid up close to her on the loveseat. "*You* are an indescribably *beautiful* woman. Your *blonde* hair and deep *blue* eyes. I find myself quite *intoxicated*." He raised one of her hands to his mouth to kiss it. "Have you ever felt *passion* for a *man* before?" He sent her a crafty smile, though it was meant to appear romantic.

"50-83 told me I shouldn't trust you."

1-13 leaned his elbow on the back of the couch and gazed at her in a seductive manner. "50-83 is a *childish* boy. *You* and *I* have *more* grown-up *mentalities*." He gently brushed a strand of her hair from her face. "There is *something* I want to *show* you." Starting with the top button, 1-13 began unbuttoning his shirt. "*Look . . .*" Around his neck he wore a silver necklace sporting a circular pendant with a large turquoise gem in the center. "An exquisite piece, wouldn't you say? A lovely blue gem that resembles your eyes. Keep your eyes focused on it." He removed the necklace from around his neck and held it by its chain in front of 4,021's eyes. The turquoise gem radiated.

"It is beautiful." She gazed at the pendant entranced.

"Yes . . ." 1-13 lightly swung the pendant before her. "Look deep within the gem. Feel yourself drawn into it. It is as if you and the pendant were one." The pendant hummed hypnotically with each swing.

4,021 felt as if her body were swinging back and forth with the gem. A sleepy sensation spread itself throughout her mind.

"Good . . ." 1-13 murmured softly. "You are sleepy. Let your eyes rest."

4,021's eyes fell shut.

"Now, *tell* me . . ." 1-13 demanded in a subtly sympathetic tone, ". . . is it *true* the *Prince* of the *Planet* of *Light* is coming *here*?" He hid the excitement that simmered within him as he pondered what power he had within his grasp to be the one and only Persuader privy to vital information on a potential invasion. *Maybe then the Dark Tyrant would realize how invaluable my services are, especially when compared with a certain nincompoop who calls himself 1.*

. Still in a hypnotic trance, 4,021 shook her head, bewildered. "Who? . . . I don't understand . . ." She only knew Infinity as a friend and rescuer. *But who was this Prince of the Planet of Light?* Her thoughts crisscrossed and became more confused.

1-13 stood to his feet and abruptly faced her. "I am talking about Infinity," he raised his voice impatiently. "Is it true? Is he really coming? . . . And what is he plotting to do here?"

Like someone trying to escape a nightmare, 4,021 shifted uneasily at his confrontational tone. She instinctively grasped her rose tighter. As she did so, the thorns on the rose pricked her hand and brought her out of her trance. "What happened . . . ?" she asked, blearily. ". . . I must have fallen asleep."

Surprised, 1-13 thought to himself, *Something must have gone wrong . . . She woke up too quickly.* 1-13 grit his teeth and clenched his fists while still trying to maintain a calm façade. "Yes . . . But not for long . . ."

4,021 looked down at her hand and saw the indentations where she had been pricked by the rose's thorns. However, remembering that 50-83 had warned her not to trust 1-13, she said nothing to him about it.

Noticing 4,021's mistrustful look, 1-13 smiled down at her reassuringly and stroked her golden hair. "You *appear* to be a *little* uptight. You should *relax*." He slithered over to a bookcase near the window and pressed a button. The lights in the room dimmed and the ceiling lit up in swirling star-like lights meant to dazzle and intrigue their observers. Seductive lights, spinning, flying, falling, casting weird and fantastic shadows that danced about the room in wild profusion. "*So . . . you must be *tired*. Go ahead and *relax*." Coolly, he made his way up behind the loveseat and placed his hands on her shoulders. "*Relax* . . ." his words dripped down to her ears like puffy clouds of cotton. He massaged her shoulders rhythmically. "You know, *my dear,* I am *genuinely* interested in this *Infinity* . . . could you *tell me* a little more about *him?*"

4,021 smiled. The warmth and gentle sound of Infinity's name circled around her like a comforting blanket. 1-13's reassuring tone made her feel secure enough to talk about her favorite topic. "Oh, he's kind, and handsome, too."

"How *interesting* . . ." 1-13 maneuvered himself around the loveseat to sit directly in front of her on the coffee table. "And is he a *friend* of *yours?*" He arched an eyebrow, not unlike a scientist who analyzes his specimen.

She noticed how stern his eyes were and again doubted whether she could trust him. "Well . . . uh . . . yes . . . and he said . . ." Her mind attempted to find answers that might shield her from 1-13 and yet at the same time satisfy him.

Her questioning eyes at once informed 1-13 that she was slipping from his grasp. "You can *trust me*," he attempted to smile comfortingly. "Just go ahead and tell me . . . *what* is it that the *two* of *you* are planning?"

Confused, she knew her only recourse was to hold her rose close to her heart. *Oh, Infinity,* she whispered within herself, *what should I do?*

Then, she heard Infinity's strong, reassuring voice come softly from within the rose. *"Don't tell him anything. I will protect you. He cannot hurt you."*

1-13 noticed the rose. "What is that you have in your hand?" Beguiled by her attachment to this beautiful and yet simplistic object, he wondered what mysterious hold it possessed.

She lowered her eyes to the rose and said nothing.

His impatience mounting at her continued stubbornness, 1-13 stiffened but masterfully forced a smile upon his lips. "Tell me, what is it?" He tried to reach for it, but she pulled it away from him.

1-13 hovered over her, as a hawk after its prey. He raised his hand to slap her. However, as he did, he noticed her lovely, frail features and changed his mind. He knew all too well how ineffective 6-96's barbaric methods were in the long run ... but he wondered if there were certain moments when inflicting a little pain might be justified. "You have not been very cooperative," he snapped. "Most Slump-Bumps eagerly answer my questions. Particularly when I warn them that being uncooperative could lead to painful consequences." He smiled cruelly. "So, are you ready to tell me about your plots with Infinity?"

4,021 shook her head unwaveringly.

He narrowed his eyes and sneered. "Very well, perhaps a little torture might change your mind." He took her firmly by her wrist and pulled her to her feet. He dragged her over to a wall and pushed her hard against it. "When you feel the sharp pain jolting throughout every inch of your body," he ground out the words, "you will willingly tell me everything I want to know."

Tears streamed down her cheeks. "No . . . please . . . I just can't . . ." She focused once more on her rose. Once again she sensed she was not alone. "Oh, Infinity, help me." A warm, comforting feeling emanated from the rose and spread itself throughout her whole body. She knew she was about to faint, but inwardly a stronger force was gently laying her to rest upon a soft cloud. She fell to the ground.

1-13 stared down at 4,021 irritated that he was not going to learn anything now that she was unconscious. He knelt beside her, in an almost motherly fashion, and patted her cheek hoping she would come to.

Pale but angelic, 4,021 continued to slumber peacefully.

He looked at the rose in her hands. He had not seen anything like it, and it intrigued him. He reached out to take it and study it more closely. However, as soon as his hand touched the rose, it sent a painful burning sensation throughout his body. He pulled his hand back and rubbed it petulantly. Like a small boy who had once again been deprived of a toy, he sulked and angrily stomped out of the room.

Perhaps the best method to get her to talk is to send her to one of the Manual Labor Rooms, 1-13 mused. *After a week of hard labor, she will be so exhausted she will tell me anything I want to know.* He examined himself in a mirror and pondered his own cleverness. *After all, I am more powerful than she is, and as for this mysterious object of hers, it could not possibly be possessed of omnipotence. I will find some way to eliminate it.*

Chapter Twenty-Seven

The *Ghost III* sent out a loud, resonating alarm. Infinity and the Way-Guide raced to the control room, where Infinity switched on the viewing screen. The alarm went silent. The screen in front of them displayed the star-strewn path ahead now blocked by a red, glowing web of electricity stretching upward, downward, to the left, and to the right as far as the eye could see.

The Way-Guide stared at the phenomenon with trepidation. "What is that?"

Deep in thought, Infinity leaned forward against the control panel as he studied the barricade on the screen. "Someone has blocked our path with a powerful electromagnetic barricade, no doubt under the Dark Tyrant's orders. Until I can locate the projection amplifier of this barricade and dismantle it, it will be impossible for the *Ghost III* to pass through."

"But we *have* to get through." The Way-Guide pounded his fist into the palm of his other hand. "What about 1-05 and the others? We don't have time to waste on something like this."

Infinity nodded calmly. "The *Ghost III* is monitoring 1-05's situation. In fact, it has already held back several attacks on her. Between the *Ghost III* and Alpha 3-0-3, she is safer than most people on that planet. Still, we must get through . . . and we *will* get through." Next to the control board was a small vase that held a red rosebud. Infinity gazed down at it with concern. "And remember the hopeful one. She still has the rose I sent her, but she will need a rescuer soon. The *Ghost III* has warned me that, in a short while, something evil and disgusting will try to destroy her." Turning to the Way-Guide directly, he sighed soberly. "That is why I am sending you to go on ahead of me."

The Way-Guide looked incredulously at Infinity. "But if the *Ghost III* can't get through, how can I?"

With a smooth sweep of his hand, Infinity directed the Way-Guide's attention to the viewing screen. "That electromagnetic barricade is not a solid force of electricity. It is a string of webs. Between each web is a small zone of safety." He adjusted a dial. The viewing screen zoomed in to a detailed picture of one of the openings between the webbing. "The *Ghost III* is too large to make it through the openings, but a small, well-navigated ship could. And you're going to be the one to navigate that ship." He looked at the Way-Guide with fixed determination.

The Way-Guide took a faltering step backwards, trying to accustom himself to the prospect of heading to the Planet of Darkness alone on such a dangerous mission. He grimaced, but deep inside he knew it would be selfish to insist he could not do it. Then an encouraging thought sustained him: *At least Infinity has faith in my abilities.*

"Follow me." Infinity led the Way-Guide out of the control room.

The high-powered elevator took Infinity and the Way-Guide down to a launching platform in seconds. A small, bullet-shaped spaceship with tapered wings was docked on the platform. "This solo ship's name is the *Forerunner*." Infinity pat the nose of the ship fondly. "You will go on ahead of the *Ghost III* and prepare for me. Most importantly, you must go to the Shadow-Shield. I want the two of you to rescue the hopeful one and guide her to the Shepherdess' Valley." He knitted his eyebrows and pressed his lips together firmly to emphasize how vital the mission was.

Conveying his understanding with a nod, the Way-Guide opened the door to the ship and prepared to enter it. He was uneasy on his own, and, before entering, turned back to face Infinity with concern. "Will you be all right without my help?" he asked, nervously trying to hide the fact that he was the one who was looking for help.

Infinity gave him a strong, steadfast look. "It shouldn't take me long to find the source of the barricade . . . *and* the fiend responsible for it being there." His eyes flamed at the thought of someone so cruelly interfering with his mission of mercy.

"What if I run into trouble?" The Way-Guide's hand shook as he pulled himself into the ship.

"Tell the *Forerunner* what you need," Infinity informed him. "It constantly keeps communications open with the *Ghost III*. I will know where you are at all times and what your situation is. I will join you as soon as I can." After a benedictory uplift of his hand, Infinity turned toward the door of the elevator.

Feeling alone, the Way-Guide quipped under his breath, "Could we make that immediately?" He closed the ship's doors and took his seat in the cockpit. In just a few minutes, he was able to launch the ship off toward the electrical barricade.

Infinity returned to the control room and watched with pride as the Way-Guide maneuvered through one of the small openings in the webbed barricade and zoomed off on his way to the Planet of Darkness. Infinity closed his eyes. Sensing the closeness of his father, he silently prayed the Way-Guide would have success on his journey.

After laboring for hours over several lengthy matrices involving complicated economic situations, 2,040 decided it was time to take a break. He put his pen and paper away in a desk drawer and made his way to the far side of the room and exited through a door into his bedroom. Closing the door behind him, he removed his jacket and tossed it, with a theatrical flair, onto a nearby chair. The room, although small, was luxuriously decorated. Silken red and gold curtains pulled back with matching golden cords lavishly draped the walls. Elegant hanging lamps with stained-glass shades illuminated the corners of the room with a soft kaleidoscope of colors.

Dominating the room was a large bed. Embellishing its marble headboard and footboard were graceful carvings of nude men and women in romantic embraces. Colorful silk and satin pillows were precariously piled like a rich mountain at the head of the bed. The shimmering blue silken sheets clung casually to the golden jacquard coverlet in disarray.

2,040 stretched out a kink in his back and unbuttoned the top buttons of his shirt. He sank back languidly into the comfortable bed and reclined on the mound of pillows. Keeping his eyes focused on a beaded doorway right across from the bed, he sighed contentedly when he noticed the approaching form of 34,000. She pushed aside the curtain of beads. 2,040 smiled at her invitingly. As she made her way toward him, he scanned her alluring shape accentuated by her curve-hugging red silk negligee. Her lithesome movements captivated 2,040 like a cool, refreshing breeze. She glided up to him and lounged seductively beside him.

He embraced her warmly. "Oh, my dear . . . you're more beautiful than ever."

Mesmerized, 34,000 gazed into 2,040's deep-blue eyes. "My fondest wish is that you will always think of me that way," she sighed as she held herself to him as close as she could. "I just feel fortunate to have you love me."

2,040 kissed her several times on her neck, allowing each kiss to bring him closer to her shoulder. He moved the thin, silk strap of her negligee gently downward and continued kissing her shoulder.

Smiling down at him fondly, she stroked a tassel of his hair, then caressed it gently.

He kissed her lightly on her nose then held her to himself and let his hand slide down her side to her waist.

She embraced him lovingly. "Oh, I just . . ." She pulled herself even closer to him and kissed him passionately.

After the kiss, 2,040 burst into such a riotous laughter he was thrown backwards and had to pound the bed hard with his fist to keep himself under some type of control.

34,000 sulked and leaned her chin on the palm of her hand. "So," she murmured sarcastically, "that's what you think of my kisses."

Trying to curb his laughter, he patted her on her upper arm to reassure her. "No . . . no . . ." he said between giggles, "no, no. I was not laughing at your kiss." He stroked his hand down her hair and her cheek.

"Oh, I see," she pouted with her arms crossed in front of her. "Well, then, I might forgive you a little, if . . ."

"If what, my dear?" he asked, bringing his face closer to hers, preparing to kiss her.

She pushed him away playfully. "If you tell me what it was you were laughing about."

"Just some thought that came into my head."

34,000 blushed and tried to keep from being annoyed. "A thought," she repeated incredulously, "a thought that was brought on by my kiss and ended up making you laugh?"

"No, a thousand times no," he reiterated and gave her a kiss on her forehead. "It was just one of those thoughts that start out by flying around and around over your head waiting for the opportune moment to jump right in and force you to think about it whether you like it or not."

"All right, so I forgive you." She tickled him behind his ear. "But you still have to tell me what the thought was."

"Very well." He leaned his elbow on the pillows. "I was thinking about 1."

"1? While kissing me?" Her eyes widened as her face grew red.

"Well, I was thinking of 1 up here in my brain, dear one." He accentuated the words with brief taps of his pointer finger to his temple. "But my lips were completely absorbed with thoughts of you." He gave her hand a comforting pat. "But, the reason 1 was on my mind is just a little while ago he asked me to take charge of the efficiency of a new manufacturing project, manufacturing shape-shifters." He laughed again but curtailed it, trying to keep it in check.

34,000 looked at him skeptically. "I don't see what's so funny about that."

"My sweet little thing." He tweaked her chin. "That is the very reason I am the great intellectual and you are only my assistant. I know what is so hilarious about 1 wanting to manufacture shape-shifters."

"So, why?"

He stared at her in disbelief. "Because it is impossible to manufacture shape-shifters on our planet. Shape-shifters are created on the Planet of Light. That is the only planet that contains litho-stones, and litho-stones are an essential component of shape-shifters."

34,000 shrugged her shoulders. "Perhaps he's planning to trade with the Planet of Light for these litho-stones."

"Perhaps," 2,040 pursed his lips thoughtfully. "Perhaps, but unlikely. The Dark Tyrant has tried repeatedly to set up a trade agreement for litho-stones and the Planet of Light has always refused. Don't you see, it's ridiculous. I consider it completely impossible, completely impossible for the Planet of Darkness to ever require someone to be in charge of production efficiency for the manufacture of shape-shifters, because, there can be no shape-shifters to manufacture." He beamed proudly.

"Oh, you are so brilliant," 34,000 whispered, stroking his cheek and gazing at him.

2,040, satisfied once more at the recognition of his own genius, embraced her again and they kissed.

An entry announcer box on a table beside the bed beeped. 2,040 pulled himself reluctantly away from 34,000 and pressed a button on the announcer. "Yes, who is there?" he asked brusquely, trying to mask his annoyance.

"9-85 to see you in the entry hall," the announcer stated in its stilted, mechanical voice.

2,040 frowned. "Well, at least it's him and not 1 again." He put his arm around 34,000's waist and brought her to himself. He kissed her one last time. "Just this one brief interlude, my lovely little thing, and I'll be back here with you." He patted her cheek with a warm smile and reluctantly left the room.

2,040 found 9-85 waiting for him near the electrical fountain.

"Sorry if I woke you from a nap," 9-85 said, uneasily noticing that 2,040's clothes were askew and his hair mussed. "It's just that when I got your message, I came as fast as I could."

"Oh, no need to worry about that." 2,040 waved an unconcerned hand.

"There was something that you wanted to talk to me about?"

"7,500 told me he has a job for you," 2,040 informed him with a clever raise of an eyebrow. "He told me it was something very urgent. It's essential you see him right away."

9-85's face fell into a frown. "7,500 wants me for one of *his* jobs? I work for you, not him." 9-85 could not accustom himself to 7,500's ambiguous and scattered manner of thinking. After years of studying math and statistics, he wanted things more logical and concrete.

"Of course you work for me," 2,040 agreed flippantly. "And, since you work for me, you will do this for him because I ask you to . . . Understand?" 2,040 waved his hand in the cascading waters of the electrical fountain, causing its brilliant colors to burst forth like fireworks.

9-85's attention was momentarily drawn to the dramatic display in a brief fixation of wonderment. "If you say so."

"He will tell you what he wants you to do," 2,040 informed him in a businesslike manner. "You know where to find him?"

9-85 nodded. "I better go see him then." After one last hesitation, he headed for the door.

"Good luck," 2,040 called out after him, his voice full of cheerful optimism. He then turned and eagerly headed back to his bedroom and to 34,000.

Pushing open the thick, heavy door to 7,500's work suite and entering, 9-85 came face-to-face with several stacks of books piled high on top of a large metal desk.

"Greetings to you," said a melodic voice that seemed to be coming from the books.

9-85 raised a perplexed eyebrow. "Yes . . . and, hello . . . ?" He shifted uncomfortably at having a conversation with the books. "Is there someone there?" He tried to peek around them.

"Oh, you silly," the voice called again through a chuckle. "Of course. Over here." A hand popped up over the top of one of the stacks, waved, and gestured for 9-85 to come over to the other side of the desk.

9-85 rounded the large desk and found he was in the front office of the work suite. Other than the desk partially hidden by the monstrous stacks of books, the room contained a plethora of file cabinets and several ceiling-high bookshelves overflowing with books. On the far wall of the office loomed a set of double doors leading to 7,500's private office.

Turning his attention from the double-doors, 9-85 found, seated at the desk, 93-73, 7,500's research assistant. "Hello."

9-85 was relieved the voice really did come from a person. "I am here to see 7,500. My number is—"

Buoyantly, 93-73 sprung from his chair and held out his hand to shake 9-85's. "You must be 9-85. How nice to meet you. I'm 93-73 — you know, 7,500's research assistant. You work for 2,040, right? Yes, that's right. Wonderful, wonderful." He searched through some papers on the desk. "7,500 has been expecting you." He found what he was looking for and took up a stack of papers then glanced back to 9-85. "All right and here, come with me — right this way." With a graceful, sweeping hand motion, he gestured for 9-85 to follow him through the double doors.

They found themselves in 7,500's private room. This room contained a large, L-shaped desk behind which were several bookshelves piled with books. In front of the desk was a cushioned, mauve chaise lounge. The walls were decorated with paintings of splattered colors and scattered throughout the room was a menagerie of bizarre statues in contorted poses.

With his hands clasped behind his head, 7,500 lounged on the chaise lounge. When he noticed 9-85 entering the room, he languidly raised one hand and waved a half-hearted greeting.

9-85 gave him an efficient nod. "2,040 told me you wanted me to help you with something."

"Absolutely," 7,500 murmured, giving no indication he was about to move from his chaise lounge at any time in the future.

93-73 sprited over to the desk and placed the papers in a folder on the desk.

7,500 pushed himself up to lazily lean on his elbow. "Ah, 93-73 . . . Efficient as always." He grinned brightly.

"This is the analysis I put together on those books covering the Grubian wars," 93-73 brushed his bangs from his eyes and shrugged his shoulders. "I just wanted to make certain you had everything you needed before you started working on those presentations." He gave 7,500 and 9-85 both a friendly smile and headed back toward the door.

7,500 covered an indifferent yawn with the back of his hand. "You know, 93-73, you really are an indispensable jewel," he said in an off-the-cuff manner that lacked sincerity. He laid his head back once more. "I can't imagine how I would survive without you."

Stopping in his path, 93-73 beamed and faced 7,500. "Why, thank you. That's very kind of you."

Smirking, 7,500 stood. "Oh, no, not really kind at all."

"Of course, you are kind." 93-73 swung his hands out enthusiastically. "You've always been kind to me, You're just being too modest."

"But I can't help it." 7,500 remarked as he polished his nails on his shirt. "I am just naturally a modest person." He flippantly gestured for 93-73 to leave.

93-73 sighed in disappointment. With his head lowered, he edged his way past 9-85 and out the door.

7,500 shook his head disparagingly. "I often worry about that young man," he said aside as if in strict confidence to 9-85. "I sometimes wonder . . . perhaps there was something wrong with the tests . . . you know, the ones that determined his career as a Historical Researcher." Nonchalantly, 7,500 moved over to a tray held by a moronically smiling statue, on which a bottle and several glasses awaited. He poured himself a drink and looked at 9-85. "Do you notice anything wrong with him? 93-73, I mean?"

"No." 9-85 was a little irritated and confused with the way the conversation was turning. "But of course, I've just met him."

Carrying his glass, 7,500 intently moved closer to 9-85. He tilted his head with surprise at 9-85's answer. "But wouldn't you say he's a bit . . . effeminate?"

9-85 bit his lip to keep from displaying annoyance at 7,500 avoiding telling him why he wanted him here in the first place. 9-85 cleared his throat. "2,040 told me you were needing my help."

Taking a drink, 7,500 nodded and raised his hand in reluctant acknowledgment. He set the glass on the desk. "Of course, we'll get to that." 7,500 glanced into a nearby mirror to adjust the curls of hair around his forehead. He sashayed over to the chair behind the desk and sat down. "Tell me, 9-85, what are your thoughts on the Dark Tyrant and 1?" Tapping the side of his mouth with his index finger, 7,500 looked at him pensively.

9-85 frowned and knitted his eyebrows, secretly questioning 7,500's motives. "Well, of course, I think that they . . ." he made an attempt to reply.

7,500 waved off the question. "No need to answer. Whatever you really think, I know what you would say. The same old rigmarole they taught us all of our lives. Do you know what I think of the Dark Tyrant and 1?" He watched 9-85 for a moment as if expecting a response but quickly resumed without allowing him a chance to speak. "They are fools. Fools to think they can be gods." He examined one of the ostentatious rings he was wearing and wiped a smudge off of it. "They are only human, just like you and me. Humans have knowledge, yes. But that knowledge is only accumulated from one lifetime. Think of it, one lifetime compared to the knowledge acquired in an eternity of lifetimes." He paused once more to allow his point to sink in. "It makes you realize that there must be a god, even if that god is time itself." 7,500 absent-mindedly leaned an elbow on the desk and rested his head in his hand becoming lost in deep thought.

9-85 was rarely inspired by philosophical conversations and could not find any connection between the orders for his presence and 7,500's babble. "Perhaps . . . but there was something you wanted me to do?"

With wide eyes and a forced smile, 7,500 faced 9-85 with an indecipherable look that some would interpret as innocent and others as empty-headed. "Very well then, let's get down to business." Displaying an air of competence, he clasped his hands on the desk. "I have been informed by certain people that the workers in manual labor room 15 have been displaying rebellious attitudes. 1 has enlisted me to give these workers little pep talks to encourage their cooperation and pinpoint the workers that are stirring up the others. This evening, other duties demand my attention, so, I was hoping you could oversee the meeting for me."

While he had been on his way to 7,500's office, 9-85 had tried to decide what various tasks 7,500 had in mind for him. He had come up with ideas like organizing the statistics for past events or calculating work level efficiencies over several consecutive years. The last thing he had expected was for 7,500 to ask him to do something so remotely distant from his expertise. After pausing a moment to make certain he had heard 7,500 correctly, 9-85 responded, "But I wouldn't even know where to start . . ."

"I will have 93-73 accompany you," 7,500 stated nonchalantly with an uplifted eyebrow. "If you don't know what to do, just ask him. Basically, all you need to do is to have them tell you what they like and what they don't like. Plus, you can reassure them their needs and wants will be addressed in due time, that sort of thing. 93-73 will take any notes I might require and that's all there is to it." He exhaled and a broad smile spread itself across his blank expression.

Seeing no possible way of escaping the unpleasantness of his new orders, 9-85 sighed. "When is the meeting?"

7,500 glanced at a clock on the wall. "You still have a few hours." He stood and jovially patted 9-85 on the shoulder. "When it's time, I'll have 93-73 meet you at your room and he can take you there. How's that?" he asked with a smile which faded too quickly.

Attempting to hide the uneasiness creeping up his spine, 9-85 laughed and nodded. "Very well. I think I can handle it."

"Excellent." 7,500 gestured sharply, guiding 9-85 through the double doors and back into the front office.

Once 7,500 had waved 9-85 out to the hall and had closed the door quietly behind him, he moved back around and leaned leisurely against 93-73's desk. "93-73, is there anything that bothers you about 9-85?" he asked seriously.

93-73 frowned thoughtfully and shook his head. "No, not really. Only that you were very quick to get me out of the office when he was there." He gave 7,500 a perturbed expression. "I thought you told me *I* was doing a good job. You're not considering replacing *me,* are you?"

"Of course not," 7,500 murmured soothingly, patting him on the shoulder. "I'm just a little worried about him. Would you say he seems a little dense, perhaps even slow in grasping the simplest instructions?"

"Oh, no." 93-73 waved his hand to accentuate his point. "I've heard that he is extremely intelligent."

"Excuse me. I didn't ask you what you've heard. I'm talking about his appearance." Self-consciously, 7,500 straightened his collar and smoothed his well-groomed curls. "Why, he even had difficulty comprehending the simple little task I laid before him."

93-73 held his hands up questioningly. "Oh, I see . . . But how am I supposed to judge the matter when I'm still in the dark myself? What is it you want him to do?" He tried hard to disguise his annoyance at what he hoped was an oversight.

Turning aside, 7,500 fingered his drink contemplatively. "It just has to do with our little meetings, you know, the ones the Dark Tyrant set up for us to placate the workers."

93-73 chuckled in wonderment. "—Did you say *placate* the workers? I doubt the Dark Tyrant knows what's *really* going on."

7,500 groomed his eyebrows with his finger. "I've heard it said that a little rebellion is good for any society." To illustrate his point, he quickly brushed aside a tall and unstable stack of books and watched them with interest as they tumbled to the floor. "The danger is that the Dark Tyrant could learn what is going on at these meetings sooner than we'd like. Sources have informed me that this evening the Dark Tyrant is sending in a spy, who will be reporting any hint of rebellious activity."

Throwing a hand to his forehead, 93-73 moaned in frustration. "Oh no. That could ruin everything. And this was supposed to be a pivotal meeting."

"Not only that, but 1-13 has questioned one of the workers. And he told the Dark Tyrant that the workers are in a volatile state and on the verge of rebellion." He set aside his drink with a somewhat anxious look. "I don't think it would be wise to try to convince them to put on a show at this stage of the game, not for one of the Dark Tyrant's spies."

Color drained from 93-73's face as he imagined the dire consequences of this evening's meeting, especially since he, himself, was involved. "What are you going to do?"

"That's where 9-85 comes in." 7,500 sat in a chair next to the desk. "I am sending him in to take over the meeting." A complacent smile played on his lips. "It would be a good experience for him, don't you think?"

"Ah." 93-73 waved an enlightened finger in the air. "And if the workers get out of hand, 9-85 will take the blame." He tapped his chin as he considered the matter.

"A good plan." 7,500 polished the nails of his right hand on his shirt as he envisioned the ultimate outcome.

"Absolutely."

Abruptly, 7,500 stood and for a second he stared at another towering stack of books. "Besides all that, I am interested in finding out 9-85's reaction to the workers. You never know, he might prove to be a beneficial ally . . . or on the other hand . . ."

Chapter Twenty-Eight

The massive viewing screens that served as backdrops to the stage in manual labor room 15 flickered off and on relentlessly as a cold, domineering voice announced over the speakers: "Shift 3 will now leave. Shift 4 will now begin working . . . Shift 3 will now leave. Shift 4 will now begin working." The large, suffocatingly hot room echoed with heavy breathing, muffled groans, shuffling, and clattering as the exhausted workers put away their tools and dragged their tired frames along as they vacated their work stations. At the same time, an efficient clean-up crew carried out the dead bodies of two workers who had died from exhaustion. As they exited, the Shift 4 workers filed in.

85-27, 38-95, and 17-07 plodded out of the manual labor room together. On the way, 85-27 leaned furtively over to 38-95. "Are you going to be at the meeting?"

"Yes, aren't you?" 38-95 unrolled his sleeves and finished buttoning his shirt.

Anxiously, 17-07 moved up on the other side of 85-27. "Have either of you heard anything from 7,500 on what's going to happen at this meeting?"

38-95 shook his head. "No, have you?"

85-27 hesitated, but then spoke up, attempting to keep his voice calm. "He told me."

All eyes focused on him.

85-27 gulped, but then boldly lifted his head and continued, "He told me that our plans are coming together without a glitch and soon—"

17-07 apprehensively clutched 85-27 by the shoulder, stopping him a moment in his tracks. "Shhh. You don't want the guards to hear you. Save it for the meeting." Cautiously, he glanced about the room.

There was a loud crash as a large pile of bloquious rocks fell directly in front of 85-27's path. Stunned, 85-27 looked over and saw 4,021 standing near the metal container which had toppled over, the last remaining rocks falling out of it. She swayed dizzily, her weak hands dropping the heavy bucket of rocks she had brought to dump into the mental container.

85-27 rushed to her side and held her to keep her from falling.

"Hey, are you okay?"

"I think so." She breathed out an exhausted sigh. "I'm just so tired."

85-27 glanced down at her sympathetically. He could see how frail and delicate she was. "You don't look like you belong here."

"They brought me here to punish me, because I couldn't tell them what they wanted." She wiped sweat from her forehead. "I really don't see why . . . why they have me working here, I mean." Her blue eyes stared upward questioningly.

17-07 and 38-95 edged in closer. "Of course not," 17-07 agreed, having overheard the last part of their conversation. "You must be a Slump-Bump. They're not supposed to work." He bent down, almost without thinking, and gathered the bloquious rocks that had fallen.

"That's right," 38-95 looked about suspiciously. "Who brought you here?"

Continuing to steady her, 85-27 noticed the rose peeking out of 4,021's pocket. "Hey, what is that?"

"Beautiful, isn't it?" 4,021 whispered, taking it in her hands. The rose reinvigorated her with a new strength. "I look at it whenever I'm discouraged."

17-07 glanced up from his task and stared at the rose in awe. "It looks phenomenal. What is it? Where did you find it?"

"It's a rose. Someone gave it to me," 4,021 replied proudly. "The One from the Planet of Light. He's coming to rescue us." She smiled, her face aglow with hope.

"Really? To be rescued," 17-07 said, awestruck. "Now that's a profound thought." Triumphantly, he lifted his right fist in the air. "You know, guys — that feeling I had that something momentous was about to happen — that feeling was dead-on." His eyes widened as he stared in the distance at something unseen but, to him, completely spell-binding.

85-27 sensed a connection between the rose and his inward longing for light. "Do you mind if I hold it, just for a minute?" He reached toward the rose.

"If you would like." 4,021 handed the rose to him. She then remembered how the rose had hurt 50-83, and she hesitated in releasing it to 85-27. But he grasped hold of the rose so quickly there was nothing else she could do but let him take it.

Entranced, 85-27 stroked the rose's petals and leaves. Unexpectedly, he became inspired by a great wisdom that exuded from the rose. "There's something powerful within this rose. Those who are your true friends don't have to fear that power," 85-27 told 4,021 sincerely. "But the power will destroy those who are your enemies."

Laughing, 38-95 gave 85-27 a good-natured shove. "Okay, now tell me how you came up with all that?"

85-27 looked up thoughtfully. "I heard it. The rose told it to me."

"It talked to you?" 17-07's mouth fell open. "That is so mindboggling."

"I wish I could keep it." 85-27 held the rose tightly. "But I think it wants to go back to you." Reluctantly, he held it out to 4,021.

As 4,021 reached out to take it back, two petals fell from the flower. Following the two petals with her eyes as they floated downward, 4,021 took the rose and knelt to pick up the petals. "Here." She handed them to 85-27. "I think these were meant for you."

85-27 clasped the rose petals in his hands protectively. "Now, together, we'll wish hard that all of us will be rescued soon." With a new determination, 85-27 walked out of the manual labor room. Compelled by both a growing curiosity mingled with fascination, 38-95 and 17-07 edged up on either side of him, trying to procure a peek at the rose petals.

One older, grey-haired worker not far away dropped a crate of ezocane crystals. He gasped, trying to catch his breath and, with his sleeve, weakly dabbed his forehead that was sweating profusely. He swayed faintly, losing his balance, and fell onto one of the orange tiles on the edge of the workroom. A pillar of orange light beamed up from the tile which disintegrated the worker into nothingness.

"Ha Ha Ha." A gruff voice laughed uncontrollably behind 4,021. "That's what he gets for trying to leave before his shift was up."

"But he wasn't trying to leave. He was sick and fainted." 4,021 looked back in concern and saw 366, the manual labor room's overseer behind her.

"So now . . ." he shouted, directing his attention away from the disintegrated worker to 4,021. ". . . what's going on here?"

"I wasn't doing anything wrong," she told him hesitantly.

He glared in her direction with bulging eyes and a sweaty brow. "Huh, not doing anything wrong. Just talking and avoiding work. You should be punished severely for that alone." He punctuated the threat by spitting angrily. It splattered uncomfortably close to her feet.

Her questioning blue eyes widened. "But I'm really not supposed to work." She diverted her gaze to the ground, not out of shyness, but because 366 had such a repulsive face it disgusted 4,021 to look at him. "I'm a Slump—"

"You were brought here to work, SO WORK." Wiping his nose with his shirtsleeve, he sneered at her. "And don't forget, everything you do or don't do is recorded by cameras. All they have to do is watch."

4,021's face became ashen.

366 interrupted his tirade long enough to rub his hand across his red beard and to eye 4,021 lustfully. "But, there is a slight chance I could forget your rebellious slacking. That is, if you were cooperative . . ." He ran the back of his greasy hand down her soft cheek as if examining the quality of a purchase.

4,021 tried to take a step back. "But . . . I told you, I didn't do anything wrong . . ."

He grabbed her by her arm to prevent her from moving away from him. "So you say. But rules have been broken, and we better discuss it — right over here in my office where we can talk — privately." His mouth curled into an eager grin.

4,021 struggled as 366 dragged her forcefully toward his office.

A shadow loomed beside him and 366 felt a sudden, sharp pain in his shin. "Ow," he cried out as he released 4,021 and clutched his swelling leg.

1-13 stepped in front of him and glared at him in annoyance.

366 looked down sheepishly, realizing that 1-13, a person of such high rank, was the one who had kicked his leg.

"I *told* you 4,021 was to be kept *working* . . . I should *report* you for disobeying my *orders*." 1-13 eyed him narrowly with intently raised eyebrows.

366 attempted to jut his weak chin forward but his face only fell into a pout. "I wasn't disobeying your orders," he whined. "She was going against the rules . . . and I only wanted to question her in my office."

1-13 shook his head unable to comprehend 366's childish outburst. "I would be more apt to believe your story if you had been conducting yourself more responsibly." He snapped his fingers toward the ground and one of the Dark Tyrant's spies slithered up beside him. "I brought my little friend with me. Since you are not to be trusted, YOU will be watched." 1-13's eyes gleamed at his own cleverness. He squatted beside the spy-creature and gave it a fatherly pat on the head. "Keep a good eye on him and 4,021. Report to me the second any of my orders are disregarded. *All right*?"

The spy-creature chirped eagerly and nodded its head. It adjusted the focus of its mechanical eyes on 366.

1-13 rose and inhaled deeply, a sneer spreading across his aristocratic face as he glared condescendingly down at 366.

366 shrunk away uneasily.

The room where the meeting was to be held was not at all what 9-85 had expected. He had anticipated one of those seemingly cloned meeting rooms, simple and sterilized, comprised of little other than a long metal table and its corresponding chairs. Instead, he was led through a storage closet with a hidden back door to an excavated underground chamber. The chamber had obviously been dug out in a hurry — the rock walls had been unevenly chiseled and the ceiling sloped considerably. Still, this room did not display a primitive appearance. It was lit by eerily glowing red lava which flowed through ezocane tubing that ran down the walls and were spaced five feet apart. In the center of the room was a large round pearlescent table surrounded by a connected curved bench. Near what was supposedly the front of the table, stood a rectangular writing board behind which was a large oval monitor built into the stone wall.

9-85 disliked being faced with the unknown, so he gestured 93-73 into the room ahead of him. 93-73 scuttled his way to the front of the table while balancing a large stack of books, folders, papers, and pens in his arms. With an exhausted sigh, he let them drop to the table. "Well, finally . . ." 93-73 brushed his bangs out of his eyes. "Here we are at last."

9-85 followed him into the room and surveyed it. "An unusual place for a meeting." He gave 93-73 a sideways glance. "I hope the workers can figure out how to find us."

Swinging out his arms in an exaggerated motion, 93-73 indicated the room. "This is where we always hold the meeting." He went about separating his books and papers into stacks, busily fussing with every page, pen, and folder to ensure that each was in its proper place. "The workers will be here any second now. Do you have everything prepared?" He stopped and eyed him intently as he waited for his reply.

9-85 shrugged nonchalantly in an attempt to disguise his growing uneasiness. "I was assured by 7,500 that all that was necessary was for me to ask them what they needed and reassure them that it would be taken care of." He casually took a seat at the table and tapped his fingers on the table top. "So . . . that's all I'm going to do."

93-73 knitted his eyebrows. He stepped away from the table and frowned. "You know, I would feel terrible if I didn't confide something to you."

"What?"

"Don't place too much confidence in what 7,500 tells you." 93-73 lowered his eyes to a pen he was toying with.

9-85 was perplexed. "You mean, I am expected to do more than what 7,500 told me?"

"No . . ." 93-73 still focused on the pen. He tossed it onto a stack of papers and faced 9-85. "That's not what I'm saying . . ." He stood and slid over to 9-85 and leaned over so that his mouth was right next to 9-85's ear. "But there *is* one thing I should warn you about."

Suddenly, the room was filled with the hustling and bustling sounds of the workers approaching the chamber door.

9-85 tensely looked at 93-73, hoping that the entrance of the workers would not prevent 93-73 from letting him in on what he was about to say.

93-73 gave 9-85's shoulder a quick pat of encouragement and whispered, "There are times when the workers can get out of hand." He then walked back to his books and papers.

His words left 9-85 both puzzled and uneasy. *Puzzled,* because the way 93-73 said the words made 9-85 wonder whether they were the warning he was going to give him or just an extra bit of information he thought 9-85 needed to know now that the workers were coming. *Uneasy,* because 9-85 now found himself standing before a huge group of strong, formidable workers who could likely get out of hand.

Fighting off the shaky feeling, 9-85 stood and faced the workers. The workers ignored him as they wandered about the room muttering and mumbling to themselves. He waited several uncomfortable minutes and then decided he had better speak. He cleared his throat and pounded the table, two actions he had seen one of his professors perform at the beginning of a class. "May I have your attention please?" he said loudly, although it did not seem loud since it was overpowered by the workers' conversations. 9-85 glanced helplessly in 93-73's direction, but all 93-73 did was blankly tilt his head while biting nervously at a hangnail. With a burst of determination, 9-85 reached over and grabbed one of 93-73's books and pounded it on the table.

The workers fell silent for a moment, but noticing 9-85, they returned to talking among themselves. Every now and then they would point out 9-85 and shake their heads disapprovingly.

9-85's eyes fired up with exasperation, and he swallowed hard to suppress his anger. He pounded the table once more. "Will you PLEASE take your seats," he shouted.

The workers ignored 9-85 as their mutterings grew even louder.

9-85 resolved not to put up with anything else. Decisively, he threw the book hard at the writing board causing one side of the board to shatter into pieces.

The workers immediately fell silent.

"As — I — said," 9-85 spoke with sharp emphasis, trying to quell his frustration, "sit — down."

The workers reluctantly moved to the table to take their seats.

85-27 looked over at 93-73 with skeptically knitted eyebrows. "What's he doing here?" He jabbed a defiant thumb toward 9-85.

38-95 stood next to 85-27 and nodded. "That's right. We don't know him. How do we know we can trust him?"

"And why isn't 7,500 here?" 85-27 adamantly asked.

93-73 grimaced at 85-27's forceful interrogation. Having been warned by 7,500 that a spy would be among the workers, he came to a mental conclusion that 85-27 had to be that spy. Resolving to follow what he considered the best approach, 93-73 acted as naturally as possible. "Unfortunately," he replied, "7,500 is away on business at the moment." He stepped over to 9-85 and, in a signal of full support, placed an arm around his shoulder. "And 9-85 was kind enough to agree to preside over this meeting in his place."

While still distrustful, 85-27 gave a curt nod to indicate he understood. He twisted his face into a frown as he reluctantly took a seat.

"So," 93-73 said in an orderly manner, "let's now give 9-85 our complete attention." While 93-73's words were directed toward the workers, they were meant more to encourage 9-85. 93-73 swept a hand in 9-85's direction dramatically. "9-85, the floor is yours."

As 93-73 moved back to his seat, 9-85 took his place at the front in the most centralized spot. Before 9-85 could open his mouth to speak, the chamber door creaked open and a dark-haired, overweight man unapologetically entered the room. He glanced in 9-85's direction and narrowed his eyes distrustfully. The back of the room was cast in shadows and many of the workers were forced to stand there because of the limited number of seats. The man slipped over to this part of the room where he was swallowed by the shadows. 9-85 had a strange feeling he had seen this man somewhere before. He wracked his brain to remember where, but his brain refused to tell him. Finally, 9-85 forced himself to accept the uncomfortable mystery-not-solved feeling and compelled himself to continue on with the meeting.

"Very well," 9-85 addressed the workers. "My primary purpose for being here is to find out from you your evaluation of the manual labor room you work in — Manual Labor Room 15, I believe. Those in charge want to know if you are pleased with the way things are running and what you would like to see changed." He looked around at the bewildered faces of the workers.

38-95 attempted to make some sense out of 9-85's words. He knitted his eyebrows and drew his head back in confusion. "'Pleased'? What do you mean 'pleased'?" he questioned with sharp skepticism. "Have you ever seen the manual labor room? How could anybody be *pleased* working in a place like that?"

9-85 started to reply but was forced to pause a moment as a group of other workers shouted in agreement. Their shouts kept increasing in intensity and might have continued ad infinitum had 93-73 not stood and gestured for silence. Once the workers fell silent, 93-73 gave 9-85 the go-ahead. "So, you're saying you're *not* pleased," 9-85 replied matter-of-factly to 38-95, "and that there *are* things about the manual labor room you would like to see changed."

With a bitter laugh, 85-27 slammed the palms of his hand on the table and stood to his feet. "Things we'd liked to see changed?" he repeated in a mocking tone. "Of course there are things we'd like to see changed. Just ask any of the workers here and they'll tell you how tough it is to work in that stinking death hole called a manual labor room. It's so bad most of us would stop working . . . if it wasn't for the fact that they'd kill us if we did."

A grey-haired man sitting near the front gave 85-27 a nod of approval and turned to 9-85 with a serious demeanor. "There's the heat," he told 9-85 with wide eyes. "It's deadly. Every day workers collapse from it."

Several of the workers joined in to voice their deep-seated resentment at working in the boiling hot manual labor room.

9-85 motioned for the workers to quiet down. "So," he said, trying to understand the chaotic outburst from the workers, "you want me to ask them if they can do something to cool the room."

A middle-aged blonde-haired worker shook his head. "They've tried that. It doesn't help. Parts of the room turn freezing cold, but most of it stays boiling hot. We just get sicker."

9-85 took a notebook and pen. "I see." He jotted some notes down. "I'll still make a note of the temperature issue." He turned to the blonde-haired man. "I'm sure that if I present this problem to them, they will come up with some solution."

"Ha," 85-27 shouted, unconvinced, "That's what they always say. They say they'll fix it, but they never do." He drooped in his chair and lowered his eyes.

"Well . . ." 9-85 tried to stay calm. "They will certainly do what they can. Of course, there will always be problems that are impossible to fix. And we have to go about it the right way. There is no constructiveness in merely complaining about something. When something does not meet a certain standard, you have to think of 'why?' and consider if there is some purpose for it being that way. For example, you're upset about knives because they are sharp and you could cut yourself on them, but an inability to cut would cause knives to no longer have a purpose for being. So, if we can pinpoint the true problem and find a way to fix it without negating the purpose of the machinery and, if I can convince those in charge that by addressing the problem there will be an increase in the production of ezocane — I'm positive they will do everything they can to remedy the situation." He tapped his notebook emphatically with his pen.

17-07 bit his lip thoughtfully. "I don't know much about this 'increase production' nonsense, but what I want you to tell them is to give us shorter hours. I mean, sixteen hours. Working, eating, and sleeping. No time to do anything fun."

The grey-haired man shook his head. "The long hours is not the problem. Everyone who works on in the City of the Dark Tyrant works sixteen hours a day. The problem is the heat."

Another worker with bulky shoulders and heavy-lidded eyes cocked his head, trying hard to think. "That's right . . . If I didn't work sixteen hours a day, I wouldn't know what to do with the extra hours."

A dark wavy-haired man stood up. "The problem isn't the hours or the heat. The problem is the machines. They are difficult to operate and are constantly breaking down."

"No," shouted a short chubby man, "what really needs to be changed is the manager. He yells and harasses us. Even beats us for no reason at all."

9-85 was becoming overwhelmed with the compounding number of problems the workers were throwing at him. He tried to continue taking notes, but his scribbles were becoming unintelligible. Finally, in exasperation, he closed the book and tried to make sense of the muddled voices of the workers. *Before coming to this meeting, I was convinced that the workers — all being workers — would have one clear idea of what they wanted improved. Now here they are arguing and disagreeing with each other. Not one of them has the same viewpoint as the other . . . It's going to be impossible to placate them all.*

He concluded what he needed to do was to just appease them a bit and end the meeting tactfully. "All right." He sighed in a 'fed up' manner. "I have all of your concerns written down and I can assure you I will put them through the proper channels and they will be taken care of as quickly as possible."

85-27 shook his head and pounded the table with his fist. "Absolutely not. We don't want any more of these 'proper channels'. If these problems aren't fixed immediately we'll stop working all together. And you'll see how much *that* 'increases production'."

The workers shot to their feet and roared their rousing support for 85-27's plan.

An uneasy tenseness built inside 9-85's already agitated brain. *Was it even possible to appease the workers and at the same time not jeopardize his own position with the Dark Tyrant?* 9-85 decided that, before he let them leave, it would be best to educate the workers on the point of view of their superiors. "I understand how you feel . . ." 9-85 hoped his psychological approach would pacify the workers somewhat. ". . . but the people you work for have reasons for doing what they do. As I said before, their goal is to either maintain or increase the production of ezocane." 9-85, in a methodical manner, moved to the half-smashed writing board and drew out several graphs, charts, and matrices. "Let's take, for instance, the idea that we want to shorten the hours you work. This line here," he pointed to a line on the graph, "represents the amount of ezocane produced when you work the present number of hours a day, sixteen." He then drew in several other lines and filled in boxes on the charts. "Now I don't know the exact number of workers or precisely how much ezocane is produced each day, but we will say it is roughly 250. Now each worker produces this percentage of ezocane and each worker needs to be working this number of hours each interval. Either that or each worker will need to work extra hard and produce more in each interval and that way we could cut his hours. Now we have mentioned making improvements on the machines. That would also increase the amount of ezocane produced in each interval and would be an incentive for them to upgrade the machines, if possible." He tapped his chalk against the board pointedly.

85-27 was watching incredulously as 9-85 wrote frantically on the writing board. "What's all those scribbles you are making? It doesn't make any sense at all."

9-85 exhaled in disbelief. "I am trying to show you everything involved in adjusting the hours you work each day. It is not something that can be done just like that." He loudly snapped his fingers to accentuate the word 'that'. "By looking at it mathematically, we can verify what factors are involved, such as tools of production, number of workers, incentives to work, comfortableness of work room, etc. and pinpoint the factor that is easiest to improve. When that factor is improved, output should go up and *then* they may consider cutting your hours."

"It's just a bunch of gibberish to me," 17-07 shook his head in a confused daze.

9-85 fixed his eyes on 17-07 in an attempt to send some kind of reasoning ability his way. "Whether you understand it or not, these are the steps your superiors will go through before any changes will be made. In order for me to try to speed the process along, I *must* give them concrete, mathematical data — data that demonstrates that improvements made to the work room and the machinery will result in maximum efficiency and greater output of ezocane."

17-07 raised his hands dramatically in the air to beckon attention to himself. "Hey, everyone. I'm starting to understand it now. . ." he said with a far-off, hint-of-the-supernatural manner. When he noticed all eyes were on him, he jumped onto the table as a man who had just seen the light and now had embarked upon a mission. He clapped his hands rhythmically and tapped his feet hard on the table top. "The only way they will 'improve' things for us is if they are convinced we will work harder for them. So that they can get more ezocane — MORE MONEY." He swept a hand theatrically across the room towards the workers. "To put it simply — we will always get less. Doesn't that just grip you right here." He slapped his hand to his chest with pathos. "Why should we have to work so hard? Just to make those higher-ups rich?"

17-07's words stirred up frustration and anger in the workers. The workers chanted in protest to the grueling work they were forced to do.

"But there is another way out. We won't have to work hard any longer." 17-07 continued enthusiastically. He gestured with gusto toward 85-27. "Come here. Show them what we found." 17-07 gave a hand to 85-27 and helped him up beside him onto the meeting table.

Hesitating at first, 85-27 finally held the rose petals up for the workers to see. "These are from an amazing thing called a rose. It's powerful. And would you believe? The rose spoke to us. It told us that soon — very soon — we are going to be rescued from this horrible place." His face glowed with a hopeful light.

The workers cheered wildly.

"That's right." 17-07 concurred eagerly. After a disdainful glance at 9-85, 17-07 continued, "We're going to be rescued. We'll leave this rotten hole forever and go someplace where we won't ever have to work again. And just you wait and see, we'll get everything we want and be treated like gods." He pounded the air with a fist of triumph.

Shocked by how quickly the workers fell out of control, 9-85 looked over at 93-73 with an expression that pleaded for help.

93-73 nodded his realization of the situation and stepped forward. "The meeting is now ended," he announced loudly and conclusively. "You are now free to leave."

The workers continued to roar in excitement as they lifted 17-07 and 85-27 onto their shoulders and carried them out of the meeting room in a riotous show of their appreciation.

The overweight man who had been quietly lurking in the shadows at the back of the room stepped forward to 9-85. "As you can see, those workers can be hard to manage," he spat out the words in a business-like manner as he held out a hand to 9-85.

9-85 shook the man's hand as a smile of recognition spread across his face. "Well, now it comes back to me. 67. I haven't seen you in such a long time. I think the last time was in that logic class. You know, the one taught by that stodgy professor with the long beard."

"Of course, how could I forget?" 67 replied in his nasally voice. "You were one of his top students. He was constantly bragging about you." He chuckled at the recollection.

"Perhaps," 9-85 laughed heartily. "But there was a student who was far better than me — one he bragged about even more — and that was you." He nodded conclusively.

"Very well, I'll admit it." 67 smiled broadly. "It didn't come easy for me, though. I had to work hard. But I've reaped the rewards of my hard work. I'm now 1's personal logician."

"That *is* impressive." Although 9-85 was glad to see his old acquaintance, he had an uneasy feeling as he wondered why 67 was at this meeting in the first place.

93-73 efficiently stacked together his books and notes while keeping a subtle eye and ear on 9-85 and 67. With 67 being the only non-worker that attended the meeting, 93-73 quickly put him at the top of his list of spy suspects to report to 7,500. Raising an arched eyebrow, he silently congratulated himself on his own unfailing ability to continually remain on guard.

"By the way," 9-85 continued to 67, "I don't see how a formulated method can be used to control those workers. It's impossible to satisfy them because every one of them wants something different."

67 laughed. "Relax . . . you've always been one to go above and beyond." He leaned in close to 9-85's ear. "Remember, if it's not your job, don't worry about it." He chuckled mischievously and waved a hand in farewell. As he passed by 93-73, 67 gave him a curt nod and made his way out the meeting room's door.

In the hall, 67 cautiously slipped over to a stoical guard who stood in wait. "Tell 1 that I have a report to make to him." He informed the guard surreptitiously. "There was someone at that meeting who was acting in a suspicious manner. His number, I believe, was 93-73."

The guard nodded to 67 and marched off to relay the message. 67 looked back in the direction of the meeting room as he tapped his chin in thought.

The Way-Guide had traveled for some time in the *Forerunner* when a slew of gorslanchers blocked his path. They quickly covered the entire ship, scratching at and gnawing on the ship's machinery. The Way-Guide's heart skipped a beat but he swiftly switched on the *Forerunner's* electronic repellant shield, setting it at the highest level of power. The gorslanchers groaned in pain as they hammered hard on the ship in retaliating rage. Eventually, the gorslanchers, exhausted by the futility of their attack, concluded that the ship's repellant shield was not going to weaken. They reluctantly released their hold on the ship and turned to search out another target. The Way-Guide took just a moment to breathe a sigh of relief, but set his attention back on his ship and his mission.

The Way-Guide programmed the ship to scan for any damage. The ship reported that its left wing had been loosened and needed repair. Noticing a small planet nearby, the Way-Guide headed his ship in its direction.

After landing, the Way-Guide put on his out-of-ship gear and exited the *Forerunner* to make the necessary repairs. He set up his equipment and went straight to work on the wing. He replaced the necessary casing and tightened it securely with several bolts. As soon as he was done, he gathered the tools together and was about to reenter the ship when he heard a hypnotic humming in his ear.

The Way-Guide turned around and saw a huge, phosphorescent, grayish cloud skirting eerily along the ground, slowly coming toward him. Inside the cloud, lightning sparked in a mesmerizing pattern. The Way-Guide stared, entranced by the cloud. His arms grew numb and he unknowingly dropped the equipment. The cloud drew closer and brushed against the Way-Guide's feet. A stronger magnetic pull drew him toward the cloud. The cloud billowed up to him, raising itself as if to look the Way-Guide straight in the eyes.

The Way-Guide irresistibly reached out for the cloud and touched it. As his hand was covered by the cloud, his hand grew larger and was imbued with strength. The cloud floated around him, embracing him and the Way-Guide looked down at the cloud. As the lightning sparked within it, he noticed shadows, which resembled a large, almost friendly, smile on what he took to be the cloud's face. Everywhere the cloud touched him, his body grew larger and stronger. The Way-Guide heard Infinity's steadfast voice calling to him from the microphone within his helmet. "Get away from the cloud. Get away from it. The cloud is evil."

The Way-Guide shook his head, forcing his mind free from the hypnotic trance. He immediately stepped back away from the cloud. He struggled to pull his arms and legs out from the cloud's grasp, desperately scraping off every last clinging fleecy tendril of the cloud. Looking back, he could see that the cloud was still reaching out, determined to envelope him again. He raced into the *Forerunner* and securely closed the ship's door behind him. Once he had clambered into the pilot's chair, he started the ship. As the ship was leaving the planet, the cloud continued in pursuit. As it tried to engulf the ship, the Way-Guide, with a resolute determination, put the ship into an ultra-high speed in order to pull away from the cloud.

When he had escaped from the cloud, the Way-Guide established a link with the *Ghost III*. "What was that?" he asked Infinity in bewilderment. He closely examined his arms and hands, making certain he was indeed free from the cloud's strange powers.

"That," Infinity told him matter-of-factly, "was the Cloud of Deception. It may give you power, but those are ephemeral powers. It covers you, engulfs you and tricks you into believing you are omnipotent. But the cloud is fickle. After it sucks from you every last ounce of your strength, it slips away quickly. You are then left weak and helpless."

Chapter Twenty-Nine

Overwhelmed by the activities of the day, 2-45 decided to retreat to the seclusion of his bedroom. Although this room was simple in design, it was a simple that mirrored the exquisite taste of the wealthy owner. While the furniture, lamps, pictures and ceramics were of a high quality, they were not ornate or gaudy. The room, being without windows and containing few doors, was relatively closed off from the rest of the house, and therefore the rest of the world. The walls were made of a drab grey stone marbled with a green crystal-like substance. While cold to the touch, the stone kept the room warm and cozy. Boasting row after row of portraits of 2-45's ancestors, some even predating the great migration from the Planet of Light, only a small percentage of which 2-45 knew anything about, the walls held a power over 2-45 by ensuring that he always felt watched. He piled the pillows high on his bed and lounged back to relax as best as he could with an audience. He was aware that 1-13 would soon be contacting him for an update, but he figured that would not be for some time. So, right now, he decided to settle into bed with a good book and concern himself with 1-13 later.

2-45 had barely read the first words his eyes landed on when a movement out of the corner of his eye distracted his attention. Despite a nagging foreboding, he hesitantly looked up over his book to discover he was not alone. It defied reality for 2-45's ancestors to be hovering down from their portraits to surround 2-45's bed, but he accepted this unusual event as normal because his exhaustion had already transported his brain to that point at which the unusual makes more sense than the usual.

Once each ancestor had taken their place around 2-45's bed, much like mournful relatives attending a funeral, 2-45 managed to recognize the one who stood directly to his left. "Ah, grandfather," 2-45 blurted out in a surprise that was mixed with apprehension. His apprehension did not stem from a fear of ghosts but from concern that his grandfather would scold and punish him as he was wont to do while alive. "Is there some special occasion that brings you here?"

2-45's ghostly grandfather was a tall, heavy man with a full grey beard. He scrunched his nose in disdain. "An occasion . . . ye-e-esss . . . a very . . . depressing . . . occasion."

Standing beside his grandfather was a shorter relative 2-45 could not place, but he recalled how his full head of dark hair that seemed to fly everywhere had annoyed him. "You know what occasion we are talking about," he told 2-45 with a knowing tilt of his head.

Another relative . . . some great-great grand uncle, 2-45 assumed . . . stood to the right. He was tall and thin with an extremely long neck. He leaned over the bed to look straight at 2-45. "It is not a funeral, because you are not dead." He looked back at the other ancestors. "But, we would be better off if it were a funeral . . . this occasion is much more dismal."

2-45 sunk deeper under his covers as he tightened his grip on his book. "W-w-what do you mean?" The sudden appearance of his ancestors was enough to make him forget the dismal occasion to which they were referring.

2-45's grandfather grabbed him by the hair as he had often

done when 2-45 was a child and used the hair to tilt 2-45's head to look at him. "You know what we are talking about . . . and it is not just your demotion . . . you are humiliating us with your constant efforts to leave this planet and its opportunities for family wealth and honor."

"But, I don't—" 2-45 started to stammer the reasons the Planet of Darkness was not a place of opportunities for honor and how the Planet of Light was a much better place to accumulate wealth, but he knew he could not argue with his ancestors. Instead, he drew their attention to something else. "Well, I have been given an invitation to meet with the Mystic of the Vale . . ."

2-45's ancestors paused and looked at each other in scrutinizing thought. 2-45 at first thought their exchanged expressions were critical, but when he saw his grandfather nod approvingly, he exhaled a relieved sigh.

"Yes," his grandfather agreed. "I have heard of this Mystic of the Vale. She is a wise woman. See that you do exactly as she says." After these words, the ancestors dispersed back to their portraits and 2-45 tried to refocus his attention to his book.

Unfortunately, just as 2-45 had flipped to the page where he had left off, his butler butted into the room.

After enduring so many aggravating events one right after another all day long, 2-45 found that his butler popping in so unexpectedly was the stick that toppled the stack. He pressed his lips together in a perturbed frown as he looked up. "What is it?"

"1-13 has arrived. He says he must speak with you." The butler raised his balding head in defiance. "He informs me that he was expected." One side of his mouth curled with contempt.

2-45 recognized in his butler's intonation the subtext of "If 1-13 was expected, what are you doing in bed?" 2-45's eyes wandered to the ceiling wearily, as he set aside his book. "Tell him I'll meet him in the antechamber." It was only out of sentiment for his father that 2-45 had not yet fired the butler, but moments like these he came close. *Yes,* 2-45 agreed with himself, *this would have been the perfect time to give that butler a lecture on the proper etiquette of servants – but how many times have I already done so with no results.*

The butler tilted his head, disapproving the use of the dusty antechamber for a meeting, but finally nodded and left to deliver the message to its intended destination.

2-45 pried himself out of his comfortable bed. *The most inopportune time for him to come,* he mumbled to himself with growing exasperation. *In fact, if 1-13 had not come, a few minutes from now I might have even had time for one of my revitosaline baths.* He extracted his dressing gown from where it had made itself cozy on the back of a cushioned chair. After throwing it on, he slammed his way out of the door to the antechamber adjacent to his bedroom.

Just as 2-45 entered the antechamber, 1-13 followed the butler into the room through the opposite door. This spacious room was cluttered with antique furniture, dusty bookshelves, and untamed climbing plants that conquered every corner, forming a veritable jungle in all directions. Even a few of the portraits – those with the most disapproving glares – had lost their way in this wilderness. 2-45 often wondered if an exploration of this room would turn up any valuable pieces of treasure . . . but, the only time he attempted it resulted in a book falling on his head and a nearly unstoppable sneezing fit.

1-13 carried one of his spy creatures in his arms. 2-45 looked down at the creature and assumed the appropriate action was to give it a smile and a wave of the hand. The spy creature's response was an infuriated hiss.

2-45 smiled graciously and attempted to ignore the creature's outburst.

Either 1-13 had not noticed the creature's reaction or chose to ignore it. Patting it on its head, 1-13 opened the conversation matter-of-factly: "So, are you ready to begin . . .?"

As the butler left, the door banged shut behind him and the spy creature leapt out of 1-13's arms with a whoosh and a whiz. 1-13 chased after it while it weaved its way behind a large cabinet. The darkness the spy creature was plunged into forced it to readjust the settings of its binocular-like eyes. After doing so, it could see every cobweb, dust ball, and dirt speck that had been hidden here for years. It wiggled its way from behind the cabinet to underneath a table. Its tiny ear openings now tuned in on 1-13's irritated voice, "You fiendish little creature, you. Get back over here at once or you will be in serious trouble." The spy creature poked its head out from under the table and could see 1-13 glaring down at it. It chirped at him questioningly, with hopes that if it made its plea as pitiful as possible, 1-13 would let it continue its exploration.

"Now is not the time for this nonsense," 1-13 scolded. "Get back here at once."

The spy creature sighed and slinked its way out from under the table, its mouth curved down into a pout.

1-13 gently scooped up the creature and stroked its head. "We'll play later," he assured it and added with a peeved expression, "Right now there's work to be done."

2-45 eyed the spy creature nervously. "I hope he's under control now." While he intended it to be more of a casual comment, it came off much brusquer. At this point there was no doubt in his mind that everything was trying to infringe on his time of rest.

1-13 turned to 2-45 with an arched eyebrow and a self-aggrandizing smirk. "I keep *everyone* who works for me under *control*." He carried the creature to a sofa where he sat and gestured for 2-45 to sit beside him.

2-45 was tempted to remind 1-13 that, as a guest in his mansion, he should not be the one giving orders. But, he refrained and casually moved over to sit where he had indicated.

"Now *tell* me . . ." 1-13 scratched the spy creature under its chin. ". . . have you found out anything of *interest* about 2,040?" He said it in a relatively bland manner, although it was obvious to 2-45 he was attempting to mask his curiosity.

With the intent of keeping his guest in suspense, 2-45 took a deep breath and smiled mischievously before continuing. "Absolutely," he blurted out and then fell silent. He determined to let him wait a bit . . . and wonder.

1-13 nodded to 2-45 to proceed.

2-45 nodded to 1-13 his acknowledgment of 1-13's nod.

1-13 nodded to 2-45 his acknowledgment that 2-45 was trying to put him off. "Very *well*, 2-45," he smiled a smile that was for the moment good-natured but possessed a time bomb ready to go off if pushed too far, "*are* you going to *tell* me what I want to *know,* or do I need to find *other methods* to *convince* you to *do so*?" 1-13 raised an eyebrow that could have been the match ready to light the fuse.

Since he had been forced into working for 1-13, 2-45 wanted to get even with him in some way. He hoped he had just now succeeded at that, but realized he did not want to push 1-13 too far. "No need. I'll tell you . . ." 2-45 replied nonchalantly. ". . . as soon as you ask." He was pleased he had succeeded in making 1-13 annoyed.

"Then . . . I'm *asking.*"

After pausing a few more tantalizing seconds . . . "It's about 2,040's model." 2-45 fingered the dust on the side table right next to him. "The one the committee is planning to put into operation. I found out that there *is* something wrong with it.

1-13 knitted his eyebrows. "Are you *sure?* What *is wrong* with it?"

"Of course I'm sure." 2-45 tried to appear calm even though he was irritated that 1-13 would question his word. "I was sitting right next to 9-85, 2,040's assistant, when he was looking over the model." In a confident manner, he flicked the dust off his fingers. "He kept on repeating over and over to himself that the model was wrong and contained errors he had missed."

A clever smile spread across 1-13's face as if defusing the time bomb. "*Perfect,*" he exhaled with contentment. His eyes glimmered with excitement at the anticipation of his approaching triumph. As he absorbed the information 2-45 had provided him, 1-13 ran his finger from the top of the spy creature's head down to where its shoulder would have been if it had any. Finally, he stood to leave, but, decided to ask one last question first. "I *suppose* you have no idea *what errors* the model contains?"

2-45 had to keep himself from choking with surprise at the thought that anyone would even expect him to understand a mathematical model well enough to recognize errors in it. "Absolutely not." He tried to hide his surprise. "But, if I saw it again, I might be able to recognize the page 9-85 was looking at."

"Well, that's something," 1-13 said slightly perturbed. "Your assistance is appreciated, and I will contact you again when your assistance is needed further."

As 1-13 left the antechamber, his spy creature glared over his shoulder at 2-45.

2-45 pursed his lips in annoyance, but recalled that the perfect way to retreat from life's irritations was in the relaxing waters of his revitosaline bath.

Passing through the foyer, 1-13 waved off the butler's offer to guide him to the front door. "I can find the door *without* your help," 1-13 told him and added a "thank you" which functioned more as an exclamation point than an expression of gratitude.

As he was exiting the mansion, 1-13 nearly ran into 7,500 approaching the front door. Taken aback at running into 1-13, 7,500 smiled an apology and sidestepped out of his way.

As if he had not even noticed him, 1-13 continued on past him toward the walkway leading from the mansion. But, before he had gone too far and before 7,500 had entered the mansion, 1-13 turned around. "I almost forgot," he called to him abruptly, eying him as he would any other intriguing specimen. "I must let you know how *sorry* I am about your *losing* your assistant. It must be difficult." He mentioned this not because he was 'sorry', but because he was curious about how 7,500 would react.

7,500's smile froze as he allowed himself time to adjust to this unexpected remark. "I . . . uh, well," he stammered, unsure of what to say because his mental filing system lacked dialogue for this particular circumstance. Finally, he pulled out a well-used file that could serve multiple tasks. "Thank you . . . that's very kind of you." He paused a moment and tugged on his earlobe as he added, "You don't mind me asking how you found out?" He laughed in a nervous, good-natured way, almost too nervous and too good-natured.

"Not at all," 1-13 replied knowingly. "I am the *Persuader* who was assigned the duty of interrogating your former apprentice in regards to his *rebellious* behavior."

7,500 shrugged unaffectedly. "Can't understand how he turned out that way." Trying to appear genuinely perplexed, he continued, "I hope next time I am given a more trustworthy apprentice." He waved an all-too-eager 'good-bye' and abruptly turned to enter the mansion.

As he walked away down the path, 1-13 analyzed 7,500's reaction. *The way his face tightened, the way his voice fluctuated, and the way he kept shifting away from me,* he pondered to himself with the calculating rationale of a mathematician, *these all indicate that he has something to hide. Definitely suspicious,* he concluded. *No doubt 7,500 had some involvement in 93-73's rebellious actions. I wouldn't even be surprised if he had a hand in his arrest.* But, 1-13 decided not to act on his suspicions at the moment. *Right now the most important thing to do is to gather some concrete evidence of the error in 2,040's model,* he reminded himself as he stroked his spy creature on the head. "And that is where you come in." He smiled down at it. The spy creature responded with an enthusiastic chirp.

Inside the mansion, 7,500 glanced about the room with a

voracious glimmer on his face. He enjoyed his frequent visits here, not necessarily because he liked the family, as most people thought, but because he liked the wealth. His family and 2-45's family had been close for years, and the prestige of 7,500's family and the wealth of 2-45's family kept them close. In fact, while it had not yet been officially announced, 7,500 and 5-07, 2-45's sister, were, more or less, engaged to be married.

The butler approached 7,500, eager to offer his assistance. "It is nice to have you here again, sir." His chubby face and bushy eyebrows jiggled with each syllable. He emphasized the bow he gave to 7,500 as if he could transport the visual to 2-45 to prove his disdain for him.

7,500 slipped off his cape. "It's nice to be here," 7,500 agreed as he carelessly tossed his cape to the butler.

The butler quickly caught the cape and turned to hang it up. "I've been hearing many compliments about you lately," he told 7,500, in a manner that was an uncomfortable combination of forceful emphasis and off the cuff.

"Oh, really?" 7,500 replied with a tone that indicated he knew it too well. "From whom?"

"Oh, just here and there."

"I see." 7,500 glanced at a golden timepiece hanging gracefully on the wall. "I believe 5-07 is waiting for me." He moved past the butler in his eagerness.

"Yes, sir," the butler agreed. "5-07 and her mother are in the drawing room."

7,500 waved for the butler to take the lead, when the mother of 2-45 and 5-07 entered the room and scurried up to him.

"Ah, 7,500, I am so glad you are here," the mother blurted out. In reality, she did not look like she was 'glad' but looked like she was trying hard not to burst into tears.

Shifting uncomfortably, 7,500 forced himself to pat her on the shoulder. "So, now, tell me, what is the matter?" Actually, he could care less 'what the matter was,' and was just simply annoyed at the way her tears had smeared her eye-makeup.

The mother wiped the moistness from her eyes. "It's my daughter. She just told me that she has changed her mind and does *not* want to marry you. Oh, what I've had to put up with. A son that flies off to distant planets on joy-rides and a daughter who—" she gulped, unable to say anymore until she had caught her breath. "And I have been so looking forward to the big wedding."

7,500 chuckled a chuckle meant to appear sympathetic but displayed instead a distinct arrogance. "Don't let that bother you." His voice exuded an air of confidence. "She has said that before and changed her mind again." He paused to look into a nearby mirror and carefully adjusted the curls that framed his forehead and ensured that his own eyeliner had not smeared. "I'll go and speak with her now."

"Yes, you do that. I know you're the one who can talk some sense into her silly little head." Her face beamed with a revived hope.

7,500 nodded succinctly and slipped into the drawing room where he found 5-07 leaning back against the wall with a pout on her face. She wore a long flowing dress of gossamer material with an attached cape. The colors in the dress shimmered with the light, varying from a dark bronze to a light ivory. When 5-07 noticed 7,500 entering, she turned away from him, facing the wall with a resolute aloofness.

Sighing wearily and acquiring an even blanker look, 7,500 approached her with an assumed consideration. "You look a little upset," he stated the obvious.

"I don't want to talk to you. The wedding's off." She lifted her chin and pulled her shoulder away from him.

"Yes, your mother told me that," 7,500 agreed routinely. Annoyed by a strand of her hair that had flipped out of place, he dutifully smoothed it in a pretense of thoughtfulness. "So, what is it you would like this time to keep the engagement on?" He dully pressed his lips together and waited expectantly.

5-07 turned back around to face him. "It's my brother. I'm

worried about him." Her eyes widened with concern. "He's been so unhappy since he's come back. I think it's because he's lost his position as a Propaganda Specialist." Her fingers fidgeted nervously with the edge of her cape. "Of course it may also have something to do with this Mystic of the Vale he keeps mumbling about. Could you do something to help him?"

7,500 laughed, primarily because he was relieved that what she wanted this time was relatively simple and inexpensive. Not only that, but the mention of the Mystic of the Vale piqued his interest. "Certainly I'll do something. Whatever needs to be done to please my pretty little thing," he said, with more pride in his acting ability than his bride-to-be.

"Oh, thank you." She embraced him. "And we will announce the wedding soon."

"Naturally," 7,500 agreed as he counted in his mind the gold coins he would soon possess. "You care a lot about your brother, don't you?" His face took on a ponderous expression as he filed away in his brain this bit of information for some future use.

She glanced away with melancholy. "Well, he and mother are all I have." She twisted a wispy strand of hair near her face.

7,500 gave her a look that indicated his pride had been dealt a blow.

Taking his hint, she quickly added, "besides you, of course."

"So, that's *all* you have?" He tried to stifle a laugh. He fastidiously pulled the wisp of hair out of her hand.

5-07 reluctantly gave in, "All right . . . there's the mansion and the money, too. You know what I'm trying to say." She breathed out a puff of air to ease her frustrations.

"Of course," 7,500 agreed with an amused chuckle. "And if all *I* had was what *you* have, I wouldn't have a care in the world." He indulged himself in a momentary daydream of future wealth.

5-07 joined him in his laughter, both to be polite and

because she wanted him to stay happy enough to do what he could for her brother.

He patted 5-07 affectionately on her cheek. "Perhaps I should talk to your brother now?"

"Yes, I think he's in his room." She led him back into the foyer.

Chapter Thirty

The bubbling turquoise streams of water swelled over like a waterfall down the glazed sandstone sides lining the spacious circular bathtub. The water of this revitosaline bath possessed a gel-like consistency because it contained molecules of parsaline, a substance that when absorbed by the skin sent messages to the muscles via the nervous system, telling the muscles to relax. The results were that, no matter how stressed someone was, a revitosaline bath was guaranteed to settle them down.

2-45 dipped a finger into the water, testing the temperature. *Just a tad too warm.* He adjusted the thermostat on the wall that regulated the water's temperature. He was just preparing to toss his robe aside and step into the water when he heard decided footsteps and voices in the hall. He retied his robe and stepped out into the hall to see what was happening.

"Well, well." 7,500 approached 2-45, hoping his remark would appear laid back, "don't you look cozy." He indicated 2-45's robe with a playful smile.

Feeling uneasy, 2-45 pulled his robe tighter together. "So, what's this about?" he asked his sister who came up behind 7,500.

"7,500 promised to help you get your job back," 5-07 told him eagerly.

"Really?" 2-45 eyed 7,500 skeptically. "How does he plan to do that?"

7,500 patted 5-07 on the shoulder and eyed her paternalistically. "I didn't exactly promise that." He then quickly turned to 2-45 to avoid 5-07's glare. "But, I will certainly do something."

"If you don't . . ." 5-07 told him threateningly.

"I will," 7,500 tried to reassure her. "But . . ." He condescendingly gestured for 5-07 to leave. "Now, my dear, leave the men to take care of this puzzle. I'm sure you have some little this or that to attend to like women always do." He then steered 2-45 out of the hall and accompanied him back through the bathroom and into the antechamber. Here, 7,500 lounged on the couch, sinking deeply on its soft pillows, relaxed but acquiring a thoughtful pose.

2-45 stood with his arms crossed, annoyed and perplexed. He had not personally invited 7,500 into his room and he almost wished the couch was on wheels so he could swoosh him out of the room and down the stairs. The reason he *almost* and not *for certain* wanted to do this was because he was a little curious about what that *something* was that 7,500 was planning to do for him. "I suppose you want me to hand over a substantial amount of money on the pretext that there is a slight chance you might be able to get my old job back, is that it?"

Sitting up slightly, 7,500 waved off 2-45's remark. "Not at all. I just told her I would help you so she would keep the wedding on." He then smiled cleverly with a let's-get-busy-with-what-is-really-important attitude. "Now, what I want you to answer me is — what do you know about the Mystic of the Vale?" His eyes glowed eagerly.

2-45 looked at 7,500, a little surprised. "What do *you* know about her?" he asked as he sat on the coffee table facing him, just as eager to discuss the Mystic of the Vale as 7,500.

7,500 became suddenly animated knowing his little bit of information would tease 2-45's curiosity. "I know she's clever and can do some amazing things. Perhaps she can even help you regain your position." He eyed the fingernails of his right hand and polished them on his left sleeve. "But I've heard you can't see her without an invitation." He looked back at 2-45 with an anticipative sideways glance.

"Well, I have an invitation. It's right over here." 2-45 moved over to a desk, opened a drawer, and pulled out the letter the wolf had given him. He brought the letter back and sat on the couch next to 7,500, handing it to him.

7,500 read over the letter carefully. "This *does* seem like it's written in her style." Satisfied, he handed the letter back. "To tell you the truth, I've always wanted to meet her but was afraid to go there alone and uninvited." He tapped the letter confidently, "With that, I'm sure we could get in."

Folding the letter, 2-45 nodded. "I was thinking about going to see her, but these directions the Duke of Distraction gave me are pretty sketchy." He held up the notes the Duke had made for him.

"That's where a historian proves useful." 7,500 could not restrain himself from rubbing his hands together in anticipation. "I have some accurate and detailed maps. With them, we could find her without any problem. Once we get an audience with the Mystic of the Vale, even if she doesn't help you, I'll see that you get your position back, all right?" He smiled, trying to appear good-natured, but 2-45 noticed something in his expression that reminded him of a gorslancher he had just recently dealt with who hungrily swallowed up a spaceship.

"All right," 2-45 reluctantly agreed.

7,500 stood and clasped his hands together, eager to start working. "Then I'll find those maps and we'll leave first thing tomorrow." He waved enthusiastically and left the antechamber.

Looking at the letter, 2-45 was overpowered once more with

a desire to leave the Planet of Darkness. *Perhaps the Mystic of the Vale knows how I can get to the Planet of Light.* As he glanced over the letter, his eyes fell on the signature. He puzzled over why the Mystic of the Vale would sign her name the Shepherdess of the Valley, but he quickly tossed the thought from his mind. Not wanting to deal with any more puzzles, he opened the drawer and dropped the letter in. He knew what he needed now was the peaceful, calming waters of his revitosaline bath. And he hoped that this time he would not be interrupted.

There existed a region in space between the Planet of Light and the Planet of Darkness, a gray area, slightly lit by the light emanating from the Planet of Light but, also, slightly darkened by the shadows from the Planet of Darkness. It was in this area where Infinity's path was blocked by the red, glowing web of electricity, a web energized by a space station maintained by a powerful and sinister man known as the Guardian.

Even though the Guardian was being paid by the Dark Tyrant to oversee the web, the Guardian was so conceited that he maintained the space station as if it were his own little kingdom. In fact, the control center of the space station was set up like a veritable throne room with a golden rug leading to a massive throne near which sentries stood at attention on either side like rows of replicated uniforms. He even commanded his men to address him as 'your majesty'.

The control center was oval-shaped. One half was focused on the technology of maintaining the web and the space station while the other half focused on the Guardian's leadership. The top half of the maintenance side was made of clear ezocane which permitted a view of the area surrounding the space station. The bottom half provided room for a large number of control boards which maintained the glowing web and the life support and security devices for the space station. The other half of the control center was the Guardian's little throne chamber. The walls of this half were covered with a black and red velveteen material. Six marble columns lined the walls and held gold planters. These planters were home to an unusual form of sentient plant which watched the activities that took place in the control center with eager anticipation. Oval shaped leaves hugged the side of the planters as the plants pulled their spherical, mushroom-like heads up to peak over the edge. The "heads" seemed to bobble in laughter at the chaotic world of humans.

The Guardian lounged confidently on his throne with one leg swung over the arm rest and his hands clasped behind his head. He was tall with dark hair and narrow, cagey eyes. He wore a beige cotton shirt that, instead of being buttoned up, was wrapped about him then tied together and his pants were a dark brown with hems tucked into dark gray boots. He looked over at a short, rounded man, one of many men who acted as lookout, watching the viewing screen and operating the controls. "Do you see anything?" the Guardian asked expectantly.

"No, your majesty," the lookout replied.

"Good," the Guardian grinned. While relieved to hear that all was clear, he still looked toward the viewing screen with a growing agitation as he rubbed his hands along the arms of the throne. He knew something was about to happen and he needed to be ready. Since the screen was clear, he was pleased that he had more time to prepare.

"Are we expecting anything, your majesty?" the lookout asked.

"I was told by the Dark Tyrant that *Infinity* might be passing by." He emphasized the word 'Infinity' in a manner that gave credence to his enemy. "I personally suspect that once Infinity sees the web, he will change his mind, turn around and race back to where he came from." While he had a measure of confidence in this happening, he still had a premonition that he would eventually have to face Infinity himself.

"But what if he doesn't, your majesty?" the lookout wondered with wide eyes. "What if he decides to take over this space station?"

"Then . . ." the Guardian stood, assertively, assured that his lifetime of acquiring skill and power were about to pay off. ". . . I will show him who's in charge here. If he's smart, he will leave quickly. If not," he clutched his hands together to demonstrate his strength, "he won't leave at all." A pale, grim determination swept across his steel, icy face.

"He could never win in a fight against you, your majesty," the lookout agreed with loyal enthusiasm.

"Damn well he couldn't." The Guardian strode over to a nearby steel door decorated with gold filigree and looked at the door — or, more appropriately, mentally looked at what was behind it — fondly. "Especially since I have my little pet on hand . . ."

The lookout shrank back. "You're not going to let it out again, are you, your majesty?"

"I sure as hell will," the Guardian chuckled self-confidently. A sadistic glimmer played about his eyes. "I miss it." He pressed some buttons on the door to unlock it. The door slid open.

A pale and astonished expression spread across the lookout's face as he stood and took a few steps back. The others in the room followed his example.

Into the room flowed a phosphorescent, grayish cloud. "Ah, my pet, come to me." He held his arms out to the cloud. The cloud sparked with flashes of lightning as it skirted toward the Guardian. The Guardian embraced the cloud and the cloud wrapped itself around the Guardian. As the cloud increased the Guardian's size and strength, he grinned a smug grin. "With all this power the cloud gives me, no one — not even Infinity — can stop me."

◄◆◆◆►

In his office, 7,500 found and dusted off several old, leather-bound books containing maps and information about places now kept in clandestine shadows since the Dark Tyrant came into power. 7,500 was certain the maps would lead him to the Mystic of the Vale. He stuffed the books into a pouch and slung it over his shoulder. He then headed for manual labor room 15. There he scanned the workers and noticed, among them, 17-07 tediously sorting through the freshly processed sheets of ezocane. 7,500 casually made his way to the table where 17-07 was working and pretended to inspect one of the sheets of ezocane.

"There's work to be done," 7,500 mumbled under his breath, after which, he surreptitiously slipped a piece of paper into 17-07's hand.

While 7,500 wandered out of the room in as nonchalant a manner as possible, 17-07 peeked at the note, which read: "The rebellion must take place tomorrow." 17-07 glanced over his shoulder and noticed 7,500 postponing his departure in the doorway. He gave 7,500 a furtive nod of understanding and moved over to the ezocane processors and tossed the paper to its fate of destruction in the burning inferno.

Following his self-made agenda, 7,500 next met with 2-45 at his mansion and from there they both drove off on their Barso-Cycles in search of the Mystic of the Vale. The endless, tedious surroundings were filled with rocky hills and jagged cliffs.

2-45 was amazed at how, with the use of 7,500's maps, they were able to find the Mystic's house without getting lost. The route was labeled out in a straight-forward manner. Still, their journey would not have taken as long as it did if the path, itself, had not been in such disrepair. More than once they had to stop to clear boulders or fallen trees out of their way, and at one point they had to lug their Barso-Cycles over a dilapidated bridge held together by frayed ropes and slats of rotting wood in order to make it across a gaping gorge. As they approached their destination, there was no doubt in their minds that they had arrived at the Mystic's house. It was a large well-lit dome brightly painted in a pie-plate of alternating colors. At first glance the grounds seemed pleasant and fun. The well-manicured 'lawn' was sprinkled with 'flowers' that appealed to the senses. Upon closer examination, they realized the 'lawn' was nothing more than green-painted slate and the 'flowers' were colored stones of red, blue and yellow.

Approaching the front door, they found their path blocked by what 2-45 at first took for a large statue of a bald man sitting on the ground cross-legged. It suddenly moved, turning, glaring, and pointing its finger at them threateningly. 2-45 jumped back, startled.

7,500 tried to appear unfazed. "We are here to see the Mystic of the Vale."

The bald man's face contorted into an even more threatening sneer as he jabbed his finger at them once more.

Pulling out the letter that the wolf had given him, 2-45 gathered his courage and approached cautiously. "Perhaps you're upset because you assume we don't have an invitation . . . well, here it is." He held out the letter.

The bald man ignored the letter. He narrowed his eyes, shook his head in disdain and, again, scornfully poked his finger at them.

2-45 looked over at 7,500, hoping to find some clue as to the meaning behind the man's unusual behavior and what they should do in response to it.

The total amount of knowledge 7,500 had for this situation was summed up in a shrug. With a blasé-fare expression, 7,500 sauntered up to the bald man. "Would you mind explaining what you mean when you—" He pointed a finger at the man. "—do this?"

The bald man angrily shook his head once more, snarled, and stabbed 7,500 in the chest with his finger so hard that 7,500 was pushed backwards.

7,500 had to catch his breath, but tried to appear unintimidated. "Are you capable of speaking?"

The bald man's glare darkened.

2-45 questioned in his mind the wisdom of their excursion altogether. He tugged at 7,500's sleeve. "Maybe we should just leave."

7,500 nodded as he muttered, "We will get nowhere with this mental case."

Just then a bouncy, bumbley-puff of a woman popped out the front door.

"What is it — what is it? What's going on out here?" she asked in an effervescent manner, while looking about everywhere except at the two guests.

2-45 could not conceal his disappointment. "Are you the Mystic of the Vale?"

"Yes, yes. What do you want, young man?" she asked as she adjusted her shawl around her chubby shoulders. Turning to glance at 2-45, she blinked in a distracted manner, as if her eyes refused to focus on any one thing.

2-45 determinedly held the letter out to her. "We have this invitation, but this man here still wouldn't let us in." He eyed the bald-headed man with growing impatience.

The Mystic of the Vale narrowed her eyes while looking over the letter. "Never mind about him." She waved her hand as if she were swatting at a fly. Even though her attention was on the letter, she was referring to the bald man. "He's just very, very jealous of you. Would you believe, he found his way to me only after years and years of searching through perilous regions, suffering starvation, and enduring vicious beatings. When he landed on my doorstep, he was a thin, bruised, bleeding skeleton of a man. I would say you two had an easier time of it." After her last comment, she peeped at them from over the letter with a slightly out of place giggle.

7,500 stepped gingerly past the bald man and to the Mystic. "You will see us, won't you?" His beseeching face radiated a genuine eagerness.

As she continued to read the letter, the Mystic of the Vale's face scrunched into such a quizzical expression that 2-45 assumed she would certainly send them away. But, on the contrary, after she finished reading, her face beamed with a sudden pleasant smile aimed directly at 7,500. "Of course, of course, of course." She promptly guided them inside.

Bouncing along in her high-heeled shoes, she bubbled her way along the entry hallway like a bouquet of balloons. 7,500 and 2-45 followed her with anxious anticipation. The continuous, star-studded hallway twisted and turned and turned and twisted, going on for what seemed to be several miles. But, no matter how long they continued on this unending hallway, the Mystic of the Vale never lost her breath and her bounce was as consistently bouncy as it was when they started. Finally, they reached an alcove that housed a large double door decorated with giant rainbowed pinwheels.

With great enthusiasm, the Mystic of the Vale danced her hands in the direction of the doors and, with a magical force, the pinwheels spun and the doors flew open. "I am sure this is what you've been waiting for," she announced, bobbling her head back and forth in excitement.

2-45 craned his head around the corner, curious to know exactly what it was that he had been waiting for. The Mystic of the Vale gestured vigorously for 2-45 and 7,500 to go ahead and enter the room ahead of her. The gesture coincided with the lighting up of something inside the room which, in this otherwise dark room, would draw the attention of the visitors.

Making his way inside, 2-45 noticed in front of him the most unusual 'something' he had ever seen in his life. It was a glowing conglomeration of hundreds of three-dimensional shapes (rectangles, triangles, spheres, etc.) that twisted and turned until they formed larger three-dimensional shapes. The rearrangement of the shapes was not robotic, but their movement was so close to being lifelike that 2-45 wondered whether the shapes were indeed alive.

7,500 pushed his way past 2-45 and to the glowing shapes. When he stood in front of it, he held his arms out in a pose of respect. "Ah, now I know what this is," he announced with a gasp of excitement as he stared at it with amazement. "This must be . . ."

The Mystic of the Vale finished for him, "Yes, this is my oracle." She twirled, she beamed, and she finally fluttered down next to the oracle in a meditative pose.

"Yes," 7,500 said, holding his hands toward it as if hoping to absorb some of its energy, "the Oracle of the Vale. The answer to all questions, the solution to all problems, and the guide into the future. How I have longed for this moment." He shook his head several times, having difficulty believing that after all of this time he had finally reached his lifelong goal.

2-45 looked at 7,500 with a questioning sideways glance. "So, you knew the Mystic had an oracle all this time?" he asked him with a slightly irritated look.

Incredulous surprise fell over 7,500's face. "Of course," he replied with a hint of disdain. "Certainly you have heard about it too."

2-45's agitation grew. "Rumors about an oracle . . . yes, but I had no idea where . . ." 2-45 shook his head. "You could have at least told me that was why you wanted me to help you get in to see her."

"You helped me?" 7,500 protested, angrily, "I was the one with the maps."

"And I had the invitation," 2-45 reminded him with a rigid stare suggesting he was coming to the end of his patience.

The Mystic of the Vale buoyantly bounded up to admire her oracle. "So magnificently beautiful, wouldn't you agree?" she squealed with joy as if completely unaware of 2-45 and 7,500's brewing arguments.

2-45 turned his attention once more to the oracle and studied it trying to understand how something like the oracle could be considered beautiful. He tapped his lower lip with his index finger in thought. "I suppose you could say that it does have some artistic quality," 2-45 was finally able to find one aspect concerning the oracle's appearance to which he could agree.

"It knows everything. It answers anything you ask. For example:" She leaned in close to the oracle. With a suddenly deep and dramatic intonation, she asked, "Oracle, look into the minds of these two gentlemen and tell me what reason they had for journeying here to see me?"

The oracle's shapes swiveled and spun until they formed a resemblance of a man wearing a hat. "To learn something," the oracle replied in a flat, unemotional voice. In finality, the shapes tipped their 'hat'.

Holding her hands palms upwards, on either side of her head, the Mystic of the Vale smiled in a 'now isn't that the most amazing thing you have ever seen' manner. 7,500 nodded, thoroughly impressed.

While 2-45 sincerely hoped it was true that the oracle could help to guide him, he was still not convinced. "So what is it?" he asked, tapping his chin in thought. "Is it some type of computer? And is it limited in the types of questions it can answer?"

The Mystic of the Vale wiggled a bit, trying to hold back a chuckle. "A computer only knows the information it is given." She opened her eyes wide to emphasize her next remark. "The oracle knows everything: past, present, future. You can ask any question you like." And lifting a finger of suggestion, she added in a slightly condescending tone, "It is especially good at answering questions asked about the future."

2-45 massaged his neck as he thought over what question he would ask. It was difficult to decide whether he wanted to ask a question simply because he was curious to know the answer or if he wanted to come up with an extremely hard question in hopes of fooling the oracle.

But, before 2-45 could make up his mind, 7,500 nudged him aside. "I'll ask the first question." Staring deep into the revolving hypnotic shapes, 7,500 reached his hands out once more toward the oracle. "Oh, oracle," he said in an overly reverential tone, "tell me, what should I do to ensure that I can acquire wealth and influence?"

The oracle fountained into a diamond shape, and rotated with vibrancy as it gave its profound answer:

> *Wealth is where*
> *Wealth you find it*
> *And influence comes*
> *When you no longer hide it.*

7,500 appeared a trifle downcast as he bit his lip with confused contemplation. "I see . . . I . . ." He pondered once more and finally at a complete loss, he turned to the Mystic and blurted out, "What is that supposed to mean?"

The Mystic of the Vale leaped over to him and patted him on the back. "Now, now, now," she scolded him. "Don't give up so easily. It's given you a clue. Think. Deliberate. Search your mind with that bit of wisdom the oracle gave you. There you will find the answer to your question." She nodded her head once firmly with a 'so there' pursing of her lips.

Trying to hide his disappointment, 7,500 stepped aside to allow 2-45 access to the oracle.

2-45 had finally come up with a question, but nearly forgot it when he fixed his eyes on the shapes that were constantly forming and un-forming themselves. For a moment, he wondered whether the oracle was taking control of his mind, dragging him into another world, a world where thoughts were no longer vague and intangible but concrete living beings. His thoughts swirled and skipped, hopping from one place to another until they were imprisoned by the oracle. 2-45 shook his head to regain some control over his mind. "Oracle, here is my question: Who can help me get to the Planet of Light?"

The oracle unfurled into a shape resembling a dragon with eyes glowing bright red. Fire and smoke spewed from its mouth.

In alarm, 2-45 turned to the Mystic of the Vale. "Is it me or the question that the oracle is upset with?"

The Mystic gave him an unconcerned smile. "Neither one," she reassured him calmly. "The oracle can become emotional, but it will answer your question, don't worry."

The oracle lowered its dragon head, and forced itself to settle down. It then answered 2-45 in a voice that was low and grating.

> *If you search for the Planet of Light,*
> *Then meet with the one who rules the Desert of Night.*

"The Desert of Night?" 2-45 asked, visibly puzzled. "Where's that? I've never heard of it . . . And have no idea who rules it."

The Mystic of the Vale beamed like a bundle of begonias. "Oh, the Queen of the Desert of Night. Such a wonderful, beautiful, kind woman. She is also known as the Queen of the Night. You will like her." She gave 2-45 a loving pat on the shoulder. "And she does have a fondness for handsome, young men." She scrunched her nose and waggled her head playfully.

2-45 was a bit overwhelmed. The letter he had received from the wolf suggested he would be provided with the solution that would free him from his "overpowering difficulties" when he reached the Mystic of the Vale, but now everything was becoming more confusing and more difficult than before. He hoped the Queen of the Night would be easier to locate than the Mystic of the Vale. "How do I find her?"

7,500 decidedly grabbed some books from his bag. "I'll find it on my maps." He thumbed through them. "Now, that place was the 'Desert of Night'?"

The Mystic shook her head as if pitying a fool. "You won't find it in there."

7,500 looked up from his books baffled. "If it's not in here, how are we supposed to find it?"

The Mystic took an iridescent pearl wand from a shelf. Using the wand, she directed their attention to the floor in front of them. "There."

"On the floor?" 7,500 asked quite perplexed.

"Keep looking," the Mystic instructed him with a mischievous light in her eyes. With her wand still aimed at the floor, she skipped about in a circle. As she did, the wand radiated a brilliant light towards the floor until the circular area glowed with the light from the wand. Once she had completed her trip, the circular area of the floor lifted with a volcanic force from below and transformed itself into a globe. The globe spun energetically and hovered in the air before them. 2-45 soon realized it was a three-dimensional representation of the Planet of Darkness.

The globe's spinning slowed and then suddenly stopped. One area on the globe glowed a fiery red. The Mystic poked her wand toward that area. Her eyes sparkled with a wild excitement. "There — that is where you need to go."

2-45 stepped closer to the globe and studied the area she pointed out. He was surprised it was not the type of desert he had expected. It was actually a wilderness area infested with deadly monsters and volcanoes.

"Not really the kind of place I would like to go," 7,500 told 2-45 in an entre nous fashion.

Bopping up between them, the Mystic shook her head scoldingly. "No more looking at those scary things," she told 7,500. "Look at this." She pointed out a magnificent mansion that eventually became visible in the area on the globe. "The Queen of the Night is wealthy and powerful. She could help you so many ways. You should both go and visit her. She knows everything — including secrets only the wise are aware of."

7,500's eyes lit with a sudden realization. "Isn't she the one who knows something about someone . . . and, I believe, that knowledge leads to some type of power?"

The Mystic of the Vale smiled in a sort of condescending

way. "Of course, my dear." Her nose twitched in a homey manner. "You are thinking about the Six Secrets of Saphi. As they say, those who know all six possess the most powerful of tricks."

7,500 moved next to 2-45. "Then we will definitely need to go there."

While the Six Secrets of Saphi impressed 7,500, they were not a motivating factor for 2-45. What did convince him that the Queen of the Night was worth searching for was that all indicators pointed toward her being the one to help him reach the Planet of Light, and he was willing to risk everything to find a way there.

Chapter Thirty-One

The engineering section was situated in the damp, dark subterranean stratum of the City of the Dark Tyrant. This was where most of the experimental projects were conducted. Being so deep below the planet's surface with layer upon layer of hard rock and mernolith gel-stones, this was the best location to contain experiments should they go wrong. An impervious tranolite metal had also been embedded around the engineering section for added protection. The grey, rocky walls blended with the shadows that permeated the area creating a contradictory feeling that was both agoraphobic and claustrophobic. The area was relatively bare, including only those tools, machines, and tables engineers required for their tasks. Other than this, the room was as sterile and empty as a Murkushian Vacuum Pod. Most of the room was dark. The only light was from four directional phosphorescent lamps aiming their beams solely at the middle of the room where five engineers were at work on a humanoid form lying on a cold, metal lab table. All available light and tools were focused on this project: it was considered a priority by 1.

2,040 entered the room and cocked his head, curious about what the engineers could be working on. While he had been summoned to this room on orders from 1 and had been to the engineering section many times before, the reception he received this time made him feel like an unwelcome outsider. He did not understand what had caused this sudden change. He knitted his eyebrows at the mystery and, in search for clues, approached them. Peeking over the shoulder of the nearest engineer, he noticed that their project was hidden under a white silken sheet.

2,040 took an indirect approach. "I was sent here by the Human Resources department. They told me you would require my help," 2,040 explained to the nearby engineer in an attempt to open a conversation.

The engineer's only response was to turn slowly from his work and look at 2,040 with a piercing disdain.

2,040 tried to ignore the disdain. They were probably intent on some delicate part of their work and needed to place extra focus on what they were doing. "Well, do you need my help?" he asked with sincere curiosity without receiving a reply. He then decided it was time to toss in the numbers of his higher ranked connections. He arched a resolute eyebrow. "They told me that 1 personally wanted me involved in this project."

Another engineer pointed 2,040's attention toward a dark corner of the room. With marked curiosity, 2,040 looked in the direction indicated. At first, all he could make out was a shapeless form only half a shade lighter than the shadows. Slowly, the form emerged, moving closer toward the light, becoming more and more distinct. 2,040 soon recognized who it was.

"1? I had no idea you were here," 2,040 exclaimed, trying to adjust the surprised expression on his own face so that it more closely resembled awe.

The light now fell directly on 1, causing sharp shadows, like many demonic beings, to dance unnervingly on his face as he moved. 1 stepped to 2,040 with his head held high and his mouth stretched low.

Eager to ensure that his superior realized he was dedicated in carrying out his duties, 2,040 rushed to him. "I came immediately, just like you requested."

1 gave him a slight nod of acknowledgment.

Out of habitual imitation, 2,040 also nodded his head. "So, what is this the engineers are working on?" He concluded now was the time to be blatant with his inquiries. "Don't tell me they are going ahead with that shape-shifter project?" He pursed his lips in disappointment. "You would probably have better luck if you just seized 1-05's shape-shifter for yourself instead of creating one of your own. After all, didn't I inform you—?"

1 interrupted by curling up his nose at him. "—that we can't make shape-shifters here because we don't have litho-stones. There is no need for you to repeat it."

"All right, very well." 2,040 brushed off his annoyance with a wave of his hand. "But it *is* an indisputable fact we cannot ignore."

1 gave 2,040 a sideways glance in which the eye closest to 2,040 seemed to bulge twice as large as the other eye. "There is *one* substitute for litho-stones."

Incredulously shaking his head, 2,040 sighed, "If there is, *I* haven't heard of it. And if *I* haven't heard of it, it must not be a workable substitute."

"Think about it, 2,040 . . ." 1 spoke with purposeful eeriness. "What are litho-stones themselves a substitute for?"

2,040 answered quickly as if being quizzed for a class exam, "Life energy."

"Well, then," 1 spread his arms out and wobbled his head with finalized certainty, "instead of *litho-stones*, we will use *life energy*."

2,040 struggled to puzzle out the conclusion 1 had come to. "Sooo . . . let me get this straight . . . you're *not* using litho-stones, but instead you *are* using a living human being?"

2,040 shook his head in disbelief. "Turning a living person into a shape-shifter . . . I don't think that has ever been done before."

1 waggled a finger at 2,040 with a sneer of a smile. "You're not up on the latest research . . . We know someone who has done this very thing and done it quite successfully."

"Who would that be?"

A voice from the shadows hissed in his ear, "Usss..."

2,040 jolted anxiously within himself and glanced around, but could see no one.

1 thoroughly enjoyed 2,040's surprised expression and laughed, his double chin jiggling as much as his belly. "You have heard of the Grubian Ghouls. They fought alongside the Planet of Darkness against the Jorgandans in the Battle of the Batolan Moon. Unbeknownst to most people, their *experimental* shape-shifters were part of the reason we won that battle. Their shape-shifters were able to slip into the Jorgandans' power cubicles and disrupt their energy source, putting them at the disadvantage. And, now, their creator is right here in our midst at this very moment." He waved an arm toward a dark, seemingly empty space in the center of the room.

With an intense amount of squinting, 2,040 managed to make out the faint lines of something that resembled a misshapen human being. 2,040 shifted nervously, uncomfortable with the idea of having someone nearly invisible in the room with him. "What process do they use to create shape-shifters?"

A low gurgling growl emanated from the center of the room. "While we are dedicated allies of the Planet of Darkness and even many citizens of this planet share ancestry with usss . . . Still, we do not share our process." 2,040 assumed that since the response came from nobody he saw, it must have come from a Grubian Ghoul. "But we will assist our ally in creating a shape-shifter." A sound that could have been a choke or a chuckle erupted from the shadows. "Especially if this shape-shifter will be used against our greatest enemy, Prince Infinity of the Planet of Light."

Several crackling voices shouted out of the shadows in agreement, making it clear that more than one Grubian Ghoul was in the room. Something slimy brushed against 2,040 and by following the sound of sloshy footsteps, he determined that the ghouls were moving over to the lab table. Dutifully but in no way enthusiastically, 2,040 followed them.

1 approached the table, and the engineers stepped aside to give him a clear view of the still-sheeted project. 1 puffed out his chest in pride which succeeded in only puffing his belly out further than it was already.

In the center of the light from the four directional lamps, the slimy, decaying form of the Grubian Ghoul was more distinct. "Once we have harvested the life force from one of the souls the Dark Tyrant keeps in the lake of lava, we will be ready for the final steps of the process."

"Good." 1 waddled his way to the door. Before reaching his destination, he turned around and looked directly at 2,040. "Don't let this take too long. Speed the engineers up." Before heading out the door, he turned back with one last remark, "I want it ready by tomorrow." And he bounced his way out the door.

A sense of helplessness fell over 2,040 with the last demands being directed entirely to him. After all, the time of completion fell as much on the shoulders of the Grubian Ghouls as on him and the engineers. 2,040 looked at the engineers. They returned his gaze by haughtily raising their heads. 2,040 was not convinced the Grubian Ghouls' shape-shifter process would be successful. In a way, 2,040 pitied the engineers. They would no doubt suffer the horrible consequences of their failure once the faulty shape-shifter came to life and proved to be a disastrous mistake.

"Please, continue your work." He pulled out a notepad and pencil from his pocket. As he did, he decided that aloofness would be the best approach with this group of 'stuck-up' engineers and unpredictable ghouls.

With hesitation, 50-83 placed his hand on the palm identifier outside 1-13's workshop. The cold steel door opened, and he cautiously entered the workshop.

Inside, he came upon 1-13 who was lounging on a satin cushioned couch, calmly smoking a cigar. He gave 50-83 a casual glance of recognition. "Ah, 50-83." He sat up a bit and smiled in a friendly manner. "You're looking very well. No doubt just getting away from 6-96 for a moment improved your health one hundred percent," He chuckled casually, but quickly concealed it when he saw that 50-83 was not laughing. This pause allowed 1-13 a chance to analyze 50-83's appearance. He now realized that 50-83 was *not* 'looking well' but instead appeared extremely ill and depressed.

Irritated that 1-13 had the nerve to display such a nonchalant attitude while he was feeling so miserable, 50-83 lowered his eyes and tightly clenched the crystal pendant on his necklace. "I hope you're not calling me here to do some more of your spy-work," he grumbled.

1-13 smiled, more to suggest that 50-83 should smile as well than to express his own happiness. "Not at all," he tried to assure him with a congenial manner, "I actually called you here to inform you of something I thought you ought to know."

50-83 looked up with a mixture of curiosity and foreboding, uncertain whether this 'something he ought to know' was going to be some warning or just some friendly advice. "Inform me of what?"

To drag out 50-83's interest, 1-13 leisurely brushed some lint from his own mauve silk shirt. "You are a friend of 93-73, are you not?" He raised a questioning eyebrow.

"Yes." 50-83 eyed 1-13 suspiciously. "Why?"

"Well," 1-13 began as he made his way to a table against the wall and poured himself a glass of wine, "he was arrested and sent to me. They want me to interrogate him concerning some rebellious activities he is supposedly involved in." He took a sip of wine while watching for 50-83's reaction over the lip of the glass.

"Him? . . . It's hard to believe he'd take part in anything like that." 50-83 remembered when they were teenagers, 93-73 was the cautious one. On occasions, 50-83 would encourage the others in their group to skip lessons and slip off to a little-known spot near the wilderness area to play the gambling game, Tassular. While 93-73 warned his friends they should not do anything that went against the Dark Tyrant's rules, everyone else insisted on going ahead with the plan. Still, 93-73 refused to join them. 50-83 and three other boys slipped away to their secret location to gamble. His thrill over winning a large handful of coins was cut short when Enforcers raided the spot before they had even finished their first round of Tassular. 50-83 often wondered if 93-73 could have been the one who informed the Enforcers of where they were and what they were doing. He was convinced 93-73 could not of his own choice be involved in a rebellious plot and if 93-73 had been, in fact, taking part in rebellious activities, someone of higher rank must have encouraged him in that direction.

1-13 took another sip of wine and nodded. "My feelings exactly." He moved back to 50-83 and stroked him sympathetically on the arm. "So, I think there's a way you can help him."

Despite 1-13's façade, 50-83 glared at him distrustfully. "What do you mean?" The forceful gaze 1-13 sent him in response was much stronger than his own, and 50-83's eyes fell to the floor.

Raising his chin confidently, 1-13 replied, "Well, if he were involved in rebellious activities, who would he be most inclined to discuss them with?" 1-13 gestured toward 50-83 with his wine glass.

Although 50-83 thought the question was too obviously leading, he chose to answer it. "His friends."

1-13 set his glass on an end table and folded his hands in front of him as if preparing for business. "So, the little method of persuasion I came up with was to let you question him." His mouth spread itself into a smile that was clearly pleased with his own plans. "This will provide you with experience in your future career as well as an opportunity to help your friend. After all, since we both know he is innocent, he will have nothing to tell, and then he will naturally be cleared." 1-13 waved a hand in a 'voila' fashion.

It sounded too simple to 50-83. From what he knew, if the leaders were convinced of a person's guilt, it would take a massive amount of evidence to induce them to even consider the possibility the person was innocent. "Are you sure the leaders will go for it?"

1-13 unhesitatingly nodded his conviction. "Of course, they will."

1-13's self-assurance gave 50-83 more faith in his plan. "Very well. Where is he?"

With a flurry of decisiveness, 1-13 led 50-83 to the hallway of cells. After making their way past several jailed prisoners, they came to 93-73's cell. The heavy metal door was flung open by a guard, and 1-13 entered followed by 50-83.

93-73 sat dejectedly in a corner of the small, unfurnished cell with his arms hugging his legs to his chest. His eyes were fixed on the blank metal wall in front of him and he failed to notice anyone entering.

Upon seeing 93-73, the first thing 50-83 noticed was how much different he looked from how he remembered him. He was usually so animated and talkative. Seeing him unreactive and silent caused 50-83 to cringe.

Placing a gentle hand on his shoulder, 1-13 acquired 93-73's attention. "A visitor has come to see you," he informed him softly.

93-73 looked at 1-13 but failed to focus his eyes. "A visitor?" he asked apathetically.

"Yes." 1-13 fixed his eyes on 93-73's eyes and drew his gaze to himself. "A friend of yours." 1-13 took a step to the side to reveal that 50-83 was in the room. With a directing nudge at 50-83's back, 1-13 drew him forward. "After hearing about the trouble you were in, he wanted to come and see if he could help you."

With a weak wave of his hand, 93-73 gestured his appreciation. "It's good of you to come." He managed a weak smile. "I hope you didn't have to give up your time at the recreation hall to see me."

Before he replied, 50-83 glanced over at 1-13 to ensure it was all right. 1-13 nodded and proceeded to slip out of the cell with his guard following. Once the cell door was slammed shut, 50-83 could hear the jangling of the key securely locking him and 93-73 inside. 50-83 had thought it would be more frightening to be locked inside a prison cell, but he found it more of a comforting feeling. It reminded him a bit of his room off of 6-96's workshop. What he did miss was the panoramic view of the night sky. He took a moment to accustom himself to the darkness. He assumed there must be some type of audio and/or video device hidden somewhere in the cell enabling 1-13 to listen in on their conversation even though he could not locate where these were hidden. Working to overcome his nervousness, he concluded that what made him the most uneasy was that his skills as a Persuader would, no doubt, be criticized and that what he said and did now would impact whether 93-73 would be set free or not.

As he sat next to 93-73, 50-83 smiled casually, in much the same manner as 1-13 had smiled when 50-83 had entered the workshop. "Oh no," he said as he would if he were preparing to invite him to join him in watching the latest competition games, "you're not putting me out of my way at all. I really did want to see you." He leaned back against the cold cell wall, realizing how much better his small underground room was. "You know, it's puzzling. You of all people being arrested. I can't believe it."

93-73 shrugged his shoulders. "I guess you never know what's going to happen."

Noticing once again the dramatic change in 93-73 and how weak and listless he appeared, 50-83 angrily knitted his eyebrows. "1-13's been torturing you, hasn't he?"

93-73 shook his head emphatically. "No, on the contrary, he has treated me very well."

"Really?" 50-83 could not help but stare at his friend in disbelief. "But you seem so . . ." He was going to say "traumatized" but was afraid it would make 93-73 feel worse than he was.

"I'm not surprised." He let his gaze fall to the grimy stone floor. "Being betrayed by someone you've trusted can be hard."

50-83's eyes widened in surprise. "Betrayed? Who betrayed you?"

93-73 raised his attention back to 50-83. "I don't know if it's my place to say."

Tightly clutching 93-73's forearm, 50-83 looked him in the eyes. "I'm your best friend and I ought to know."

"Perhaps . . ." 93-73's mind was on some far-off thought. "But, in order for you to understand, I will have to give you some background information first." He rubbed his shoulder in thought as he decided where he should begin his report. "A little while back, 7,500 and I were doing research over the events which lead to the destruction of that small planet, Bercolar."

"That's right. I remember you telling me they asked you to do that," 50-83 agreed recalling how it had been around the time when 1-13 kicked him out of his workshop. After losing his position, 50-83 wanted 93-73 to join him at the Dive of

Distraction for a drink, but the heavy late-night research requirements prevented 93-73 from being able to extricate himself from his work. "They wanted you to find out more about it because that planet was destroyed two years ago, and they still can't understand the reason."

93-73 nodded, took a breath, and continued, "Well, I found the readings very interesting and eventually I came to a section covering the history of the Planet of Light. The book was very old. If I didn't handle it with extreme care, the pages would crumble. It was written in an ancient form of Bercolese and must have dated hundreds, if not thousands, of years before the destruction of Bercolar. Still, it described in detail everything that led up to, and included, that destruction. What I found unusual was how when the author described the events, he or she used verbs like 'erlof', the future tense, as if he or she knew what was 'going' to happen.

"One evening, I mentioned this to 7,500 and he appeared quite perplexed. 'Are you sure you are reading it correctly?' he asked with that particular peeved expression on his face.

"I nodded and handed the book to him for his evaluation. 'See,' I said, pointing it out, 'the author uses future tense verbs: erlof, vertof, masof and so forth, and even specifies the present year as 4029 — 1029 years before Bercolar was destroyed.'

"He remarked how unusual that was and that the author must have made some error. He then passed it off as an anomaly and told me to research a different book. So, I thought no more about it. That is until the next book proved to be just as puzzling. This one was a Bercolan biography on Infinity, the prince of the Planet of Light. The book was also written in that same ancient form of Bercolese and it was called *Naloson Alinda, Tho Abondet Enfenity* which translates to *To Bring Light, The Life of Infinity*. Now the verbs they used when describing Infinity's actions astonished me. Why? Because they would switch so drastically from past tense verbs like erloni to present tense verbs like erlit then suddenly everything is in the future tense. And it wasn't written in a subjunctive form. They were positive — Infinity will do this and that." 93-73's eyes widened as he remembered his amazement at reading the unusual text.

50-83 was stunned at once more hearing Infinity's name. "I met a girl who's convinced that Infinity will come here," 50-83 interjected trying to overcome his astonishment and return back to the state of calm control which was expected of Persuaders.

"The book mentioned he would come to the Planet of Darkness," 93-73 went on thoughtfully. "But the puzzling part was that the book was so old it must have been written before Infinity was even born."

50-83 sat up with interest. "So, what did 7,500 have to say about that? Another anomaly?"

93-73 shook his head. "When I told him about it, he was furious. He forced the book out of my hands and pored over it like an angry beast."

"Why should he be so upset?"

93-73 waved his hands upward, expressing he was equally perplexed. "I thought maybe it just frustrated him to find something he couldn't explain." He pursed his lips as he pondered the moment. "I mean, it *was* confusing. But it certainly wasn't something to get that angry about." He flipped his hand back as if tossing off the thought. "Anyway, I asked him if it was possible that certain members of the Bercolan population had the gift of foresight. Perhaps they did know what *was going to happen*. After all, there were rumors that a small segment escaped from Bercolar just days before the destruction. I believe they went to the Planet of Light." He nodded as if convinced he had solved the dilemma satisfactorily.

"Was anybody able to ask them how they knew they needed to escape?" 50-83 asked, sincerely curious.

"I believe so, but we don't have any record of it. Our information from the Planet of Light goes through so many

channels, that when it becomes available, it's hazy at best."
93-73 shrugged his shoulders. "I think they could have had the
gift of foresight. But, 7,500 didn't agree with that possibility.
When I suggested it, his face turned a heated red and he hurled
the book right back at me. I quickly caught it or the book
would have been horribly damaged. While I was trying to un-
crease some pages, he stormed over to me and shouted, 'I
suppose you think this is some prophetic book and you believe
all the events in it will happen.' And, before I could answer,
he had stomped out of the room."

50-83 knew someone in leadership was involved in 93-73's
arrest, but he was surprised it was 7,500. To him, 7,500 was
friendly and good-natured. "So, he had you brought here."

93-73 nodded but raised a finger to encourage 50-83 to
patiently listen to the rest of what he had to say. "Note that he
said 'will happen'." He tilted his head meaningfully.

"You mean, the book talks about events that haven't
happened yet?" 50-83 whispered in awe.

"Remember the book said that Infinity would come to our
planet?"

Everything in and around 50-83 paused for over half a
minute as his mind worked to recall 93-73's words about the
book and Infinity. After he managed to remember that the
book did indeed say that Infinity would come to the Planet of
Darkness, 50-83 was finally able to take a deep breath of air
since he had even stopped breathing as he was focused on
remembering. Then the reality of 93-73's statement hit him.
"Oh, and that has never happened." This reality hit him
doubly hard because 93-73 was the second person to mention
Infinity coming to the Planet of Darkness. 4,021 could not
have read the book that 93-73 was mentioning. Slump-Bump's
are not taught to read. She had told him that she had met
Infinity in a dream. 50-83 wondered what connection there
could be between the book and 4,021's dream.

"No, it has never happened and neither has the destruction of the Planet of Darkness," 93-73 explained with a significant foreboding.

As 50-83 and 93-73 were having their discussion, 1-13 was watching and listening to them on a viewing screen. He raised a curious eyebrow as 93-73 discussed what the Bercolans claimed would happen.

He smiled a clever smile. *Infinity will come and our planet will be destroyed. I wonder how many of our councilmembers and legal examiners know about that. I would certainly like to get my hands on that book.* In his mind, he constructed a plot in which he managed to extract the location of the book from 93-73 and, afterwards, convinced the councilmembers and legal examiners that his own valuable discovery meant that he ought to be given a more prestigious position. But, he reminded himself that that was for another time. First he must finish the missions assigned to him by the Dark Tyrant.

Knowing that his number one mission was to find out what rebellion 2,040 was concocting, he snapped his fingers to summon the aid of one of his spy creatures. It affectionately slithered up to him. He patted it on the head and looked down at it fondly. "Are you eager to get started with your mission?"

The spy creature chirped and nodded its head.

"All right then. No need to wait any longer." 1-13 carried the spy creature to a wall grating for the ventilation system. He removed the grating and set the spy creature inside. "Now, written into your memory is the map you are to follow. When you reach your destination, record everything you see and hear and bring it back to me." He smiled at the creature encouragingly before releasing it to its task.

The spy creature nodded and after rubbing its head against 1-13's hands in a loving goodbye, the creature disappeared into the ventilation ducts.

While tidying the room after 2,040 had left, 34,000 noticed something that troubled her. *His glass of wine is still half full. He always finishes his drink when he is happy. Something must be worrying him.* She carefully picked up the glass along with its contents and set it on a centralized tray on the bar. Placing her hands reverently around the glass, she looked deep into the wine, as if into a crystal ball, hoping it would unfold some secret. Unable to decipher the wine's varying tones of red, she turned from the glass and slipped downstairs to find 9-85, hoping he knew more about what was happening.

9-85 was at a nearby table feverishly scribbling out mathematical calculations in a notebook. Haphazard stacks of paper barricaded him from the world around him. 34,000 silently moved up behind him to see what he was working on. "*That* model again," she said with annoyance. "Why must you keep working on it?"

Lost within the cavernous clandestine world of numbers, 9-85 jolted at the sound of an outside voice, but settled down when he noticed it was 34,000. "I must." His voice came across harsher than he intended. "It has to be corrected." He refocused his attention on the model.

34,000 took a seat next to him. "It doesn't help. By insisting the model is wrong, you're only upsetting 2,040."

9-85 faced her directly. "Of course we're all upset about it. But we can't ignore the fact that it has errors." he insisted. "Or should I say, it did. I've made the corrections." In a sudden change of mood, he smiled proudly as he held up the notebook containing the corrections.

9-85's words were nothing but a mumble to 34,000. She focused her attention on the table's uneven surface to disguise a moment of sorrow. "He was so upset, he didn't even finish his wine." She felt as if she was a mist floating far away from everything. "1 called him to some meeting. Do you know what it is about?"

"He mentioned it was about shape-shifters, but, I suppose it could be about anything."

34,000 turned her attention sullenly away from 9-85 to the edging of her sleeve. The more 9-85 talked about 2,040 and the mistakes in the model, corrected or not, the more she worried some terrible fate was in store for 2,040. All of her life, 34,000 knew nothing but insecurity and unhappiness. Her parents were only faint blurs in her memory. Her teachers were strict, unsympathetic thunder clouds that loomed over her entire childhood. When she became an apprentice, she worked for a series of masters who could not care less whether she existed or not except for when she was needed to perform some task or another. It was not until she finally began working for 2,040 that she felt needed and appreciated. She would not forget the first moment they met. The second he laid eyes on her, he exclaimed that he had never been so lucky as to have a research assistant so beautiful and so intelligent at the same time. Suddenly, her heart came to life and had consistently beat to that same thrilling love song every time she was in the same room as 2,040. But now her heart was as silent and still as a grave.

When 9-85 realized that 34,000 was determined to remain dejected, he decided to keep the conversation serious. "Hopefully, the meeting will help 2,040 to start realizing the seriousness of the situation we're in." 9-85 turned back to the paper he had been working on and, in his mind, recalculated a portion of the model.

A tear trickled down 34,000's cheek. "But there's nothing we can do," she said through a sob. "So, why should we even think about it?"

9-85 looked from his paper, noticing her tears. He lightly patted her hand in an effort to comfort her. "The key is to focus on our situation. We must pinpoint the source of difficulty and neutralize it." He tapped his pencil hard on the table to emphasize his point.

Close by, in a ventilation duct, 1-13's spy creature slithered out of the shadows into a position where it could easily watch and listen in. It focused its binocular-like eyes on the papers 9-85 was working on and began taking a recording of them through the grating.

34,000 stared at 9-85 in bewilderment. "If 2,040's model *is* wrong, once the Dark Tyrant realizes it, he will certainly punish us. There's nothing we can do to prevent it."

"I told you I fixed the model." 9-85 shuffled through his papers, with determination. "Look for yourself." He pointed out the corrections, scanning through the functions, constraints, and his calculations.

The spy creature zoomed its eyes even closer to create a clear recording of the model as 9-85 flipped through the pages.

9-85 held the papers in front of him in a gesture of decisiveness. "Now all we have to do is replace the wrong one with this corrected version before the Dark Tyrant notices the errors."

Seeing the corrected model in 9-85's hands was like being tempted by a jewel that would forever be out of reach. She knew it was too late for the corrections to make any difference. "The model is at this moment in the Dark Tyrant's master computer. How could you possibly manage to replace it when the Dark Tyrant knows everything that happens in that high-security zone?" 34,000 studied 9-85's features, trying to decide whether she should be impressed by his sudden bravery or frustrated by his reckless foolishness.

9-85 tapped his pen on the table in thought. "Right now, I don't know, but I'm certain there is some way. We just need to plan it out."

She shook her head hopelessly. "That's one miracle you'll never manage to pull off." She stood, accepting the unhappy situation, and walked out of the lab.

After she had left, 9-85 looked once more over the model. He knew 34,000 was right, but he wished there was a way he could transport the corrections to the master computer. His eyebrows drew down and he clenched his teeth, but concluded it was an impossible task. He placed the papers neatly into a file and turned to place the file in a drawer. As he did, he caught a glimpse of a shadowy movement in the ventilation duct. A deep foreboding fell over him.

Chapter Thirty-Two

Finding their way back to the City of the Dark Tyrant was much quicker for 2-45 and 7,500 than it had been for them to search out the Mystic of the Vale. When they arrived within the city's limits, they agreed they would return to their homes, complete any necessary tasks, then meet at 7,500's quarters to prepare for their journey to locate the Queen of the Night.

Though he was exhausted, 2-45 hoped he could slip into his mansion, pack his bags, and slip out unnoticed and avoid irritating inquiries from his mother and sister. He was grateful he was able to pass through the entryway without encountering the butler; however, as soon as he started to mount the stairs toward his room, a hand clasped his arm tightly. He turned around and came face to face with his sister, 5-07. She was wearing a light blue gossamer negligee and her eyes appeared red and moist, as if she had been crying.

"You've been gone a long time." Her sentence was punctuated with a hint of a hiccup, which may have been an attempt to hold back a sob. "Where were you?"

2-45 turned to her with a stern look, but tried to tone down the sternness. He did not want her to suspect he was angry with her. If she did, she might become so emotionally upset it would take him hours to calm her down. "I was taking care of a task for 1-13, naturally." He continue up the stairs and hoped his business-as-usual manner would convince her.

Refusing to allow 2-45 to slip away from her, 5-07 followed him closely with determination. "Why are you lying?"

2-45 stopped and turned back to her. "Lying?" he asked with a well-acted honest expression. "What gives you the idea that I am lying?"

"1-13 came here and was looking for you," 5-07 explained to him directly. "He said he hasn't seen you this entire work session." She shook her head with a pitying expression. She stopped on the stairs and kept her eyes focused on her brother as she leaned an elbow on the railing. "Why are you lying to me? You know I would help you if I could."

Breathing out a quick sigh of frustration, he slammed a fist on the railing. While he cared quite a bit for his sister, he knew there were some things he could not trust her with. He remembered the day when they were still in school and she caught him slipping into their father's hidden money vault in the bookshelf. He only took a couple of gold coins to pay off a debt, but she still insisted on telling on him. Mother applauded 5-07 and gave her a raise in her allowance. 2-45 was punished by having to spend the night in the damp dark dungeon-like basement and forced to accept a decrease in his allowance. "This is just something I can't tell you anything about right now." He whipped back around and climbed the rest of the stairs to his room.

5-07 raced after him and slipped into his room before he could shut her out. "Listen. You keep racing off into all types of dangerous situations. And it's just not worth it. You're wasting your money and ruining your career for this crazy idea. Not only that, but you're making me so worried about you." She looked him in the eyes with an emotional quivering that was like an earthquake to her but could only be detected by those who knew her well.

Without acknowledging her presence, 2-45 pulled a suitcase out from his closet, tossed it on the bed and threw it open.

Taking a breath to calm down, 5-07 stifled her emotions with a mind-body awareness technique she had diligently practiced. "So where are you going now?"

2-45 kept his attention focused on packing his clothes and personal items. "If you are really interested, I spoke with the Mystic of the Vale." 2-45 tossed into his suitcase a pair of shoes, some socks, and a hairbrush. "She told me that the Queen of the Night would like to help me. She is a wealthy and powerful woman."

5-07's eyes widened in concern and if she had not caught the wall for support, she might have fallen to the floor from shock. "Is she the same Queen of the Night who is known for giving room and board to criminals who have been banned from the City of the Dark Tyrant?"

After carefully folding some shirts into the suitcase, 2-45 faced her dispassionately. "That's fitting. Since, just a while ago I too was close to being banned from the city."

"Your situation was different."

"Not really." He closed the suitcase and lifted it from the bed. "I know you think I am crazy for putting our family in danger, but I have my reasons." He closed his eyes, trying to block an image that refused to be blocked. After a breath, he opened his eyes and continued, "Every night I sleep, I keep having this dream . . . not dream, more like a nightmare. Our tower is surrounded by flames and crumbles to the ground." He moved to the door and with a gentle nudge, moved her out of his way. "I will not let that happen." He gave her a quick hug and turned to leave.

It suddenly dawned on 5-07 that 2-45 really meant to leave. She now felt as if she were looking at him through the wrong end of a telescope and he seemed so far away and distant. "You're going without me?"

"It's too dangerous for you."

5-07 moved in front of him and blocked the door. "If it's too dangerous for me, it's too dangerous for you." Her eyes widened with determination.

Gently shoving her out of the way, 2-45 managed to open the bedroom door. "7,500 will be with me. We'll manage." He stepped past her and made his way down the stairs.

Feeling doubly deserted, 5-07 whirled around after him. "7,500's going too?"

2-45 reached the bottom of the stairs. "Yes."

Following behind him, 5-07 insistently reminded him, "But he promised to marry me."

Turning back for a second, he reassured her, "I'm certain he'll be back in no time." Then he made his way out the front door and toward his Barso-Cycle.

5-07 reached the doorway and watched him leave dejectedly, wondering what type of woman the Queen of the Night was and whether she should be jealous of her or worried about the safety of 2-45 and 7,500. For a second she thought she should just resort to a life of loneliness away from those she cared about the most. But then she remembered there was someone who might be willing to help her, if she was able to help him first.

As the *Forerunner* approached the area of space bordering the Planet of Darkness' interplanetary zone, it detected in the vicinity a fleet of patrolling Control Craft on its port side. While hoping that if he kept his distance he would not be noticed, the Way-Guide still knew he could not take a chance on being caught. His mission was too vital. He recalled Infinity's words concerning the open communications link the *Forerunner* kept with the *Ghost III*. "The *Forerunner* calling the *Ghost III*. Infinity, can you hear me?" the Way-Guide called, even though he was doubtful the *Ghost III* could pick up the signal at such a distance.

"Yes, I am listening," Infinity's clear voice came to the Way-Guide. "And I can see the Control Fleet patrols on either side of you."

The Way-Guide started, both because he did not realize Infinity was receiving visuals of his situation and because he, himself, had not yet seen the Control Craft on his starboard side. "There's too many," the Way-Guide groaned. "I've got to leave this area."

"You do not need to leave," Infinity assured him.

The Way-Guide bit his lip nervously as the Control Craft moved in closer. "Then what can I do?"

"Just continue on your course to the planet."

With marked hesitation, the Way-Guide set his ship to continue on toward the Planet of Darkness. The Control Craft increased their speed following him. His heart beat faster as his hand instinctively hovered over the weapons controls. He then noticed a large spaceship in front of him blocking his view of the Control Craft. As the *Forerunner* moved closer toward the large ship, he could see past it and noticed that the Control Craft had increased their speed not because they were honing in on him, but because they had observed this other ship and were rapidly closing in on it. The Way-Guide directed his attention once more on this new ship and realized that the ship was the *Ghost III*.

"Infinity. You made it here." The Way-Guide laughed, concluding that the reason Infinity knew the details of his situation was because he was close by the entire time.

"Not exactly," Infinity's voice corrected him calmly over the communications link. "What you and the Controllers are seeing is not the *Ghost III* of the present but the *Ghost III* of the future. Since we know the *Ghost III* will reach the Planet of Darkness eventually, the *Ghost III* can pull its image from that time in the future and bring it to the present to block the image of the *Forerunner* from the Controllers' view. Since it is just an image, the Control Craft cannot damage it, but *being* an image, you can set your course through it and you will be invisible to them. However, be sure that you keep to the lower portion of the *Ghost III,* since the Control Craft will focus their weapons on the propulsion mechanisms of the ship located above."

The Way-Guide took a moment to digest everything Infinity told him. He took a breath to calm his head which was whirling and proceeded to direct his ship through the image of the *Ghost III.* The narrow misses of the Control Craft's quark blasters almost unnerved him, but the Way-Guide focused on his goal. By the time he had exited the image, the Control Craft were concentrating on the *Ghost III* and did not notice the *Forerunner* slip past them and make its way toward the Planet of Darkness.

Not all of the means The Dark Tyrant used to ensure his workers put forth as much work as possible were violent or threatening. Some of them were almost pleasant. Research proved that workers who kept a relatively high level of caffeine in their systems worked harder and longer than those who did not, so the Dark Tyrant saw to it that the City of the Dark Tyrant contained a large number of coffee stations and several coffee bars. The coffee stations served plain coffee at the press of a button. The coffee bars served a variety of coffee and lattes which were ordered through a monitor at the bar and served on a conveyor belt that ran from a back room in which the drinks were mixed by programmed androids.

The Planet of Darkness had no means of growing coffee itself, so coffee beans were grown and processed on the planet Grubia. The Planet of Darkness' need for coffee beans and the Grubian Ghouls' need for financial wealth led to a longtime alliance between these two planets. Still, Grubian coffee beans were by no means the highest quality. These coffee beans had a muddy, sour, moldy flavor that was difficult to hide no matter how much sweetener and cream was added. Most people realized that the highest quality coffee came from the Planet of Light. Still, no one on the Planet of Darkness dared to admit it. They continued to force down the disgusting coffee, accepting that it was the best available.

1-13 entered one of these coffee bars. When walking into this bar, one first comes to a seating area with several tables placed there for workers, who have the time, to relax and enjoy their coffee. The walls of this area were plastered with propaganda posters, several of which had been designed under 2-45's orders. One read, "Keep up your work for the Dark Tyrant and Ensure Security for our Planet." Another one read, "The Dark Tyrant Knows What You Need Better than You Do." And yet another read, "Those Who Resist the Dark Tyrant Learn Their Place." 1-13 continued further inside and past a black and turquoise banister to the bar. The back wall of the bar curved backward and the bar itself curved forward creating an oval-shape between them. The back wall was a mottled blend of black and red which swirled into seemingly random shapes. However, one soon noticed that the shapes actually resembled the Dark Tyrant torturing and tormenting the workers to ensure a high output of work. The bar itself was a glossy black, but would have been glossier if it was not in need of washing. 1-13 sat at this bar and grimaced when his hand fell on a sticky spot.

Earlier, 1-13 had contacted 6-96 and asked her to meet him here. While he made certain she knew it would be to her benefit, he was still unsure whether she would come. He punched into the monitor his order and waited for his mulcandor latte. After a few moments his drink was before him and he took a sip. He glanced over his shoulder at the door just as 6-96 marched in and up to the bar.

6-96 leaned an elbow on the bar and shot a glare dead center into 1-13's eyes. "What is this all about," she asked with an irritated snort. "I have several people in need of my persuasion and I hate to leave them waiting." She laughed at a joke that only she was aware of.

1-13 drank down the last sip he could manage from his cup and set the rest aside. He faced 6-96 with a deadly serious expression. "I know we both were given our own assignments by the Dark Tyrant, but I think it is time for us to pool our resources."

6-96's mouth curled down into a contorted frown which 1-13 presumed meant she was giving the proposition serious thought. Instead it meant she could in no way fathom what gave 1-13 such a preposterous idea. She shook her head condescendingly. "I cannot see why I would ever need *your* help."

"Listen," 1-13 quickly interjected to ensure that 6-96 would not leave. "You may have information that could be somewhat condemning for 2,040. I have seen your little lackey rushing about on your little tasks. But, I have something on him too. Plus, I know the source of this rebellion. If we worked together, we can ensure that 2,040 faces the Dark Tyrant's judgment."

6-96 tapped her chin thoughtfully. "Perhaps," she looked at 1-13 with a mistrustful raise of the eyebrow. "But how did you find out about the source of the rebellion."

"I've done some research. The source of the rebellion does not come from any person on our planet. It was supposedly foretold in some books. They claim someone called Infinity will come here to the Planet of Darkness and when he does our planet will be destroyed. A book containing that type of information could certainly guarantee the rebellion of a certain segment of any society."

"Yes. Dangerous, indeed." She turned to 1-13 and to his surprise nodded. "All right. I'll agree to a truce. We will work together — for the moment."

Chapter Thirty-Three

Even before 2,040 spoke a word, 9-85 could tell his superior had drunk too much wine. 9-85 had been waiting for hours while 2,040 was occupied overseeing the development of some secret project, and now that the economic efficiency expert was finally allotted a short break, 9-85 was dismayed to find his superior using the break to become intoxicated. Despite the fact that 2,040 put on a façade of being in complete control, 9-85 noticed him overreaching his hand to pick up a glass and missing 34,000's cheek when he leaned over to give her a kiss. Normally, 9-85 would graciously tell 2,040 that any necessary discussions could wait until later, but 9-85 knew something had to be done immediately about the errors in the model. It annoyed 9-85 that 2,040 had either intentionally or unintentionally twisted the conversation around to poetry pertaining to romance.

". . . That is the most passionate — the most beautiful poem in the world," 2,040 smiled as if he had at that moment blissfully entered into the idealistic world of the author's poem. "How does it go? . . .

> *A woman stands where life is born in a world that freezes yet burns,*
>
> *Lit by a light from a diff'rent sphere, she passionately sighs and turns,*
>
> *Once facing me, she reaches out her soft, gentle hands toward mine,*
>
> *Resolute eyes of enchanting brown, lips of roses and sweet wine,*
>
> *Shimm'ring of stars, she speaks these words, while wind blows her hair soft and free,*
>
> *"Enter my garden and this love belongs always to you and me"*

"I can't remember how the rest of the poem goes . . . Something about lakes bubbling with life and trees dancing with blossoms . . . but I'm not sure . . ." After a grimace which was meant to activate his brain, 2,040 shook his head and rubbed his forehead in hopes that the words would come back to him. "No, it's gone. But I think it's in a book around here." Tipsily losing and then regaining his balance, he stood to search for it.

"Right now is not a time to go searching for books," 9-85 reminded him flatly. "We were supposed to be discussing a plan for correcting the model in the master computer." He brandished the file of the revised model like a flag meant to call all patriots to their duty.

Giving 9-85 an irritated glare, 34,000 retrieved from a shelf the book 2,040 was looking for and handed it to him defiantly. "I don't see anything wrong with discussing poetry," she said assertively to all who would listen, "especially if 2,040 wants to."

2,040 took the book and looked at it sadly. "Spending several hours deciphering the subtle meanings of poetry would have been so pleasant." He turned to 9-85 and shook his head pityingly. "You really should learn to appreciate it." Then, after giving 9-85 the sad expression of a man who would never forget he had just cold-bloodedly murdered all happiness, he resolutely tossed the book on the coffee table. "But, 9-85 is right." He raised a decided finger. "We must face this problem like determined scientists who refuse to turn away from it until the solution is found." He attempted to massage his forehead to facilitate his ability to think, but, unfortunately his drunken brain did not send his fingers to the right destination and they instead jabbed him in the eye. To appear less inebriated, he pretended it was what he meant to do and he transformed the jab into a rubbing of his eye.

Ignoring the fact that 2,040's gestures were shaky from drink, 9-85 smiled gratefully and moved closer to him, sitting on the coffee table to face him. "As I said earlier, I have corrected the model. We just need to find a way to replace it in the master computer without anyone finding out."

"Oh, yes, that," 2,040 flippantly replied, waving an index finger in the air, "and I told you there's nothing to worry about. If worse comes to worse, we can make our way out of the City of the Dark Tyrant in that escape vehicle I showed you. We will be fine." He then grabbed a half-empty bottle of wine and shook it to determine how much was left.

For 9-85 the thought of venturing off into the unknown was worse than trying to appease the Dark Tyrant. He had heard rumors about what it was like in the wilderness area, and what he heard made him determined to avoid it. "Yes, fine. Suffocating from the putrid air and steam of the wilderness, being strangled to death by carnivorous plants, and surviving on the wild Carconin rats we kill." 9-85 nodded in a humoring manner. "That is perfectly fine for an emergency. But, if there is any chance at all, we've got to try to bypass the system and get into the master computer to replace the model."

Placing a weary hand to his forehead, 2,040 groaned. "I know very little about computers."

9-85 refused to let up on 2,040. "Do you know anyone who does?"

Feeling uncomfortable with being forced to face the problem, 2,040 nervously rubbed the back of his neck. "I don't know," he responded dejectedly.

34,000 placed a protective arm around 2,040 and allowed him to lay his head on her shoulder. "You shouldn't ask him anymore questions."

"We've only started discussing this," 9-85 replied, pulled 2,040 from her, and shook him while looking him directly in the eyes. "You work with people from all sorts of fields. Certainly you have encountered someone who knows about computers. That light source you showed me and even your emergency vehicle — they both required computer programing. Who provided you with their expertise on those projects?"

2,040 knitted his eyebrows as he tried to guide his brain past the haziness of the wine. "Oh, yes." He managed to mentally clear the path to thought-land. "His number is 81-4-60. He's a good friend of mine. Me and him and 7,500 often enjoyed a bottle of wine together at the Duke of Distraction's lair. A computer expert, and very loyal."

"To you?" 9-85 wanted to be certain that by 'very loyal' he did not just mean to the Dark Tyrant.

"Of course, to me," 2,040 reaffirmed as he laughed out his tension and felt more relaxed. "As you said, he helped me with the emergency vehicle, and we agreed that was to be kept 'top secret'. He's a close friend and he would practically give his life for me." Then, like a sheepdog, he herded his mindlessly scattered thoughts and brought them to the present task. "But even though he's a computer expert, what can he do with the model since it is in the master computer?" He paused in thought, then a smile broke out on his face as he chuckled. "Of course, why didn't I think of it? The master computer. Of course." He rubbed his hands together in excitement and made his way to the electrical fountain. After taking a stimulating moment to watch the fountain's splendor, he turned back around to face 9-85. "What a clever plan. Break into the Dark

Tyrant's master computer, replace the model, and sneak back. Nobody, not even the Dark tyrant, will know the difference. That will pull one over on them. I like it."

9-85 could not help but frown a bit at 2,040 stealing his plan and claiming it as his own. Still, with 2,040 convinced it was his own idea, he knew it would be easier to move forward with it. 9-85 forced his frown into a smile and nodded his support for 2,040.

A shiver of concern traveled up and down 34,000's body. "It sounds too dangerous."

9-85 walked over near 2,040 and sat on the ledge of the fountain with determined readiness. "If this friend of yours agrees to help, I'm willing to take the risk."

"Well, then." 2,040 ran his fingers in the fountain's display and the lightning sparkled with fervent colors. He then turned to 9-85 with a thoughtful, Socratic expression, "our first step will be to contact him; after that, everything will fall into place like clockwork."

Chapter Thirty-Four

As the *Forerunner* entered the heavy atmosphere of the Planet of Darkness, the Way-Guide adjusted his course to come down close to the safe house. Following the directions dictated by Infinity, he set down near an icy mountain ledge where an overhanging cliff provided cover for his ship. He had also been told where, under the snow, he would find the entrance and, after knocking with a secret pattern on the hatch, he was admitted inside by the Dream-Saver. The Dream-Saver led him through the passageway to the safe house. Just as the Way-Guide stepped into the foyer, four children jumped out from opposite hallways with a chorus of giggles and shouts that were contrived to produce both surprise and challenge. The Way-Guide took a step back to steady himself from the unexpected greetings.

"Oh, hello," he said, uncertain whether he should step further out of their way or give each of the children a handshake. "What are you all up to?" It was only recently that the Way-Guide had started to become accustomed to interacting with children. The only people living on the Planet of Darkness who had dealings with children were the medical caregivers, teachers, and occasionally Enforcers. During his time on the Planet of Darkness, the Way-Guide worked as a pilot and rarely saw children; however, his years on the Planet of Light brought him into more contact with them. A group of children often played in the park not far from his house and several boys worked part-time at the transport hangar to help with repairing the ships. Still, the Way-Guide knew the Planet of Darkness' strict policy on children and as he landed his ship, he had set himself into the frame of mind that he would not run into them.

The Dream-Saver noticed the surprised look on the Way-Guide's face, so, to set him at ease, he gave him a friendly smile. "In case you weren't told before you headed here," he leaned in close to inform him, "we do care for a number of children here."

"I see that now," the Way-Guide laughed good-naturedly.

One of the children, a little girl wearing a garland of flowers draped around her neck, leaned against the wall while spinning a lock of her hair around her finger. "We just wanted to surprise you."

Another girl took the first girl's hand, pulled her back, and looked her in the eyes while shaking her head. "No, don't tell him that. It will ruin everything."

One of the boys stepped closer to the Way-Guide. "Were you surprised?" he asked with a more serious tone than the Way-Guide expected from a child his age.

"I can honestly tell you, I *was* surprised."

The Dream-Saver noticed another boy lagging behind the others, so he took that boy by the hand and led him to the front. That was when the Way-Guide noticed the boy was leaning on a pair of crutches. "What happened? Was he hurt in some type of accident?"

"No." The Dream-Saver tousled the boy's hair. "The children brought here had been declared by the Dark Tyrant's evaluators unfit for any of the city's categories of work. And you know what that means?" He gave the Way-Guide a meaningful look.

The Way-Guide nodded with serious realization. A wave of rage flowed through his body at the thought that if the Dark Tyrant had had his way, these children would have been killed as babies. "How did you manage to get them away safely? From what I remember, the city employs extremely advanced and complex security measures."

"We have the Shadow-Shield to thank for that," the Dream-Saver told him proudly. "I believe you are already well acquainted with him, so I am sure I don't need to remind you of his impressive stealth skills."

In a reserved manner, the Way-Guide tilted his head and waved a hand in acknowledgement. "That's right. If anyone could manage it, he could." He turned his attention back to the children. "But these boys and girls, most of them look intelligent, smart, and healthy. I don't see why they didn't easily fit into some career regime . . ."

The Dream-Saver cut him off, "It doesn't have to be something major for the Dark Tyrant to toss someone aside. Little Flower-Weaver here . . ." He gestured toward the girl leaning against the wall. "She is only slightly deaf in her left ear. The other girl has a mild heart murmur and this boy, we call him Dark-Breaker, finds it difficult to interact with others."

"I never would have guessed that." The Way-Guide smiled at the serious boy.

The boy averted his gaze to the floor and moved behind the boy with the crutches.

The Dream-Saver patted the other boy on the shoulder. "Our little Goal-Reacher here was born with weak muscles in his legs. Still, we are all confident that, with enough exercise and practice, he will someday be able to walk without the crutches."

The boy looked at the Way-Guide and beamed. "And the Wisdom-Giver told me that if I can make it to the valley and visit with the Shepherdess, I could get completely well."

"Of course," the Dream-Saver agreed proudly.

The Soul-Guard entered into the hall and knelt in the midst of the children. "Okay, I think you all have spent enough time away from your lessons." She gave them a slight hug, smiled, and nudged them toward their classroom. "Your teacher is expecting you back at your desks, so go on, and no lagging behind." As the children gave the Way-Guide a wave goodbye and slipped down the hall, the Soul-Guard watched them proudly. She then looked the Way-Guide straight in the eyes and breathed in as if preparing to tell someone the inspiring news that they had been waiting to hear. "There will come a day when these children will join us and Infinity in a full-scale battle against the suffocating suppression being carried out by the Dark Tyrant, and the entire planet will see what they are truly capable of." She gestured for the Way-Guide and Dream-Saver to follow her to the living room where they each took a comfortable seat on the cushioned couch. The Soul-Guard pulled up a chair near them and sat down.

The young woman who chose to care for the new baby girl sensed a guest had joined them. On cue, she brought in a tray piled high with coffee, cakes, and cookies. She poured the Way-Guide a cup of coffee. "I am afraid that the Shadow-Shield has not yet returned from his latest rescue mission."

"I can wait a few minutes to talk to him." The Way-Guide took a gulp of coffee. He noticed the faraway look in the young woman's eyes and sensed something ethereal about her. He tried to unsuccessfully make eye contact with her. "After all, I don't even know what your name is?"

She touched him gently on his shoulder as she moved past him. "Your voice sounds as if it is directed toward me." She took a seat on a nearby ottoman. "They call me the Light-Defender and I can promise you that no matter how much the

Planet of Darkness tries to dim the light from Infinity's planet, I will not let them do it."

"She tells the truth," the Dream-Saver told the Way-Guide. "She has given everyone here lessons in fighting and I can honestly say, she fights as well as any of the Dark Tyrant's Enforcers."

The Way-Guide was surprised by what the Dream-Saver said because the Light-Defender appeared small and withdrawn. "But, doesn't she . . ." Not wanting to say the word, he gestured toward his own eyes, to indicate his concern.

The Soul-Guard glared at him disapprovingly. "Just because she can't see doesn't mean she can't be a powerful fighter." She noticed the Light-Defender lowering her head in frustration and gave her a firm and determined pat on the arm. "If I was being targeted by Enforcer fire, I would trust her to protect me over a score of trained soldiers who could see."

"Thank you." The Light-Defender bit her lip to keep back a tear. "But people have fixed in their minds what others are capable of. I will not force my help on anyone." Not letting her face become more than an unemotional mask, she stood and walked silently out of the room.

Aware that he had taken the conversation in the wrong direction, the Way-Guide stood ready to follow her to apologize. The Dream-Saver stopped him. "She'll be fine. She seems shy and helpless, but her strong, fiery nature makes her the perfect protector. Between the Soul-Guard and the Light-Defender, the children are in good hands. And we have several others here who would give their lives to secure this safe house."

"So, you're not the soldier around here?" the Way-Guide laughed.

"No," the Dream-Saver said shyly with a slight chuckle, "my help is more in baby-sitting and dish-washing."

The Way-Guide sat down again and took another gulp of coffee. "Do you have any idea when the Shadow-Shield will be back? Infinity sent me to assist in safely conducting the hopeful one out of the City of the Dark Tyrant to the Shepherdess of the Valley."

The Soul-Guard's eyes lit up in surprise. "The Shepherdess of the Valley?"

Setting down his cup, the Way-Guide tilted his head in incredulity. "That's what I was told. Is there something I should know about this Shepherdess?"

The Soul-Guard laughed good-naturedly. "You think we doubt whether we should trust her. On the contrary, she is the most trustworthy person on this planet. My surprise was because I have not heard anyone mention her in connection with Infinity in a long time. The fact that Infinity is calling her to action now could only mean one thing . . ." She gave the Way-Guide a meaningful look.

The Way-Guide was still puzzled. *Could Infinity be planning something more than just the rescue of certain people from this planet?* "What *does* it mean? Is there something that Infinity hasn't told me that I should know?"

The Dream-Saver shook his head. "I'm sure when you volunteered you knew this would be a dangerous mission. And the risk of an outbreak of war is part of the danger when coming to the Planet of Darkness."

"War?"

"Naturally," the Soul-Guard replied calmly. "At one time the Shepherdess lived much closer to the City of the Dark Tyrant under an established agreement between both of them. The agreement stated that if people in the City of the Dark Tyrant chose to leave it, they could go with the option of living in the Shepherdess' mountaintop cottages. The wilderness area flourished then, and the trees were lush and green. She is a natural caregiver of plants and animals, and even though the light of the sun does not reach this planet, she knows what to do to balance the ecosystem of whatever land she tends and makes that place ideal to live in. Eventually, the Dark Tyrant realized that more people were drawn to her pleasant community than were willing to live in his smoggy, dirty city. He placed a huge bounty on her head and sent people into the community to sabotage it. Perhaps you have heard of the man-eating plants and birds of that area? All results of the Dark Tyrant's work to destroy the Shepherdess' community. Finally, thirty years ago, the Shepherdess decided to separate herself completely from the City of the Dark Tyrant. She left for a secluded valley, unknown to most people. Before she left, she told a few of her followers that when she is called back by Infinity to assist him, they should not be surprised when war breaks out between the Planet of Darkness and the Planet of Light."

The Way-Guide rubbed his pant leg in concern. "And that is why we need to get as many people to safety as possible."

"True," the Dream-Saver agreed, "but how do we know where is the safest place? We may be safer in the middle of a battle than hiding in a cave. But don't worry. The Shadow-Shield is an expert at rescuing. He sneaks in and out in no time. Even if he runs into trouble, they never stay on his trail longer than a few minutes. He becomes practically invisible to his enemies."

The Way-Guide shifted at the mention of the Shadow-Shield and took another sip of coffee. He heard a rattling of the ceiling hatch that led outdoors. The Dream-Saver moved out of the room as he raised his hand to indicate that he would be right back. Instead of waiting for the Dream-Saver, the Way-Guide followed him and stood watching him in the doorway to the hall. He noticed that the Dream-Saver was approaching someone who was coming from the room with the outside hatch. The Way-Guide moved in closer when he recognized him as the Shadow-Shield.

Upon seeing the Way-Guide, the Shadow-Shield took on a serious expression and nodded in his direction. "Glad to see you got here safely." The Shadow-Shield held a welcoming hand out to him. "Sorry I wasn't here to meet you when you first arrived, but I had work to take care of in the City of the

Dark Tyrant, preparing for the rescue," he explained as he took off his coat and handed it to the Dream-Saver.

"What are your plans?" the Way-Guide asked anxiously.

The Shadow-Shield moved past the Way-Guide and into the living room. "The focus of the rescue is on labor room 15." He helped himself to a cup of coffee.

"Labor room 15?" The Way-Guide frowned in frustration, following the Shadow-Shield into the room. "But what about the prison? 1-05 is still captured. We need to get her out."

The Shadow-Shield sat comfortably in a cushioned chair, unmoved by the Way-Guide's outburst. "Yes, and we *will* get her out. Just not right now."

"Why not?" The Way-Guide stepped up to the Shadow-Shield and pounded his fist on a nearby table.

"1-05 is safe where she is and there are more pressing matters that demand our attention," the Shadow-Shield explained and took a sip of coffee before continuing. "The important thing about this mission is that it hinges on three steps, which are also three locations in the City of the Dark Tyrant. Step One focusses on Manual Labor Room 15 and is a pivotal point of our mission. The hopeful one is being held there, and she will be held there as long as the Persuader in charge deems it necessary. As long as she stays there, we have a chance to get her out. If the Persuader moves her somewhere else, that somewhere else will most likely be armed with higher security, making her extraction much more difficult." He looked the Way-Guide in the eyes meaningfully.

"All right," the Way-Guide sighed reluctantly in agreement, "we concentrate on manual labor room 15 first."

The Shadow-Shield waved his hand as if wiping false information off of a board. "No, *you* concentrate on the manual labor room while I take a group to work on the other two steps."

Shaking his head to clear it, the Way-Guide tried to adjust himself to this new overwhelming responsibility. "What? How am I supposed to break anyone out of a manual labor room I have never seen?"

"You'll have help. In fact, you won't even need to go near the manual labor room. What you need to do is much harder." The Shadow-Shield gave the Way-Guide a smile that was meant to be enthusiastic, but the Way-Guide took it as a bit sadistic. He then gestured for the Way-Guide to sit on the couch across from him. "You are a pilot and pilots rely on computer programming to guide their ships, so you know a good deal about computers, right?"

The Way-Guide nodded his head and sat on the couch. "But what does ship computer programming have to do with breaking anyone out?"

"Well," the Shadow-Shield explained, "the manual labor room is surrounded by floor tiles that prevent the workers from leaving. If they step on the tiles, they will instantly be disintegrated. These tiles are controlled by the Dark Tyrant's master computer. You need to gain access to the computer and reprogram the tiles." He then laughed so mischievously, that it made the Way-Guide uneasy, "perhaps even make the tiles so they target the guards instead. That would make our task that much easier."

The Way-Guide had a feeling the Shadow-Shield was going to elaborate further on the need to target the guards, so before the Shadow-Shield finished a breath, he interjected, "Break into the Dark Tyrant's master computer?" The Way-Guide stared at the Shadow-Shield, dumbfounded. "I honestly don't think I am the one for this job."

"I can tell you one thing, if you want to rescue 1-05, this is what needs to be done, and, frankly, you are the only one here who can do it."

The Way-Guide took a deep breath to bolster himself for the task at hand. "All right," he said, as much to build up his own determination as to voice his acceptance of the job. "You do have some architectural plans of the area that houses the master computer, right?"

Chapter Thirty-Five

2,040 watched with puzzled wonderment as the Grubian Ghouls and the Dark Tyrant's engineers created 1's shape-shifter, or shadow-shifter, the term he overheard one of the Grubian Ghouls use. It interested him that the methods used by the Grubian Ghouls in the construction were contrary to those used to make shape-shifters. While shape-shifters were made using one element, lithostones, both for life energy and as a means of affecting light waves and sub-atomic particles to change the shape of the shape-shifter, shadow-shifters required two elements to accomplish these tasks. Human souls were used for life energy and dark nefescur crystals were used to alter the shadows around the shadow-shifter to convince viewers they were seeing something other than what was actually there. Because nefescur crystals did not allow actual changes in the shadow-shifter, the perceived changes to the shadow-shifter's form were more apparent in the dark than in the light. Another difference was in the make-up of the brain. Shape-shifters used computer-based artificial intelligence for cognitive functions such as decision-making, problem-solving, reasoning, and learning, whereas the shadow-shifters had organic brains that were created from altered human brains with parts of the brain adjusted or removed to make the shadow-shifter more subservient and less empathetic.

The process the Grubian Ghouls were using reminded 2,040 of stories he read as a child about scientists who pieced together body parts from graves and created a crazed monster that became the outcast of society. Still, he reminded himself, reality had advanced much further than those books accounted for. The body parts used in this project had been created from stem cells under careful sterilization in a clean laboratory and the only part that came from anything resembling a grave was the life energy. Even so, as the engineers and ghouls tinkered on the Shadow-Shifter, 2,040 pondered a moment in reverential silence as he wondered whether the human soul being used was anybody he once had known.

The part 2,040 played in the creation of the Shadow-Shifter, or what he considered a tragic opera with a predictably catastrophic ending, was to see that it was completed in a timely manner. Thus, he sent for a couple more computers and several assistants to free up the engineers to focus on the more complex tasks. He also periodically reminded the engineers and Grubian Ghouls, in as polite and urgent a manner as possible, of the deadline that loomed on the horizon. Still, 2,040 did not have to be so worried, since the Grubian Ghouls were just as eager to quickly complete the creation of the Shadow-Shifter as 1 was. With this being the case, the moment that 1 poked his nose into the engineering workshop to see if the deadline was being met, the engineers and Ghouls were making the final adjustments on the Shadow-Shifter.

As 1 made his way to the lab table which held the Shadow-Shifter, the engineers backed away to permit 1 a view of their project. It was obvious, though, that the Grubian Ghouls continued to stand close due to the noticeable hazy fracturing of the light surrounding the Shadow-Shifter. As 1 tilted his head with his analysis of what seemed like nothing more than a body on the table, his flab-filled chin followed the pull of gravity one way then the other. "What is this? Where's my shape-shifter?"

"Shape-shifter?" one of the Grubian Ghouls gurgled and snorted, "yes . . . this is your shape-shifter . . . it will begin functioning . . . yes . . ."

1's mouth twisted up in determined skepticism causing every bulge in his face to become even more pronounced than it already was. In an attempt to avert his skepticism, one of the engineers pulled back the lab sheet covering the Shadow-Shifter. 2,040 wondered how the engineer could have imagined this could change 1's mind, because the newly created shadow-shifter looked like nothing more than a dead body lying on a table in the morgue. Still, this was the first time that 2,040 was able to acquire a clear view of the Shadow-Shifter. While it had the appearance of a sturdy yet slender man with firm shoulders and determined eyebrows, there was something feminine in its high cheekbones, waist, neck, nose, and mouth. *Perhaps Grubian Ghouls have little understanding of the differences between human males and females,* 2,040 surmised. What gave the Shadow-Shifter an even more bizarre appearance was its wild full-bodied blond hair which reached just past its shoulders.

"Your Shadow-Shifter," one of the Ghouls said with a hiss that seemed as if it was flowing over a bed of sharp rocks.

As he examined the shadow-shifter, 1's nose curled up in disdain. "Are you sure it is alive? Make it turn into something," he demanded.

"It will," the Ghoul gurgled. "You will sssee."

The faint outline of the other Ghoul tapped the shoulder of one of the engineers. "Go ahead," the Ghoul told him, sounding much like the air escaping from a worn-out lead pipe.

The engineer grabbed a syringe and filled it with a light green glowing liquid. He depressed the plunger of the syringe to empty the barrel of air and jabbed the needle into the Shadow-Shifter's arm.

As the liquid entered its body, a mild green glowing light illuminated from the Shadow-Shifter. Its eyes flew open, and it looked directly at 1. Its mouth curled in an evil sneer.

"Shape-shifter, I want you to turn into . . ." 1 rubbed his cheek in thought as his eyes wandered upon 2,040 standing in the shadows. 1 remembered 2,040's claims that making a shape-shifter was impossible and smirked at him mischievously. "Turn into 2,040 there."

The shape-shifter (or shadow-shifter) deliberately stood to its feet, its back to 2,040, and turned its head to look over its shoulder at 2,040.

2,040 did not like the feeling of having this odd-looking shadow-shifter's eyes on him. There was something not right about its eyes, as if they were unbalanced or, maybe, opposites in color or size. Its unblinking, fixed gaze made 2,040 feel almost helpless and invaded. 2,040 shifted nervously. "Can't you think of something else for it to shift into?" 2,040 took a step back into the shadows.

A pleased chuckle was 1's only response.

The Shadow-Shifter turned back to 1 and a cloudy dark haze engulfed it. It scrolled through a series of faces, much like dice rolling across the table. As the haze dissipated, what was left was a replica of 2,040.

While this replica was much like 2,040 in its general shape and likeness, 2,040 noticed a number of differences. It was an exaggerated and distorted version of himself. Upon first glimpse of it, 2,040 became extremely dejected because he had no idea that his own eyes were filled with such hatred nor that he sneered in such a disgusting manner. Earlier he had looked at himself in the mirror and, despite the fact that he had been under the influence of Winchian wine at that time, he thought for sure he had looked much more amiable. Upon realizing the faultiness of the Shadow-Shifter's ability and the embarrassing image it presented of him, 2,040 built up a strong dislike for the Shadow-Shifter. His dislike increased when he saw what he could have sworn to be his nose on the

Shadow-Shifter growing much longer and dipping even deeper. Then, the Shadow-Shifter laughed with intense disdain as its eyes seemed to shoot out fire. "That doesn't look a thing like me," 2,040 insistently shouted out.

"No, no." 1 jiggled with pleased laughter, "It looks *exactly* like you. It's perfect."

2,040 shook his head in disbelief wondering how 1 could find the Shadow-Shifter's interpretation of him in any way believable.

The Grubian Ghouls, however, were thrilled to hear 1's approval of their Shadow-Shifter. They gurgled with ecstatic laughter and announced that Grubia and the Planet of Darkness should work together more often in the future.

With 2,040's directions in hand, 9-85 made his way to the workshop of 81-4-60. 9-85 discovered that this workshop was not at all what he had expected. 9-85 had imagined 81-4-60 as a grey-haired, scatter-brained man living in the lower levels of the City of the Dark Tyrant bent over wires, circuits, and gutted-out computers, surrounded by mechanical mishmash which littered every table, chair, and walkway. In reality, 81-4-60's workshop was located not far from the Duke of Distraction's cavern and actually held a surprising amount of flair. The first thing 9-85 came to when he approached the workshop was the front door which fell away from him and formed a ramp much like a gangway leading to a sea ship. The ramp led to a rectangular area surrounded by a railing, past which was the wooden landing to a large oval-shaped room. When 9-85 stepped into the rectangular area, he realized it was an open elevator which dropped down to take 9-85 to a lower-level floor.

The railing parted, moving away to allow 9-85 to enter the lower level of the oval-shaped room which was lined by computers and monitors. The computers by no means made the room look impassive or sterile, because the monitors displayed travelogue-like images from various planets, most of which showed scenes of nature and ocean life. Looking up, 9-85 saw the level he had first come to, an upstairs landing surrounded by a wooden railing which resembled the railing found on a wooden pirate sea ship. From where he stood, 9-85 felt as if he was the southern point on a compass and on the upper-landing both to the west and east were large computers working on complex calculations at lightning speed. At the north compass point of the room on the upper landing was a large open desk at which sat a man with light brown hair and light blue eyes. He wore a neatly trimmed beard which balanced out a fairly prominent nose. He had a trim physique and did not wear the clothes usually worn by computer engineers. Instead, he wore a white silk shirt and a black velvet vest trimmed in gold. His pants matched his vest and were tucked into dark brown knee-high leather boots.

It took the man a few minutes to notice that 9-85 was there. Eventually, the man stood and came to the upper-railing and looked down at 9-85. "So, now," he asked, squinting a bit, much like a sea-captain squints at the sun when he is deciphering the markings on the flag of an oncoming ship, "what is your business here?"

"I'm here because 2,040 sent me." 9-85 hoped that by mentioning 2,040's name, the man would smile in recognition and join him downstairs. 9-85 was eager to meet 81-4-60 face-to-face so that he would no longer have to crane his head upward to continue his conversation with him.

Unfortunately, the man did not smile in recognition and only narrowed his eyes in suspicion. "Who are you and what does 2,040 want?"

"You are 81-4-60, aren't you?" 9-85 stepped forward. "2,040 told me you would be willing to help him out of a certain difficulty."

The man's eyes widened as he took on a "blown away with the thought" expression. The expression made 9-85 doubt that the man, if he was 81-4-60, would help 2,040, but, at the same time, 9-85 became a little more hopeful when the man started making his way down the stairs. "I remember the last time I agreed to *help 2,040 out*, it ended up with me and 2,040 rappelling down a rope into an active volcano to retrieve rare living crystals . . ." The man gave 9-85 a sideways look. "He isn't asking me to do something like that again . . . is he?"

9-85 took a second to adjust to the conversation going in a direction opposite of what he had expected. "So, you *are* 81-4-60?" he asked firmly in order to reorganize the conversation.

The man had reached the bottom of the stairs and, when 9-85 had finished his second inquiry, looked as if he would have pulled his hair out if it had been a long enough to grab easily. "Of course I'm 81-4-60. Who else would I be? The Corvanian monster from Margill?" He waved his hands in disbelief and moved over to collapse on a nearby couch. "So, tell me. Is he wanting to go after those living crystals again? Or does he have some other hopelessly impossible task for me to perform?" He leaned his head back on the couch and looked at the ceiling as if to say, 'heaven help us.'

Feeling relatively reassured that the man *was* 81-4-60, 9-85 followed him to the living area and took a seat on a chair next to the couch. "Well, I suppose it depends on your point of view. The task 2,040 had in mind does not carry so much the risk of falling into a volcano as the risk of being thrown into the Dark Tyrant's prisons."

9-85 was afraid that after telling him about the prisons, 81-4-60 would slam his fist, shout, "That does it," and throw him out of the room. Instead, he only shrugged his shoulders, tilted his head casually, and remarked that it sounded interesting. "So, what exactly is it he wants me to do?" he asked attentively.

9-85 was so surprised by 81-4-60's response that, had he not been holding firmly onto the arms of the couch, he might have fallen off of it. "Basically, we have to break into the Dark

Tyrant's master computer and make some changes to the data there." 9-85 proceeded to explain the whole fiasco with 2,040's economic model and the corrections that needed to be made before anyone noticed the mistakes. "2,040 told me that if anyone could break into the Dark Tyrant's master computer, it would be you."

81-4-60 looked at 9-85 with a no-nonsense expression. "No," he told him pointblank.

9-85 knew he heard him correctly but had a hard time grasping the fact that he said 'no'. "What do you mean 'no'? Are you saying that you *won't* do it or that you *can't* do it?"

81-4-60 took a deep exasperated breath. "I am not saying I *won't* do the job. It is just that I am not the one who can do it, not on my own, anyway." He sat up a little more, leaning toward 9-85 in an entre-nous manner. "To tell you the truth . . . there *is* someone who can hack into the master computer *much* better than me."

Shifting in his seat, 9-85 wrung his hands together nervously. "Perhaps you are right, but this is something we can't . . ."

". . . trust just anyone with?" 81-4-60 finished the sentence for him. "Of course. The good thing is that this *other* someone *can* be trusted." He nodded his head with confident finality, but, afterwards, sighed wearily. "People. Horrible monsters if you ask me. Avoid them whenever possible, that's my advice." He then, ran his fingers through his hair in frustration, which was more like running his fingers over his hair than through it, his hair being so short. "People overrate the usefulness of people, I say." He stood and walked over to the chair next to where 9-85 was sitting. "After all, people are the source of 99.9% of all problems in the universe — wars, pollutions, murders, famines, all have people at their source . . . so, don't deal with people, unless *absolutely* necessary." He knelt on the ground and leaned an elbow on the ottoman in front of the chair. Then, with his other hand, he caressed the ottoman tenderly.

9-85 found 81-4-60's actions strange, but just took it to mean that he was one of those brilliant men that were all the more brilliant due to their eccentricities. "But you said that this *person* you recommended could be trusted . . ." 9-85 reminded him.

"Wrong." 81-4-60 pointed a firm finger at him. "I did not say person . . . I said *someone*."

"But isn't that the same thing," 9-85 asked in frustration.

"No," 81-4-60 said with a seriousness so serious that 9-85 questioned 81-4-60's sanity. "The someone I was speaking of is *not* a person but my assistant." He tapped the ottoman a couple times to draw attention to it. "Meet my assistant, Octelix."

9-85 shook his head, finding 81-4-60's actions too far from the realm of sanity. "That's a footstool."

81-4-60 tapped his chin, frowned, and knitted his eyebrows as if ready to give 9-85 the psychological examination. "Remember," 81-4-60 reiterated, "people cause problems. If we had more 'footstools,' as you call Octelix, for assistants, our planet would be much better off." He then stood and looked 9-85 straight in the eye. "By the way . . . you really hurt Octelix's feelings when you call him a footstool."

"But that *is* a footstool," 9-85 insisted, standing in preparation to make an exit the first moment he could without upsetting 81-4-60.

"No," 81-4-60 told him firmly, "that is my assistant."

9-85 shook his head once more and was about to excuse himself from the room when his eyes fell again on the 'footstool,' but this time he noticed it moving on its own. It lowered what must have been its 'head' and took on an expression that could not have been anything other than wounded disbelief. 9-85's eyes widened in surprise. "What *is* that?" he asked, stepping closer to it. "Is it some kind of robot?"

"No . . ." 81-4-60 was astonished at such an absurd idea. "Not a robot and certainly not an android . . . Why everyone is in this obsession of making computerized assistants in the form of people is beyond me." He gave Octelix a friendly pat and gestured for it to step forward. "Octelix is far more useful than any person could be. Plus, he reads my thoughts and knows what I need even before I tell him." 81-4-60 nodded his head in the direction of a computer near the center of the room signaling Octelix to join him there.

9-85 thought he detected Octelix giving 81-4-60 an enthusiastic nod and wiggle followed by a quick bolting over to the computer. "It does follow your instructions well." 9-85 was impressed with the quick and accurate reactions of Octelix and was eager to learn more about it. Most robots he had worked with were sluggish and needed such precise directions it took so long to program them it would have been quicker for him to complete the task himself.

"Of course," 81-4-60 agreed as he waved his hands outward in a conductor-like fashion. "Octelix is obedient, smart, and much more companionable than a human or a pet." Indicating he had one more thing to add, he held up one finger. "Most people and pets can't read your mind which leads to countless confusions and misunderstandings. Octelix *can* read anyone's mind, so he will always know what needs to be done." He turned to Octelix as if indicating that the time had come to move on from the *sales-pitch* to a practical *demonstration*. "All right, Octelix, talk to this computer. Tell it to forget the entry I inputted yesterday after my coffee break and tell it to remember the conversation you and I had over lunch."

Octelix jumped up next to the computer. 9-85 expected Octelix to attach itself in some way to the computer to relay the information to it, but Octelix just 'stared' intently at the computer. After a few minutes, it turned to 81-4-60 and moved what 9-85 assumed was its head up and down to indicate that it had completed its task.

81-4-60 gave Octelix a friendly pat and sat in front of the computer. "Okay," he declared, much like a proud father ready to show off the talents of his son, "let's see how this turned out." He pulled up on the computer all of yesterday's entries. He pointed out to 9-85 where the entry was deleted. He then scrolled down to further in the day and drew attention to an added dialog between Octelix and 81-4-60 covering the need to procure more computer hardware to upgrade certain computers. "You need to transmit data . . . Octelix can definitely take care of that for you."

9-85 rubbed the back of his neck in thought. "I know you mentioned telepathy," he said in a tone of skepticism, "But, how was it *really* able to do that? Some sort of radio waves?"

"Of course not," 81-4-60 replied, bluntly bucking at 9-85's doubt. "Radio waves are far too limited. People don't realize computers really do want to have conversations with each other. And they *have* advanced much further than people would like to believe. Just take it from me, telepathy is not a power beyond Octelix's ability."

9-85 shook his head in disbelief, "I don't believe in telepathy in humans, let alone robots. I mean, how would it work when robots don't even have real brains?"

81-4-60's jaw dropped, astonished at 9-85's lack of understanding. "I told you, Octelix is *not* a robot. Furthermore, telepathy has been proven to exist and occurs both in people and in computers *and* in compiled assistants," he explained. "If you don't believe me just read any of the 20 scientific papers I wrote on it." He gestured emphatically toward a stack of books and magazines on a nearby table, the top book of which was titled *Telepathy. Still Skeptical? Here's the Facts'* by 81-4-60.

Not because he was convinced, but because he wanted to move on from the conversation, 9-85 nodded in agreement. "So, you are telling me that Octelix is capable of telepathically communicating the economics model to the master computer without any problem?"

"Sure," 81-4-60 agreed with a far-away look that could be taken as extremely brilliant or extremely brain-dead. "The main thing is he needs to be within a certain range . . ." He waved his hands in front of Octelix to indicate the roughly three feet range. "You know . . . computers need to have a little space . . . need to meet each other . . . before they have that connection."

9-85 frowned. *For being so against humans, it is strange how many human characteristics his little robot friend has.* "So, all we really need is Octelix and all we need to do is get it to the master computer, and it will take care of the rest." He knelt next to Octelix and gave it a quick pat on the head for emphasis. Octelix shied away from him and sulked over next to 81-4-60. "That makes the main challenge, then, getting it there undetected?" 9-85 looked at 81-4-60 hoping he would agree and declare the simplicity of that part of the mission.

81-4-60 stood and shook his head again.

9-85 sighed exasperatedly. "So, what am I leaving out now?"

"Well, I will also need a few other things." 81-4-60 pulled out of his pocket a notebook and listed items which he made a point of keeping a mystery to 9-85. "While Octelix is good at communicating to other computers, I need some tools in order to get through to the master computer and introduce Octelix to it. That entails both getting past the security guarding the computer itself and the security programmed into the computer as well. I know for a fact they put a lot of barriers into that particular computer, and I will need to find the means to bypass those. To do that, I will need to buy some supplies. 5,000 coins should do it." He made one final scribble in his notebook and tucked it back in his pocket.

2,040 had foreseen the possibility that 81-4-60 would require money, and had provided 9-85 with plenty before he came. 9-85 him the bags of coins. "So, when do you think we can take care of this?" He looked at 81-4-60 expectantly to emphasize the need for getting the job done quickly.

81-4-60 pocketed the coins, carefully checking each bag as he did. When he had assured himself he was not being short changed, he replied, "Just give me two hours and then we can meet outside the master computer."

"All right then," 9-85 agreed. "I'll see you there in two hours." As he turned to leave, his mind ran through the many possible activities he could engage in to prepare for the upcoming task. After pondering whether reviewing mathematical calculations, reading up on computer programming, or physical exercise were the best ways to prepare, he finally settled on visiting a nearby coffee shop and taking a moment to let his brain completely relax.

Once 9-85 left, 81-4-60 sat on the floor next to Octelix in a confidential manner and looked it straight in what one could imagine were its eyes. 81-4-60 shook his head and sighed, "Thank God, he's gone."

Chapter Thirty-Six

The Guardian stood before the viewing screen and stared fixedly at the *Ghost III* suspended motionlessly not far from his space station. His orders were to prevent that ship and its captain, Infinity, from passing his web. He was determined to carry out his mission. After all, if he succeeded to stop Infinity's invasion of the Planet of Darkness, he would be hailed as a brilliant and powerful leader. On one hand, he was confident in his ability to win against Infinity. His new pet made him unbeatable. Still, he had his misgivings. A conviction deep within him warned him it would be a mistake to confront Infinity.

"Your majesty." The Guardian's chief guard approached him. "What is your plan of attack?"

Without taking his eyes off the *Ghost III*, the Guardian responded with confidence, "We'll outsmart him with an unexpected tactic . . . one that I managed to pull off when I smuggled the Chamoleena Wine into Zandosia." He held his chin higher to emphasize how certain he was they would win. The confidence was just an act. If he played the part compellingly enough, though, he hoped he might be able to convince his men, as well as himself, that he *was* confident. "To start with, play it subtle and keep your men restrained. We'll wait for him to make the first move." He narrowed his eyes to emphasize his determination for success.

The chief guard nodded, "Yes, your majesty." He turned to command the guards and ensure that weapons and engineers were properly prepared and the pilots were ready to board their ships on command.

After the chief guard had left, the Guardian thought he heard an eerie croaking voice calling his name. He shifted uneasily and let his eyes scan the command center for anything unusual. The voice came from an area close to the room where he kept his pet. He pulled himself away from the viewing screen and ensured he had his gun ready. With eyes alert, he made his way to the room. He was about to press the button to open the door to the room, when he heard his name called again, this time the voice came from down the nearby hallway. The Guardian cautiously walked down the shadowed hallway wondering what type of unusual mystical being had invaded his space station.

At the end of the hallway sat a man wrapped in a rough-woven grey cape and hood crouched on the floor against the wall, his face tucked into his arms. When the Guardian moved to stand in front of him, the man slowly raised his hooded head to reveal plastered black hair and a smooth black beard. His face had a faded orange-bluish tint and he had wide, blood-shot eyes. "Why are you hesitating?" the man growled in a voice that reminded the Guardian of a pack of vicious dogs gnawing on old, rotting bones.

The Guardian's heart skipped several panicked beats, and he took a step back, his hand hovering over his gun. "Who are you?" he asked.

"You know me," the man replied with bulging, insistent eyes. "I may look different to you because, being so far from the dark energy generated by the souls of the lava pit, I am unable to alter my form for long." He held his hands in front of him and they transformed for a brief moment into long, leaf-less tree branches. However, the image quickly faded into ghostly smoke, leaving him with his orange-tinted hands once more.

The Guardian moved his hand away from his gun, to ensure his intentions would not be misinterpreted. "The Dark Tyrant?" the Guardian trembled as he gasped.

"Yeeessss," the Dark Tyrant tossed aside his cloak and stood up. The movement seemed to exhaust him and leave him out of breath. When standing, he remained hunched over and the effort to move caused his blood-shot eyes to become a deeper shade of red, even spreading to his eyelids.

"We are planning the attack," the Guardian assured the Dark Tyrant. "I had decided to use a strategy that worked well when—"

The Dark Tyrant sneered and shook his head. "It won't work with Infinity." As he spoke Infinity's name, his mouth curled in disgust, and his voice choked like dogs gagging on the bones they had devoured. "Infinity is too uncooperative, too unpredictable, too infuriating to be destroyed by simple strategies." His face took on an even deeper shade of orange as he struggled in vain to contain his deep resentment of Infinity. "That is why I took the effort of coming here to advise you." The Guardian noticed that the angrier the Dark Tyrant became, the more his eyes resembled twin spiders walking around in red and orange goo.

The Guardian tensely scanned the Dark Tyrant. "It might have been easier to send the message over the communications link."

The Dark Tyrant shot the Guardian a glare. "Brainless fool. And have it picked up by Infinity?"

The Guardian shifted his weight and wiped his clammy forehead. "You are right, of course."

After a shiver that stemmed either from hatred or weakness, the Dark Tyrant drew back on his cloak and turned his back on the Guardian. "You must destroy Infinity, but you cannot do this by attacking him." He heaved away from the Guardian in a bobbing, slithering movement accompanied by a screeching and gasping of his throat.

"I don't get it," the Guardian puzzled, "the only way to kill somebody is to attack them someway or other."

The Dark Tyrant snorted in disgust at the Guardian's stupidity. He turned his head to look at the Guardian over his shoulder, his eyes seeming to transform from spiders to vampire bats. "There is only one way to destroy Infinity and that is to destroy *The Ghost III*. Once the ship is gone, you can easily put an end to Infinity." He grinned, revealing crowded crooked teeth that gleamed yellow in the shadows. His eyes bulged further and his orange face seemed to expand like a ready-to-burst balloon. He then turned back to face the end of the hall. He took several steps away from the Guardian and then disappeared into a hazy smoke.

The Guardian thought over the Dark Tyrant's commands and concluded that they must be the best strategies. Anyway, he had to assume they were the best strategies, since he had no choice but to go by the Dark Tyrant's orders.

Chapter Thirty-Seven

9-85's training was in mathematics, not military or strategic planning, so his organization of the task to replace the file in the master computer was uninspired at best. All he focused on was the actual replacing of the file. While he considered the possibility of a few electronic alarms or traps leading to the computer, he figured 81-4-60 would have no trouble in spotting and disarming them. What he had not foreseen or planned for was the presence of Enforcers. He would have been surprised enough had there been two or three, but he was in no way prepared for twelve armed Enforcers pacing the hallway to the entrance to the master computer.

When he peeked around the corner and counted the twelve Enforcers, he considered scrapping the entire plan. He reminded himself, though, that he would be facing the same consequences for sneaking into the master computer as he would if the Dark Tyrant found out the economics plan was wrong. So, he took a deep breath and determined to continue to wait for 81-4-60, hoping he would have a plan for getting past the Enforcers.

While 9-85 had only been waiting ten and a half minutes, the tension stemming from his quandary with the Enforcers made the time pass much slower. By the time 81-4-60 and Octelix finally did show up, 9-85 had managed to run through his mind at least twenty-two possible plans for getting past the Enforcers, all of which he quickly tossed as completely useless.

To 9-85's surprise, 81-4-60 was not taken aback when he saw the Enforcers. "Mhm, looks like they doubled security," he blandly acknowledged as he turned a blaming eye on 9-85. "Were they expecting you?"

Even though he tried not to show his irritation at being blamed for the extra Enforcers, 9-85 could not help but grimace a bit and clench his fists. "Of course not," he replied. "No one other than you and 2, 040 knew about this."

"Hmm." 81-4-60 was not convinced. He gestured for Octelix to come closer. Octelix bounded over to him and rubbed itself affectionately against 81-4-60's pant leg. "Ok, enough of that," he told Octelix as he moved it to where it could stand between him and 9-85. "Octelix, I need you to listen in on the Enforcers' intercom system."

Octelix nodded and carefully sneaked up close to the corner leading to the hallway patrolled by the Enforcers. It scooted to the point where what could have been its face was just inside the other hallway. The Enforcers may have even seen part of Octelix, but, as 9-85 concluded, they probably thought nothing of it, since it only looked like some type of footstool.

81-4-60 dipped his hand into a satchel he was carrying and pulled out and unfolded a small computer. "Now to see what's going on in Octelix's brain . . ." He examined the visuals displayed on the computer screen. The computer was connected wirelessly with Octelix and could capture everything that was going through what 9-85 assumed was Octelix's memory bank. 81-4-60's computer screen was divided into twelve separate visuals, displaying what each Enforcer was seeing. Beneath the visuals ran a text description of the audio input and output of the Enforcers' intercom systems. 81-4-60 scrolled through each of the conversations.

9-85 glanced over 81-4-60's shoulder at the screen. He was unfamiliar with this type of computer, but from what he gathered most of the conversations concerned times for scheduled cleanings and repairs. The only mention of possible break-ins was in reference to potential sabotage by some insurgents connected to a certain manual labor room 15.

81-4-60 looked back at 9-85. "Well, it sounds like it's not us they are after . . . but they are on the watch for intruders, so we have to proceed with caution." Even though he was away from his nautical workshop, he still brought a bit of it with him in his demeanor of a sea captain on the lookout for a chest of gold. He slapped his computer closed and crammed it into the satchel he slung over his shoulder.

"But how *can* we proceed?" 9-85 asked.

81-4-60 tilted his head and slowly waved a hand as if to say, *what's to worry about?* "We get them to leave, of course," he replied and wagged his head at the simplicity of it all.

"All right." 9-85 still wondered how they were going to accomplish it.

Raising one hand mechanically, 81-4-60 snapped his fingers once for Octelix to return. It eagerly came back and *looked* expectantly up at 81-4-60, waiting for its orders.

"Octelix," 81-4-60 told it with a straightforward, no-room-for-misinterpretation manner, "there are twelve Enforcers in this hallway. I want you to connect with their intercom and send them emergency orders that they are needed to help guard the Dark Tyrant's executive hall." He nodded once to ensure that Octelix understood the importance of completing the task correctly. "Now, go on and take care of it." He gruffly gestured toward the hallway with his thumb, encouraging Octelix to move quickly to carry out its job.

While Octelix was sending the emergency messages to the Enforcers, 9-85 was distracted by a dark shadow moving at the opposite end of their hallway. By the time he could focus on it, it had ducked around the corner. 9-85 hoped what he saw was either someone who was just going about their own business or some distortion from his own imagination.

However, the shadow was the spy-creature 1-13 had sent to spy on 2,040. After ducking into the shadows, it waited and then craned its head around the corner, focused its binocular-like eyes on 9-85 and 81-4-60, and continued to record their movements from a safe distance.

A few minutes after 81-4-60 had given Octelix its directions, 9-85 heard the Enforcers' communication devices relaying the orders for them to report to the Dark Tyrant's executive hall. 9-85 eagerly watched, counting the moments to when the hallway would be completely clear of Enforcers.

The Enforcers gathered around the lead Enforcer who, in a firm voice, clarified the orders for the rest of them. The lead Enforcer gestured for four of the Enforcers to take up posts surrounding the entrance to the main computer while he and the other seven Enforcers marched off, most likely to the executive hall.

9-85 turned to 81-4-60 and gave him a disappointed expression.

As if placing his final bet in a game of Tassular, 81-4-60 waved his hands outward in the air. "What do you expect, we got rid of eight. I'd call that rather good."

9-85 had to nod in agreement, but gestured toward the remaining Enforcers. "But what do we do about them . . . They will still be impossible to get past."

81-4-60 ran one hand down his face in thought. "Impossible? Certainly not impossible." He pulled Octelix in on the conversation. "Octelix will take on two of the Enforcers and you and I will handle the other two."

9-85's eyes widened nervously. "What am I supposed to do?"

"Just follow my lead," 81-4-60 replied as he *handed* Octelix a small metal canister.

9-85 could not pull his eyes away from Octelix, because he was curious as to how it would be able to take the canister from 81-4-60. To his amazement, Octelix reached one of its front legs up to grasp the canister firmly. It then managed to stuff the canister into some unseen compartment underneath itself. In spite of his curious amazement, 9-85 forced his eyes away from Octelix and turned to follow 81-4-60 who was already several steps ahead of him. The two slipped into the shadows of a nearby archway while Octelix proceeded up to the Enforcers.

Octelix could not help but draw the attention of the Enforcers as it scuttled up to them.

One of the Enforcers moved to stand in its path. "Stop."

Octelix stopped and tucked its head down, playing it cagy.

The Enforcer bent over Octelix, examining it to determine what it was. "This is rather strange." He gestured for one of the other Enforcers to come and assist him.

"What do you think it is?" the first Enforcer asked as the other one approached.

The other Enforcer knelt next to Octelix for a closer examination. "I've never seen anything like it. I think I see something here, though. Look." He gestured for the other guard to bend down closer to see a compartment he found underneath Octelix.

Octelix took this opportunity to open the compartment and let the canister fall to the ground. The second it hit the ground, the canister popped open and the entire area filled with a bluish gas. The two guards choked and gasped and fell to the ground unconscious. One of the last two Enforcers started to move toward them to offer aid but the other Enforcer stopped him. "Wait until the smoke clears. And keep your gun aimed at that thing."

81-4-60 took this as a cue for him and 9-85 to move into action. He casually strolled up to Octelix and looked from it to the two Enforcers who were cautiously making their way to their unconscious comrades. The first Enforcer saw him and covered him with his gun.

"It appears you've had a bit of a run in with that adorable little Octelix there," 81-4-60 told them in a more nonchalant manner than they were expecting.

"Octelix?" the first Enforcer repeated, unused to the term.

"Well, I could explain everything to you, but, unfortunately you would not understand a word of it, since you have never read any of my research papers . . . here . . ." He pulled the computer out of his satchel. "Let me show you this." He unfolded the computer, pulled up one of his papers on the screens and handed it to the Enforcer. "Read the first few paragraphs and you will know everything you need to know about this situation." He clasped his hands behind his back as he waited.

Unconvinced, the Enforcer read the paper on the computer, which was a difficult task because, first, Enforcers are taught only basic reading and, second, the paper was written in a complex and convoluted style.

The last Enforcer moved up, glanced at the computer screen which the other Enforcer was staring at. "Stop wasting your time," he belligerently told the first Enforcer.

81-4-60 gestured subtly to 9-85 to take his place behind the belligerent Enforcer.

The belligerent Enforcer tapped the other on the arm. "Come on, let's take these two to the Persuaders for questioning."

But the other Enforcer had become figuratively glued to the computer screen. Once he had finished the first paragraph, a countdown took over the screen and once it had reached zero, the screen burst into irresistible, three-dimensional hypnotic images. After trying to see what had caught the other Enforcer's interest, the last Enforcer took one look at the screen and became captivated by the images as well. 985 watched the Enforcers fall into their trance, and smiled, impressed by the extent of 81-4-60's computer skills.

81-4-60 gestured with his head toward the two Enforcers and gave 9-85 a '*we got them*' nod. He then turned back to the Enforcers, rubbed his chin in thought, and walked around them as he spoke. "You do realize, you two, that you're in a difficult situation," he told them in a friendly monotone used to keep them at ease and in a semiconscious state. "The most difficult part of your situation is that you happen to be people. People are horrible, nauseating creatures that this world would be better off without. Unfortunately, there is nothing we can do about that. But, what you can do is drift off in your mind to a calm, contented world in which you don't have to think, because I will do your thinking for you." He took the computer out of the one Enforcer's hands and put it back into his satchel and, instead pulled out of the satchel four cords of grimseen wire. He handed one to 9-85 and used another to start binding up one of the Enforcers. "This wire is extra strong and should hold them for quite some time."

As 9-85 started to tie up the other Enforcer, the Enforcer jerked himself free and attempted to reach for his gun. 9-85 remembered reading in a book that the best place to hit someone to knock them out was on the back of the head just above the neck. After a short pause of doubt, 9-85 tightened his fist and hit the Enforcer as close to the correct spot as the Enforcer's helmet would allow. To 9-85's surprise, the Enforcer fell unconscious to the floor.

"I wasn't sure that would work," 9-85 announced, hoping for a few accolades.

81-4-60 was not the type to dole out compliments and all he could notice was that the fingers of the Enforcer's right hand were twitching. "I think you better either hit him again or get him tied up real fast," he replied.

After 9-85 and 81-4-60 made certain all four Enforcers were secure and propped against the wall, they made their way to the entrance to the Master Computer. Beside the entrance was a square box with three red flashing lights, indicating that the door was locked and secured with an alarm. 81-4-60 stepped to the door and attached an electronic tracker over this box so he could find all electric currents connected to the door. He then placed another small circular device on the wall next to the first to redirect the current. He opened the door and gestured for 9-85 and Octelix to follow him clandestinely into a hall that led to the master computer.

Once inside, 81-4-60 paused in the shadowy hallway and looked around cautiously.

"Okay, let's go." 9-85 started to walk past him.

81-4-60 held him back. "Don't be in a hurry. We will more than likely run into traps. And we won't be going forward very quickly if we slip into one of those."

9-85 glanced about the empty hall uneasily. *How could any traps be hidden in such emptiness?* 9-85 gestured for 81-4-60 to precede him. "Then you first. Disarm the traps."

81-4-60 shook his head. "I would if I could, but I can't tell a trap from a bump in the road."

9-85 exhaled. "Why didn't you tell me that before?"

81-4-60 looked at 9-85 in disbelief. "I did not say I couldn't disarm the traps. I just said I couldn't recognize them. Octelix is the one that lets me know where the traps are. So Octelix is the one that should go first." He knelt next to Octelix and gestured for it to go forward carefully, communicate with all computer-like devices, and alert him to any traps. Octelix weaved forward, hopping occasionally to take in the readings of any hidden wireless traps. While Octelix was scanning for traps, 81-4-60 turned to 9-85 confidentially. "Computers can be very rude with each other. And their language can be appalling. If you knew what they were saying about you to each other, you would be shocked." 81-4-60's eyes widened in a 'believe it or not, but it's true' expression. When he noticed 9-85 watching Octelix nervously, he moved closer to 9-85 to reassure him. "Don't worry, Octelix will let me know when the computer is being mean or saying anything unacceptable."

When Octelix located a trap, it tucked its *head* down and stared intently at the trap. 81-4-60 gestured from Octelix to 9-

85 indicating Octelix had done exactly what he said it would do.

9-85 tried to stay calm while 81-4-60 worked on the trap. It did not help that at a few points the trap sizzled and even once beeped loudly. Finally, 81-4-60 stood and announced that it was safe to continue on.

As they continued down the hall, 81-4-60 pointed out where he predicted the next traps would be. "I would say they are setting these traps in what the notoriously clever 9-60-52 claims as the MCP or the MUMS Contradictory Pattern. You know, middle, under, middle, side." He waved his hand like haphazard brush-strokes demonstrating the pattern. "Once you know the pattern, disarming the traps is child's play." They ran into several other traps, and, despite a few more close calls, 81-4-60 managed to disarm each of them.

The hallway eventually led them to the room that housed the main computer. The walls of this room were a rusty red and straight in front of them as they entered was the only thing in the room: the master computer. While the computer filled the entire wall, it was not as big as 9-85 expected. The center portion of the computer housed six computer screens and on either side of the screens were metallic boxes containing various buttons, touch-screens, and input ports.

81-4-60 made his way to the computer and connected a rectangular metal connector to one of the ports and used this to attach his smaller computer to the master computer. "Now to check for any barriers that need to be broken down in order for it to accept a conversation with Octelix." He flipped through incoming data on his computer screen.

In the gray area of space, The *Ghost III* continued moving slowly along the red, glowing electric web which blocked the path to the Planet of Darkness. The web was fully powered and Infinity could not find any weak points that would allow the *Ghost III* to slip through.

Infinity shook his head soberly. "We won't be able to make it through without locating the energy source for the electric web and taking it down," he told the *Ghost III*. "And I am fairly certain of where that energy source is . . ." He narrowed his eyes as he looked through the viewing screen at the distant space station ahead.

"We will have to find the energy source later," the *Ghost III* informed Infinity. *"There are those on the Planet of Darkness who are searching for truth."* The *Ghost III* dropped a small video screen over the larger viewing screen. The video screen displayed images of 9-85 and 81-4-60 as they were breaking into the Dark Tyrant's master computer. *"It is important that they know the way to escape the Planet of Darkness."*

Infinity raised an eyebrow and nodded. "Yes. We should let them know the way of escape." His eyes focused on Octelix. "And I know the perfect way to send them that message."

81-4-60 had been working on pinpointing a pathway of communication in the master computer for so long that 9-85 was wondering whether they should quit and leave before being discovered. As a buffer, he stood with firm footing at the entrance of the room, eyes and ears focused on the hallway, ready to announce the presence of any intruders.

In a huff, 81-4-60 gave the master computer a forceful kick. "This is unquestionably the nastiest computer I've ever worked with." He rubbed his forehead and allowed himself a moment of meditation. "I am beginning to doubt that there is any way to get through to it."

Octelix hurried to 81-4-60 looking visibly animated, which was not easy for something like a footstool. It nudged 81-4-60's hand and *looked* up at him excitedly.

"What is it?" 81-4-60 asked it. "What do you hear?"

Octelix shifted in anticipation and *stared* up at 81-4-60, trying hard to concentrate.

9-85 moved up from the hallway. "What's going on with Octelix? Did he find a way to transfer the data to the master computer?"

81-4-60 shushed 9-85, closed his eyes, and, through his mind, listened to what Octelix was telling him. After a few seconds, he opened his eyes and looked at 9-85 in astonishment. "Octelix said he's made a friend . . . ?"

"So, he's made friends with the master computer?" 9-85 asked, uncomfortable with the thought of computers making friends.

Ponderously, 81-4-60 tilted his head. "I don't know." He reached over to his computer and opened a new screen. "But, it might help if we can find out what he learned." He turned back to Octelix. "All right, Octelix, tell my computer what you've learned from your new friend."

Octelix sprang close to 81-4-60's computer and *looked* at it intently as it relayed the information it had gathered.

The information was soon displayed on the computer's screen. The first thing that appeared was a picture of a determined wolf carrying a letter in his mouth. The wolf dropped the letter, which opened and filled the screen. The letter read:

To the skeptical engineer and the cunning assistant,
The Planet of Darkness is in danger and will soon be no more. Infinity is on a quest to rescue those who want to escape this danger. Mistakes that have been made cannot be undone. Covering them up is just a distraction. Instead, for your safety, make your way to the Shepherdess' Valley.
Your friend and guide,
Infinity

After the letter folded up again, a map opened showing the path to the Shepherdess' Valley.

81-4-60 and 9-85 exchanged perplexed expressions. "Did that come from the master computer?" 9-85 puzzled.

81-4-60 flipped through some screens on his computer and shook his head. "I don't know, but it saved itself on my computer. And guess what . . ." He looked back at 9-85 with the most excited grin 9-85 ever saw him give. "I have a pathway into the master computer."

With the door open for a conversation between Octelix and the master computer, it did not take 81-4-60 long to enable Octelix to replace the old incorrect economics model with the new corrected one. Unfortunately, as soon as the model was replaced, 81-4-60's computer started screaming an alarm and a message popped on the screen in large blood-red letters: THE MASTER COMPUTER HAS BEEN HACKED. 9-85 gasped. "They know."

81-4-60 quickly disconnected his computer from the master computer. "I knew the master computer was mean. It tattled on us." He stuffed his computer in the satchel with a huff. "Now, the Dark Tyrant knows what we've done."

Chapter Thirty-Eight

ix ghostly, glowing white balls hovered in a row in front of 2,040. He sat on the couch and leaned forward toward the coffee table over which they floated. Instead of speculating the outcome of 9-85's undertaking, he chose to bury his thoughts in a little game he had created once in his spare time. The objective of the game was to keep as many glowing balls floating at the same time. To do this, he had to tap the metal discs under each floating ball, one after another in the correct sequence and without allowing more than 3 seconds between taps. The more glowing balls he had floating in the air the harder it was to keep them floating. He was up to ten glowing balls when 9-85 and 81-4-60 entered the room with unmistakably glum faces. 2,040's concentration was broken and the glowing balls fell to the table and evaporated into nothingness.

34,000 noticed a spasmodic shaking of 2,040's hand and rushed to sit beside him.

2,040 looked at 9-85 and 81-4-60 with sad eyes that resembled a mournful puppy dog who dared its owner to give him nasty vegetable treats instead of yummy meaty treats. "So," he frowned, "what went wrong?"

Sitting around the coffee table, 9-85 and 81-4-60 gave 2,040 a rundown of events involving the replacement of the file in the master computer. They showed him the message they received through Octelix, the announcement that the master computer had been hacked, and the inescapable consequence of the Dark Tyrant knowing the economic model had been replaced.

To 9-85's surprise, 2,040 merely cocked his head to one side and asked, "Are you sure about that?"

"He must know," 81-4-60 slammed the coffee table, rattling 2,040's game. "The master computer told on us. I am sure of it."

With a casual scratching of his beard, 2,040 sighed. "Of course the Dark Tyrant knows the computer has been hacked . . ." He paused briefly for a quick pouting of his lips. "But what makes you think he blames *you* for the hacking." He waved his hand in their directions. "Didn't you just say you received a message from that Prince of the Planet of Light . . . what was his name . . . Infinity. Some letter about the notorious Shepherdess of the Valley?" He looked at them with intense meaningfulness. "I am confident," he pointed an insistent finger at 9-85, "that it is this Infinity that the Dark Tyrant will blame for the hacking."

9-85 frowned in thought. "The Shepherdess of the Valley is notorious? . . . I haven't heard of her."

2,040 shook his head pityingly. "Of course you haven't," he snorted with a hint of disdain. "You're of the younger generation."

Intently analyzing the threads woven into the arm of the couch, 81-4-60 nodded in a half-here and half-there manner. "Yes, about fifteen years ago she was quite a fad topic for debate."

"That's right," 2,040 agreed. "That was a time when people of intelligence spent more time sitting around and discussing important events of the past. And many of them pertained to this Shepherdess of the Valley and the Planet of Light." He took a moment to let his eyes wander to the ceiling as he remembered those times. He eventually snapped himself out of his reverie. "But you certainly must know about the Planet of Light and that conspiring Prince Infinity."

9-85 replied, "I didn't consider it all that important, since it has nothing to do with math."

2,040 was visibly irritated with 9-85's apathy. "The Planet of Light is obviously conspiring against our planet, so it is the duty of all of us to know about the history of that planet and the horrible atrocities they have done to ours." He made his way to a bookshelf and pulled out a book. "It shocks me that you have never even heard about the Shepherdess of the Valley. She was the one who connived with Infinity to start an uprising against the City of the Dark Tyrant."

9-85 knit his eyebrows in perplexity. "But why should that upset you? You often complain about the atrocious way the city is being run." He did not mean his comment as an attack on 2, 040 and was surprised it sounded more contemptuous than he had intended.

Walking up to 9-85, 2,040 shook his head at his ignorance. "Yes, our planet is in need of political repair, but that does not mean I am unpatriotic." He dropped the book on 9-85's lap.

9-85 read the title. "*The Evil Plot of the Shepherdess of the Valley.*" He then thumbed through the book, not so much to read it as to look interested enough to keep 2,040 happy.

Before 9-85 could even offer a comment, 2,040 was bent on reciting his rampage against the Shepherdess. "I mean, even her name tells you she is up to no good. The Shepherdess of the Valley — the Shepherdess of Evil — they sound so much alike. At one time, the Dark Tyrant was sympathetic toward the Shepherdess and even allowed her to live not far from the city. Even permitted people to live in her small town. But then . . ." He shook his head to emphasize the tragic consequences he was about to describe. ". . . she turned more and more people against the Dark Tyrant. Even sent spies into the city to lure them to her town. What started out as a small town eventually rivalled the City of the Dark Tyrant in size." He moved back to the couch and sat down as if the thought of the Shepherdess's appalling actions exhausted him. "Naturally, the Dark Tyrant had to do something to protect himself and his people. He was forced to banish her farther from the city and made it a crime to move to her valley." He waved his hands out in a grand finale. "So, I am sure the Dark Tyrant's focus is more on the Shepherdess and Infinity than about any of our minor blunders." He chuckled.

An intercom on the end table beeped and 2,040 leaned over to answer it. "Yes?"

"This is 1," a voice squawked over the intercom. "You are being summoned to the Dark Tyrant's executive hall. Be there immediately." The intercom went silent.

All eyes in the room focused nervously on 2, 040.

"All of you look so worried," 2,040 laughed flippantly. "The Dark Tyrant may be giving me a new project to work on . . . Or perhaps he wants to compliment me on the work I did on the shape-shifter." He chuckled lightly once more, but nothing he said could allay the uneasiness that filled the room. "If it would make you feel better, I will take this . . ." 2,040 grabbed an automatic exterminating gun and tucked it into one of his pockets.

An even more profound feeling of doom pulled within 34,000 as she saw the gun swallowed up in 2,040's pocket. She wrapped her arms around him. "Stay safe, my love."

9-85 and 81-4-60 exchanged apprehensive expressions, hoping their premonition was wrong.

Chapter Thirty-Nine

While 2-45's sister, 5-07 was set to marry 7,500 and live a pampered life, her childhood training had been much different. Upon examination of all data concerning 5-07, the Labor Executive had set her on the training path of an Enforcer. She was taught military strategy, weapon training, and physical fitness. However, through the use of connections and bribes, her father managed to move her onto the life-track of the upper-class and to arrange for her a profitable match in 7,500. She had not used her Enforcer skills often but now she knew they would come in handy. When she learned that 93-73 was a prisoner of 1-13, she wondered if she could break into the prison so she could to talk to him. While she did not want to tarnish her family's reputation, her number one concern was her brother, and if anyone knew how to find him and 7,500, it was 93-73.

A bit of a pack rat, 5-07 kept, in the far back of her closet, all of the gear she had used in her Enforcer training. Her black tight fitting suit was a little shorter on her legs than when she first wore it; but, after putting on her knee-high boots, she concluded no one could tell. Her keys into the prison cells were three valuable tools: her electronic stun gloves, several lengths of rappelling rope, and a couple of bags of gold coins for bribes which she *borrowed* from the safe.

When 5-07 first arrived at the complex that housed 1-13's workshop, she waited in an adjacent hall for several minutes, surveying the doorway. To her surprise, 1-13 was away. She heard the guards mention he was taking care of important business at the executive hall. She was pleased to hear this. 1-13 was the one she was most apprehensive about running into. Her opportunity for action arrived when the two guards finished their conversation and one withdrew into the workshop. Before she moved forward, she ensured her stun gloves were on securely and the glowing red band around her wrists was lit, indicating they were functioning.

5-07 crept up behind the remaining guard and touched both of her gloves to the back of his neck. The guard stiffened, winced in pain, and fell to the ground, unconscious. She grabbed him by the arms and dragged him next to the doorway. Lifting his hand to the palm identifier next to the door, she placed his hand onto the reading plate and the door opened for her. She stepped over the guard and slipped into the workshop.

The workshop was in darkness. As she cautiously made her way through the room, she strategized a method for unlocking the door to the prisoners. However, before she reached the door, the room filled with an eerie green light, just enough for her to see 93-73 in the center of the room hunched over, his hands tied to posts on either side of him by a ropes of blue energy.

"93-73 . . ." she whispered in surprise. "Is that you . . ?"

93-73's eyes fell to the ground and he shook his head. At first 5-07 thought the shake of his head meant he was not 93-73, but she knew that would be absurd because she was positive he *was* 93-73. She then noticed that the green glow emanated from six pillars of light surrounding him. Looking deeper into these pillars of light, she saw they were ghostly skeleton-like forms and concluded 93-73 was shaking his head to warn her she was being led into some type of trap.

"Sooo . . . you did come . . ." the closest skeleton-ghost grumbled in a grating growl.

"Yesss . . ." another one chimed in. "After executing the enchantment of the doomed and speaking with the demons of the Planet of Darkness's underworld, we were warned you would be coming." It moved up and scowled down at her.

A third skeleton-ghost shrieked. ". . . And were warned that you would try to stop usss."

5-07 had heard about 1-13's skeleton-ghosts but had doubted they were real. Even now she wondered if they were an illusion created out of puppets and light. She moved around the ghosts in a half-circle, checking for wires or hidden lamps. When she was unable to find any, she had to admit to being unnerved for a moment as an eerie feeling deep within warned her they were real. But she refused to let the ghosts know she was frightened. She raised her head confidently. "Stop you from what?" she asked as she took an unwavering step forward.

The skeleton-ghosts each laughed in an unplanned and uncoordinated moment of unsettling laughter. "Killing 1-13's prisoner here." 5-07 could not tell if one or more than one skeleton-ghost replied.

The skeleton-ghost's response caught her off guard. She had considered 93-73 relatively safe because, unlike 6-96, 1-13 had the reputation of letting his subjects live. "You mean, 1-13 ordered you to kill him?"

"Noooo,"the skeleton-ghosts crackled in unison.

"This was our idea," the first one continued swooshing down next to 5-07. "The prisoner keeps talking about Infinity . . . and every time he mentions his name . . ." the skeleton-ghost groaned in pain. "We HATE the thought of Infinity."

"Yessss . . ." another skeleton-ghost moaned. "Let's kill him."

5-07 tried to puzzle out what they were talking about, but it all was so vague. In fact, she had to remind herself they meant kill 93-73, not kill the concept of infinity. "What do you mean, he talks about infinity? What infinity? And why does that make you want to kill him?"

93-73 leaned weakly against one of the poles trying to pull himself upright. "These ghosts are creatures of the dark caverns of our planet. Infinity is the prince of the Planet of Light. They are afraid Infinity will bring light to our planet and destroy them." He shook his head to keep from fainting. "But I was just reciting portions of historical texts. These creatures are excessively paranoid and won't listen to reason."

"QUIET," a skeleton-ghost nearer the back howled bitterly. "Or you will die at once."

5-07 turned to what she considered the lead skeleton-ghost. "Is that true? You want to kill him just for reciting history?" She narrowed her eyes in inquiry.

The skeleton-ghost's breath slowed in thought, sounding much like a death rattle. "No matter what reason we have for killing him, there is nothing you can do to stop us."

5-07 hated anyone telling her she could do nothing to stop something. She took it as a challenge. If the skeleton-ghosts had simply said she was not welcome because 1-13 was still questioning 93-73, she might have apologized and left. But now that she had been challenged, she refused to leave without accomplishing her objective. "But why should you kill him?" she asked. "It doesn't change history. It won't keep Infinity from coming here." She looked them straight in the open sockets of their heads which she considered to be their eyes. "And even if you did kill him, what's to stop others from coming in here and reciting that same bit of history? I think your best option is to let me take 93-73 out of here. That way you won't have to hear him." She took several determined steps to 93-73. "If you don't, I will join him in talking about Infinity and you'll have to kill us both." 5-07 had no idea what the skeleton-ghosts would do. In fact, after she finished, she closed her eyes, half-expecting to feel the final death blow. To her surprise, all she heard was silence. She cautiously opened her eyes again and noticed the lead skeleton-ghost touching its bony finger to the energy that bound 93-73, causing the energy to fade. 93-73 collapsed to the ground and 5-07 raced to assist him to his feet.

"Leeeeeave," the lead skeleton-ghost commanded in disdain. "Or we *will* kill you both."

5-07 and 93-73 directly ducked away from the skeleton-ghosts' reach and 5-07 guided 93-73 out of the workshop.

The other skeleton-ghosts surrounded the first. "Must we let them live?" they grumbled.

"Yessss. We must," the lead skeleton-ghost replied. "At least her. The demons of this planet want her alive because soon she will feed them." Its eye sockets widened in emphasis.

The skeleton-ghosts then skulked back into the dark corners of the workshop.

5-07 had expected to sneak into 1-13's workshop, ask 93-73 how to find her brother and slip back out. She had not expected to actually break him out of prison. *Time for a change of plans,* she reevaluated her situation. She had to quickly come up with a quiet, out of the way place to take him so they could talk privately. The only place that came to mind was her home.

Once they reached the towering mansion, 5-07 realized it would not be wise to just pop in through the front door. She did not want to meet up with her mother and have to explain 93-73 being with her, and she was determined to avoid the butler. He was annoying and unpredictable. She decided her best option was to sneak 93-73 in through the back door and guide him to the lower-levels of the tower, which were not used as frequently as the rest of the house.

Once inside the shadowy, cobwebbed basement corridors of the tower, she found an empty storage room off of the stairway. After turning on the muted glowing light that made the room appear even emptier than it was, she led 93-73 inside. The dirt-laden mottle-green rocks that made up the walls of this room seemed to exude every depressing memory of years gone by. 93-73 was mentally and physically exhausted and, since the room had no chairs, he sunk to the ground and leaned his back against the wall. "I appreciate you helping me." His shoulders sunk weakly. "But no doubt I will have to go back. At least I won't be killed by those horrific creatures." He brushed a strand of hair from his face and let his eyes meet 5-07's in gratitude.

5-07 knelt beside him. "I don't know," she sighed as she ran her fingers across the edge of her sleeve. "I hope I didn't make it worse for you."

93-73 waved a hand in the air to wipe away her concern. "No, you were such an angel getting me away from them."

"Not really." She averted her eyes. "There is something I hoped you'd help me with."

"What?"

She took a quick breath before continuing. "7,500 and my brother are going to see the Queen of the Night. I want to know how to get there so I can stop them." She tugged at his sleeve in her eagerness to do something about the situation.

93-73 nodded. "7,500 and I tried to find her castle once. He has always been obsessed with her and the Mystic of the Vale. You see, he is determined to learn the Six Secrets of Saphi."

5-07's eyes widened in surprise. "Did you find the Queen of the night? Is it safe to see her?"

Tilting his head in thought, 93-73 recalled the events of their expedition. "I wouldn't say it is really safe. You see, we didn't actually find her. She lives in the middle of a dangerous wilderness full of mountainous rocks and deep pits. It is also scattered with active volcanos. All sorts of vicious monsters live there. We were chased away by a giant grey creature with deadly claws and teeth. We had a guide with us. The poor thing was eaten by it in just a few bites." He looked down either not wanting to remember a painful memory or out of respect for the dead.

In desperation, 5-07 clenched her fists. Her brother's journey to the Queen of the Night sounded worse than she had thought. "Then, give me directions on how to get there."

93-73 tapped his chin in thought. "Actually, I can't."

"Why not?"

He widened his eyes and blinked. "It's one of those places that's impossible to find just by directions. If you want to go there, I would have to lead you."

She looked at him pleadingly. "Would you?"

"Of course."

A ghastly scream broke the silence and 5-07 and 93-73 exchanged alarmed expressions.

93-73's heart raced in a rush of panic. He grabbed 5-07's hand in both of his and kept his eyes fixed on her.

5-07 patted 93-73's hands and returned them to him. "Wait here," she whispered and rushed out of the room. She looked through the dark stairway to determine which room the scream had come from. She saw a hazy reddish light emanating from the half-open doorway to one of the rooms higher up the tower. Her eyes narrowed as she tried to penetrate the darkness and puzzle out what had happened. She climbed the stairs as fast as she could toward the room. The stairs were steep and narrow and the railing was only on the side close to the wall. The other side of the stairs led to a large open cavity with a drop into the depths of the tower, the dark, damp, and boiling sublevel chambers below. In her desperation to reach the room in time, her foot slipped from one of the steps. She would have toppled off of the staircase, if 93-73 had not disobeyed her orders and followed her up the stairs. He caught her as she was about to fall.

"What do you think it is?" He looked with dread at the red glow oozing from the room now eerily still.

"I don't know," 5-07 gasped. "Let's hurry." She made her way up the rest of the stairs between her and the room.

She crept to the door that was ajar, and came upon, in the doorway, the body of the butler lying face upward, his head to the side. His mouth still hung open as if he was about to explain the absurdity of the situation and his eyes were wide and staring, fixed upon a large spider intent on crawling away from the one who had intruded upon its web. Blood oozed to the floor from a deep wound on the back of his neck. 5-07 forced her eyes from the dead butler to look about the room. The red glow came from some communications equipment that was softly humming and beeping on a small wooden table. She looked up from the equipment and saw her mother stepping out of the shadows holding a heavy metal sword stained with blood.

"Mother," 5-07 shouted in astonishment. "What happened here?"

"I was saving us from total ruin," she said with a rational straightforwardness as she held several wires from the equipment she had disconnected. She yanked out a few more wires and it went silent, causing the red glow to fade. "Our butler has been recording everything that has been going on around here and sending those recordings to someone connected to the Dark Tyrant . . . I haven't yet figured out who." She glanced over the equipment as if they might hold the last clue she needed.

5-07 nearly fainted in shock. "Our butler told you this? And you killed him?"

"I had to." She tossed the wires to the ground as if they were as much to blame as the butler. She then scrunched her nose up in disdain. "As I was confronting him with my suspicions, he confessed everything so proudly. My only concern is that I did not kill him soon enough. Enforcers no doubt are on their way here now." She sighed as if the Enforcers coming was as minor an inconvenience as a neighbor being late for a party.

5-07 dropped her face into her hands in frustration. "Oh no. They can't come here."

Her mother stroked her cheek to calm her child. "You know they will."

"But when they discover his body, they might find--" 5-07 waved her hands at her whole world going awry.

"Find what?"

"93-73."

"Who?" her mother asked, in exasperation.

93-73 stepped out from the shadows behind 5-07. "She was referring to me. She rescued me from some awful skeleton creatures, but I am supposed to be 1-13's prisoner."

To 5-07's surprise, her mother beamed at seeing him. "Aren't you 7,500's assistant?" she asked, as if the dead body and the Enforcers no longer existed. "How is he doing?"

"5-07 tells me he is off to find the Queen of the Night—" he started to politely reply.

"We don't have time for this," 5-07 cut him off abruptly. "We need to get out of here before the Enforcers arrive." She turned to her mother. "Mother, do we still have those trechirs in the tunnels below the tower?"

Her mother frowned at the thought of the creatures. "You mean those awful giant rodents you and your brother used to play with at night when you should have been sleeping? I hired someone to come in and clear the tunnels, but I think they were too elusive for him."

"I hope you are right," 5-07 replied in a rush. "Because, they're our best way out of here. The tunnels under the tower lead to a stream outside of the city, and the trechirs can lead us to that stream." She turned to 93-73 in earnest. "And you are coming with us. You can take us to the Queen of the Night."

93-73 shook his head as he remembered the last moments of the guide. "Are you sure you want to go there?"

"She harbors criminals, doesn't she?" asked 5-07, bluntly.

"I believe so."

"Then we will be in like company." She turned to the door.

93-73 stepped back nervously. "But I've never ridden anything like a giant rodent before."

"It's easy," 5-07 answered, "you just hold on and they do the rest." She then took her mother by the arm. "The only thing we should take with us is the gold."

"All right," her mother replied as she stepped over the body of the butler. "I will go get it from the safe and meet you two in the basement." She made her way out of the room and climbed the stairs to the safe.

5-07 and 93-73 hurried down the stairs to the tunnels below in hopes of finding a few trechirs. The molten magma which warmed the surface of the planet flowed through tunnels within the planet's crust. Still, it did not stayed bottled-up in one area for long. It was constantly moving from one area to another and as it moved, it left behind a network of tunnels which would become occupied by a variety of wild animals, the most frequent of which were the giant rodents known as trechirs. Around 6 feet from head to tail and around five feet at the withers, trechirs were large enough for a human to ride. In fact, some covert groups would use trechirs in races, encouraging people to place bets on which trechir would win. The trechirs' large furry bodies, big eyes, and wide ears made them appear helpless and friendly. However, they had sharp claws and a powerful bite and had been known to kill people when defending their young.

It took 5-07 at least half an hour to round up three trechirs. The exterminators must have frightened and drove most of them into the deeper tunnels. To encourage them out of the deep tunnels and calm them, 5-07 used presline grain, a favorite of the trechirs. She tossed a thick layer of it just outside the deeper tunnels and once they came near, she continued to spread more to keep the trechirs occupied with eating until her mother was able to rejoin them.

93-73 cautiously stepped up to an arm's length away from one of the trechirs and examined it cautiously. "Are you sure it would be safe to ride them? They are wild, aren't they?" He stepped back from it uncomfortably.

In a carefree manner, 5-07 moved to another trechir and scratched it behind its ear. The trechir leaned into the scratching and joined in by using its back leg to scratch its own back. 5-07 tossed her hair back and met 93-73's eyes reassuringly. "Trechirs are social creatures. While they shy away and hide from danger, when they know you mean them well, they are tame enough." She laughed at a surprising thought. "Me and my brother would come down here all the time to play with them. One trechir even dragged 2-45 by his leg all the way to its nest."

93-73 shied away from the trechir. "It wanted to eat him?"

"Of course not," 5-07 laughed. "She wanted him to play with her children. They had so much fun."

5-07's mother followed the sound of her daughter's voice to the tunnel, carrying over her shoulder a large bag containing the gold from the safe. "The Enforcers are right behind me," she shouted her warning to them with a panicked gasp. "That bop on the head I gave them with this bag of gold won't keep them down for long."

"Let's hurry," 5-07 exclaimed. She gave her mother a boost and pushed her up onto the Trechir.

"What about me? Do I get any help?" 93-73 asked in a panic as he noticed the shadows of the Enforcers making their way down the stairway.

"Get on that trechir," 5-07 yelled to 93-73, grabbing a backpack from the corner. She swung it over her arms and, in one leap, she sprang onto her trechir and urged it on to follow her mother through the tunnels.

93-73 had hoped for a lesson in trechir-riding, but, now alone, he was forced to teach himself. He grabbed hold of the trechir's fur and used it to climb up and, with some effort, managed to pull his leg around the trechir's body. "Okay, trechir, let's go." He shook the creature urgently.

The trechir's beady yellow eyes rolled back at 93-73 as if wondering why he was on its back. 93-73 scrunched his eyes shut, bracing himself to either be captured or shot by the approaching Enforcers.

To his surprise, the trechir leapt into action, not because of 93-73's prodding but because the clamoring of the Enforcers sounded so much like the deadly exterminators that it had to deal with some time back. On his way through the tunnel, 93-73 heard one of the Enforcers telling another to bring in the drones.

Flying down the tunnels on trechir back, 93-73 only saw a blur of the light brown walls with their jagged, uneven surface marbled with red, steaming veins. In a few minutes, 93-73 was able to catch up to 5-07 and her mother and maintain a steady scamper alongside them and their trechirs. "Do we have any chance of eluding them?" he asked.

"These tunnels are very complex," 5-07 replied. "It could take them hours to find us."

93-73 examined the complex arrangement of the tunnels within tunnels as they passed and nodded a bit more reassured, but he had one more question. "Even if they are using drones?"

"Drones?" 5-07 asked in a manner that was not as surprised as 93-73 had expected.

"I heard them mentioning them just a minute ago."

"Good," she laughed. "Drones are drawn to heat and there is a lot of it down here. We just need to find it." She reached one hand out and felt the walls as she passed. "The magma still flows in adjacent tunnels. If you find a warm wall, chances are magma is on the other side."

93-73 worried he would fall off his trechir if he unclenched one hand from the creature's fur. However, to test the walls for warmth he forced himself to let go with one hand, continuing to keep his balance by reinforcing his other hand's hold by taking some of the trechir's fur into his teeth.

A sudden whizzing sound behind them drew 5-07's attention. She looked back and saw the drones following not far behind them. The drones maintained a speed much faster than the trechirs were capable of reaching.

5-07's mother touched the wall, screamed in pain and pulled her hand away. "Definitely hot there."

"We got them." 5-07 reached into her backpack and pulled out an explosive device. She attached it to the wall of the tunnel as they continued to race on. A few minutes after they had passed, the device exploded.

The rocky wall burst and crumbled away as a gush of lava splurted through the gash, swallowing the drones in a sizzling, sulfurous flood.

After several hours, 5-07, her mother, and 93-73 reached a juncture in the tunnels that opened to an area several miles away from the City of the Dark Tyrant. The gloom outside was broken by the gentle sound of a rippling brook and the cooling shadows of a majestic forest of towering rocks.

"I don't think the Enforcers will find us here." 5-07 encouraged her Trechir to help itself to a drink from the brook.

93-73 took an exhausted breath and sunk to a rock near the brook. He was mesmerized by the clear brook and how it reflected the trechirs and them in perfect likeness. "We are lucky to happen upon this place," he sighed. "We needed the rest."

"Yes," 5-07 agreed. The trechir turned from the brook and looked at her as its tongue passed over its muzzle to slurp up the last drops of water that dripped from its mouth. "Now," she turned from the trechir and fixed her eyes on 93-73, "let's find the Queen of the Night."

Chapter Forty

A s 2,040 entered the executive hall, he managed to maintain as positive an attitude as possible. In his mind, the black marble contained tints of rose, the suffocating humidity was a warm, cozy blanket, and the echoing goo creatures were fluttering mincha birds. When he crossed over the bridge, the only thing he could not drown out were the wails of the victims in the lava lake below him. He tried to compare their groans to the rippling of the electrical light-display of his fountain, but the low moans and the sparkling sizzles had little in common. Despite his best efforts, the moans continued to be a nagging reminder of an impending threat.

Standing in the center of the archway, 1 dominated the front of the executive hall with 6-96 to his left and 1-13 to his right. As 2,040 approached, 1 protruded forward, more to distinguish himself from the Persuaders than to move closer to 2,040. 1 raised his chin and pushed his right hip forward in a way that was a bit disconcerting since he was an overly-rounded man and not a well-shaped woman. "Me and the Persuaders have been discussing your work." He raised his nose higher with a haughty lift of his chin and, his nose being too high to look past, he was forced to look down and to the side to see 2,040. "We feel we owe you something."

2,040 let his eyes fall with a contrived coyness. "You owe me nothing. All I wish is that your new shape-shifter is serving you well and . . ." He took a breath, preparing to continue a wish-you-all-the-wonderfulness-in-the-world speech, but 1 cut him off.

1 stepped forward and, when face-to-face with 2,040, he bolted a hand up indicating 2,040 should cease talking. 2,040 fell silent and 1 abruptly turned his back on him and marched up to a dark corner of the room. He hit a spot on the wall with the back of his hand, and the corner lit up to reveal 1's Shadow-Shifter standing with its eyes closed as if it were a sleeping statue. 1 ran his fingers down the Shadow-Shifter's face, and as he did, the Shadow-Shifter opened its eyes wide and fixed its pinpoint accusing pupils on 2,040. "You did well in overseeing the completion of MY Shadow-Shifter." 1 jiggled with laughter as if what he said was a hilarious joke.

2,040 looked up with a clueless what's-so-funny tilt of his head. "Thanks to my direction, they completed it at least 120 hours earlier than . . ."

1 raised his hand to cut 2,040 off again and turned to address his Shadow-Shifter. "Is it true that 2,040 satisfactorily directed your creation?"

The Shadow-Shifter replied with a dispassionate nod. "Yes, he has earned his reward," the Shadow-Shifter said in a more succinct and silky tone than 2,040 expected.

1 pressed his frog-like lips together, making them look even more frog-like, and gave a nod that almost hinted at a father's pride for the Shadow-Shifter's response. Then, as if on a tight schedule, he promptly turned to 1-13. "So, 1-13, what do you think?"

With a convincingly genuine smile and nod, 1-13 began to give his input. "His economic plan for manual labor room 15 was pure genius."

2,040 took this moment to break into the conversation and add his own embellishments. "I calculated and plotted every detail of that plan with mathematical care and precision, testing and retesting each variable and . . ."

"Yeess." 1 rubbed his flabby chin. He raised a finger in front of 2,040 so close 2,040 was worried it would poke his eye out. "Plus," 1 continued, "You organized well the scheme to exchange the incorrect model housed in the master computer with the correct one."

"What?" 2,040 squealed as his heart missed a panicked beat. "I had nothing to do with that," he protested, with an emphatic wave of his arms across his body and to either side.

1-13 nodded in 2,040's direction with a humoring smile. "Of course. And he has certainly earned his reward." He bowed in 1's direction and stepped back into the shadows of the archway.

2,040 shook his head in confusion. While he felt as if he was on some type of trial, more than once they had mentioned a reward. *Is this just some sort of silly game that, once it's all over, everyone laughs at its ridiculousness?* 2,040 wondered with a weak chuckle of hope. *Perhaps they just want to make me as nervous as possible and then pull out the balloons and confetti and shout 'Surprise. Here's your reward.'"*

Without even looking where he was going, 1 sidestepped over to 6-96. "6-96," he addressed her while his eyes were fixed disconcertingly on 2,040. "What is your impression of 2,040's work performance?"

6-96 boldly marched to 2,040 and studied him with a half-impressed and half-contemptuous smile. "He does do an excellent job on whatever he puts his mind to. Even projects that are not particularly condoned by the Dark Tyrant."

2,040 felt as if her words jabbed into his chest like a dagger. "I do not involve myself in projects that are not condoned by the Dark Tyrant."

6-96 raised one eyebrow sharply. "That escape vehicle hidden in a secret room in your workshop is an amazing creation and is especially deserving of a reward." Her nod of finality was as powerful as a blow to the chin.

1 twisted his mouth in thought in such a way that 2,040 supposed a long tongue would pop out to catch a fly. "Yeess," he agreed. "You do deserve a reward."

2,040 fixed his eyes on 1 unseeingly as if trying to understand a work of literature written in a language that did not exist. "I-I . . . I don't understand. What reward?"

1 swung his arm to the left and pointed his finger toward an arched open doorway. The sandstone frame was etched with vining roses and leaves. Over the doorway was a placard with one word, 'Welcome', written in decorative font. "Your reward," 1 answered casually. "Right through there. Go on to your reward."

Two Enforcers flanked 2,040 to guide him to the doorway. Still confused about what 1 meant by the word 'reward,' 2,040 did not resist the Enforcers, but his feet dragged and he was unable to snap himself out of a puzzled daze.

When they reached the doorway, the Enforcers prodded him to enter. 2,040 looked through the door and was sincerely surprised. The sky was blue and clear. A large yellow sun beat down a warming heat into a lush green garden with beautiful yellow, pink, and blue flowers. Even though flowers did not grow on the Planet of Darkness, they fascinated 2,040. He had read stacks of poetry on all types of flowers and seeing them before him was a poetry-lover's feast. A cool lake stood in the middle of the garden and in the center of the lake was a tall marble fountain that shot out like an overflowing pagoda composed of dozens of cascades of water.

2,040 continued into the garden, his eyes drinking in every object of beauty. "I never knew such a glorious garden existed in our city." He exhaled as he took in the garden's splendor. Eventually, his eyes fixed on an exceptionally exquisite orchid growing near the bank of the lake. He bent down to examine it more closely, but as he did, he tripped on some sharp blades of grass. He fell forward and landed on what he thought was going to be the lake. Pulling himself up on his hands and knees, he looked around and noticed that he was not wet and the lake was a large sheet of ezocane. He stood and touched the orchid. It was not soft, delicate and scented, but shaped and painted metal. He looked about and realized all of it was just a painted illusion.

As 2,040 stared at the garden, stunned, the Enforcers moved back toward the entrance and slipped out of the room. 2,040 heard the door slam shut with a loud bang and blippity-bleep as it locked. He knew he was alone in the room, but he did not race for the door or scream to be let out. He was still drawn into the garden, longing to explore its exotic complexities. Though they were not real, the yellow sun and rainbow of flowers became for him a kaleidoscope world with colors shifting and swirling all around him. In the distance, he could hear stilted mechanical music and wondered where it came from. He walked in the direction of the music and the closer he came, the more tinny, robotic, and monotonous it sounded. Eventually, the music seemed to be playing all around him and no matter how far he moved away from it, it followed him.

Out from behind faux trees, bushes, and brick walls, popped bizarre, floating ghosts. They wore colorful, polka dotted outfits that flowed behind them as they swirled about. Their faces were eerie masks with wide staring eyes and painted smiles. They looked like grotesque playthings, but their flamboyant gestures were so comical 2,040 could not help but laugh. *A reward . . .* he thought in delight . . . *Yes . . . This is beyond a doubt the best reward I could have possibly expected.* With genuine enjoyment, 2,040 laughed as the ghosts spun over his head, floated down in front of him, and waved their arms about in enthusiastic glee.

When the ghosts noticed they had 2,040 entranced, they motioned for him to follow them. 2,040 nodded, smiled, and wandered after them as a boy eager for a second piece of candy. The ghosts exchanged pleased expressions and led him

461

toward a distant towering pyramid formed from giant glistening black cubes and separated into three levels. As they moved closer to the pyramid, the music became more discordant and hectic and the ghosts' laughter became more evil and demonic, like cries from the world of the damned.

When 2,040 reached the foot of the pyramid, he noticed a stairway carved into the pyramid's black cubes. This stairway rose to the top, almost disappearing into the blue vastness above. In a trance, 2,040 automatically started to climb the staircase. Despite his dreamlike state, he noticed that a crowd of people surrounded the pyramid to watch him. They filled the ground reaching back as far as he could see. As he came to the intermittent levels, he could even see crowds teeming on these levels as well. The people did not move and were unaffected by everything around them. They simply stared straight ahead at him. Continuing up the staircase, 2,040 smiled and waved to the people, assured they had come to see him. His actions did elicit a response from the audience. They applauded and cheered him ecstatically, even though they continued to stand motionless, staring and impassive. What puzzled 2,040 the most was that they did not even move their hands or open their mouths. Still, 2,040 did not let that trifle bother him. He shrugged his shoulders and continued on to the top of the pyramid.

When 2,040 reached the top, he waved his hand in the air and the crowd fell silent. He had never ceased to have their full attention, since they had never ceased staring at him from the moment they had sprung out of nowhere. The strangeness of the scenery, the music and ghosts, and the baffling appearance of the audience did not dissuade 2,040 from giving his acceptance speech. He clasped his hands together in a feigned gratefulness. "Dear friends," he began with enthusiasm, "when I first came here, I had no idea I would be receiving such an astonishing award. In fact, I had no idea I would receive a reward at all." He casually laughed and the sound of the audience joined in even though the audience itself simply stood staring. "But, honestly, I really am overwhelmed with gratitude at being selected for this reward. A lot of hard work and dedication went into the projects I have coordinated, and I believe that work and dedication shows in their quality. Quality is the key to success and success leads to magical moments like these." He paused and smiled at the audience in a way that could fool the audience into believing he was thinking of them but he was in reality thinking of his own magnificence. "Thank you." He nodded a bow and added one more, "Thank you." His smile spread itself even wider as it crinkled his eyes almost shut until they fell on 6-96 on his level of the pyramid, stepping from around its corner out toward him. His smile faded and his eyes widened in spell-broken surprise.

"What are you doing here?" He tried to maintain a polite unsuspecting manner even though his suspicions were rising. "Are you here to congratulate me on my reward?" he asked in hopes of keeping the conversation business-as-usual.

"No," she replied with a sneer as she pulled out from behind her two long razor sharp swords. "I came to ensure that you received your reward." Her eyes flashed her deadly intentions. She brought her right sword forward and approached him in determination until the sword was less than an inch away from 2,040.

2,040 ducked to avoid the sword plunging into him. He reached into his pocket and pulled out his automatic exterminating gun. He slipped behind her, avoiding the sword. He aimed his gun and shot twice in her direction. 6-96 leapt to the side and seemingly disappeared into the shadows. Her disappearance and the screams and shrieks from the emotionless audience disoriented 2,040 and he shot randomly into the crowd. He then noticed that in the back past the audience was a glowing red sign with the word 'Exit' on it. He determined that the most important thing was to avoid whatever fate 1 and the Dark Tyrant had in store for him. He needed to escape. He raced down the pyramid and headed in the direction of the sign.

When he reached the exit, he was stopped by six Enforcers who prevented his escape and forcibly dragged him to a stark black corner of the room. Here, the floor ended, leading to a great abyss. As he fought to free himself from the hold of the Enforcers, 2,040 leaned over and looked down into the abyss, seeing that deep below the ground was covered with bloody, smashed, and mutilated bodies. He heard above him an unexpected grinding, screeching sound and saw, descending into the abyss, a huge, heavy, cylindrical metal crusher. Once it hit the bottom of the abyss with an earth-rattling thud, flattening the bodies below, it rose and 2,040 could see that, as it rose, another cylindrical crusher next to this one began to descend. The bottom of each crusher was red with blood and clinging to them were the pulp and limbs of the bodies it was crushing.

"No, no, NOOOO." 2,040 struggled to break from the Enforcers' grasp. But, the Enforcers were too strong for him, and with one powerful shove, they easily thrust him into the abyss. However, as 2,040 fell, he managed to reach out and grab hold of the closest crusher as it was coming down. Holding on desperately, he took a deep breath and, with all of his strength, swung himself from the one crusher to the other. As this crusher rose, he watched for a path from it to the floor to come into view. Once he saw this path, he leapt from the crusher to the floor. He skinned his palms and bruised his chin as he fell, but he did not take time to nurse them. He scrambled to his feet and raced to the exit, desperately avoiding all Enforcers and their gunfire.

The world became a blur as 2,040 ran faster than he thought he could possibly run. He found his way through the halls of the City of the Dark Tyrant to his suite. He was greatly relieved to find he had managed to arrive safely. He rushed inside where he was surrounded by 34,000, 9-85, and 81-4-60 all eager to know the details of the meeting. 2,040 fell against the door he had just closed and sunk against it to the floor in exhaustion. 34,000 knelt beside him and dabbed his forehead with a handkerchief.

"You look terrible." She noticed his bruised chin and sweaty brow. "Are you alright?"

"What happened? Is someone after you?" 9-85 demanded in a tone that, though meant to convey concern, made 2,040 feel a bit threatened.

Before 2,040 could answer, a thumping and clattering filled the halls. Its chaotic echoing constantly increased in loudness "Hurry," 2,040 panicked a gasp. "They're coming."

"Sounds like Enforcers." 81-4-60 matter-of-factly gestured at the hall with his thumb.

34,000 assisted 2,040 to his feet as she tenderly rubbed his back. "You should rest. Tell me what to do, I'll protect you. You need to lie down."

Once he was steady on his feet, 2,040 waved her away. "No . . . no, I must do this myself." He shot his look straight into 9-85's eyes. "We need to secure this suite."

9-85 replied with an abrupt nod and stationed himself by the statue of 2,040. He pressed the hidden button at its base. Once the panel in the wall opened revealing the plate of black glass, 2,040 held his hand on the glass allowing the bright blue line to read the information from his hand. As the banging and rumbling in the hall grew louder, the heavy, thick metal wall fell with a thud blocking the noise and providing a momentary sense of security. 9-85 pressed the series of buttons below the plate of glass, and the humming of the wall's protective heat filled the room.

"What is it?" 34,000 clung to his side. "What *are* they wanting?"

2,040 grabbed her hands in his and penetrated her eyes with a grave expression. "They want to kill me."

34,000 had to cover her mouth with her hand to prevent herself from screaming. "They can't." She grabbed him by his shirt and shook him desperately. "I won't let them."

"Listen." 2,040 stroked her hair to calm her. "The only way out of this is to leave."

"I agree," 81-4-60 nodded.

There was no need for 2,040 to rethink the actions he had rehearsed many times before. He flew across the room to the other side of the fountain and moved aside the file cabinet that concealed the hidden metal door. He tapped the buttons on the narrow panel in the correct order and the metal door opened. "Come on," he urged the others as the sound of the Enforcers in the hall indicated they were ramming the wall of the suite to break through.

9-85 and 34,000 were the first into the hidden room. 81-4-60 grabbed his satchel with one hand and Octelix with the other and brushed in past 2,040.

One thing 2,040 refused to leave behind was his magnificent light source. He gestured a quick return to the others and dashed off to the lab. He packed the light source model into a cloth-lined wooden box, took it into his arms, and raced back with it. "Don't want to forget this," he told 9-85 as he set it next to the glass-enclosed escape vehicle. But, just as he was about to raise the glass around the vehicle, something called him back to his suite. As if being urged from another world, he unseeingly pushed his way passed the others back to the suite. Once there, he looked about the room with a fond smile upon his lips. He found it hard to say good-bye to his awards and paintings, but the hardest thing for him to leave was his fountain.

Don't leave . . . Not now . . . 2,040 was certain he heard the fountain calling to him . . . *You know you can't leave . . . We need you . . .* The ghostly voice came from his fountain and lured him toward it. With his eyes fixed on the dancing lights, he moved with methodical deliberation away from the hidden room and to the fountain.

"What is he doing?" 81-4-60 asked in bewilderment. "The Enforcers will break through any time now."

"2,040," 34,000 screamed. "Come back. We need to leave."

"Don't worry. I'll see that he comes." 9-85 moved past her back to 2,040.

2,040 stared at the glowing lights of his fountain. He held his hand out and let the lights play on his palm. *That's right,* the fountain seemed to say, *we look forward to you joining us.*

9-85 came up behind 2,040 and whipped him around by his shoulder to face him. "You said we have to get out of here. Come on."

"No . . ." 2,040 said in a drug-like haze. "I have to stay . . ."

9-85 shook his head as he tried to make sense of this confused puzzle. His concentration was broken by a hissing, blubbing, and murmuring sound from the fountain. He craned his neck to look past 2,040. The basin of the fountain was filling with lava. As the lava deepened, it crested up and reached out for 2,040. 9-85 grabbed 2,040's arm, in hopes of dragging him away from the fountain before the lava could take a hold on him.

2,040 shook his head and pulled his arm out of 9-85's grip. "I told you. I can't leave. I need to stay . . . They want me . . ." His face was unemotional yet determined.

"Stop it," 9-85 grabbed 2,040's arm once more. "You know we need to leave."

But 9-85's grip was not strong enough. In a powerful burst, the lava extended out of the fountain and wrapped itself around 2,040's other arm. Before 9-85 could get a firmer grasp on 2,040, the lava sucked him into the fountain. The more the lava touched his body, the more 2,040 became a part of the lava. As the lava reached the arm 9-85 was holding, 9-85 quickly let go to avoid becoming part of the lava himself. The lava retreated, pulling 2,040 with it down the drainage hole in the bottom of the basin.

34,000 shook all over in panic as she saw 2,040 disappear into the fountain. 81-4-60 tried to hold her back, but she pushed him from her and ran to the fountain in search of any sign of 2,040. He was gone. Even the colored streams of light had vanished. She broke into uncontrollable sobs as she crumpled to the floor.

9-85 jerked her to her feet. "Stop it. Get ahold of yourself. We have no time for this."

"No," she moaned through tears, "we can't leave without him."

"We tried," 9-85 told her firmly, "but there is nothing we can do now. If we don't get out, we will be joining him down that fountain or worse."

34,000 pulled away and dropped again to the ledge of the fountain. "I want to join him. Let me join him." She gasped as tears streamed down her face which was red from weeping.

9-85 waved a hand in the air to signal he had, for the most part, given up on her.

With a focused power of command, 81-4-60 pushed a palm toward him, indicating for him to have patience. He joined 34,000 on the ledge of the fountain. He stroked her hair. "I know how you feel. It's tough to lose someone you love. I've lost several people who I cared about deeply." His eyes moistened.

9-85 watched in amazement. He did not expect 81-4-60 who had been so insistent that he hated people to be so compassionate.

"But the most important thing to remember is . . .," 81-4-60 lifted her chin so he could look her straight in the eyes, "that 2,040 did love you very much and would not want anything to happen to you. He would want you to leave."

34,000 sighed more from the exhaustion of crying than from 81-4-60's words. "Yes, I suppose you are right." She wiped her tears even though more tears still streamed from her eyes.

81-4-60 wrapped his hand around hers, helped her gently to her feet, and guided her to the hidden room.

9-85 looked back at the metal wall covering the front entrance. The humming which indicated the protective heat was active started to become more sporadic and a blue glow formed on the wall from the laser device the Enforcers were using to break through. "It's time to leave." 9-85 stood at the door as they passed him into the hidden room. As 34,000 stopped before entering, she looked at 9-85 questioningly.

"Go on," he told her. "I will stay out here and hold them off." He gave her a firm shove into the hidden room. Once they were in, he pressed a code into the keypad which closed the door. He then replaced the file cabinet and, hearing a loud room-shaking crash, decisively turned to face the front door just as a crack spread from top to bottom.

In the hidden room, 81-4-60 punched a code into a keypad in the wall and the glass that covered the escape vehicle rose. He then guided Octelix to the vehicle. "It's up to you, Octelix. You know the way, so you need to tell it where to go."

Octelix saluted with its front leg and jumped to take its place at the front of the vehicle.

After seeing that 34,000 had boarded, 81-4-60 climbed in beside her. She looked at him, puzzled. "How does Octelix know where we need to go?"

"He downloaded a map from Infinity," 81-4-60 replied. "2,040 tried working with the Dark Tyrant and you see where that got him. Now I'm inclined to try the other side."

Octelix started up the escape vehicle and drove it into the tunnel and out of the City of the Dark Tyrant just as they heard the Enforcers break through the metal wall.

Chapter Forty-One

5 0-83 wandered aimlessly along the dark paths outside the city. His goal was not to reach any particular destination but to escape everywhere and everything because everywhere and everything depressed him. When his foot sloshed several inches into a puddle of thick clinging mud, he realized he had somehow wound up in the Slump-Bump area. The hovels plastered in thick mud and the drooping limbs of leafless trees confirmed his location. This depressed him even more. Extracting his foot from the mud, he noticed his clean white boot now encased in the muck, and his eyes moistened with tears. He thought about when he had built the mud fort with the Slump-Bump boys. Then, the dead trees were backdrops to adventures, and the mud and stones were sources for challenging competitions. Now the trees wept mud and were surrounded by lifeless stones and boulders, like omens of death.

Looking overhead, 50-83 noticed a portentous shadow moving across the starless sky like a black cloud, leaving him in a world darker than he had ever experienced before. Still, he continued to stumble along, unsure of where he was, where he wanted to go, and where he had just left. Eventually, he found himself in a particularly boggy spot and his boots were clamped in a tangle of twigs, vines, and mud. The more he tried to free himself, the more ensnared he became and the more ensnared he became, the more furious he grew at the situation. Finally, by using every bit of his bottled-up anger, he kicked the whole mess off his feet but lost his balance in the process and fell face forward into the mud. In irritation, he leaned on his elbows and sunk his chin onto the palms of his hands.

"I should just stay right here," he mumbled to himself as he turned on his side and brushed the mud from his vest. "What's the use? It doesn't matter where I go."

A cheerful humming and the bright voice of his crystal interrupted the gloom. "You should go back to 6-96 and apologize. Displaying a remorseful attitude will give you the best chance of her welcoming you back with open arms."

50-83 touched his chest, expecting to find the crystal there, but when he did not feel it, he looked around. He finally noticed it a few feet in front of him, almost disappearing into the mud. He stretched his hand out and grabbed it up. After pushing himself into a sitting position, he wiped the mud off the object and noticed the crystal was detached from the chain. He searched around in the mud for the chain, but failed to find it anywhere.

"Anyways," he confided to himself, "I hated wearing that stupid crystal. Its answers never make any sense." He stood and stuffed the crystal into his pocket. After an unsuccessful attempt to clean the mud from his clothes, he fatalistically trudged on into the Slump-Bump area.

It was still not clear to 50-83 where he was going and what made him choose to head in any particular direction, but he found himself approaching 4,021's hovel. Strangely, though, when he stood still and surveyed the mud-drenched area, even though every path and hovel looked alike, he still could tell something was missing. Facing the hovel of 4,021's neighbor, he realized the missing something was the unnerving creaking sound of 5-68's rocking chair. 50-83 took a look around 5-68's front door to see if he was nearby. However, as he was walking to the door, not half-way there, he nearly tripped over something in his path. He could not tell immediately what this something was because it was lodged in the ground and covered in mud. With a hesitant curiosity, he knelt next to it and scooped away handfuls of mud from the object. As the mud was cleared away, 50-83 discovered the hair, face, and ears of 4,021's neighbor and even the top back railing of his rocking chair. The rest of him was so deep in the mud it would take more than one person to pull him out. Shaking him and slapping his face, 50-83 tried to bring him to, but there was no response from 5-68. He just sat there, relaxed and immobile. The cold blue tint to 5-68's face told 50-83 there was nothing more he could do.

Not wanting to dwell on it any longer, 50-83 scrambled to his feet and faced away from 5-68's hovel. He was standing on a towpath made of cemented stones and rocks on the edge of the sewage river. There was no fencing or railing lining the towpath and the only thing that separated the towpath from the river was a single row of sand-colored bricks. He rushed to the river and looked into the waters. The reflections in the water took on the forms of wide-eyed, half-decayed corpses, snakes with venom dripping from their fangs, and the morphing form of the Dark Tyrant reaching out to stab him with inferno darts. "I can't take it any longer," he choked on the words, but even though he wanted to cry, he would not allow the tears to form. "I just want to die." He took a step closer to the edge of the towpath and convinced himself that suffocating within the reeking waters would be better than the dismal and hopeless life that loomed before him.

In the grey area of space, a heavy, unnatural mist clung to the castle-like fortress of the Guardian's space station. Through the mist, Infinity aboard the *Ghost III* observed something that resembled glowing bat-like eyes staring out at him. This eerie glow was the light exuding from the lookout window of the control room located in the center of the space station. The citadel glared forebodingly down on all who imposed themselves too closely.

Infinity sensed an unnatural presence in the Guardian's space station, but continued to pilot the *Ghost III* towards the back entrance. This was the most logical spot for the energy source of the electric web. *"The energy source will have to wait,"* the *Ghost III* announced, directing Infinity's attention to 50-83's dilemma. *"The young fighter is overwhelmed. Too many forces are closing in on him."* Unsurprised but concerned, Infinity nodded his head in thought as he proceeded to formulate a plan to remediate the situation.

Infinity climbed down a ladder into the lowest front room of the ship. In this room, three glowing red machines hummed, generating and regenerating the invisible soul of the *Ghost III*. "I knew it would not be easy for the young fighter to find his way to the Shepherdess' Valley." Infinity turned on a screen and watched 50-83 as he stood by the river. "Fighters often fight against everything but what really needs to be destroyed," Infinity told the ship. "While he must go through his present struggle . . ." He secured his helmet and took hold of the sword of sacrifice which his father had given him. ". . . he will not have to go through it alone." He stepped over to a red glowing pillar in the center of the room which was connected to the three machines by a glowing cross-like beam in the floor.

"I cannot remove all challenges from his path. They were set in place to prepare him for the vital task he must accomplish in the future. However, I will go and carry him through this particular ordeal." With pronounced purpose, Infinity stepped inside the glowing pillar. The pillar held his body within its glow, while it transported his image to the Planet of Darkness.

The last step 50-83 had taken toward the river was so close to the towpath's edge the front of his boot extended off the ledge. He looked into the water at how dark it was and determined that the only difference between the dark world in which he lived now and the dark world into which he was about to plunge was that in the river's depths his depression would eventually be over.

"It does not end there," he heard a confident voice behind him say.

50-83 turned around and was struck by a light that transcended the darkness and enveloped his existence. Eventually, he could discern a man standing within the light. "Who's there?" he asked, curiosity pulling his mind away from thoughts of suicide.

"I am Infinity," the man told him directly. "You have heard of me, so you should not be surprised at my presence."

It was a few seconds before 50-83 was able to remember his doubts of 4,021's *imaginary* Infinity, after which his eyes fell uncomfortably to the ground. "I suppose I shouldn't be surprised, but—"

"—but you did not believe I existed?" the man completed 50-83's sentence with a questioning tilt of the head.

"I guess." 50-83 pressed his lips together to hide how frustrated he was with himself.

"But you *did* believe," the man corrected him.

50-83 looked up in surprise.

With a focused look that shot deep into 50-83's mind, Infinity sent 50-83 on a mental reencounter with his own past. With Infinity's help, 50-83 was able to unpack several well-buried boxes in his mind. He soon realized 4,021 was not the first person to tell him about Infinity. After brushing the dust off of a box that had been buried especially deep, he finally opened it and remembered how, when he was young, he would often slip away from studies and spend time with his friend and his friend's family. His friend's grandfather worked as a jeweler. He was tall and thin and had a dark complexion that allowed the clever light in his eyes to stand out. Even though he was old, he was still agile and had not slowed down in his ability to form beautiful works of art out of gems and strips of metal. 50-83 would become entranced, watching him twisting shiny bits of gold around sparkling diamonds. The old man noticed 50-83's fascination and began to teach him the basics of making jewelry.

One time, while helping 50-83 link a star-shaped charm onto a bracelet, the old man drew his attention to the way it reflected the light. "See how the star glistens . . . sends its light everywhere . . . to the table, to the walls, even to you and me . . ." He moved the star so the light it cast from a nearby lamp flickered into 50-83's eyes. 50-83 playfully shielded his eyes from the light, while watching the star in fascination. ". . . just like the real stars in the sky . . . it is hard to see the stars clearly from this planet, but if you look closely you can see one particular light that shines brighter than all the others. They say that is not a star but a planet. The Planet of Light." The old man smiled with excitement and a reverential awe in his eyes.

With curious interest, 50-83 looked up from the bracelet. "A Planet of Light? On that planet do they put lamps outside so you don't have to play in the dark?"

The old man laughed in amusement and with his hand brushed 50-83's bangs back from his eyes. "No. They don't need lamps. It's bright outside without them."

50-83's eyes widened, "Wow." He tried to compare the planet he lived on now with the Planet of Light, but found it difficult because he could not even imagine what a planet with light would be like. Still, he believed it must be better, because it was so hard to do anything but hide wherever it was dark.

"Yes, it is a planet that is ruled well," the old man continued while taking out a buffing cloth and polishing the bracelet, "by a man called Infinity. They say that he is the only one who can pull anyone out of this darkness." He nodded his head once in emphasis.

Even as a child, 50-83 had been warned that the Dark Tyrant was to be feared and obeyed without question. When his friend's grandfather spoke of Infinity, 50-83 could not help but find him a much more admirable and dependable leader than the Dark Tyrant. 50-83 decided he liked Infinity.

The old man took the bracelet and latched it around 50-83's wrist.

After searching through a few more of the boxes in his mind, 50-83 remembered that a few weeks after his friend's grandfather had given him the bracelet, the grandfather disappeared. 50-83's mind would race, wondering whether he had been taken prisoner, had died, or possibly had flown off to the bright, far-off star in the dark sky, the Planet of Light. He and his friend spent hours searching for him. His friend had told him that his grandfather often mentioned a place past the wilderness area, so their search often led them there. Each search inevitably proved unsuccessful, however, and in order to keep his friend from becoming too sad, 50-83 made up games to distract him. It was during one of those games that they were captured by Enforcers and brought before the Dark Tyrant. He concluded that he must have lost the bracelet he had been given there, because he could not remember having it after that.

50-83 stepped closer to Infinity. "So you came all the way from the Planet of Light?"

"I am not here yet." Infinity held out his hand to demonstrate that he was translucent. "But I will be here soon."

"So you *are* coming like 4,021 said." 50-83 nervously remembered he had told 4,021 that he and Infinity were friends and knew she would inevitably find out he had lied.

After a moment of silence, Infinity lifted his chin and asked, "Is there something wrong?"

"Uhhh, well," 50-83 tried to formulate his question. "Would you mind telling 4,021 that you and I are friends and we are working together?" 50-83 wondered if, since Infinity came there just to talk to him, he would not mind saying he was his friend. He was surprised to see that Infinity stiffened and clenched his fists in anger.

"So that I can back up the lie you told her?" he said with marked irritation. "Do you know what a lie is?"

"A lie?" 50-83 asked as if he had never heard the word before.

Infinity stepped forward and held up a finger in instruction. "A lie is an altered reality. Do you think you have the power to alter reality? One reality is connected to another reality and that reality connects to yet another. When you alter one reality, you must alter them all. Do you really think you have the power to keep track of all those realities?"

Infinity's words overwhelmed 50-83. He was a bit dizzy as if he just climbed off a rollercoaster. "I've messed up on everything. It's all falling apart and I don't think I can find a way to fix it."

"It's not up to you to fix everything or to do everything on your own," Infinity told him pointedly. "We are not gods. There is nothing wrong in admitting our need for help and reaching out to others. Our inabilities can be our strengths if we know how to use them correctly. What *is* wrong is to pretend we are smarter, stronger, and more powerful than we are. That is hypocrisy and that is something that is practically impossible to fix."

50-83 paled as he remembered the conversation he had had with 93-73. "Is it true that when you come here our planet will be destroyed?"

"The destruction of the Planet of Darkness does not hinge on me," Infinity responded. "The Planet of Darkness is already on a path spiraling toward destruction, so it will be destroyed whether I come there or not. The reason I am coming is to rescue those who want to be saved."

50-83 could not focus on what Infinity said because he was overwhelmed by an incessant buzzing in his ears that drowned out all other sounds. This buzzing culminated into a huge pressure that crashed so loudly and with such force that 50-83 was convinced several planets had collided overhead. Afterwards, a sudden wave of depression hit him so hard his eyes fixed once more on the mud at his feet. He bit his lip hard to stifle a sob.

"The venom of the seven-headed snake has only one antidote."

"You know that I was bitten?"

"The fact *is* that you were bitten. The fact *is* that you need to be cured." Infinity pulled out his sword and brandished it before him. "And there is only one way to do that."

50-83 gasped and stepped back, wondering whether that one way was to drive the sword deep into his heart.

Infinity tilted his head and looked directly at 50-83 for a meaningful minute.

For thirty seconds of that minute, 50-83 instinctively considered running off somewhere far away, but for the last thirty seconds he looked into Infinity's determined eyes and concluded that Infinity knew what had to be done. He gave Infinity a nod of agreement.

"Follow me." Infinity led the way out of the Slump-Bump area.

50-83 did not know why, but for some reason the way back was easier and much quicker. The mud was not as sticky and sloshy, but more buoyant. The atmosphere was not as humid, but more refreshing and magical. The entire area was not so dark and shadowy, but was brighter, lit by a shining glow that radiated from Infinity's armor.

Soon they reached the City of the Dark Tyrant. Within just a few minutes, Infinity led 50-83 right back to the main complex and guided him into 6-96's workshop.

50-83 had an eerie emptiness inside and wished they had not returned. Having Infinity with him did not alleviate the deep fear of encountering 6-96 again. "I hope she is out," 50-83 whispered as he glanced about the room with a nervous apprehension.

The silence was broken by an echoing hiss as if each of the snake's seven heads had decided to start its hiss at a different time. 50-83 glanced through the dark room to discover where it was hidden. Looking through the shadows, he could see that one of the snake's heads was watching them from around a corner. After a few seconds, the rest of the heads popped around the corner and laughed among themselves as if plotting some trap.

"See. It's over there." 50-83 pointed out the snake to Infinity, wanting to make sure he gave him enough of a warning so he would not fall prey to the snake.

"I know," Infinity told him with an unexpected calmness. "I called it to meet me here."

50-83 paused as Infinity stepped toward the snake. "Why do you want to meet it?"

Infinity did not answer but continued to advance toward the seven-headed snake.

A shadow of hopelessness fell over 50-83. "Be careful," he warned Infinity, "You don't want to get too close to it . . . it's dangerous . . . and it can bite without warning." He wanted to move forward to help Infinity, but fear and depression kept his feet glued where he was.

The snake had crept around the corner and its hiss now crescendoed into discordant laughter. Its tongues hung out hungrily, eager to sink its fangs into Infinity.

50-83 was worried Infinity was unaware of the snake's plot, because he steadily continued up to the snake. Even though he was tempted to close his eyes, 50-83 forced them to stay open, in case he needed to pull Infinity out of danger.

Seeing that Infinity did not hesitate in their presence, the snake cowered its heads as he approached them.

"I am fully aware of the danger." Infinity stood over the snake. "This snake draws its strength from you, leaving you weakened by its depression." The centermost head lashed out at Infinity. Its fangs jabbed into nothing but air, since only Infinity's image was present. However, with the energy of the *Ghost III*, Infinity wrapped his gloved hand around the snake's throats. "Because of this, it must die before it inflicts its venom on others." Infinity raised his sword and dropped it firmly just below the snake's heads, cutting off all seven heads with one blow.

As soon as the snake's heads had been severed, 50-83 felt as if he had been pulled out of a sinking, binding mud pit. He could breathe and move more freely and his mind was no longer obsessed with thoughts of suicide. He raced forward to thank Infinity, but Infinity's image had already returned to the *Ghost III*. He was about to leave the room when he heard the slamming of the front door and 6-96's footsteps entering the workshop. He gulped and looked around for a place to hide, but decided the best option was to go forward and meet her before she noticed the dead snake. Before he could move, he heard her cackle in triumph and lost his nerve. Instead, he stepped back into the shadows of the room and hoped she would not see him.

She came in and hung her swords on the wall. "Well, well, that went better than expected," she chuckled. "2,040 thought he would get away, but forgot the Dark Tyrant has ways to ensure cooperation."

50-83 wondered who she was talking to, but remembered she was unaware the snake was dead and was probably talking to it.

6-96 grabbed her staff from a corner of the room and polished the obsidian stone against her sleeve. "I personally think he let 2,040 off too easily. He should have been tortured a few days before being sucked into the lava pit." She grinned as she thought of the tortures she would have enjoyed using. "What torture do *you* think would have worked the best on him?" She turned around to see the snake's reaction.

Still hoping to remain invisible, 50-83 stopped breathing as she looked around for the snake. In agitation, he reached into his pocket and toyed with his crystal nervously.

Unfortunately, 6-96 noticed him immediately. "So," she snorted gruffly, "you returned, as I expected." Her eyes then fell on the decapitated snake on the ground, like a splayed mess of wires torn from their socket. "You despicable monster. You killed my snake." She grabbed 50-83 by his hair and shoved him against the wall. "This time, you won't survive your punishment." Still holding him against the wall with one hand, she reached over with the other and grabbed a sword from its wall mount. She pulled the sword back ready to plunge it into his chest.

Before she was able to, though, 50-83 held up his hand that was holding the crystal. The sword collided with the crystal and the crystal sent a powerful electrical shock throughout 6-96's body, causing her to scream and convulse wildly. The bolt of electricity enveloped her entire body and pulled her to the crystal and she was immediately sucked into the center of the crystal.

Alarmed, 50-83 tossed the crystal away, but the crystal did not drop. It floated before him forging a crystal chain it used to latch itself around his neck. He tried to take the necklace off, but it would not let him. He held the crystal up, and inside it, he saw 6-96 glaring back at him. Pulling harder on the latch of the necklace, he tried more desperately to remove the necklace, but the crystal sparked him with a mild jolt to prevent him from removing it.

When they find 6-96 missing, 50-83 thought in a panic, *they will no doubt blame me for her death. I need to get away and hide somewhere.*

"You've just destroyed everything." 5083 heard 6-96's voice screaming from the crystal.

Oh no, he thought as she glared back at him, *she can still talk to me through the crystal.*

"You'll never be a Persuader now," she shrieked. "You'll be nothing but an outcast."

50-83's heart sunk. His whole life had been devoted to becoming a high-ranking Persuader. Now, all of that work would be for nothing. But, no matter what, he had to leave. He looked toward the elevator that led out of the workshop, and, in the elevator, he noticed one of the Dark Tyrant's spy-creatures. It whirred as it relayed the video images it had just recorded. 50-83 raced to the spy creature to do to it what Infinity had done with the seven-headed snake. Unfortunately, the spy-creature was much too fast and quickly slithered on its way to the Dark Tyrant with the information it had collected.

50-83 looked once more at the crystal around his neck.

"It looks like you're in a big mess, my apprentice," 6-96 laughed derisively.

Trying to ignore the voice, he weighed in his mind what he should do. He was tempted to escape the city and hide out in the wilderness area, but he remembered that did not go well when he tried it before with 4,021. At a loss of what else to do, he decided to seek advice from someone he figured would be glad to see 6-96 neutralized. He decided to pay 1-13 a visit.

Chapter Forty-Two

As Infinity continued his search for the web's energy source, he once more perceived a disturbing presence emanating from the space station. He closed his eyes and connected mentally with the presence to understand it more thoroughly. "Who mans that space station?" he demanded of the *Ghost III,* his eyes nearly penetrating the space station to see within.

In less than a second the *Ghost III* acquired the information. *"The Guardian. The Dark Tyrant pays him well to secure this area."*

Infinity knitted his eyebrows and tapped his temple in serious contemplation. "Yes, the Dark Tyrant wants to prevent me from passing this place. But there is something even more devious at work here." He closed his eyes once more and searched for the connection. Directly, in his mind's eye he saw what it was: "The Cloud of Deception. It rules here."

The Cloud of Deception was highly infectious, and Infinity knew this. He promptly directed the *Ghost III* to envelop itself in an extra layer of solectrostatic protection. The *Ghost III* proceeded to produce a golden wall of electrons which enveloped the area just outside the spaceship. Infinity climbed down a nearby ladder and proceeded straight to the ship's armory to acquire his own protection. He put on his highly durable and virtually impenetrable armor. It was made from a resilient but lightweight metoline material. Within the armor was an infallible electrical programing, which could read everything Infinity thought and could act upon those thoughts as if the armor were an extension of Infinity's body. All of the actions the armor could perform were so numerous that nobody, other than Infinity and, perhaps, the armor's designer, could list each one. The armor was of a deep black with the edges lined with a blood red. Lastly, Infinity fitted on his helmet, its mask-like face protector completely covering his face. The viewing area of his mask was covered with black ezocane which prevented his combatants from seeing in but enabled Infinity to see out. This area formed a horizontal line that covered his eyes and intersected with a vertical line from his chin to the top of his mask to form a cross-shape. The edges of the cross-shape were lined in the same blood red. Inside the armor, Infinity took on the appearance of a stealthy, robotic shadow.

Infinity returned to the *Ghost III's* controls to secure communications with the space station. While the *Ghost III* promptly set up a communications link between it and the space station, Infinity did not immediately grant the final approval for opening the link. Instead, he first gave the *Ghost III* instructions for one more task. He gave the orders to "activate Operation Covert Spies." Once the *Ghost III* put the operation into action, Infinity pressed the final sequence into the command station to establish the communications link.

The Guardian's image appeared on the viewing screen. "Well . . ." he laughed, ". . . Here already. And I didn't expect you until tomorrow." His face boasted a self-confident grin. "Anyway, I am flattered that you went through all the trouble to hurry over here just to talk to me. But, certainly you now realize that there is no way you can get past the webbing."

In response, Infinity tilted his head calmly.

The Guardian grew edgily eager to face Infinity in a fight, but, realized it would be unwise to let Infinity observe his eagerness. Instead, he let his tension flow to his tightening fists, and otherwise tried to appear forceful yet calm. "Go back to your pampered planet and your spoiled citizens. Don't waste your time here among real men who know how to fight."

The glint in Infinity's helmet glared fiercely. "I have set my course for the Planet of Darkness and I will not stop until I get there."

The Guardian shook his head in disbelief. "Damn it, you know you'll never get through. You position your ship within a mile of my web and you and your ship will be fried to cinders."

The cross on Infinity's helmet was fixed on the Guardian. "You will let me through."

The Guardian was overtaken by a fit of laughter. "Don't be ridiculous." When Infinity was unmoved, the Guardian forced himself to once more become serious. "I am being paid a lot to keep you from passing that web. Do you really think for one minute I would let you through?"

Infinity lowered his chin, unamused. "You will."

"The hell I will," the Guardian persisted. "The Dark Tyrant must really hate you, the amount of money he is willing to spend on keeping your hide away. You won't live two seconds on that planet, so you might as well turn tail now."

"I *am* going to the Planet of Darkness, and you *will* let me through."

The Guardian stood. He filled the screen with his stature and his muscles flexed with an indomitable strength. "Think what you will, but you are NOT going to get past me. This is a powerful space station and I am a powerful warrior. You haven't got a chance." To add finality to his remark, the Guardian cut off the communications link and the screen went black.

Infinity pressed a button on the *Ghost III's* console. A detailed three-dimensional map of the Guardian's space station appeared on the viewing screen. While Infinity was in conversation with the Guardian, Operation Covert Spies was in action. The *Ghost III* had launched several small robotic spider-like cameras that were incapable of being spotted by the space station's radar. These robotic cameras invaded the space station through exhaust vents. They worked at top speed and were able to spy out the entire space station, return to the *Ghost III*, and create the map in the amount of time it took Infinity and the Guardian to hold their conversation.

Infinity pored over the map. "And now to formulate the strategy for taking on and defeating the Guardian."

2-45 pushed the doors open and entered 7,500's private office. He had hoped that 7,500 would by now have his suitcases packed and be ready to embark on their journey. He passed several statues that made their home in the office and came upon one particular statue of a young man with a face that looked as though he had swallowed something sour. The statue held a pile of fallen drapery that represented his clothes and pointed to the left. 2-45's eyes followed the direction the statue was pointing and fixed upon 7,500 still at work packing. 2-45 puzzled over the fact that, instead of clothes and toiletries, 7,500 was shoving several exterminating guns into his suitcase. 2-45 shifted from one foot to the other once as he mentally questioned this unusual action. He decided to pretend it was not unusual and cleared his throat to give 7,500 time to hide the guns in case he was not supposed to have seen them.

"Ready to head out?" he more commanded than asked.

7,500 quickly threw a few shirts and pants into the suitcase to cover the guns and turned to face 2-45. He rubbed his nose casually before raising his eyes to 2-45's. "Uh . . . hmm?" He tilted his head, pretending to have missed what 2-45 had said.

"Are you packed?" 2-45 raised an eyebrow and fidgeted his fingers at his side to give a slight insinuation that he knew 7,500 was up to something.

With one quick movement, 7,500 swung over and closed his suitcases. "Yes." He smiled finding 2-45's suspicions amusing. "But, before we head out, we need to stop off at manual labor room 15."

2-45 was tired of playing it cagey. "Does it have to do with the guns?"

To 2-45's surprise, 7,500 simply turned to him as a smile spread itself across his face. "Why, yes." He grabbed his suitcases and headed for his front office. "You worked in propaganda so you should understand. Rebellion is what it takes to draw out some people's real character. Am I not right?"

To avoid being committed to his response, 2-45 half-nodded and half-shook his head. "I suppose it could work that way."

"So, one can provide people with the tools . . ." 7,500 set one suitcase down as he used his free hand to pat the other suitcase, ". . . they need to rebel and then, after a little prodding, we step back and note which ones rebel."

Opening the door to the hall for 7,500, 2-45 turned to him with a shrug. "Perhaps." The corners of his lips rose in an amused smile. "So, does that make you the leader of a rebellion?"

7,500 grabbed both suitcases again and made his out, ensuring his suitcases did not bang on the doorframe. As they stepped out into the halls of the City of the Dark Tyrant, 7,500 shook his head with a supercilious lowering of his eyelids in response to 2-45's question. "I wouldn't say that." 7,500 thought a moment and as he did his mouth dropped and his eyes rose so far upward that 2-45 wondered if he would faint. Finally, 7,500's moment of meditation paid off and he burst out in a short, loud laugh. "Ha, not in the least. More of a gem collector seeking to toss out the fakes that were surreptitiously slipped into the collection."

2-45 noticed that as 7,500 spoke his eyes fell to the ring 2-45 wore on the small finger of his right hand. It was a family heirloom that had been handed down to his father after being in the family for several generations. It was gold and engraved with an emblem compiled of petrified trees and an erupting volcano. The vent of the volcano was graced with a 2-carat ruby. When 2-45's father gave it to him, he reminded him it was over a thousand years old and represented the wealth and respect their family had earned. 7,500's focus on his ring made 2-45 a bit uncomfortable. He twisted the ring on his finger so the gem faced inward. He wondered if 7,500's new role as *gem-collector* played a part in his interest for the ring.

"You're thinking how unlike the workers you and I are, aren't you?" 7,500 commented. "Of course, you and I are much different from them. They are struggling to survive, so something like a rebellion brings out their true natures. We are in a much different class. To bring out our true natures, one would have to send us into the burning hot lavas in the center of the planet." He laughed as if what he was saying was not to be taken seriously. However, 2-45 knew him too well. Whenever 7,500 laughed at what he said, 2-45 knew he really meant it.

Chapter Forty-Three

The *splitch-splotch drip-dolopity slosh* of the mud-soaked dampness streaming down the stone walls of 1-05's prison cell made it impossible to sleep. A cold shiver ran through her body and she knew even trying to sleep was hopeless. She laid back and stared at the walls. They were brick. She knew that from feeling them. But, in the darkness of the cell she could not really tell their color patterns. *Perhaps a marble mixture of red, black, and brown.* The shadows formed strange figures on the wall. In one corner, a giant bird carried a carcass over a volcano. Near a center crack in the wall, a mountain grew out of a tall, nearly toppling tower. On the door, a one-legged man stood with an insolent puckered-up face. She closed her eyes to stop the onslaught of the shadows and turned her thoughts to the man who visited her earlier. *What was it that letter said?* 1-05's teeth chattered as she thought. *That I would be safe here? Yes, safe . . . safe and miserable.* She furrowed her brows in a silent grumble as she glanced about the cell trying to determine what shadow or crevice Alpha 3-0-3 was hiding in. *Is it still a mouse? Or has it turned into a pebble or bug or dust particle,* she wondered as she slid herself to a dark corner of the cell where she noticed a faint light-colored something.

"Alpha 3-0-3, is that you?" she asked as she poked the something with her finger.

A mouse hopped onto her shoulder and whispered in her ear. "I'm here," it giggled. "That thing you are poking is the stivel toad whose croaking has been annoying us so much." It tilted its head in concern. "I finally convinced it to be quiet. But you still can't sleep?"

"No." She watched the stivel toad sluggishly hop away from her. "It's freezing in here. Aren't you cold?"

Tapping its chin in thought, Alpha 3-0-3 nodded its reply. "Well, I am cold, but I can still function in the cold, so it is only an inconvenience to me."

1-05 crossed her arms in front of her and tucked her hands under her arms to keep them warm. "So can I." She pouted in a stoic frown which was interrupted by a shiver. "I just can't sleep in the cold."

Alpha 3-0-3 waved its hands upward, ready to perform whatever magic was needed. "Then I shall keep you warm."

"How?" she asked perplexed.

"A fire should do the trick." Alpha 3-0-3 scurried down her arm to the floor. Once it was several inches away from her, it transformed itself into a mass of sparkling particles that reformed into a warm, bright, crackling fire.

1-05 knelt next to Alpha 3-0-3 and held her hands close to the fire, rubbing them to spread the warmth. "Alpha 3-0-3, I am always amazed at what you can do."

"The most important thing is that you are warmer," it flickered brighter as it replied.

"Warmer? Yes," she replied. "Happy? No. It is completely unreasonable that I have to stay in prison." She twisted the ring the Shadow-Shield had given her. "That man who came here with the wolf. He snuck in here didn't he. I'm certain he could have found a way to sneak us out. But he says I will be safe here, so I have to stay." She snorted her displeasure.

"The ring has kept us safe." Alpha 3-0-3 reminded her.

"Yes, but I can't stand it here much longer. He didn't even say how long I would have to stay." She was so furious that her hands shook and would have burned in the fire if Alpha 3-0-3 had not pulled itself out of the way.

Alpha 3-0-3 beamed brighter in hopes that the extra light would cheer her up. "But you did find out that 8-23 is still alive. That was good to know."

"Of course," 1-05 sighed and let her head drop dejectedly. "But the way they described him. He seems so different. He even has a new name. What was it he calls himself now?"

The flames of fire tilted to the side as Alpha 3-0-3 pondered the question. "The Way-Guide, I think."

1-05 nodded impassively. "And how can we be sure he will get us out of here?"

"Because the Shadow-Shield told us he would." Alpha 3-0-3's flames stretched high in confidence.

"Ideally we could trust him to keep his word, but I can't," she told Alpha 3-0-3 with a marked irritation. "I can't trust him. There is something Grubian about him and I don't know him and even if his best intentions were to rescue us, something may have gone wrong." She pounded the wall of the cell to express her frustration. "No, we won't wait." She stood in determination. "We will do this ourselves."

Alpha 3-0-3's brightness waned as it expressed its concern. "But what if there's a good reason we need to wait. I am sure they will rescue us when the time is right."

"No, no, no," 1-05 fumed. "I am tired of waiting and I *will* get out of this prison. We just need to come up with a plan to get out. I am certain you could think of something."

"Well, yeeess, I suppose so." The fire wavered a bit as Alpha 3-0-3 deliberated over the best plan. "I could transform myself so I look like you. When the guards see me in the cell, they will think I am you and that you are still here, when you are actually slipping out of the prison."

In a stark transformation, 1-05 beamed at Alpha 3-0-3's suggestion. "That is a brilliant plan." She wished she could give Alpha 3-0-3 a warm hug, but just patted the air around the fire instead. "You have done more for me than anybody."

1-05 took a deep breath as she reminded herself there were still details about the plan that needed to be worked out before they could be put into action. "The guards' fifth inspection round would be a good time for the escape. We should have everything ready by then."

The Way-Guide was aware his presence added an extra burden to the safe house. He did not expect regal treatment or a room the size of a meeting hall, but he had hoped for a room at least big enough to lie down and walk around in. Instead, the Dream-Saver led him to a room just a few inches bigger than a broom closet with a ceiling that dripped and sagged downward because the porenthian foam was failing and needed to be replaced. Trying to avoid becoming too paranoid, he convinced himself he was given the room because space was limited and not because the Shadow-Shield was annoyed at his arrival. The Way-Guide lifted one hand above his head to push the drooping ceiling upward so he could move from one end of the room to the other without taking a face-full of ceiling in the process. Surveying the room from the other side, he contemplated the best plans for sleeping. The overstuffed chair was the closest thing to a bed, and he had just collapsed into it when the Shadow-Shield knocked on the door and let himself in.

"Come on in." The Way-Guide was unable to hide a slightly bitter tone. "Why not invite a few other people to join us. Maybe with enough of us here, we might be able to keep that ceiling horizontal instead of parabolic."

The Shadow-Shield leaned his back on the wall so casually it seemed to the Way-Guide he did not even notice the room's defects. "We are preparing another room for you," the Shadow-Shield explained nonchalantly. "But, in the meantime, I wanted us to have a clear understanding of how we are going to carry out the rescue plan."

"From what I understand, all I'm supposed to know is my part of the plan," the Way-Guide shrugged his shoulders. "And that is one, two, three," he held up one finger after the other as he counted, "break into the master computer; reprogram the computer; and, break out."

The Way-Guide thought the Shadow-Shield would be irritated at his sarcasm, but, instead, he chuckled and nodded. "I guess that about sums it up." The Shadow-Shield pulled a sheet of paper out of his inside jacket pocket. "Here," he handed the paper to him. "The architectural plans you asked for. While comfortable room accommodations take a little longer, requests connected to important tasks can be accomplished much quicker."

The Way-Guide took the plans and looked them over, genuinely impressed. "If there is anything else I need, I'll let you know."

"Not me," the Shadow-Shield replied flatly, "the Dream-Saver. In just a few minutes, I will be off on my part of the rescue plan."

The Way-Guide noticed a hint of sadness in his voice that made him suspect the mission would be dangerous. "Is anyone going with you?"

Moving his head from the right to the left in such a way that could have been both a 'yes' and a 'no', the Shadow-Shield glanced down for a second then back at the Way-Guide. "You need help breaking into the room that houses the master computer. The Dream-Saver will organize your team. Be sure to take them with you."

"You know I work best on my own, but, alright, I'll go with a team."

"And take your ship," the Shadow-Shield reminded him. "The Dream-Saver can show the best place to hide it while you are working on the master computer. You need a quick escape."

The Way-Guide was still irritated the Shadow-Shield was dodging his question. "But what about you? If you're heading into danger, I'm willing to help you out."

The Shadow-Shield smiled and shook his head. "You may be a loner, but not as much as me. You come from the Planet of Darkness, so you have some connections here. I don't come from the Planet of Light and I don't come from the Planet of Darkness. I'm a little out of place wherever I am. So, even more than you, I work best on my own." The Shadow-Shield turned and left the Way-Guide's room.

The Way-Guide followed him into the hall. "You're going to need help." He held out a hand and blocked the Shadow-Shield. "It's not wise to try this alone."

"You're right," the Shadow-Shield replied. "And I won't be alone." He moved passed the Way-Guide down the hall.

The Way-Guide continued to follow him. "So, you want me to come with you?"

Grabbing an extra coat from a rack hanging on the wall, the Shadow-Shield bundled up for his journey. "Don't worry. The Shepherdess is sending help." He took a bag of supplies and swung it over his shoulder.

With the Way-Guide following, the Shadow-Shield made his way to the hatch that led outside. He climbed the ladder and opened the hatch. Slipping through the opening, he found himself outside in the snow-covered coldness.

The Way-Guide followed him through the hatch to see him off and, hopefully, convince him to let him come along. Once through the opening, the bitter cold wind struck against his face. A swarm of snow blurred his vision and, for a moment, he could not even see the Shadow-Shield who was right beside him. Eventually he could make out the Shadow-Shield looking into the freezing wind as if the bitter cold was a refreshing breeze. "You should get back inside where it is warm," the Shadow-Shield told him. "You're not even geared up for this weather."

"But you need someone to go with you," the Way-Guide insisted. He looked deeper into the blizzard and saw the Shadow-Shield was not alone. Surrounding him was a pack of at least twenty-four wolves.

The Shadow-Shield noticed the astonished look on the Way-Guide's face. "I told you the Shepherdess would send help. You should go inside and prepare for your part of the mission."

The Way-Guide watched as the Shadow-Shield turned and headed on his way to the City of the Dark Tyrant. The pack of wolves walked confidently on every side of the Shadow-Shield and it was clear he was well protected. The Way-Guide shook his head at how foolish he was to have been concerned. He sunk back into the opening and the warmth below, closing the hatch once he was inside.

Chapter Forty-Four

The portion of the ezocane ceiling over the City of the Dark Tyrant covering a flight departure tube dilated, permitting a towering semi-sphere-shaped spaceship to depart the city and hover in the planet's atmosphere. A stark purple glow emanated from the ship's thrusters as it loomed over the city like a portentous plague.

Inside the ship's command center, the Dark Tyrant hung from the ceiling over the pilot and copilot's shoulders, his shadowed form in the shape of a giant bat-like creature. "Rebellion," he screeched out, his mouth stretching open so wide, the pilot and copilot shrank down fearing they would be swallowed alive. "How dare any of my subjects even contemplate rebellion?"

1 bobbled up behind him as he peered out the viewing screen with bulging eyes. "They won't rebel for long, Great Incomparable Dark Tyrant."

The Dark Tyrant dropped from the ceiling and swayed from side to side like a misplaced amoeba. "Of course they won't," he declared in a crescendo that was half grumbled and half roared. "The dead cannot rebel."

Sitting further back to the side, inconspicuous and unconcerned, was 1's Shadow-Shifter. "Destroying the entire city should be an easy task for you," it said with a grunt of indifference. "The city does not appear to be much more than a speck from up here."

1 held his head high in excitement. "Yes," he agreed with panting enthusiasm. "Destroying the city *would* be so simple for you."

The Dark Tyrant grew larger and more human. His hands formed fists that swelled as he brought them down to emphasize his disapproval of the suggestion. "NO," he bellowed. "I am the Dark Tyrant and in order to be a ruler I need a population to rule." He shrank down to a relatively normal human shape, albeit one with a hint of an anorexic shadow. "The people rebel because they have heard rumors that Infinity is coming to our planet."

"Rumor?" 1 asked, both of his eyes quizzically protruding so much they nearly bumped into each other. "Then he isn't really coming here?"

The Dark Tyrant rubbed his chin back and forth in nervous thought. "Oh, he *is trying* to come." He breathed out in frustration. "Yes, he wants to come . . . but he *must not* come."

The Shadow-Shifter cocked its head in thought-filled interest. "Yesss." It stood to its feet and stepped forward from the back shadows of the ship. "There is a prophecy that Infinity would come before our planet would be destroyed."

Stunned at his display of knowledge on Infinity, 1's mouth dropped open.

The Dark Tyrant glared down at the city, wrapping himself around the viewing screen as if to gobble it up with his arms. "But I will not let this prophesy be fulfilled," he growled. "He must not come. And to keep him from coming we must prevent the citizens from leaving the city and joining the Shepherdess of the Valley in her rebellious activities."

The Shadow-Shifter raised its head in subdued surprise. "Soooo the Shepherdess of the Valley does exist?"

Fuming at hearing the Shepherdess' name once more, the Dark Tyrant's form compressed lower. "Unfortunately she does."

"Is she really so dangerous?" the Shadow-Shifter asked as it moved to the viewing screen, looking toward the horizon and the direction of the valley belonging to the Shepherdess.

1 stared at the Shadow-Shifter, his mouth still open like a toad trying to swallow something much bigger than himself. "Yes," he said with slow deliberation. He then added another, much more confident, "yes." Then, with excitement, he turned to the Dark Tyrant. "She once was *too* dangerous, but not anymore."

The Dark Tyrant's eyes narrowed with skepticism.

"It's true." 1 turned eagerly to the Dark Tyrant. "We now have the key to defeating the Shepherdess." He laid his short fat fingers on the Shadow-Shifter's shoulder. "The one thing that could defeat the Shepherdess. I am sure of it. My Shadow-Shifter."

"Yesss," the Dark Tyrant agreed. "The perfect rival for her."

"I would gladly destroy the Shepherdess for you," the Shadow-Shifter bowed its head toward the Dark Tyrant. A second later, though, it shifted uncomfortably and took several steps back to allow the shadows of the ship to engulf it.

"But now," the Dark Tyrant told them, "the center of immediate concern is the manual labor room 15."

The Dark Tyrant's ship hovered over the northeast sector of the city and sunk close to an entrance tube in the ezocane ceiling. The portion of the ceiling covering this tube dilated, allowing the ship to enter. Once the ship was inside the tube, the ceiling closed and the ship followed the tube until it came to the huge work station. The ship landed on the area of the roof just over manual labor room 15 and locked itself onto it. The ship was now attached to the roof and when the ship's door slid open, the portion of the roof attached to it also slid open, allowing the Dark Tyrant, 1, and the Shadow-Shifter to enter into manual labor room 15. Entering from the roof, they stepped onto an open catwalk that ran across the entire upper portion of the room. As they followed the catwalk, they surveyed the workers busy with their tasks.

1 leaned in close to the Dark Tyrant and spoke to him under his breath. "What is it that is so special about this manual labor room?" He blinked nervously when he noticed the Dark Tyrant glaring at him with a sideways look. "I mean . . ." 1 stammered, "I have heard about the rebellion taking place here . . . But I am sure it must be taking place in all the labor rooms."

"More so here . . ." the Dark Tyrant told him with a heavy breath. "Infinity has already had an influence on this place. He must have spoken directly to someone here." His eyes scanned the room . . . looking for something. They fell on 85-27 and narrowed with a shrewd malicious awareness. "Or . . . Given someone something." He abruptly turned back to 1. "The workers here. They *will* try to escape. They will try it soon. But they must *not* get away."

The Shadow-Shifter took a decided step up to the Dark Tyrant and bowed its head obediently. "They will not get away," it affirmed.

With his chest swelling like a proud father, 1 nodded. "Go on. Put a stop to this rebellion."

The Shadow-Shifter turned and met 1's eyes with its own to determine if he meant what he said. After 1 wobbled his head in confirmation, the Shadow-Shifter swooped down from the catwalk to mingle with the workers.

Tilting his head and transforming more and more into a sickly, half-human, half-feline creature, the Dark Tyrant scrunched his nose up, unimpressed. "It will take more than one Shadow-Shifter to keep these workers from escaping."

1 tapped his fingertips together in agitation. "Of course," he agreed. "But I am sure the Enforcers will stop them."

"Perhaps . . . Perhaps not." The Dark Tyrant's head sank further into his body and his shoulders moved higher. "But when Infinity is involved, we need to be sure. Force cannot be the only means of stopping them."

1 frowned in confusion. "But what method is there of stopping them other than force?"

"Dissuasion." The Dark Tyrant lifted his head higher. "We can use the punishment others endured for trying to escape to dissuade the workers from trying it themselves." A dark, mottled, literal shadow of a smile spread itself on the Dark Tyrant's face. "And we have recently come across the perfect example." He swung a deliberate hand toward the viewing screens and seemingly at his command the screens played images of 2,040 trying to escape from the crushing machines, being sucked into his fountain, and becoming a part of the lava lake.

1 watched the screens, impressed. "Yes, YES. This method will be most effective."

"I will be watching from my ship as you and your Shadow-Shifter stop the rebellion." The Dark Tyrant swung back to his ship.

1 looked about the room and a sudden nervousness spread itself throughout his body. "But this room," he choaked. "It makes ezocane. Ezocane is our chief commodity. What if it . . ." The final words of his sentence were snuffed out by panicked gasp.

The Dark Tyrant turned to him as his face transformed into a banderwile bear ready to kill. "Preserve the ezocane if you can. Destroy it if you must. I want this rebellion stopped."

The Way-Guide leaned back in his chair and stared at the still-drooping ceiling. The Shadow-Shield had assured him a new room would be available eventually, but that 'eventually' was yet to arrive. In the meantime, the Way-Guide was convinced the sagging of the ceiling had increased by at least one inch. While he pondered fetching a measuring stick to start a regular data log on the ceiling, the Dream-Saver knocked on the door and entered.

"Welcome to the royal suite," the Way-Guide greeted him in a sarcastic tone. "Watch your head. The ceiling ensures that everyone who enters bows."

The Dream-Saver laughed good-naturedly and gave the ceiling a firm shove upward, which, to the Way-Guide's amazement, caused it to stay somewhat horizontal, at least temporarily. "Your new room is ready," he announced.

The Way-Guide nodded, his eyes still fixed on the recently 'repaired' ceiling. He then turned to the Dream-Saver. "I have been studying the architectural plans of the city. I am still trying to determine the best way in."

"Perhaps your planning will go quicker if you planned with your team," the Dream-Saver suggested.

The Way-Guide sighed wearily. "The Shadow-Shield told me that you would be organizing my team." He stood and shook his head in annoyance. "I could use, perhaps, one or two people, but definitely no more than that."

To the Way-Guide's surprise, his remark did not dampen the Dream-Saver's spirits. He just chuckled and waved the remark away. "Yes, I know. But, still, we have some people here you could really use. Like me for instance."

"You? I thought all you did was wash dishes and baby-sit."

The Dream-Saver blushed. "Okay, yes, for the most part." He then pointed to the architectural plans in the Way-Guide's hand. "But who do you think drew up those plans?"

Holding them up, the Way-Guide looked at the Dream-Saver in surprise. "You?"

"That's right. Before the Shadow-Shield convinced me to join him here at the safe-house, I was a drafter and records-keeper. I either drew, edited, or safe-guarded all the plans for the City of the Dark Tyrant."

The Way-Guide thought over what the Dream-Saver had told him. "Alright. Then it's you and me working on this mission."

"And the Sword-Wielder," the Dream-Saver added.

The Way-Guide's face screwed up in confusion at a name he had never heard. "Who?"

"The Sword-Wielder," he repeated. "He is our best war strategist and fight specialist. We really should have someone on our team who understands battle in case we run into Enforcers."

"But I haven't event met him. How can I work with someone I don't even know?"

"Well, come with me and I'll introduce you to your team." The Dream-Saver led the Way-Guide down the hall until they reached an open room with a long conference table. Around the table sat eight people, including the Light-Defender and the Soul-Guard.

Standing in front of so many unfamiliar people, the Way-Guide shifted nervously. "I really think we should keep this team small," he told the Dream-Saver aside.

"They won't all be on the team. I was thinking it was important that we have input on the plan from as many people as possible, then just a few of us would carry it out."

"Very well," the Way-Guide agreed, willingly dropping his control of the mission to the Dream-Saver. "Does everyone know the mission's objective?"

"No harm in reiterating it." The Dream-Saver turned from the Way-Guide to everyone at the table. "We need to break into the Dark Tyrant's master computer and reprogram it so that the tiles of the manual labor room 15 will not disintegrate the workers there when they escape."

"First of all," the Way-Guide broke in, "we need to get to the outskirts of the city. We will use the *Forerunner* to get there but we need a safe place to hide the ship while we are working. The Shadow-Shield told me you would know of the best place."

"Yes." The Dream-Saver set a stack of maps on the table in front of the Way-Guide and pointed to it. "This area, just a few miles from the city's own docking bay, is full of crags and tunnels. There are plenty of places to hide a ship in there."

The Soul-Guard rose to her feet. "Is it true that from there you are planning to tunnel into the City of the Dark Tyrant?"

The Way-Guide nodded and sat down. "We thought that would be the safest way to get into the master computer."

"But wouldn't tunneling take a long time?" she asked in concern.

"If we don't have the right tools it could." The Way-Guide looked to the Dream-Saver for a response.

The Dream-Saver grabbed a blueprint and placed it on an easel at the head of the table. The blueprint was of a machine on wheels containing a cone-shaped laser gun at the front and a rectangular soil disintegrator throughout its center. "We have recently acquired this tunnel excavator from a shipment heading to the City of the Dark Tyrant. With this it should only take a few minutes. This medium-sized machine contains a strong laser. Also, while it is powerful it is also quiet. I estimate we should get from the tunnels near the ship to below the room that houses the master computer in less than half an hour."

"Once inside," the Way-Guide took over, "I will work with the master computer to complete the reprogramming. Hopefully, we can complete that in less than an hour. It could take longer depending on how difficult it is to get past the Dark Tyrant's computer security. What I need are people who can operate the machinery and people who can fight in the event we meet up with Enforcers."

The Light-Defender moved to the Dream-Saver. "You said you wanted me to come. Why?"

A tall, elderly man set a hand on her shoulder. "Because we will need you."

She laid her fingertips on his hand and smiled. "Sword-Wielder? Are you coming too?"

"Of course," the man told her firmly. "I told the Dream-Saver that both you and I are coming. We are the only ones who could defend this mission against Enforcers. Without us, it would be doomed to failure."

She patted his hand. "In that case, I will come."

Chapter Forty-Five

The darkness hid the Shadow-Shield as he crouched behind close to the ground just outside the City of the Dark Tyrant's prison. The Shepherdess' wolves surrounded him and sniffed the air for any hint of danger. From his spot, just around the corner from the entrance, the Shadow-Shield could see the Enforcers making their rounds along the prison's perimeter. He counted four Enforcers but knew more were not far away. He gestured to four wolves, who approached and awaited orders. With a smooth wave of his hand, he directed their attention to the Enforcers.

The wolves leaped to attack, and as they did, the Shadow-Shield kept his body low as he moved closer to the prison and knelt near the wall. He moved his hand along the wall feeling every change in texture and temperature. The flowing of heat in one area indicated to him an electric current was inside the wall. After detecting the location of a particularly strong current near the base, he attached a square, black, handheld box at that spot. Once the box made contact, it enabled the Shadow-Shield to open a portion of the wall with one strong pull of the box. Inside the wall he found a set of wires and connections. The opening was too small for him to reach in and adjust the connections. He closed his eyes and concentrated on them. With a deep inward thought, he ordered his body to fade and reform. His hand could now reach through the wall to the wires. He adjusted the connections within the wires and the large metal door of the prison slid open.

The four wolves had burst from the shadows so rapidly the Enforcers did not have a chance to draw their weapons. Two of them sunk their teeth into closest Enforcers' wrists and confiscated their weapons. The others leaped at the Enforcers' chests, knocking them to the ground, and pierced their eyes with a relentless stare. When the Enforcers made eye contact with the wolves, they were overcome with fear. One rolled away from the wolves, buried his head in the ground, and waved his hands in the air screaming for them to leave him alone. The other sunk into the shadows. The doorway now stood open for the Shadow-Shield and the wolves.

Once inside, the Shadow-Shield found a hallway just off the entrance and ordered the wolves to guard it. He proceeded in the direction of 1-05's prison cell. When he noticed several Enforcers marching toward him, he slipped into the shadows, becoming nearly invisible as they passed by. After the guards turned into another hallway, he detected movement in the opposite direction. He could not tell what it was. It appeared as only a flicker of light and a fluttering of cloth. He crept forward cautiously, but as he moved into the shadows he collided into 1-05 who fell backward and landed on the stone floor.

"Why aren't you in your cell?" he asked as he helped her to her feet.

"I was escaping," she snapped. "We decided that Alpha 3-0-3 would impersonate me while I got away. It's a good plan. By the time they figured it out, I would be miles from here." She heaved a sigh when she saw the fall had drenched her clothes in more mud than had covered them the whole time she had been in prison.

The Shadow-Shield groaned in frustration. "You were to stay in the cell."

"I don't have to do what you tell me," she told him firmly. "If you aren't going to help me out of here, I will do it myself." The raised voices drew attention to their presence. A siren sounded in the hall and the Shadow-Shield heard the shuffling, stomping, and clanking of Enforcers heading their way.

The Shadow-Shield pulled her into a shadowy spot along the wall, pushed her against the wall, and covered her with his body which blended with the shadows. They remained unnoticed as the Enforcers passed through the hall. He kept his eyes focused on the hallway to the right until the Enforcers had moved on to another hall. Once he was certain the Enforcers were out of hearing range, he faced her. "I am going to help you out of here, but we need Alpha 3-0-3. I am going to have to go back and get him. You continue down this hall. Turn left when you reach the end of it. You will be met by a group of wolves who will lead you to safety."

After just avoiding a group of Enforcers, 1-05's realization of the seriousness of the situation sent a moment of panic throughout her body. The directions the Shadow-Shield gave her were muddled and confused in her head. She hoped she could remember when to turn left and how to recognize the wolves. She took a deep breath to calm herself but before heading off, she turned back to the Shadow-Shield.

"You don't happen to have an extra exterminating gun, I could borrow?" she asked.

To her surprise, the Shadow-Shield detached a gun from his belt and placed it in her hand. "Now, hurry," he told her with marked concern.

She took the gun and raced in the direction the Shadow-Shield had pointed out to her.

Keeping hidden in the shadows, the Shadow-Shield raced to 1-05's prison cell. Once there, he looked through the bars and found Alpha 3-0-3 appearing as 1-05 in the cell. The Shadow-Shield made himself visible enough for it to see him and tapped gently on the door.

Alpha 3-0-3 turned to the door and smiled brightly. "Is 1-05 safe?"

"Yes," he told it in a hoarse whisper. "But you need to get out of here too." He glanced up and down the hallway and, seeing it clear, he held his hand upward and waved his fingers away from the cell, indicating that Alpha 3-0-3 was to come.

Alpha 3-0-3 nodded and transformed into a swirl of particles that reformed into a stivel toad much like the one that had been hiding in the cracks of the cell wall. It hopped through the bars and landed onto the Shadow-Shield's boot. "All right," Alpha 3-0-3 croaked, "let's go."

The Shadow-Shield raced down the hall, but as he was leaving, he heard guards and Enforcers scuttling about behind them and raising the alarm.

The Shadow-Shield would have raced faster to the exit, but he was distracted by a whimper. One of the Shepherdess' wolves lay on the ground facing a prison cell. He turned to the Shadow Shield pleadingly and pawed the door.

The Shadow-Shield knelt next to the wolf and stroked his neck. He leaned his ear to the door and listened. He heard the voices of several children.

"What is it?" Alpha 3-0-3 asked.

"The wolf senses danger for the children inside." The Shadow-Shield stood to his feet. "We should rescue them as well." He looked through the bars of the cell and saw, huddled inside, four young boys, one was red-haired, another was dark-haired, another was tow-haired, and the last was curly-haired. By their manner, he assumed they were Slump-Bumps. He tapped on the door. "We are going to get you out of here," he told them softly.

The tow-haired boy pulled himself up to look out past the bars. "We don't dare," he told the Shadow-Shield "The Enforcers are furious at us."

The red-haired boy pushed his way forward. "We worked too hard cause we were building a mud fort."

"All the more reason we should get you out." The Shadow-Shield pointed out the lock to Alpha 3-0-3.

Alpha 3-0-3 hopped up to the handle of the cell and reached its small but sturdy arm into the lock. It pulled and twisted the cylinders and pins until they gave way with a clatter and the cell door opened.

The Shadow-Shield guided the boys out of the cell. "Get them to the entrance," he told the wolf who herded them toward the hall where the rest of the wolves were waiting for them.

They had almost made it to the entrance, when they were overtaken by several Enforcers coming up behind them. The Shadow-Shield and the wolf pushed the boys out of reach of the Enforcers. The Shadow-Shield forced the Enforcer aside with his left lower arm and pounded him with several blows.

Another Enforcer came to the first one's aid and beat the Shadow-Shield back. The Shadow-Shield could hear more Enforcers flooding in from all directions.

The red-haired boy turned to the tow-haired boy. "Do you think it would help to build a mud-fort."

The tow-haired boy felt the ground and noticed it was covered in mud. He pointed to several wooden beams that were stacked along the wall. He nodded.

The wolves heard the commotion at the entrance, and the lead wolf lifted his chin and howled the call to join the fight. When they saw the boys building the mud-fort barricade, three of the wolves moved in to guard them with their bodies. With several effortless leaps, the other wolves had surrounded the Enforcers.

The Shadow-Shield was struck several times by the Enforcer. The final blow sent him colliding in sharp pain against the stone wall. His head hit it so hard he could feel the blood trickling down into his ear.

One of the wolves recognized the danger the Shadow-Shield was in and leapt between him and the Enforcer. He growled fiercely at the Enforcer, his head held low and ears alert. The wolf's fur bristled as he bared his teeth. The Enforcer grabbed his annihilation gun from where it hung on his back and swung it at the wolf. The wolf took the Enforcer's wrist by its teeth, bit down hard, and thrashed it about. The Enforcer took his gun in his other hand and used it to strike the wolf hard. The force of the gun knocked the wolf back and to the ground. With a painful effort, the wolf tried to raise its body to once more join the fight, but the Enforcer aimed his auto-targeting annihilation gun at the wolf and a bullet ripped through the wolf's chest. As blood spread across the floor around him, the wolf's eyes met with the Shadow-Shield's. He lifted his right front paw weakly and gestured for the Shadow-Shield to escape quickly. The wolf's head became too heavy and fell to the floor, lifeless.

A rush of anger spread itself throughout the Shadow-Shield's body. With unshakable rage, his eyes fell upon the Enforcer who killed the wolf. He grabbed the Enforcer and whipped him around in front of him so that he could hold the Enforcer firmly around the chest. He then wrenched the gun from the Enforcer's grip and aimed it at the Enforcer's head.

"There *is* a life after death and you will spend it on your knees begging this creature for forgiveness." The annihilation gun went off, rattling the Enforcer's helmet. The Shadow-Shield still kept a firm hold of the Enforcer as the Enforcer's body convulsed.

Alpha 3-0-3 hopped from the Shadow-Shield's boot and onto his shoulder as the Shadow-Shield continued to grip the convulsing body of the Enforcer.

"Time for me to do something desperate, right?" Alpha 3-0-3 asked.

The Shadow-Shield forced the gun deep into the Enforcer's helmet. He heard the Enforcer's skull crackle as the muzzle pushed through it and entered the brain tissue. The Shadow-Shield pulled the trigger and the Enforcer's body went limp.

"Yes," the Shadow-Shield replied flatly to Alpha 3-0-3. He let the Enforcer's body drop to the ground with his eyes fixed on another Enforcer trying to take down another wolf.

In two leaps, the Shadow-Shield was next to the Enforcer. The Shadow-Shield forced him to the wall and rammed his knee against the Enforcer's right hand, forcing him to drop his gun. He then pressed his right arm against the Enforcer's neck until he felt the Enforcer's wind-pipe collapse. While still holding the Enforcer in place, he touched his own head gingerly with his left hand and, drawing his hand down before his eyes, he noticed the drops of blood from his head wound. He raised the hand higher, signaling that the wolves should stop their attack. When the Enforcer weighed lifeless against his arm, the Shadow-Shield stepped back and let him fall. "Time for something desperate," he said aside to Alpha 3-0-3 as he raised his hands to indicate surrender.

Assuming the Shadow-Shield and the wolves were surrendering, the Enforcers moved in with caution. One of the Enforcers jabbed his gun at the Shadow-Shield's neck. "On your knees, freak." The Enforcer nudged the body of the Enforcer near the wall to confirm he was dead. "What is that trick you have?" the Enforcer asked. "In the darkness, you're almost invisible." He sauntered back to the Shadow-Shield and craned his head forward to look into his eyes. "I bet 1 would like to experiment on you to learn your secret. He will no doubt give me a nice big bonus when I take you in to him."

"I don't think so." The Shadow-Shield picked Alpha 3-0-3 off of his shoulder and tossed it behind the mud-fort barricade the boys had built.

Alpha 3-0-3 croaked its understanding and let its image fade into a sparkling haze. As it reformed its image, the Shadow-Shield and wolves had completely disappeared to the

Enforcers. The Enforcers heard the sound of a powerful high-powered engine and felt a hot gust of air as something passed them, but they could not tell what it was. Alpha 3-0-3 had transformed itself into an enclosed barso-cycle constructed of trantonine metal which both absorbed and reflected images, using the same principle that cloaked EEVs. The Shadow-Shield, boys, and the wolves hid themselves inside Alpha 3-0-3, just before it broke through the barricade and sped down the hall from the Enforcers. The cloaking method was not perfect though, and a few of the Enforcers managed to see their own image reflected in the barso-cycle as it raced out of the prison.

"It's the shape-shifter 1 warned us about," one of the Enforcers shouted. He fired his exterminating gun at the nearly invisible mass. The other Enforcers joined him in aiming their annihilation guns and firing several shots in the same direction. Still, their shots did not manage to stop the cloaked barso-cycle and it was soon lost in the darkness that loomed everywhere outside of the prison. The Enforcers agreed with each other that since it was nearly impossible to see the barso-cycle and that they only had a vague idea of what had happened, they would report the prison break and leave out the confusing details about the shape-shifter.

When Alpha 3-0-3, the Shadow-Shield, the boys, and wolves had reached a safe distance from the prison, Alpha 3-0-3 returned to its form of a stivel toad and hopped to 1-05. She was resting on the ground in the middle of the group of wolves who were assigned to guard her.

"What's going on?" she asked Alpha 3-0-3. "I heard fighting."

Alpha 3-0-3 heaved a sigh and lowered its head. "One of the wolves gave its life to rescue us."

The wolves who had remained protecting 1-05 exchanged alarmed expressions when they heard what happened and noticed a missing member. They let out a mournful howl and sunk to the ground in somber reflection.

The four boys moved next to the wolves. A tear fell down the dark-haired boy's cheek and the curly-haired boy stroked a grey wolf's side.

The Shadow-Shield scratched one of the wolves behind his ear and nodded at him gratefully. He then followed Alpha 3-0-3 to 1-05. "I will need to leave you here," he told her. "There is a task I need to do." He turned and gestured for four of the wolves to stand ready.

1-05 could not keep the confusion of the moment from screwing up her face. "But what about 8-23? You will take me to him?"

The Shadow-Shield looked at her perplexed for a second, and he had to remind himself that 1-05 had not been briefed on the mission. "8-23, the Way-Guide, is busy working on a mission to help transport some workers who are in danger. We will take them to a protected location past the wilderness. We will need your help, too. We will get you to the *Journey* so you can transport them to the safe house."

"What?" 1-05 stood and stomped a foot in insulted frustration. "Nobody told me anything about this. You just assume I will help without even asking me. Maybe I don't want to."

"Oh," the Shadow-Shield nodded. "Well, the Shepherdess told me you would help with the mission. But, if you do not want to . . . I guess we will just make the necessary adjustments." He rubbed his chin in thought. "But we do need to use the *Journey*. People's lives are at stake."

1-05 crossed her arms over her chest and snorted her irritation. What bothered her the most was that he was so congenial about her not wanting to help.

The Shadow-Shield knelt and patted Alpha 3-0-3 on the head. "And thank you, Alpha 3-0-3, for protecting 1-05.

Infinity told me that you were created to help her until she could once again be with the Way-Guide."

Alpha 3-0-3 tilted its head and turned a slight orange as stivel toads often do when worried. "I only wish I could have been more help."

The boys moved to surround 1-05. "If you need our help," the red-haired boy volunteered, "we will definitely do what we can."

"Oh, all right," 1-05 groaned. "I'll do the mission. But, I want you to know, I would have liked more information about it ahead of time."

"Those who work with us require a good deal of trust," the Shadow-Shield told her. "We couldn't risk you knowing too much. Persuaders might have forced the information out of you."

The Shadow-Shield turned to the four of the wolves waiting near him. "You four, take 1-05 to the hangar and help her ready the *Journey* for takeoff." He patted the red-haired boy on the shoulder. "You boys can join her." He picked Alpha 3-0-3 up and set him once more on his shoulder. "The rest of you, come with me. We are going to stir up trouble for a certain manual labor room."

Chapter Forty-Six

When they reached manual labor room 15, 7,500 told 2-45 to wait in the hall while he went inside to hand over his suitcase. Normally, 7,500 would not have minded 2-45 joining him in his little rebellion, but at the moment he was not in the mood for extensive questions and explanations. He wanted to complete the task and be on their way to the Queen of the Night as soon as possible. 2-45 was not insistent on joining him anyway. He leaned against the wall in his blasé-faire manner and simply told 7,500 not to take too long. 7,500 was tempted to pat him on the cheek and tell him to wait patiently like a good boy, but refrained from doing this. "I'll be quick," he told him with the smooth upward raise of one hand.

Once inside, the suffocating heat sent a stream of sweat down 7,500's face. He pulled out a handkerchief and dabbed his forehead, trying hard not to disturb his curls. Once he located 17-07, he slipped over to him as casually as possible to avoid the notice of the larger than usual number of Enforcers. He slid the suitcase under the table 17-07 was working at. "These tools should be of use," 7,500 whispered aside to him.

"Yeah. Should help immensely." 17-07 grinned without looking up from his work.

Even though 17-07 tried to remain focused on the sheet of ezocane he was smoothing out, 7,500 noticed him chuckle a bit as if eager to start blasting away Enforcers as he escaped from the manual labor room. "You should get started right away," 7,500 told him. "My assistant was captured by Enforcers but has gotten away. This could complicate things."

17-07 smiled at 7,500. "We're going to make this happen, and we're going to make this happen soon," he said as if reciting poetry. Noting the smile that spread itself on 17-07's face was the type that indicated not a care in the world was in the head attached to the smile, 7,500 knew the rebellion should go smoothly.

2-45 was under the impression 7,500's side task would take under half an hour. But, the waiting went on and on. After finding it necessary to shift his position several times to ease the stiffness in his back and noting that it had been over an hour, 2-45 decided not to wait any longer. The sides of his mouth dropped in an irritated pout and he jabbed the wall with an agitated fist. He moved towards and pushed his way through the doors, entering the manual labor room.

While 2-45 did not expect the manual labor room to compare with his tower, he was surprised at the stifling atmosphere and the mold-ridden rusty equipment. He chose not to focus on the unpleasant surroundings and, instead, took in the viewing screens straight ahead of him. The images on the screen were replaying the last moments of 2,040, the man 2-45 had been sent to spy on. 2,040 was being sucked through his fountain and into the lava lake that ran through the Dark Tyrant's executive hall. A cold sweat broke out on 2-45's forehead and a shudder ran through his body. 2-45 was aware of the Dark Tyrant's methods for disposing of uncooperative citizens, but seeing someone dragged into the lava from their own home without the formality of a structured trial, deeply disturbed him. He forced his eyes from the viewing screen and scanned the room for 7,500. Instead, his eyes fell on the ominously present 1 and someone beside him who managed to blend in with the room's shadows. They spoke furtively amongst themselves and gestured often toward a blonde-haired woman whose frailness looked out of place in the manual labor room. The woman's otherworldly presence and the fact that 1 appeared uneasy about her drew 2-45's attention to her.

2-45 knew he was taking a risk by approaching her in front of 1, but he was irresistibly drawn to her, and since he did not even know who she was and was not guaranteed he would ever see her again, he was willing to take that risk. He weaved his way to her through a littering of equipment, tools, and bloquious rocks. He was about to introduce himself, when her hand fell weakly to her side and dropped a red flower that wafted to the ground. The flower mesmerized him. While he had never seen one before, that was not what drew his attention to it. The flower had an aura so overpowering he could not pull his eyes from it, but it was this same aura that made him hesitant to pick it up.

"Oh," the woman nervously choked back a sob. "I didn't mean to drop it." She was about to pick it up when 2-45 braved his uneasiness and raised the flower to her fingers.

"Lovely flower. You know, I don't think it grows on our planet. If it does, it must grow outside the city. In fact, this is the first time I've seen a flower, other than in those pictures in books."

She tilted her head and narrowed her eyes in mistrust. "Who are you? Are you trying to get me to tell you about Infinity?"

"Infinity?" 2-45's eyes met hers as he raised an eyebrow, confused. "What infinity?"

"You don't know him?"

"Him?" He puzzled over Infinity being a man. He shook his head. "I was going to ask you if you were connected with the Queen of the Night."

"Queen." She lifted the rose to her shoulder in thought. "No. But could she be related to Infinity? Since he is a prince."

The notion grabbed 2-45's attention. "Perhaps." He tapped his lower lip in thought.

She shook her head as she reconsidered. "No, they couldn't be related . . . I mean, Infinity brings light and the queen is of the night."

Her reasoning did not make sense to 2-45, but he did not want to tell her that because she appeared sincere. He just nodded a slight nod before responding. "Oh, well. I can ask her when I see her." He looked at her with a grin that was eager to impress. "I am going to see the queen soon. I could put a word in for you. You might want to visit with her too. I hear she has some good connections." He then was struck once more by the glowing aura that surrounded her. "Have you been to the Planet of Light?"

She pondered his question, setting her finger to the side of her face. "No," she replied simply. "But Infinity is from there and he's going to be coming soon."

Before 2-45 could ask another question, 7,500 dropped a meaningful hand on his shoulder to let him know that silence was required. "Now's not the time to talk with the workers," he whispered to 2-45 with his mouth so close to 2-45's ear it was difficult for 2-45 to refrain from shivering from the tickling sensation.

"I suppose you're right," 2-45 told him. Before he left, he nodded politely to the woman. "If I see you again, I will let you know what the Queen of the Night told me."

"All right. My number is 4,021." She smiled a little, finding his polite nod charming.

2-45 was about to give her his number, but 7,500 nudged him away too quickly.

As 2-45 was leaving, 1 pointed out 4,021 to his Shadow-Shifter. "Notice the rose she holds in her hand. It is unusual and reeks of the Planet of Light."

The Shadow-Shifter nodded. It resisted an unusual pull from the rose. While that pull was a bit intoxicating, it left him with an empty feeling of doom. "Yes," the Shadow-Shifter agreed. "It must be from the Planet of Light. We have found the source of the rebellion."

The *Forerunner* circled over the area where the Way-Guide had anticipated landing, near a cliff overhang just off the underground tunnels. Looking at the viewing screen, he noticed the majority of the tunnels had collapsed and were sinking in a sea of smoking lava. The Way-Guide shook his head in frustration. "We won't be able to land here," he told the Dream-Saver.

The Dream-Saver scrambled up from the back and stood behind him. He surveyed the area with a somber frown. "Sometimes these areas erupt spontaneously, but the damage is too extensive for that. It looks like it was done on purpose."

"It really doesn't matter who did this. The fact is it's done and we will have to adjust the plan." He spotted in the distance a crevice in the cliff. "I will land the *Forerunner* there. Hopefully, we can find some tunnels. If not, we will have to make them."

After landing, the Way-Guide and the Dream-Saver climbed down to the hold of the ship to prepare the tunnel excavator. While the Dream-Saver was unclamping the front wheels of the excavator from the floor, the Way-Guide circled around to reach the back wheels. As he rounded the left of the excavator, his foot ran into an unexpected object which nearly tripped him.

"What is it?" the Dream-Saver craned his neck to see if the Way-Guide was hurt.

A dark beige cloth covered something, but the shadows that encompassed the area made it impossible to tell what it was. The Way-Guide knelt to investigate. He pulled back a cloth covering, and found a young boy sleeping against the excavator.

The Dream-Saver noticed the boy. "Dark-Breaker," he gasped. "He's not supposed to be here."

The boy stretched and rolled over. His eyes opened a bit and realizing that he had been discovered, he clambered to his feet. "I-I-I . . ." He backed up to the wall. "I just thought . . ."

"You thought you would stow away because you thought it would be fun," The Way-Guide concluded and shook his head in disappointment.

"No," Dark-Breaker insisted. "I came because you need my help."

"Okay," the Way-Guide conceded. "You can help then." He pointed out the clamps holding down the excavator's wheels. "Unclamp the excavator and help us get it ready."

"All right," the boy agreed as he raced to get started.

After the excavator was prepared, the Light-Defender and the Sword-Wielder returned from scouting the area for tunnels. The Way-Guide looked into the Sword-Wielder's eyes hopefully.

The Sword-Wielder shook his head. "The longest tunnel we could find was two miles in length, but it was too narrow. We will have to settle for the one over there." He pointed out a wide tunnel not far to the left from the *Forerunner*. "That tunnel heads toward the city but it is less than a mile long."

The Way-Guide bit his lip in thought and moved toward the excavator. "It will have to do, then." He turned to start up the tunnel excavator but stopped when he felt a hand on his arm.

The Light-Defender tightened her hold on the Way-Guide's arm to encourage him to wait. "There is something I must warn you about." While she could not physically look him in the eye, her mind looked deep into his thoughts. "A dangerous creature lives within that cave. While it is not a huge creature, it is ready to drive us out if we come too close. I heard its movements, smelled its breath, and felt its determination. And, yes, it is intelligent."

At first the Way-Guide thought the Light-Defender could have been exaggerating the danger, but when he felt the hand on his arm shake, he knew the danger must be formidable. "We'll be cautious," he told the Light-Defender.

The Way-Guide started up the tunnel excavator and, walking along beside it, he used the hand-held guiding system to lead it toward the tunnel. Dark-Breaker watched as the Way-Guide flipped levers and twisted dials to control the excavator. The Way-Guide smiled at the boy's interest and handed him the guiding system. "Why don't you try it?"

An eager grin spread itself on the Dark-Breaker's face as he grabbed the guiding system the Way-Guide offered. The boy's hands dropped a bit since it was much heavier than he had expected. During the transfer of the system, the excavator had powered down. The boy pointed toward a lever on the left side of the system and looked at the Way-Guide for his approval. The Way-Guide nodded and the boy flipped the lever, starting up the excavator again. The Way-Guide gave Dark-Breaker a run-through on the rest of the guiding system and the boy managed to maneuver the excavator deep into the tunnel in no time.

The Way-Guide heard a sudden faint moan past the whirring of the excavator. With a rapid up and down wave of his hand, he gestured for Dark-Breaker to power it down. After the engine went silent, a louder and shriller moan filled the tunnel. The Way-Guide whipped around and grabbed the Light-Defender by her upper-arm. "Is that the creature you warned me about?"

She nodded. "Yes," she sighed as a shiver ran through her body. She raised her hands in front of her to connect with the creature's thoughts. "We are getting too close to its lair . . . and its master . . . its master orders the creature to prevent us from getting too close."

"You know what it is thinking?" The Way-Guide tilted his head in surprise.

"Its thoughts are too strong to miss," she replied. "Its thoughts come from the left. We should move more right."

"Agreed." The Way-Guide and Dream-Saver calculated the direction and distance necessary to reach the room housing the master computer.

"5.45 miles to the master computer from here," the Dream-Saver announced.

The Light-Defender shook her head. "That couldn't be right."

"The calculations are based on the plans," the Way-Guide insisted, "so they must be right."

"That's what's wrong." She grabbed the plans from the Way-Guide's hands and waved them in his face. "The plans are not accurate. Yes, it's 3.25 miles to the city, but it is much farther than a little over two miles to the master computer from there. I know. I have been there. I have a sister who lives close to the master computer."

"How much farther?" the Way-Guide asked, uneasy with the delay. "Can you give us the exact calculation?"

The Light-Defender lowered her head. "No. I cannot calculate it precisely. All I know is that it is farther."

The Way-Guide looked at the Dream-Saver in hopes of a suggestion of what he should do. The Dream-Saver simply shrugged and took the plans from the Light-Defender. "The plans should be accurate," he told him. "They are used by those who work for the Dark Tyrant."

The Way-Guide gave the Dream-Saver the order to program the tunnel excavator with the calculations from the plans. They once again heated up the excavator's laser. The heat from the laser and the dust from the dirt spraying out from the laser's blast made it difficult to breathe. The walls became increasingly hot to the touch and a couple of times Dark-Breaker wanted to rest his back against the wall, but the heat from the wall quickly changed his mind. They eventually reached a point approximately a mile from where the calculations put the floor of the room housing the master computer above them. At this point, the excavator's laser sputtered, sparked and failed.

The Way-Guide tried making adjustments on the laser, but nothing could restart it.

"Can't you fix it?" the Dream-Saver asked.

The Way-Guide shook his head.

The Sword-Wielder helped the Dream-Saver move the excavator back, to allow access to the wall they wanted to break through. "This mission is too important. We can't give up," the Sword-Wielder declared.

"We won't," the Light-Defender told him. "There are shovels on the ship. It will take longer, but if we all work together, we can still dig our way through."

"It won't be easy to break through the floor," the Way-Guide told them grimly. "But we can still try."

Chapter Forty-Seven

7,500 and 2-45 were just leaving manual labor room 15. 2-45 saw the door a few steps ahead and reached out to pull the door open when his foot ran into something metal and sturdy, preventing his exit. It was a spy-creature. Its eyes narrowed and glared up at 2-45 as it gave a low, threatening growl. 2-45 took a confused step back and turned to 7,500 for an explanation. But, 7,500 was no help. He was busy scratching his chin in bewilderment as he surveyed the room, as if in search of some custodian to clean out the trash.

At that moment, 1-13 entered the manual labor room, blocking the doorway to prevent 7,500 and 2-45 from exiting. He scooped up the spy-creature and smiled at it proudly. "You were absolutely right," he told it, "there *are* some miscreants here in the labor room and you *led* me to them *just* in time." His eyes met 2-45's with a meaningful glint.

7,500 did not notice 1-13 was speaking directly to 2-45 and took what he said personally. His face turned a fiercer red than 2-45 had ever seen, as one who is ready to challenge an opponent to a duel. "Who are you calling a miscreant?" he demanded. "I know people who work directly with 1. I have worked with 1, himself. You will regret calling me a miscreant."

1-13 ignored 7,500's demands and grabbed 2-45 firmly by the shoulder, swinging him around and back into the manual labor room. "No matter what *clever* explanations you contrive and what *money* you *manage* to toss about, you are not wriggling out of *this*."

While 2-45 was strong enough to break free from 1-13's grasp, he knew resistance would be interpreted as guilt. "What brought this on?" 2-45 insisted in a tone that would have been considered under his breath if it was not so forceful. "Don't tell me you were *that* desperate to find someone to toss to the Dark Tyrant just to cover up your own meddling?"

"Watch it," 1-13 snarled. "You're on dangerous ground and that ground will soon swallow you up."

"I guess all that information I provided you earlier doesn't mean much now," 2-45 mumbled half to himself.

"I have him," 1-13 shouted in 1's direction and gestured toward his prisoner. "The rebellion, you are investigating. 2-45 was the one who orchestrated it." No one was more surprised at hearing 1-13 suspected him of being in charge of the rebellion than 2-45. He had assumed 1-13 seized him because of his attempts to leave the planet. Just a few moments ago, he was discussing 7,500's involvement in the rebellion and now he was being accused of it.

While 1, the Shadow-Shifter and a group of Enforcers gathered around, 7,500 attempted to slip discreetly toward the exit. Unfortunately for him, he could not reach the door in time and found himself jostled back into the room by the crowd.

1 looked over at 2-45 with his head leaning one way and his frown leaning the other, unsure of why 2-45's capture was important. "He orchestrated the rebellion?" he asked.

2-45 jerked his shoulder from 1-13's grasp and faced him in defiance. "I am in no way involved in any rebellion."

1-13 laughed and held his head high in confidence. "You are involved," he insisted. He reached into his front shirt pocket and pulled out a recording device. He had earlier hidden this recording device in the bracelet he was wearing when he had met 2-45 in the Duke of Distraction's dive. "If you listen to this recording," he told 1, "you will know his tendencies are rebellious and he would definitely be the one who would lead this rebellion."

1 gestured for the Enforcers to hold 2-45. "Bring him to 366's office for questioning."

As two Enforcers took charge of 2-45 and pushed him toward the office, 2-45 noticed 1-13 stand taller and take a deep, self-satisfied breath. 2-45 glanced about to determine whether 7,500 had left him, but saw him following nearby, not out of comradery, but because his attempts to slip passed the crowd of Enforcers were unsuccessful.

After setting a bag of bloquious rocks near a large boiler, 4,021 caught sight of the Enforcers pushing 2-45 into the 366's office. She turned to 17-07, her eyes screwed up in confusion. "Why are the Enforcers taking him? He's done nothing bad."

17-07 moved uncomfortably close to 4,021 and pierced her eyes with a warning look that would frighten a ghost. "The Enforcers take everyone. No one's safe with all these Enforcers about. But we'll take care of them soon. Don't you worry."

His 'don't you worry' was unsuccessful at making her not worry. In fact, it made her worry even more. She left the bloquious rocks and followed 2-45 and the Enforcers, slipping quietly into the office in hopes of protecting him.

Even though the wolves seemed to know where they were going, 1-05 felt silly following them. She had never met a wolf before in her life until just a few minutes ago and now she was letting them take her wherever they chose to go.

"Do you know anything about these creatures?" she asked the Slump-Bump boys.

"No," replied the tow-haired boy. "But they seem to know what they are doing."

"Yeah," grinned the curly-haired boy. "I like them. They're nice."

The boys' confidence in the wolves was not enough to reassure her. Still, she continued to follow the wolves. They were supposed to be taking her to the *Journey* and she did miss her ship. Eventually, she recognized the horizontal yellow and blue zigzag stripes on the walls indicating they were close to the City of the Dark Tyrant's primary hangar. She breathed a sigh of relief and was more confident about following the lead of the wolves. However, she was not relaxed enough to ask them what they should do when they entered the hangar.

The lead wolf skulked up to the hangar's entrance, ensuring he remained hidden in the shadows. He watched the hangar for a few moments, making note of the layout of the hangar and the number of workers inside. Even from where she was, 1-05 could see that at least ten workers were scattered throughout the hangar. The wolf crept back and with a turn of his head, gestured for the other wolves to follow him back to the hangar.

1-05 and the boys assumed they were to follow as well, and they started to join them. The lead wolf raised a paw indicating they were to stay.

"Why can't I help?" 1-05 pouted in frustration as she knelt and faced the wolf.

The wolf shook his head and struck the ground forcefully with his front paw. He then leaned forward and licked her face and looked her in the eye with concern.

"But what if you get hurt?" the tow-haired boy insisted. "We could help."

While its eyes were still focused on 1-05, the wolf tilted its head in concern and then left to join the other wolves. 1-05 hit the wall once with her fist. She turned to the boys. "It feels odd being ordered about by wolves, doesn't it?"

The dark-haired boy shrugged. "I guess they know better than us what to do."

"I hope so," 1-05 grumbled. She crossed her arms and lowered her chin, as she waited.

The wolves snuck into the hangar, keeping to the shadows to avoid being seen. The lead wolf looked toward the wolf to his right and lifted his head upward, indicating that the wolf was to circle around from the right. He then turned to the wolf to his left and lifted his head upward in the opposite direction. The wolf to the left circled around the workers from the left. Soon, before the workers knew what was happening, they were completely surrounded by wolves.

The workers, unprepared for having the hangar overrun by wolves, stepped back and exchanged questioning looks with one another. Before any of them could sound the alarm, though, the wolves reached into their pouches and pulled out small metal balls. They rolled these balls toward the workers.

The workers, impressed with the clever agility of the wolves, watched them, fascinated. They became even more fascinated with the balls that rolled toward them, wondering what they were. When the balls reached the workers, they blip-beeped a short melodious tune and clicked open. A purple smoky gas escaped from the balls and filled the room. The wolves were unaffected by the gas, but the workers coughed, choked, and fell unconscious to the ground.

The lead wolf stepped forward and tapped each of the workers with his paw to ensure they were unresponsive. When he was certain that the gas had done its job, he turned and headed toward the hangar's entrance. As he passed the entrance, he spotted a bag of gas masks and grabbed it up in his mouth. He raced back into the hall and dropped the bag in front of 1-05 and the boys.

"What is this?" the tow-haired boy asked.

1-05 opened the bag. "Gas masks."

The wolf lifted its muzzle from the gas masks to her face.

1-05 pulled them out and passed one to each of the boys. "Evidently they want us to put these on." She put the gas mask on, demonstrating the process to the boys and assisting them on with theirs. She turned to the lead wolf. "I saw what happened. You are not affected by that purple smoke, but it affects humans. That is why you didn't want us to join you." She scratched the wolf behind its ear and smiled. "You are brilliant."

The boys and 1-05 followed the wolf into the hangar to prepare the *Journey*.

Chapter Forty-Eight

The escape vehicle powered between the caverns, dodging pillars of stalactites and stalagmites, as Octelix transmitted the necessary directions to the vehicle's control system. Tears still streamed down 34,000's face and she coughed and gasped, unable to catch her breath. The loss of 2,040 weighed on her so much, she sunk from the seat of the escape vehicle to the floor. Octelix noted she was in danger and moved between her and the edge of the racing vehicle to prevent her from falling out.

81-4-60 stood from his seat to survey their surroundings. It was difficult to see in the darkness, but something in the distance puzzled him. He was about to suggest that Octelix guide the vehicle closer to that something for closer inspection, but, before he could, he felt Octelix's movement. He turned and saw 34,000 on the floor crying. "It will be all right," he told her. "We'll be out of danger soon."

34,000 choked back a sob. "It doesn't matter. He's gone and nothing matters."

Shaking his head, 81-4-60 moved next to her and lifted her back into her seat. "Well, no. Not really. I mean, technically he's not really gone. Not for good, anyway." He knew what he was saying was not going to help, but he was uncomfortable about leaving an untruth uncorrected.

34,000 shoved 81-4-60 away from her. "I don't want to hear it. Just go away."

81-4-60 frowned, raised his hands in surrender and moved back to the driver's seat to refocus his attention on the puzzle that had attracted his attention earlier, a spaceship hidden a short distance from them under a rock overhang. He normally would have assumed the ship belonged to the Dark Tyrant and taken off in the opposite direction. But upon adjusting the viewing screen for a closer look, he noticed on the side of the spaceship the same image that appeared on the message they received on the master computer, an image of a wolf.

Wiping her eyes, 34,000 finally noticed that 81-4-60 was driving closer to the spaceship. "What are you doing?" She grabbed his sleeve to ensure he heard her. "There could be Enforcers on that ship."

"I don't think so," was all 81-4-60 replied.

The Way-Guide and his crew were just heading back to the *Forerunner* for the shovels when they spotted the approaching escape vehicle. The Way-Guide pointed it out to the Dream-Saver. "Any idea what type of vehicle that is? What is doing so far from the city."

The Dream-Saver just shrugged but the Light-Defender listened carefully. "That vehicle does not sound like the type the Dark-Tyrant uses."

Before they could analyze the vehicle further it had pulled up next to them. The first one out was Octelix. 81-4-60 then clambered out and raced to the *Forerunner* and pointed at the wolf design. "Who's Infinity?" he demanded.

The Way-Guide and the Dream-Saver exchanged incredulous expressions. "What do you know about Infinity?" the Way-Guide asked.

81-4-60 pointed more emphatically to the image of the wolf. "That image is connected with Infinity, right?"

"Yes, but . . ." the Way-Guide was still unsure of 81-4-60's intentions and found his behavior erratic.

"Who is Infinity?" 81-4-60 demanded once more.

The Dream-Saver decided to take a risk. "He is the Prince of the Planet of Light."

81-4-60 tilted his head in thought and pulled once on his ear. "That explains it." He walked back to the escape vehicle and drummed his fingers on its door frame.

"Explains what?" the Way-Guide asked.

"I received a message from Infinity. He said that this planet was going to be destroyed, so, him being a prince explains how he would know that, right?" 81-4-60 was convinced he knew what he was talking about, until he got to the last few words, then he began to doubt his confidence and looked down a bit confused. He looked back at the spaceship and turned to the Way-Guide. "Are you using that spaceship to get out before the planet is destroyed?"

The Way-Guide ignored his question because his attention was focused on 81-4-60's escape vehicle. "Does this vehicle drill into the earth for energy?" he asked as he examined it.

"Why?"

"Could we use your vehicle?" the Way-Guide continued.

"Well, it's not exactly mine . . . but why?" 81-4-60 was beginning to feel a bit touchy about the escape vehicle. After all, it was the last thing he had to remind him of his friend, 2,040. "I will be needing it myself. The message mentioned going to the Shepherdess of the Valley, so I will need it to get there."

"We know where she is," the Dream-Saver told him. "We can get you there. Right now, we need the vehicle to break into the Dark Tyrant's master computer."

81-4-60's chin would have drop to the floor it could have. "The master computer? Again?"

"Again?" asked the Way-Guide.

"Never mind," with an abrupt wave of his hand, 81-4-60 brushed off the question. "Go ahead and use it. Why shouldn't we break into the master computer? We could do this all day."

34,000 forced herself out of the escape vehicle and moved close to 81-4-60. "Perhaps 2,040 would not want you to let them use it?"

81-4-60 shook his head firmly. "I think he would. Anything to unnerve those in control, right?"

His response gave 34,000 a sense of relief. *Yes,* she thought, *2,040's heart would be in this project.*

With 81-4-60's help, the Way-Guide moved the escape vehicle into the tunnel. After turning a dial and pulling a lever, the vehicle's drill was breaking through the tunnel wall. 81-4-60 thought he heard a rumble followed by the wail of some forlorn beast in the distance. He shifted in concern, and glanced over his shoulder. In the shadows down the tunnel behind a pile of rocks appeared two red flaming eyes, glaring at the group. 81-4-60 was about to alert his colleagues when the flaming eyes disappeared followed by a swift shuffling of the shadows and stirring of the rocks as the creature made a quick retreat.

In less than an hour the drill had broken through the floor of a room in the City of the Dark Tyrant. The Way-Guide and 81-4-60 climbed up through the floor.

"This isn't the room housing the master computer," 81-4-60 told him as hoisted himself into the room.

The Way-Guide looked around in frustration. "Does anyone know where we are?"

The Light-Defender felt the walls. "This room controls the electrical grid of the city. I did mention that the maps were often inaccurate. The Dark Tyrant does this on purpose to keep others from using the plans to his disadvantage."

Dark-Breaker withdrew a small black box from his jacket pocket and held it out to the others. "We can still hack into the computer."

"What do you mean?" the Way-Guide asked.

"If we are within sixty feet of the master computer, we still can hack it," Dark-Breaker told him.

The Way-Guide took the box and examined it. "Are you talking about radio waves?"

"Not just regular radio waves, bur silvastronic radio waves." Dark-Breaker moved up to the Way-Guide. "Most people don't know how to transmit and send silvastronic radio waves, but that is the type of radio waves the Dark Tyrant uses with his master computer. These radio waves deflect off of the silvasphere portion of the atmosphere of our planet. These waves are extremely short and most people find it difficult to pick them up."

The Way-Guide listened in amazement. "So, how did you learn to transmit and send these radio waves?"

"I read about them, of course." The boy took back his black box. "The master computer can read certain signals sent by silvastronic radio waves that are within the sixty foot radius. You just need the right type of transmitter to send the signals. I have it in this box."

"Are we within a sixty-foot radius of the master computer?" the Sword-Wielder asked.

"Yes," the Light-Defender told them. "If my memory serves me correctly, this room is only a few rooms down from the master computer."

The Way-Guide drew a chair next to a table and offered it to Dark-Breaker. The Way-Guide grabbed another chair nearby and sat next to the boy. He then unpacked pieces of a small computer from a hand-held bag. "All right. In just a few minutes we will start testing that little box of yours." He turned to the Dream-Saver. "And I certainly hope it works."

The Light-Defender heard a nearly silent sob and stepped back toward the feeling of sorrow. "Times are troubling, but know that there are those nearby who care."

34,000 wiped her tears, feeling uncomfortable that her grief was noticed by a stranger. "I am sorry," she apologized. "I just today lost someone very close. I mean, I believe he is gone. At least he is out of my reach."

The Light-Defender put a caring hand on her shoulder. "I know how you feel. Me and my sister were close as children. There were times she literally saved my life. I worked as an Enforcer then until an explosion near the lava pits took my eyesight. My sister was furious at the accident because she knew the City of the Dark Tyrant had no use for someone who could not see. The Shadow-Shield helped me get out of the city before it was too late, but I did not dare tell my sister where I was going. Recently something terrible has happened to her. I can sense it. It is as if she has fallen into some deep pit and is trapped within glass."

Chapter Forty-Nine

When 50-83 arrived at 1-13's workshop, he was surprised to find it open. He slipped inside and closed the door behind him. The room was dark, but, at the moment, the darkness provided him with the comforting feeling of being isolated from everyone and everything. He touched the crystal warming against his chest. He drew it from under his vest and examined it once more to confirm that 6-96 was truly trapped in the crystal. She glared back at him from within, confirming the incident was not just a persistent nightmare.

"Ah, 1-13's workshop . . . you think that he can help you out of this mess?" 6-96 asked in a condescending tone. "You think he can help you when he can barely help himself out of the disasters he keeps stumbling into."

50-83 examined the crystal on all sides, hoping to find some switch that could silence 6-96. He knew the crystal never had one, but hoped that with the series of strange things that had been happening with the crystal, one had miraculously appeared. When he found no way of silencing her, 50-83 sighed and checked to see if the crystal still possessed a little of its old self.

"Crystal," he called to it, "can you still answer questions?"

"Crystal, ha," 6-96 retorted. "There is no one in here but me."

50-83 moaned and put the crystal back under his shirt. He sat in an armchair to wait for 1-13. He shivered slightly, as he sensed several ghosts surrounding him.

After playing his recording in which 2-45 admitted he was in search of a way off the Planet of Darkness, 1-13 turned it off and pointed an accusing finger at 2-45. "So, you see," he announced to 1, "he wants to leave our planet. It is only natural to assume someone wanting to leave our planet is also organizing a rebellion with plans to transport the whole lot of them to the Planet of Light."

"I did not start this rebellion," 2-45 protested. "And what I said in that recording is not related to it either."

1 moved in between 1-13 and 2-45. "I am inclined to agree with 2-45." He pulled on his double chin in thought. "I know you have been jealous of the wealth of 2-45's family, but we already know the source of rebellion and it is right here in this room." He grabbed 4,021's wrist and dragged her to the center of the room. He lifted her arm high so everyone could see the rose in her hand. "This is the source of rebellion. Have you ever seen a rose like this on our planet? No. There is only one place it could come from. The Planet of Light."

"Yes," the Enforcers agreed as they shot their fists in the air. "The rose is the source of rebellion and must be destroyed."

366 edged up behind 4,021 and reached around her for the rose. "I'll destroy that rose," he told them. "Here. Give it to me."

As he reached for the rose, he gripped her wrist so tight that she winced in pain. When she refused to release it, he hit her hard against the side of her head causing her ear to ooze blood. Still, she refused to drop the rose.

2-45 broke free from the Enforcers and rushed forward to help 4,021. He sent his fist at 366's jaw. 1-13 directed two Enforcers to restrain 2-45. "Now is not the time to get involved," he told 2-45 as the Enforcers held 2-45 firmly on either side. "This situation does not concern you."

While 2-45's blow did unbalance 366 for a moment, he quickly regained his balance and once again had 4,021 in his grasp. "Do as I say," he demanded. "I am the only one here who can get you out of this." Furious at her unwillingness to obey, he wrapped his hand around her throat. "I suppose you think that the one who gave you that rose is going to rescue you . . . Well, there's no one here to help you now."

"Infinity will rescue me," 4,021 announced with conviction as she held out the rose. She did not hold it out to hand it over to 366, but as if it were a shield of defense. The closer the rose came to him the more the power within the rose forced him away from her.

"Put that thing away," 366 screamed and slunk back behind several Enforcers.

The Shadow-Shifter watched in fascination and slipped into the shadows, shifting to appear as part of the wall. "There is some magic at work here. Magic that is unusual but familiar," it thought to itself. "It is time to watch and learn."

Fighting the repelling force around the rose, 366 again reached for 4,021's wrist to force her to put away the rose. Before his hand could come close to hers, a billowing form emerged from the center of the rose's petals. Like a growing storm cloud, the image overshadowed the room until the form solidified into a large wolf. The wolf leapt from the rose and as his front paws touched the ground, he took 366's wrist in his teeth. With one firm yank of his head, the wolf hurled 366 against the metal wall in the corner of the room.

The Enforcers surrounded the wolf, with their guns aimed at his head. As they fired on the wolf, the force from their annihilation guns was so strong, their combined blast glowed a fiery, smoking orange. The blast, however, did not touch the wolf, but died right outside the rose's force field. 1-13 laid a hand on one of the Enforcer's shoulders. "Do not waste your weapon's energy on the wolf," he said with a solemn tilt of his head. "This magic is too strong for you to fight." The Enforcers lowered their weapons and turned to 1 for guidance.

1's jaw was closer to his feet than to his head, but when he saw that a command was needed, he regained a semblance of composure. He pointed an urgent yet impotent finger toward 4,021. "Don't let her get away."

The wolf placed his head under 4,021's hand and looked up at her with determined eyes. 4,021 heard the wolf's voice within her telling her that he would guide her from the city. "Lead on," she whispered as a contented smile formed on her lips.

1 grabbed 366's arm and pulled him to a standing position. 366 groaned as the movement intensified the throbbing pain in his bleeding wrist. 1 shot him a fierce glare. "You had better remedy this situation or the Dark Tyrant will have another soul in his lava lake."

366 averted his eyes from 1 and they fell on the Shadow-Shifter. The Shadow-Shifter only confirmed 1's threat with a solemn nod of the head. With resignation, 366 slipped out of the office to secure 4,021.

Outside the office, 366 came upon 1-13 who had his eyes fixed on 4,021 and the wolf who were walking over the orange tiles and exiting the manual labor room. 366 grabbed 1-13 by his sleeve and shook him. "How could this be happening? The tiles must be malfunctioning. Workers can't pass over the tiles without being killed."

1-13 removed 366's hand from his sleeve and brushed out the wrinkle his grip had left. "She is not a worker. She's a Slump-Bump." He then turned from 366 and hastened to 4,021, intent on preventing her from leaving. He grabbed her shoulder before she could step out of the manual labor room's door. "You can't leave. You'll never make it."

She turned back with a calm, unconcerned expression. "I'll be fine," she told him, but 1-13 did not release her.

He looked into her eyes, entering deep into her soul through her pupils. There was a deep magic he once learned that could enable him to convince someone to do whatever he wished, if only he could enter the soul. He took the first step into her soul. Now all he had to do was enter deeper and close the door behind him. He was almost there, but a strong force knocked him to the ground.

When 1-13 looked up to determine what it was, he saw the large wolf glaring down at him. He stood on 1-13's chest, pinning him to the ground to prevent him from moving. The wolf's eyes overpowered 1-13 as his glare penetrated deep into 1-13's soul. 1-13 was not certain of whether he had fainted or slept, but he was certain he heard the wolf speaking to him. *This message is for you, unassuming espionage agent. You want to learn the secrets to power, but you will only learn those secrets when you escape from the power within. That destructive power is hurtling this entire planet to its destruction. There is only one person who can teach you the secret to true power — Infinity. Go to the Shepherdess of the Valley and learn more from her.*

Once the wolf had relayed his message, he bared his teeth, snorted once, and turned away. He moved to 4,021, nudged her hand with his muzzle, and guided her out of the room.

113 breathed deeply and sat up stunned and amazed. He ran his hand across his face to ensure that he was awake. When he was convinced what had happened had really happened, he knew there was no sense in staying where he was. He slipped out of the labor room and headed for his workshop.

The workers noticed 4,021 and the wolf pass over the orange tiles and escape out of the room. They stopped their work and exchanged amazed expressions, whispering among themselves that they the tiles must be off. A few even murmured that the time was perfect to rebel.

When 1-13 failed to stop 4,021 from leaving, 366 determined to stop her himself. He raced toward the door, but was stopped by a strong grip on his upper arm. 2-45 spun him around and pinned him against a nearby metal cabinet.

"Stay out of this," 2-45 informed him with an insistent narrowing of his eyes. He let 366 drop to the floor then turned to follow after 4,021 out of the manual labor room

7,500 came up right after 2-45. He squatted next to 366 and patted him on the shoulder. "There are some moments in life that are rougher than others," he said with a casual lift of an eyebrow. Upon noticing the gaping wound on 366's wrist, he winced. "I'd tend to that if I were you. It looks nasty." He then lightly touched 366's cheek in a contrived moment of sympathy, pulled himself to his feet and exited the room with 2-45.

366 grumbled a curse and tried to stand but the pain was to much for him. He fell back to the floor and passed out.

1-13 slipped into his workshop, closing the door behind him. He leaned his back against the closed door, pulled his ventualine handkerchief from his pocket and wiped the sweat from his forehead and wrung his hands in thought. *Infinity. The wolf told me I should talk to Infinity.* He recalled that his prisoner, 93-73, had done research on Infinity. After taking a deep breath to regain his composure, he entered the prison hall. As he approached 93-73's cell, he gestured to one of the guards in the hall. "Open this cell," he ordered. "I must talk to the prisoner."

The guard's eyes widened in confusion. "But the prisoner is not there."

"What?" 1-13's head heated up in fury. He touched the cell door. It was not locked. When he flung the door open, he found no one inside. He turned back to the guard in rage. "Where is the prisoner? Why did you let him escape?"

The guard trembled in fear. "I did not let him escape. Your ghosts took him."

"My ghosts? What would they want with him?"

The guard forced himself to speak past the fear that obstructed his throat. "They said they wanted to kill him because he mentioned Infinity."

1-13 slammed the prison door shut and powered down the hall to his room determined to face down his skeleton-ghosts. When he stepped in, he was surprised to find 50-83.

50-83 stood to his feet and, upon noticing 1-13 was upset, shifted nervously. "I am sorry. I can leave if you're busy."

"No, you don't have to leave." 1-13 averted his attention from 50-83 to the corners of the ceiling. He knew his skeleton-ghosts were in the room, but they were hiding.

"I was wondering if you could help me with something." 50-83 noticed that 1-13 was obviously busy and uninterested in anything outside of whatever problem distracted him at the moment. Still, since he was here, 50-83 decided to at least present his problem to him. He forced his shaking hand to clasp the crystal.

1-13 had barely heard 50-83. It annoyed him that the skeleton-ghosts refused to show themselves. He knew they would remain hidden as long as 50-83 was present. To encourage 50-83 to leave as soon as possible, he feigned attention to 50-83's problem. "What is it you want me to help you with?"

50-83 stepped closer to 1-13 and pulled out the crystal from underneath his vest. "It was an accident. Her knife struck the crystal and she was sucked into it."

1-13 took the pendant to look at it more closely. His first thought was that 50-83 had contrived some bizarre practical joke. However, 1-13 knew 50-83. 50-83 was clever and imaginative, but he did not have the skills to put together something as complex as this. 1-13 could not help but smile a little at seeing 6-96 struggling to find a way out of the crystal. "This is strange." He handed the pendant back to 50-83.

"But what should I do?" 50-83 found it difficult to read 1-13's reaction to the crystal.

To 50-83's dismay, 1-13's only response was a shrug.

50-83 concluded that his only option was to be completely honest with 1-13. Normally he would not even consider honesty an option, but Infinity had made it clear that hiding the truth would not solve problems, and right now, what 50-83 wanted most was a solution. He took out the letter the wolf gave him. "Some huge creature gave me this letter. Perhaps you can figure out what it means?"

1-13's interest was piqued. He snatched the letter from 50-83. "You mean you have seen the magical wolf creatures from the ancient times?"

"Perhaps," 50-83 replied with a confused tilt of his head. "I have no idea what the wolf creatures look like."

Still clutching the letter, 1-13 weaved his way to his bookcase and pulled out a book on the early history of the Planet of Darkness. He tossed the book on a table.

The picture on the front cover was identical to the wolf that 50-83 had seen. "Yes, that was the creature," 50-83 agreed as he shifted his attention to 1-13 in amazement. "He gave me that letter. It says it's from a Shepherdess of the Valley."

"Yes," 1-13 nodded in thought. "And there seems to be some connection between the Shepherdess and Infinity."

"Infinity. He does exist, you know." He looked straight into 1-13's eyes. "I met him."

It irritated 1-13 that his lips tugged in an eager grin and he was unable to control it. He was not sure why this should happen, but he decided it was because he was excited to find proof that Infinity existed. If Infinity existed and he could meet him, perhaps he could learn more about the secrets of power. "You mean Infinity is here?"

50-83 groaned a bit, wondering how he could explain the situation. "No, not really. But he did talk to me."

"He sent you a message?"

50-83 let his head sink. He knew he could not form a believable explanation. "I guess."

A startling, raspy voice rattled above them. "Do not mention Infinity."

Upon hearing this voice, 1-13 clenched his fist and fumed. "Stop hiding."

The six skeleton-ghosts precipitated down to the center of the room. They formed a circle between 1-13 and 50-83. Each of their heads was lowered, but their eyes burned toward whichever human was closest to them.

"What have you done with my prisoner?" 1-13 demanded.

The skeleton-ghosts laughed a laugh that sounded like air escaping into a vacuum. "We wanted to kill him because he talked about Infinity."

50-83 gasped. "You killed 93-73?"

One of the skeleton-ghosts sneered at him. "No, he was taken by a very infuriating woman."

1-13 slid carefully to stand next to 50-83.

50-83 remembered when he assisted 1-13 in their search for the skeleton-ghosts. They were just as frightening then, but in their search, he had learned a few of their weaknesses. "There is only one way to stop them," he whispered to 1-13.

1-13'a response was a quick nod and a raise of the hand to indicate silence. He stepped casually away from the skeleton-ghosts and furtively snatched his silver wand from his desk. "Very well," he told the skeleton-ghosts with his back to them. "I can understand your reasoning completely. But," he turned abruptly to face them and as he did, he used his wand to set every light in the workshop to full brightness. The skeleton-ghosts moaned and creaked as they swooshed to the corners of the room where the only shadows could be found. 1-13 called after them, "You are the destructive power from within the planet that is leading our planet to its destruction and you are wrong to hold such animosity toward a man as powerful as Infinity." 1-13 knew the light would only keep them hidden for a short time. He reached over and took his snoozing spy-creature into his arms and pointed 50-83's attention to a bag next to the bookcase.

The short time he had worked for 1-13 enabled 50-83 to decode 1-13's gesture toward the bag. 50-83 grabbed the bag and followed 1-13 into the hall of the city.

Once in the hall, 50-83 turned to 1-13. "They might try to attack you when you return."

"I am not returning. At least not for some time," 1-13 told him as he led 50-83 down the halls of the city.

50-83 noticed the letter he had shown him still in 1-13's pocket. "Are you going to the Shepherdess of the Valley?" he asked 1-13.

"No," 1-13 told him flatly and turned to face 50-83. He held up the letter from the wolf. "I know all about these letters. I received one myself that warned of the destructive power within our planet. Yes, we will eventually search out the Shepherdess and Infinity, but first we must learn all we can about this power."

"But aren't the Shepherdess and Infinity the ones who would know the most about it?"

1-13 placed a determined hand on 50-83's shoulder. "They are powerful, but in a different way. We are going to my mentor, a sage named Thoravin. He is an expert on the destructive magic of the Planet of Darkness."

50-83 noticed a resolute light in 1-13's eyes that struck him with an inexplicable awe. Before he had found 1-13 devious and irritable, but now 1-13's words caused a wave of inspired trust to leap up within him. "Of course," 50-83 agreed. "We should go to him."

1-13 beamed as 50-83 followed him out of the city. "I believe Thoravin will even be able to tell us what to do about 6-96."

Chapter Fifty

hen the Shadow-Shield entered manual labor room 15, the room seethed with confused noises and chaotic movements. As the guards and Enforcers were trying to push the workers back to their stations the Shadow-Shield noted underpinning vibrations of a rebellion in the workers' hesitation to work. As he surveyed the room from entrance, the wolves held back in the shadows of the hall just outside. Alpha 3-0-3, still in the form of a stivel toad, hopped onto the Shadow-Shield's shoulder.

"Will we rescue all of them?" Alpha 3-0-3 asked with a gleam of hope in its eyes.

"Anyone who wants to come with us is welcome . . . but . . ." He rubbed the back of his neck as he noted that something was not right. His eyes fell on the orange floor tiles that bordered the room.

A worker broke free from an Enforcer and shouted to the other workers. "That girl with the creature . . . If she was able to cross the tiles we can too." He evaded two other Enforcers who tried to restrain him and raced for the tiles. As soon as his foot met the tile he was zapped into a pile of ashes.

546

The Shadow-Shield's eyes fell on Alpha 3-0-3 as he rubbed his neck in frustration. "The tiles are still functioning," he groaned, then slipped back into the hall and took from his pocket a communication device. He opened a link to the Way-Guide.

"Have you reached the master computer?" the Shadow-Shield asked as he reattached his gun to his belt. "The rescue cannot move forward until the tiles are disabled."

"I know," the Way-Guide's muffled response came through, "we tunneled through, but are in the wrong room. We have a plan for something that might work, but it will take time."

The Shadow-Shield's eyes flashed in irritation, but one look into the lead wolf's eyes calmed him down. "Alright, you have an hour." He slapped his hand against the wall to revert his frustration. "But once that hour is up, we are going in whether those tiles are down or not." He switched off the communication device before the Way-Guide could answer.

Alpha 3-0-3 shifted its weight in concern. "But what about the workers?"

The Shadow-Shield look down at Alpha 3-0-3 with narrow pensive eyes. "If the tiles aren't down . . ." He took the shape-shifter in his hands. ". . . we will just have to work out another plan, won't we."

The Way-Guide pocketed his communication device and moved to Dark-Breaker and 81-4-60 who were using Dark Breaker's black box to locate the radio waves emitted from the master computer. Octelix stood by eager to help.

"Is it working?" the Way-Guide asked 81-4-60.

"I think it will," 81-4-60 replied. "But it is a good thing we have Octelix with us. He is the only computer communicator we have. The main trouble I see is biding time. The Enforcers will know we are here before we have established a stable connection."

The Sword-Wielder unleashed two swords from his scabbards and the Light-Defender followed his lead, readying her sword. They marched to the door, but before leaving, they turned to the Way-Guide. The Sword-Wielder raised his head, resolutely. "We will hold the Enforcers off," he told the Way-Guide past a troubled breaking of his voice. "We can at least hold them back long enough for you to disable the tiles."

The Way-Guide shook his head. "No, you will not last long against them. There will be too many." He pulled out a gun from a holster under his coat. "Perhaps if I join you . . ." He turned to 81-4-60 ready to tell him to ensure the mission was completed, but he noticed 34,000 dropping a shaking yet determined hand on 81-4-60's shoulder. She stared straight ahead at the door in thought.

81-4-60 looked up at her. "Is something wrong?"

"Don't go," 34,000 told the Light-Defender and Sword-Wielder.

"We must," the Light-Defender said with a gentle smile meant to reassure her.

34,000 suppressed the nervous tremblings inside herself, transforming her entire being into one that was steadfast and unmoving. "There is no reason for you to go." She stepped forward. "I will go . . . and 81-4-60, you will come with me."

81-4-60 frowned, his eyes wide and clueless. "Should I bring Octelix?"

She shook her head. "The rest of you, hide as far back in the shadows as possible."

As 34,000 and 81-4-60 exited the room, 81-4-60 took her by the upper arm. "You do have a plan, right?"

34,000 waved off his question and directed his attention to five Enforcers marching toward them.

The tallest Enforcer stepped to 34,000. "We have detected several life forms in this room, yet no one is scheduled to be using it."

34,000 reached into a pocket in her jacket and pulled out a pass. She held it out to the Enforcer. "I am sorry that I forgot to schedule the room, but I do have a pass."

The Enforcer took it and ran it through a hand-held verifier. When he found the pass valid, he handed it back to 34,000.

"After everything that happened today, I wasn't thinking clearly," 34,000 continued. "But, I was wanting to carry on the experiments 2,040 was working on. There were some of them that were brilliant and would be so benefit our city. 81-4-60 here was assisting me in testing them."

The Enforcer held up a hand for silence. "But why do the sensors indicate that there are more life forms inside." He moved to the door. "We should look inside."

"No need," 81-4-60 told the Enforcer. "Your sensor doesn't indicate life forms inside."

"Of course it does," the Enforcer held out the sensor to show 81-4-60 the display screen indicating in red the four life form in the room. "See."

81-4-60 took the sensor and looked at it closely. "What this sensor is actually indicating is a serious need to be calibrated." He took the sensor from the Enforcer and a fond I-remember-you-old-friend smile spread itself on 81-4-60's face as he looked down at it. He had worked with this same type of sensor so many times that he knew it inside and out. A double on and off of one switch and a rough tap on the left side and it ceased working. Afterwards, he let his left hand fall to his side as he snapped his fingers twice.

Octelix heard the signal and rose to its feet. It honed in on 81-4-60's brain waves and knew what it needed to do. It focused its attention on the sensor to inform it that there were *no* life forms in the room.

When the sensor displayed the *corrected* number of life forms as zero, 81-4-60 handed it back to the Enforcer. "See," he told the Enforcer, "after the calibration it reads no one else is inside."

The Enforcer scratched his head confused and put away the sensor. "Ok," he conceded. "Finish what you are doing and leave the room. Next time be sure to schedule the room."

The Enforcer turned to leave but was not completely convinced. 81-4-60 left the door open a crack and watched the Enforcer go straight up to another Enforcer and start a serious discussion in which they gestured toward the room more than once.

81-4-60 closed the door and on his way back to the table, he passed the Sword-Wielder and Light-Defender. "Stay positioned there." He gestured their attention back to the door with his thumb. "If those Enforcers return, stop them." When he sat at the table, Octelix hopped up and looked at him steadily. "What is it, Octelix?"

Octelix hopped over to the Dark-Breaker's black box and shoved it toward 81-4-60.

81-4-60 nodded to Octelix and looked up at the Way-Guide. "Octelix says they can't get through the master computer's programming."

The Way-Guide threw his hands in the air. "All we can do is keep trying."

The Light-Defender stepped to the table and laid a hand on the black box. "Most people run into challenges because they complicate things. We need to simplify the situation."

"How can we do that?" the Dream-Saver asked.

"To break the problem to its simplest element is to break it down to humanity," she told him. "What are the most important things to humans? Ego and impatience. Who is in charge of reprogramming the master computer? 1. If he is reprogramming it what would he be thinking of? 1. He is wanting to reprogram it quickly so he will have no time to be inventive. I would recommend that you add 1 to each of the passwords to gain access."

81-4-60 dropped his head to the table to look Octelix in the 'eyes'. "Did you hear that? Go ahead and try it."

Octelix nodded and ran over to the black box and relayed the message. The edges of the black box glowed green indicating the program was working.

The Sword-Wielder gestured for the Light-Defender to join him at the door. "The Enforcers are returning," he told her.

The Light-Defender stood in front of the Sword-Wielder and held a hand outstretched toward the hall in front of her, to feel the vibrations in the air. "Yes, but we can stop them temporarily." She pointed the Sword-Wielder's attention to the rafters overarching the hall.

"Understood," the Sword-Wielder agreed. He readied a sword in each hand and the Light-Defender aimed her crossbow at the hall's ceiling. "Now," shouted the Sword-Wielder. He swung his swords upward and they flew up and spun one on each side of the rafters, sawing away at the loose fittings. The Light-Defender sent six arrows to complete the weakening of the rafters so that they dropped creating a barricade which blocked the path of the Enforcers.

"Good job," the Way-Guide told them. "That will hold them for a few minutes, but we must hurry." He moved over to Dark-Breaker and 81-4-60. "How's the programming coming?"

"Not bad." 81-4-60 scratched his beard. "We've established communication with the computer, but we're in a bit of a disagreement."

"Yes." Dark-Breaker frowned as he kept his eyes on the edge of the table. "81-4-60 wants to reprogram it to turn off the tiles, but I don't think we should."

81-4-60 groaned and waved his hands outward. "I mean, well . . . Isn't that the objective?"

"Of course." Dark-Breaker tapped the black box as his mouth stretched down in disbelief. "But if we turn them off it will be obvious that they had been tampered with."

"That's right," the Way-Guide sighed. "We have to keep it running so that the reprogramming is not detected."

"In other words," 81-4-60 joined in, grasping the challenge that needed to be overcome. "We have to program the tiles to target something."

The Sword-Wielder heard the thumping and clanging of the Enforcers outside. "We could target the Enforcers," he suggested.

"Good idea," 81-4-60 agreed, turning to Octelix to have him relay the message.

The Light-Defender laid a hand on his shoulder to stop him. "There are too many Enforcers in that area and they would catch on that something is wrong too quickly. Target the Overseers."

Like the jarred lurching of a boat predicts an oncoming storm at sea, the clattering of equipment and tense whispers among the workers left no doubt that a rebellion was fomenting within manual labor room 15. A weaving of workers consistently slipped up to 17-07's station where he surreptitiously handed each one an exterminating gun. "Watch the Enforcers," 17-07 whispered to the worker receiving the gun. "When they change shifts. That's when we force them to switch off the tiles and then we break out."

The Shadow-Shield marched into the midst of the confusion in the manual labor room, jerked out his communicator and switched it on. "Way-Guide," he spoke into the communicator with a determined seriousness, hoping the hubbub would not drown out the relay. "Tell me the tiles are off."

"They have . . . been reprogrammed to target . . . the Overseers," the Way-Guide's voice came over the communicator in the midst of crackling, clambering, and thuds. "We'll have to cut off communication . . . We need to get out of here before the Enforcers break through." The Shadow-Shield heard a few more seconds of clattering and banging then a round of gunfire. The communicator went silent.

The Shadow-Shield held Alpha 3-0-3 up to face him. "They claim the tiles are reprogrammed. You have to test them for me. Before the workers storm the tiles. Shape-shift into a worker and cross the tile."

Alpha 3-0-3 cocked its head. "If it hasn't been fixed will it target a shape-shifter? Does it work that way?"

"Yes," the Shadow-Shield told him. "When you shape-shift into anything you take on its identity. Go, now. I will try to keep the workers away from the tiles until we know they have been fixed."

Alpha 3-0-3 let its image of the stivel toad fade and the sparkles reformed into a bulky dark-haired worker. While the Shadow-Shield kept the workers who were nearest away from the tiles, Alpha 3-0-3 thrust itself forward past a frenzied slew of rebelling workers and raced over the tiles.

Upon seeing Alpha 3-0-3 make it safely past the tiles, the rest of the workers shouted eagerly that the tiles were off. They pushed and shoved their way forward anxious to cross the tiles and exit the manual labor room. Enforcers hurried into position and surrounded the perimeter. They hurled workers back inside and kicked and dragged them back to their stations. Still, several workers managed to dodge the Enforcers and slip out of the manual labor room.

366 came to, his jaw still pulsing with pain. With effort, he pushed himself to his feet. He expected the manual labor room to be in chaos, but the chaos he woke up to far exceeded his expectations. He could not tell whether the frenzied scenes around him or the pain and loss of blood had caused his wobbly unsteadiness.

The Shadow-Shifter lunged up at him. He pulled 366 forward and gripped him by the back of his head, physically turning his head to see the workers escaping. "It looks like you failed in preventing the rebellion." He then shoved 366 aside and turned from him.

"I'll put a stop to this," 366 grunted as he gestured for a group of Enforcers to join him in regaining control. He pulled a nearby lever, setting off a deafening continuous alarm that blared out like a dying gorslancher. He climbed on the stage and stood in front of the screens which displayed the ongoing demise of 2,040. "Workers," he shouted. "Get back to work. If you try to escape you are only ensuring your own death. Even though the tiles are not working at the moment, those who escape will be tracked down and killed. Get back to work now."

366 leapt from the stage and joined the Enforcers in pushing workers back to their stations. His eyes fell on three workers exiting the manual labor room. "Stop those workers," he screamed, waving his arms in the directions of the workers as if his movement would send a swarm of Enforcers to block their path. Enforcers were racing toward the workers, but not fast enough for 366. He snorted with impatience and grabbed a whip from the wall and snapped it near his leg in preparation. He then stormed toward the escaping workers. His eyes were so fixed on the workers, he did not even notice the moment his foot fell on the tile. The next moment a pile of ashes rained onto the orange tile and the whip clumped to the ground right next to it.

During the chaos, 17-07 had slipped under his workstation table to watch for the perfect moment to join the rebellion. When he saw 366 disintegrated by the tiles, his mouth and eyes widened in amazement. "This is so a sign," he breathed. He jumped out from under the table with the clattering of tools and brandished his exterminator gun. "Workers. It is time." He raised his gun high over his head, pulsing it up and down to generate excitement. "We are not helpless. These guns will speak for you and the Enforcers will have to listen." He threw the suitcases open and tossed guns to the workers who pushed their way towards him. "Take your weapons and claim your freedom." He tossed some more guns to nearby workers, knocked over tables, and smashed equipment.

After pulling an Enforcer off a staggering worker and throwing the Enforcer against the wall, the Shadow-Shield moved to Alpha 3-0-3. "Go out in the hall with the wolves. Direct any workers there to join the wolves in heading for the Journey. I will help the workers here. Tell the lead wolf to wait for me."

Alpha 3-0-3 kicked and punched out a nearby Enforcer. "All right," it agreed and slipped out into the hall to carry out its orders.

The Enforcers guarding the perimeter shot at the workers, but the workers shot back. A group of workers took up long thin sheets of ezocane and used them as battlesticks and swords to fight the Enforcers, knocking the Enforcers' guns away and cutting through their armor. Other workers fixed up ropes, connecting them to pulleys. They dropped the ropes down on the Enforcers to lasso them and pull them from the catwalks. The Enforcers were then sent down into the smoking and boiling ezocane, with horrifying shrieks.

17-07 grinned in ecstasy as he watched the rebellion unfold. In one leap, he flew onto the stage and raised both hands in the air as if giving the workers his blessing. The Enforcers' bullets flew close on either side of him but missed him. "Fight on. It is happening. We are on the verge of something so profound. It is a reawakening of the dignity of personhood. We will now be rich in everything: Freedom, Justice, and Money. Look." He held up the rose petals and gestured at them wildly. "You saw it. 4,021 had the rose and was given the power to walk over the tiles and survive. Our overseer tried it and he was obliterated. We have the victory." He swayed back and forth on the stage, singing and shouting at the top of his lungs that their rebellion would succeed.

A young blond worker broke into 366's office and managed to readjust the controls for the video images on the screens behind the stage. They now flashed on and off in a hectic display of varying angles of the rebellion taking place, workers fighting with Enforcers, workers smashing the machines, Enforcers shooting workers, and 17-07 singing on stage.

A shadow grew behind the worker controlling the video images and brought its fist down hard on the back of his head. The Shadow-Shifter reformed itself from the shadows and stepped back as the worker fell to the floor.

1 waddled up behind the Shadow-Shifter and pulled on his own ear. "This rebellion has gotten out of hand," he moaned. "They have failed to destroy that rose and now the Enforcers can't even control the workers. You have to bring back some order."

The Shadow-Shifter's eyes were fixed on the video images. "Something is wrong," it murmured as it searched the images for the disturbing factor. "There." It pointed out the Shadow-Shield. "He holds strange magic and talks of the Planet of Light. I think he's at the bottom of it all."

1 pulled his mouth to the side and ran his finger down his own nose in thought. "Perhaps you are right." He stroked his Shadow-Shifter once down its back and nodded. "Go and confront him."

The Shadow-Shifter slipped out of the office and kept to the shadows along the edge of the manual labor room. It came to the exit and peeked out, noticing several wolves waiting in the hallway. This gave it an idea, and it let the shadows engulf its image and transformed itself into a wolf. It swung itself around and crept up to a group of workers. "If you want to be free follow me," it told them with a sly gleam in its unbalanced eyes.

The workers connected the wolf with the one that guided 4,021 out of the manual labor room. They followed the wolf as it led them to 366's office. Several Enforcers were waiting in the office and when the workers entered, they surrounded the workers and tossed them into a burning furnace in the back of the room. The workers' screams quickly faded.

The wolf returned to the manual labor room in search of more workers when the Shadow-Shield noticed the strange darkness surrounding the wolf and pushed his way past the Enforcers and up to it.

The Shadow-Shifter wolf found another group of workers and slunk up to them. "If you want to be free, follow me."

"Don't follow that wolf," the Shadow-Shield moved in between it and the workers. "He'll send you to your death."

"What makes you say that," the Shadow-Shifter snarled as it let the shadows transform its image back to its original form.

"Because you work for the Dark Tyrant," the Shadow-Shield told him firmly. "And all who work for the Dark Tyrant are swallowed up by the fire of death within this planet." The Shadow-Shield turned from him but the Shadow-Shifter set a firm hand on his shoulder to stop him. The Shadow-Shield looked down at the hand and saw how it faded in the shadows. "You are Grubian . . ." He noted a burning under the shadows. "But not completely," the Shadow-Shield said mostly to himself.

"I am a Shadow-Shifter." It spun the Shadow-Shield around and pinned him to the wall with its forearm. "But you . . . there is something strange and familiar about you." The Shadow-Shifter breathed in thought. It could not place the familiar moments in his mind. It was a either a faint feeling or a swirl of magic in his memory. "Are you from the Planet of Light?"

The Shadow-Shield jerked his knee up and jabbed it into the Shadow-Shifter's ribs. He swung himself off the wall and pushed the Shadow-Shifter off of him with his forearm.

The Shadow-Shifter slipped into the shadows to disappear, but the Shadow-Shield knew this Grubian trick. His eyes penetrated the darkness and could clearly make out its form. He joined the Shadow-Shifter in the darkness and also disappeared. The Shadow-Shield knocked the Shadow-Shifter to the ground and dropped a foot onto its chest to hold it there. He looked into the Shadow-Shifter's eyes and saw something there he did not expect. "Who are you?" the Shadow-Shield asked.

"I told you. I am a Shadow-Shifter and I work for 1." It struggled to free itself from the ground, but the Shadow-Shield's foot was firm.

"Yes," the Shadow-Shield agreed. "But deep inside you have a soul. The soul was changed by the Grubian Ghouls. I can sense this. My mother moved to the planet Grubia. She met my father, a Grubian Ghoul, there. I never knew either of them well, but I know this: It is not who or what you are that determines what you become. I am not your enemy. Someone else started this rebellion even before we came here. He is the one you are after." The Shadow-Shield released the Shadow-Shifter and raced off for the manual labor room exit.

The rebellion had slowed. Some of the workers made it to the exit while several held up hands in surrender. When 17-07 noticed the workers surrendering, he stopped singing. "Hey, don't surrender. I mean, this rebellion has just started. We won't stop until they treat us like kings." At that moment, several Enforcers aimed their guns at 17-07 and fire on him. He jerked with the blows and fell to his knees. "We will be free," he mumbled through a sputter of blood as he fell face forward on the stage.

While the attention was on the stage, 85-27 adjusted the settings on the boilers so that the pressure inside increased to a point beyond its capacity. The boilers heaved in and out spasmodically until they erupted into a tremendous explosion, spewing out steaming hot ezocane and metal. The distraction enabled a number of workers to escape out into the halls.

85-27 searched through the rubble until he came upon 38-95 buried in the debris. He helped him to his feet. "Can you walk?" he asked 38-95.

"I think so." 38-95 became steadier on his feet.

"Let's get out of here," 85-27 told him. "I heard there was a safe house to the north. We can try and make it there."

"Agreed. Let's go." Avoiding the hail of debris, they weaved their way past the dazed Enforcers, and finally found their way out of the manual labor room.

Reinforcements joined the Enforcers in the room, who were now starting to recover sufficiently to focus once more on their objective. The Dark Tyrant wiggled and wobbled in behind the reinforcements, in the form of gelatinous seaweed. The Enforcers surrounded the remaining workers, and the Dark Tyrant waved a green tentacle in approval.

Upon noticing the Dark Tyrant, 1 marched out of 366's office and strode up to the gelatinous seaweed. "As you see we are successful. The rebellion has been quelled and we have captured or killed most of the instigators."

The seaweed tremored, splattering seawater everywhere. "But many of them have escaped," the Dark Tyrant pointed out. "Plus 366 has been killed. You and your Shadow-Shifter have failed me in this event. I am assigning you a new associate. Perhaps together, you and he will not fail me next time. Follow his lead and do as he says. It will take some time to get the manual labor rooms back to full capacity. But his skills as an economics specialist will come in handy." The Dark Tyrant gestured for the new assistant to enter.

9-85 walked in and up to 1. "So, you and I will be working together." He held out his hand to 1. 1 hesitated. With a low frown, he stepped back. However, after shifting in thought, he brought himself to accept the outstretched hand.

"Like I always say," 9-85 told 1 as he gave his hand a firm shake. He took a step forward and pivoted to assess the extent of damage the manual labor room endured. "We need to consider all variables. The reason we were not completely prepared for this rebellion was because several variables escaped us. When I was calculating the degree of threat from each particular variable, the one that kept coming up as the most dangerous to our planet was a certain Shepherdess of the Valley. That's where we should focus our attention first."

Out from behind a muddle of shadows and debris wriggled a spy-creature. Upon noticing the creature, 9-85 moved to it and, ignoring its squeak of surprise, he scooped it up for all to observe. "Where did this spy-creature come from?"

"1-13 has creatures like that," 1 stammered. "We noticed him here, but he left before the rebellion broke out. That is not the one that came in with him."

"This creature could tell us who is behind the rebellion." 9-85 yanked a table back to its feet and dropped the creature on top of it. "It must have observed quite a bit." He pulled a dangling wire attached to one of the viewing screens and jabbed the other end into the back of the spy-creature.

Upon recognizing the connection, the viewing screen displayed the images the spy-creature had observed over the last 24 hours. 9-85 pulled open a panel in the creature's back and adjusted a knob so the video played through at a quicker pace. Eventually, the creature's visual displayed 50-83 in 6-96's workshop. 6-96 entered and 50-83 destroyed her with his crystal.

1 gasped and waved a finger at the viewing screen. He snorted and mumbled, unable to speak.

"Yes," 9-85 said, as if he had no trouble translating 1's indecipherable babbling. "50-83 does have a connection to 2,040. He must have a link to this rebellion. Our first step, then, is to find 50-83."

Chapter Fifty-One

The Guardian stood from his throne and followed the black and red tambrelian rug from his throne to the viewing screens monitored by his men. His eyes turned a fiery red as he jabbed a finger toward the *Ghost III* just visible through the viewing screen. "Infinity must not escape us. The only way to stop him is demolishing his ship. I want the *Ghost III* blasted out of existence." The Guardian's weapon specialist was sauntering to his station when the Guardian grabbed him by the upper arm and pushed him down to the controls. "Quark blasters should do the trick. Start charging them now." The Guardian's eyes fixed on the weapon specialist, and he pointed a warning finger at him. "If that ship gets away, I'll hold you responsible."

The weapon specialist switched a lever and carefully watched the countdown, prepared to fire on the *Ghost III* the second the quark blasters were equipped.

On board the *Ghost III*, Infinity sensed the tension building within the Guardian's space station. He guided the *Ghost III* in closer, slipping to the side, a blind spot for the Guardian's viewing screens. When the *Ghost III* was alongside the docking port, he used the information provided by Operation

Covert Spies to enable the *Ghost III* to connect to the docking port.

"*Ghost III*," Infinity addressed his ship, "meld with the space station."

The *Ghost III* connected itself with the docking port and the ship and the space station melded into one making it impossible to determine where the *Ghost III* ended and the space station began. The *Ghost III* appeared only as an extension of the space station.

The Guardian's weapon specialist looked out of the viewing screen, prepared to fire, but could not find the *Ghost III*. "Locate the enemy ship," he told the radar expert.

"The ship no longer appears on the radar."

"The ship must be there. It cannot just vanish." The Guardian scowled at the radar expert. But then a smile spread itself on his face. "Or perhaps it can." He pivoted around with a thoughtful look and made his way back to his throne. He settled into it with self-satisfaction. "I have heard that Infinity's ship can be rather unusual. He must have rethought my threats. His ship is fast, so he must have raced back to the Planet of Light where we won't have to deal with him again."

Infinity ensured his armor was secure and climbed down from the *Ghost III's* control room to the port leading into the space station. The *Ghost III* unscrewed the hatch and pushed it open. Infinity leaned in on the shadowed walls of the entrance, staying hidden as he scanned the port. He noted four guards and calculated their projected movements. By keeping his own path to the left, he skulked through the shadows toward the port and out of sight of the guards.

Infinity and the *Ghost III* maintained a connection and Infinity could still speak with it even though he was inside the Guardian's space station. "*Ghost III*, where is the main power generator for the web?" Infinity asked.

"*You will find it easily,*" the *Ghost III* responded. "*The plans we acquired from Operation Covert Spies are familiar since they are identical to the space station designs created on the Planet of Light."*

"Stolen plans. I am not surprised," Infinity nodded as he slipped around a corner, undetected. "While that may have been easier for them when building the space station, it gives us the advantage now."

On the adjacent hallway, Infinity located a ladder built into the wall. He ascended the ladder and lifted an access door in the ceiling to climb through the scuttle hole. He quietly crept through the crawlspace designed to allow just enough room for mechanics to enter and complete repairs. He came to a T-intersection where one part of the crawlspace led up and another led down. Infinity climbed the ladder leading up and found the circuit board controlling the web. He took from a pocket in the left arm of his jacket a ball of blue energy small enough to fit in his hand. The ball had four small legs which Infinity attached to four of the circuits on the board. Afterwards, Infinity slid down the ladder and pressed a red button on his wrist. The ball of energy exploded taking the circuit board with it.

"Tell me, *Ghost III*, is the web down?" Infinity asked as he returned to the access door.

"Yes, the web is down."

"Prepare for us to leave." Infinity slipped out of the scuttle hole. "I will be there soon." He marched with firm determination through the hall toward the Guardian's throne room. "I just have one more thing to take care of."

One of the Guardian's men gasped as they noticed the readings on their control board. "Your majesty, the web is malfunctioning."

"Malfunctioning? That's impossible. We ran a diagnostic check on it yesterday." The Guardian moved to the viewing screen and looked out. His mouth dropped open in astonishment when he saw no electric web in his view of space. "Who turned off my web?"

One of his men gulped before responding. "Your majesty, it just turned off on its own."

"Webs don't turn off on their own." The Guardian punctuated his sentence by kicking the man's shin. "Get it back on immediately or I will let you explain everything to my pet."

Infinity found his way to the Guardian's throne room. He held his back as close to the wall as possible as he surveyed the activity within. He sensed a strong malicious presence from a room nearby.

Keeping his voice down, Infinity contacted the *Ghost III*. "I have located the Cloud of Deception. It is in the security room behind a locked steel door. Open the door."

"The door will be unlocked within the next few seconds."

Infinity heard the sound of metal sliding against metal as the cylinders and pins within the locked door settled into an unlocked state. The door opened and the Cloud of Deception billowed out as lightning branched within itself from one side to the other. As soon as it saw Infinity, it raised itself up and jolted back. It convulsed, its eyes and mouth widening as a scream of static filled the room.

The Guardian turned on his heels and faced Infinity. "So, you haven't left." He shook his head, annoyed that he had one more problem to deal with. He then noticed his "pet". "So, you accidently released my pet." The Guardian laughed in amusement. "That saves me the trouble. Come here, my pet."

Infinity looked back at the Guardian over his shoulder. "It wasn't an accident."

Infinity pulled out a metal cylindrical container from his jacket. He opened it with a whoosh as the vacuum sucked the cloud into the container. As it was pulled in, the cloud tried to grasp for the pillars and walls, but the pull was too strong and with one last hiss and spark the cloud was locked inside. Infinity closed the container, capturing the Cloud of Deception.

Infinity approached the Guardian. "I have not released it. I have contained it."

"Release it or . . ." The Guardian lifted his hand and directed the attention of his guards toward Infinity. ". . . my guards will destroy you." He unholstered an annihilator gun and aimed it at Infinity. The Guardian's guards did the same.

Infinity held out the canister as if about to release the cloud. Instead, he pressed a button on his glove which filled the room with a blinding red light. The Guardian and his guards fell back stunned.

Infinity lifted the container that held the Cloud of Deception. "You have been deceived by the Cloud of Deception. It promises you power but it will leave you weak and helpless. The cloud is helpless on its own. If you don't believe me, I am willing to release it and let you call on the cloud now."

The Guardian squinted past the darkness in his own eyes at Infinity. "Release it."

Infinity unlocked the container and the cloud cautiously slipped out and up to the Guardian. It enveloped him and increased the Guardian's size and strength. The cloud then hesitated as it turned and noticed Infinity.

Infinity pulled out of a pouch on his belt a large red vial and opened it. Out of the vial burgeoned a red, nebulous gas. The gas filled the room upward, downward, and to the left and right. When the Cloud of Deception saw the red gas racing at it, the cloud shrank back in fear, shrinking so small, it eventually disappeared.

When the Guardian realized his pet was gone, he dropped to his knees and pounded the floor with his fists. "You destroyed my pet. You will pay for this."

"Your 'pet' was destroying you," Infinity told him. "It convinced you into thinking it gave you strength and courage, but it was really using you to help it appear strong and brave. And as it did it was draining you of your strength and courage."

The Guardian hit the ground one last time and stood to his feet. "I suppose I should thank you for that." He grimaced and shook his head. "But I can't. I still must destroy you because the Dark Tyrant has ordered me to. I must keep you from getting to the Planet of Darkness and corrupting the planet." He held a hand up, ready to order his men to fire on Infinity.

"The Dark Tyrant told you I would be corrupting the Planet of Darkness?" Infinity took another step to the Guardian. "Evil sees evil everywhere and the corrupt consistently see corruption. I have been called evil because I help others, even when they attack me. I have been called corrupt because I refuse to take advantage of the helpless. I am not going to the Planet of Darkness to corrupt it but to save it."

The Guardian lowered his head and nodded. "Perhaps. But it really doesn't matter what your plans are. I have to stop you or the Dark Tyrant will destroy me."

"He won't destroy you," Infinity told him as he turned to leave. "The Dark Tyrant will be destroyed before he can destroy you."

"You are going to kill him?" the Guardian asked in disbelief.

Infinity shook his head. "He is already on a path heading toward destruction. It is only a matter of time . . ."

The Guardian sighed and looked down to avoid facing Infinity. "So, you are causing the destruction of both the Dark Tyrant and me. You are leaving me here helpless."

Infinity stood in the shadows and faced the Guardian one last time. "In reality I am giving you a second chance." He slipped out of the space station and into the *Ghost III*. *The Ghost III* detached itself from the space station and set a course for the Planet of Darkness.

When Infinity was in his ship, one of the Guardian's men turned to the Guardian. "Your majesty, should we fire on his ship?"

The Guardian sat on his throne and rubbed his chin. "No, let Infinity pass."

"But what about the Dark Tyrant's orders?" the Guardian's weapon specialist asked.

"Perhaps we should prepare for the Dark Tyrant's retribution," the Guardian agreed as he scratched the back of his neck. "But, then again, we may not have to worry about the Dark Tyrant at all, after Infinity has dealt with him."

Chapter Fifty-Two

Life struggled to exist in most areas of the Planet of Darkness; however, there was one place where human, animal, and plant life flourished. The Valley of the Shepherdess was enclosed by towering conical grey-green rocky cliffs that formed a barricade of protection. At one end of the cliffs, a refreshing aquamarine waterfall cascaded into a stream which flowed into a stone fortress watering the valley and cooling the boiling heat emanating from within the planet. Overhanging the waterfall were elegant boughs of flowering trees that dropped white and blue blossoms into the stream below. The valley was also populated by the massive Bercolan trees which clung to the walls of the rocky cliffs throughout the region. The limbs of these trees branched out to such an extent that a whole family of topan deer could shelter beneath them. The leaves were pale green and each was composed of three interlocking oval lobes. Its bark was smooth and emitted a luminescent glow that lit the entire valley.

The Shepherdess rowed a light green boat from a tunnel hidden by the waterfall. As she passed through the waterfall, it lightly sprinkled her long black hair with a refreshing shower.

She filled her lungs with the clean air that swept through the plant life surrounding her. The flat-bottom boat she stood in was built from the leaves of the Bercolan trees which when layered with ezocane dust were resilient and watertight. The Shepherdess' black hair was held back with a muslin yellow scarf. Her bandeau dress was yellow with vertical leaf-like strips of green and came down to just above her knee. Her skin was a soft bronze and her eyes were a sparkling blue. Tiny glowing birds flit about the stream lighting up her path. Small mammals scampered about ducking in and out of the foliage that covered the valley. The Shepherdess stood toward the rear of her boat and used long oars to glide it along the edge of the stream. A group of villagers raced to the stream to greet her.

"Is the crop improving?" a grey-haired female villager called to her.

"Yes," the Shepherdess replied as she passed a basket of berries to each of the villagers. "The temperature for the underground farm has been ideal. The waterfall has been providing the right balance of moisture. There will be a bountiful harvest this year." She guided the boat to a nearby wooden dock and was helped out of it by a short young man with reddish-brown hair that framed his face like a mane. "You're here early, Harmony-Keeper." She secured the boat to the dock. "Is something wrong?"

The Harmony-Keeper adjusted the collar of his woolen jacket. "It's Infinity," he explained. "A message is coming in from him."

"We do need some good news." The Shepherdess handed him the oar and passed him to join a flock of sheep who were being guarded by a pack of wolves. One of the sheep nudged the Shepherdess, slipping his head under her hand to be petted. As the Shepherdess stroked the sheep a wolf licked his ear to ensure they were clean. Another wolf directed the Shepherdess' attention to several thorns in the lamb's coat. The Shepherdess dropped to her knees to remove them.

"Dear, Amber, you so often are watching out for others. I know it is heartbreaking that you have recently lost some of your brothers in the fight. They were brave and the mission was so important. They are heroes. Yes, one day this planet will be destroyed, but we will preserve the beautiful parts of it. Like this valley. It will live on, because of the sacrifices you and your family have made."

Amber moved closer to the Shepherdess and snuggled closer to her side. She lowered her eyes and whimpered then looked into the Shepherdess' eyes in search of hope.

"It is hard to have faith when members of your family are responsible for leading a group from the city to this valley. They may need more help." The Shepherdess stood and gestured for a group of wolves near the stream to come forward. "Three of you need to go through the caves and find the wolves that were sent to bring the hopeful one here. Back them up as they complete their task."

A large grey wolf nodded with a snort. He turned to the group and dropped his paw on the shoulder of a wolf who stood near him. Another dark wolf moved forward, eager to join them. The grey wolf growled his approval and gestured for them to join him. They raced off and disappeared into a cave in the rocky cliff.

Amber looked up at the Shepherdess with a glow of hope in her eyes. The Shepherdess stroked her in encouragement and moved on toward the stone fortress that overarched the stream. She entered through a door in the right tower and ascended the spiraling stairs to its top floor. She opened a plain, large wooden door and stepped into a stone-tiled room at the top of the tower. She walked to a wall that was covered in thick red drapes. After pushing back the drapes to reveal an arched window, she looked out and noticed the dark sky which was marbled by the clouds in varying shades of grey and black. She sighed and lowered her head in thought.

A small glowing bird landed on her windowsill carrying the sapling of a glowing plant.

The Shepherdess took the sapling. "You have found another Bercolan tree. Thank you. These will continue to light our valley."

She took a pot from a shelf below the window, filled it with soil, and gently planted the sapling. Taking a nearby pitcher, she poured water from it onto the plant and the young tree glowed brighter, lighting up her room.

The Shepherdess turned from the plant to a control center at a desk to her right. She flipped a switch on a monitor and Infinity appeared on the screen.

"Infinity." She sat in front of the control center. "It is good to hear from you."

Infinity smiled and nodded. "I have made it out of the Guardian's space station and am now on my way to you."

"While we have had some losses, the mission has so far been successful here as well." The Shepherdess sighed as she remembered the wolves who had lost their lives. She took a breath and continued with her report. "The Shadow-Shield and Way-Guide are leading many of the workers to the safe house. Also, the wolves are guiding the hopeful one to my valley."

"Tell our workers to continue to ready themselves for what is to come. I will be there soon. And while my arrival will include a rescue, it will likely also include a battle. We must prepare for that battle now."

"I understand." The Shepherdess turned off the viewing screen and moved to the window. Setting her hands on the sill, she looked out upon the valley she ruled.

Rock scraped against rock as the walls of the cavern shifted with instability. 4,021 shook in concern and her eyes fixed on the wolf. He nudged her arm with his nose, encouraging her onward. She laid a hand on his back and continued by his side.

2-45 and 7,500 still followed from a distance. 2-45 noticed the irregularities of the marbled textures in the walls of the cavern. An unstable shifting caused him to lose his balance for a moment and a shower of dirt fell from the walls.

"These underground tunnels appear to be a disaster in the making," 7,500 commented as he brushed the dirt from his sleeves. "I would not be surprised if we ended up colliding with an oncoming stream of hot magma." A cluster of rocks plunged down the edge and landed in his path. He sidestepped the rocks and turned to 2-45 who had just dodge them. "As I said, unsafe."

The tunnel reminded 2-45 of those that mazed underneath his tower. He remembered when he and his sister would sneak through the shadows of the tunnels to catch trechirs. Trechirs are alert and he and his sister often ended up involved in a full-scale trechir-chase. Being much faster than people, though, trechirs are nearly impossible to catch in chase. However, with a few well-placed food lures throughout the tunnels, they managed to catch a few. 2-45 soon learned the best lures for capturing the fastest trechirs so that when he raced his sister, he often won. He was snapped out of his reverie by a mournful wail that filled the tunnel. 2-45 leaned into 7,500's ear. "That doesn't sound right."

"Probably one of the Shepherdess' more violent wolves," 7,500 murmured back.

The wolf whipped a glare back at 7,500 and bared his teeth.

"He says it's not a wolf." 4,021 told him and swallowed a nervous lump in her throat. "It's something dangerous . . . A guardian that works for the Queen of the Night."

2-45 focused deep into the shadows, hoping to catch a glimpse of the creature. "If we catch it, we could convince it to lead us to her?"

The wolf bounded to face 2-45 and block his path. He pushed forward forcing 2-45 back.

4,021 took 2-45's hand and held it tight until 2-45 looked at her. She directed him back on the path the wolf indicated. "That creature is dangerous and the wolf warned us not to go anywhere near it," she told him.

2-45 raised his hands in surrender to demonstrate he no longer intended to follow it.

The wolf once again lead the way.

Even though 2-45 and 7,500 continued to follow, they fell several steps behind. "You're right," 7,500 told 2-45. "I believe that creature would lead us to the Queen of the Night."

2-45 scratched his ear in thought. "Yes. But we can't just leave."

Some rock debris fell on 7,500's shirt and he fastidiously brushed it off. "Perhaps, but the first opportunity we find we should slip away." He ran his fingers through the curls in his hair to ensure they were not decorated in dust.

2-45 tapped a finger to his lips as he considered 7,500's proposition. "Maybe," he replied. "But let's stay long enough to learn more about 4,021's rose. It's from the Planet of Light. It was given to her by Infinity."

7,500 grimaced at the mention of Infinity. "So what? We can get away from this planet without concerning ourselves with Infinity and his Planet of Light."

"Perhaps." 2-45's foot slid on the uneven water-slick stone of the cave floor. He caught his balance and continued. "But I don't want to end up on another planet plunged in darkness."

The wolf guided them to an open cave where he was pleased to meet three members of his wolf pack. The wolves had anticipated their arrival and had built a large campfire which lit the cave in a warm orange flickering light. He nuzzled each of them and nipped at their ears, then directed their attention to the three humans he was leading to the Shepherdess.

7,500 screwed up his face. "Not more wolves."

The large gray wolf sniffed 7,500, snorted, and shook his head.

The lead wolf crinkled his nose and nodded with his disapproval. He back away and joined the other wolves in surrounding 4,021 in a circle of protection.

2-45 chuckled. "I don't think they like you."

7,500 shrugged and dusted off a nearby boulder and sat down. "From our lead wolf's reaction earlier, they really hate you." His eyes focused on the ceiling of rock above him, bored with the conversation.

4,021 returned to 2-45 and 7,500. She shifted upon locking eyes with 7,500 and stepped closer to 2-45. "Sorry to interrupt, but I just wanted to let you know that the wolves have agreed to lead all of us to the Shepherdess of the Valley. They just insist that we rest for a while before we continue."

2-45 sank to sit on the ground and leaned an arm on one knee. "How long? Wouldn't that give the Enforcers a chance to find us?"

"The Enforcers don't know about this tunnel." She set a hand on his shoulder. "We will be safe here."

7,500 snorted. He gave 4,021 a condescending look as if she were a Zeento spider at a Sopline feast. "How is it you always know exactly what those wolves are saying? Do you speak wolfese?"

4,021 looked at him confused. "I just know."

2-45 nudged 7,500 so he would not press the point. "It probably has something to do with that rose. I told you it was unusual."

4,021 ignored their remarks and turned to leave. "I will help the wolves prepare our dinner."

7,500 scooted closer to 2-45. "I am really troubled with the idea of going to that Shepherdess of the Valley."

2-45 tilted his head in surprise. "Why?"

"Well, think about it," 7,500 shrugged his shoulders and spread out his hands in front of him as if magically creating a world of confusion in front of him. "She calls herself the Shepherdess of the Valley. Then why is she connected with wolves? You know she is considered a villain by practically everyone in the City of the Dark Tyrant."

2-45 leaned against the wall to rest his back. "I have heard quite a few claim she is a protector of those in need."

"Well, it's true. She is a villain," 7,500 quickly chimed in. "I would be for sneaking out of this cave immediately if it wasn't that I have no idea how to find the Queen of the Night from here."

1-05 looked out of the window of the *Journey*. The workers for the hangar were still unconscious. "I hope they don't wake up before we leave."

"The wolves know what they are doing," the tow-haired boy told her.

"You're right." 1-05 had not meant her earlier comment for anyone but herself. For the most part, she was a loner, but she knew how to work with others when necessary. "Yes, they know what needs to be done. And they told us to prepare the *Journey*, so let's prepare it."

Even though the Slump-Bump Boys knew little about spaceship mechanics, with 1-05's guidance, it was not long before the *Journey* had every system checked, rewired, recalibrated, and refueled. Just as they were replacing the last tubing for the auxiliary power system, several wolves entered the hangar.

As the wolves boarded the *Journey*, 1-05 noticed a slew of workers pressing in behind them. Upon realizing that the wolves had brought them to a spaceship, they pushed upon each other, desperate to ensure their place on the *Journey*. 1-05 and the boys rushed out of the ship to help. She told the boys to wait at the ship's entrance as she exited to help the worker's board. She squeezed through the throng, holding her breath most of the way to shrink herself small enough to squeeze in the almost nonexistent spaces between the workers. With the help of 1-05, the boys, and the wolves, everyone made it onto the ship safely.

The lead wolf looked 1-05 in the eyes with a steady gaze. 1-05 took this as her cue to navigate the ship out of the hanger.

She marched to the cockpit and dropped into the chair in front of the pilot's controls.

She had been so focused on completing her tasks that she had failed to notice that the tow-haired boy had followed her. "Where are we going," he asked.

1-05's hand hesitated over the lever to start the engine. "Off the planet, I suppose," she replied. She turned to face the boy, but before she could say another word, the lead wolf strode in. He shook his head, blinked once and met her eyes with his.

She rubbed her temple with her fingers as she readjusted her thoughts. "We're not leaving the planet?"

The wolf shook his head once more. He moved toward the console and placed his paw on the digital map.

1-05 noted the location. She shivered as she recalled the location as being frozen and desolate. She read the coordinates out loud, to ensure they were correct.

The wolf nodded and left the room.

The tow-haired boy watched as 1-05 readjusted their destination. "So, we are *not* going to leave the Planet?"

"No," she grumbled, but then looked back at the boy's eager excitement. "Oh, never mind me." She tapped the co-pilot's chair. "Go ahead and sit here."

The boy smiled in excitement as he sat beside her.

"You can help me make sure we get there safely," she told him as she pointed out the button he was to push.

The *Journey* moved toward the hanger's exit and the tow-haired boy faced 1-05. "Do you have any idea where we're going."

"I just hope it's someplace safe," she replied as the *Journey* climbed into the night sky.

Chapter Fifty-Three

It was a never-ending cycle. The fire within the planet scorched its way to the surface, smog-filled smoke escaped the fire, and new ghostly creatures were born. At least it appeared this way to 5-07 as she approached a mountainous region just off a forest of rock pillars. Coming to the ledge of a cliff, 5-07, her mother, and 93-73 scanned the region that stretched out before them, looking as if it had been decimated by ghostly smog. "Where is it coming from?" she asked under her breath.

93-73 evidently heard her, because he pointed out the horizon.

5-07 squinted deep into the darkness. At first all she could see was a large plume of lava-encrusted smoke, but that smoke had to be living off of something. Below the smoke was the burnt remnants of her family's tower. She took a deep breath and lowered her head. It used to be their home. A place where her family and all they owned was protected. Now, the tower could not even protect itself from the destructive flame.

She turned to her mother and noticed her hands shaking unsteadily. Her mother batted her hands about in search of her daughter's arm to lean on. 5-07 moved in the path of her mother's hand. Her mother gripped her arm and 5-07 steadied her.

"Why must they destroy it?" 5-07's mother moaned and reached her other hand out in hopes that if she found the right button or switch, she could turn the fire off. "My husband was a top advisor to the Dark Tyrant . . . Why would they destroy his home?"

Lowering her head to avoid confronting her mother's question, 5-07 wrapped her arms about herself and sighed.

"Let's go back," her mother wailed. "We need to see what we can salvage."

5-07 hesitated. She did not want to dash her mother's hopes, but at the same time she did not want to promise her mother something that could not come to pass. She decided instead to redirect her mother's attention. "2-45 needs our help. We must find him."

5-07's mother pulled her focus from her home and moaned. "They promised our family a comfortable life." Her hand flew to her forehead as a migraine overtook her. "This is not what I would call a comfortable life."

93-73 draped an arm around the shoulder of 5-07's mother. "We'll see it's all put right. Now, you need to rest." He fixed 5-07 with eyes that meant what he said.

While 5-07 was in complete agreement that they needed a break, she doubted that they could find shelter anywhere nearby. She noticed the smog conspiring with the clouds and knew a downpour was in the making. *At least we are close to the mountains,* she thought. *Perhaps there's a cave or an overhang.* She glanced about and her eyes fell on a peculiar sight. Against a vertical side of one of the smaller mountains stood a dead tree. The tree was encased in a buildup of black, hardened lava rock. 5-07 concluded that it had battled several times in vain with the reoccurring lava flow and was left charcoaled and petrified.

A hollow opened within the tree near its roots and provided an entrance into a cave. As they stepped toward the entrance, a man exited. He just stood there, his dark wild curls dancing in the wind and his icy blue eyes which contrasted starkly with his dark skin fixed on them. His tunic and loose-fitting pants were embroidered with an edging that depicted indecipherable words and images. Acquiring a life of their own, his clothes rippled like the waves of the sea as the wind thrashed against them. The smog-like creatures 5-07 had seen earlier swirled out of the hollow behind him. It was now evident she had not imagined them.

The man appeared so bizarre that 5-07 took an unsteady step away from him. However, he was not so easily put off. He rushed toward the group. With a crazed glow in his eyes and an emphatic scooping of his arms, he gestured them toward the entrance through the tree.

93-73 and 5-07's mother took hesitant steps toward him, but 5-07 stood her ground. "Who are you?" she demanded.

For some reason, he chuckled at her question and held out his arms on each side of his body as if he were about to perform a juggling trick. "I am Thoravin. My affinity with the magic of this area is unrivaled. The magic here is powerful and was meant to be used." Again, he gestured them toward the entrance at the hollow of the tree. "Come in, come in. Enter my workshop and I will show you wonders that would baffle the most skilled magician."

They were inclined to leave, but an intoxicating bitter-sweet, citrusy scent drew them in. It was as if they were drowning in darkness until a light-yellow glow wrapped itself around them and ushered them into Thoravin's workshop. The glow lit the workshop in a dim yet comforting brightness. The warmth of some unseen fire and the intoxicating scent lulled them into complacency.

Thoravin gestured for them to sit in a pile of pillows on the floor. They looked comfortable and 5-07 was eager to sink into them. They were so puffy and deep it seemed she was falling into a cloud. However, the puffiness was not as comfortable as she hoped. They left her feeling unsteady, trying to balance herself within inches of the floor. Sinking so deep, she felt abandoned within a formidable barricade of pillows.

Once all his guests were boxed inside their pillows, Thoravin turned and took several purposeful steps away from them. He let a hand fall onto the table beside him and faced them. The table beside him housed a makeshift chemistry set. Near his feet was an odd compilation of scrolls, crystals, clay creatures, and jars of dismembered bits of insects and weeds. "You seem surprised to find me here. Whom were you seeking?" Thoravin asked with his eyebrows scrunching down and his nose scrunching up. He looked like a perplexing combination of a friend that was too good-natured and a murderer that was too murderous.

"We were searching for my brother," 5-07 told him. "He was trying to find the Queen of the Night."

Thoravin's eyes lit up at the mention of the Queen of the Night. "Ah, yes," he mumbled, his mind someplace else. "She lives around here . . . Doesn't she?" His hand waved about as if it had no idea where it was going. His eyes then widened, remembering that he had no idea what he was talking about. "Somewhere around here?"

"So, can we reach her from here?" 93-73 asked. He ran a flustered hand down his own sleeve.

Thoravin tilted his head as if ready to laugh any moment at 93-73's foolishness. "Perhaps . . . Perhaps not." He lifted a portentous finger. "Her guardian will not allow most to pass this area." He hovered over 5-07 and looked down his nose at her. "For your own good, I recommend you stay here awhile."

5-07 peaked over her pillows to determine 93-73's expression. "But we have to find my brother."

An archaic smile formed on Thoravin's lips. Setting a finger on top of his nose, Thoravin leaned in towards 5-07 and nodded a condescending head. "Let me search the area with my magic before you set out. It would be safer, yes?"

5-07 shifted. "I suppose," she replied, more to the floor than to Thoravin.

Thoravin turned his back to his guests and took a few steps toward the table. He paused, scratched his ear, and spun back to face them. "You know what's interesting about this place? We are at a crossroads. Head south and you find the Queen of the Night . . . or, more likely, her beast. Head east and you will enter the Valley of the Shepherdess."

93-73 looked up in interest. "I read that she's an agent for Prince Infinity."

Thoravin's face stretched in a thoughtful meditation that had yet to produce a thought. "That's possible."

"But aren't Infinity and the Shepherdess dangerous?" 5-07's mother clasped her hands together in concern.

Thoravin tilted his torso to the side and swung a finger in her direction as if she had won the party prize. "Exactly. Everyone knows they are not to be trusted. But still, the whispering tongues wag and people grasp at straws of hope."

"But what if they are right?" 5-07 asked. "What if she is here to help?"

Heaving a long sigh, Toravin shook a pitying head. "There is only one thing that will help anyone on this planet." He let his arms go limp at his side and his face fell, his eyes fixed on the floor. A thought jolted him back to life and his hands flew to grasp the air on either side of his head. "That is magic."

93-73 stood and looked Thoravin straight in the eyes. "You have talked a lot about magic, but you still haven't shown us anything." He laid his hands out before him as if begging for them to be filled with answers. "How do we know you are as powerful as you claim?"

Thoravin dropped a hand on 93-73's shoulder and rubbed it as if trying to relax his concerns. "I like you. I like your directness. Yes, you deserve to see my power . . . So . . ." Thoravin grabbed a spear that was naively napping within one corner of the room. He lifted it high over his head with the spearpoint directed downward. With one powerful thrust he slammed the point into the floor. The point cracked open the stone tiles and zig-zagging crevices opened in three directions. A green glow oozed out of the crevices and swirled around his feet. The glow was accompanied by the smell of sweet apple and burnt wood.

5-07 shot to her feet and ducked behind the pillows. "That looks like 1-13's skeleton-ghosts."

"Yes." Thoravin bent down and scooped up a handful of the green glow. "The skeleton-ghosts were found deep within this planet." He carried the glow over to 5-07's mother. "Something concerns you, doesn't it?" he asked in such a calm manner that it was impossible to determine whether or not he cared.

5-07's mother was pleased with the attention. "Concerns me?"

"Something has been troubling your mind," Thoravin repeated with careful precision.

"Well, yes . . . Our tower . . . They destroyed our tower." She was about to go on with a detailed description of the destruction, but Thoravin held a calming hand out before him. His other hand, the one holding the green glow, raised on the left side of her head. As his hand touched her head, the green glow entered her head, calming her concerned thoughts.

"Ohhh," 5-07's mother gazed deep into Thoravin's eyes. "Yes, everything will be fine." She flustered and twisted her left sleeve with the fingers of her right hand. "Yes, you truly are an amazing man."

Thoravin raised his head several inches higher. "There is so much this Planet of Darkness has to offer and so many choose to ignore it." He stroked 5-07's mother down her cheek. "But at least we can appreciate it."

5-07's mother stared at him in awe. "Of course."

93-73 turned to 5-07. "We are lucky he happened by."

"What do you mean," 5-07 grumbled as she kept a distrustful eye on Thoravin.

"We needed a place to rest, and," 93-73 shrugged, "he seems nice enough."

5-07 released a frustrated sigh. "Perhaps, but I don't trust him."

The uneasy mixture of rumbling from deep within the planet and the splitter, splatter of moisture dripping on several sides of him joined forces with the cozy crackling of the fire near the wolves to relax 2-45 to the point where his exhaustion sent him to a quick sleep. He was so tired, he did not even notice the point when his head dropped to the cave floor.

He woke when a booted foot jabbed the back of his leg. He sat up and stretched the aches out of his back. He looked up and found 7,500 looming over him.

"The wolves are ready to leave," 7,500 told him. "They are ready to take us to the Shepherdess of the Valley."

2-45 stood to his feet. "So, you've decided we should go with them to the Shepherdess?"

7,500 shifted his weight and analyzed a stalactite in the ceiling of the cave. "Not exactly," he murmured. "We don't have a choice . . . But, I mean, anything to get out of this dark, disaster of a cave."

A whirl of refreshing air swirled in and was followed by 4,021. "Are you ready to continue?"

"Yes," 2-45 replied as he grabbed his cloak from a jagged boulder. "However, if it is all right with your wolf-friends, we are thinking of continuing on to the Queen of the Night once we are out of the cave."

To 2-45's surprise, 4,021 simply shrugged her shoulders. "If you insist." Her eyes focused a moment on a trio of stalactites off a nearby cliff, but then she looked into 2-45's eyes. "I think you should see something though." She gestured him to follow her.

The path guided them up a steep incline. The cave ceiling remained unmoved on its horizontal path, but the floor was set on meeting the ceiling. Eventually the ceiling of the cave was so close to the floor that 2-45 and 4,021 had to duck down on all fours to make it through the path. They reached an opening in the cave so small, neither of them could fit through it. However, 2-45 had a clear view of the City of the Dark Tyrant and knew they were a good distance from it.

"So, we have escaped them," 2-45 concluded.

"Not completely," 4,021 told him. "But look." She pointed in the distance past the city. "The wolves said you would want to know about that."

2-45 looked in the direction she pointed out. It was the tower of his home, but there was no tower, only a pillar of flames. He jolted towards the flames and would have jumped through the opening to reach his home if the opening was big enough. Instead, he drove his fingernails into the loose stone surrounding the opening. "It's too late. Everything's gone. And my mother . . . and sister . . . Are they . . ." he groaned.

4,021 shook her head. "The wolves say they're alive. We may find them with the Shepherdess."

"I . . ." 2-45 dropped a hand on her shoulder. "Are you sure?"

4,021 looked deep into his blue eyes. "Of course. The wolves know these things. Also, the Shepherdess works for Infinity and he is the one who gave me this rose." She handed the rose to 2-45.

2-45 took the rose and looked deep into its petals. He was certain he heard the rose. In a soft, almost undetectable voice, it told him that his mother and sister were safe. "Yes," he said past the tightness in his throat. "You are right. The rose . . . the wolves . . . the Shepherdess . . . they all know the truth." He looked into her eyes. They glowed with an eagerness to help. His head dropped and he focused on the damp patterns of the cave's slate floor. He handed the rose back to 4,021 and momentarily touched his hand to her hair. "Thank you."

Chapter Fifty-Four

Even though it had been years since 1-13 had visited Thoravin's workshop, he still had no trouble locating it. He navigated the stone forest with the ease and precision of a pre-programmed pantor-indictor, with 50-83 trudging a distance behind him. 1-13 looked back and gestured 50-83 onward. "We need to reach Thoravin quickly. I know he could neutralize the power within. He's the only one who could."

50-83 dug his hand into his pocket and touched the crystal to confirm it was still there. "Do you think it was the power within that trapped 6-96 into my crystal?"

"Perhaps." 1-13 stalled for 50-83 to catch up with him, but his body energy still shifted onward. "Whatever it is, Thoravin will know what to do."

To 1-13's dismay, 50-83 stood still and surveyed the horizon. 1-13 followed 50-83's gaze to a dark Shlampine bird breaking free from a cage of dead overgrown twigs into the dark cloudy sky. "That bird is too busy to be worried about us," 1-13 assured him.

"You remember when we were here before," 50-83 breathed, his eyes still fixed on the horizon. "Our search did not turn out so well that time."

"I wouldn't say that. I secured the skeleton-ghosts." 1-13's eyes crinkled as a casual smirk lit his face. "They did prove useful for a while."

"There's a dark oppression here." 50-83 clenched his crystal harder as if hoping that by breaking the crystal the oppression would dissipate. The crystal fought back, though. One of its pointed edges dug into his palm and several drops of blood escaped. He groaned.

1-13 had not heard him. His eyes locked on the black stone encrusted tree along the mountain. He ran to it. "We are here," he beamed and gestured 50-83 next to him.

50-83 reached the door and shifted uneasily. "It's the same feeling of oppression I sensed whenever we were near the power within."

1-13 waved away 50-83's concern. "It is just the magic you feel. This whole area is permeated with it." He laid his hand on the largest branch of the tree near the trunk and it opened to allow them to enter.

The ghostly smoke that spiraled out of the tree and the thick scent of musty decay reminded 50-83 of their last visit to Thoravin's workshop. "It hasn't changed much."

"In some ways it has changed," 1-13 commented as he passed the threshold. "I believe the power is stronger."

The walls and ceiling of the entranceway were a meld of petrified tree growing within mountain rock. A green glow marbled its way through the walls as if on a tour to inspect the strange phenomenon of a marriage between wood and rock. The glow guided their path inside.

The absence of Thoravin made 50-83 uncomfortable about entering too deep into the workshop. On purpose, he lagged, waiting for Thoravin's appearance. Once inside the actual workshop, 50-83 paused to adjust his eyes to the light, but before he knew it, the weight of arms surrounded him in a hug. He took a step back to see who it was.

50-83 could not hold back a grin. "93-73, it's you? How is it you are free?"

"Yes," 93-73 laughed and tugged playfully at 50-83's hair. 93-73's laugh faded when he noticed 1-13 glaring at him.

Realizing that he was standing between 93-73 and 1-13, 50-83 moved out of the way.

93-73 turned pale and slapped his hand to his face. He hesitantly stepped up to 1-13. "I guess I am going back now."

A smirk played on 1-13's lips. He pulled out his pocket watch and swung it before 93-73. "Hmmm . . . Maaybee . . . But," 1-13 shrugged his shoulders, "I personally blame my skeleton-ghosts. If they can't keep you, you are free." He dropped his watch back in his pocket and waved 93-73 away.

50-83 paused 93-73's back-track. "How do you happen to be here?"

93-73 swung his hands toward a corner of the room where 5-07 and her mother were resting. "They brought me. I'm here to help 5-07 find her brother."

5-07 recognized 1-13 and leaned in towards her mother. Her hand unconsciously fell on her mother's shoulder and tightened with her annoyance.

Her mother recognized her daughter's frustration but did not draw attention to it. She moved her hand away and pointed out 1-13. "Isn't he the one 2-45 has been reassigned to?" Her voice was calmer than 5-07 had expected.

"Yes," 5-07 snarled. She sprang to her feet and stormed up to 1-13. She gave him a firm shove toward the wall. "Was it you who talked my brother into going out to find the Queen of the Night?"

"Me?" 1-13 dodged her second attack. "Why would I? I don't care anything about this Queen of the Night."

Thoravin appeared, seemingly out of nowhere, and stood next to 1-13. "You should care. The Queen of the Night is considered by many to be the most powerful person on this planet – perhaps even more powerful than the Dark Tyrant himself."

"Master Thoravin," 1-13 lowered his head in respect. "It has been a long time. It is good to be here with you again."

Thoravin embraced 1-13 and patted his back three times as if to accept his compliment and brush it aside at the same time. He then turned from 1-13 and faced 5-07's mother, as if about to say something.

1-13 spoke first. "The wolf broke the spell."

Thoravin met 1-13's eyes and curled up his nose. "What spell?"

"The spell to read minds," 1-13 continued with an emphasis and speed that indicated the urgency he gave his message. "They threw me to the ground and entered my mind. They told me that I had to escape the power within or this whole planet would be destroyed."

Thoravin held a crooked finger to his lips in thought. "Did they mention the Shepherdess of the Valley?"

"I believe so."

With a shake of his head, Thoravin dismissed 1-13's urgency. "The Shepherdess of the Valley has been up to strange magic — steer clear of the wolves as they could bring you under her power."

1-13 took an unsteady step back. "So, she is dangerous?"

Thoravin shook his head and chuckled in a way that seemed contrary to what he was about to say. "1-13, you need to stop drifting into muddy waters. If you are not careful you will surely perish."

50-83 let his thoughts stray to the green glow that marbled the walls. "Does the Shepherdess also tap into the power within?"

"Ahhh, 50-83 . . ." Thoravin brushed 50-83's bangs from his eyes and smiled with a momentary congenial smile. "You were much shorter when I saw you last time."

Unsure of how to respond, 50-83 simply nodded.

Thoravin half-sat and half-leaned against a table and faced his guests with clasped hands before him. "The Shepherdess uses a different kind of magic. It is not from within but from without. It is from another world." He snorted in such a serious manner it disturbed 50-83. "I would be cautious around it if I were you."

50-83 wondered about showing Thoravin his crystal but thought better of it. There was something too unreal about Thoravin.

Thoravin knew what 50-83 was thinking. "So, you have a very unusual crystal?"

Thoravin's words caught 50-83 off his guard, and the air caught in his throat and choked him with surprise. Sensing all eyes on him, he reached into his pocket, brought out the crystal, and presented it to Thoravin.

Thoravin took the crystal and dangled it before his eyes by its chain. Discovering 6-96 was trapped inside did not seem to faze him. Instead, he chuckled in amusement. "Ah, the power within holds her hostage."

"This has happened before?" 50-83 leaned in to join Thoravin in his examination of the crystal.

"Not often." Thoravin wagged his head at 50-83's amateur inquiry. "But the power within controls what it wants to control."

5-07 pressed pass 50-83 to confirm there was a living person inside the crystal. "You keep talking about this 'power within.' What is it and why is it so important?"

Thoravin tapped a finger on her forehead. "We call it the power within because the power lies within the Planet of Darkness. The power within controls this planet and without that power we are all basically helpless." He next tapped her on the nose. "That is why it is so important."

5-07 huffed at Thoravin's rudeness. She looked to her mother for back up, but she was just chuckling at his playful joke.

Thoravin handed the crystal back to 50-83 who took it gingerly with one finger and thumb, letting it swing as far from himself as possible. "I will not deny that she deserved to be imprisoned," 50-83 told him as he shoved it back toward Thoravin, "but is there any way to get rid of her and the crystal?"

Thoravin took the crystal and opened his hand flat before him, palm up with the crystal in the center of his palm. The crystal flew out of Thoravin's hand and landed on the ground right before 50-83. "It doesn't want to leave you," Thoravin commented as he squatted next to the crystal and craned his neck to look at it closer.

50-83 groaned. "Just my luck to be stuck with it."

Thoravin held a negating finger before 50-83's eyes. "Not necessarily. We were talking about the Queen of the Night. If anyone could control this crystal, it would be her. She deals with the same power I do, but she has delved deeper into its power than I have. I can wield the conscious power from within. She has gone further, conquering the subconscious power within."

"The subconscious power?"

Thoravin replied with an emphatic nod of the head. "The thoughts in our dreams hold more power than the thoughts when we are awake." After heaving a can-only-do-what-one-can-do sigh, Thoravin swung on his heels to face the large filigree-engraved front door. A long metal pole, black from its many encounters with the lava of this area, stood vigil next to it. Thoravin wrenched the pole from its lookout and in three forceful steps, stood next to the opening in the floor. He plunged the pole into the opening and the home of the underground pool of lava and ghost spirits that lived off the power within.

1-13 sunk to his knees before the underground pool and hovered his hand above it. "The power has grown exponentially." His face glowed with excitement as he raised his eyes to Thoravin.

Thoravin put all his strength into driving the pole in several wide stirs of the lava. "Yes . . . There is enough power here to bind the crystal and make it more easily controlled."

"What about 6-96?" 50-83 asked. "Is there any way to get her out?"

"I don't think we want her out," 1-13 mumbled mostly to 50-83.

Thoravin clanged the pole back into its corner. "The power wants her in the crystal, so in the crystal she must stay." He placed his hand on the middle of 50-83's back and, with firm pressure, guided him to the edge of the lava pool.

The pulsing orange and green light emanating from the pool drew his focus with such power, 50-83 was afraid he would unconsciously answer its call to join the power within. As the heat rose from the lava so also rose the smell of burnt flesh. A sweat broke out on 50-83's forehead as he wondered whose body Thoravin had buried in the pool. He broke from the magnetic pull and backed away. He directed his focus from the pool to Thoravin. "What am I supposed to do?"

Thoravin mimicked holding the crystal by the chain and dunking it into the lava.

50-83 knelt at the edge of the pool and let the crystal dangle, half-submerged, into the lava. He ignored the screams of 6-96 that erupted and left the crystal under for several minutes. When he lifted it out, the lava had hardened, coating the crystal in a strong black rock. 6-96's screams were now silenced, and she was imprisoned by both crystal and rock. "Is she dead?" 50-83 asked.

"She is silenced, but the crystal is still bound to you." Thoravin noticed 50-83's quizzical look, so he elaborated. "There is only one person who could possibly free you completely from 6-96, and that is the Queen of the Night."

A low rumbling shook the workshop and a haze of smoke hovered up from the lava pool. A ghostly voice moaned out of nowhere.

"The power within speaks?" 1-13 wondered.

Thoravin responded with a firm shake of his head. "I speak with the power within often and that does not sound like it at all."

At the first rumblings, 50-83 had taken refuge under a table. But there was something familiar about the voice and, out of curiosity, he now pulled himself out. "I know that voice."

Thoravin and 1-13 exchanged puzzled expressions.

50-83 fixed his eyes on the pool and threaded past 1-13 and Thoravin back to the edge. "Is that you?" His voice almost broke.

"I guess that trip up to the mountains did not turn out quite the way we planned," the voice replied with less rumbling.

Even though his eyes were focused on the cobblestone floor, 50-83's mind was in the past. The boxes in his mind were creaking open on their own. The conflicting memories awoke conflicting emotions. However, the most pronounced emotion was sadness, and he did not want to cry. It took a greater effort than before to stuff the tears back into the boxes in his mind. "I thought we'd find your grandfather. He often roamed that area."

"That's all right. I haven't found him here either."

"Where are you?" 50-83 dropped to his hands and knees before the pool and looked as deep into it as he could. "I don't see you. Where are you?"

"You remember where," the voice replied. "I've never left. I'm still in the city."

"You're still there?" 50-83 almost reached into the pool but pulled his hand back in time. "I'll come and find you. I'll get you out." He clambered to his feet and pushed his way passed 1-13 and 93-73 on a set course for the door.

"Where are you going?" 1-13 demanded.

50-83 pulled the door open. "I'm going back to the City of the Dark Tyrant."

Grabbing his upper arm, 93-73 held him back. "You know your friend's dead. You told me you saw him die. It's too dangerous to go back."

"But you heard him." 50-83 threw a wild wave of the hand toward the pool. "He's alive and I need to get him out of the city."

"By now the Dark Tyrant knows what happened to 6-96." 1-13 trained his serpentine eyes on 50-83 wondering whether a bit of hypnosis might change his mind. "You could be arrested or killed."

"I've got to go back and get him out." He crossed the threshold and was on his way once more to the City of the Dark Tyrant.

Chapter Fifty-Five

9 3-73 looked into the lava pool half-expecting the voice to call out after 50-83, begging him to stay. "Was the voice real?" he asked of no-one in particular.

Thoravin's face hung in a frown. "There is something sinister about this voice."

"Perhaps it's the Queen of the Night?" 5-07 wondered as she gazed into the pool. "My brother was coming here to find her."

Thoravin edged between her and 1-13. "It could be the Queen." He paused. His eyes strayed upward and widened in thought as he focused on the mad maze of tree and stone that made up the ceiling. "You know, it's not such a bad idea."

93-73's hands clamped on his hips as he huffed at the directionless course the conversation was taking. "What's not a bad idea?"

"Visiting the Queen of the Night." Thoravin wondered why 93-73 failed to infer his meaning. "She could clarify this mystery voice and tell us how to find 2-45 at the same time."

5-07's mother pressed toward Thoravin with the shy eagerness of a new devotee. "But I'm sure you can find those answers as well as she can." Her hand almost touched his shoulder, but a self-conscious moment convinced her to lower her hand and blush.

"I appreciate the compliment," Thoravin replied with a beneficent squeeze of her hand. "But, she could find the answers much more quickly than I could." He extracted a cape from a peg on the wall and swung it about himself. "So, shall we go?"

93-73 hung back as a shadow of dread fell over his face. "It's impossible. The path is too dangerous."

"Only for those who are unwelcome." Thoravin waved him to join him on his way out. "Her beast can be deadly and the atmosphere of her castle can be suffocating since the magic is so strong, but, I am always welcome, so you have nothing to fear."

1-05 had talked herself into accepting the fact that the *Journey* may set down in an unexpected location. However, after running through a list in her mind of all the least expected places to set down, the place they landed had been nowhere on this list. The bitter cold penetrated the ship's isolation and the frozen wasteland that she stared at through the viewing screen sent another shiver up her spine.

"This can't be right," she breathed. Steam followed the words out of her mouth.

"Did we land in the wrong place?" the Slump-Bump boy asked, his eyes widening in concern.

1-05 shook her head but her words did not coincide with the shaking of her head. "I sure hope so." She turned and marched out of the cockpit area to find the wolf. "Why did we land in such a . . ." She cut her sentence off with a gasp when she found herself face to face with 8-23. She only hesitated a second to convince herself he was real. Once she felt the warmth penetrating from his body, she threw her arms around him. "You are alive," she exclaimed, but most of the volume was muffled by the cascade of kisses she lavished on his neck.

The Way-Guide pulled her even closer. "Your safe." He warmed more and more with every kiss.

1-05 framed the Way-Guide's face with her hands. "I wish you would have told me you were in such an unlivable place," she told him. Her eyes glistened with a stern light. "I could have flown here and shipped you out."

The Way-Guide only laughed. "I thought you would at least be pleased I am alive."

"Of course, I am." 1-05 pushed him playfully against the wall of the ship. "But you can't blame me for wanting to keep you safe after your disappearance almost scared me to death."

The Way-Guide was about to respond, when he was interrupted by a shadow that fell on them. He glanced to the right and saw they had been joined by the Shadow-Shield.

The Shadow-Shield looked straight into 1-05's eyes. 1-05 leaned closer to the Way-Guide but listened with attention. "You find this place discouraging?" he asked her. "You probably thought that when we left the city we would take you to some secure place away from all danger."

Her eyes lowered as she grimaced at how close he came to the truth. "I had hoped we would at least have a few moments of peace."

The Shadow-Shield took her hands and rubbed some warmth into them. "There is no place secure from *all* dangers. It may be a challenge to live here because of the lack of heat, but at least for now, that is the only challenge." He sent her a slight smile that showed more in his eyes than the rest of his face. "You will have those few moments away from danger."

The Way-Guide kissed the top of 1-05's head. "Come on. Let's get everyone into the safehouse."

1-05 let her head nestle a moment on his shoulder as her arm embraced his waist. "A safehouse sounds like a good place to stay for a while."

Her eyes strayed up to his and she no longer felt cold.

Chapter Fifty-Six

As they trudged through the cave, 2-45 noticed the air turning musty. His feet were sore from walking and he could not put from his mind the thought that his mother and sister were either dead or in danger. He considered stopping and turning back, but finally chose to complain to 7,500 instead. "The air smells awful in this part of the cave."

7,500 returned the complaint with an uncharacteristic bright smile which, perhaps, blossomed from his friend's misery. "We're nearly there. That smell indicates an opening nearby." His smile faded at the sound of a loud rumbling whine which resembled a mixture of a rockslide and the screams of someone in their death throes. "That creature again," he grimaced.

"We better be almost through this cave." 2-45 quickened his pace for a moment, but a pebble chose to make its home in his boot. He stopped to remove it.

7,500 was tempted to continue without 2-45 but concluded that waiting was the generally accepted action. To ensure the world knew he would not wait forever, he exaggerated a moment of fidgeting with his shirt buttons and sleeve.

As he tossed out the pebble, 2-45 turned once more to 7,500. "5-07 and mother . . . I am sure they are in danger."

2-45 was surprised by his friend's reaction. 7,500's hand flew to his forehead, and he gargled both a moan and a laugh at the same time. "What should you be worried about? They don't need you to watch over them. Let them enjoy their little time away from you."

7,500's response annoyed 2-45 to such an extent that if he could breathe out fire he would have. Instead, he shoved him against the cave wall with one strong jab to his chest. "Something destroyed my tower, perhaps my mother and sister too. Of course I'm going to be worried and of course you better watch how you talk about my family."

The wolves and 4,021 paused to observe and ensure the fight did not escalate.

2-45 thought his response would have made a bigger impression on 7,500 than it did. His friend merely shrugged his shoulders and held his hands up in a half-surrender, half-wave. He shook his head and sighed. "You could have told me that part first." Then, to affix an official stamp claiming his side had won, he added an old adage. "You can't blame the pallbearer for smiling if he wasn't informed about the funeral."

2-45 would probably have groaned if he had not noticed the cave opening ahead.

4,021 tugged at 2-45's sleeve and pointed. "We are almost there."

"Yes," 2-45 said more to himself than anyone else. His determination quickened his pace.

Once outside the caverns, he saw the path before him leading to a crossroads with three paths to choose from. His focus was on the paths, but he soon felt 7,500's breath on his neck. "Which way?" 2-45 asked.

7,500 tilted his head and inflected an up and down grunt as he thought how sorry 2-45 should be that he ever laid a hand on someone so indispensable. "Well, you could randomly pick either one."

2-45's fists tightened, but he took a deep breath. "But *you* know where they all lead."

7,500 could not resist a smug smirk. "Yes." He moved in front and pointed out each path. "That flat empty path to the left leads back to the City of the Dark Tyrant. The path before us filled with a forest of towering pillar-like rocks leads to the Queen of the Night. The path to the right framed by trees and vines leads to the Shepherdess of the Valley."

While the cool, clean breeze from the Shepherdess's Valley drew 2-45's attention, he was distracted by a bright glow on the horizon in front of him. It started barely visible like a thin line of hazy light that separated the ground from the dark sky. Soon it dazzled through the pillars of rock and seemed to pull 2-45's gaze toward it. Past the glow, he could make out the spectacular castle of the Queen of the Night which spanned an area twice the size of the City of the Dark Tyrant and was framed by golden gates, crenelated walls, and lofty towers.

"Perhaps the Dark Tyrant feels threatened by the Queen of the Night," 2-45 wondered under his breath.

"Why?" 7,500 followed 2-45's gaze.

"She is obviously powerful."

7,500 nodded, face fixed on the path ahead of them.

After leaving the cave, 4,021 blinked with concern at 2-45 and 7,500 moving toward the center path. The lead wolf nudged 4,021 toward the path to the right. The rest of the wolves bounded ahead of her as she followed the path leading to the Shepherdess.

4,021 passed beautiful multicolored flowers and plants with green leaves as tall as herself. The wolves paused and she saw that they had brought her to an area overgrown by vining flowers and overlapping leaves. Snuffling their noses through and pawing back the plants, the wolves prodded open the path. A hand reached out from the other side and the Shepherdess pushed through as she guided the vines back up a sturdy tree.

Nestling against the Shepherdess' knee, the largest grey wolf gazed up into her eyes and growled a low bark.

"We have three potential guests," she interpreted the wolf's meaning. She paused upon noticing the direction 2-45 and 7,500 were facing. "But I sense only one will stay."

The Shepherdess redirected her attention to 4,021 as she approached her.

"You must be the Shepherdess of the Valley." 4,021 lowered her head and remembered the rose she held. "You can take me to Infinity?"

"I can show you where he will be soon." The Shepherdess gestured for 4,021 to follow her down the path.

4,021 took a few steps then paused. She turned back, concerned that 2-45 and 7,500 remained at the crossroads. "What about them?"

"Perhaps they will join us later," the Shepherdess told her without wasting a moment to look back at them. She instead led 4,021 to a stone bench in a hidey-hole surrounded by the thicket. "Rest here. It is easier to breathe in this part of the planet since it is unaffected by the corrupting power within."

As 4,021 sat on the bench, the Shepherdess half-knelt, half-lounged in front of her on the ground.

A large grey wolf brought a basket to the Shepherdess and from it she pulled out a bottle of berry juice. "Thirsty?" She presented it to the Slump-Bump.

"Yes. Very." 4,021 reached for the bottle.

The Shepherdess held it away from her and brought out a glass. 4,021 was fascinated with how beautiful the glass was with its delicate crystal etchings of flowers and molding of gold trees wrapping their way around the glass. She was eager to take it and once it was in her hands, the Shepherdess filled it to the brim with the juice. The juice was more flavorful and refreshing than anything she had ever drunk before. The only way she could describe it was sweet happiness.

The Shepherdess next presented her with a platter of bread and fruit.

The food looked perfect and after guiding a strand of hair back from her face, 4,021 took the bread which was warm and soft, unlike the hard, dry morsels she was lucky enough to receive on occasion in the city.

The wolves reclined near the entrance, staying alert but taking the opportunity to restore their strength.

The Shepherdess stood and took a seat next to 4,021 on the bench. "There is something I need to warn you about," she told the Slump-Bump in a voice so serious that even the wolves were silent.

4,021 let a hand drop to the bench to ensure she was well balanced just in case the warning would cause her head to spin. "Was I wrong to leave the city?"

"No." The Shepherdess lifted the Slump-Bump's sinking chin. "What I am warning you about is generally considered a good thing . . . but it can be tricky."

"Tricky?"

"Yes," the Shepherdess nodded. "You've lived all your life in the same old village near the City of the Dark Tyrant. Even though it was not a perfect life, it may have been a relatively comfortable one. If you continue to my valley, your world will become much larger. That could be a scary thing."

While 4,021 did not completely understand what it was like to have worlds become larger, she was willing to let the Shepherdess guide her. There was one thing she wanted to know. "What do you mean by scary?"

The Shepherdess' smile told 4,021 that whatever was scary must not be too scary. "You will shoulder more responsibilities than you ever have in your entire life."

4,021 remembered her rose. She drew it from her pocket and held it close to her chest. "Is Infinity staying in your valley?"

"His journey from the Planet of Light has taken longer than he anticipated. But he told me that he wants you to help me prepare the Planet of Darkness for his arrival."

4,021 drew in a gasp. Her hands shook involuntarily at the thought of such a responsibility. "How could I help?"

"You already have," the Shepherdess explained as she set her hand out palm upward to draw 4,021's attention to her rose. "While Infinity sent you this rose, it was not intended for you alone. You could have hidden it in your hovel, but you didn't. You were willing to share its power. Because of this many workers are right now finding their way to the safehouse where they are meant to be when Infinity arrives."

4,021 smiled. She could imagine him walking to her through the thicket. "When will he come?"

"It won't be long," the Shepherdess reassured her. She looked her deep in the eyes and squeezed her hand to send her the confidence she possessed. "In fact, he will be here very soon. Rescuing us is his priority." She stood and took two steps away from 4,021 and toward the entrance of the hidey-hole. Before returning to the cross-roads, the Shepherdess turned back to her. "I must return to the others for a moment." Her eyes lowered in thought, and she took in a deep breath of preparation. "There is something evil that lurks out there . . . but I will be back." She swept her hand from two wolves who stood nearby toward 4,021 to indicate that they were to protect her. Afterwards, she sent 4,021 a reassuring nod and left to return to the crossroads.

Chapter Fifty-Seven

With just a few determined steps, the Shepherdess soon stood at the point where all roads met. She turned to 2-45. A resolute gust of wind blew in from her valley billowing her dark locks off her shoulders.

2-45's eyes were drawn to hers and her gaze cut deep into his soul. While the wealth of the Queen of the Night tempted him to follow the path toward her castle, he now worried that his greed was laid bare to the Shepherdess. He thought he should ask her about it but did not want to confess for all to hear. Instead, he chose to ask something else. "Is there danger on this path?"

To 2-45's surprise, the Shepherdess's first response was a slight smile. *Can she read my thoughts?* She reached over her shoulder and grabbed a spear from the pouch on her back. She jabbed its point into the ground at her side and lowered her chin as her eyes rose to meet his. "More danger than you can handle," she replied. Two of her wolves moved forward to stand on either side of her.

Taking her words as a fair warning, 2-45 turned to catch 7,500's response. 7,500 moved his neck back and forth to stretch out a stiffness and waved off the Shepherdess. Without one more thought, he stepped out on the path toward the Queen of the Night ready for 2-45 to follow. 2-45 was set to join him but pivoted back toward the Shepherdess. He touched a finger to the side of his mouth in thought and then convinced himself to ask the question that was preying on his mind. "I suppose you advise against us visiting the Queen of the Night?"

The Shepherdess took a breath before answering. "You, yourself, do not believe it is the right thing to do." She swept her hand out before her to direct 2-45's attention to the cave.

2-45 followed her gesture to a rock that jutted out near the cave's entrance. Not far from the rock grew an unusual tree with bark that emitted a luminescent glow. Several lush bushes thrived under the tree, but one small bush barely clung to life. This bush was sheltered by the rock and the shadow of the rock blocked it from the tree's light.

"The soul longs for light," he repeated out loud as he recalled the book he had read.

7,500 groaned and turned back to 2-45. "The soul longs for what?" His nose scrunched up in irritation. "And soul . . . What kind of word is that? It has no meaning."

2-45 stepped toward the Shepherdess and looked to her for guidance. She nodded her approval. Giving 2-45 the confidence to respond. "By soul, I mean the life that lives within the body. Certainly you have heard about the 'judgement beyond death'."

7,500 crossed his arms before him and grimaced. "It's a fable. A scientific impossibility."

2-45 shook his head. "You cannot prove it one way or the other. But one thing I do know, people need light to flourish."

"That's debatable," 7,500 mumbled.

2-45 ignored his disdain. "So, of all the directions we could take, only one path leads to light. The City of Darkness and the Queen of the Night both take us back into darkness. The

Shepherdess' Valley leads to light." He pointed out the Bercolan trees and the light emanating from the valley.

7,500 shook his head. "Wrong. We saw a glow in the direction leading to the Queen of the Night."

The Shepherdess raised a knowing eyebrow. "Yes. She does toy with simulated lights and luminous illusions. She is skilled in deception."

7,500 noticed that 2-45 was seriously weighing the Shepherdess' words. He knew that if he did not intervene immediately, 2-45 would side with the Shepherdess and remain in the valley. "All the more reason we should visit the Queen of the Night," he blurted out as he grabbed 2-45's arm and pulled him toward the path he planned on taking.

2-45 took back his arm. "You're not making any sense."

"You remember when you and I were talking about gem collecting?" 7,500 spun a finger in the air to help 2-45 visualize the thought process. "You and I are the ones with the task of tossing out the fakes. Well, if the Queen is a fake, it is up to us to determine that."

2-45 agreed that 7,500 reasoning made sense. He turned from the valley and took the path leading to the Queen of the Night. After only a few steps, the ground quaked, and he struggled to catch his breath. Boring its way upward from under the ground, a giant stone-like slug broke through and blocked their path. It was so large it loomed over them like a massive obelisk. Its lower body resembled a huge earthworm, yet it crawled around on numerous small, claw-like feet. It tilted its immense golem-like face to examine 2-45 with its red flaming eyes. Its mouth formed a grin displaying rows of sharp fangs. "The Queen of the Night is expecting you," it roared in a voice that resembled rocks scraping against rocks. "But you will not live to see her."

7,500 sidestepped backwards behind 2-45. "It must be the creature that was following us in the cave." He waved an accusing finger at the Shepherdess. "You sent it after us, didn't you?"

The Shepherdess shook her head, unfazed. "I do not tend to creatures that are unnatural. This creature was born from the evil magic within this planet and was drawn from it by the Queen of the Night."

"Maybe the creature is friendly." 2-45 took several cautious steps back. "It did say the Queen is expecting me. But if she expects me, why would her creature want to kill me?"

The Shepherdess tightened her grip on her spear. "The Queen does have a strange form of hospitality."

The creature gurgled in response and sprang from the ground like a sprouting boulder and dove down upon 2-45. 2-45 rolled out of its path. 7,500 raced back toward the cave and ducked behind a stack of petrified logs beside its opening.

Upon missing 2-45, the creature burrowed back into the rocky ground it landed on to tunnel its way back underneath.

The Shepherdess' wolves stirred and moved forward, ready to attack the creature. The Shepherdess, herself, was eager to take on the creature. Sweat formed on her hand that held the spear. After surveying the crossroads and the cave, she gestured her wolves to keep calm. "Not yet," she told them. "Just wait for my signal."

Across from the cave, a group of people approached through the forest of rock pillars. Thoravin reached the crossroads first. His eyes fell on the Shepherdess. She met his gaze, but raised her chin, wary of his intentions. Thoravin sensed her distrust and lowered his eyes.

93-73 came behind Thoravin and noticed 2-45. He waved 5-07 forward and with a quick toss of his hand directed her attention to her brother.

5-07 breathed in an excited gasp. "Mother, look. We found him." 5-07 threw herself into a sprint toward him but was jerked back by a grip on her arm.

"Careful," Thoravin whispered in her ear.

She felt an unsteady shifting of the ground at her feet. The grains of gravel took on a life of their own as they seemed to scurry away from something that forced its way out of the earth. The giant rock slug rose and hunched its head down, glaring at 5-07.

Thoravin pulled her back. "The Queen of the Night is up to her mischief," he told her. "Best not to upset her creature."

5-07 brushed off Thoravin's hold. "Is it after us or 2-45?"

A cold hand fell on her shoulder. She looked back and noticed 1-13 standing behind her. "Perhaps the creature's after her." He pointed out the Shepherdess standing at the crossroads surrounded by her wolves.

"I wouldn't blame the Queen for sending her creature after the Shepherdess," Thoravin snorted.

"Shepherdess?" 1-13 asked in surprise. "As in, Shepherdess of the Valley?"

"The same. One thing the Queen of the Night and the Dark Tyrant agree on is their dislike of the Shepherdess of the Valley."

The giant rock slug shifted its attention to Thoravin. It roared, lunged toward him, but wrenched past him and spun around. When its stubby tail faced Thoravin, the creature whipped it at him.

Thoravin would have been knocked a dangerous distance if he had not ducked behind a nearby rock-pillar in time. The force of the creature's movement forced 93-73 to fall back where he joined Thoravin behind the pillar.

93-73 rubbed his bruised shoulder. "I think it's after us."

The giant rock slug turned from Thoravin and now faced 2-45.

5-07's mother screamed. "No, it's after my son." She grabbed Thoravin by the upper arm. "Do something." She shook him several times in a panic. "Use your magic powers."

7,500 dropped a hand on 2-45's back. "I suppose you've already noticed, but your mother and sister are alive." He jabbed a thumb in their direction.

2-45 ground his fingers into the boulder he leaned against. "Yes, but now that thing is going to kill us all." He felt a gust of moist hot air across his face and looked up. The giant slug creature was glaring down at him. "The Shepherdess claims the creature comes from the Queen of the Night. Are you sure we still want to go to her?"

7,500 leaned in to 2-45's ear. "Perhaps you just have to say the right thing to it. There are places around here where that sort of thing works."

2-45 wanted to snarl at 7,500 and tell him that since it was his idea, he could carry out that experiment on his own. Before he could say anything, he noticed that his sister did not hesitate. She rushed out to distract the creature. In a half-circle spin close to the ground, she slid in front of it. She waved an explosive device in the air, brandishing it above her head. "Leave my brother alone," she belted out at the creature.

The creature groaned and turned to face her.

Timing was vital. 2-45 could not give the creature the opportunity to lash out against his sister. He pushed himself to his feet and rushed over the barrier of petrified logs to face the creature. He had just jumped the barrier when he felt the ground give out beneath him and his left foot sink into a hole. He lost his balance and fell backwards. He tried to pull his foot from the hole, but several rocks lodged themselves on top of his foot and refused to budge.

The creature grunted when it noticed the explosives in 5-07's hand. "You cannot frighten me with your human weapons." It sneered at 5-07 sideways, focusing on her with only its left bulging eye. "My power comes from within this planet and that power is stronger than anything humans could create." Its mouth widened as it reached down for her.

2-45 located a rock nearby and stretched toward it, but since his foot was trapped, he could not reach far enough.

7,500 noticed the rock and, after a moment of hesitation, slipped out from the barrier to grab it up. 2-45 gestured for him to throw it at the creature, but 7,500 was not in the mood for angering it.

"Come on," 2-45 shouted at him as he jerked his hand forward and back in a more emphatic demonstration of throwing the rock. "Now!"

Realizing he would have enemies on both sides if he did not act, 7,500 decided to prove his worth. He pulled the rock back and threw it with as much force as he could muster.

The rock bounced off the creature's back without even distracting it. Without hesitating, the creature swooped its head down to grab up 5-07.

5-07 dropped to the ground and squeezed between several large boulders to avoid the encounter. She pressed hard on the button to activate the explosive device and threw it toward the creature. The creature dug its way down into the earth, dodging the subsequent explosion. The explosion broke loose a rockslide next to the cave which torrented toward 2-45 and 7,500 and almost buried them alive.

5-07 was about to race over to help 2-45 free his foot from the hole, but the creature erupted out of the ground again, this time adjacent to the cave. It wriggled up to 2-45 and 7,500.

"It's after us again." 7,500 glanced about for an escape route.

"I know," 2-45 moaned while digging out scoops of the earth and rock keeping his foot prisoner. He heard racing footsteps approaching. He glanced up and saw, in the shadow of the creature, his sister. "Get out of here. Get to someplace safe," he snapped at her.

She crouched next to him. "Where's that?" She aimed her annihilation gun toward the creature's head and fired it. The creature only quickened its movement toward them.

With a furious huff, 5-07's mother slammed her fist against Thoravin's shoulder. "Why aren't you doing something?"

Thoravin pulled at his ear in thought. "We can't just storm over haphazardly. We must first have a plan."

After a second of thought, 93-73 stood to his feet. "I've got a plan."

Thoravin moved in front of him and placed a hand on his chest to prevent him from passing. "There is nothing you can do out there."

93-73 brushed Thoravin to the side as if parting the curtain to begin a stage play. "My friends are out there, and I won't let that creature kill them." He raced passed Thoravin and up to a tree with copious branches. Using the branches as a ladder, he managed to climb to one of the tree's highest branches. This placed him alongside the creature. He grabbed a weaker branch and broke it off the tree. When the creature came close enough, he jabbed the limb into the creature's eye. As the limb sunk in, a green viscous goo splattered from the eye.

When 5-07's shot failed to stop the creature, 2-45 took out his fury on the rocks confining his foot. He dug his fingers in with such aggression they bled. "Get back there with 7,500. He can protect you," he shouted to his sister.

She looked straight into his eyes and shook her head. She reattached her gun to her belt and worked to help 2-45 dislodge several rocks surrounding his foot.

The Shepherdess noticed the green goo and glow of power emanating from the creature. "The Queen of the Night is determined to have them. Especially that one," she directed the wolves' attention toward 2-45 with her spear. "We must not let her let her win easily."

The creature loomed so close over 2-45 that a drop of its saliva wetted his hair. He pushed his sister back out of the creature's reach, but its attention was fixed on 93-73.

1-13 had been attempting to remain neutral in hopes of avoiding the creature's notice. However, when he saw the creature's eyes on 93-73, he puzzled out a way to rescue him. He felt the watch in his pocket and took a tense step up to Thoravin. "We have to do something. Do you think it's possible to control the creature's mind?"

Thoravin shook his head. "Its mind is too powerful for us." Thoravin let his brain digest the thought until the light of a five-pointed star sparkled in his eye. "I have an idea." He lifted one hand and nodded as if to say he had been planning on acting but was too busy formulating a plan. He pulled from his pocket a brown bottle stained green near the cork. He marched out from behind the stone pillar and raised his hands on either side of his head. Waving them side to side and forward and back, he warded off whatever he wanted warded off. He then took several confident steps up to the creature.

The creature rotated its head and looked at 93-73 with its good eye. It wrinkled its muzzle and snarled.

93-73 reached for another limb but could not free it from the tree. In a panic, he realized there was little else he could do and searched for the quickest way down the tree. The creature, however, did not give him that opportunity. It grabbed him up between its teeth and slurped him into its mouth. When the creature turned and bared its teeth to 2-45, 93-73 was no more. 5-07's mother paled and, in a panic, looked all around to locate her two children.

While her wolves surrounded the creature on all sides, the Shepherdess raced up the rockslide. She kept up her pace and did not lose her balance even though pieces of rock and dust unsettled and shifted as she made her way up. Once at the top, she thrust her spear between the top rock and the outside wall of the cave and used the spear to direct the rocks toward the creature.

The creature lunged down on 2-45. It picked him up between two of its fangs. 2-45's heart rate increased as he was pulled higher. His mother screamed. While he had been unpunctured by the creature's teeth, his shoulder was pinched between them and he was pained by a deep bruise that was forming. As he was lifted, his foot was forced out of the hole with an immense shot of pain.

The ground shook and the rumble of the rocks pierced the air. The pack of wolves converged to form a barricade to prevent the creature from escaping while managing to avoid the rocks themselves. A dust cloud choked the air over the rocks as the wolves penned in the creature.

7,500 and 5-07 noticed the rocks tumbling toward them and moved across the path to join her mother.

Thoravin raised an amused eyebrow as he acknowledged to himself that it would be much easier to use his magical powers on a creature that could not get away. "Creature," he proclaimed as he marched up to it, "put down your captive now."

The creature's fiery red eyes narrowed and it lifted its chin in disdain. "Use your magic," it growled past the victim it still held in its mouth. "Your powers are sure to leave me helpless."

2-45 felt the blood rush to his head. He was unsure of how anything anyone did could help. If he was released, it was a long drop to the ground. If he was swallowed, he wondered how long it would take him to be fully digested.

The creature's disdain for his magic led Thoravin to be that much more determined to use it. He unstopped the bottle and poured a handful of the green glowing goo onto his hand. As he rubbed his hands together, he chanted with a loud and determined air. *"Cantodoluf entolmartof mantodoluf entolmartof intilodus. Mar mor mir. Sar sor sir. Dan don din. Dalos dilos din."* The green glowing mixture in his hand rose before him and floated toward the creature.

Without hesitation, the creature moved its head into the green glow and it engulfed it completely. The creature sneered and raised its head in a frenzied excitement. "The extra energy is welcome." It bellowed a laugh and tossed 2-45 into the air to catch him in its mouth.

Before he could reach out to catch him, the tip of a spear emerged out of its throat. It convulsed and its head fell limp. The Shepherdess removed the javelin she had just stabbed into the creature's throat.

As 2-45 plummeted downward, two of the wolves leaped into the air and used their bodies to knock him to the side.

Two other wolves used their paws to push him toward the branches of a widespread tree. He landed as comfortably as expected on the branch.

5-07 raced over to help him down. As he touched ground, she gave him a tight embrace. 2-45 took an uncomfortable, shallow breath to help stifle a groan of pain from his bruised ribs. "Did you see that," 5-07 told him excitedly. "The Shepherdess killed the creature."

Thoravin navigated up to 2-45 and helped him to his feet. "I don't believe the creature is dead," he told 5-07. "It lives by the power within, so it would be very hard to kill."

As he spoke, the creature lifted its head with effort and sent the Shepherdess a malicious glare. "If you kill me, the Queen will destroy your valley. You are only permitted to stay here out of her compassion."

A wolf pulled out a cloth from the pouch it carried and gave it to the Shepherdess. She used it to clean her spear. "Our valley is well protected and *that* is why the Queen has not yet destroyed it. The Queen has no compassion, but out of *my* compassion, I will permit you to return to her."

The creature tucked its chin down, either out of defeat or disgust and slithered away on the path leading to the Queen of the Night.

The Shepherdess reached her spear over her shoulder and dropped it into the pouch on her back. Her eyes surveyed everyone who had survived the encounter, but landed on 2-45. "You should not tarry too long at the crossroads. This is one of the most dangerous places on the planet. You should make up your mind quickly which way you will go."

2-45 considered following the Shepherdess, but noticed his family stood near the path that led to the Queen. "I appreciate what you have done," he told the Shepherdess. "If it wasn't for you, I would be dead."

The Shepherdess took his right hand and patted it once. "You have chosen your path, and it is not my place to judge your choice." She turned away from him and followed her wolves toward the valley.

2-45 noticed that he held something in his hand that must have been given to him by the Shepherdess. He opened his hand palm upward and realized she had given him a wooden ring that glowed with the bark of the Bercolan trees.

Chapter Fifty-Eight

7,500 guided the others away from the valley. At one point a trail branched off from the path and Thoravin sidestepped the others to take it. "This trail leads back to my workshop, so I will be leaving you here." He half-shrugged and half-stretched out a stiffness in his shoulders then detoured down the trail away from the path.

1-13 considered the seemingly unending path ahead, and he veered to intercept Thoravin. "But I thought we were going to the Queen of the Night. She was going to teach us more about the power within."

Thoravin drew one side of his mouth down in a thoughtful frown and shook his head. "My only intention for going to the Queen was to help this mother and daughter find 2-45. Now that they have found him, there is no need for me to entangle myself with someone so powerful." 1-13 studied Thoravin's expression to determine if he too should remain with his old master, but he threw a questioning look back at 2-45.

2-45 mumbled something to himself then raised a finger as he faced 5-07. "You and mother should stay with Thoravin."

5-07 readjusted the gun on her belt. "Why?" She raised a defiant chin.

2-45 shook his head with more emphasis. "Because 7,500 and I area going to the Queen of the Night, and that path is too dangerous for you. I know you have some skills, but . . ."

Their mother stood between 2-45 and 5-07 and swatted the disagreements away. "I've had enough of all this. 2-45, you have been taking too many risks." She faced 5-07, raising her head sternly. "And, 5-07, you have been just as bad." She turned to Thoravin. "What do you recommend?"

Thoravin raised his hands palms upward before him as he let his eyes stray to some obscure bit of dirt floating nearby. "Well, anyone who so wills is welcome to stay at my workshop for a few days if necessary."

While 2-45 considered this a generous gesture, he wondered whether he meant it or not. He noticed Thoravin shift uncomfortably when everyone exchanged glances of gratitude at the offer. Even so, he believed his family would be safer with Thoravin than taking the dangerous journey to the Queen of the Night. "You should stay here," he told them.

7,500 adjusted some wrinkles out of his sleeve and noticed a smudge on it. "We have already wasted a lot of time." He rubbed the smudge in hopes of making it disappear. "We need to be on our way."

5-07 took her brother's hand in hers. "Do you want us not to join you?"

He smiled at her, even though the smile did not extend to his eyes. He rubbed the back of her hand with affection. "I want you and mother to be safe."

"Okay," 5-07 replied as if concluding the argument. "Then stay here with us. We only leave if you leave."

2-45's grip on his sister's hand tightened. "I don't want you to go with me. It's not safe."

5-07 raised her nose several inches. "Then it's not safe for you as well."

2-45 looked to 7,500 seeking advice. The only advice he received from him was a shake of the head indicating he was not happy with the idea of having women join them on the journey. He then turned to his mother in hopes that she might reprimand his sister.

2-45's mother just huffed. "If you insist on visiting that Queen of whatever, then you just have to accept the fact that we're coming too."

2-45 turned once more to 7,500 to determine if he was still against bringing along his mother and sister. While 7,500 did groan to display his displeasure, he shrugged his shoulders admitting he was outvoted.

"Very well," 2-45 told his mother and sister.

5-07 threw her arms around her brother. "You know you need us."

"Whoever is leaving," 7,500 announced, "we start now." Without waiting for a reply, he plunged down the path as if leading a parade. Outpacing the others by several meters, he believed he was being more than considerate by moderating his speed as much as he did to allow those who would hurry to keep up with him.

5-07 and her mother moved to follow 7,500, but 2-45 hesitated. "Are you coming?" he asked 1-13.

1-13 shook his head. "Eventually . . . maybe." He raised his eyes to meet Thoravin's. When Thoravin nodded, 1-13 continued with more confidence. "I do want to better understand the power . . . but right now I have lost too much of my control over it. I don't think I could handle learning from anyone too powerful until I regain that control."

Thoravin and 1-13 took the trail to Thoravin's workshop. 2-45 raced to join 7,500 and his family on the path that led to the Queen of the Night. When he was just within a few paces of them, he thought he heard a slithering behind a rock just off the path.

When he had passed, a spy-creature raised its head over the rock and adjusted its binocular-like eyes to take in the group just ahead. It relayed the information and continued following behind, just out of sight.

P.O.D Official IDs

Notice: All residents of and travelers to the Planet of Darkness shall be required to carry their P.O.D ID with them at all times and display it upon request by any Enforcer of the Dark Tyrant

--- Official decree of 1

50-83

Persuader
Apprentice

ALPHA 3-0-3

Shape-Shifter

4,021

Slump-Bump

9-85

Economic Researcher
Assistant

WAY-GUIDE

Pilot for Infinity

Shadow-Shield

Agent for Planet of Light

1-13

Persuader

6-96

Persuader

7,500
Historical Researcher

93-73
Historical Research Assistant

Glossary of Names and Terms

A

Alpha 3-0-3 (Alpha Three-Oh-Three) A shape-shifter. Co-pilot to 1-05.

B

Barsian Rock A rock found in the tunnels of the Planet of Darkness. When heated it can be used for fuel.

Barso-Cycle A type of motorcycle that is fueled by barsian rock.

Batolan Moon A moon of Grubia where a historic battle took place in which Grubia and the Planet of Darkness fought against the Jorgandans.

Bercolar A planet that was destroyed. Historical manuscripts suggest that there were prophecies before the destruction of Bercolar that it would happen.

Bloquious Rock A type of igneous rock, found in the walls of volcanoes on the Planet of Darkness. It is used in the development of ezocane.

C

Camboline Stone A type of stone found on the planet Zeento, which has the ability to insulate buildings from both extreme cold and extreme heat.

Chorondi A planet known for its artistic achievements, particularly in architecture and food.

Cloud of Deception A creature that can live anywhere, even in space. It is a parasite that looks like a cloud and drains strength from its host.

Control Fleet A fleet of ships that the Dark Tyrant uses to retrieve anyone trying to leave the Planet of Darkness without permission.

Crystal Pendant A crystal sphere that can detect the exact feelings and thoughts of the one who wears it.

D

Dark-Breaker A boy who lives in the safehouse. He had been rescued from the City of the Dark Tyrant.

Dark Tyrant The dictatorial, shape-shifting ruler of the Planet of Darkness.

Desert of Night An area deep in the wilderness of the Planet of Darkness where the Queen of the Night lives.

Dive of Distraction A dive hidden in a cavern. It is run by the Duke of Distraction. Here, he provides all types of technically illegal distraction for the citizens of the Planet of Darkness, for a price.

Dream-Saver A young man who helps the Shadow-Shield and Soul-Guard at the safehouse.

E

EEV An escape vehicle that is constructed of trantonine metal which both absorbs and reflects images to make it difficult for other vehicles to detect it.

Ezocane Crystals that, when hammered into clear glass-like sheets, are strong enough to be used in the production of windows, viewing screens, flooring, and even weapons.

F

Forerunner A small, bullet-shaped spaceship that is a companion vessel of the *Ghost III.*

G

Ghost III Infinity's triangular spaceship. It contains two floors. Stretching between the two floors and encircled by a protective railing is a brilliant ball of energy that shoots out power to all electrically run devices on the ship.

Goo Creatures What is left of subjects of the Planet of Darkness after going through the lava pit and realizing their place in society as absolute nothingness. They then bubble up as spineless, shapeless goo and live around the Dark Tyrant's throne to agree with everything he says.

Grey-Marrow A planet to which Infinity and the Shadow-Shield went in order to dismantle an enemy tracking center. The Shadow-Shield earned his name in recognition for his heroics during a battle that broke out during their mission.

Gorslancher Green lizard-like creatures that live and breed in space. They have pointed teeth and huge red composite eyes. They have two muscular forelegs which contain fingers tipped with sharp claws. They also have a long tail with no back legs. They search out and devour any energy sources, including spaceships.

Grubia The dark, swampy planet which is home to the Grubian Ghouls. Grubia is a staunch ally of the Planet of Darkness.

Guardian A man hired by the Dark Tyrant to rule a space station in the gray area of space. His primary duty is to ensure that Infinity does not pass the space station on his way to the Planet of Darkness.

I

Infinity The prince of the Planet of Light. His duty is to watch the galaxy for those who want to escape to the Planet of Light. When he discovers an individual needing help in their escape, Infinity embarks on a rescue mission to aid them.

J

Jorgandans The Grubian Ghouls fought alongside the Planet of Darkness against the Jorgandans in the Battle of the Batolan Moon. With the help of the Grubian's experimental forces, the Planet of Darkness overpowered the Jorgandans.

Journey 1-05's spaceship used to transport merchandise and people for a price.

Judgment Beyond Death A philosophical concept that argues that individuals exist in some form after death to face additional consequences. This concept has been dismissed by most of the intellectual community of the Planet of Darkness.

L

Light-Defender A young woman who was rescued by the Shadow-Shield and now provides the safehouse with her skills as a warrior.

Lithostones The stones used in the process for creating shape-shifters. Lithostones provide the shape-shifters with their abilities.

M

Mernolith Gel-Stones A type of stone found on the Planet of Darkness that helps to absorb sound and heat.

Mud-Crawler A vehicle that uses propulsion to lift itself above the muddy terrain to enable transportation in environments such as the Slump-Bump area.

Mystic of the Vale A woman known for her sixth sense and ability to provide insight into the future. People embark on pilgrimages to the Mystic of the Vale to consult the Oracle of the Vale.

N

Nefescur Crystals A type of crystal used by the Grubians to construct a Shadow-Shifter without the use of lithostones.

O

Octelix An ottoman-shaped entity that is mostly computer and is loyal to 81-4-60. Octelix has the unique ability to communicate with others using a type of telepathy.

Oracle of the Vale An unusual mechanism found at the residence of The Mystic of The Vale. The oracle presents riddles that provide clues to the future.

Orfoid A planet known for its giant air-breathing piranhas.

P

Planet of Darkness A planet that is so far from its sun that it has no concept of day and relies on electric lights and lava flow for heat and light sources. The planet is ruled by the Dark Tyrant.

Planet of Light A planet that is closer to its sun than the Planet of Darkness is. The Planet of Light produces lithostones and has an abundance of natural, light-producing planet life that supplements the light from the sun. The Planet of Light is ruled by a wise king whose son is Infinity.

Porenthian Foam A material used in underground buildings. When solidified, the Porenthian foam can channel oxygen.

Power Within A power propounded by the mystic Thoravin and the Queen of the Night. The Power Within is claimed to be a magical force that can create, influence, and sustain elements on the Planet of Darkness.

Q

Queen of the Night A powerful woman who rules the Desert of the Night. She is credited with the ability to channel and control the Power Within.

R

Revitosaline Bath A therapeutic bath that possesses a gel-like consistency because it contains molecules of parsaline, a substance that when absorbed by the skin sends messages to the muscles via the nervous system, telling the muscles to relax.

S

Schlampine Birds Giant, flesh-eating birds who circle the wilderness area in search of prey. They have been described as resembling the shape of a giant stomach with wings.

Seven-Headed Snake A pet of 6-96. Its venom is claimed to enslave its victim into a state of deep depression.

Shadow-Shield An agent for Infinity. He helps run the safehouse on the Planet of Darkness and is indispensable in espionage missions because he possesses the ability to be undetectable in the shadows.

Shadow-Shifter A form of a shape-shifter created with the help of the Grubian Ghouls.

Shepherdess of the Valley A powerful woman who oversees a realm on the Planet of Darkness. Her realm uses natural processes to provide light and natural resources to those who are sheltered in her valley.

Six Secrets of Saphi Secrets that are sought after by those who crave power. When all six secrets are possessed, it is claimed, the possessor can perform the most powerful tricks of all.

Skeleton Ghosts Ghosts that resemble skeletons and are maintained through the Power Within.

Slump-Bump A segment of society on the Planet of Darkness that is ordered to only do what is absolutely necessary for existence. They are not allowed to work, play, party, or think.

Soul-Guard A woman who helps in the safehouse on the Planet of Darkness.

Sword-Wielder An older man who lends his abilities as a warrior to help guard those who live in the safehouse.

Spy Creature A cybernetic creature that is part snake and part robot. It spies on the inhabitants of the Planet of Darkness and is able to record anything it sees or hears.

T

Thoravin 1-13's mystic mentor from whom he learned his persuasive powers of hypnotism. Thoravin lives in the wilderness area and studies the Power Within.

Trantonine Metal The metal that is used in EEVs. This metal both absorbs and reflects images.

Trechirs Giant rodents that, when full grown, reach a size of 6 feet from head to tail and five feet at the withers. The trechirs have large furry bodies, big eyes, and wide ears that make them appear helpless and friendly. Nevertheless, they have sharp claws and a powerful bite and at times are reported to have killed people when defending their young.

W

Way-Guide Formerly known as 8-23, the Way-Guide was co-pilot to 1-05 and currently serves as an assistant to Infinity.

Z

Zeento A planet not far from the Planet of Darkness, most known for its caves, spiders, and building materials.

Numbers

1 (One) Ruler of the Planet of Darkness under the Dark Tyrant.

1-05 (One-Oh-Five) Pilot of the *Journey*.

1-13 (One-Thirteen) Persuader who uses more mystical methods of persuasion such as hypnotism and his skeleton-ghosts. He also was instrumental in the creation of the Dark Tyrant's spy creatures.

2-45 (Two-Forty-Five) Propaganda specialist in search of a way off the Planet of Darkness.

366 (Three-Hundred-Sixty-Six) Overseer of Manual Labor Room 15.

5-07 (Five-Oh-Seven) 2-45's sister. Ex-Enforcer who is engaged to 7,500 and is trained in the arts of dance and combat.

5-68 (Five-Sixty-Eight) A Slump-Bump and neighbor of 4,021.

6-96 (Six-Ninety-Six) Persuader who uses violent forms of torture to acquire information and cooperation.

7-43 (Seven-Forty-Three) Prison Warden and friend of 2-45.

8-23 (Eight-Twenty-Three) Pilot. Also known as the Way-Guide.

9-85 (Nine-Eighty-Five) Apprentice to 2,040. Highly trained in math and economics.

17-07 (Seventeen-Oh-Seven) Manual labor worker.

38-95 (Thirty-Eight-Ninety-Five) Manual labor worker.

50-83 (Fifty-Eighty-Three) Apprentice to 6-96. Formerly apprenticed to 1-13.

81-4-60 (Eighty-One-Four-Sixty) Computer specialist.

85-27 (Eighty-Five-Twenty-Seven) Manual labor worker.

93-73 (Ninety-Three-Seventy-Three) Apprentice to 7,500.

2,040 (Two-Thousand-Forty) Economics Efficiency Specialist.

4,021 (Four-Thousand-Twenty-One) Slump-Bump.

6,025 (Six-Thousand-Twenty-Five) See Duke of Distraction

7,500 (Seventy-Five-Hundred) Historical Researcher and friend of 2,040.

34,000 (Thirty-Four-Thousand) Lab Assistant to 2,040.

Acknowledgments

It took a universe of support to see this book to completion. One of the most helpful and supportive humans in this effort was Julie Burris, an author in her own right, who provided in depth feedback on early drafts and had faith that this work is something other readers would love.

I would also like to thank Kathleen Cuyler of Mocha Wave Publishing for her advice on editing and formatting. She was always there when I had questions and needed a sounding board.

A huge thanks to Jody Cantrell Dyer of Crippled Beagle Publishing who provided mentoring on the writing and publishing process, without which this book may never have seen the light of day.

Thank you also to Sarah Jo Wrinkle of Blue Betty Photography for her encouragement and professional author photographs.

Finally, I want to send a big thank you to my family, to my mom who first encouraged me to write and to my sisters who joined me in midnight writing sessions and provided a much needed support group throughout the entire book-writing journey.

--Tirzah Darnell